DARK NEST I
THE
JOINER KING

By Troy Denning

WATERDEEP
DRAGONWALL
THE PARCHED SEA
THE VERDANT PASSAGE
THE CRIMSON LEGION
THE AMBER ENCHANTRESS
THE OBSIDIAN ORACLE
THE CERULEAN STORM
THE OGRE'S PACT
THE GIANT AMONG US
THE TITAN OF TWILIGHT
THE VEILED DRAGON
PAGES OF PAIN
CRUCIBLE: THE TRIAL OF CYRIC THE MAD
THE OATH OF STONEKEEP
FACES OF DECEPTION
BEYOND THE HIGH ROAD
DEATH OF THE DRAGON (with Ed Greenwood)
THE SUMMONING
THE SIEGE
THE SORCERER

STAR WARS: THE NEW JEDI ORDER: STAR BY STAR
STAR WARS: TATOOINE GHOST
STAR WARS: DARK NEST I: THE JOINER KING
STAR WARS: DARK NEST II: THE UNSEEN QUEEN
STAR WARS: DARK NEST III: THE SWARM WAR
STAR WARS: LEGACY OF THE FORCE: TEMPEST

STAR WARS

DARK NEST I
THE
JOINER KING

TROY DENNING

LUCAS BOOKS

DEL REY

BALLANTINE BOOKS • NEW YORK

A Del Rey Books Mass Market Original

Copyright © 2005 by Lucasfilm Ltd. & ® or ™ where indicated. All Rights Reserved. Used under authorization.

Included is the following previously published e-book: "Star Wars: The New Jedi Order: Ylesia" by Walter Jon Williams copyright © 2002 by Lucasfilm Ltd. & ® or ™ where indicated. All Rights Reserved. Used under authorization.

Published in the United States by Del Rey Books, an imprint of The Random House Publishing Group, a division of Random House, Inc., New York.

Del Rey is a registered trademark and the Del Rey colophon is a trademark of Random House, Inc.

ISBN 0-345-46304-8

Printed in the United States of America

www.starwars.com
www.delreybooks.com

OPM   9 8 7

For Curtis Smith
Who invited me to play in the Galaxy Far, Far Away
A long, long time ago

ACKNOWLEDGMENTS

Many people contributed to this book in ways large and small. Thanks are especially due to: Andria Hayday, for advice, encouragement, critiques, and much more; James Luceno for being such a fun target for idea-bouncing; Enrique Guerrero for his suggestions and our many useful Chiss discussions; Shelly Shapiro and all the people at Del Rey who make this so much fun, particularly Keith Clayton and Colleen Lindsay; Sue Rostoni and the wonderful people at Lucasfilm, particularly Howard Roffman, Amy Gary, Leland Chee, and Pablo Hidalgo. And, of course, to George Lucas for opening his galaxy to the rest of us.

THE STAR WARS NOVELS TIMELINE

33 YEARS BEFORE STAR WARS: A New Hope

Darth Maul: Saboteur*

32.5 YEARS BEFORE STAR WARS: A New Hope

Cloak of Deception
Darth Maul: Shadow Hunter

32 YEARS BEFORE STAR WARS: A New Hope

**STAR WARS: EPISODE I
THE PHANTOM MENACE**

29 YEARS BEFORE STAR WARS: A New Hope

Rogue Planet

27 YEARS BEFORE STAR WARS: A New Hope

Outbound Flight

22.5 YEARS BEFORE STAR WARS: A New Hope

The Approaching Storm

22 YEARS BEFORE STAR WARS: A New Hope

**STAR WARS: EPISODE II
ATTACK OF THE CLONES**

Republic Commando: Hard Contact

21.5 YEARS BEFORE STAR WARS: A New Hope

Shatterpoint

21 YEARS BEFORE STAR WARS: A New Hope

The Cestus Deception
The Hive*

Republic Commando: Triple Zero

20 YEARS BEFORE STAR WARS: A New Hope

MedStar I: Battle Surgeons
MedStar II: Jedi Healer

19.5 YEARS BEFORE STAR WARS: A New Hope

Jedi Trial
Yoda: Dark Rendezvous

19 YEARS BEFORE STAR WARS: A New Hope

Labyrinth of Evil

**STAR WARS: EPISODE III
REVENGE OF THE SITH**

Dark Lord: The Rise of Darth Vader

10-0 YEARS BEFORE STAR WARS: A New Hope

The Han Solo Trilogy:
The Paradise Snare
The Hutt Gambit
Rebel Dawn

5-2 YEARS BEFORE STAR WARS: A New Hope

The Adventures of Lando Calrissian

The Han Solo Adventures

STAR WARS: A New Hope YEAR 0

**STAR WARS: EPISODE IV
A NEW HOPE**

0-3 YEARS AFTER STAR WARS: A New Hope

Tales from the Mos Eisley Cantina
Galaxies: The Ruins of Dantooine
Splinter of the Mind's Eye

3 YEARS AFTER STAR WARS: A New Hope

**STAR WARS: EPISODE V
THE EMPIRE STRIKES BACK**

Tales of the Bounty Hunters

3.5 YEARS AFTER STAR WARS: A New Hope

Shadows of the Empire

4 YEARS AFTER STAR WARS: A New Hope

**STAR WARS: EPISODE VI
RETURN OF THE JEDI**

Tales from Jabba's Palace
Tales from the Empire
Tales from the New Republic

The Bounty Hunter Wars:
The Mandalorian Armor
Slave Ship
Hard Merchandise

The Truce at Bakura

*An ebook novella

DRAMATIS PERSONAE

Alema Rar; Jedi Knight (female Twi'lek)
Ben Skywalker; child (male human)
C-3PO; protocol droid
Cal Omas; Galactic Alliance Chief-of-State (male human)
Cilghal; Jedi Master (female Mon Calamari)
Gorog; mastermind (Killik)
Han Solo; captain, *Millennium Falcon* (male human)
Jacen Solo; Jedi Knight (male human)
Jae Juun; captain, *XR808g* (male Sullustan)
Jagged Fel; commander, Chiss task force (male human)
Jaina Solo; Jedi Knight (female human)
Leia Organa Solo; copilot, *Millennium Falcon* (female human)
Lowbacca; Jedi Knight (male Wookiee)
Luke Skywalker; Jedi Master (male human)
Mara Jade Skywalker; Jedi Master (female human)
R2-D2; astromech droid
Raynar Thul; crash survivor (male human)
Saba Sebatyne; Jedi Master (female Barabel)
Tahiri Veila; Jedi Knight (female human)
Tarfang; copilot, *XR808g* (male Ewok)
Tekli; Jedi Knight (female Chadra-fan)
Tenel Ka; Queen Mother (female human)
Tesar Sebatyne; Jedi Knight (male Barabel)
Welk; crash survivor (male human)
Zekk; Jedi Knight (male human)

PROLOGUE

The feeling had returned, a sense of desperation that burned in the Force like a faraway star, clear and bright and beckoning. Jaina Solo found her gaze straying through the justice ship viewport, out into the blue-flecked void that hung behind the slowly spinning cylinder of Detention Center *Maxsec Eight*. As before, the sensation came from the direction of the Unknown Regions, a call for . . . what? And from whom? The touch was too wispy to tell. It always was.

"Jedi Solo?" The inquisitor stepped closer to the witness rail. "Shall I repeat the question?"

A tall, stiff woman with a shaved head and deep lines at the corners of her gray eyes, Athadar Gyad had the brusque demeanor of a retired military officer. It was a common affectation among petty Reconstruction Authority bureaucrats, even when the only notation in their service record was a decades-old planetary conscription number.

"When you boarded the *Night Lady* with Jedi Lowbacca and—"

"Sorry, Inquisitor. I did hear the question." Jaina shifted her gaze to the accused, a massive Yaka with an expressionless, near-human face. He wore an engraved Ithorian skull on the lateral cover of his cybernetic implant. "Redstar's crew tried to turn us away."

A glint of impatience showed in Gyad's gray eyes. "They attacked you with blasters, isn't that correct?"

"Right."

1

"And it was necessary to defend yourselves with your lightsabers?"

"Right again."

Gyad remained silent, tacitly inviting her witness to elaborate on the battle. But Jaina was more interested in the sense of desperation she felt in the Force. It was growing stronger by the moment, more urgent and frightened.

"Jedi Solo?" Gyad stepped in front of Jaina, blocking her view out of the inquest salon. "Please direct your attention to me."

Jaina fixed the woman with an icy stare. "I thought I had answered your question."

Gyad drew back almost imperceptibly, but continued her examination as though there had been no resentment in Jaina's voice. "What were you wearing at the time?"

"Our cloaks," Jaina said.

"Your Jedi cloaks?"

"They're just cloaks." Jaina had stood at enough witness rails in the last few years to know that the inquisitor was trying to bolster a weak case with the mystique of her Jedi witnesses—a sure sign that Gyad did not understand, or respect, the Jedi role in the galaxy. "Jedi don't wear uniforms."

"Surely, you can't mean to suggest that a criminal of Redstar's intelligence failed to recognize—" Gyad paused to reconsider her phrasing. Tribunal inquisitors were supposed to be impartial investigators, though in practice most limited their efforts to presenting enough evidence to lock away the accused. "Jedi Solo, do you mean to suggest the crew could have legitimately believed you to be pirates?"

"I don't know what they believed," Jaina said.

Gyad narrowed her eyes and studied Jaina in silence. Despite Luke Skywalker's advice after the war to avoid involving the Jedi in the mundane concerns of the new government, the challenge of rebuilding the galaxy obliged much of the order to do just that. There were just too many critical missions that only a Jedi could perform, with too many dire consequences for the Galactic Alliance, and most Reconstruction Authority bureaucrats had come to view the Jedi order as little more than an elite branch of interstellar police.

Finally, Jaina explained, "I was too busy fighting to probe their thoughts."

Gyad let out a theatrical sigh. "Jedi Solo, isn't it true that your father once made his living as a smuggler?"

"That was a little before my time, Inquisitor." Jaina's retort drew a siss of laughter from the spectator area, where two of her fellow Jedi Knights, Tesar Sebatyne and Lowbacca, sat waiting for her to finish. "And what would that have to do with the price of spice on Nal Hutta?"

Gyad turned to the panel of magistrates. "Will you please instruct the witness to answer—"

"Everyone knows the answer," Jaina interrupted. "It's taught in half the history classes in the galaxy."

"Of course it is." The inquisitor's voice grew artificially compassionate, and she pointed to the Yaka captive. "Would it be possible that you identify with the accused? That you are reluctant to testify against a criminal because of your father's own ambivalent relationship with the law?"

"No." Jaina found herself squeezing the witness rail as though she meant to crimp the cold metal. "In the last five standard years, I've captured thirty-seven warlords and broken more than a hundred smuggling—"

Suddenly the sense of desperation grew more tangible in the Force, more clear and familiar. Jaina's gaze turned back to the viewport, and she did not finish her answer.

"Wait."

Tahiri Veila raised a hand, and the two Yuuzhan Vong standing before her fell silent. The two groups of spectators watched her expectantly, but she remained quiet and stared into Zonama Sekot's blue sky. Over the last few weeks, she had begun to sense a distant foreboding in the Force, a slowly building dread, and now that feeling had developed into something more . . . into anguish and panic and despair.

"*Jeedai* Veila?" asked the smaller of the speakers. With one blind eye and a lumpy, lopsided face, he was one of the Extolled, a disfigured underclass once known as the Shamed Ones. They had earned their new name by rising up against their upper-caste oppressors to help end the war that had nearly destroyed both the Yuuzhan Vong and the civilized galaxy. "Is something wrong?"

"Yes." Tahiri forced her attention back to the group. Their blue-rimmed eyes and leathery faces seemed more familiar to her than the reflection of the blond-haired women she saw in the mirror every morning—but that was hardly a surprise, considering what had happened to her during the war. She was as much Yuuzhan Vong now as she was human, at least in mind and spirit. "But it doesn't have anything to do with this. Go on."

The Extolled One—Bava, she remembered—bowed deeply, intentionally lowering himself to her height.

"As I was saying, *Jeedai* Veila, four times this week we have caught Sal Ghator and his warriors stealing from our gardens."

Tahiri cocked her brow. "*Your* gardens, Bava?" La'okio was supposed to be a communal village, an experiment where the contentious castes of Yuuzhan Vong society would learn to work together—and to trust each other. "I thought the gardens belonged to everyone."

"We have decided that every grashal is also allowed to plant an extra plot for itself." Bava sneered in Ghator's direction, then continued, "But the warriors are too lazy to work their own ground. They expect us to do it for them."

"We cannot do it for ourselves!" Ghator objected. Half a meter taller than Tahiri and nearly three times her mass, he still bore the tattoos and ritual scarrings of a former subaltern. "We are cursed by the gods. Nothing we plant will grow."

Tahiri fought back a sigh. "Don't tell me you've separated by caste again. You're supposed to be living in mixed groups."

As Tahiri spoke, she felt the familiar touch of a Chadra-Fan searching for her in the Force, wanting to know if she also sensed the growing strength of the *feeling*. She opened herself to the contact and focused her thoughts on the mysterious fear. Tekli was not particularly strong in the Force, and what Tahiri perceived as a clarion call would seem barely a whisper to the little Chadra-Fan. Neither of them bothered to reach out for their companion Danni Quee; Force-sensitive though she might be, so far Danni had proven numb to the sensation.

"Living in mixed grashals is unclean," Ghator said, drawing Tahiri's attention back to the problems in La'okio. "Warriors cannot be asked to sleep on the same dirt as Shamed Ones."

"Shamed Ones!" Bava said. "We are Extolled. We are the ones who exposed Shimrra's heresy, while you warriors led us all to ruin."

The blue rim around Ghator's eyes grew wider and darker. "Beware your tongue, raal, lest its poison strike you dead."

"There is no poison in truth." Bava sneaked a glance in Tahiri's direction, then sneered, "You are the Shamed Ones now!"

Ghator's hand sent Bava tumbling across the rugrass so swiftly that Tahiri doubted she could have intercepted it had she wanted to, and she did not want to. The Yuuzhan Vong would always have their own way of working out problems—ways that Danni Quee and Tekli and perhaps even Zonama Sekot itself would never fully comprehend.

Bava stopped rolling and turned his good eye in Tahiri's direction. She returned his gaze and did nothing. Having risen from their outcast status through their efforts to end the war, the Extolled Ones were proving eager to find another caste to take their place. Tahiri thought it might be good to remind them of the consequences of such behavior. Besides, the *feeling* was growing stronger and clearer; she had the sense that it was coming from someone she knew, someone who had been trying to reach her—and Tekli—for a very long time.

Come fast . . . The voice arose inside Tahiri's mind, clear and distinct and eerily familiar. *Come now.*

The words seemed to fade even as Jacen Solo perceived them, sinking below the threshold of awareness and vanishing into the boggy underlayers of his mind. Yet the message remained, the conviction that the time had come to answer the call he had been feeling over the last few weeks. He unfolded his legs—he was sitting cross-legged in the air—and lowered his feet to the floor of the meditation circle. A chain of soft pops sounded as he crushed the tiny blada vines that spilled out of the seams between the larstone paving blocks.

"I'm sorry, Akanah. I must go."

Akanah answered without opening her eyes. "If you are sorry, Jacen, you must *not* go." A lithe woman with an olive complexion and dark hair, she appeared closer to Jacen's age than her own five standard decades. She sat floating in the center of the meditation circle, surrounded by novices who were trying to imitate her with varying degrees of success. "Sorrow is a sign that you have not given yourself to the Current."

Jacen considered this, then dipped his head in acknowledgment. "Then I'm not sorry." The call continued in the Force, a needle-sharp pang that pulled at Jacen deep inside his chest. "And I must go."

Now Akanah opened her eyes. "What of your training?"

"I'm grateful for what you have shown me so far." Jacen turned to leave. "I'll continue when I return."

"No." As Akanah spoke, the meditation circle exit vanished behind a vine-strewn wall. "I cannot permit that."

Jacen stopped and turned to face her. "Illusions aren't necessary. If you don't wish me to return, I won't."

"What I don't wish is for you to leave." Akanah floated over to him and lowered her own feet. She was so immersed in the White Current that even the delicate blada leaves did not pop beneath her weight. "It's too soon. You're not ready."

Jacen forced himself to remain patient. After all, he was the one who had sought out the Fallanassi. "I have completed many trainings, Akanah. What I have learned is that every order believes *its* way is the only way."

"I am not speaking of monks and witches, Jacen Solo. I am speaking of you." Her dark eyes caught his gaze. "Your feelings on this are unclear. Someone calls, and you go without knowing why."

"Then you feel it, too?"

"No, Jacen. You are as clumsy in the Current as your uncle. Your feelings leave ripples, and ripples can be read. Does the call come from your brother?"

"No. Anakin died in the war." It had been eight years, and

Jacen could finally speak those words with some measure of acceptance, with some recognition of the purpose his brother's death had served in the Force. It had been the turning point in the war, when the Jedi finally learned how to fight the Yuuzhan Vong—and not become monsters themselves. "I've told you that."

"Yes, but is it *him*?" Akanah stepped closer to Jacen, and his nostrils filled with the scent of the waha plants that grew in the temple bathing pool. "After someone sinks beneath the Current, a circle of ripples remains behind. Perhaps it is the ripples you sense."

"That does not make what I feel any less real," Jacen countered. *"Sometimes, the effect is all we can know of the cause."*

"Do you remember my words only so you can use them to spar with me?" Akanah's hand came up as though to bat him across the ear, and his own hand reflexively rose to block. She shook her head in disgust. "You are a dreadful student, Jacen Solo. You hear, but you do not learn."

It was a rebuke to which Jacen had grown accustomed during his five-year search for the true nature of the Force. The Jensaarai, the Aing-Tii, even the Witches of Dathomir had all said similar things to him—usually when his questions about their view of the Force grew too probing. But Akanah had more reason than the others to be disappointed in him. Striking another would be anathema to any Adept of the White Current. All Akanah had done was lift her hand; it had been Jacen who interpreted the action as an attack.

Jacen inclined his head. "I learn, but sometimes slowly." He was thinking of the two apparitions he had already seen of his dead brother, the first when a cavern beast on Yuuzhan'tar used one to lure him into its throat, the second on Zonama, when Sekot had taken Anakin's form while they talked. "You think I'm giving form to this call, that I impose my own meaning on the ripples I feel."

"What *I* think is not important," Akanah said. "Still yourself, Jacen, and see what is really in the Current."

Jacen closed his eyes and opened himself to the White Current in much the same way he would have opened himself to the

Force. Akanah and the other Adepts taught that the Current and the Force were separate things, and that was true—but only in the sense that any current was different from the ocean in which it flowed. In their essential wholeness, they were each other.

Jacen performed a quieting exercise he had learned from the Theran Listeners, then focused on the call. It was still there, a cry so sharp it hurt, in a voice he remembered and could not identify . . . *come . . . help . . .* a male voice, but one he recognized as not belonging to his brother.

And there was something else, too, a familiar presence that Jacen *did* know, not sending the call, but reaching out along with it. Jaina.

Jacen opened his eyes. "It's not Anakin . . . or his ripples."

"You're certain?"

Jacen nodded. "Jaina senses it, too." That was what his sister was trying to tell him, he knew. Their twin bond had always been strong, and it had only grown stronger during his wanderings. "I think she intends to answer it."

Akanah looked doubtful. "I feel nothing."

"*You* aren't her twin." Jacen turned and stepped through the wall-illusion hiding the exit, only to find Akanah—or the illusion of Akanah—blocking his way. "Please ask the Pydyrians to bring my ship down from orbit. I'd like to leave as soon as possible."

"I am sorry, but no." Akanah's eyes caught his gaze again and held it almost physically. "You have the same power I once sensed in your uncle Luke, but without the light. You must not leave before you have found some."

Jacen was stung by her harsh assessment, but hardly surprised. The war against the Yuuzhan Vong had brought the Jedi a deeper understanding of the Force—one that no longer saw light and dark as opposing sides—and he had known before he came that the Fallanassi might find this new view disturbing. That was why he had hid it from them . . . or thought he had.

"I'm sorry you disapprove," Jacen said. "But I no longer view the Force in terms of light and dark. It embraces more than that."

"Yes, we have heard about this 'new' knowledge of the Jedi."

Akanah's tone was scornful. "And it troubles my heart to see that their folly now rivals their arrogance."

"Folly?" Jacen did not want to argue, but—being one of the first advocates of the new understanding—he felt compelled to defend his views. "That 'folly' helped us win the war."

"At what price, Jacen?" Akanah's voice remained gentle. "If the Jedi no longer look to the light, how can they serve it?"

"Jedi serve the Force," Jacen said. "The Force encompasses both light and dark."

"So now you are beyond light and dark?" Akanah asked. "Beyond good and evil?"

"I'm no longer an active Jedi Knight," Jacen answered, "but yes."

"And you do not understand the folly in that?" As Akanah spoke, her gaze seemed to grow deeper and darker. "The arrogance?"

What Jacen understood was that the Fallanassi had a rather narrow and rigid view of morality, but he did not say so. The call was continuing to pull at him inside, urging him to be on his way, and the last thing he wanted to do now was waste time in a debate that would change no one's mind.

"The Jedi serve only themselves," Akanah continued. "They are pompous enough to believe they can use the Force instead of submitting to it, and in this pride they have caused more suffering than they have prevented. With no light to guide you, Jacen, and the power I sense in you, I fear you will cause even more."

The frank words struck Jacen like a blow, less because of their harshness than because of the genuine concern he sensed behind them. Akanah truly feared for him, truly feared that he would become an even greater monster than had his grandfather, Darth Vader.

"Akanah, I appreciate your concern." Jacen reached for her hands and found himself holding only empty air. He resisted the temptation to find her real body in the Force; Adepts of the White Current considered such acts intrusions just short of violence. "But I won't find my light here. I have to go."

ONE

Evening had come to Unity Green, and the first hawk-bats were already out, dipping down to pluck yammal-jells and coufee eels from the rolling whitecaps on Liberation Lake. On the far shore, the yorik coral bluffs that marked the edge of the park had grown purple and shadowed. Beyond them, the durasteel skeletons of the rising skytowers gleamed crimson in the setting sun. The planet remained as much Yuuzhan'tar as Coruscant, and in many ways that would never change. But it *was* at peace. For the first time in Luke Skywalker's life, the galaxy was truly not at war—and that counted for everything.

There were still problems, of course. There always would be, and today several senior Masters were struggling to address the chaos that Jaina and four other young Jedi Knights had caused by abruptly abandoning their duties and departing for the Unknown Regions.

"Lowbacca was the only one who completely understood the biomechanics of the *Maledoth,*" Corran Horn was saying in his throaty voice. "So, as you can see, the Ramoan relocation project has ground to a complete standstill."

Luke reluctantly shifted his gaze from the viewport to the council room's speaking circle, where Corran stood using a laserwand to highlight the holographic projection of a huge Yuuzhan Vong slaveship. The Jedi order had been hoping to use the vessel to evacuate the population of a dying world.

Corran flicked the laserwand, and the holograph switched to the image of blast-pocked asteroid miner. "The situation in the Maltorian mining belt is deteriorating as well. Without Zekk there to lead the hunt, Three-Eye's pirates have the run of the system. Raw material shipments have fallen by fifty percent, and RePlanetHab is trying to buy them off."

"That's one circuit we need to kill now," Mara said. Seated in the chair next to Luke's, she was—as usual—the first to cut to the heart of the matter. That was one of the things Luke most admired about her; in a time when the smallest decision carried ramifications that even a Columi dejarik champion could not predict, his wife's instincts remained steady and true. "If rehab conglomerates start buying off pirates, we'll have marauders popping up all over the Core."

The other Masters voiced their agreement.

"Fine," Corran said. "Where do we find a replacement for Zekk?"

No one rushed to answer. The Jedi were spread too thin already, with most Jedi Knights—and even some apprentices— already assigned three tasks. And as the ranks of the greedy and the selfish grew ever more adept at manipulating the Galactic Alliance Senate, the situation seemed increasingly desperate.

Finally, Kyp Durron said, "The Solos should be finished on Borao soon." Dressed in threadbare cape and tunic, wearing his brown hair long and shaggy, Kyp looked as though he had just come in from a long mission. He always looked like that. "Maybe RePlanetHab will be patient if they know they're the Solos' next assignment."

The silence this time was even longer than the last. Strictly speaking, the Solos were not available for assignments. Han wasn't even a Jedi, and Leia's status was completely informal. The council just kept asking them to help out, they just kept doing it, and every Master in the room knew the order had been exploiting the Solos' selfless natures for far too long.

"Someone else needs to contact them," Mara finally said. "It's getting so bad that Leia cringes whenever she sees Luke's face on the holocomm."

"I can do it," Kyp offered. "I'm used to making Leia cringe."

"That takes care of Maltoria," Corran said. "Now, what about the Bothan ar'krai? Alema's last report suggested that Reh'mwa and his fundamentalists had a line on Zonama Sekot's location.

They were provisioning the *Avengeance* for a scouting mission into the Unknown Regions."

A subtle eddy in the Force drew Luke's attention toward the entrance. He raised a hand to stop the discussion.

"Excuse me." He turned toward the foyer and immersed his mind completely in the Force until he recognized one of the presences coming toward them, then said, "Perhaps we should continue this later. We don't want Chief Omas to know how concerned we are about Jaina's departure."

"We don't?"

"No." Luke rose and started toward the door. "Especially not when he's bringing Chiss."

Luke stopped in the foyer area, where a simple wooden bench and two empty stone vases sat opposite the door, arranged to subtly calm visitors and make them feel welcome. Barely a moment passed before the door hissed open and a young apprentice came to a surprised halt directly in front of Luke.

"M-master S-skywalker!" the young Rodian stammered. He turned and raised a spindly-fingered hand toward the door. "Chief Omas and—"

"I know, Twool. Thank you."

Luke nudged the youth back into the corridor with the other apprentice, then stepped into the doorway and found himself looking at Chief of State Cal Omas and a trio of blue-skinned Chiss. With a wrinkled face and sagging jowls, the Chiss in front was probably the oldest Luke had ever seen. The two in the rear were clearly bodyguards—tall, strong, alert, and dressed in the black uniforms of the Chiss Expansionary Defense Fleet.

"Chief Omas," Luke said. The strains of Omas's office showed in his hollow cheeks and ashen complexion. "Welcome."

"You're expecting us." Omas cast a pointed glance into the conference room. "Good."

Luke ignored the hint and bowed to the elderly Chiss.

"And Aristocra . . ." It took a moment for the name to rise to the top of Omas's mind, where Luke could sense it without being overly intrusive. "Mitt'swe'kleoni. It's a pleasure to make your acquaintance."

The Chiss's red eyes narrowed to crimson lines. "Very impressive. It's not easy to gather identity files on Chiss aristocracy."

"We haven't." Luke smiled and continued to block the door. "You and your bodyguards are welcome to come inside, once you have removed your hidden weapons."

Omas cringed visibly, but Luke did not move. Even had he not perceived the concealed weapons through the Force, he still would have made the request. These *were* Chiss, after all.

"As you know," Luke continued, "the only weapons allowed in the Jedi Temple are lightsabers."

Mitt'swe'kleoni smiled like an old man caught sipping something against his doctor's orders, then pulled a small hold-out blaster from his boot and passed it to a bodyguard.

"My bodyguards will wait in the corridor," he said. "I can see they wouldn't be of much use in a room full of Jedi."

"There would be no need." Luke stepped aside and waved the two statesmen toward the conference circle. "Please join us."

As they crossed the room, Mitt'swe'kleoni kept sneaking glances at its appointments—the automated service kitchen, the small forest of rare trebala plants, the flowform chairs—and the arrogance vanished from his demeanor. It was not a reaction Luke liked to see. The new Temple had been a gift from the Galactic Alliance, pressed on the Jedi when—in a desperate attempt to manufacture a symbol of progress—the faltering Reconstruction Authority had moved the seat of government back to Coruscant. In most regards, the relocation had failed as spectacularly as it had deserved. But the Temple, a stone-and-transparisteel pyramid designed to harmonize with the new face of postwar Coruscant, never failed to impress with its regal scale and Rebirth architecture. It also served as a constant reminder to Luke of his greatest fear, that the Jedi would start to perceive themselves through the eyes of others and become little more than the guardians of a grateful Galactic Alliance.

At the conference area, the Jedi Masters rose to greet their guests.

"Everyone knows Chief Omas, I think." Luke motioned Omas into a chair, then took Mitt'swe'kleoni by the elbow and guided him into the sunken speaking circle. "This is Aristocra Mitt'swe'kleoni from the Chiss empire."

"Please use my core name, Tswek," the Aristocra instructed. "It will be much easier for you to pronounce correctly."

"Of course," Luke said, continuing to look at the council. "Tswek has some disturbing news for us, I believe."

Tswek's wrinkled brow rose, but he no longer seemed surprised by Luke's "intuition." "Then you know the purpose of my visit?"

"We can sense your apprehension through the Force," Luke said, avoiding a direct answer. "I assume it concerns our Jedi in the Unknown Regions."

"Indeed it does," he said. "The Chiss Ascendancy requires an explanation."

"An explanation?" Corran was not quite able to conceal his indignation. "Of what?"

Tswek pointedly ignored Corran and continued to stare at Luke.

"The Jedi have many voices, Aristocra," Luke said. "But we speak as one."

Tswek considered this a moment, then nodded. "Very well." He turned to Corran. "We demand an explanation of your actions, of course. What happens on our frontier is no concern of yours."

Despite the wave of confusion and doubt that rippled through the Force, the Jedi Masters remained outwardly composed.

"The *Chisz* frontier, Aristocra?" Saba Sebatyne, one of the newest Jedi Masters, asked.

"Of course." Tswek turned to the Barabel, his brow furrowed in thought. "You don't know what your Jedi Knights have been doing, do you?"

"All of our Jedi are well trained," Luke said to Tswek. "And the five under discussion are very experienced. We're confident they have good reason for any action they've undertaken."

A glint of suspicion showed in Tswek's crimson eyes. "So far, we have identified *seven* Jedi." He turned to Omas. "It appears I have no business here after all. Obviously, the Jedi involved in this matter are acting on their own."

"Involved in *what* matter?" Kyp asked.

"That is of no concern to the Galactic Alliance," Tswek said.

He bowed to the council at large. "My apologies for taking so much of your time."

"No apologies are necessary," Luke said. He considered dropping the name of Chaf'orm'bintrani, an Aristocra he and Mara had met on a mission some years earlier, but it was impossible to know how this would be received. Chiss politics were as volatile as they were secretive, and for all Luke knew Formbi's had been one of the five ruling families that had mysteriously disappeared while the rest of the galaxy fought the Yuuzhan Vong. "Anything in which our Jedi Knights involve themselves concerns this council."

"Then I suggest you do a better job supervising them in the future," Tswek said. When Luke did not step out of his way, he turned to Omas. "I'm quite finished here, Chief."

"Of course." Omas shot Luke a look imploring him to stand aside, then said, "An escort will meet you at the Temple entrance. I believe I need to have a word with these Jedi."

"In that case, I'll thank you for your hospitality now." Tswek bowed to the Chief, then started for the door. "I'll be returning to the Ascendancy within the hour."

Omas waited until the Aristocra was gone, then scowled at Luke. "Well?"

Luke spread his hands. "At this point, Chief Omas, you know more than we do."

"I was afraid of that," Omas growled. "Apparently, a team of Jedi have involved themselves in a border dispute with the Chiss."

"How can that be?" Mara asked. Luke knew that she meant the question literally. Before departing, Jaina had sent the council a set of destination coordinates that she and the others had calculated by triangulating the direction from which the mysterious call had come. An astronomical reconnaissance had revealed not even a star in the area, and certainly no indication that the coordinates would be of interest to the Chiss. "Their destination was over a hundred light-years from Ascendancy space."

"Then our Jedi *are* out there," Omas said. "What in the blazes for? We can't spare *one* Jedi at the moment, much less seven."

Mara's green eyes looked ready to loose a stream of blaster bolts. "*Our* Jedi, Chief Omas?"

"Forgive me." The Chief's voice was more placating than apologetic; Luke knew that, in his heart, Omas considered the Jedi as much servants of the Galactic Alliance as he was. "I didn't mean to imply anything."

"Of course not," Mara said, in a tone that suggested he had better be serious. She turned to the rest of the council. "Mitt'swe'kleoni said *seven* Jedi. What do we make of that?"

"This one only countz five." Saba lifted her hand and began to raise her taloned fingers. "Jaina, Alema, Zekk, Lowbacca, and Tesar."

Kyp added two fingers. "Tekli and Tahiri?"

Omas frowned. "How could you know that? I thought they were with Zonama Sekot in the Unknown Regions."

"They're supposed to be," Corran said. "But, like the others, they're also Myrkr survivors."

"I don't understand," Omas said. "What does this have to do with the Myrkr mission?"

"I wish we knew," Luke said. Undertaken in the middle of the war with the Yuuzhan Vong, the Myrkr mission had been as costly as it had been successful. Anakin Solo and his strike team had destroyed the enemy's Jedi-killing voxyn. But six young Jedi Knights had died in the process—including Anakin himself—and another was missing and presumed lost. "All I can tell you is that for several weeks, Jaina and the other survivors of that mission reported feeling a 'call' from the Unknown Regions. On the day they left, that call became a cry for help."

"And since we know Tenel Ka is still on Hapes," Mara explained, "it seems likely the extra Jedi are Tekli and Tahiri."

Nobody suggested that Jaina's brother, Jacen, might be one of the extras. The last anyone had heard, he had been somewhere on the far side of the galaxy, sequestered with the Fallanassi.

"What *about* Zonama Sekot?" Omas asked. Zonama Sekot was the living planet that had agreed to serve as home to the defeated Yuuzhan Vong. "Could the call have come from it?"

Luke shook his head. "Zonama Sekot would have contacted me directly if it needed our help. I'm convinced this has something to do with the mission to Myrkr."

Omas stayed silent, waiting for more of an explanation, but that was all Luke knew.

Instead, Luke asked, "What did Mitt'swe'kleoni tell you?"

Omas shrugged. "He demanded to know why the Galactic Alliance had sent its Jedi—*his* words—to interfere in a Chiss border dispute. When he saw how surprised I was, he demanded to speak to you."

"This is bad," Mara said. "Very bad."

"I agree," Omas said. "Either he thinks we're all lying—"

"Or he believez our Jedi Knightz have gone rogue," Saba finished. "In either case, the result will be the same."

"They'll try to solve the problem themselves," Omas said. He ran a hand through his thinning hair. "How hard will this be on them?"

"Our Jedi Knights can take care of themselves," Luke said.

"I know *that*!" Omas snapped. "I'm asking about the Chiss."

Luke felt Mara's ire rise, but she chose to overlook Omas's tone and remain silent. Now was a poor time to remind him that the Jedi did not expect to be addressed as though they were unruly subordinates.

"If the Chiss take action against them, Jaina and the others will attempt to defuse the situation . . . for a time," Luke said. "After that, it depends on the nature of the conflict."

"But they won't hesitate to meet force with force," Mara clarified. "Nor would we ask them to. If the Chiss push things, sooner or later Jaina is going to bloody their noses."

Omas paled and turned to Luke. "You need to put a stop to this, and soon. We can't let it come to killing."

Luke nodded. "We'll certainly send someone to—"

"No, I mean *you* personally." Omas turned to the others. "I know the Jedi have their own way of doing things. But with Jaina Solo leading those young Jedi Knights, Luke is the only one who can be sure of bringing them home. That young woman is as headstrong as her father."

For once, nobody argued.

TWO

A silver splinter shot across the *Falcon*'s bow, three kilometers ahead and hanging just below the clouds, then disappeared into a fog bank almost before Han Solo realized what he had seen.

"Did you see that?" As Han spoke, he kept both hands on the control yoke. With fangs of gray mist dangling beneath a low gray sky and spires of vine-covered yorik coral rising from a floor of undulating forest, Borao was a dangerous planet to map. Deadly, even. "What's another ship doing here? You told me this planet was abandoned."

"It is abandoned, dear." Leia glanced at the console in front of the copilot's seat, then shook her head in disgust at the static-filled array. "The sensors can't get a reading through these ionized clouds, but we *know* what kind of vessel that was."

"And you say *I* jump to conclusions!" Despite Han's protest, his heart was sinking. Since the Derelict Planet Reclamation Act had passed, there seemed to be more survey ships in the galaxy than stars. "It could have been a smuggler or a pirate, you know. A place like this would make a good hideout."

Leia studied her display screen for a moment, then shook her head. "Not a chance. Have a look."

The view from the stern vidcam appeared on his display, showing the knobby little cone of a Koensayr mapping skiff. It was in the middle of his screen, dead center.

"He's following us!"

"So it would seem," Leia answered. "The good news is he hasn't been there long, or I'd have seen him. With our long-range sensors blinded, I've had the exterior cam views rotating across my display."

"Good thinking." Han smiled at Leia's reflection in the cockpit canopy. She had thrown herself into her role as the *Falcon*'s second in command with the same devotion she brought to everything she did, and now a finer YT-1300 copilot could not be found anywhere. But there was an uneasy tension beneath her regal bearing, a restlessness in her big brown eyes that sometimes made the post seem too small for her. And Han understood. Any woman who had inspired a rebellion and shepherded a galactic government through its infancy might find life a little cramped aboard a tramp freighter—even if she had too much class to say so. "That's what I love about you."

Leia smiled brightly. "Smart as well as beautiful?"

Han shook his head. "You're a really good copilot." He pushed the throttles forward, and the forested ridges below began to flash past in a verdant blur. "Maximize the rear shields. Koensayr just delivered a fleet of armed mappers to RePlanetHab, so things might get rough."

Leia only stared at the throttles. "Han, what the blazes are you doing?"

"I'm tired of getting kicked around by these RePlanetHab pilots. It makes me look old."

"Don't be ridiculous," Leia said. "You're barely in your midsixties."

"That's my point," Han said. "Just because a guy goes a little gray at the temples, people think he's slowing down. They think they can push him around—"

"Han, nobody thinks you're slowing down." Leia's voice grew soft. "You have at least forty good years left. Maybe even fifty, if you take care of yourself."

A prim electronic voice sounded from the comm station behind Leia. "And may I point out how difficult it would be to see the gray in your hair from another vessel?" C-3PO leaned forward, pushing his golden head into Han's peripheral vision. "Whatever the reason other pilots have for thinking you've slowed down, sir, I'm quite sure your hair color has nothing to do with it."

"Thanks, Threepio," Han growled. "Maybe you ought to disconnect those vocabulator circuits before someone probes them with a plasma torch."

"A plasma torch!" C-3PO cried. "Why would anyone do that?"

Han ignored the droid and took the *Falcon* into a wisp of low-hanging cloud. Normally, he would have circled around it to avoid the small risk of hitting one of the strange spires the Yuuzhan Vong had left scattered across the planet. But that would have required a second mapping run around the other side, and they simply did not have the time—not if they wanted to beat these claim jumpers at their own game.

When the *Falcon* came out the other side without crashing into anything, their passenger gasped in relief and pushed his T-shaped head between the seats.

"Captain Solo, there is no sense placing your ship at risk." Ezam Nhor spoke with the mouths on both sides of his arched neck, giving his Ithorian voice a mournful stereo quality. "DPRA regulations state that when two parties file simultaneous claims, the Reconstruction Authority must give preference to the one with greater resources. My people do not have the means to match even a small rehabitation conglomerate, much less one like RePlanetHab."

"You're young, so maybe you don't know this," Han retorted. "But I don't usually obey regulations."

An uneasy wheeze shot from both sides of the Ithorian's throat.

Leia laid her hand over Han's. "Han, I hate losing to these world grabbers as much as you do, but Ezam is right. The Ithorians don't have—"

"Look, we can do this," Han said. A vast fog bank appeared on the horizon, its misty hem dragging in the treetops. "Borao isn't an easy world to map, and we have a big head start."

"And?"

"And the Reconstruction Authority has to log every claim it receives." Han eased the control yoke back and started to climb above the oncoming fog bank. Risking a small wisp of cloud was one thing, but even he would not fly blind through who-knew-how-many kilometers of dense fog. "If I can talk Lando into sponsoring us, we still have a chance. All we have to do is transmit our map first."

Leia remained silent.

"Okay, so it's a small chance," Han said. "But it's better than nothing. And it's not like we haven't bet on long-shots before."

"Han—"

"Besides, maybe Luke can swing us some support from Cal Omas," he added. "That would—"

"Han!" Leia laid her hand on his and pushed the control yoke forward again, ending their climb. "We don't have time to waste recalibrating the terrain scanners."

"Are you crazy?" He studied the atmosphere ahead with a nervous eye. "You are. You're crazy."

"I thought you wanted to win this thing?"

"I do," Han said. "And to do that, we need to stay alive."

"Captain Solo makes an excellent point," C-3PO said. "Without our sensors working properly, our chances of hitting an abandoned watchtower in those clouds are approximately—"

"Don't quote me odds, Threepio," Leia said. "I need to concentrate."

She focused her attention on the gray curtain ahead, and whorls of fog began to peel away from the center. Han started to make a wisecrack about having a weather-Jedi for a copilot, then recalled what Leia had said to C-3PO and thought better of it. Her training was still casual at best, and if she said she needed to concentrate, it was probably smart to believe her.

By the time they reached the fog bank, Leia had opened a long channel down the center—a very narrow channel, not much wider than the *Falcon* itself.

C-3PO's electronic voice split the tense silence. "Oh, my!"

"Quiet, Threepio!" Han barked. "Leia needs to concentrate."

"I'm aware of that, Captain Solo, but the route she is clearing has opened a small path through the ionic interference. We seem to be receiving an insystem comm transmission from Master Durron."

"Take a message," Han ordered. In the canopy reflection, he

saw a furrow crease Leia's brow, and blankets of fog started to spill back into the channel. "And stop bothering us!"

"I'm sorry, Captain Solo, that's quite impossible. The ionic interference seems to be returning, and our reception is too distorted for me to record. If you were to climb a few hundred meters, I could use the static scrubbers to enhance the signal."

"Not now!" The fog closed in completely. Unable to see past the end of the cockpit anyway, Han looked over to Leia. "If this is too much—"

"It's not too much, if you'll just leave me alone!" she snapped. "Do you want to win this thing or not?"

"All right. No need to get touchy."

Han turned his gaze forward, and the fog parted again.

"Much better," C-3PO said. "Thank you, Princess Leia. Master Durron seems quite upset."

Kyp's voice came over the comm speakers, scratchy and distorted. ". . . melt your circuits from the inside!"

"Take it easy, kid. You're on," Han said. "And this had better be good."

"When are you going to stop calling me kid?" Kyp asked.

"Soon," Han promised. "Look, we're kind of busy here, so if that's all you need to know—"

"Sorry," Kyp said. "I wish this could wait, but I'm only passing through on my way to Ramodi."

"The baradium ring?" Han asked. "I thought Tesar Sebatyne was supposed to handle that."

"*Supposed to* is right." Kyp paused a moment. "Something came up."

"Bigger than smuggling baradium?"

"Hard to say," Kyp said. "When you're done here, the council needs you and Leia to take over in the Maltorian system."

"Nice of them to ask," Han grumbled into the comm mike.

"That's what I'm doing now," Kyp said. "The council doesn't give orders—especially to you two."

"Could've fooled me," Han said. "What happened to Zekk? Is he okay?"

There was a long pause, and Han thought they might have lost the signal.

"Kyp?"

"Zekk's fine," Kyp said. "But something came up, and he had to leave."

Alarms started to go off inside Han's head. Jaina had told them about the mysterious call that she and the other strike team members had been feeling from the Unknown Regions.

"Listen"—Kyp's voice crackled over the comm—"we didn't want to ask you again, but this is important. RePlanetHab is about ready to start paying Three-Eye off."

"I'll have to talk it over with Leia." Given who was currently trying to steal Borao out from beneath them, Han was not sure either one of them would be eager to help RePlanetHab with its pirate problem. "Redstar's tribunal ought to be just about over, and we were hoping to catch up with Jaina for a few days before she goes out again."

There was another long silence, and this time Han decided to wait Kyp out. A blurry sliver of green murk appeared at the end of the fog channel that Leia was holding open. Her gaze remained dead ahead. Han hoped that she was actually seeing; that she had not sunk so deeply into her trance, she would fail to notice the hazy stripe of darkness ahead.

Finally, Kyp said, "Uh, seeing Jaina might be a problem."

"Don't tell me," Han said. "Something came up." The hazy strip ahead thickened into a sharp, distinct streak. "Something in the Unknown Regions, I'll bet."

"Well . . . yes."

"Thanks for letting us know," Han snorted. Normally, he tried not to worry about Jaina's assignments. As a top fighter pilot and leading Jedi Knight, his daughter could handle almost anything the galaxy threw her way. But the Unknown Regions were different. The Unknown Regions were home to a hundred terrors too terrible to imagine—or so he had been told. "What's the situation?"

"We don't know, exactly," Kyp said. "But there's no reason to worry. Master Skywalker has taken Mara and Saba to investigate."

Now Han *was* worried. To draw three Masters away when the Jedi were already spread too thin, the problem had to be serious.

"All right, kid," Han said. The dark streak at the end of the fog channel had grown sharp enough to identify as a yorik coral spire. "What *aren't* you telling us?"

"Nothing."

Han remained silent, and finally Kyp asked, "Did I mention the Chiss?"

To Leia's credit, she did not look away from the forward viewport—but she did lose her concentration. The fog came rolling back into the channel ahead of the *Falcon,* and Han lost sight of the spire. He jerked back on the throttles . . . then felt a sudden stab of neck pain as something slammed the ship forward. A cacophony of damage alarms erupted from the control console. Han's gaze flew to the status lights of the most critical systems.

"What was that?" Nhor asked from behind him. "Did we crash?"

"Not exactly," Han answered. Over the comm, he said, "Stand by, kid. We're a little distracted here."

"Copy." Kyp sounded relieved to have a few moments to formulate his explanation. "Take your time."

Once Han had confirmed that all vital components were still operational, he called up the view from the stern vidcam and saw nothing but static.

"Something hit us from behind."

"The mapping skiff?" Leia asked.

"It *was* following us," Han said. "I hate that."

"Oh, dear," C-3PO said. "I hope there aren't any casualties!"

"It would serve them right," Han growled. He activated the intercom and ordered Leia's Noghri bodyguards, Cakhmaim and Meewalh, into the cannon turrets. "Don't shoot anything. Just tell me what you see back there."

Han glanced over at Leia and saw by the tension in her lips that she had heard every word of the conversation between him and Kyp. He closed the intercom, then returned to his comm mike.

"Okay, kid. Tell us about the Chiss."

"It's not as bad as it sounds." Kyp told them about Aristocra Tswek's visit and Cal Omas's "suggestion" that Luke handle the matter personally, and then said, "Master Skywalker knew you'd be worried, so he asked Cilghal to fill you in when you asked for the Maltorian dossier. I really wasn't—"

The *Falcon* shuddered, and another damage alarm sounded. Cakhmaim reported that, despite its damage, the mapping skiff was firing at them.

"Then shoot back!" Han ordered. "Kyp, you'll have to—"

"Standing by," Kyp acknowledged. "Be careful."

"I've got a better idea." Han pushed the throttles forward and accelerated into the fog, then asked Leia, "Can you do that fog thing again?"

"Yes," Leia said. A low rumble reverberated through the *Falcon* as Meewalh and Cakhmaim unleashed the big laser cannons. "But why not climb out of here and fight where we can see?"

Han allowed himself a sly grin. "Didn't you see that spire up ahead?"

"I saw it," Leia said. A smile as sly as Han's came to her lips. "I like the way you think, flyboy."

"How does he think?" Nhor asked. "What are we doing?"

"You'll see," Han said. "Just hold on."

Leia turned her attention back to the fog, and soon the verdant finger of a vine-covered spire could be seen jutting up at the end of the channel. If Han did not break until the last second, the mapping skiff following them would have no time to avoid a crash.

Nhor finally saw what they were planning.

"No!" He shrieked the word with both mouths. "You mustn't! Tell your gunners to stop firing!"

"Stop firing?" Han repeated. The spire was as wide as his hand now, and he was beginning to see dark patches of coral showing through the curtains of vine. "Are you crazy? They're shooting at *us*."

"It doesn't matter." Nhor's voice remained shrill with panic. "My people could never inhabit a planet won through murder."

"It's not murder," Han objected. "They started this. We're just defending ourselves."

"There is a difference between defending and killing," Nhor said.

Han began to grow impatient. "Look, if that's the way you feel, the Ithorians are never going to find a planet." The spire had grown as large as his arm; another five seconds, and the mapping skiff wouldn't have a chance. "In this galaxy, you've got to fight for what you need."

"My people believe there has been too much fighting already." Nhor paused, then said, "This isn't your choice to make, Captain Solo. If you kill our rivals, the Ithorians will not come anyway."

"Han, Ezam's right," Leia said. Her gaze remained fixed on the fog, but she reached over and gently clasped his arm. "We just can't win this one."

Han could hear in the edginess of Leia's voice that she wanted to keep going as much as he did. The war had made both of them harder—less forgiving and more determined to win at any price—and sometimes that made him wonder if the Yuuzhan Vong had won after all. Certainly, they had changed more in the galaxy than a few thousand planets.

"Okay." Han pulled the control yoke back, and the *Falcon* began to climb free of Borao's clouds. "The world grabbers win again."

"Sorry to hear that," Kyp said over the comm. "But you'll have a freer rein in the Maltorian belt. There are no gray areas with Three-Eye."

"Not so fast, kid. We haven't said we're going."

"But Jaina—"

"Is in the Unknown Regions," Han said. "That's the point. Give us a second."

Leia muted the comm mikes, then asked, "What are you thinking?"

"You *know* what I'm thinking," Han said. Though he would never have said so, Han wished he had gone after Anakin to Myrkr. He knew it would have made no difference and maybe even gotten them both killed, but he still wished he had tried. "You're thinking the same thing."

"I suppose I am." Leia sighed. "You know there's no sense going after them."

"Them?" Han asked. "Jaina and Lowie and—"

"And Jacen." Leia's eyes were closed, and her face was raised toward the stars. "It feels like he's on the move, too."

"*Another* reason to go," Han said. "Five years is too long."

"You know we'd just be going for ourselves," Leia said. "Our kids are better at this sort of thing than we are now."

"Yeah," Han said. "But what else do we have to do? Stick our necks out for RePlanetHab? Look for another abandoned planet just so they can steal it out from under the Ithorians?"

Leia closed her eyes, perhaps reaching out to their children through the Force, or maybe only searching her own heart for guidance. Finally, she opened her eyes again and reactivated the channel.

"Sorry, Kyp, we can't help you," she said. "Han and I have other plans."

THREE

The unknown object lay directly ahead of *Jade Shadow,* a crooked oval of darkness the size of a human thumb. Sensor readings suggested a body about as dense as ice, which would have been a rare—though not impossible—thing to find floating around loose in the interstellar void. But infrared measurements placed the core temperature at somewhere between warm and sweltering, and the spectrograph showed a halo of escaped atmosphere that suggested living inhabitants.

Mara had already sensed as much through the Force. She could feel a strange presence within the object, diffuse and ancient and utterly huge. There were also other, more familiar lifeforms—smaller, distinct, and somehow enclosed within the haze of the larger being. But there was no hint of Jaina or the other strike team members, nor of the urgent summons they had reported from these coordinates.

Mara glanced at an activation reticle in the front of the cockpit. A small section of the *Shadow*'s plexalloy canopy opaqued into a mirror, and she turned her attention to Luke and Saba Sebatyne, who were seated high behind her in the copilot's and navigator's chairs.

"Time to reconnoiter?" she asked.

"What's reckon . . . recoin . . . wreckoy . . . ?" The question came from behind Luke's chair, where a freckle-faced boy with red hair and fiery blue eyes stood peering around the edge of the flight deck hatchway. "What's that?"

"*Reconnoiter,* Ben. It means take a look." A smile came to

Mara's heart at the sight of her son, but she forced a stern tone. "Aren't you supposed to be playing with Nanna?"

"Nanna's game module is for little kids," he complained. "She was trying to make me play Teeks and Ewoks."

"And why aren't you?" Luke asked.

"I turned her off."

"How?" Mara asked. "Her power switch is hidden under her neck armor."

Ben looked away as casually as a young boy could. "I tricked her into bending down and showing it to me."

"Turning Nanna off wasn't very nice," Mara said. "Her circuits are pulse-shielded. How do you think she's going to feel after an emergency shutdown?"

"Stupid." Ben's answer was almost gleeful. "I've only done it to her three times before."

A loud siss of amusement escaped the pebbled lips of Saba Sebatyne, causing Ben to shrink back through the hatchway—and almost muffling Luke's exclamation of alarm. "You have?"

Ben nodded, but his wide eyes remained fixed on Saba's lumpy face. Luke reached around the corner and pulled him onto the flight deck itself.

"Promise me you won't do that again," Luke said. Mara could feel how worried he was by Ben's mischievousness. They had long ago decided against having someone else raise their son while they crisscrossed the galaxy attending to their duties as Jedi Masters, but they both knew their choice would require an extraordinary amount of discipline from their young son. "Nanna can't protect you if you shut her down."

"If she's that stupid, how can she protect me anyway?" Ben countered. "A Defender Droid's not supposed to be dumber than her kid."

Rather than explaining the complexities of utter-devotion programming, Mara said, "Ben, answer your father. Or would you rather stay at the academy next time he and I go on a trip?"

Ben pondered his decision for a moment, then blew out a long breath. "Fine." He turned to Luke. "I promise."

"Good," Luke said. "Maybe you should go reactivate her."

"But we're *there*!" Ben pointed out the forward viewport,

where the unknown object remained hidden in its darkness. "I want to see Jaina!"

"Jaina isn't here anymore," Mara said.

"How do you know?"

"The Force," Mara explained. "If she were here, your father and I would feel it."

"Maybe not. You don't feel everything."

"We would feel Jaina," Luke said. "She's not here."

"Now do as your father says." Mara hooked her thumb toward the main cabin. "Go power up Nanna and stay with her until we figure out where Jaina is."

Ben didn't argue, but neither did he turn to go.

"If Ben doesn't wish to go, this one will watch him." Saba spun her chair around and winked a slit-pupiled eye at him. "He can sit on her lap."

Eyes widening, Ben spun on his heel and disappeared down the access corridor. Saba sissed in amusement, but softly and slow, and Mara thought maybe the Barabel's feelings were hurt. Maybe.

"Don't let it bother you, Saba," Mara said. "Even we don't understand what's happening with him these days."

Saba blinked at Mara's reflection—twice. "He is hiding from the Force," she said. "This one is surprised you and Master Sky-walker have not noticed."

"We have," Luke said. "What we don't understand is why. He started to close himself off after the war."

"Ben says he wants to be like his uncle Han and do things the hard way," Mara added. "But I think there's more to it than that. This has lasted too long to be a phase."

Mara did not add *and he's gotten too good at it,* perhaps because of how much that thought frightened her. She had to concentrate hard and long to find the Force in her son, and sometimes Luke had trouble sensing Ben's presence at all.

"Interesting." Saba licked the air with her long tongue, then turned to look down the access corridor. "Perhapz he did not like how the war felt."

"Perhaps not," Luke said. "We tried to shield him from it, but it just wasn't possible."

"There was too much happening in the galaxy," Mara said, surprised to find herself feeling almost defensive. "The Force was too filled with anguish."

"And so were we," Luke said. "That's what really worries us, Saba . . . maybe he's hiding from *us*."

"Then you have nothing to worry about," Saba said. "Ben will not hide from you forever. Even this one can see how attached he is to his parentz."

Luke thanked her for the reassurance, then asked R2-D2 to bring up an infrared image of the unknown object. What looked like a collection of palpitating blood cells appeared on Mara's display screen. Each cell had an irregular white heart surrounded by a pink halo, and they were all connected by a tangled web of flowing red dashes.

"It looks like a network of housing modules," Mara observed.

"And it feelz like a rangi mountain," Saba added.

"Now we're getting somewhere," Luke said. "By the way, what *are* rangies?"

"Very tasty—and the feeling is mutual!" Sissing hysterically, Saba rose and turned to leave the flight deck. "This one will take the StealthX and reconnoiter."

"Better hold tight," Mara said. On the infrared display, a string of tiny white circles was flaring to life near the center of the unknown object. "At least until we know what those are."

The circles began to swirl and grow larger. Mara didn't even try to count the number, but there had to be over a hundred of them. More tiny circles blazed into existence and shot after the others. She initiated a series of automated systems checks to warm the *Shadow*'s battle circuits.

"Lower—"

The *Shadow*'s retractable laser cannons dropped into firing position as Luke anticipated Mara's order. She armed the proton torpedoes and opened the firing-tube doors.

"Artoo, tell Nanna to put Ben in his crash couch," Luke ordered.

R2-D2 tweetled a protest.

"Nobody said they *were* shooting," Luke said. "We just want to be ready."

R2-D2 added another warning.

"Really?" Luke responded. "That many?"

Mara glanced at the corner of her display and saw a counter quickly adding numbers.

"Five hundred?" she gasped. "Who sends five hundred craft to investigate one intruder?"

R2-D2 chirped testily, then Mara's screen displayed a message telling her to have some patience. He was still trying to assemble vessel profiles. Identifying who had sent them would have to wait.

"Sorry," Mara said, wondering when she had started to be intimidated by astromech droids. "Take your time."

R2-D2 acknowledged, then added a note about the propulsion systems the vessels were using.

"Rockets?" Luke asked in disbelief. "As in old nuclear rockets?"

R2-D2 tweeted irritably. The note on Mara's display read, *Chemical rockets. Methane/oxygen, specific impulse 380.*

Luke whistled at the low number. "At least we can run, if we have to."

"Jedi?" Saba began to siss again. "Run?"

The image on Mara's display melded into a single infrared blob. She looked up and saw a small cloud of twinkling stars between the *Shadow* and the unknown object. As she watched, the swirling cloud grew steadily larger and brighter. Soon the stars resolved into two parts, yellow slivers of rocket exhaust and brilliant green bursts that looked a lot like strobe beacons.

Mara engaged the ion drive actuator. "Does this make sense to *anyone*?" She began to turn, giving the *Shadow* some running room. "With all that evasive maneuvering, that *has* to be a combat—"

R2-D2 began to whistle and trill urgently.

Mara checked her display, then asked, "What old blink code?"

R2-D2 buzzed in impatience.

"Imperial?" Mara looked out the side of the canopy. The swarm had drawn close enough now to reveal the sleek, dart-shaped hulls of a small fighter craft stretched between the green

nose strobes and the yellow rocket tails. In the closest vessel, she could barely make out a pair of curved antennae pressed against the interior of a low cockpit canopy, and there were two bulbous black eyes peering out at her. "As in *Palpatine's* Empire?"

R2-D2 squawked a peevish affirmative.

"Then tell us what they're saying," Luke ordered. "And stop talking to Mara that way."

R2-D2 warbled a halfhearted apology, then the message appeared on Mara's display.

Lizil welcomes you . . . Please all arrivals may please enter through the central portal please.

FOUR

The nearer the *Falcon* drew to her destination, the more mystified Leia became. The thumb-sized oval of darkness they had found when they emerged from hyperspace—at the coordinates they had wheeled out of Corran Horn, who was supervising operations in Luke's absence—was now a wall of murk that stretched to all edges of the cockpit canopy. But the terrain scanners showed a jumble of asteroids, iceballs, and dustbergs ranging from a hundred meters across to several thousand, all held together by a web of metal struts and stony tubes. Though the structure had not yet collapsed under its own gravity, a rough guess of its mass was enough to make Leia worry.

The *Falcon*'s escorts—a swarm of small dartships being flown by *something* with antennae and big, bulbous eyes—suddenly peeled off and dispersed into the surrounding darkness. A jagged array of lights came to life ahead, hooking along its length toward a single golden light at the end.

"That must be the guidance signal the dartships told us to watch for," Leia said. The terrain schematic on her display showed the lights curving over the horizon of a small carbonaceous asteroid located on the cluster's outer edge. "Follow the amber light. And slow down—it could be dangerous in there."

"In where?"

Leia sent a duplicate of the terrain schematic to the pilot's display. Han decelerated so hard that even the inertial compensators could not keep her from being pitched into her crash webbing.

"You sure about this?" he asked. "It looks about as safe as a rancor's throat down there."

The image on their displays was that of a jagged five-kilometer mouth surrounded by a broken rim of asteroids, with dark masses of dust and stone tumbling down into the opening in lazy slow motion. Though the scanner's view extended only two thousand meters into the chasm, the part it did show was a twisted, narrowing shaft lined by craggy protrusions and dark voids.

"I'm sure." Leia could feel her brother's presence somewhere deep inside the jumble of asteroids, calm, cheerful, and curious. "Luke knows we're here. He wants us to come in."

"Really?" Han turned the *Falcon* toward the lights and started forward. "What'd we ever do to *him*?"

As they passed over the array, Leia began to catch glimpses of a black, grainy surface carefully cleared of the dark dust that usually lay meters thick on carbonaceous asteroids. Once, she thought she saw something scuttling across a circle of light, but Han was keeping them too far above the asteroid to be certain, and it would have been too dangerous to ask him to go in for a closer look. She trained a vidcam on the surface and tried to magnify the image, but the shaft was too dusty and dark for a clear picture. All she saw was a screenful of gray grains not too different from sensor static.

They were barely past the first array when two more came to life, beckoning the *Falcon* deeper into the abyss. The ship bucked as Han avoided—only half successfully—a tumbling dustberg, then a frightened hiss escaped Leia's lips as the jagged silhouettes of two small boulders began to swell in the forward viewport.

"Don't sit there hissing." Han's gaze remained fixed on his display, where the resolution of the terrain schematic was not fine enough to show the two objects. "Tell me what's wrong."

"There!" Leia pointed out the viewport. "Right there!"

Han looked up from his display.

"All right, no need to get all worried." He calmly flipped the *Falcon* on her side and slipped between the two boulders an instant before the pair came together, then went back to watching his display. "I had my eye on them."

Han's voice was so cocky and sure that Leia forgot for a moment that this was not the same brash smuggler who had been running her defenses since she was still fighting the Empire— the man whose lopsided grins and well-timed barbs could still raise in her a ruddy cloud of passion or a red fog of anger. He was wiser now, and sadder, maybe a little less likely to hide his goodwill behind a cynical exterior.

"Whatever you say, flyboy." Leia pointed at the light arrays, the ones she had decided would be too dangerous to investigate. "I want to do a close pass on one of those."

Han's eyes widened. "What for?"

"To see what kind of technology we're dealing with here." Leia put on a flirtatious pout, then asked in an innocent voice, "That isn't too risky for you, is it?"

"For me?" Han licked his lips. "No way."

Leia smiled and, as Han angled toward the array, shunted extra power to the particle shields. Maybe the challenge of nap-of-terrain flying down a dark, twisting shaft filled with flotsam would help snap Han out of his touchy mood.

Han weaved past a dozen obstacles, working their way across the abyss toward the second array of lights . . . and that was when C-3PO, returning from a postjump hyperdrive check, arrived on the flight deck.

"We're crashing!"

"Not yet," Han growled.

"Everything's under control, Threepio." Leia's attention was focused on the asteroid ahead, where the lights had begun a slow flashing as the *Falcon* approached. "Why don't you go back and continue supervising the maintenance checks?"

"I couldn't possibly, Princess Leia!" C-3PO placed himself in the navigator's chair behind Han. "You need me in the cockpit."

Han started to reply, but stopped when a ball of frozen gas came floating across the *Falcon*'s path.

"You see?" C-3PO demanded. "Captain Solo nearly missed that object!"

"I *did* miss it," Han snapped. "Otherwise you'd be plastered across the canopy right now."

"What I meant was that you failed to see it until the last moment," C-3PO explained. "Do be careful—there's a rather large one coming toward us from forty-seven point six-six-eight—"

"Quiet!" Han swung around an oblong megalith the size of a heavy cruiser, then added, "You're distracting me."

"Then perhaps you should have your synapses checked," C-3PO suggested. "Slow processing time is indicative of aging circuits. There's another object at thirty-two point eight-seven-eight degrees, inclination five point—"

"Threepio!" Leia spun around to glare at him. "We don't need help. Go to the main cabin and shut down."

C-3PO's chin dropped. "As you wish, Princess Leia." He stood and half turned toward the exit. "I was only trying to help. Captain Solo's last medical evaluation showed a reaction time decrease of eight milliseconds, and I myself have noticed—"

Leia unbuckled her crash webbing.

"—that he seems to be growing—"

She rose and hit the droid's circuit breaker.

"—rather hesiii t a a a."

The sentence trailed off into a bass rumble as C-3PO lost power.

"I think it's time to get his compliance routines debugged." She pushed the droid into the seat in front of the navigation station and strapped him in. "He seems to be developing a persistence glitch."

"No need." The *Falcon* shot to the right, then shuddered as a dustberg burst against its shields. "Nobody listens to droids anyway."

"Right—what does Threepio know?" Leia kissed Han on the neck, then returned to her own seat.

"Yeah." Han smiled the same hungry grin that had been making Leia's stomach flutter since Palpatine was Emperor.

Han swung the *Falcon* in behind the lights and began a steep approach toward the surface. The array began to flash more brightly, illuminating the rough, silvery surface of a metallic asteroid. On the ground behind the first beacon, Leia saw the swirling lines of a closed iris hatch, made from some tough membrane that bulged slightly outward under the pressure of the asteroid's internal atmosphere. The light itself was held aloft on the end of a conical, meter-long stand that seemed to be crawling across the surface of the asteroid on six stick-like legs. At the forward end of the apparatus, the lenses of a large ovoid helmet reflected the glow of the next beacon in line.

"Bugs!" Han groaned and shook his head. "Why did it have to be bugs?"

"Sorry," Leia said. Han normally avoided insect nests—something to do with a water religion he had once started on the desert world of Kamar. Apparently, a mob of angry Kamarian insects had tracked him down months after his hasty departure, taking him captive and demanding that he turn Kamar into the water paradise he had shown them. That was all Leia knew about the incident. He refused to talk about how he had escaped. "It'll be okay. Luke seems to feel comfortable with them."

"Yeah, well, I always knew the guy was a little strange."

"Han, we have to go in," Leia said. "This is where Jaina and the others came."

"I know," Han said. "That's what *really* gives me the creeps."

They reached the end of the array and passed over the insect holding aloft the amber light; then Leia glimpsed a second iris hatch and they left the asteroid behind. Far ahead, spiraling down the walls of the ever-narrowing passage, three more beacon lines flared to life. Han stayed close to the walls, showing off for Leia by following the contour of the conglomeration's unpredictable topography.

After a time, the arrays began to grow hazy and indistinct as the dust, being slowly drawn inward by the conglomeration's weak gravity, thickened into a gray cloud. Han continued to hug the wall, though now it was to make it easier for the terrain scanner to penetrate the powdery fog.

A nebulous disk of golden light appeared at the bottom of the shaft. As its glow brightened, Leia began to see meter-long figures in insect-shaped pressure suits working along the passage walls, dragging huge bundles across asteroid surfaces, repairing the stony tubes that held the jumbled structure together, or simply standing in a shallow basin and staring out at her from behind a transparent membrane.

"You know, Han," she said, "this place is starting to give *me* the creeps."

"Wait till you hear a pincer rap," Han said. "Those things will really ice your spine."

"Pincer rap?" Leia glanced over at the pilot's seat, wondering if there was something Han wasn't telling her. "Han, do you recognize—"

Han cut her off. "No—I'm just saying . . ." He raised his shoulders and shuddered at some memory he had kept buried their entire married life, then finished, "It's not something you want to experience. That's all."

The dust cloud finally began to thin, revealing the disk of light below to be a bulging hatch membrane more than a hundred meters across. Several dozen insects were scuttling away from the middle of the hatch, oozing a thick layer of greenish gel from a valve at the rear of their pressure suits. Han eased back on the throttles, then—when the portal showed no sign of opening—brought them to a stop twenty meters above the center.

The insects reached the edge and turned around, the lenses of their dark helmets turned up toward the *Falcon.* Soon, the gel began to bleed off in green wisps.

"What are they waiting for?" Han turned his palms up and gestured impatiently. "Open already!"

Once the gel had evaporated, the insects returned to the center of the portal and began to mill about aimlessly.

"Is there *anything* on the comm channels?" Han asked.

Leia double-checked the channel scanner. "Only background static—and not much of that." She did not suggest trying to comm the *Shadow.* Some insect species were sensitive to comm waves, a fact that had led to some tragic misunderstandings in the early days of contact between the Verpine and the rest of the galaxy. "I could wake Threepio. He might be able to tell us something about who we're dealing with here."

Han sighed. "Do we have another choice?"

"We could sit here and wait for something to happen."

"No," Han said, shaking his head wearily. "You can't outwait a bug."

Leia rose and flipped the droid's circuit breaker. After the light had returned to his photoreceptors, he sat turning his head back and forth as he calibrated himself to his surroundings, then finally fixed his gaze on Leia.

"I *do* wish you would stop doing that, Princess Leia. It's most disorientating, and one of these times my file allocation table will be corrupted. I could lose track of my personality!"

"Wouldn't that be too bad," Han replied.

"Threepio, we need your help," Leia said, allowing the droid no time to process Han's sarcasm. "We're having trouble communicating with the indigenous species."

"Certainly!" C-3PO responded cheerily. "As I was saying before you debilitated me, I'm always happy to help. And you are certainly aware that I'm fluent in—"

"Over six million—we know," Han interrupted. He pointed outside. "Just tell us how to communicate with the bugs."

"Bugs?" C-3PO stood and turned toward the roiling mass of insects. "I don't believe those are bugs, Captain Solo. They appear to be a sentient hybrid of coleoptera and hymenoptera, which often use complex dances as a means of communication."

"Dances? You don't say!" Han returned his hands to the control yoke and throttle. "So what are they telling us?"

C-3PO studied the insects for a moment, then emitted a nervous gurgle and moved forward to the control console.

"Well?" Han demanded.

"How odd." C-3PO continued to study the creatures. "I have no record of this happening before."

"Of *what* happening?" Leia stepped to the droid's side. "What are they saying?"

"I'm afraid I can't tell you, Princess Leia." C-3PO kept his photoreceptors focused below her eyes. "I have no idea."

"What do you mean, *no idea*?" Han demanded. "You're always bragging about how many forms of communication you're fluent in!"

"That's quite impossible, Captain Solo. Droids are incapable of bragging." C-3PO returned his attention to Leia. "As I was explaining, my memory banks contain no record of this particular language. However, syntactic analyses, step comparisons, and pattern searches do suggest that this is, indeed, a language."

"You're sure?" Leia asked. "It couldn't be random wandering?"

"Oh no, Mistress Leia. The pattern and period of circulation bear a statistical correspondence that is quite significant, and the recurring oblique head bobs suggest a syntax far more sophisticated than Basic—or even Shyriiwook." C-3PO turned back to the viewport. "I'm quite sure of my conclusions."

"Then let's hear 'em," Han demanded. "Who are these guys?"

"That's what I'm trying to explain, Captain Solo," C-3PO said. "I don't know."

They all fell quiet, C-3PO carefully documenting the mysterious dance while Leia and Han tried to see how this fit into the mystery of why the survivors of the Myrkr mission had been summoned here. None of it made any sense. It seemed almost impossible that the insects could have any tie to the Myrkr strike team. And even Leia could feel that they were not strong enough in the Force to send the call Jaina and the others had reported.

C-3PO suddenly stepped away from the canopy. "I've identified the basic syntactical unit! It's really quite simple, a matter of positioning the abdomen at one of three levels to indicate whether a step is—"

"Threepio!" Han interrupted. "Can you tell us why they're not opening the door?"

C-3PO tipped his head slightly. "Why, no, Captain Solo. To do that, I'd have to understand what they're saying."

Han groaned. "What's wrong with the Imperial blink code those dartships were using?"

"Unfortunately, their pressure suits don't seem to be equipped with strobes," C-3PO explained. "But I *am* making progress with their dance-language. For instance, I've established that they're repeating the same message time after time."

"*Exactly* the same message?" Leia asked.

"Of course," C-3PO said. "Otherwise, I would have said similar—"

"Long or short?"

"That's quite impossible to say," C-3PO said. "Until I can establish the average number of units it requires to express one concept—"

"How long does it take to repeat the message?" Leia peered out at the bulging hatch, studying its membranous segments. "Seconds? Minutes?"

"Three point five-four seconds, on average," C-3PO said. "But without a context, that datum is entirely worthless."

"Not *entirely* worthless." Leia returned to the copilot's seat. "Edge us ahead, Han. I want to see something."

As Han complied, Leia stared out at the bulging hatch, looking for any flaw in her thinking. The insects suddenly arranged themselves in the center of the membrane, then started to scuttle toward the edge and ooze green gel again.

"Keep going," Leia said. "I know what they've been saying."

"That's quite unlikely!" C-3PO objected. "Even I don't have enough data to establish a grammar—much less attempt an accurate translation."

Instead of arguing, Leia reached for the glide switches that controlled the *Falcon*'s shields. Han eyed her hand warily, but continued forward. When the hatch began to bow inward, Leia lowered the shields, and a moment later the flexible membrane was sucked tight against the *Falcon* by the external vacuum.

Han let out a breath, then said to Leia, "Good call."

"Yes, Princess Leia, it was quite an extraordinary translation." C-3PO sounded crushed. "In how many forms of communication did you say you are fluent?"

FIVE

Luke felt as though he had swallowed a jug of minnows. Ben had turned an alarming hue of green. Mara, who could normally whirl-dance for hours in weak gravity, held her jaws clamped tight against the possibility of an embarrassing eruption. The Skywalkers were hardly micro-g novices, but their stomachs were rebelling at the utter *strangeness* of the asteroid colony— at the sticky gold wax that lined the corridors, at the constant thrum of insect sounds, at the endless parade of six-limbed, meter-high workers scurrying past on the walls and ceiling.

Saba, however, seemed entirely comfortable. She was moving along in front, trotting along a wall on all fours, her head swinging from side to side and her long tongue licking the sweet air. Luke suspected that the heat and mugginess reminded her of Barab I, but maybe she just liked the way her hands and feet squished into the corridor's wax lining. Barabels, he had noticed, took pleasure in the oddest things.

They came to a cockeyed intersection, and Luke stopped to listen to a strange pulsing sound that was rumbling out of a crooked side tunnel. It was muted, eerie, and rasping, but there was a definite melody and rhythm.

"Music," he said.

"If you're from Tatooine, maybe," Mara said. "The rest of us would call that a rancor belch."

"This one likez it," Saba said. "It makez her tail shake."

"I've seen squeaky thrust impellers make your tail shake," Mara said. She pointed at the floor, where a steady flow of booted feet had worn the wax down to the stone. "But it is popular. Let's check it out."

They started up the passage, and Ben asked, "Is this where Jaina is?"

"No," Luke said. Ben had been repeating the same question since they had emerged from hyperspace. "I told you, she's not in the asteroid colony."

"Then where is she?"

"We don't know." Luke looked over his shoulder at Ben. "That's what we're trying to find out."

Ben considered this a moment, then said, "If you don't know where she's at, then maybe she *is* here, and maybe you just don't know it."

This sent Saba into a fit of sissing. "He has you there, Master Skywalker."

Ben retreated behind his mother, and Luke found himself worrying about the boy's strange fear of Saba. They had made a point of exposing him to friends of many species early in his life, and only Saba still seemed to frighten him.

Luke smiled patiently, then explained, "Ben, if Jaina were here, I would feel her in the Force."

"Oh."

Surprised that Ben was willing to drop the matter with that, Luke added, "But I do feel Aunt Leia. She's here with Uncle Han."

Saba stopped on the wall ahead and peered back down at Luke. "The Soloz are *here*? This one thought they were going to hunt Three-Eye."

"So did this one." Luke could not quite keep the displeasure out of his voice. "Apparently, they decided it was more important to join us."

"And they have every right," Mara said. "*We've* seen Jaina more than they have in the past year, and with Jacen still off chasing Force-lore . . . Han and Leia must be lonely." She ruffled Ben's hair. "I would be."

"I know," Luke said, feeling guilty now for his irritation. He had grown so accustomed to everyone doing as the council asked that he tended to forget that it had no formal authority;

everyone—especially the Solos—served at their own pleasure. "They've already done more than we have a right to ask."

"And what of Three-Eye?" Saba asked. "Who will stop her?"

"It might not be a bad thing to let the Reconstruction Police handle that one until we find Jaina," Luke said. "After that, the council can send her and Alema back with Zekk. It shouldn't take the three of them long to clean up the problem."

"*If* they will go." Saba continued up the corridor shaking her head. "This one is beginning to doubt the wisdom of our council. Every pack needz a longfang, or itz hunters will scatter after their own prey."

"The Jedi are a different kind of pack," Luke said, following after her. "We're an entire pack of longfangs."

"A *pack* of longfangz?" Saba let out a trio of short sisses and disappeared around a bend. "Oh, Master Skywalker . . ."

As they continued up the passage, the music grew clearer. There was an erratic chirping that struck Luke as singing, a rhythmic grating that passed for percussion, a harsh fluting that provided the melody. The overall effect was surprisingly buoyant, and Luke soon found himself enjoying it.

After about fifty meters, the passage opened into a cavernous, dimly lit chamber filled with rough-looking spacers. The music came from a clear area in the center of the room, where a trio of stick-like Verpine stood playing beneath the chemical glow of a dozen waxy shine-balls. Luke found himself studying their instrument, trying to imagine how they made so many different sounds sharing only one string.

"Astral!" Ben left Mara's side and started into the cantina. "This is gonna blast!"

Mara caught him by the shoulder. "Not a chance."

He gave her a knowing smirk, for they had left Nanna behind to help R2-D2 watch the *Shadow.* "You can't leave me out here alone. I'm only eight."

"What makes you think you'll be alone?" Mara nodded Luke toward the cantina, then said to Ben, "You and I will stand watch out here."

Luke and Saba stepped through the door. The usual assortment of riffraff spacers—Givin, Bothans, Nikto, Quarren—

were gathered in the middle of the room, sitting on synthetic stone benches and holding their drinks in their laps. A few hard cases, such as the Defel "shadow Wraith" hiding in the corner and a Jenet hoodlum holding court on the far side of the chamber, sat apart from the group. Many of the patrons were listing in their seats, but there was none of the latent hostility that usually permeated the Force in spaceport cantinas.

Luke followed Saba to the service area, where a distracted Duros stood at the end of a long bank of beverage dispensers. There was no counter or ordering station, nor anything that looked like a payment terminal, but a soft clicking noise was coming from a darkened alcove beneath the middle dispenser. As they drew near, the clicking stopped and a worker insect emerged from the alcove. It stared up at them for a moment, then handed an empty cup to both of them and retreated into its alcove.

Luke and Saba studied the unmarked dispensers for a moment, then Saba hissed in frustration. She walked over to the inattentive Duros and thrust her mug into his hands.

"Bloodsour."

The Duros swung his noseless head around sharply, then saw he was being addressed by a Barabel. The blue drained from his face.

"Don't have bloodsour," he said in his flat Duros voice. "Only membrosia."

"Will this one like it?"

The Duros nodded. "Everyone likes membrosia."

"Then I'll have the same," Luke said, passing his mug over.

The Duros studied Luke's face for a moment, clearly struggling to place it in some context other than a pair of well-worn flight utilities.

"I'm just a pilot," Luke said, reinforcing the Force illusion he was using to disguise himself. "A *thirsty* pilot."

"Sure."

The Duros turned to the nearest dispenser and filled both mugs with a thick amber liquid, then returned the cups. Luke pulled a ten-credit voucher from his pocket, but the Duros waved it off.

"Nobody pays here."

"Nobody payz?" Saba echoed. "This one doesn't believe you."

A hint of indignation permeated the Force, then the Duros shrugged and looked back to the Verpine musicians.

Saba studied him for a moment, then glanced at Luke. "This one is tired. She will find a seat."

She took a sip from her mug, then started to work her way deeper into the cantina. The Duros looked as though he wished Luke would join her, but Luke remained where he was, pouring camaraderie and goodwill into the Force. The Duros' aloofness did not melt until Saba raised a storm of angry jabbering by taking an empty seat in front of an Ewok.

"*This* should be interesting." The Duros grinned. "That little Ewok has a death mark in ten systems."

"You don't say." Luke took a sip of membrosia. It was sweet and thick and potent, warming him from his toes to his ear tips. He allowed himself a moment to savor the sense of well-being that came with the intoxicating heat, then asked the Duros, "Have you been here long?"

"Too long," the Duros said. "Turns out Lizil doesn't use processing chips, and now I can't get a cargo out."

"Is that a common problem?"

"Common, but not a problem." The Duros waved his hand vaguely in the direction of the membrosia dispensers. "Everything's free, and you can stay as long as you want."

"Very generous," Luke said. "What's the catch?"

"Isn't one," the Duros said. "Except you get used to it, and then you don't *want* to leave."

"That sounds like a catch to me," Luke said.

"Depends on how you look at it," the Duros admitted. "Especially if you have obligations at home."

"Why don't you just take your chips back to the known galaxy?" Luke asked. "With so many manufacturing worlds destroyed by the war, the Galactic Alliance is desperate for processing chips."

"Too dangerous." The Duros cocked his big head toward Luke. "You wouldn't want some kriffing bounty hunter to catch you with these particular chips."

"Ah," Luke said. Lando and Tendra had put up a million-credit reward for a load of specialized processing chips that had been hijacked on its way to Tendrando Arms' new rehab-droid factory. "That makes sense."

"Void-breathing right it does," the Duros said. "Already had five Jedi come through on my tail. That's when I decided to dump the load."

Luke tried not to wince at the loss of the vital chips. "You're sure the Jedi were looking for *you*?"

"Who else would they be looking for?" The Duros shook his head, then said, "I knew Calrissian had pull with the Jedi, but who'd have guessed it was *that* strong?"

"Not me," Luke answered. He stepped closer to the Duros and lowered his voice. "Were they fairly young? A couple of humans with a Barabel and a Wookiee?"

"And a Twi'lek." The Duros' voice grew suspicious, and he began to ease away from Luke. "How'd you know?"

"I've got a little problem of my own with them," Luke said. "And I don't want to find them waiting at my next stop. Know where they went?"

The Duros watched the Verpine band for a moment, no doubt trying to find a way to work an angle for himself. Luke poured a little more goodwill into the Force, and finally the Duros shook his head.

"Sorry," he said. "You'd need to ask Lizil."

Before Luke could ask how to find Lizil, he realized someone new was coming up behind him. The person seemed both to have her own presence in the Force and to be a part of the larger, diffuse essence that permeated the entire asteroid colony. He turned to find a striking Falleen female approaching, her scaly skin almost as green as a male's. She acknowledged Luke with a polite nod, then stopped before the Duros.

"Tarnis, we have a cargo for you," she said.

The Duros took a sip of membrosia and tried to appear calm. "To where?"

"The Horoh nest," the Falleen answered. "You'll be given a load to take home, of course."

Tarnis's eyes grew round—at least by Duros standards. "Done."

When the Duros did not instantly start for the exit, the Falleen said, "It requires immediate departure. Lizil is already loading the *Starsong*."

"No problem." Tarnis placed his mug on the floor. "I'll just gather my crew—"

"We're gathering them now." The Falleen started toward the exit. "They'll meet you in the hangar."

"Right behind you," Tarnis said. He started after the Falleen, shaking his head in amazement. "Finally!"

Seeing that he had been forgotten in the excitement, Luke used the Force to slow the Duros down, then cleared his throat.

"Oh, yeah." Tarnis took the Falleen's arm and gestured toward Luke. "This fellow wants to talk. I can find my own way to the hangar."

The Falleen barely slowed. "We're very busy." She glanced over her shoulder, but avoided Luke's eyes. "Enjoy the hospitality of the nest."

When Luke reached out to probe her feelings, he experienced a deep sense of worry. Her scales rippled in alarm; then an enormous, murky presence rose inside her mind and pushed him out so forcibly that he stumbled into a membrosia dispenser.

As Tarnis and the Falleen walked out the exit, Mara peered around the corner, checking to be certain the surprise she had felt was nothing to be alarmed about. Luke smiled and turned around to display the new membrosia stain on the back of his utilities, then watched intently as Tarnis and the Falleen disappeared down the corridor.

Once the pair were far enough ahead that she would not be noticed following, Mara took Ben's hand and started down the corridor, talking as though they were just a mother and son returning to their vessel.

Luke worked his way to the cantina center and sat on a bench next to a pair of Ishi Tib. He remained quiet for a few moments, pretending to listen to the music but actually reaching out in the Force to search for eavesdropping devices. He was not quite certain what had happened over at the membrosia dispensers, but he felt certain that the Falleen's arrival had been no coincidence. Lizil—whoever that was—had not wanted Tarnis to talk about Jaina and the others.

After a few minutes, Luke finally felt confident that he could ask his questions in peace. He began to pour out feelings of comradery and goodwill, and it wasn't long before the nearest Ishi Tib turned toward him.

"My name is Zelara." She pointed at her companion, who swiveled her eyestalks around and gently clacked her beak. "This is Lyari. She likes you."

Luke smiled back. "Thank you."

Zelara batted the lids of her yellow eyes. "*I* like you."

"That's very nice." He eased off the good feelings, then said, "Actually, I'm looking for some friends—"

"*We'll* be your friends," Lyari said. She came around to Luke's other side, then slipped her stubby hand through the crook of his arm. Her breath smelled heavily of membrosia. "I've never felt this way about a human before."

"Me, either." Zelara took Luke's other arm. "But this one is cute, even with the recessed eyes."

"Ladies, that's just the membrosia talking." Luke sensed Mara already returning to the cantina. She did not feel angry or frightened, but she was frustrated; she had lost the Duros and his escort. "I'm looking for a group of young travelers who came through here. There would've been at least two humans, a Twi'lek, a Barabel—"

"And a Wookiee?" Lyari asked.

"Then you've seen them," Luke said.

Lyari opened her beak in a sort of smile. "Maybe."

"Maybe not," Zelara added. She began to tug at the chest closures on Luke's utilities. "Let us have a look inside, and we'll tell you."

Luke caught her hand. "It probably wouldn't be a good idea for us to—"

"Come on, bright boy." Lyari reached for closures a little farther down. "Give us a chance."

"No." Luke put enough Force behind the word to prevent Lyari from ripping open his utilities. "That would never work."

"Why not?" Zelara demanded.

"Because I have lips and you have beaks, for starters."

Zelara spread her eyestalks. "You'd be surprised what a girl can do with her beak."

"Let me show you," Lyari said. She caught Luke's nose in her beak and gave it a tug.

"Ouch!" Luke reached up and freed his nose. Other people were starting to look in their direction, and that was exactly what he *didn't* want. "Please, ladies. Just tell me what you know about my friends."

Zelara ripped his chest closures open, revealing Luke's undershirt. "First you show, then——"

Mara's astonishment hit Luke like a Force hammer, and he failed to hear the rest of Zelara's comment. He turned toward the exit and saw Mara swinging her hand down to cover their son's eyes.

"Who's that?" Lyari asked, following his gaze.

"My wife."

"Wife?" the Ishi Tib repeated in unison. They jumped to their feet, Zelara crying, "You didn't tell us you were mated!"

"And he's got a fry, too!" Lyari exclaimed.

The outburst caused the Verpine musicians to fumble over a string of notes, and several annoyed patrons turned to suggest that Luke and the Ishi Tib take their personal lives to a quiet corner.

Mara rolled her eyes, then shook her head and dragged a very reluctant Ben around the corner.

Luke sent her a feeling of reassurance, trying to make sure she knew there was a good explanation. He received an impression of amused doubtfulness in reply, then he heard Saba sissing from across the room and realized he might never live this one down. He shook his head in disgust, then closed his utilities and looked up at the Ishi Tib.

"Will you *please* sit?"

Zelara put a hand on her hip. "I don't think so."

"You just forget about us, you double-spawner." Lyari shooed him toward the exit. "You'd better go catch your mate and that little fry."

"As soon as you answer me." Luke grabbed both Ishi Tib by

their wrists and pulled them down. "When did you see my friends? The Wookiee and the Barabel and the others?"

"When they were here," Zelara answered coolly.

"Which was?" Luke put the Force behind his question, pressuring her to answer.

"I don't know." Zelara turned to Lyari. "When was that?"

"Who can remember? They only stayed a day."

Luke started to pressure Lyari to think back, then realized that someone else was approaching. As with the Falleen who had led Tarnis away, the newcomer appeared to have a double presence in the Force, except that the individual essence felt much more menacing and powerful than had the Falleen's. Luke turned and, when he saw a blocky shadow with red eyes and white fangs approaching, nearly reached for his lightsaber.

The Defel watched Luke's hand until it dropped back to his side, then turned to the Ishi Tib. "The nest has secured a barrel of fresh Tibrin salts," he rasped. "We are preparing an immersion tank now."

"For us?" Zelara gasped.

"Where?" Lyari demanded.

The Defel offered a shadow-furred arm to each of them. "We'll escort you."

"First, answer my question," Luke said, putting the weight of the Force behind his command.

Lyari started to stop and look back, but the Defel pulled her forward.

"Come, ladies." His eyes flared red. "The immersion tank is growing cool."

The same murky presence Luke had felt before rose against him. It was not a Force attack, merely an enormous exertion of will. Had he wanted to, Luke could have found another way to maintain his hold, but that would have meant drawing even more of the mysterious entity's attention to himself than he already had.

Besides, Saba was on her way over, a furry little Ewok at her side. It was the Ewok she had sat in front of earlier, with a single white stripe running diagonally across a stocky body that was otherwise as black as space. They stopped in front of Luke and stood there sissing and chortling together.

"Go ahead," Luke said. "Get it out of your system now. Who's your friend?"

"Tar . . . Tarfang," Saba laughed. "He sayz he can help us find our friendz . . . if you are finished chasing Ishi Tib."

SIX

Save for the lining of golden wax, the rows of shine-balls stuck to the ceiling, the random tunnel openings, and the lack of even a vague sense of up or down, the interior of the spherical hangar resembled all the spaceports Han Solo had visited on a thousand unknown, out-of-the-way planets scattered across the galaxy. There was the usual collection of battered transports, the usual cargo of stolen goods on open display, the usual dregs-of-their-species smugglers bustling in and out of their vessels, working harder to make dishonest livings than they would have at honest jobs.

Han felt a swell of nostalgia rise inside, and he found himself missing the days when he could debark in such places and know that nobody was going to mess with him and the Wookiee. Of course, now he had a Jedi Knight wife, a pair of Noghri, and a refitted battle droid to back him up, but it just wasn't the same. Chewbacca had been his co-conspirator as well his best friend, a pain-in-the-neck conscience at times but also a comrade-in-arms who understood the betrayals and disappointments that had turned Han into the wary, bitter smuggler he'd been when Leia came along and rescued him from that aimless life.

"At least we've solved one mystery," Leia said. She pointed at a duraplast pallet filled with crates labeled RECONSTRUCTION AUTHORITY—SANITATION. "That may explain why it's been so hard to track down the RA supplies shrinkage."

"I don't know," Han said. He eyed the giant bugs that seemed to be crawling across every surface. "This pile of rocks isn't big enough to take everything that's disappearing."

The more Han watched the activity around the transports, the more he felt his skin crawl. The bugs were marching in and out of the vessels completely unescorted, off-loading cargo, foodstuffs, even vital ship's tools, and stacking them at the base of the boarding ramps. Instead of stopping the insects, the crews were doing the same thing in reverse, on-loading huge stoneware crocks, balls of multicolored wax, and many of the same tools and foodstuffs the bugs were unloading. And nobody seemed upset about working at cross purposes. In fact, save for the care they took to avoid crashing into each other, they barely seemed to notice one another at all.

Han spied the sleek gray wedge of a *Horizon*-class space yacht resting about halfway up the "wall" of the docking vault, its landing struts sunk well past their feet in the waxy substance that coated the chamber. The boarding ramp was lowered and a big Tendrando Arms Defender Droid was standing beside it, her massive torso and systems-packed limbs at odds with her cherubic face and smiling mouth.

"There's the *Shadow*," Han said. He brought the *Falcon*'s nose around and started toward an open berthing space on the wall next to Mara's ship. "Let's go say hello."

Leia shook her head. "It doesn't feel like there's anyone aboard."

"No?" Han scowled; it wasn't like Mara to leave the *Shadow* open and unattended—although with Nanna there, that wasn't really the case. Basically a bodyguard version of Lando's successful YVH battle droid crossed with a TD Nanny Droid, the Defender was more than capable of guarding the ship. Even the bugs seemed to realize that; every now and then, one would stop by and sweep its antennae across the ramp, but they never attempted to enter. "Probably in the cantina already."

Han swung the *Falcon*'s stern "up" along the wall and landed in the open berth. The struts sank into the wax and seemed to hold the ship fast, but he fired the anchoring bolts anyway. Microgravity could be tricky; it was impossible to tell which way it was pulling until something started to slide.

Han rose and strapped on his blaster. "Okay, let's go see Nanna. Maybe she can fill us in."

They lowered the boarding ramp and reeled back as a wave of warm, too-sweet air rolled through the hatchway. The vault was filled with a blaring cacophony of ticking that immediately sent a rivulet of sweat rolling down Han's spine. Half a dozen bugs appeared at the bottom of the ramp and started to board. They had deep orange thoraxes, pale blue abdomens, and feathery, meter-long antennae. Han's stomach turned queasy, but he started down to meet them.

Leia caught him by the arm. "Han? What's wrong?"

"Nothing." Han swallowed hard, then continued down the ramp. He was not going to be intimidated by a memory of the Kamarians. Besides, these guys were only about waist height, with four skinny arms, scrawny legs, and a stubby set of mandibles better suited to steadying loads than rending flesh. "I'm okay."

Han stopped midway down the ramp. He folded his arms across his chest and assumed a stance wide enough to block the ramp, then forced himself to glare down at the lead bug. In addition to the smooth green balls of its two main eyes, it had a trio of ocular lenses atop its head, leaving him uncertain as to which set of eyes he should meet.

"Where do you fellows think you're going?"

The lead bug stared up, ticking its mandibles nervously, and emitted a soft drumming from its chest.

"Burrubbubbuurrr, rubb."

It dropped to all sixes, lowering itself to about knee height, then dipped its antennae politely and shot between Han's legs.

"Hey!" Before the bug could continue up the ramp, Han spun around and caught it by the undersized wings on its back. Some insects had a habit of hiding eggs wherever they could, and he didn't want any infestations aboard the *Falcon.* "Hold on!"

The bug spun its head around to meet Han's gaze, then pointed at his hands and gently clacked its mandibles. *"Ubburr buurr ub."*

"Captain Solo," C-3PO said helpfully, "I do believe the insect is requesting that you release it."

"You understand this stuff?" Han asked.

"I'm afraid it's only an educated guess," C-3PO said. "This form of their language is as obscure as the dance—"

"Then not a chance."

"Han," Leia said, "I don't sense any danger here. Until See-Threepio figures out how to communicate—"

"I *am* communicating." Han fixed his gaze on the nearest of its eyes and said, "I don't know who you think I am, but no one boards the *Falcon* until *I* say so."

The other five bugs dropped to all sixes, then slipped to the underside of the ramp and continued toward the hatchway.

"No!" Han flipped the insect he was holding off the ramp, then started after the others. "Stop them!"

The Noghri stepped in front of Leia and placed themselves squarely in the door, crouched for action. The bugs swung back to the ramp's upper side and tried to squeeze aboard the *Falcon* anyway. The first pair were knocked away by a pair of quick Noghri kicks.

The remaining trio of insects stopped where they were and dropped into a six-limbed crouch. Their antennae fell flat against their heads, and a soft little *"rrrrrrr"* began to come from their chests. Someone else might have described the sound as meek, but Han knew better than to assume. Bug minds did not work the same way as those of other species.

BD-8, the Solos' battle droid, appeared behind the Noghri and pointed his blaster cannon over Meewalh's shoulder. "Do not be alarmed!" With the full jacket of laminanium armor and red photoreceptors in a death's-head face, he still resembled the YVH droid from which he had been refitted. "Intruders identified. Permission to fire?"

"No!" Leia snapped. "Stand down! Return to leisure station."

"Leisure station?" BD-8's tone grew doubtful as the other bugs continued up the ramp. "Ma'am, we're being boarded!"

"We're *not* being boarded," Leia said.

"Not if I can help it!" Han said.

He snatched another of the bugs and, in the low gravity, sent it spinning twenty meters across the hangar. Cakhmaim and Meewalh removed the last two, grabbing a mandible and executing quick twists that sent the insects tumbling away.

Han nodded his approval. "See?"

A bitter odor began to waft up from the floor. Han looked

down to see two of the dislodged bugs standing beside the ramp on their four front limbs, their abdomens raised so they could squirt greenish fluid on the sides of the ramp.

"What the garzal?" Han cried.

"Ubbub bubbur," the bugs drummed.

"Bubbur yourselves!"

Han raised his arms to shoo them away. They continued to squirt, and C-3PO picked that moment to interrupt.

"Captain Solo, we seem to have another visitor."

The droid pointed past Han's shoulder.

Han turned around to find a tall, bald-headed figure with large, buggy eyes and a pair of thick tusks approaching the *Falcon*'s boarding ramp. In his hands, he carried a rag and a spray canister.

"Great," Han said. "Now an Aqualish."

"That can't be good," Leia said. The Aqualish were an aggressive species known across the galaxy for picking fights—and jumping into the middle of them. "What's he want?"

"To wash the viewports, it looks like," Han said. The Aqualish reached the base of the ramp and started forward toward the bugs. "What do you want, Fangface?"

The nickname was despised by Aqualish, but it was better to take an aggressive tone with them. They were less likely to start a fight with someone who did not intimidate easily.

"Nothing, friend." The Aqualish spoke in the gravelly voice typical of his species. "Just to help you out."

Han and Leia exchanged puzzled glances. *Friend* was not usually a word you heard from an Aqualish.

"We're not your friends," Han said.

"You will be."

The Aqualish waited until the bugs finished squirting, then shooed away the one on his side of the ramp and sprayed a harsh-smelling foam over the same area.

"That stuff better not be corrosive," Han warned.

Aqualish could not smile—the need had probably never arisen during their evolution—but this one lifted his head and managed to seem like he was.

"It's not." He tossed the spray canister to Han. "You need to clean that mess up."

The Aqualish pointed at the far side of the ramp, where the other worker had squirted its goo, then started to wipe the area he had already coated. Han sprayed a thick layer of foam over the side of the ramp, filling the air with a smell somewhere between rotting fruit and burned synfur.

"Tell me again what I'm doing?"

"When you tossed the workers off, they marked you," the Aqualish explained. He tossed Han the rag. "Now you have to start over, or they'll call their soldiers and tear your ship apart to see what you're hiding."

"Start over?" Leia asked.

"Transacting," the Aqualish explained. "Isn't that why you're here?"

"Uh, maybe," Han said. "You mean like trading, right?"

"More like taking," the Aqualish said. "They take what they want. You take what you want. Everybody's happy."

The insects started up the ramp again.

"Boarding imminent," BD-8 reported. "Permission to—"

"No!" Leia said. "Stand down."

Han finished wiping the foam away, then stood up to find the six insects lined up on the ramp below.

"They're not going to lay eggs or anything?" he asked.

"No, they only do that in the heartcomb," the Aqualish assured him. "Just let them bring out whatever they want, then take back whatever you want to keep. It's a lot easier—and safer."

"If you say so." Han stepped aside to let the bugs pass. "Okay?"

The lead worker responded with a single mandible clack, which was simultaneously echoed by the rest of the squad.

"That would be an affirmative," C-3PO offered helpfully.

The bugs started up the ramp.

Han jumped down beside the Aqualish and returned the spray canister and rag. "Sorry about that Fangface stuff." He reached for his money. "What do I owe you for the help?"

"Nothing, friend." The Aqualish waved a dismissing hand. "It happens to everyone the first time."

"Really?" Han's mind began searching for angles, trying to figure out what kind of swindle the Aqualish was trying to pull. "Hope you don't mind me saying so, but you're a pretty helpful guy for your kind."

The Aqualish watched the last bug disappear into the *Falcon,* then nodded. "Yeah. I don't get it, either." He turned and started back toward his own vessel. "This place just makes me feel good."

Han, Leia, and the others spent the next hour returning to the *Falcon* most of what the bugs carried off. At first, the work was confusing and frustrating—especially after they had carried the same crate of protein packages aboard for the seventh or eighth time. But eventually order emerged, with the ship's crew leaving anything they could bear to part with at the foot of the ramp and stacking whatever they wanted to keep in the forward hold. Toward the end, the bugs even started to add balls of wax and jugs of some amber, sweet-smelling spirit to the *Falcon*'s stack.

Finally, the only item under contention was *Killik Twilight,* a small moss-painting that had once hung outside Leia's bedroom in House Organa on Alderaan. Designed by the late Ob Khaddor—one of Alderaan's foremost artists—the piece depicted a line of enigmatic insectoid figures departing their pinnacle-city home, with a fierce storm sweeping in behind them. Han had no idea why the bugs were so taken with it—apart from the subject matter—but every time he put it on the *keep* stack, an insect would deposit a jug of spirits or a shine-ball in its place and carry it back down the ramp again. Han was about ready to start exterminating. The painting was Leia's most prized possession, and he'd almost died trying to recover it for her on Tatooine.

A bug emerged from the *Falcon* carrying *Killik Twilight* in its four arms and stopped about halfway down the ramp, peering over the top of the frame. Han, waiting at the bottom, folded his arms and sighed.

"Come on," he said. "Let's get it over with."

Instead of continuing down the ramp, the worker jumped to the floor and disappeared behind the disordered heap of crates and spare tools stacked next to the *Falcon.*

"Hey!"

Han rushed to the other side to cut off the bug's escape, but it was nowhere to be seen. He glanced back at its buddies—waiting for this last bit of "transacting" to be completed—but they only turned their oblong eyes away and pretended not to notice. Han sneered, then knelt down to peer behind the *Falcon*'s landing struts.

Nothing.

"Blast!" Han slowly turned, his pulse pounding as he searched for the bug. Halfway up the hangar wall, he saw the Skywalkers emerging from a passage with Saba Sebatyne and a black-furred Ewok, but no sign of the thief. "Huttslime!"

"Han?" Leia appeared at the top of the boarding ramp, her arms loaded with provisions that she and the others were stowing again. "What's wrong?"

"Nothing," Han answered. "The bugs are getting sneaky."

Leia put her load aside. "Define *sneaky,* Han."

"Nothing to worry about." A soft rustle sounded from the transaction pile. Han peered over a stack of raw protein packages and saw a slender insect foot sliding behind a crate of Endorian brandy. "I've got everything under control."

Han slipped around the stack of packages, then pulled the crate aside and found the worker bug cowering with *Killik Twilight* in its four hands.

"Uub urr," it thrummed.

"Yeah? Two can play that game."

Han pulled the painting from its grasp, then turned to find Ben rushing up ahead of Luke and the others.

"Uncle Han!" He raised his elbow in an old smuggler's greeting Han had taught him. "Dad said you were here!"

"Good to see you, kid." Han touched his elbow to Ben's. "I'd love to talk, but I'm in the middle of a contest of wills."

Leaving Leia to slow down the bug and greet Luke and the others, Han carried the painting onto the *Falcon,* then knelt on the floor and opened a smuggling compartment.

"That's a funny place to put Aunt Leia's painting," said Ben, who had followed him aboard.

"Tell me about it," Han said. He slipped the painting into the compartment, closed the cover, and stood. "Now let's go see your mom and—"

The bug appeared in the corridor, sweeping its antennae along the floor. It passed Han with a polite rumble, then stopped and began to pry at the secret panel. When the compartment would not open, it sat down and began to clack its mandibles.

"All right! You don't have to call your buddies." Han knelt on the floor beside the bug. "Just get out of my way."

Han opened the panel. The insect pulled the painting from the compartment and turned to leave, then let out a startled rumble when it found Saba and her Ewok companion coming up the corridor. The Ewok snatched the painting from the bug's hands, turned it over, and spat on the back.

"What the blazes!" Han turned to Saba. "Is this guy a friend of yours?"

"Tarfang and I have made no killz together," Saba said. "But he can help us."

"Yeah?" Han watched doubtfully as Tarfang placed the painting on the floor. "How?"

The Ewok glared up at Han and jabbered something in the squeaky language of his species, then motioned Han and the others toward the boarding ramp.

"Listen up, Cuddles," Han said, "I don't know who you think you are, but on the *Falcon*—"

"Uncle Han, look!"

Ben pointed at *Killik Twilight*. The bug stood holding the painting in its hands, running its antennae over the back where the Ewok had spit. It repeated the gesture several times, then emitted a sad little hum and returned the painting to the smuggling compartment.

Han looked back to Tarfang. "How'd you do that?"

The Ewok's only answer was an indignant snort. He spun around and started for the boarding ramp, no longer seeming to care whether Han or anyone else followed.

"Touchy little fellow, isn't he?"

"Tarfang is not a nice being." Saba started after the Ewok. "But his captain can help us find Jaina and the otherz."

Han caught up to her outside, where C-3PO informed them

that Luke and the others had gone on ahead with Tarfang. Despite Saba's assurances that *Killik Twilight* was perfectly safe now that someone had spit on it, Han asked the Noghri to stay with the painting.

They dropped Ben at the *Shadow* with Nanna, then joined Luke, Mara, and Leia outside the blast-pocked, carbon-scored disk of a small YT-1000 transport. A smaller cousin to Han's own YT-1300, the YT-1000's cockpit sat atop the hull where the *Falcon*'s upper laser cannon turret was located; there was no lower turret at all. For defense, the vessel had only four short-range blaster cannons spread evenly along the rim of its hull.

"That thing *flew* here?" Han gasped.

An indignant Ewok voice chuttered from inside the vessel's shadowy entrance.

"He says it came straight from Regel Eight," C-3PO translated.

Tarfang stepped into the light and jabbered at Han some more.

"I'm certainly glad we don't fly on this ship!" C-3PO said. "He says not everyone has credits to waste on repairs!"

Leia stepped to Han's side. "We apologize, Tarfang." She flashed one of her old diplomat's smiles, a bland show of teeth that could have meant anything. "Han didn't mean to insult you."

"Yeah," Han said. "I was just amazed by your bravery."

Tarfang eyed Han for a moment, then growled deep in his throat and waved them up the ramp.

Han turned to Luke and Mara. "You sure about this?"

"Not really," Luke said. He smiled and clapped Han on the shoulder. "We weren't expecting you and Leia."

"Yeah, well . . . *anybody* can bust up a pirate ring," Han said. "But Jaina—we figured you'd need the help."

"We might," Mara said with a laugh. She kissed him on the cheek. "Good to see you, Han."

They exchanged greetings all around, then climbed the boarding ramp into a surprisingly tidy air lock with all proper emergency equipment neatly stowed in a transparisteel rescue locker. Beyond the hatch, the interior of the main access corridor was lit only by two of the waxy shine-balls the bugs used for illumination. By the green glow, Han could see that the durasteel floor panels had been sanibuffed a little *too* well. There was a telltale shadow where the "invisible" seams came together over the smuggling compartments.

Tarfang was waiting a few steps up the corridor. He grunted and waved them into the main cabin. Given the ship's dim lighting, Han expected to find some fierce, dark-loving being like a Defel waiting inside.

Instead, kneeling in front of an open engineering panel was a little jug-eared Sullustan in a set of carbon-smeared utilities. He was busy soldering powerfeeds to a new master control board, though Han could not imagine how even a Sullustan could see to work by the light of the single shine-ball stuck to the wall above him.

Tarfang went to the Sullustan's side and, coming to attention, cleared his throat.

"Go on." The Sullustan spoke without looking away from his work. "I'm listening."

Tarfang launched into a lengthy explanation, gesturing at Saba and Luke even though the Sullustan's attention remained fixed on the control board. Finally, the captain finished the attachment he was working on and turned to his visitors.

"I'm Jae Juun, captain of the *XR-eight-oh-eight-g*."

"XR-eight-oh-eight-g?" Han asked. "What kind of name is that?"

"It's a Galactic Alliance registration number, of course." Juun frowned and squinted in the direction of Han's voice, but Han was standing well back in the shadows, where even a Sullustan's sensitive eyes would have trouble with the contrast between light and darkness. "You haven't heard of the *XR-eight-oh-eight-g*?"

"Should we have?" Leia asked.

Juun pasted on a small Sullustan smirk. "Not if I've been doing my job."

"You're succeeding beyond your wildest dreams," Han said.

Leia grabbed the back of his elbow and squeezed in warning, but the Sullustan merely smiled in pride.

"Tarfang tells me you're looking for someone to help you catch your friends."

"To find them," Luke corrected.

"I see. Well, it makes no difference." Juun cast an annoyed glance in Tarfang's direction. "I'm afraid my first mate sometimes exceeds his authority."

Tarfang asked something in a disbelieving tone.

"It's not the mate's responsibility to raise funds," Juun replied. "You let me worry how we're going to pay for that vortex stabilizer."

"A warp vortex stabilizer?" Han asked. "For a YT this old? It can't be easy to come by one of those out here."

"Not at a fair price," Juun agreed. "I've had one brought in, but I'm two hundred credits short of the shipping fees."

"Not if you help us, you're not," Han said, stepping into the light. "We can pay you the two hundred credits."

Juun's mouth fell. "I knew that was your voice!" He turned to Tarfang. "Why didn't you tell me Han Solo was with them?"

Tarfang sneered in Han's direction and prattled an answer.

"Yes, but this is *Han Solo!*" The Sullustan rose and thrust a hand out. "The *XR-eight-oh-eight-g* follows all your procedures, and I've memorized all your combat maneuvers from the history vids."

"Uh, I wouldn't trust everything I see in those holovids," Han said, allowing the Sullustan to shake his hand. "Now, about that help . . ."

"I'd like to help you." Juun's voice grew disappointed, and he turned back to his work. "But it wouldn't be proper."

"Proper?" Han echoed. That particular word encompassed everything he hated about Sullustans. "Why not?"

"Because I have an arrangement with our hosts, and evidently they don't want you to find your friends."

Tarfang groaned and slapped his brow.

"We can't ignore the wishes of our business partners," Juun said to the Ewok. "We have a deal."

"A deal you can't keep until you find two hundred credits," Han said. "How long are they willing to wait?"

"We *are* facing a bit of a dilemma," Juun admitted.

"What if we were to buy a copy of your charts?" Luke asked.

Juun shook his head. "My charts wouldn't help you. Your friends went to Yoggoy."

"And you don't know where Yoggoy is?" Luke asked.

"Nobody does," Juun said. "The Yoggoy are very proud and secretive. They hide the location of their nest from outsiders."

Saba glared down at Tarfang. "Then why did you say you could help us find our friendz?"

Tarfang jabbered an answer.

"Because the *XR-eight-oh-eight-g* has been assigned a cargo for Yoggoy," C-3PO translated, "and when a ship is assigned a cargo for Yoggoy, it is also assigned a Yoggoy to serve as its navigator for the trip."

"Fine," Leia said. Even she seemed to be losing patience. "Help us get a cargo, and we'll pay you for consulting."

Tarfang rattled off a long response, which C-3PO translated as, "Tarfang suggests you simply give Captain Juun the money. They'll check on our friends and give us a report when they return."

"Sure they will." Han turned to the others, then nodded toward the door. "We're wasting our time here."

Luke motioned Han to wait, his gaze fixed on Tarfang. Han realized for the first time that Mara was no longer with them; under circumstances like these, she had an uncanny knack for slipping away unnoticed.

Finally, Luke turned back to Han. "Tarfang's not trying to swindle us, Han. He really does want to work out an honest deal."

Tarfang snarled something at the Jedi Master.

"He wasn't stealing your thoughts," C-3PO said to the Ewok. "Master Luke is not a thief."

Tarfang whirled on the droid and yapped a command.

"Very well. But I wouldn't blame him if he used his lightsaber on you." C-3PO turned to Luke. "Tarfang is threatening to remove your eyes if you do that again."

"Oh, *that* scares him," Han said to the Ewok. "You want to make a deal? Here it is: two hundred credits to get us a cargo."

To Han's surprise, it was Saba who answered. "He can't."

"Why not?"

"Because Lizil wouldn't allow it," Luke said. "He—or she—doesn't want us to find Jaina and the others."

"They," Juun corrected.

Luke frowned. "What?"

"They," Juun said.

The Sullustan continued to work, soldering what looked like the rear hold powerfeed onto the main cabin output. Han would have said something, but he had long ago learned never to tell another captain how to maintain his own ship. Besides, anyone who looked at the *Falcon*'s main control board would probably have just as many doubts about his work as he was having about Juun's.

"Lizil isn't their leader." Juun looked up from his work, dragging the hot tip of his soldering iron across the flux-inhibitor circuitry. "Lizil is *them*."

"They all share one name?" Leia asked.

"In a sense, but it's more than that. The way they think of it, they're all Lizil together. Lizil is the nest, but so are all of the members."

"They don't have an individual sense of identity?" Leia asked.

"I think that's so," Juun said. "But I'm not really current on my xenobiological definitions."

Tarfang chortled something helpful sounding.

"Master Tarfang says that it's only important to remember that when you say *Lizil,* you might be talking about the entire nest or any of its members."

Tarfang chattered something impatient.

"And you'll never be sure which," C-3PO added.

"Cozy," Han said. "So why doesn't Lizil want us to find Jaina?"

When Juun hesitated, Tarfang let out a long, urgent chitter.

"But nobody said it *wasn't* secret," Juun countered.

"You are being rockheaded," Saba rasped. "Something is only secret if—"

"Hold on," Han said to Saba. The Sullustan mind was as stubborn as it was methodical, and the Barabel would only delay things by browbeating Juun. "It *is* a bit unclear."

Saba glared at Han out of one dark eye.

"There are your implied agreements and your tacit obligations." Han turned to Juun. "Am I right?"

The Sullustan nodded rapidly. "Only captains understand these things."

"True," Han said. "But aren't you smugglers, too?"

Tarfang grunted an affirmative.

"There you have it, then," Han said. He looked back to Juun. "You have to answer me."

"I do?"

"Yeah." Han allowed some of the impatience he was feeling to show in his voice. "The Smuggler's Code says so."

Juun looked back to his work and casually asked, "The Smuggler's Code?"

"Item seven?" Han prompted. *"I swear to help other smugglers, as long as it don't cost* me*?"*

"Yes, of course." Juun's beady-eyed gaze flicked back and forth across the master control board. It was impossible that he actually knew the Smuggler's Code—Han was making it up—but nothing embarrassed most Sullustans more than admitting they did not know proper procedures. "Item seven. I'd almost forgotten."

"I think that clears things up," Leia said. She flashed Han an approving smile, then sat on her haunches beside Juun. "So what's Lizil trying to hide?"

Juun began to solder the forward loading door's powerfeed to the forward loading door's control circuit. "You have seen the Joiners?"

Han expected Leia to shake her head, but she seemed to sense something from her brother and allowed Luke to respond for her.

"You mean Lizil's translators?"

"Not translators," Juun said. "*Joiners.* They're Lizil, too."

Saba lowered her scaly brow. "How can that be?" she rasped. "Most of them do not even have six limbz!"

"It doesn't matter," Juun said. "They've been absorbed."

"Absorbed?" Han was having trouble following the conversation now, probably because he had not yet seen any of these "Joiners." "Absorbed *how*?"

"Mentally, I suspect," Luke said, keeping his eyes on Juun. "Is it some sort of brainwashing?"

Juun shrugged. "All I know is that when someone spends too long in a nest, he gets absorbed."

"You're saying that my daughter thinks she's some kind of bug?" Han demanded, taking a step forward. "And you *weren't* going to tell me?"

Juun jumped up and stepped behind Leia. "It's not my fault!"

"Take it easy, Han," Luke said. "We don't know that has happened."

"Do we know it hasn't?" Han countered.

"Now *you* are being a rockhead," Saba said. "We know nothing, not even where they are."

Saba's intervention reminded Han that he and Leia weren't the only ones with a child at risk. Her son, Tesar, was one of the Jedi Knights who had followed Jaina into the Unknown Regions.

"Sorry. I don't know what came over me." Han touched Saba's back—then swallowed hard, remembering that touching a Barabel uninvited was a good way to lose an arm. "Sometimes, I forget they're Jedi."

"Not to worry." Saba thumped a scaly hand down on his shoulder. "This one forgetz sometimez, too."

A moment of silence hung in the air as they recalled all they had lost at Myrkr, Anakin and Bela and Krasov and the others, and Han thought he could almost feel Saba reaching for him in the Force, trying to lend him the strength to have faith in his daughter's abilities, to recall that she was a Jedi Knight and an ace star pilot and a hero as big in her war as he and Leia had been in theirs. It was not an easy thing for a father to keep in mind, but it was true, and—as Leia always said—in truth there was strength.

"All right already," Han said, motioning Juun back to the control board. "You can go back to work. I'm better."

Leia gave him an understanding wink, then turned back to Juun. "What does Lizil need with a group of Jedi Knights?"

"I don't know," Juun said. "But they left with Unu."

"Unu?"

"The central nest," Juun said. "Your daughter and the others were met by an escort of Unu guards."

"*More* bugs?" Han had a sinking feeling. "Great."

"Then there's an *organization* of nests?" Leia asked Juun.

The Sullustan nodded. "The Colony."

Han thought he was beginning to understand. "How big?"

Juun pulled a datapad from beneath his utilities, then began punching keys. "I have heard three hundred and seventy-five names."

Luke whistled. "Enough to stretch from here to the Chiss frontier. Now this is beginning to make some sense."

"How do you figure?" Han asked.

"The situation isn't complicated," Leia said. "The Colony is rubbing borders with the Chiss empire. It's pretty clear why the central nest might want a team of Jedi Joiners on their side—especially this particular team."

"Jedi commandos are good equalizers," Han agreed. "But what I want to know is how the Colony got them to come out here in the first place."

Several moments passed with no answer, and finally their gazes began to drift toward Juun. Tarfang's eyes darted from one to the other of them, and finally he jabbered an angry denial.

"Tarfang asks that you stop looking at them," C-3PO said. "He denies any involvement."

"That's not what we were implying," Leia said.

"But we do need your help," Luke said to Juun. "*Han* needs your help. We must find our Jedi Knights."

Juun considered this for a moment, then said, "Perhaps there *is* a way. There's room in the forward hold. If we hide you in there—"

"Forget it," Han said. "We're flying our own ships."

"I'm afraid this is the only practical way," Juun said. "I'll be relying entirely on the guide myself."

Han shook his head.

"Han, I know it'll be crowded," Luke said. "But it sounds like the best plan."

"No, Luke," Han said, discreetly eyeing the control board. "It really *doesn't*."

Luke's gaze darted to the board and away again almost immediately, but he was not quick enough to escape Juun's notice.

"Why are you looking at the control board?" he demanded. "You don't trust me to maintain my own ship?"

"Well, you did slip with your solder." Han stooped down and pointed at a silver line angling across the board. "You're going to have a short running across your flux inhibitors."

Juun studied the line, then said, "It's nothing to worry about. I followed all the proper procedures."

"Yeah, but you slipped—"

"It's more than adequate. I'll demonstrate." Juun slipped the master plug onto the supply prongs, then waved Tarfang to the far side of the cabin. "Close the main breaker."

"Juun, I don't think that's a good—"

A sharp *clack* echoed across the room. Han barely managed to close his eyes before the ship erupted into a tempest of bursting lamps and sizzling circuits. Leia and the others cried out in shock. When the crackling continued, Han pulled his blaster and, opening his eyes to what looked like a indoor lightning storm, shot through the wire array just above the master plug.

The popping and buzzing quickly died away, and the main cabin was again plunged into its previous green dimness. Juun dropped to his knees in front of the control board.

"Not again!"

"What did I tell you?" Han asked.

Tarfang returned to the group and studied his crestfallen captain a moment, then looked Han in the eye and spoke sharply.

"He says the cost just doubled, Captain Solo," C-3PO said. "You must pay for the damages you caused."

"*I* caused?" Han protested. "I told him not to—"

"We'll be glad to replace the wire array Han destroyed saving the *XR-eight-oh-eight-g,*" Leia interrupted. "And we'll do anything else we can to help Captain Juun complete his repairs . . . per item seven of the Smuggler's Code."

"You bet," Han said, catching Leia's strategy. "It's not as bad as it sounded, or the smoke would be a lot thicker."

Juun looked up, his small eyes round with wonder. "This is covered under item seven?"

"Oh, yeah," Han said. "But we're flying our own ships."

"I'm sure we can think of a way to follow Captain Juun." Luke spoke in a tone that suggested he had already solved this problem. "We may need to install a couple of pieces of equipment when we repair the wire array."

Tarfang raised a lip, then jabbered a demand.

"What kind of equipment?" C-3PO translated.

"The secret kind," Luke said, glaring at the Ewok.

Tarfang lowered his furry brow and glared back for a moment, then finally said something that C-3PO translated as, "Captain Juun will be taking a big risk. It'll cost you."

"Fine," Luke said. He stepped close to Juun and Tarfang, and suddenly he seemed as large as a rancor. "But you know who we are. You understand what it will mean if you try to double-cross us?"

Tarfang shrank back, but Juun seemed untroubled.

"Double-cross Han Solo?" the Sullustan asked. "Who'd be crazy enough to do that?"

SEVEN

Down in the valley, the Taat were scavenging along the flood-plain, their thoraxes glowing green in Jwlio's hazy light. With the rest of their foraging territory brown and withering from a Chiss defoliant, the workers were stripping the ground bare, leaving nothing in their wake but rooj stubble and mud. It was a desperate act that would only deepen their famine in the future, but the insects had no choice. Their larvae were starving *now*.

In the midst of such poverty and hardship, Jaina Solo felt more than a little guilty eating green thakitillo, but it was the only thing on the menu tonight. Tomorrow, it would be brot-rib or krayt eggs or some other rarity more suitable to a state dinner than a field post, and she would eat that, too. The Taat would be insulted if she did not.

Jaina spooned a curd into her mouth, then glanced around the veranda at her companions. They were all seated on primitive spitcrete benches, holding their bowls in their laps and using small Force bubbles to keep the dust at bay. Despite the gritty winds raised by the tidal pull of Qoribu—Jwlio's ringed gas giant primary—the group usually took their meals outdoors. No one wanted to spend more time than necessary in the muggy confines of the nest caves.

After the curd had dissolved, Jaina tapped her spoon against the bowl. "Okay," she asked. "Who's responsible for this?"

One by one, the others raised their gazes, their faces betraying various degrees of culpability as they examined their thoughts over the last week or so. Shortly after arriving, the team had discovered that whenever they talked about a particular food, the

Taat would have a supply delivered within a few days. Concerned about squandering their hosts' limited resources, Jaina had ordered the group to avoid talking about food in front of the Taat, then to avoid mentioning it at all.

Finally, Tesar Sebatyne flicked up a talon. "It may have been this one."

"*May* have been?" Jaina asked. "Either you said something or you didn't."

Tesar's dorsal scales rose in the Barabel equivalent of a blush. "This one *said* nothing. He thought it."

"They can't eavesdrop on thoughts," Jaina said. "Someone else must have slipped."

She glanced around the group, waiting. The others continued to search their memories, but no one recalled talking about food.

Finally, Zekk said, "I'm just happy it's thakitillo instead of some skalrat or something." Seated on a bench next to Jaina, he wore his black hair as long and ragged as he had in his youth, but that was all that remained the same. A late growth spurt had turned him into something of a human giant, standing two meters tall, with shoulders as broad as Lowbacca's. "I thought Barabels liked to catch their own food."

"When we can, but this one was thinking of our last meal aboard *Lady Luck,* and he alwayz tastes thakitillo when he rememberz Bela and Krasov and . . ." Tesar trailed off and glanced briefly in Jaina's direction, quietly acknowledging the bond of grief they had come to share through the Myrkr mission. ". . . the otherz."

Even that gentle reminder of her brother's death—even seven years later—brought a pained hollow to Jaina's chest. Usually, her duties as a Jedi Knight kept her too busy to dwell on such things, but there were still moments like these, when the terrible memory came crashing down on her like a Nkllonian firestorm.

"So maybe the Taat *are* eavesdropping on our thoughts," Tahiri said, bringing Jaina's attention back to the present. "If we're sure no one said anything, that has to be it."

Lowbacca let out a long Wookiee moan.

"I suppose we *will* have to avoid thinking about food," Jaina agreed. "We're Jedi. We can't keep eating like Hutts while the Taat larvae starve."

"It certainly takes the fun out of it," Alema Rar agreed. The Twi'lek slipped a spoonful of thakitillo into her mouth, then bit into a curd and curled the tips of the long lekku hanging down her back. "Well, *most* of the fun."

Zekk ate a spoonful, then asked, "Does it bother anyone that they're listening to our thoughts?"

"It *should,*" Jaina replied. "We should feel a little uneasy and violated, shouldn't we?"

Alema shrugged. "*Should* is for narrow minds. It makes *me* feel welcome."

Jaina considered this for a moment, then nodded in agreement. "Same here—and valued. Zekk? You brought it up."

"Just asking," he said. "Doesn't bother me, either."

"I feel the same," Tekli agreed. The furry little Chadra-Fan twitched her thick-ended snout. "Yet we avoid the battle-meld now because we dislike sharing feelings among ourselves."

"That's different," Tahiri said. "*We* get on each other's nerves."

"To put it mildly," Jaina said. "I'll never forget how that blood hunger came over me the first time Tesar saw a rallop."

"Or how twisted inside this one felt when Alema wanted to nest with that Rodian rope-wrestler." Tesar fluttered his scales, then added, "It was a week before he could hunt again."

Alema smiled at the memory, then said, "*Nesting* wasn't what I had in mind."

Lowbacca banged his bowl down on the bench next to him, groaning in distaste and weary resignation. After the war, Jaina and the other strike team members had begun to notice unexplained mood swings whenever they were together. It had taken Cilghal only a few days to diagnose the problem as a delayed reaction to the Jedi battle-meld. Their prolonged use of it on the Myrkr mission had weakened the boundaries among their minds, with the result that now their emotions tended to fill the Force and blur together whenever they were close to each other.

Sometimes Jaina believed the side effect was also the reason so many strike team survivors found it difficult to move on with their lives. Tenel Ka was doing well as the Hapan queen, and

Tekli and Tahiri seemed to regard Zonama Sekot as both a friend and a home, but the rest of them—Jaina, Alema, Zekk, Tesar, Lowbacca, even Jacen—still seemed lost, unable to maintain a connection with anyone who had not been there. Jaina *knew* that was why she had failed to reconnect with Jagged Fel during their desperate rendezvous when he had still been serving as Chiss liaison to the Galactic Alliance. She loved him, but she'd just grown increasingly distant from him. From everyone, really.

Sensing that she had let her dour mood affect the others, Jaina forced a smile. "I *do* have some good news," she said. "Jacen is coming."

As she had hoped, this lifted spirits instantly—especially those of Tahiri, who shared a special kinship with Jacen by virtue of the time they had spent in Yuuzhan Vong torture dens.

But it was Alema—always quick to take an interest in males— who asked, "Can you tell how soon?"

"It's hard to say," Jaina answered. No one bothered to ask if she had actually spoken to her twin brother; there was no HoloNet in the Unknown Regions—and even if there had been, they were too close to the Chiss frontier to risk being overheard by a listening post. "But it feels like he's made it past whatever was delaying him."

"How will he find the Colony?" Tahiri asked. Though she could certainly sense Alema's interest in Jacen as clearly as Jaina did, she seemed more amused by it than irritated. "Tekli and I would have been lost without Zonama Sekot's help."

"I left a message for him with the coordinates of the Lizil nest," Jaina said. "So, assuming he tries to comm . . ."

She let the sentence trail off when she felt a sudden alarm. The sense did not ripple or grow or rise. It simply appeared inside Jaina, instantly full-blown and strong, and at first she thought she was feeling something inside her brother. Then bowls of thakitillo began to clack down on the spitcrete benches, and her companions started to rise and reach for their lightsabers.

"You feel it, too?" Jaina asked no one in particular.

"Fear," Zekk confirmed. "Surprise."

Lowbacca rawwled an addition.

"Resolve, too," Jaina agreed.

"What the blazes?" Tahiri asked. "It's like the Taat were a part of the meld, too."

"Maybe they're more Force-sensitive than we thought," Alema suggested.

Jaina gazed around, searching the faces of her companions for any indication that the sensation had felt even remotely like a normal Force perception to someone else. She found only looks of confusion and doubt.

A familiar rumble rose deep inside the nest. Long plumes of black smoke began to shoot from the exhaust vents above the hangar cave, then a cloud of dartships poured into the air above the valley and began to climb toward Qoribu's ringed disk.

"Looks like another defoliator squad coming in." Jaina was almost relieved as she started toward their own hangar. After the unexpected feeling of alarm, she had feared something worse. "Let's turn 'em back."

EIGHT

The wreck was a CEC YV-888 stock light freighter. Jacen could see that much from its tall hull, and from the stubs of the melted maneuvering fins on the rear engine compartment. The crash had occurred sometime within the last decade. He could guess that much from the faint odor of ash and slag that still wafted down the flowery slope from the jagged crater rim. But the vessel's hull was too thickly covered in insects for him to be certain this was *the* ship, the one that would explain why he and Jaina and the others had been called so deep into the Unknown Regions.

Jacen waited for a throng of thumb-sized insects to scurry past on the enclosure wall, then placed a hand on top and vaulted over. A harsh rattle rose behind him as other, larger visitors pulsed their wings in disapproval. He paid no attention and started up the slope, feeling his way with the Force to avoid stepping on any tiny beings hidden in the flora. The Colony species came in an enormous variety of sizes and shapes, and any insects he happened to crush on monument grounds were more likely to be other visitors than foraging bugs.

Jacen's guide, a chest-high insect who had been waiting at the Lizil nest to serve as his navigator, scurried to his side and began to rumble objections.

"You're the one who said we didn't have time to wait in line," Jacen reminded him.

"Rububu uburu," the guide responded. With a yellow thorax, green abdomen, and bright red head and eyes, it was one of the more colorful strains that Jacen had seen. *"Urb?"*

"I told you," Jacen answered. "I might know this ship."

Jacen reached the crash crater and climbed to the rim. Ten meters below, in the crash bottom, a sagging tangle of heat-softened durasteel so covered in crawling insects that it took a moment to realize he was looking at a small starship bridge. The vessel had crashed upside down.

The guide thrummed impatiently.

"Not yet." Jacen pointed at a place near the bow where a dozen Jawa-sized insects were sticking their antennae through a twisted rip in the hull. "Ask the ones near that breach to clear a space. I need to see if I can read its name."

"Ub Ruur." [The Crash.]

"I need to know the name of the *freighter,*" Jacen explained. "It's written on the side of the hull. In letters."

Like most species of intelligent arthropods in the galaxy, the Colony insects recorded their language in pheromones instead of writing, but Jacen felt certain the Joiners would have explained the concept of letters.

"U." The guide curled its antennae forward. *"Burubu ru?"*

"Maybe," Jacen said uncertainly. He was relying the Force and his empathic connection with other life-forms to infer his guide's meaning, and he could not always be sure that he understood all the nuances. "But we'll certainly be on our way sooner than if I have to piece the letters together through their legs."

The guide clacked its mandibles in frustration. It drummed its chest loudly, then the insects near the rip began to mill about in confusion. Jacen did not understand what they got out of crawling over the wreck, but insects were very tactile creatures, and he suspected they were establishing some sense of connection to it. Finally, a space began to clear where Jacen had requested. The durasteel was so caked with carbonization that he could barely make out a handful of dark, upside-down letters.

. . . ACH . . ON F . . . ER

"Tachyon Flier," Jacen said. It was the ship in which the strike team had planned to depart the Myrkr system—until they were betrayed by two Dark Jedi they had rescued from the Yuu-

zhan Vong. Jacen turned to his guide. "What happened to the people aboard that ship?"

"Bu ruub ubu buubu," the guide said.

"And he'll keep waiting until I have my answer."

"Ubu buubu ru ruubu." [Unu must not be kept waiting.]

"Your rules," Jacen answered. "Not mine."

Seeing no easier way down, Jacen stepped off the rim and used the Force to slow his descent. The insects on his side of the *Flier* watched in stunned silence as he caught hold of the rip in the hull and brought his fall to a gentle stop.

The guide boomed a question from above.

"The people who brought this ship here had a friend of mine with them," Jacen said. "I'm not leaving here until I know what happened to him."

"Rur ruru rr ubu buubu bub!" the navigator drummed.

"*I* don't wish to see Unu at once." Jacen knew he was being rude, but he had learned from the Fallanassi to see through the illusion of authority, to free himself of the expectation of blind obedience by respecting his own desires first. "It makes no difference to me if Unu can't wait."

Jacen pulled himself up and peered through the hull breach. The *Flier*'s presence certainly lay at the heart of the mysterious summons that had brought him here, but that told him little. Before he allowed himself to be drawn farther along this current, he needed to find out what had happened aboard the ship. He needed to know *who* had called the strike team survivors here . . . and why.

The interior of the vessel was dark and acrid smelling, lit only by the shafts of light pouring through several dozen hull breaches. A few of the holes were large and twisted, like the rip beneath the vessel's name, and had probably resulted from the crash. The rest were oblong, small, and surrounded by the metal spatter-beads associated with hits from Yuuzhan Vong plasma cannons. The *Tachyon Flier* had clearly taken a beating as it left the Myrkr system. It was surprising the ship had held together long enough to fly into the Unknown Regions.

As his eyes grew attuned to the dim light, Jacen realized that he was looking into the hold area. The adjustable cargo decks had left their tracks in the crash and fallen into what had been the top of the ship, burying the bridge and crew quarters beneath a tangle of twisted, half-melted durasteel. Seeing that no insects were crawling over the inside of the ship, he closed his eyes and listened for any stirrings in the Force that might explain their reluctance to enter. He heard the whisper of a long-spent inferno and the faint scream of twisting metal, but nothing to alarm him now.

Jacen swung a leg up and slipped into the *Flier*'s hold. The acrid smell grew stronger. It was more than just ash, it was carbonized synthplas and iron slag and charred fibercrete. He slid down the hull, calling on the Force to hold himself against the wall and slow his descent. About two-thirds of the way to the bottom, he came to the jumble of decks and stopped, then used a Dathomiri Force spell to kindle a sphere of bright light.

A chorus of sharp *clacks* sounded above, and Jacen looked up to see a carpet of insects large and small crawling down the hull behind him, their feathery antennae sweeping the surrounding durasteel. Worried his invasion of a sacred site might be considered an outrage, Jacen touched them through the Force. He felt astonishment, curiosity, a little wariness, but no anger or indignation.

"Be careful," Jacen called, a little puzzled by their willingness to follow *him* into the vessel. "It might not take much to shift the debris down here."

The insects answered with the full range of thrums, chirps, and thuds.

Jacen used the Force to slide several tons of cargo deck into a secure position, then walked over to the edge and discovered the reason for the insects' earlier reluctance to enter the wreck. Several large exoskeletons lay crushed beneath a twisted crossbrace. Though the rest of the jumble was every bit as tangled as it had appeared from above, Jacen could now see that many decks had fallen against each other, creating a tent effect that might have protected the bridge from being crushed—at least from above.

Jacen turned to the insects. "I'd appreciate it if everyone stayed here for now."

The insects gave a confirming *clack*. Floating his sphere of Force light behind him, Jacen threaded his way down to what had been the underside of the bridge, where the metal was buckled and discolored from a conflagration below.

Jacen began to fear the worst.

Seeing no convenient hatch in the vicinity, he ignited his lightsaber . . . and was startled by the sudden clicking of mandibles behind him. He glanced over his shoulder and found a long ribbon of golden eyes reflecting the glow of his Force light and green lightsaber.

"I asked you to wait," Jacen said.

"Uu rrrruub." The thrum set up a sympathetic vibration in the jumble above, inducing a long metallic scream as a deck edge slid down an underbrace. *"Brrr brru!"*

"I am being careful." Jacen used the Force to stabilize the twisted metal above their heads. "Just be quiet."

The swarm rustled its agreement—then clicked madly as he plunged his lightsaber blade into the floor of the bridge.

"I'm sorry to disrespect the Crash," he said. "But my friend may be down there."

"Bru bur, ruu," a ghostly pale insect informed him.

"Obviously." Jacen continued to cut. "I still need to find him."

This occasioned a flurry of thrumming and clicking among the other insects.

"No." Jacen began to feel sick, though it was impossible to say whether this was from the smell of melting metal, the stale stench rising from below, or the insects' question. "I'm not going to eat his remains."

The insects continued to clack and drum. They seemed to be debating whether he should be allowed to continue if he wasn't going to return his friend to the Song. But Jacen was inferring as much as translating, and there was so much he did not know about the Colony that it was equally possible they were talking about eating *him*. He shut the words out and tried to hear through the Force, as the Theran Listeners had taught him, and was relieved to sense that they were arguing over whether *they* should eat the dead.

Jacen finished cutting, then used the Force to lift two disks of metal out of the hole he had cut in the double-floored deck. The smell of ash grew overwhelming, and rustling filled the air as the insects eased forward behind him. Jacen lowered his light through the hole and felt his heart sink.

The cabin below had been so incinerated that only the twisted remains of a row of double bunks, hanging upside down on the far wall, identified it as the crew's quarters. What had once been the ceiling lay barely two meters below, blackened, crumpled, and strewn with ash and twisted metal. The remains of several mattresses lay in the corner beneath the bunks, half burned and covered in black mold.

Being careful to avoid touching the white-hot edges, Jacen dropped through the hole and found several shattered tranqarest vials under one of the half-burned mattresses. Under another, he found a melted lump of casing and circuitry that might once have been Lowbacca's translation droid, Em Teedee. He tried to pick it up and discovered it had been fused to the floor.

Under a third mattress, he found the singed remains of one of the molytex jumpsuits the strike team had worn on their mission to Myrkr. There were four slashes across the chest, where Raynar had been wounded before being put aboard the *Flier.*

A series of soft patters sounded from the middle of the cabin. Insects began to swarm over the "floor" and walls, sweeping their antennae over the bunks and other debris and raising a choking cloud of ash. Jacen made his way forward through the galley and wardroom, dropping into a crouch as the space between the crumpled ceiling and the old floor grew too short for him to walk upright. The walls and other surfaces in these rooms were covered with a thick layer of pink powder, the residue of a fire-fighting foam.

On the bridge, the foam lay so thick that he kicked up clouds of pink dust as he moved. The canopy that had once enclosed the flight deck on three sides was buckled and broken, with dirt spilling through long rents in the transparisteel. A string of gray emergency patches ran diagonally across the forward viewscreen, roughly parallel to a line of destruction that had left the navicomputer, sublight-drive control relays, and hyperspace guidance system in a burned shambles. It was no wonder the ship had crashed; the Dark Jedi crew had done well to escape the Myrkr system at all.

The crash webbing at all the flight deck stations hung down beneath the chairs in a melted tangle, but a faint drag mark beneath the pilot's and copilot's seats led through the foam residue toward the engineering cabin. Jacen dropped to his knees to peer through the cockeyed hatchway, and his nostrils filled with the caustic stench of charred bone.

Jacen began a slow breathing exercise. The harsh smell burned his nostrils at first and threatened to make him nauseous, but as he centered himself in the Force and slowly detached from his emotions, the odor grew less biting, its implications less painful. He placed a hand on the wall and imagined it growing warm under his touch.

The staleness seemed to fade from the air inside the wreck, then the smell of old soot turned to the acrid bite of smoke. Jacen's eyes started to water as he looked back through the Force. His lungs were racked by an endless fit of coughing, and the cabin grew hot and orange. Where he was touching the wall, his palm began to sting and blister. He held it in place and looked over his shoulder.

The flight deck was hidden behind a curtain of smoke and rolling flame. Geysers of fire retardant rose from the ceiling nozzles, creating swirling ghosts of pink fog. Howls of human anguish drowned out the scream of buckling metal.

A single figure crawled out of the smoke, hairless and coughing and blistered raw. His face was unrecognizable, but four gashes ran diagonally across his chest, the wound hanging half open where the fleshglue had dissolved in the heat. One hand trailed behind, dragging a pair of levitated shapes along by their cloak collars. The two shapes were still burning, writhing in the air and flailing against each other in their pain.

Smoke began to rise from beneath Jacen's palm, and the smell of cooking flesh filled the air. He kept his hand pressed against the wall. Pain no longer troubled him. Pain was his servant; he had learned *that* from Vergere.

The crawling figure reached the hatchway and paused, turning in Jacen's direction. The face was too scorched and swollen to recognize, but the eyes belonged to Raynar, questioning and proud and so terribly naïve. The two of them locked gazes for a moment, then Raynar cocked his head in confusion and started to open his mouth . . .

Jacen pulled his hand from the wall. The figures vanished instantly, returning him to a flight deck filled with the stale smell of ash and clouds of pink dust.

An insect brushed its antennae over his scorched hand. *"Rurrrrruu,"* it drummed in concern. *"Urrubuuuu?"*

"Yes, it does hurt." Jacen smiled. "It's nothing."

He removed a small canister from his equipment belt and sprayed a coating of synthflesh over his palm. Raynar had been the misfit of their childhood group, trying a little too hard to fit in and often the butt of jokes for his arrogance and showy clothes. He had never impressed anyone as exceptional Jedi material, and there had been a few conversations in which fellow candidates had expressed reservations about his judgment and initiative. Yet what Raynar had done on the *Flier,* risking his own life to save those who had betrayed his friends and abducted him, was the essence of being a Jedi Knight. Jacen doubted he would have done the same thing—and *Jaina* would have stayed to watch them burn. Given what the theft of the *Flier* had meant—that Anakin would certainly die of his wounds—Jacen might even have joined her.

Floating his Force light ahead of him, Jacen crawled into the engineering cabin and followed Raynar's trail through a cramped maze of toppled equipment. The stench of charred bones grew stronger, and Jacen feared he would only find their burned remains trapped in some dead-end corner, or simply lying in the middle of the aisle where Raynar had succumbed to smoke inhalation. His fears began to seem justified when he started to find scorched bones in the middle of the aisle—first, a few finger and toe and hand bones, then a forearm and a shin, then finally a femur. The space between the floor and ceiling grew smaller and smaller, and he had to drop to his belly, and he began to sense the residue of Raynar's panic in the Force.

Then Jacen came to the shoulder blade, lying half buried in a pile of dirt that had poured in through a rent in the hull, and he knew. He began to dig, pulling the soft dirt under his body and pushing it back with his feet, and a moment later he felt a welcome draft of fresh air. Raynar had reached an exit—but in what condition? Had he survived? Had either of the others?

His chest tight with hope and fear, Jacen belly-crawled through the hole, out into the bottom of the crater . . . and was surprised to find his guide waiting. In its hands, the insect held a new starfighter helmet and flight suit.

"Ubu rrru ubb." Without waiting for Jacen to stand, the guide offered the helmet and suit to him. *"Urru bu."*

Jacen stood. "Why would I need a starfighter helmet?" Instead of taking either item, he began to brush himself off. "I fly a skiff."

The guide raised one of its four hands toward the crater rim, where one of the Reconstruction Police's new XJ5 X-wings sat with an open cockpit.

Jacen had a sinking feeling. "I'm *happy* with my skiff."

The guide thrummed a long explanation, which seemed to assert that he would be much happier serving the Colony in a ChaseX than his skiff, which the Colony was already using to ferry a group of Togot pilgrims back to the spaceport.

Jacen did not bother to demand its return. He had already learned that the Colony insects had no real understanding of private property. The skiff would be put to use—and, fortunately, well maintained—until he was ready to track it down again.

"Why would I want to serve the Colony?" Jacen asked. "Especially in a combat craft?"

A membrane slid over the guide's bulbous eyes and rose again, and it continued to hold the helmet and flight suit out to Jacen.

"It's a simple question," Jacen said. "If the Colony expects me to kill people, you'd better be able to tell me why."

The guide cocked its head in incomprehension, and Jacen knew he was asking too much. As social insects, Colony residents obviously had a very limited sense of self—and absolutely no concept of free will. He might as well have been asking a beldon to take him fishing.

Always the preacher. The voice was the same that had come

to Jacen back in Akanah's teaching circle—save that now the words were raspy and booming instead of faint and wispy. *You still think too much, Jacen.*

"I usually find it preferable to catastrophic blunders," Jacen said. The voice was so harsh and deep he found it even more difficult to place. It might have been Raynar—or it might have been Lomi or Welk or someone else altogether. "You seem to know me. You couldn't believe I would just start killing for you."

We do know you, Jacen, the voice said, not unkindly. *We know what you will fight for.*

As the voice spoke, an immense murky presence rose inside Jacen's mind, overwhelming his defenses so quickly he had no chance to shut it out. In the midst of the presence, he saw Jaina and the others, their faces filled with surprise and revulsion and pity. They were all in their flight suits, haggard and travel-worn, but healthy enough and unafraid.

They *serve the Colony, Jacen,* the voice said. *Will you join them? Will you help your sister?*

Jacen did not answer, even in his thoughts. A day ago, he had felt Jaina growing small and cold in the Force, the way she always did before a battle. But there had been no indication afterward of anything alarming, not even the usual weary sorrow that always came of taking lives. He reached out to her, probing to see if there was anything amiss. She responded with a welcoming warmth that let him know she was looking forward to seeing him.

But there was more, just a hint of the murky presence that had pushed its way into Jacen's mind—not hostile or ominous or threatening, just there.

The guide drew Jacen's attention back to it by pressing the helmet and flight suit into his hands. *"Buu buur urub ruuruur."*

Jacen pushed the equipment back into the guide's hands. "I haven't said I'm going."

"Buu rurr. Ubu ur."

"Perhaps," Jacen allowed. The murky presence had withdrawn from his own mind, once again leaving him solely with his guide. "Once I've found out what happened here."

He squatted on his haunches and ran his fingers through the dirt, searching for any sign that Raynar and the others had died here. When he found no more large bones, he pictured the raw and blistered face he had seen on the flight deck, then called on the Force again, trying to reach into the past and learn what had become of Raynar.

But this time, the Force opened itself to him in its own way. Instead of the smoke and scorched flesh he had smelled on the flight deck, the odor it brought down to him was fresh and fragrant and familiar, a smell he had known since childhood.

Jacen looked up at the crater rim and was puzzled to find an image of his mother there, frowning across the gap at the *Flier*'s blast-pocked hull. She was wearing a white blouse with a brown skirt and vest that reminded Jacen of his father's swashbuckling style, right down to the holstered blaster hanging on her hip. There were some new strands of gray hair and a few more laugh lines around her mouth, but she looked healthy and content, and Jacen's heart leapt at the sight of her. The last time he had seen her face had been over five standard years ago, before leaving on his odyssey of self-discovery, and he was astonished at the joy even a vision of it brought to him.

Jacen swallowed his surprise and tried instead to simply concentrate on what the Force was revealing to him. He knew that she was not actually standing there *now,* but at some other time. And, since his mother was the only figure he could see, she was probably the link to discovering what had become of Raynar.

She turned to someone he could not see, then asked, "What happened to the crew?"

There was a pause while she listened to the reply. Jacen could imagine only one thing that would bring his parents this deep into the Unknown Regions, the heart of the Colony itself. They had to be looking for the strike team.

His mother looked back to the *Flier.* "I mean the rest of the crew. We *know* Raynar survived."

Jacen had his answer, but he was not ready to release the vision—not yet. He looked up at his mother's image, reaching out to her in the Force to strengthen their contact.

"Hello."

Her gaze dropped toward Jacen's voice, then she furrowed her brow and reached out, as though grasping for someone's arm. "Jacen has been here."

Has. So they were still behind him.

The guide snapped its mandibles next to Jacen's ear. *"Bubu ruu bu?"*

"No one. Sorry." Continuing to hold the vision through the Force, Jacen finally took the helmet and flight suit. "Okay. Where am I going?"

The guide replied that Jacen wouldn't recognize the name of the system. It was on the Chiss frontier.

Up on the crater rim, the vision of his mother frowned. "Jacen? I'm having trouble hearing you."

Jacen ignored her and continued to speak to the guide. "Humor me. In case something happens and I need to find my own way."

The navigator spread its antennae. *"Burubu,"* it answered. *"Ur bu Brurr rubur."*

"Jacen?" His mother's face grew pale. "How? You're not—"

"I'm fine, Mom," he said. "I'll see you soon."

The guide turned a bulbous eye toward the crater rim.

"Qoribu," Jacen said, looking up at his mother. "In the Gyuel system."

NINE

As the *Falcon* dropped toward the mottled pinnacles below, Leia found herself straining against her crash webbing, almost gasping at the bustling vastness of the Colony's central nest. The Yoggoy towers, brightly adorned in wild splashes of color, stood hip-to-hip across the entire planet, and the air was so thick with flying vehicles that she could barely see the surface.

"Kind of looks like old Coruscant," Han said, speaking to Leia and—over the comm—to Luke, Mara, and everyone else aboard the *Shadow*. "So big—and all that bustle."

Leia continued to strain forward over her controls, peering out the lower edge of the canopy. As the *Falcon* descended, she began to see that while the pinnacles came in every size, they were all distinctly cone-shaped, and they all had horizontally banded exteriors—like the insect spires in *Killik Twilight*.

She started to say as much, then decided she was letting her imagination run wild. Cones were a basic geometric form. Creating them out of mud rings was probably as common among intelligent insects as was erecting stone rectangles among social mammals.

"I'm gonna blast that can of corrosion back to quarks!" Han said.

Leia glanced over to find Han frowning at his tactical display, then checked her own screen and saw that the *XR808g*'s transponder code had disappeared. "Did Juun land already?"

Han shook his head. "The little earworm shut off his transponder."

Knowing better than to ask if Han had remembered to run a code search, Leia activated her throat mike.

"We've lost the *Exxer.*"

The report was greeted with a troubled silence. Right now, the *XR808g* was their only hope of locating Jaina and the others.

"Any ideas?" Han asked. "I'd like to find these kids *before* they become a bunch of bughuggers."

"That's not going to happen." Even over the cockpit comm, Luke's voice was calm and reassuring. "They're Jedi."

"What's that have to do with the price of spice on Nal Hutta?" Han demanded.

"They're too strong, Han," Mara said. "Especially Jaina."

"Yeah?" Han asked. "If they're so strong, how'd that Force-call drag them all the way out here in the first place?"

The troubled silence returned.

Leia reached over and laid her hand over Han's. "It'll be all right, Han. I can still feel them out there. They're not Joiners."

"Yet," Han grumbled. Over the comm, he asked, "How about those ideas?"

"Try a code search," Luke suggested helpfully.

Han rolled his eyes.

Leia smiled at him, then said to Luke, "Thanks for the suggestion. We've already tried that."

"No need to worry," Mara said. "We haven't lost them."

"We haven't?" Leia asked. Before the *XR808g* left Lizil, Han and Juun had hidden a subspace transceiver beneath the cockpit and linked it to the navicomputer. Each time the *XR808g* initiated a jump, the transceiver automatically encoded the galactic coordinates and broadcast them to the *Shadow* and *Falcon*—but that didn't help them now, when they were already *at* those coordinates. "I don't understand."

"Give me a second." Mara remained silent for a moment, then said, "Be ready to take a fix, in case Juun is smarter than he looked."

Han raised his brow. "I don't recall planting a homing beacon on the *Exxer.*"

"Because *you're* not the sneaky one—despite all reports to the contrary," Mara commed. "Ready?"

Leia smiled and prepared a navigation lock. "Ready." A red dot began to blink in the upper corner of the tactical display. "Got it."

Leia activated the lock, and Han swung the *Falcon* around behind the red dot. Yoggoy traffic proved an unimaginable free-for-all, with muscle-powered balloon-bikes competing for airspace against dilapidated cloud cars and modern airspeeders. Thick-waisted rocket planes flashed past in all directions, packed to bursting with goggle-eyed insects and trailing oily plumes of smoke. Battered space freighters eased their durasteel hulks down into the mess, descending through the traffic toward the haze-blanketed towertops below.

A stubby little rocket plane shot out from under a cargo blimp off to starboard and began to climb, coming for Leia's side of the cockpit.

"Rodder!" Han cursed, and the *Falcon* took a sudden skip upward. "Watch where you're going!"

"Don't get so upset," Leia said. "We have plenty—"

A thirty-meter insect shuttle flashed into view from beneath Leia's side of the cockpit, headed straight for the little rocket plane.

"Oh, my!" C-3PO said from the navigator's station. "That was too close—"

"Hard to port," Leia interrupted. "Now, Han!"

"Port?" Han shot back. "You're crazy!"

Leia glanced over and saw the mountainous hull of a giant transport gliding past above the *Falcon*'s forward mandibles.

"Oh—" Leia slapped the crash alarm, bringing the inertial compensators to maximum, priming the fire-suppression systems, and setting off a cacophony of alerts farther back in the vessel. "Brace yourself!"

"Dead stop!" Luke's voice came over the comm. "Dead stop!"

Han already had his hand on the throttles—but before he could pull them back, the shuttle was diving and the rocket plane was climbing past the *Falcon* almost vertically, so close that Leia could have reached out and grabbed the pilot's antennae.

Han casually slipped his hand off the throttle and deactivated the crash alarm. "No need to get all excited." His hands were shaking as badly as Leia's, but she saw no use in pointing that out. "I've got it under control."

"Yes," C-3PO agreed. "It's fortunate that you were wise enough to do nothing. It gave the other pilots time to respond to your error."

"*My* error?" Han replied. "I was flying straight and level."

"Quite so, but the others are all following sine wave trajectories," C-3PO said. "And may I point out that any system functions optimally only when all elements use the same equations?"

A two-seater rocket plane dropped in ahead of the *Falcon* and bobbed along pouring fumes into their faces, then swerved aside to reveal the bulbous shape of a balloon-bike coming at them head-on. Han rolled into an inverted dive and spiraled past beneath it.

"Now you tell me," Han said.

"Watch it back there," Leia warned the *Shadow*. "And have Artoo plot a sine wave trajectory for us—a *safe* one."

"We'll send it up in a moment," Mara promised.

The moment went by, then two, then several. Finally, when her nerves could stand no more close calls—and no more of Han's grouching—Leia commed back to the *Shadow*.

"Uh, we didn't receive that trajectory."

"We're trying," Luke said. "Artoo's sort of locked up."

"Locked up?" Han asked. "An *astromech*?"

"He's been acting strange lately," Luke explained. "All we got before he went blank was *not safe, not safe, not safe.*"

"Oh, dear!" C-3PO exclaimed. "It sounds as though he's trying to resolve an unknowable variable. We're doomed!"

"Yeah?" Han waved at the traffic outside the forward viewport. "Then how come none of *them* are crashing?"

C-3PO was silent for a moment, then said, "I wouldn't know, Captain Solo. Their processors certainly aren't any better than Artoo's."

"They don't *need* processors." Leia was thinking of Luke's description of the cantina where Saba met Tarfang, of how the mysterious Joiners had arrived to lead away any patron with whom he struck up a conversation. "It was pretty clear that the Lizil can communicate telepathically. Maybe the Yoggoy can, too."

"Probably," Mara agreed. "And since *we* don't have any Yoggoy navigators aboard—"

"We're flying blind!" Han finished. "Better bring the shields to maximum, Leia. We're going to get some bug spatter."

"Perhapz not," Saba commed from the *Shadow.* "Leia, have you been doing your reaction drill?"

Leia felt a stab of guilt. "When there's been time."

Saba was kind enough not to remind her that she was supposed to *make* time for her training. That was the obligation of a Jedi Knight—though Leia, in all honesty, had a hard time thinking of herself as anything other than an eternal apprentice. Perhaps that was why she found it so hard to find training time.

"Do the drill now," Saba said. "But instead of stingerz, imagine the remote is shooting vesselz at you."

Leia started a breathing exercise, then closed her eyes and opened herself to the Force. She immediately felt something swooping down on them from above.

"Down and starboard," she said.

The *Falcon* continued on the same course.

"Han—"

"Are you crazy?" he interrupted. "With your eyes open, maybe. But not . . ."

The *Falcon* dropped five meters, and Leia opened her eyes to see the swollen underbelly of a big Gallofree transport gliding over them.

"*Now* you will . . . listen . . . to your nestie!" Saba was sissing hysterically. "Mara is *flying* with her eyes closed."

"Who isn't?" Han gave Leia a quick nod. "Whatever you say, dear."

Leia closed her eyes again and began to call directions. At first Han emitted an alarming string of oaths and gasps, but gradually the sensations grew more concrete—and Han's willingness to follow the blind more ready. Within the hour, they were bobbing and dodging along more or less steadily behind the *XR808g.*

Finally, Han said, "Looks like he's going to ground."

Leia opened her eyes to see the tracking blip drifting down toward the middle of the display, its color deepening to red as the *XR808g* lost altitude. She looked out the canopy and found the distinctive wafer of a YT light freighter in the distance ahead, descending into the hazy labyrinth of insect pinnacles. Traffic remained heavy above the spires, but there were only a handful of drifting balloon-bikes and slow-moving airspeeders among the towers themselves.

"We'll take point," Leia commed. "Why don't you fly top cover?"

"It's a plan," Luke answered.

As the *Falcon* descended, Leia saw that the mottled colors decorating the pinnacles had been created by pressing colored pebbles into the exterior walls. The effect was remarkably calming. If she watched them out of the corner of her eye, or allowed her gaze to go unfocused, the bright blotches of color reminded her of a meadow in full bloom—and, she realized, of the elaborate mosaics inside the spires depicted in *Killik Twilight.*

"Could it be?" she gasped.

"Could be anything," Han answered. "So let's be ready. Send Cakhmaim and Meewalh to the cannon turrets, and tell Beady to go to ready standby."

They followed the *XR808g* down to within a hundred meters of ground level, where the balloon-bikes and airspeeders gave way to rivers of racing landspeeders, speeder bikes, and dangerous-looking rocket carts steered exclusively by Yoggoy pilots. Pedestrians were forced to scurry along the tower bases, hanging on the walls sideways if they were insects or keeping themselves tightly pressed against the foundations if they were bipeds.

Juun began to fly erratically, making last-second turns and doubling back on his own trail. If not for the tracking blip, Leia would have lost him a dozen times in half an hour. Finally, they swung onto a large curving boulevard and began to circle a massive complex of fused towers sheathed in an eye-pulling mosaic done in every imaginable shade of red. The *XR808g* eased steadily toward the interior lanes, then abruptly dropped to ground level and disappeared into the dark mouth of a huge, barrel-vaulted gateway.

"That kreetle!" Han said. "I should've blasted him when I had the chance."

Leia immersed herself in the Force, then reported, "It looks more dangerous than it feels."

"You sure?" Han gave her a sidelong look. "No offense, but I *know* how much time you have to practice that Jedi stuff."

"Would it make any difference if I wasn't sure?"

Han gave her that crooked grin of his. "What do you think?"

He eased the yoke forward and swung the *Falcon* into the murky gateway. Leia activated the forward maneuvering lights, illuminating the interior of a huge, winding passage covered in a wavy pink-and-yellow mosaic. The tunnel was longer than Leia had expected, and each time the ship rounded a new bend, they sent a swarm of insects scurrying for the vault edges.

After a couple of minutes, they emerged in a small, flower-shaped plaza enclosed by a dozen fused towers. The mosaics were bright and disorienting, with solid bands of color gradually paling from deep amber at ground level to pure white at the pinnacletops. At the far side of the area, the *XR808g* sat on its landing struts, its boarding ramp already dropping into position.

Han brought the *Falcon* to within twenty meters and set her down with the missile launchers facing the *XR808g*. "Cakhmaim, Meewalh, be ready with those cannons," he ordered over the intercom. "Ready—"

"Prepared to open fire, Captain," the droid reported.

"Not *yet*," Leia said, unbuckling her crash webbing. "Only if they shoot first."

"Survival rates decrease thirty-two percent for combatants firing in reaction," BD-8 objected.

"We're not shooting first." Han strapped on his BlasTech holster. "Just stand ready to look tough."

"Look tough?" BD-8 inquired.

"Intimidation mode one," C-3PO clarified. He turned to Han. "You really should use the standardized terms with the BD series. Their tactical overlays leave little processing power for semantic analysis."

Han rolled his eyes. "Yeah, maybe I'll read the manual some-day."

He led the way off the flight deck, and they descended the boarding ramp to find Juun scurrying toward them in a torn tunic.

"Han! Princess Leia!" he called cheerfully. "I was afraid we'd lost you!"

"Sure you were," Han replied coldly. He stopped a few steps from the end of the ramp and rested a hand on his holstered blaster. "Your transponder just happened to go on the blink?"

"Of course not!" Juun said. "Our guide disabled it. After the last jump, he found the subspace transceiver."

BD-8 came up behind Leia and glared over her shoulder, clicking and whirring loudly. Juun stopped three meters away and gawked up at the battle droid. Leia tried to get a read on the his truthfulness, but she felt only alarm and confusion.

Juun raised his hands. "Please! It wasn't my fault!"

Leia glimpsed movement on the tower walls behind him, then saw several tiers of insect soldiers stepping into view. They looked much like Lizil workers, except they were the size of a Wookiee, with meter-long mandibles and scarlet carapaces covering their backs. The undersides of their thoraxes were bright gold, and their eyes were a deep, haunting purple. In their four hands, they each carried a crude electrobolt assault rifle and a short, thick-shafted trident. It took an instant to realize they were standing on small terraces instead of midair, for human eyes found it difficult to interpret the subtle interplay of hue and shadow that defined each belt of the wall mosaic.

"That does it!" Han said, reaching for his holster. "I'm gonna blast you myself."

The edges of Juun's cheek folds turned blue. "What for?"

"What for?" Han waved his blaster at the surrounding walls. "For leading us into a trap!"

Juun's eyes went wide. "I did?"

Leia reached out to the insects above, searching for any hint of hostile intentions, and felt none.

"Don't play dumb," Han said to Juun. He aimed his blaster at the Sullustan's knees. "It just makes me mad."

Leia reached over and covered Han's blaster hand. "Put that thing away!" she whispered. "It isn't what it looks like."

"Then what is it?" Han continued to glare at Juun.

"We'll have a better chance of finding out if you keep that thing in its holster."

Han allowed her to push the blaster down, but BD-8 was harder to convince.

"Situation serious," the droid reported. "Suggest withdrawal to transport. Permission to lay covering fire?"

"Denied!" Leia and Han said simultaneously.

"Okay," Han said to Juun. "Maybe it's not what it looks like. Where's Tarfang?"

Juun remained at a distance. "In the medbay. When our guide found the transceiver, there was a little fight."

Leia began to have a sinking feeling. "What about the guide? It's not—"

Her question was drowned out by the sudden thunder of insect drumming. The three lowest rows of soldiers raised their carapaces, then stepped off their terraces and added to the tumult the roar of hundreds of beating wings. Leia heard BD-8 ask something she could not understand and ordered him to stand down on general principles—though she did pluck the lightsaber off her belt and start easing back toward the *Falcon*'s boarding ramp.

Juun scurried over to join them, his round ears red with alarm. The soldiers continued to swirl overhead in a dark mass for several seconds, then glided to the plaza floor and formed a tightly packed cordon around the *Falcon* and *XR808g*.

"Situation critical," BD-8 reported. "Permission to return to stand ready?"

"G-granted," Leia said.

The soldiers thrummed their chests in a single deafening boom, then brought their feet together and snapped their weapons to the attention position against their thoraxes. On the far side of the *XR808g*, the cordon parted to admit a small parade of insects of many different body shapes, ranging in size from that of Leia's thumb to somewhat larger than an X-wing. Most seemed to be simple variations on the standard Colony pattern, with feathery antennae, large bulbous eyes, and four arms and two legs. But some had exaggerated features, such as one with slender, two-meter antennae ending in fuzzy yellow spheres, another with five large eyes instead of the usual two large and three small, and several that walked on four legs instead of two. One of the largest had a coat of sensory bristles so thick it looked like fur.

In the center of the procession walked an imposing, melt-faced man with no ears or hair and a mere bulge for a nose. His brows had fused into a single knobby ridge, and all his visible skin had the shiny, stiff quality of a burn scar. He wore purple trousers with a scarlet cape over a gold chitin breastplate.

"Who's the fashion victim?" Han asked Juun.

"I think it's the Prime Unu." Juun's voice was almost a gasp. "*Nobody* ever sees him."

"The Prime Unu?" Leia asked.

"You might consider him the chief of the Colony," Juun whispered. "He's doesn't rule it, at least not the way most species think of ruling, but he's the heart of the whole thing."

"Sort of the king bee, huh?" Han asked.

Leia felt Luke reaching out to her from above, alarmed by the growing trepidation he had been sensing in her. She filled her mind with reassuring thoughts.

The Prime Unu stopped in front of the *XR808g,* and two of his companions boarded the battered freighter. Leia reached out in the Force, trying to gauge his intentions, and found the same double presence that she had come to recognize in the Joiners of the Lizil nest. But the individual element of his presence felt stronger than most and—to her surprise—somehow familiar. Leia allowed her thoughts to roam freely over the past, seeking their own connections to that familiarity.

Her mind went first to the Jedi academy on Yavin 4, during a time when Anakin was still too young to attend and jealous of his older siblings. The memory brought with it a flood of emotion, and Leia found herself struggling to retain her composure—to avoid the torrent of grief and remembrance that always threatened to sweep her away when she thought of her lost son. Her mind was telling her that the Prime was tied to her children—particularly Anakin—and she could not help hoping that the Prime *was* Anakin; that her son had somehow survived the Myrkr mission after all, and the funeral on Hapes had been some other young man's.

But that was fantasy. Had it been Anakin standing next to the *XR808g,* Leia would have *known.* She would have felt it in her bones.

Her thoughts wandered to another memory, on Eclipse, where Cilghal and Danni had learned to jam Yuuzhan Vong battle coordinators. The Jedi were meeting in a lab, with the milky splendor of the galactic core pouring down through the transparisteel ceiling. Cilghal was explaining that she had discovered where the enemy was growing the deadly voxyn that had been attacking the Jedi across the galaxy.

. . . *a full-grown ysalamiri,* the Mon Calamari was saying, and suddenly Leia felt an enormous, murky presence in the Force pressing her away from the Prime. She looked up and found him staring in her direction, his blue eyes shining like a pair of oncoming blaster bolts. Leia raised her chin and held his gaze. Her vision grew dark around the edges, and soon she could see nothing but his eyes.

He winked and looked away, and Leia felt herself falling.

"Whoa!" Han caught her under her arms. "What's wrong?"

"Nothing." Leia allowed Han to hold her as her vision returned to normal. "The king is Force-sensitive."

"Yeah?" Han replied. "I've never seen you react that way before."

"Okay, he's *very* Force-sensitive." Leia gathered her legs beneath her. "We might know him."

"You're kidding." Han studied the Prime for a moment, then shook his head. "Who is it?"

"I don't know yet," Leia said.

A pair of insects emerged from the *XR808g* carrying the Yoggoy guide that Juun had been assigned. The chitin of its thorax was pitted and charred, three of its limbs hung beside its body loose and swinging, and both of its antennae had been broken off. The Prime pressed his melted brow to the insect's, then raised the remains of a three-fingered hand and began to stroke the stumps of its antennae.

"An *Ewok* did that?" Han asked Juun.

The Sullustan nodded. "Tarfang is not the gentle soul he seems."

A contented *boom* reverberated from the chest of the wounded guide, and the Prime stood and started toward the *Falcon*. It was impossible to read the expression behind his grotesque mask of a face, but the briskness of his pace suggested how he felt about what he had just seen.

"The king doesn't look very happy," Leia said. "Maybe you should wait aboard the *Falcon,* Captain Juun."

"That won't be necessary," Juun said. "The guide assured me there would be no—"

The Prime raised two fingers and pointed at the *Falcon*'s laser cannons. There was a *thunk* as the turrets broke their collar locks, then the muffled scream of grating servomotors.

"Hey!" Han protested.

The turrets continued to rotate—tearing up their internal maneuvering mechanisms—until the cannons faced aft.

"Hostile action under way," BD-8 reported. "Permission to—"

The Prime raised a finger toward him, and the request ended in a garbled blast of static. The harsh smell of melting circuits filled the air, then the droid crashed to the ground. Han glanced over his shoulder.

"Bloah!" he gasped. "Can *Luke* do that?"

"Maybe I'll wait aboard the *Falcon* after all," Juun said.

The Sullustan turned and raced up the boarding ramp—and the Prime surprised Leia by letting him. The ghastly figure crossed the last few steps and stopped in front of the Solos, towering over Han by a good third of a meter. For a moment, he stood glaring down, his breath coming in audible wheezes that suggested badly damaged lungs, his blue eyes sliding back and forth between their faces.

Then Cakhmaim and Meewalh appeared at the top of the boarding ramp with power blasters in hand. Leia started to order the Noghri to stand down, but she was no match for their reflexes. They shouldered their weapons and yelled for the Solos to drop to their bellies.

The Prime flicked his wrist, and both Noghri went tumbling back into the *Falcon*'s main corridor. He stared in their direction for a moment, no doubt checking to make sure they would not surprise him later, then turned back to Leia and Han.

"Captain Solo." His voice was a deep, gravelly rasp that made Leia's throat close with empathic pain. "Princess Leia. We weren't expecting you." He glanced skyward, where Luke and Mara were still circling onstation in the *Shadow*. "Nor the Masters Skywalker."

"Sorry about that," Han retorted. "We tried to comm, but it turns out there's no HoloNet in the Unknown Regions."

"No HoloNet." The Prime's upper lip quivered, straining to smile, but not quite able to break free of its scar-tissue cast. "We hadn't considered that."

He turned away and walked under the *Falcon*, craning his inflexible neck around awkwardly to inspect the ship's belly. He made a complete circuit like this, pausing beneath the cargo lift, rising on his toes to peer at the seals around the missile tube doors, kicking the landing struts. Finally, he reached up and touched the carbon-scored hull.

"We never liked the black," the Prime said. "White is better. White is your color."

Leia's mind flashed back to the Yavin 4 visit, to a handsome blond-haired boy lying unconscious on the floor after being bitten by Jacen's crystal snake—a handsome boy dressed in the haughty scarlet, gold, and purple of the Bornaryn shipping empire.

"Raynar?" she gasped. "Raynar Thul?"

TEN

"Raynar Thul is no more," Raynar said. He was squatting on his haunches in the heart of the Prime Chamber, high atop a circular dais where he would always be visible to the hundreds of insect attendants that followed wherever he went. His long arms were hanging over his knees with the backs of his hands resting slackly on the ground before him, and his blue eyes were riveted, unblinking, to Luke's face. "We are UnuThul."

"How strange, then, that I still sense Raynar Thul's presence within yours," Luke said.

He found it difficult to meet Raynar's gaze, not because of those unblinking eyes or the ghastliness of the face that held them, but because of the conflicting emotions they aroused— elation that Raynar had survived his abduction, regret over what had happened afterward, anger and anguish that so many others had failed to return at all . . . especially his nephew Anakin. He still woke up nights praying that it had been just a bad dream; that there had been a better way to stop the voxyn and he had never been asked to authorize the mission to Myrkr at all.

But Luke was careful to keep those feelings hidden, buried deep inside where they would not show in the Force and complicate a discussion already sure to be difficult and full of emotion for both sides.

"Raynar Thul may be in hiding," Luke said carefully. "But he is not gone. I feel that clearly."

"We are surprised, Master Skywalker, that you cannot feel the difference between a ghost and a man." The same murky presence that Luke had felt in the Lizil cantina rose within Raynar's body, not forcing Luke out, but preventing him from feeling anything else. "Raynar Thul vanished with the Crash."

"And then UnuThul was born?"

"The Kind are not born, Master Skywalker," Raynar said. "An egg drops, a chrysalis is spun."

"You mean there was a metamorphosis?" Leia asked. Along with Mara and Saba, she was sitting cross-legged with Luke on the dais floor. Han, of course, could not be talked into sitting. He was pacing the edge of the dais, keeping a wary eye on the attendants below and grumbling about the heat and mugginess and too-sweet smell of the nest. "Is that the story on the walls?"

Leia gestured at the colorful mosaics that decorated the interior of the Prime Chamber, and Raynar's eyes flashed in delight, a pair of blue embers flaring back to life in that melted wreck of a face.

"You are as observant as we recall, Princess," he said. "Others are not usually observant enough to perceive the Chronicle."

"The Chronicle?" Luke asked.

Raynar pointed over Luke's shoulder, where a red streak arced down the domed ceiling to a white smear opposite the main entrance to the chamber.

"A star wagon fell from the sky," Raynar said.

As Luke twisted around to look, he glimpsed the blocky hull of an overturned YV-888 light freighter protruding above the rim of a still-smoking crater. But as soon as his gaze fell directly on it, the image dissolved into the same blur of semi-random color that had been there before.

"I don't see anything," Han complained.

"Only a wall of rockz," added Saba, whose Barabel eyes were incapable of seeing nearly half the colors in the design.

"You can't look directly at it," Mara explained. "It's like one of those air-jellies on Bespin. It only shows up when you look away."

"Oh, yeah," Han said.

Saba hissed in frustration.

Luke let his gaze slide to the next image and glimpsed Raynar kneeling over a wounded insect, his palms pressed to its cracked thorax.

"No, Master Skywalker. Over there." Raynar pointed to a pinkish blotch on the adjacent wall, eliciting a loud rustle as all the insects in the chamber turned to look in the direction he was pointing. "The Kind do not order such things in the same way you Others do."

When Luke turned his head, he saw a scorched figure lying in the bottom of the crash crater, surrounded by waiting insects.

"Beside the star wagon Yoggoy found Raynar Thul, a scorched and dying thing," Raynar continued. "We climbed down to wait for the Last Note so we could share his flesh among our larvae."

Raynar pointed across the room again, to another mosaic depicting the insects carrying him toward a small enclave of spires similar to those in the city outside.

"But he touched us inside, and we were filled with the need to care for his body."

The next image showed Raynar's burned body in the bottom of a large six-sided basin, curled into a fetal position and tended by two human-sized insects.

"We built a special cell, and we fed him and cleaned him like our own larvae."

Luke had to slide his glance past the following scene three times before he could be sure of what he was seeing. The mosaic showed only Raynar's face, surrounded by the walls of a much smaller cell, his neck craned back and his mouth gaping open to accept a meal from a nearby insect.

"After a time, Raynar Thul was no more."

The picture he pointed to next showed Raynar rising from the cell much as he was now, a knobby, faceless, melted memory of a man, arms crossed across his chest, feet together and pointed downward, eyes shining beneath his heavy brow like a pair of cold blue moons.

"A new Yoggoy arose."

The following image showed Raynar splinting the leg of a wounded insect, and the one after that showed several Yoggoy tending to an entire chamber of sick and injured nest members.

"We learned to care for the infirm."

Several pictures showed the Yoggoy nest expanding and growing, with Raynar supervising the construction of irrigation aqueducts and a drying oven.

"Before, only the nest mattered. But Yoggoy is smart. Yoggoy learned the value of the individual, and Yoggoy grew stronger."

Then came the crucial set of images. The first showed Raynar trading with other nests for food and equipment, the second depicted several insects from different nests gathered around listening to him, and in the third he was leading an even larger group of insects—all different in color, size, and shape—off to start their own nest.

"The Unu was created," Raynar said.

Before he could point to another mosaic, Leia asked, "What exactly is the Unu? The governing nest?"

Raynar tilted his head and gave a short, negative click. "Not in the way you think. It the nest of the nests, so that Yoggoy may share our gift with all of the Kind."

"Yeah?" Han asked. "And how's that work?"

"You would not understand," Raynar said. "No Other would."

There was more, an attack by a disapproving nest, a time of starvation as the flourishing nests stripped their worlds bare, the beginning of the Colony as the Kind began to spread across local space. But Luke paid little attention. He was struggling with what he had learned already, with the fear that Raynar remained as lost to them as ever, and that Jaina and the others would soon be just as lost—and with the growing alarm he felt over what the young Jedi Knight had become. Jedi should not be leaders of galactic civilizations; it was too easy to abuse the power they wielded, too easy to use the Force to impose their will on others.

He felt Mara touching him through their Force-bond, urging him to keep his disapproval in check.

To Raynar, she said, "What happened to the Dark Jedi who abducted you?"

Raynar lowered his fused brow. "The Dark Jedi?"

"Lomi and Welk," Luke prompted. He was careful to keep his disapproval well buried within himself, in case Raynar could sense his feelings better than he could Raynar's. "The Jedi whom you rescued on the Myrkr mission."

"Lomi and Welk . . ." Raynar's eyes grew restless. "They were . . . trouble. You say they abducted us?"

"They stole the *Flier* with you aboard," Mara said. "You must have figured this out by now. They tricked Lowbacca into leaving the ship, then stole it while you were unconscious inside."

As Mara spoke, Raynar's gaze kept sliding away from her face, then back again, and his presence in the Force grew confused as well. The familiar part, the part Luke recognized, rose repeatedly to the surface, only to be swallowed a moment later by the murkier, more powerful essence that confronted him every time he tried to probe a Colony member.

After a few moments, Raynar said, "We remember the Crash, but not the Dark Jedi. We think they . . . they must be dead."

"You don't remember them on the *Flier* at all?" Luke asked. "You must have seen them before you crashed."

The murky presence rose inside Raynar and pushed Luke out with such power that he felt as though he were falling.

"We remember the Crash," Raynar said. "We remember flames and pain and smoke, we remember fear and loneliness and despair."

The finality in Raynar's voice brought a tense silence to the dais—a silence that Han broke almost instantly when he whirled on Raynar with an outstretched finger.

"What about Jaina and the others?" he demanded. "Do you remember *them*?"

"Of course," Raynar said. "They were our friends. That is why we called them."

"*Were*?" Han stepped toward Raynar. "Has something happened? If you're trying to make Joiners of them—"

"Han!" Leia stopped Han with a gesture—she was probably the one person in the galaxy who could do that—then turned to Raynar. "Well?"

"Jaina and the others are well." Raynar addressed himself to Han. "But they were Raynar Thul's friends. We are unsure how they feel about *us*."

"You haven't answered the question," Luke observed.

"The Colony has need of them," Raynar replied. "Only Jedi can prevent a war with the Chiss."

Han started to complete the threat he had made earlier, but Leia quickly rose and drew him to the edge of the dais.

"The Chiss have told us that there is a border conflict," Luke said. "But not why."

Raynar's scar-stiffened face showed twitches of suspicion. "We do not know why. The system we have entered is over a light-year from the nearest Chiss base, and we have established nests only on food sources. Their explorers are alone on all the ore planets. We have even offered to work in their mines, in exchange for food and supplies."

"Let me guess," Han said from the edge of the dais. "The Chiss aren't interested?"

"Worse. They have poisoned our food worlds." He tilted his disfigured head and made a clicking sound deep in his throat—a sound that was echoed by the tapping mandibles of the attendant insects below. "Our nests our starving, and we do not understand why."

Luke found Raynar's confusion odd. "You're only a light-year from their border. You don't think they might be worried about your intentions? Or want to claim the system for their own?"

"The Colony is not stopping them," Raynar said. "They are free to take what they need."

"As long as you're free to take what you need?" Leia asked.

"We do not need the same things," Raynar answered. "There is no reason to fight."

"No reason you can see," Mara said. Luke sensed that she was as mystified as he was by Raynar's blindness to Chiss territorial concerns. "Maybe we should go take a look at what's happening there. Where is this system?"

Raynar's unblinking gaze shifted to Mara. "You wish to go there?"

"You said you needed help," Luke reminded him. "Perhaps we can resolve the situation."

"We know what we said."

Raynar's eyes grew very dark around the edges, and suddenly Luke could see nothing else. The murky presence began to reach into his mind, trying to push its way inside his thoughts to read his intentions. Luke was astonished by its power and had to reach deeply into the Force to bolster his own strength. Though the probe was hardly subtle or refined, it felt as though it were being driven by a thousand Raynars, and he feared for a moment that in his surprise he would be overwhelmed by its sheer might.

Then he felt Mara pouring her own strength into him, and Saba and even Leia. Together they pushed the dusky hand back. Luke found himself looking once again into the blue, lidless eyes of their host, and he finally began to comprehend just how difficult it was going to be to reach Raynar Thul.

"What are you waiting for?" Han demanded, apparently not noticing his companions' sweaty brows and trembling hands. "Tell us where the system is . . . unless you're afraid of what we'll find."

"We have nothing to fear from you, Captain Solo. Jaina and the others are free to leave anytime they wish." Raynar floated to his feet, then tipped his head to Luke and the other Jedi. "As are you, Master Skywalker. We will assign a guide to escort you back to the Lizil nest."

"We won't be going back to the Lizil nest. Not yet." Luke met Raynar's eyes, this time ready to meet a probe with a Force wall of his own. "We came to investigate what Jaina and the others are doing."

"You're welcome to stay on Yoggoy as long as you like," Raynar said. "But we're sorry. You can't see our Jedi."

"*Your* Jedi?" Han snarled. "When the Core goes dark!"

Leia motioned Han back, then stepped toward Raynar, her chin raised in challenge. "Why not? Because we'll discover you haven't been entirely honest? Because the Chiss are more in the right than you're telling us?"

"No." Raynar's mouth straightened, perhaps in an attempt at a smile. "Because we know how good you are, Princess Leia—and because you serve necessity instead of virtue."

"Just hold on," Han objected. "Leia has been out of politics for a long time. This is just *us*."

"Really?" Raynar turned to Luke. "What do the Jedi seek?"

"Peace," Luke answered instantly.

"Peace in the Galactic Alliance," Raynar amended. "We know where the new Jedi Temple has been built."

"That doesn't mean we are the Galactic Alliance's servants," Luke said.

"Master Skywalker, remember who Raynar Thul's parents were. We *know* how money works." Raynar stood. "You must bow to the needs of those who pay your bills—and, at the moment, the Galactic Alliance needs you to turn your back on what is right."

"Right from whose viewpoint?" Luke countered, also standing. "Right and wrong, good and evil, light and dark—most of the time, they are illusions that prevent us from perceiving the greater reality. The Jedi have learned to distance themselves from these illusions, to seek the truth beneath the words. Let us go—"

"No."

Raynar stepped toward Luke, and suddenly the dark presence returned, pressing against him, trying to push him toward the edge of the dais. Luke opened himself to the Force and pushed back, standing firm until Raynar came toe-to-toe with him, and they stood glaring into each other's eyes, two strangers who had been, in another life, Master and pupil.

"We have heard about this new Force of yours," Raynar said. "And we despair. The Jedi have grown blind to the dark side itself."

"Not at all," Luke said. "We have learned to see it more clearly than ever, to recognize that the dark side and the light side spring from the same well—inside *us*."

"And which side is it that wishes to find Jaina and the other Jedi Knights?" Raynar asked. "The side that knows what is right? Or the side that serves the Galactic Alliance?"

"The side that the serves the will of the Force," Luke answered. "Everywhere."

"Then you will serve it best by leaving Jaina and the others to settle this," Raynar said. He turned his back on Luke and started toward the steps. "As we said, you are welcome to stay on Yog-goy as long as you like."

"I'll bet," Han said, going after him. "And when we get to be Joiners—"

"Thank you." Leia grabbed Han's arm and jerked him back. "We look forward to learning more about the Colony. After we have, perhaps we can discuss this further?"

Raynar stopped on the top step and glanced back, his scorched face tipped at a slight angle. "Perhaps, but you won't change our mind, Princess. We know you too well." His gaze shifted back to Luke. "We know you *all* too well."

ELEVEN

Were it not for the golden gleam of C-3PO's head—bobbing along through a forest of feathery antennae as he questioned their guide about the Colony languages—Leia would never have been able to tell which scarlet-headed insect they were following. The route back to the hangar was swarming with Kind, and at least half of them were Yoggoy, proud and bustling and identical in every way she could see to the guide that had been assigned to escort them.

The passage took a sharp bend, and Leia lost sight of C-3PO. Waving the others to follow, she started to walk faster.

"What's the hurry?" Han said, catching her by the arm. "We could use a few minutes alone."

"Alone?" Leia tipped her head at the steady stream of insects clattering past. "Take a look around!"

Han was careful to avoid doing as she suggested, but gave a little shudder anyway. "You know what I mean. Without Raynar's spy listening in. I've got a plan."

"Planz are good," Saba agreed from the back of the group.

"But we don't want to look suspicious," Mara said. She waved the group forward again, and they set off with Leia and Han in the lead, Luke and Mara next, and Saba bringing up the rear. "Let's keep moving while we talk."

"I'm pretty sure I can talk Juun into giving us a copy of that list of nests on his datapad and any charts he *does* have on the Colony," Han said. "Between that and your Jedi senses, it shouldn't take us that long to figure out where Jaina and the others are. After all, Raynar practically told us where to look—a light-year or so from the frontier."

"*If* he was being honest," Mara said. "He was always clever, but now . . . we should be careful. This new Raynar is a lot more formidable than the kid we remember. I have a feeling he's already ten steps ahead of us."

"And *that's* why we should accept his offer to stay on Yoggoy for a while," Leia said. They rounded the bend in the corridor, and Leia spotted C-3PO's golden head fifteen meters ahead—far enough away that no matter how good the guide's ears were, it should be impossible to eavesdrop over the clicking and thrumming that filled the passage. "We need to learn as much about Raynar—and the Colony—as he knows about us."

"We know enough," Han grumbled. "We know that Raynar joined minds with a bunch of bugs, and that if we don't get to Jaina and Jacen and the others soon, the same thing's going to happen to them."

"Han, we have time," Luke said. "A Jedi's mind is not easily dominated."

"Oh, yeah?" Han glanced back. "*Raynar* was a Jedi."

"A much younger and inexperienced Jedi—and a grievously wounded one," Mara said. "Luke and Leia are right. We need to answer some questions before we go."

"Yes," Saba said. "This one would like to know why they are lying about the Dark Jedi."

Mara nodded. "I noticed that, too."

"Even *I* picked up on it," Han said. "But I don't see what difference it makes to finding Jaina and the others."

"*That's* what we need to find out," Leia said. Han's mind ran as straight as a laser bolt when he was worried about his children—and she loved him for it. "Trust me, we're better off knowing if Lomi and Welk are mixed up in this."

"And we need to talk to Raynar some more," Luke added. "I don't want to leave him here like that. I'm sure Cilghal knows someone who can repair that burn damage."

"*That* choice may not be ourz," Saba said. "He is the heart of the Colony. This one does not think the Kind will let him go easily."

"Even if he wanted to, which he won't," Mara said. "Power is addictive, and he's the king bee of a galactic empire."

"If power was the only appeal, we might have a chance," Leia said. The passage divided about twelve meters ahead, and C-3PO and the guide vanished down the right branch without looking back. "But Raynar is *responsible* for the Colony. It wouldn't exist without him, and he won't abandon it lightly."

"Now I *really* have a bone to pick with those Dark Jedi," Han said. "And with Raynar, too. Why couldn't he just let bugs act like bugs?"

"Because he's a Jedi." Luke sounded almost proud. "And he was trained in our old tradition—to serve life and protect it, wherever he found the need."

"Yeah, well, he won't be protecting much life when that border conflict gets out of hand," Han said.

"Yes, now many more livez are at risk," Saba said. "Nature is cruel for a reason, and Raynar has upset the balance."

"The law of unintended consequences," Mara said. "That's why it's better not to intervene. A modern Jedi would have held himself apart and studied the situation first."

"And we're sure that's a good thing?" Leia asked. She was as surprised as anyone to hear herself asking this question, for the war had hardened her to death in a way that she would not have believed possible twenty years before. But the war was over, and she was *tired* of death, of measuring victory not by how many lives you saved, but how many you took. "How many beings would have died while a modern Jedi studied the situation?"

Luke's confusion filled the Force behind her. "Does it matter? A Jedi serves the Force, and if his actions interfere with the balance of the Force—"

"I know," Leia said wearily. "I just miss the days when all this was simple."

Sometimes, she wondered whether the tenets of this new Jedi order were an improvement or a convenience. She worried about what had been sacrificed to this new god Efficiency—about what had been lost when the Jedi abandoned their simple code and embraced moral relativism.

They came to the divide in the passage and started down the right-hand branch. C-3PO and the guide were waiting about five meters ahead.

"Buruub urub burr," the guide droned.

"Yoggoy asks that you please try to keep up," C-3PO translated.

"Rurr bururu ub Ruur."

"And she politely suggests that you start your investigations at the Crash," C-3PO continued. "That way, you can see for yourself that UnuThul is not lying about the Dark Jedi."

"Urr buub ur bubbu."

"Or anything else."

Leia's stomach tightened in surprise, but she wasted no effort trying to figure out how the insect knew what they had been discussing.

Instead, she smiled calmly and said, "That sounds like an excellent idea, Yoggoy. Thank you for the suggestion."

By the time they reached the hangar a few minutes later, another Yoggoy was waiting for them with a battered hoversled.

"Burru urr burrr ubb," it explained, pointing toward the *Shadow* with one of its four arms. *"Burrrr uuu!"*

"Oh, dear!" C-3PO exclaimed. "It seems that when Yoggoy attempted to collect Ben, Nanna threatened to open fire!"

"I apologize, Yoggoy," Luke said, addressing the driver. "But why were you trying to collect Ben?"

The driver drummed an excited explanation.

"Because you and Mistress Skywalker said it would be good for him to see the Crash," C-3PO translated. He tipped his head, then added, "As a matter of fact, Master Luke, I do recall hearing you say that only one point seven minutes ago."

"Yes, but how—"

"Collective mind," Leia said, suddenly understanding how their guide had been eavesdropping on their conversation earlier. "What one Yoggoy hears—"

"—they all do," Han finished. "Kind of a new twist on being bugged, isn't it?"

"It certainly is," Leia said. As the constant stream of insects droned past, Yoggoy had been eavesdropping on them one word at a time. She took Han's hand and stepped aboard the hover-sled. "As I said, we have a lot to learn about the Colony."

The others climbed aboard as well. They stopped at the *Shadow* to pick up Ben and Nanna, then began a harrowing ride—it was very nearly a flight—through the congested avenues that wound through the skyscraping spires of the Yoggoy nest.

An hour later, they were still in the "city," standing in a long line of insects and Joiners outside the Crash. The site seemed part tourist attraction and part shrine, with thousands of insects waiting patiently in line, looking across a low stone wall up toward a wrecked light freighter. The crater slope was mottled with wadla and lyris and a dozen other kinds of flowers that Leia did not know, and the air was heavy with the vanilla tang of bond-inducing pheromones. Even the constant drone of several thousand drumming, ticking insect pilgrims had a strangely soothing effect.

Despite the ambience, Leia was growing increasingly uneasy. She felt as though the half-buried YV-888 were still burning down through the atmosphere, as though something huge were about to come smashing down atop her head. And the other Jedi felt it, too. She could sense Luke's disquiet through the Force and see Mara's wariness in the sudden economy of her gestures. Even Saba seemed tense, watching the surrounding insects out of the corner of her eye and testing the air with her forked tongue.

Or maybe the Barabel was just getting hungry.

Leia stretched out into the Force, hoping to learn more. But reaching into the immense, diffuse presence that pervaded the insect nests was like looking into a room filled with smoke. There was something going on, but it was impossible to tell what.

The Skywalker–Solo group finally reached a gate in the stone wall, where their escort motioned them to stop and wait.

"Would anyone object to our visit, Yoggoy?" Leia asked. She still found it a little awkward to address every insect in a nest by the same name, but it certainly cut down on the need for introductions. "I keep having the feeling we're not welcome here."

Yoggoy rumbled a reply.

"Yoggoy assures you that your feeling is wrong," C-3PO said. "Everyone is welcome to partake of the Crash."

"Partake?" Han asked. "What are we going to do, eat the dead?"

"Uburu buu," Yoggoy replied. *"Bubu uu."*

"There weren't any dead," C-3PO translated. "She apologizes."

"Uh, thanks," Han said. "But no need. I wasn't hungry anyway."

Leia felt a gentle tug through the Force. She turned slowly and found herself looking at her sister-in-law's slender face.

"Do you think Ben's too young for this?" Mara asked. Her green eyes slid toward her right shoulder, indicating to Leia that she was asking another question entirely. "I don't want him to see anything that would scare him off space travel."

"I'm old enough!" a small voice said from Luke's side. "Nothing's going to scare me."

"That's a good question," Leia said, ignoring Ben's protest. "I guess it depends on what we see."

As Leia answered, she was looking past Mara's ear toward a large, single-colored insect ten places back in the line. So blue it was almost black, it stood nearly the height of a man, with short bristling antennae and barbed, sharply curved mandibles. She could not tell whether its huge, bulbous eyes were focused on the Solo–Skywalker party, but when her gaze lingered an instant too long, the creature slipped out of sight behind a tan-and-gray insect the size of a landspeeder.

"We'll just have to keep an eye out," Leia said, "and take off if this starts to look disturbing."

"How disturbing can it be?" Han asked, clearly oblivious to what the two women were really talking about. "This wreck is seven years old. I'll bet he sees worse stuff on the newsvids."

"Every day," Ben agreed. Clearly eager to be on their way before his parents changed their mind, he turned to their guide. "Why are we standing here? I wanna see the Crash!"

The guide thrummed an explanation.

"Yoggoy assures you that we'll see it soon, Master Ben," C-3PO said. "But we must wait—"

"Rurubur ur." The guide extended one of her lower hands to Ben.

"Oh. Apparently it's our turn—"

Before Nanna could stop him, Ben grabbed the insect's hand and dragged her up the slope at a sprint.

"Ben!" Nanna squawked, her repulsor-enhanced legs hissing as they propelled her enormous mass past Leia. "Stay with the group!"

Mara shook her head, then turned to Han. "You seem to be rubbing off on my kid, Solo. Were yours this headstrong?"

Han and Leia shared a glance, and they both nodded.

"Anakin," Han said. "If I said no, he had to find out why."

As Han spoke, a familiar sadness came to his face, and his eyes dropped. There was an awkward silence while everyone wondered what to say next, and Leia finally began to understand why there seemed to be such a bond between her husband and their nephew. Like Anakin, Ben was headstrong, fearless, and curious, with a clever mind and a quick wit, and he insisted on dealing with life on his own terms.

After a moment, Mara reached over and squeezed Han's forearm. "I just hope Ben grows up to be as fine a man as Anakin was. Nothing could make me more proud."

"Thanks." Han looked up the slope—probably to disguise the glassiness that had come to his eyes—then added, "He will."

They followed Ben to the rim, then found themselves looking into the bottom of the crater. Ten meters below sat a cockeyed box of heat-softened durasteel, somewhat flattened in the bottom and so covered in crawling insects that they could barely tell the vessel had landed bridge-down. The hull was pocked with the oblong holes made by plasma cannons, and there were several long, twisted rips that were probably a result of the crash itself.

"It looks like they flew through a plasma storm just leaving the Myrkr system," Luke said. "I'm surprised they made it out."

"Corellian engineering," Han said with pride. "A CEC ship will keep going until it hits something."

"Not always a good thing, especially when that something is a planet," Leia said.

She turned toward their escort, running her glance over the surrounding crowd, and noticed several dark blue insects similar to the one she had caught watching them earlier. It seemed to her that their huge eyes were all looking toward the Solo–Skywalker group, but that was hardly unusual. Most species of intelligent insect had an unsettling tendency to stare.

Leia reached out to Luke and sensed that he had noticed the blue insects, too, then asked their guide, "What happened to the crew?"

The guide used an upper hand to point at the base of the ship, where a pile of dirt lay slumped against the smashed bridge. Descending through the pile, toward a jagged rent in the hull, was a half-meter burrow that felt oddly familiar to Leia, as though she had seen it before—or somehow knew where it led.

The insect began a lengthy explanation, which C-3PO translated: "That is where Yoggoy found Raynar Thul. He was badly burned and barely alive."

Leia forced her attention back to the guide and said, "I mean, what happened to the *rest* of the crew?" She knew what Yoggoy was going to say—that there had been no one else—but when confronted with an obvious lie, a good interrogator kept asking the same question in different ways, trying to find a seam that she could pry open to expose the truth. "We know *Raynar* survived."

A familiar touch came to Leia through the Force, one that she knew instantly and certainly to be her son's, and she found herself looking away from their puzzled guide into the bottom of the crater. There, standing outside the burrow in a dirt- and soot-stained flight suit, was Jacen.

Or, rather, a vision of Jacen. The *Flier's* hull was still visible behind him, as was the mouth of the burrow.

He smiled and said, "Hello."

The blood drained from Leia's head, and she had to grab Han's arm to steady herself. "Jacen's been here."

"What?" Han peered into the crater. "I don't see anything."

Luke saved her the trouble of explaining. "The Force, Han. She's having a vision."

Han's voice immediately grew wary. "Great. Just what we need. First, Force-calls, now Force-visions."

"Quiet, Solo," Mara said. "Don't interfere."

Jacen said something Leia could not hear, then a helmet and X-wing flight suit appeared in his hands.

"Jacen," Leia said, frowning. "I'm having trouble hearing you."

Jacen spoke again, but still she could not hear him.

"Jacen?" Leia felt the color drain from her face. "How? You're not—"

"I'm fine, Mom," he said. "I'll see you soon."

"Uh-oh," Han said beside Leia. His hand tightened around her arm. "Looks like someone's been listening in."

Leia glanced over and saw three more deep blue insects pushing through the crowd gathered along the crater rim. They were clearly coming toward the Solo–Skywalker group, but Leia was not ready to leave yet. Jacen was still standing in the bottom of the crater, looking up at her.

"Qoribu," he said. "In the Gyuel system."

Leia wanted to ask him to repeat it, to be sure she had heard correctly, but Han was pulling her away, following Nanna down the crater slope through a swarm of astonished insects. Ben was in the droid's arms, while Luke, Mara, and Saba flanked her on three sides. Leia and Han were in the rear.

It took Leia a moment to see why they had suddenly grown so concerned. More blue insects had appeared, pushing through the crowd from all directions, not really attacking, just clacking their mandibles and staring. The rest of the Kind seemed unconcerned; they stepped aside politely, then continued to stare up at the Crash.

Leia drew her own lightsaber and activated it. "Threepio, what are they saying?"

"They're not saying anything that makes sense," C-3PO said. "They're just repeating *is it is it is . . .*"

Their guide rumbled an explanation.

"What a relief!" C-3PO said. "Yoggoy says they're just curious about us."

"Bugs are *never* just curious," Han said. He drew his powerful BlasTech DL-44. "Especially when they're hungry."

"Ubrub ubru Ruur!"

"They just want to see the Crash!"

"Then how come they're coming after *us*?" Mara demanded.

They reached the bottom of the slope and found the gate blocked by blue-black insects. Nanna shifted Ben to one arm and opened the other at the elbow, revealing her built-in blaster cannon.

"That means move," Han said, stepping past Nanna to confront the insects in front of them.

The insects began to crowd forward to meet him.

"The *other* way."

Han raised his blaster pistol and flicked the power setting from stun to lethal.

"Not yet, Han." Luke glanced in Han's direction, and Han's hand slowly fell to his side. "Let me handle this."

"Then you'd better handle it quick," Leia said, looking back up the crater slope. Two dozen of the blue insects had emerged from the mass and were slowly creeping closer. "It's getting crowded back here."

Leia felt a brush of reassurance from Luke, then an astonished booming erupted behind her. She glanced back to see several dozen insects hanging in midair, their legs and arms wiggling wildly as they attempted to make contact with the ground. The group began to move forward again, and she backed out the gate under the dangling insects. Luke was standing to one side, holding his hands palms-up above his shoulders.

"Not bad," she said.

"Impressive, even."

Luke winked at her, then turned toward the rest of the blue insects, who were still attempting to follow. He lowered one of his hands and stretched it toward them . . . and the insects immediately began to back away, dipping their heads and clacking their mandibles.

"They're apologizing, Master Luke," C-3PO said. "They didn't mean to make you feel hunted."

"No harm," Luke said. He waited until Leia, C-3PO, and their guide were past, then lowered the first group of blue insects down inside the gate. "As long as the feeling doesn't come back anytime soon."

They followed Mara and Nanna back to the lot where Yoggoy

had left their transport, then climbed aboard the battered hoversled. Their guide slipped behind the controls and turned her head all the way around to the passenger compartment, then thrummed a question.

"Yoggoy asks what you would like to see next," C-3PO said.

"The *Falcon*," Han said.

"Rurr ur uu buubu."

"Yoggoy suggests a stop at a membrosia vault," C-3PO said. "You seem rather tense."

"That's 'cause I am," Han growled. "And getting—"

"I think we've seen enough for one day," Leia said tersely. She could tell that the other Jedi shared the same feeling she did, for they were still holding their lightsaber handles in their hands and scanning the surrounding area. "I think we'd all like to go straight back to our vessels."

"Ububu."

The guide slipped the hoversled into motion so quickly that Leia and the others were knocked into their seats, and a moment later they were gliding onto a broad, traffic-choked boulevard flanked by looming insect spires.

The uneasy feeling Leia had been experiencing only grew worse. She slid forward and leaned over the low wall separating the driver's compartment from the passengers.

"Yoggoy, who were those blue insects?"

"Ububub bur?"

"The blue Kind who accosted us at the Crash," C-3PO explained helpfully. "Actually, they were more of a deep indigo, if that helps."

"Bubu bur ub."

"Why of course there are blue Kind," C-3PO protested. "We just saw them at the Crash!"

"Ur ub bur."

"What do you mean you don't remember that?" C-3PO demanded. "We all saw them."

The street ahead suddenly grew clear, and the unease Leia had been feeling blossomed into full-fledged danger sense.

"Stop the hoversled!" Leia cried.

Mara's approach was more direct. She was already leaping over the driver's wall, wresting the controls from their guide. She brought the hoversled to an instant halt, drawing a chorus of surprised *oofs* from Leia and the others.

"Not good," Han said, coming forward. "Bad, even. These streets never—"

Leia did not hear the rest of Han's observation, for suddenly her danger sense was turning somersaults in her stomach and Mara was backing the hoversled up the street. When their guide protested and tried to retake the controls, Mara used the Force to push the insect off the hoversled.

"Mom!" Ben cried. "You just dumped—"

A deafening crackle echoed through spiretops, then chunks of mosaic-covered wall began to rain down on both sides of the boulevard. Leia instinctively turned to protect Ben, but Nanna already had him on the deck, shielding him with her laminanium-armored body. Luke and Saba were standing beside the droid, using the Force to push falling rubble away from the hoversled.

Realizing that she still had a little honing to do before her instincts were up to full Jedi speed, Leia tipped her head back and began to look for chunks of falling building.

"Assailants at forty degrees!" Nanna reported.

The droid's arm rose and opened at the elbow. The entire hoversled shuddered as the warrior-nanny cut loose with her blaster cannon.

"Astral!" Ben yelled, peering out from under her arm.

Nanna gently pushed his head back, then fired again. More pieces of wall crashed down in the street, and Leia glimpsed the inky shape of half a dozen dark blue insects diving for the interior of the tower.

"Did you see that?" Han raised his blaster pistol and began to fire into the dust. "Kriffing bugs!"

In the next instant, the hoversled pivoted around and started up the avenue away from the ambush.

"They were trying to kill us!" Han cried from the floor of the hoversled. He hauled himself up and, as Mara swung down a side street and left the billowing dust behind, caught Leia's eye. "*Now* can we try my plan?"

TWELVE

For the first twenty minutes of the trip to the hangar, Han remained silent about Mara's piloting. She was racing down the insect-choked boulevard, using the Force to weave and jink and at times bounce through the traffic as though she were flying an X-wing instead of an ancient hoversled with a repulsor drive that sounded like it might come apart at any second, and most of the time he was just too scared to talk. But when she suddenly swung into a packed alley and slowed to a more sustainable speed, he could not help himself.

"Don't tell me you're losing your nerve," he said, leaning over the half wall into the pilot's compartment. "We've got to get back to the ships before Raynar finds out we survived!"

Mara continued at the same sane speed. "He already knows."

"The collective mind," Leia reminded him. "What one Yoggoy knows, they all do."

"Great." Han's stomach began to churn. "There ought to be a nice bunch of bugs waiting when we get back to the hangar."

"Maybe not," Luke said. "I can't believe Raynar would turn on us like that. He was one of the most earnest students at the academy."

Han and Leia shot Luke simultaneous looks of astonishment.

"Raynar Thul is no more," Han quoted. "He's one of *them* now. UnuThul. A Joiner."

"Raynar's still in there," Luke said. "I felt him."

"Yeah? Well, it's the other guy I'm worried about," Han said. They left the alley, flashed across a boulevard, and shot into another alley. Han had no idea where they were—their guide had stuck to the main boulevards on the way to the Crash—but he assumed Mara knew where she was going. Jedi were not the only ones who could trust the Force. "And if his bugs try knocking another building down on us, I'm gonna blast him."

An amused twinkle came to Luke's eye, and Han suddenly realized how ridiculous his declaration must have sounded after describing how easily Raynar had destroyed BD-8, disabled the *Falcon*'s laser cannons, and neutralized Leia's Noghri bodyguards.

"Or something."

"Of course, dear," Leia said, patting his arm. "But I don't think that will be necessary. Raynar had to know that attack would never work—not with *three* Jedi Masters aboard."

"And a Jedi Knight of much experience." Saba nodded at Leia, though it was impossible for Han to guess whether this was a gesture of agreement or to indicate whom she meant. Barabels were *blasted* hard to read. "This one thinkz it was just a warning, a way to make us to leave."

"I hate giving in to bullies," Han said. "But I'll make an exception in this case. We can use the Force and Juun's datapad to track down the twins."

Leia nodded. "I think it's time to move on. We've found what we came for."

"We have?" Han asked.

"The Force-vision," Luke surmised. "What did you see?"

"Just Jacen," Leia said. "But he gave me the name of a planet and a system. I don't recognize them, but maybe Juun—"

"Jacen *told* you the system name?" Mara asked from the pilot's seat.

"That's right," Leia said. "He looked straight at me and said it. Why?"

"That is a strange kind of vision," Saba said.

"More of a sending," Luke agreed. "But across time instead of space."

The three Masters fell silent, leaving Han and Leia to look at each other in puzzlement.

Finally, Han said, "I don't get it. What's the problem?"

"I've never heard of a Jedi using the Force that way," Luke said.

"So he's creative," Han asked. "He's my kid. What'd you expect?"

"I think I understand," Leia said, beginning to sound worried. "The future is always in motion . . ."

"But not *yourz*," Saba said. "When Jacen spoke acrosz time, you became destined to be there."

"He fixed your future," Luke said. "At least for those few moments."

Leia was silent for a moment, then said, "Well, I seem to have survived it. And my future is my own again."

"I don't like it," Mara said. "Not at all. What exactly was he learning while he was gone?"

It was a good question—one Han had been asking himself since Jacen was a teenager.

Mara brought them out of the alley onto a busy avenue of zooming landspeeders and almost managed to keep up by pushing the repulsor drive beyond its top rating. The avenue snaked through the brightly decorated insect spires for perhaps five kilometers, then spilled onto the great boulevard that encircled the Unu's complex of red towers, and a few minutes later the hoversled was sliding down the long golden throat of the Prime Hangar.

The bugs were clattering about their business, durafilling micropitted hulls, off-loading bales of some spicy-smelling resin, tapping rivets on starships that should have been scrapped when the Empire was a glimmer in Palpatine's eye. Han began to hope that Saba was right about the attack—that it had just been an impolite invitation to leave.

Then they reached the bay where the *Falcon* and *Shadow* had been left, and Mara stopped short.

A trio of rocket shuttles had been squeezed between the two vessels. Maintenance crews were busy stringing webs of fueling hoses across the entire alcove, thwarting all hope of a quick departure. Even worse, Raynar was standing at the foot of the *Falcon*'s ramp, surrounded by an entourage of bug attendants and huge Unu soldiers. He was looking toward their end of the bay, clearly awaiting their return.

"So much for thinking he was just sending us a warning," Han said. "I really hate being right all the time."

Meewalh and Cakhmaim, who had remained behind to watch the ships and begin repairs on the *Falcon*'s weapons turrets, were peering out from the top of the ramp. The pair hadn't made much progress. Both sets of the blaster cannons remained pointed at the ship's aft.

"We should send the Noghri to fetch Tarfang and Juun," Leia said softly. "Do you think I can risk a comm call?"

"We'll have to," Han whispered. "Unless Jacen gave you co-ordinates to go with that name."

"Just the name," Leia said.

"I don't think this will come to a fight," Luke said. He rose and joined Han behind Mara, hiding Leia so she could comm the Noghri without being seen. "But Ben, you—"

"I know . . . stick close to Nanna," Ben said. "I know."

"Right," Luke said, smiling. "Nanna, get Ben aboard either ship as quickly as you can."

"But don't try anything pushy," Han advised. "You'll only get a brain-melt."

"I am not programmed to be pushy, Captain Solo," Nanna said.

"Will we get to shoot that blaster cannon in your arm again?" Ben asked enthusiastically.

"Only if someone threatens your life," Nanna said. "You know all my routines are strictly defensive, Ben."

Mara threaded the hoversled through the tangle of fueling lines, but had to stop ten meters from the *Shadow* because a rocket shuttle blocked their way. Nanna immediately took Ben and headed for the boarding ramp, which was still down be-cause of the bugs' mistrust of closed doors. Everyone else re-mained on the hoversled, their hands out of sight and grasping their weapons, their gazes fixed on Raynar and his entourage.

Han felt as though he were aging a week for each second it took Ben to reach the *Shadow*. By comparison, Luke and Mara seemed downright calm. And why shouldn't they? Having seen all the times Han and Leia's kids had been kidnapped or threatened when they were supposedly hidden safely away, Luke and Mara had decided that—short of an actual battle—Ben would *always* be safer if they kept him close. So they had repeatedly rehearsed with Ben exactly what to do in circumstances like these, and weekly "protect-the-kid" drills were standard procedure for all traveling companions. Given whom they usually traveled with—Jedi Knights and veteran soldiers—Han thought they had probably made the right decision.

When Mara failed to start the hoversled toward the *Falcon,* Raynar cocked his earless head in bewilderment, then started across the hangar floor.

"That's my signal," Mara said. "I'm out of here."

She stepped out of the pilot's station and, still moving casually, started up the *Shadow's* boarding ramp. Raynar's eyes followed her progress, but he made no attempt to stop her. That was good, since it meant Han didn't have to blast him yet.

Han slipped into Mara's place at the pilot's station, then frowned as he tried to pick out a path to the *Falcon.* This was going to be difficult, at least until Mara distracted them with her blaster cannon—provided Raynar didn't twist that around as he had the *Falcon's* turrets. Han's palms started to sweat, and he began to wish he hadn't left their thermal detonators aboard the ship. Nothing distracted a big, bad, all-powerful enemy like one of those little silver balls rolling around at his feet.

Raynar stopped two paces from the hoversled. "Was anyone injured?"

"No," Han answered. "Sorry to disappoint you."

"Disappoint us?" Raynar's eyes grew confused. "When you left Yoggoy to be crushed, we thought someone must have been—"

"Yeah, well, sorry about the guide, but that's what happens when you start dropping buildings on people," Han said. Daring to hope that Raynar would actually make this easy, he gestured toward the *Falcon.* "Do you mind? We need to clean up."

Raynar lowered his melted brow, then shifted his gaze to Luke and Saba, who were waiting at opposite ends of the hoversled with their hands hidden behind the durasteel sides. His scarred lips twitched in a mockery of a smile.

"Of course." Raynar gave no discernible command, but a path opened through the soldier bugs at his back. He stepped onto the hoversled beside Han. "You believe the building collapse was an attack?"

"It wasn't exactly friendly." Trying to hide his uneasiness, Han started the hoversled toward the *Falcon*. "And we saw your killer bugs."

"Killer bugs?" Raynar asked.

"They were solid blue—dark blue," Saba said from the back of the sled. "They blasted the wallz just before we passed beneath."

"You're mistaken," Raynar said. "If any of our nests had attacked you, we would have known."

Saba rose and came forward, and Han was a little unnerved to realize that she was not large enough to loom over Raynar the way she did most beings. "This one saw the ambusherz with her own eyez. Ben's Defender droid killed two."

"The Kind did not lose anyone in the accident," Raynar said.

"It was no accident," Han snapped, beginning to grow angry. "Someone tried to kill us. You, I'm thinking."

"If we wanted to kill you, we would not make it look like an accident," Raynar said. "We would just do it."

They reached the *Falcon*. Han stopped the hoversled, then faced Raynar and found himself staring at the underside of a white-blotched chin.

"Remember who you're talking to, kid," he said. "This is *Han Solo*. I've been sticking my finger in the eyes of two-credit dictators like you since before I broke your mother's heart, so show a little respect when you threaten me. And don't lie. I hate that."

Raynar was no more intimidated than he had been by Saba. He simply glared down at Han, his breath coming in slow, angry rasps.

Luke leaned close to Leia and whispered, "Han dated Raynar's mother?"

"You'd be surprised at the women Han's dated. I always am." Leia stepped to Raynar's side, then said, "You must admit the collapse looks suspicious. If it was an accident, how did the Yoggoy nest know to evacuate the area? And what about the blue Kind we saw? The ones we *killed*?"

Raynar's breathing softened to a wheeze, and he turned to face Leia. "The only dead Kind we have found at the site was your guide."

"The otherz must have taken the bodiez," Saba said. "There were more than the onez Nanna killed."

"You were mistaken," Raynar said. "The dust was thick, the rubble was still falling. What you saw were shadows."

"Who're you trying to convince here?" Han demanded. He glanced at the attendant bugs, wondering whether they could have more say than he realized. Perhaps *they* were the reason Raynar was trying to deny the Colony's responsibility. Perhaps they didn't approve of murdering guests. "Because *we* know what we saw."

Raynar turned back to Han. "Eyes can deceive, Captain Solo. What you say you saw is impossible."

"Or our interpretation of it." Luke's voice was thoughtful. "What if it wasn't the Kind who attacked us at all?"

"Others aren't allowed to wander Yoggoy alone," Raynar said. "We would know even if someone else attacked you."

"What if you didn't know they were here?" Leia asked.

Raynar's eyes narrowed in thought, then he shook his head in a gesture that—for a change—seemed more Raynar than insect. "You said Yoggoy was warned to evacuate. Why would Others do that?"

"And if they did, you'd certainly know they were here," Luke said.

Han frowned at Luke. "Don't tell me you're buying this?"

"Not that it was an accident," Luke said. "But that Ray—er, UnuThul—believes it was."

Leia caught Han's eye, then gave a curt nod that suggested he should believe it, too. "I think we can all agree on that much," she said. "If the Colony wanted us dead, they wouldn't have given up after one try. The attack was supposed to look like an accident, which means somebody was trying to hide it from the Unu."

"We're glad you believe us, Princess," Raynar said. "But there's no evidence to support your theory."

"How could you know?" Han demanded. "There hasn't been time. The attack was less than thirty minutes ago!"

"Yoggoy workers have already cleared much of the rubble," Raynar answered. "The only body they have—Kind or Other—is your guide's. The evidence suggests the towers just collapsed. We are sorry it happened when you were about to pass beneath them."

"Does that happen often?" Leia asked. "That a spire just collapses?"

"Once, when there was a quake," Raynar said. "And sometimes storms—"

"Not what I asked," Leia said, stepping off the hoversled. "Let me show you something."

She took Raynar's meaty hand, then led him up the boarding ramp into the *Falcon*. Han followed with Luke and Saba, but fortunately only a small part of Raynar's entourage—the bug with the really long antennae and another covered in furry bristles—joined them. They caught up to Leia and Raynar in the Solos' sleeping quarters. The pair were standing in front of the bunk, staring at the famous moss-painting hanging on the wall.

"This is *Killik Twilight*," Leia said to Raynar. "Do you recognize anything?"

"Of course," Raynar said. "Lizil was very excited about the painting."

Raynar stepped to the side of double bunk—the Solos had installed it when they had realized the *Falcon* was going to be their primary home—then leaned closer to the painting and began to run his gaze over every detail.

"Thank you for showing it to us," he said. "We wanted to ask, but our meetings have gone so badly that we didn't want to presume."

Han raised his brow. Maybe there was less Raynar left in that seared body than he thought. The Raynar Thul whom Han remembered had been a decent-enough kid, but his wealthy family had never taught him to do anything *but* presume.

Leia appeared less stunned than Han by Raynar's politeness.

She smiled graciously, then said, "Sometimes, art helps us know each other better. Do you know what this painting depicts?"

Raynar nodded. "It shows an arm of the Lost Nest." He still did not look away. "We remember it well."

"The Lost Nest?" Luke asked.

"*Remember* it?" Han gasped. "It's ancient!"

Raynar finally tore his gaze from the moss-painting.

"We remember the *nest*." He fixed his eyes on Leia. "When humans came to Alderaan, they called it the Castle Lands. But we knew the nest as Oroboro. Our Home."

Han shook his head in disbelief. He liked to say that all bugs were alike, but not even he had assumed that the Kind and the Killiks were actually the same. Sure, they shared the same general body shape and had the same number of limbs, but beyond that, the Kind looked like the Killiks in the painting about as much as humans looked like Aqualish. The towers, on the other hand, were another matter. In both the painting and the Yoggoy nest, they were crooked cones with distinctly banded exteriors.

Leia did not sound surprised at all. "So the Killiks didn't go extinct, as everyone supposed. They simply left Alderaan thousands of years ago."

"You seem less surprised at that than Lizil was to see a painting of Oroboro," Raynar said.

"I've had my suspicions since we arrived at Yoggoy," Leia replied smoothly She turned back to the painting. "Archaeologists have dated the oldest of those spires to twenty-five thousand standard years."

"Correct," Raynar said. "The Celestials emptied Oroboro ten thousand generations ago—that would be twenty thousand years, as humans measure time."

Han wanted to ask who the Celestials were—and what Raynar meant by *emptied*. He also wanted to ask if a Killik generation really passed at the rate of one every two years. But he could see by the set of his wife's jaw that she was pursuing her own line of questioning.

"And yet, only three towers had collapsed before Alderaan was destroyed," Leia said. "No maintenance or repairs, exposed to the elements all that time, and only three collapse. But here, a tower just happens to collapse as we're about to pass by. Do you see where I'm going with this?"

"There is more gravity here than on Alderaan," Raynar countered. "And the ground does not make such strong spitcrete."

"This was still the first tower to collapse for no apparent reason," Luke reminded him.

"There is always a first, Master Skywalker." Raynar turned back to *Killik Twilight* and began to study it. "We cannot explain what happened. Please accept our apologies."

Han exchanged looks of frustration with Luke and Leia, but Saba—who did not truly understand the concept of apology—made a distasteful grating sound in her throat.

"This one does not want your apology, young Thul. She does not eat humanz." She glanced out into the corridor, where Raynar's duo of assistant Killiks stood waiting. "And she has never cared for the taste of insectz, either."

Raynar's head snapped around so quickly that Han feared he was about to have bloody Barabel scales flying all over his sleeping quarters.

"Take it easy, kid. You remember how Barabels are." Han took Raynar by the arm and started forward. "Sorry for the misunderstanding, but we still need to get under way. Why don't you tell us about these Celestials on the way out?"

"If you like." Raynar allowed himself to guided into the corridor. "It was after we built Qolaraloq—you Others call it Centerpoint Station. The Celestials were angry—"

Saba stumbled into Han's back as he stopped dumbfounded in the corridor.

"You're saying Centerpoint was built by *Killiks*?" Leia gasped. Finally, she sounded like something had surprised her.

Instead of answering, Raynar abruptly stopped. "We need to see the aft hold. Your Noghri are abducting Captain Juun and his first mate."

Han winced inwardly. "Abducting? What makes you say that?"

The muffled whine of an angry Sullustan drifted up the access corridor. ". . . *will* not be quiet! Let me see Captain—"

Juun's voice fell silent, but Raynar was already out the cabin door.

Han turned to Leia. *"Abducting?"*

Leia shrugged. "I told Cakhmaim to bring Juun and Tarfang to the *Falcon*. I guess they didn't want to come."

"A misunderstanding," Luke said. "We'd better go explain."

Luke led the way into the access corridor, and they caught up to Raynar and his attendants outside the aft hold. Raynar hit the touch pad, then scowled when the hatch did not open and raised his palm toward it.

"Wait!" Han leapt to the control panel and punched in the override code. "Just be patient."

The door slid open to reveal Meewalh and Cakhmaim holding the *XR808g*'s two crew members. With one of Meewalh's arms clamped around his throat and her other hand covering his mouth, Juun was at least still conscious. Tarfang was another matter. Still casted and bandaged from his fight with the Yoggoy guide, the Ewok was lying unconscious in Cakhmaim's lap, with a freshly swollen eye and two new bare patches of fur.

"It's not what you think," Han said. "I can explain."

"That won't be necessary, Captain Solo." Raynar made a humming sound deep in his throat, then turned and fixed Han with his unblinking gaze. "Just tell us why you are suddenly in such a hurry to leave."

"Uh . . ." The truth was the last thing Han could tell him, but he knew how good Jedi were at detecting lies—and whatever Raynar was now, he had *started out* a Jedi. "What makes you think we're in a hurry?"

Raynar's noseless face grew stormy, and Han began to feel a dark weight pressing down on him inside.

It was Leia, as usual, who came to his rescue. "We have no wish to insult the Colony," she said, "but we don't feel safe here."

Raynar turned to her, and the dark weight lifted.

"You are safe. We promise."

"We don't believe you," Han said. That much was completely true. "Either you're lying—"

Leia's face paled. "Han—"

Han raised a hand, then continued. "Or you have no idea what's happening. Either way, we're out of here."

Raynar's eyes grew so soft that they made Han think of the poor, confused kid whom the other Jedi trainees used to heckle for dressing so funny.

"Very well. You have always been free to come or go as you wish." He turned toward the Noghri, who were still holding Juun and Tarfang captive. "The same applies to Captain Juun and his copilot. Will you be leaving with Captain Solo?"

Meewalh glanced at Leia. When she nodded, the Noghri removed her hand and arm from Juun's mouth and throat. The Sullustan bustled to his feet and, glaring at Han, brushed himself off.

"I'll have to think about it," he said. "Tarfang doesn't care for being kidnapped."

Han's stomach turned cold. Without Juun and his datapad, their chances of finding Jacen and the others before they turned into a bunch of Joiners went way down. Their only recourse would be to make their way to the Chiss frontier and start jumping from system to system.

Luke stepped toward Juun. "We weren't trying to kidnap you." He spoke in a soft monotone. "We were just—"

One of the bristly Killiks slipped forward to block Luke's way, and Raynar said, "It would be better if Captain Juun made up his *own* mind, Master Skywalker."

"Look, we were worried about him." Han addressed Raynar, but he was watching Juun out of the corner of his eye. "We thought you were trying to kill us, and since he and Tarfang were the ones who helped us find this place—"

Juun's small mouth dropped in alarm. "Don't remind him!"

"Sorry—honest mistake," Han said. He felt guilty about forcing the Sullustan's hand, but Juun's days running Colony cargo had come to an end when their guide found the transceiver that had helped the *Falcon* follow him to Yoggoy. "We were kind of worried about you. But if you *want* to stay here—"

"I'm not leaving without the *XR-eight-oh-eight-g*," Juun said. He looked at Tarfang, who was still unconscious. "And you'll have to lend me a copilot until Tarfang's better."

Han faked a scowl. "Getting kind of pushy there, aren't you, fella?"

"You owe it to me," Juun said. "Item twenty-two in the Smuggler's Code."

Han sighed, then turned back to Raynar. "There you have it," he said. "I guess we're stuck with 'em."

THIRTEEN

The Jedi pilots rounded the brightly striped mass of the gas giant Qoribu and found themselves staring into the turquoise brilliance of the planet's huge star, Gyuel. Jaina blinked instinctively, and by the time her eyes opened again, her astromech droid had darkened the StealthX's canopy tinting. She saw the hawk-winged silhouettes of four inbound defoliators sweeping in just meters above Qoribu's dazzling ring system, racing for the gap between the moons Ruu and Zvbo on initial approach for a dispersal run. With a four-squadron escort of clawcraft, the Chiss were clearly determined to reach their targets this time.

Rather than break comm silence, Jaina opened herself to the battle-meld and immediately knew her wingmates had done the same. Sometimes they could hear one another's thoughts through the meld, but more often they simply *knew* what their fellows were thinking . . . what they were doing. And the connection had only grown stronger since coming to Qoribu. During battles, they sometimes came perilously close to sharing minds.

Jaina focused her thoughts on the impending clash. The Chiss were coming hard this time. The Jedi had to disable those defoliators quickly and withdraw before the fight turned bloody.

Jaina sensed disapproval and knew that Alema favored a more forceful approach, one that would leave the Chiss with no illusions about the consequences of attacking the Colony's food supply. And she was not alone. Others were outraged as well. Instead of attacking outright—a violation of the Ascendancy honor code, which prohibited an unprovoked first strike—the Chiss were trying to starve the Qoribu nests into retreat. Tesar,

Tahiri, even Jacen believed that the Chiss were engaged in a campaign of species cleansing and deserved to get their noses bloodied.

Only Zekk did not agree. Jedi saw similar cruelties everywhere they were called in the galaxy. But it was their responsibility to remain dispassionate, to cut through the veil of obscuring emotion and find the core of the problem. If they allowed themselves to seek retribution rather than peace, how could they bring a lasting solution to *any* conflict?

As much as Jaina wanted to make the Chiss pay for the lives they were taking, she had to agree with Zekk. So far, this had remained a low-intensity conflict. But if the Jedi turned it into a killing fight, that would end. A simple border clash would erupt into all-out war, and the carnage would be staggering.

The Chiss task force entered the gap between Ruu and Zvbo. Two of the four defoliators left the main formation with their clawcraft escorts and turned toward the moons. They were met by clouds of defenders, from the Saras nest on Ruu and the Alaala on Zvbo. Too small to be visible at even this relatively short distance, the dartships were nevertheless numerous enough to spread hazy stains of gray across Gyuel's blue face.

Jaina had barely formulated a plan to meet them before Tahiri shot ahead in the sleek little skiff that Zonama Sekot had grown for her. A living ship, its three-lobed hull glowed a deep, sea green against the star.

Jacen followed a moment later in his ChaseX, which, like Tahiri's living ship, could not be concealed from the Chiss sensors. The Jedi all understood what Jaina intended. Tahiri, who was not subject to StealthX comm restrictions, opened a channel to the Taat dartships still swarming around Jaina and the other StealthXs.

"ReyaTaat, bring the dartships and follow us. We need to make this look real."

"We are to create a diversion?" A Chiss Joiner who insisted on being called by both the nest name and her own, ReyaTaat freely admitted that she had been sent by Chiss Intelligence to spy on the Qoribu nests. Her allegiance had changed—she claimed—when the Taat discovered her hiding in near starvation and started to bring her food. "The stealth fighters will divide and strike the defoliators by surprise?"

"Something like that."

Though all of the Qoribu nests seemed to have complete faith in Reya, the Jedi were less trusting, and Tahiri was not about to reveal their plan.

When neither the dartships nor Reya's little scoutcraft started after her, Jacen added, "You need to come *now*. You're drawing attention to the StealthXs."

"Taat is not happy with this plan," Reya said. "The Chiss have changed tactics, and the nest worries they are trying to lure the Jedi into a trap."

Jaina's suspicions about Reya began to deepen, and Tahiri asked, "The nests worry, or you do?"

"We speak for the nests in this," Reya said. "And we know the Chiss."

"You *are* the Chiss." Tahiri's skiff slowed, and she added, "Maybe you're less worried about the Jedi than about your old friends."

"We are *Taat*," Reya insisted. "But we were Chiss once, and we understand how dangerous it is to underestimate them."

The Saras dartships met the first defoliator and swallowed it in a cloud of gray, whirling slivers. The defoliator continued toward Ruu's amber disk, engulfed in a halo of silver sparkles as the insect pilots hurled their tiny fighters against its shields. The Force grew heavy with anguish and admiration for their sacrifice, and Jaina was surprised to feel her own throat closing with emotion. Usually, she felt nothing when she entered battle, not fear or excitement or dread. Usually, she was too focused on the fighting to experience any emotions at all.

The Chiss clawcraft circled back and began to make runs along the length of the defoliator's hull, driving the Saras dartships off and giving the larger vessel time to refresh its shields. The StealthXs had to make their move *now*, or they would never reach the defoliators in time. Jaina pushed her throttles forward and broke for the amber moon, Ruu. Tesar, the second best pilot on the team, started for Zvbo, while Zekk, Alema, and Lowbacca all began a high arcing maneuver that would drop them down on the last two defoliators.

"ReyaTaat, the Jedi are starting their run." Jacen's voice was sharp. "And we're not going to be much of a diversion alone."

There was a moment of silence, then a vague tide of alarm rose in the Force. "Slow down!" Reya commed. "The dartships can't catch you!"

Jaina checked her tactical display and found a blue cloud of Taat dartships sweeping up from the bottom of the display, following Reya's little scout-lancet after Tahiri. At the top of the screen, both Chiss defoliators were fully engulfed in swarms of Saras and Alaala, with the curved horizons of Ruu and Zvbo hanging high in the corners. The main body of the Chiss task force remained in the center of the display, the clawcraft escorts hanging back just far enough to make the last two defoliators an inviting target.

What were they up to?

Jaina's astromech changed scale, and suddenly her tactical display was a mass of "friendly" blips—the Saras dartships—whirling around the defoliator she had targeted. The friendly blips were winking out by the dozens.

Jaina checked her estimated time to attack. Five seconds, but she sensed that Tesar needed seven. She armed two proton torpedoes, then added a sweeping curve to her approach and came in behind the battle.

Outside her cockpit, space was a tightly wound ball of orange rocket trails swirling around the blue glow of the defoliator's big ion drives. A pair of dartships blossomed in scarlet as they exploded against the shields of an oncoming clawcraft, but a third collided with its wing.

The clawcraft pilot lost control and went corkscrewing into Ruu's thin atmosphere. Assuming he survived the crash, Jaina knew, he would be taken into the Saras nest and treated as a welcome guest. Unless they were clearly being attacked, none of the Qoribu nests seemed to have any real concept of *enemy*.

Jaina tried to pick a route through the mad tangle of dartships, but it was like trying to avoid drops in a rainstorm. Two seconds from her launching point, a Saras bounced off her shields, and her canopy went black to prevent her from being blinded by the white flash of an exploding rocket.

By the time the tinting paled an instant later, three Chiss clawcraft were coming at Jaina head-on, pouring a steady torrent of cannon bolts in her general direction. She did a half-roll slip, taking two hits on her forward shield as she passed through the third fighter's stream of fire, then loosed her first torpedo.

Nothing if not well trained, the Chiss adjusted their aim instantly, targeting on the weapon's origination point. Jaina's forward shields flared into a white wavering wall of heat, and shrieking overload alarms filled the cockpit. She released the second torpedo and jinked hard to port. More Chiss brought their craft to bear, barely grazing her with a blue inferno that was nevertheless enough to bring her shields down with a final, warning screech. The air grew acrid with the smell of fused circuits, and warning messages that Jaina could not read through the smoke began to scroll down her status display.

"Just keep the masking systems up, Sneaky," Jaina ordered her droid, taking the StealthX through an unpredictable coil of reversing rolls. "If those guys get a sensor read on us, we'll really be in trouble."

The droid replied with a cynical whistle.

Jaina continued to maneuver until, a second later, the torrent of cannon fire ceased for an instant and she knew the Chiss had been momentarily blinded by her passing torpedoes. She pushed the stick up and to the left, circling out of the dartship tangle as quickly as she could and climbing for the stars, where her dark craft would not be silhouetted against Qoribu's scintillating rings.

A pair of bright dots flared through the smoke in Jaina's cockpit, and she leaned closer to her tactical display. Two shrinking circles of light indicated that her proton torpedoes had detonated where she intended, just behind the defoliator's thrust nozzles. The big ship was already beginning to swing off course, rising into a tight banking turn that would carry it into Qoribu's gravity well if the crew did not regain control soon.

Jaina allowed herself a moment of self-congratulation—just so her wingmates would know she had completed her assignment—

then the Saras swarm began to drift back toward Ruu, leaving the crippled defoliator to recover control and flee. Even now, after two months of living and fighting with the Taat, Jaina was awed by the insects' complete lack of spite. Once a threat had been turned away, they never attempted to cause it more harm.

Jaina's admiration was mirrored in the Force by that of the other Jedi, and her thoughts turned to the other three defoliators.

"Give me an overall sitrep, Sneaky. And clean this smoke out of the cockpit." Jaina finally realized that she was reflexively using the Force to keep from coughing. "I can barely see my display."

A valve hissed open and cleared the air, then Jaina was hit by a wave of shock so sudden and powerful it reminded her of the time her X-wing had been blown from under her at Kalarba. She automatically began a systems sweep, but knew before her gaze reached the life-support readout that the alarm had come to her through the meld, from the three Jedi she had sent to stop the middle two defoliators.

The tactical display showed the other three defoliators also drifting dead in space. But a new vessel had appeared on the far side of the battle, well positioned to prevent the Taat—and Jedi—from returning to their home nest. It was simultaneously bleeding clawcraft into space and sweeping the area with tractor beams, gathering up dartships like flitnats in a net.

"*Victory*-class Star Destroyer." Jaina turned toward the battle zone and poured on velocity. "Where did *that* come from?"

Sneaky let out a defensive tweet, then replayed a high-speed version of the last ten seconds of tactical record. The vessel had simply appeared a few moments ago, *after* the Jedi had disabled the defoliatiors. Jaina grew instantly cold and emotionless inside.

"Cloaked."

She wasted no time asking herself why she had failed to anticipate the tactic—capable enemies *always* surprised you—but her thoughts did leap to the implications. Had the Star Destroyer been an escort, it would have revealed itself as soon as the nests moved against the defoliators. Instead, it had waited until the

Jedi launched their proton torpedoes—betraying both their presence and their general location. It had come for *them*—using their own subterfuge against them.

It had been one of Jag Fel's favorite tactics, when they had flown together against the Yuuzhan Vong. Jaina reached out toward the Star Destroyer, searching for his familiar presence, but could not find him among all the beings on the vessel—at least not in the middle of the battle.

A burst of dismay swept through the Force, then a soft growl arose inside Jaina's head. Lowbacca was caught in one of the tractor beams. She wondered how bad, then had a brief vision in which dartships were flying past in a black, swirling wall and the cockpit was filled with the screaming whine of overloaded fusial thrust engines.

Jaina felt Tesar reaching out to Lowbacca, urging him to hold on until he and Jaina could get there. They might be able to shut down the tractor beam if they could destroy its generators. But none of the Jedi knew what the tractor beam generators on a Chiss Star Destroyer looked like . . . or where to find them.

Lowbacca thought they were being foolish; that they would only get themselves captured by trying something so risky. The best way to help him was to avoid falling into the Chiss trap themselves.

A swell of anger rose in the Force. Jaina was still too far from the battle to see anything more than a hazy cloud of dartships silhouetted against Qoribu's gleaming rings, but the tactical display showed more than a dozen clawcraft swarming Jacen and Tahiri, methodically herding them toward the Star Destroyer's tractor beams. Supported by a throng of Taat, they were fighting back valiantly, opening one hole after the other in the enemy formation. The Chiss always managed to cut them off and drive them back toward the sweeping tractor beams.

Then a clawcraft designator vanished. Another turned yellow and spiraled through the ring system and out of the system. Jaina felt Alema and Zekk urging Tahiri and Jacen to accelerate through the gap. Two of three clawcraft moving to cut them off also lost control and flew out of the battle, then Tahiri and Jacen were free, pulling away from their pursuers and weaving a crooked path among the few enemy fighters still in a position to attack.

Tahiri's gratitude flooded the Force, but quickly changed to astonishment when a clawcraft behind her exploded in a flash of static. A second one vanished an instant later, then a third turned yellow on Jaina's display and broke into two parts.

Tahiri's shock was overpowered by Alema's glee, then almost instantly by Zekk's righteous fury.

This is wrong! Zekk raged. He was furious with Alema; she was killing for revenge!

But Alema did not think so. She felt she was only killing to teach them a lesson, to make them understand there were consequences.

Jaina added her anger to Zekk's. Alema had violated the unspoken rules of the conflict. She had killed without purpose. When the Chiss reviewed their battle vids, they would feel bound to retaliate in kind.

Alema didn't care, and Taat seemed to agree. The hundreds of dartships not yet swept up in the tractor beams began to coalesce in tightly knit balls, moving with eerie precision into the path of oncoming clawcraft. Chiss fighters began to explode as though they were crashing into asteroids. The conflict was turning into an all-out battle.

Sensing Jaina's alarm, Tahiri opened a comm channel. "Reya-Taat, call off the dartships! Our last attacks were mistakes."

"They did not feel like mistakes," Reya countered. "They felt good."

"This battle is getting out of hand," Tahiri responded, echoing Jaina's feelings. "Reya was Chiss. She *knows* what will happen if you continue."

Reya fell silent, but the dartships continued to attack. Jaina found her frustration with Alema growing. The Twi'lek was a fine pilot, but she was too wild, too quick to surrender to the pearl of hatred that had been accreting inside her since the death of her sister, Numa. Now Alema's anger would spread across the Gyuel system like a nova blast.

When the Taat continued to attack, Jacen said, "ReyaTaat, the Chiss will return with bigger ships. They'll attack the nests directly, and Taat will be destroyed. *All* the Qoribu nests will be destroyed."

"What difference does it make? Our nests are already dying." Reya's voice grew icy. "But Lowbacca must not be captured."

The Force resonated with agreement—none of the Jedi wanted to see their friend captured—but Lowbacca was calling the shots. He was the one in trouble.

"Lowbacca can take care of himself," Tahiri said. "And if he is captured, what the Taat are doing now will only hurt him."

"Lowbacca *won't* be captured," Reya said. "The Colony does not wish it."

The Taat continued to place themselves in front of their enemies, but instead of pursuing Tahiri and Jacen all the more ferociously, the clawcraft peeled away, giving them a clear route to freedom. Jaina exhaled in relief. At least Jag—or whoever was commanding this task force—still had the sense to back off before the conflict escalated.

Then a new tractor beam shot out from the Star Destroyer, capturing Tahiri, Jacen, and—judging by their surprise and anger—Alema and Zekk. Jaina cursed at the same time she heard Tesar's irate hiss in her ears. It was not easy to lock on to a wildly dodging spacecraft visually, but if a beam crew knew the comm frequency being used by the target, they could follow the carrier wave straight to their victim. And while Reya had not initiated the contact with Tahiri, she *had* kept the young Jedi talking until the clawcraft dispersed.

Jaina was close enough to the battle now that she could see the laser cannons flashing inside the whirling cloud of dartships. Four waving fingers of darkness marked the areas where the tractor beams were sweeping the Taat out of space, slowly pulling them toward the Star Destroyer. The vessel itself resembled a gray version of the Empire's old *Victory*-class Star Destroyers, save that it was a little sleeker, longer, and narrower, with a conical hull that gave it a menacing, needle-like appearance. It was impossible to tell where the bridge was located—it was not in the Chiss nature to reveal such a crucial detail just for the looking—but a dome-shaped bulge amidships probably housed the cloaking equipment that had masked the vessel's approach.

Jaina dropped the nose of her StealthX and started a fast approach toward the bow of the Star Destroyer, then felt Tesar's excitement starting to mount as he initiated his own run. An image of his view of the ship appeared in the back of her mind. He seemed to be approaching from the opposite end, more or less head-on toward Jaina. They would have to be careful to avoid a collision.

"Sneaky, give me a ten-mag view of the area around the root of the nearest tractor beam," Jaina ordered.

Risky or not, she could not let the Chiss reel in four Jedi.

Over the comm, Reya said, "We will have you free in a minute, friends."

Not kriffing likely, Jaina thought. Half of the Taat were already being sucked toward the Star Destroyer's capture bays, and the rest were too busy hurling themselves in front of clawcraft to disable any tractor beams.

"Help is coming." Reya's voice was reassuring. "The Mueum are almost here."

The timely assurance raised the hair on the back of Jaina's neck. Recalling Taat's uncanny ability to sense what foods she and the other Jedi were longing for, she began to wonder what else Reya could sense.

Tesar began to think Reya was a better spy than they had thought. Projecting his thoughts openly into the battle-meld, he wondered if he should eliminate her.

Jaina had the mental image of Tesar selecting Reya's lancet as a primary target, but realized instantly that the Barabel was only trying to test whether Reya knew what was happening in the battle-meld. He was passing over the stern of the Star Destroyer and could not have targeted her if he wished.

When Reya did not fall for the ploy, Jaina checked her tactical display and found a blue storm of Mueum dartships cascading down from the direction of Eyyl and Jwlio—just as promised.

"Sneaky, do an EM sweep of the hull," Jaina ordered. She still did not see how the arrival of the fresh swarm was going to save Lowbacca and the others. "We might get lucky and locate an energy output that will tell us where those generators are."

Sneaky whistled an acknowledgment, then the image on her

display switched to a rectangular portal set into a field of gray durasteel. The tractor beam itself was invisible, save for a few distortion ripples that suggested it was a very powerful beam indeed—one designed to drag in unwilling ships. As Jaina had feared, the portal was protected by a grid of blue energy—a repulsor screen designed to prevent someone from disabling the beam by dropping a piece of ordnance into it. The Chiss were far too good to overlook something that obvious.

"Go to five mag," Jaina ordered.

The beam portal grew small in her display, and the white cave of a capture bay appeared beneath it. Jaina could see a pair of weapons turrets flanking a transparisteel viewing panel set high in the innermost wall, but no hint of the tractor beam generator.

Sneaky piped a warning, and Jaina looked up to see the Star Destroyer stretched out before her like the long gray plain of an empty speeder lot. The beam cannons, big and small, remained silent in their sunken firing pits—a sure sign that the gunners still had not detected the approaching StealthXs.

"Anything on that EM sweep, Sneaky?" Jaina asked.

The droid tootled a negative, and Jaina sensed that the same was true for Tesar. It was beginning to look like they would have to do this the hard way. The Jedi would have to eject and destroy their ships.

Tahiri did not want to leave her living ship. It was a gift from Zonama Sekot . . . and it was a friend.

But her only other choice was to let herself be captured—and Jaina forbade that. She would go EV with Jacen and everyone else. Ten seconds.

Lowbacca did not have ten seconds. Five—if he was lucky.

Three, then.

"Give us eight!" Reya pleaded. No doubt now about whether she could read their emotions in the Force. "The Mueum are almost here."

Sure—enough time for your friends to capture Lowbacca's StealthX, Jaina thought. Two seconds.

Tesar urged Jaina to wait. The Mueum *were* attacking.

Jaina glanced at her display and saw a single, tightly packed arrow of Mueum designators driving through a screen of Chiss clawcraft like a blaster bolt through a tunic. The Star Destroyer opened up with all bearing batteries, hitting the mass with a devastating fusillade that would have torn a minor moon in half.

The Mueum did not even slow down. Long furrows of dartships vanished into fiery nothingness, and the swarm simply flowed into the open spaces, shrinking a little, but continuing toward the Star Destroyer amidships.

"No, Reya!" Jaina ordered. "Stop them!"

Lowbacca went EV, and Jaina lost all hope of bringing the conflict back under control. The Mueum took another volley of laser cannons and continued on as before, coalescing into a single black harpoon aimed at the heart of the Chiss Star Destroyer. Lowbacca's StealthX detonated in the mouth of the capture bay, taking with it fifty square meters of deck and several dozen dartships, but doing nothing whatsoever to interrupt the tractor beam.

Jaina rolled away from the Star Destroyer and started firing, trying to force as many clawcraft as possible away from Tahiri and the other captured Jedi. Tesar dropped in behind Jaina, firing to kill as a string of brave Chiss pilots jumped on her tail.

Finally, the Mueum reached the Star Destroyer. On her tactical display, Jaina glimpsed the lead dartships crashing into the vessel's particle shields, vaporizing themselves in an ever-broadening circle of light and fire. She thought for one moment that the suicide attack would come to no more than that; that the entire Mueum swarm would simply smash itself against the powerful Chiss shields.

Then the shields crackled, flashed, and fell. The Mueum assault smashed into the hull in a conflagration of rocket fuel and fire and burned through within seconds. Bodies and equipment began to tumble from the breached hull, but the swarm continued to pour through, streaming through the inner hull and spreading along the corridors to all the hidden corners of the vessel. Within moments, long tongues of flame began to lick out of the gun turrets, and towers of white fire started to shoot from the discharge vents.

A wave of explosions shook the Star Destroyer, and the hull began to come apart. Jaina was shaken by an all-too-familiar wave of anguish and fear, then a rip seemed to open in the Force as the huge vessel began to disintegrate from the inside.

The tractor beams sputtered into nothingness, and a sense of relief permeated the Force as Tahiri and Alema and Zekk finally regained control of their craft. A Chiss fighter appeared in front of Jaina, coming at her head-on and pouring angry streams of blaster bolts more or less in her direction. Jaina returned fire automatically, and she did not notice how her hand was shaking until after the clawcraft exploded.

Jaina reached out for Lowbacca and felt him drifting away, frightened and awed and lonely.

We'll find you! she promised. But he would have to stay open to the meld, he would have to help them find him.

She'll be doing well, Lowbacca thought, *just to save herself.*

FOURTEEN

After a week of travel and three off-course jumps, the dark-banded surface of Qoribu's night side was finally swelling in the *Shadow*'s forward viewport, biting an ever-larger crescent from the blue-green sun behind it. The planet was girded by a spectacular ring system, and the dusky shadows of its penumbra were brightened by a litter of twinkling moons, but Luke's gaze kept drifting to the velvet void beyond, to a few bright stars where the Chiss frontier hung stretched like the web of some dark, deadly spider better left undisturbed.

The Chiss prided themselves on never being the aggressor people. By their own law, they never attacked first. Their military doctrine took the edict even farther, decreeing that an enemy must attack them within Ascendancy space before they responded. So Luke did not understand how the Chiss had ended up in a border conflict when both sides acknowledged that the Colony was still over a light-year from the border.

Perhaps doctrine had changed. After all, the war with the Yuuzhan Vong had changed almost everything else. And Luke knew from his last journey into the Unknown Regions that there were things happening out here that the Galactic Alliance still did not understand. The number of Chiss ruling houses been reduced from nine to four for some unknown reason, and the Empire of the Hand had mysteriously vanished. So it certainly seemed possible the Chiss had changed their doctrine.

Still, Luke doubted that the Chiss would abandon their most basic tenet—the prohibition against attacking first. The law had stood for a thousand years, and Thrawn—the Chiss Grand

Admiral who had nearly defeated the New Republic single-handedly—had been exiled from the Ascendancy for violating it.

To Luke, there was only one logical conclusion. The Colony had brought this conflict on itself—or Raynar had.

Just the thought of what Raynar had become filled Luke with guilt and sorrow. The Myrkr mission had cost his nephew Anakin and six other young Jedi their lives, and Raynar had suffered horribly, alone and with no reasonable hope of rescue. Could he be blamed for becoming the entity that he was now?

"It was war," Mara said softly from the pilot's seat. She glanced up at the activation reticle in the canopy, then looked at Luke in the section that mirrored over. "You're not responsible for what happened. Billions of good people were lost."

"I know that," Luke said. The blue star was completely hidden behind Qoribu's dark side now, and the yellow ring system looked as though it encircled a ghost planet. "But Raynar isn't lost. I may be able to bring Raynar back."

"You dream big, Skywalker," Mara said, shaking her head. "But it's not going to happen this time. For better or worse, Raynar is entwined with the Colony. I doubt that they *can* be separated."

"You're probably right," Luke said. "But something here feels wrong."

"Define *wrong*," Mara ordered. "Something to do with Raynar?"

"Maybe. It frightens me when Jedi become emperors."

"The galaxy had a bad experience with that," Mara admitted. "But Raynar is hardly another Palpatine. He seems very concerned about his, uh, people."

"For now," Luke said. "But how long before power becomes the end instead of the means?"

"So it's your job to set it right?" Mara asked. "We have enough to worry about in the Galactic Alliance."

"The galaxy is larger than the Galactic Alliance."

"And the Jedi can't be responsible for all of it," Mara retorted.

There was a long silence while they continued the discussion on a deeper, more intimate level, wrapping themselves around the other's viewpoint, trying to understand completely, but also searching for a way to consolidate what seemed to be opposing opinions. Such moments were one of the secret buttresses of their marriage. They understood how they fit together, how each had strengths and insights that complemented the weaknesses and blind spots of the other, and they had learned early in their relationship—during a desperate, three-day hike fleeing Imperials in a vornskyr-filled forest—that their future always looked brighter when they relied on each other.

But this time there seemed no way to reconcile their concerns. Jedi resources were already stretched too thin to try separating Raynar from the Colony, even if Luke could convince the rest of the council that it was the right thing to do. Yet he could not escape the feeling that something important had fallen out of balance; that his Jedi Knights were busy plugging vac holes while their ship flew down a black hole.

"Life was a lot simpler when we could just draw a lightsaber and cut the bad guy down to size," Luke said.

Mara smiled. "Simpler—not necessarily easier."

They were close enough to Qoribu now that its moons had begun to resolve into colored shapes, from twinkling yellow specks to creamy fist-sized disks. Luke counted twenty-five different satellites glimmering in the penumbral grayness to either side of the gas giant's murky face, and the navigation display revealed another thirty hidden in the complete darkness of umbra.

Luke reached out in the Force. A diffuse insect presence blanketed six different moons, all currently clustered together near the penumbra's outer edge. Jaina and most of the other Jedi seemed to be on a moon near the center of the group, and—to his great relief—they exhibited only a hint of the Joiner double presence. But Lowbacca was floating a little behind the group, just inside Qoribu's pitch-black umbra, frightened and alone amid a mass of Chiss presences.

One of the Jedi in the main group stirred beneath Luke's Force-touch, then extended a welcoming embrace.

Luke recognized Jacen's presence, but before he could respond with his own feeling of warmth, his nephew's voice sounded inside his head.

Hurry.

Jacen seemed more concerned than alarmed, and Luke had the clear impression that things were about to get crazy. He raised a hand to point toward the moon with their Jedi, but Mara was already swinging the *Shadow*'s nose toward it. He would have liked to open a hailing channel and raise Jaina on the comm, but there were certain to be Ascendancy listening posts all over the system—and the less the Chiss knew about who was approaching, the better.

"Faster." Saba's voice came over a vessel-to-vessel tight-beam channel that would be difficult for the Chiss to intercept; she was aboard the *XR808g* serving as Juun's copilot until Tarfang recovered. "It feelz like our Jedi Knightz are preparing a battle rage."

"You heard him, too?" Luke asked. "Jacen?"

"Yes." Saba's breathing began to grow heavy and deliberate. "It felt like they were about to go crazy. They must have found a great evil, or Tesar would never awaken the Hungry One."

"The Hungry One?" Mara echoed. "Take it easy, Saba. I don't think *crazy* means the same thing to humans as to Barabels."

Saba's breathing slowed. "No?"

"It just means unpredictable," Luke said, amazed at how little he *still* understood Barabels. "A bit out of control."

"Unpredictable?" Saba's voice returned to normal. "What a relief. This one does not like to set her mind aside."

Grimacing at the thought of a Barabel robbed of all restraint, Luke brought up a tactical display and found a trio of frigates drifting in unpowered orbit near Lowbacca's presence. They were being tended by a swarm of rescue craft, with a shield of clawcraft fighters hovering between them and the Killik-occupied moons. Floating just above the ring system were several massive chunks of flotsam that gave Luke a very bad feeling.

"Artoo, give me a composition analysis on that debris in the middle of the Chiss task force."

R2-D2 tweeted an listless acknowledgment, and a moment later the analysis appeared in an inset on Luke's screen. The flotsam was metallic, irregular, and mostly hollow. Starship pieces.

Luke started to comment that there had been a battle, but stopped when he heard a pair of small feet slapping onto the flight deck behind him.

"Hurry!" Ben cried from the door. "Jacen needs us!"

Luke turned to find his son charging forward in his night tunic, his red hair still pillow-mussed and his eyes bleary with sleep.

Luke opened his arms. "You heard Jacen?"

Nanna clomped onto the deck behind him. "I apologize. He woke and jumped up before I could get to him." She extended her hand, saying to Ben, "Come back to bed. It was only a dream."

Luke motioned her to wait. "It wasn't." He hoisted Ben onto his knee. "We heard Jacen, too."

Ben's mouth dropped open. "You did?"

"Yes," Luke answered. "Through the Force."

This brought a flash of alarm to Ben's eyes.

"It's okay, Ben," Mara said in a soothing voice. "There's nothing to be scared of. You touched the Force all the time, when you were younger."

"During the war, I know." Ben stretched his arms toward Nanna. "I wanna go back to bed."

Luke didn't lift him toward the droid. "You're sure? We're coming up on Qoribu now."

Ben's face lit briefly in delight when he glanced forward, but he quickly turned back to Nanna. "I'm still tired."

"Really?" Luke frowned inside, but passed Ben to the droid. "We'll wake you when we see Jacen and Jaina."

"Okay." Ben buried his cheek on Nanna's synthflesh shoulder and looked away.

After the droid had taken him off the flight deck, Luke said, "He's afraid of it."

"Clearly." Mara's voice was sharp, but Luke sensed it was only because she was worried about Ben. "Maybe he thinks the Force is why his cousin and so many other Jedi died?"

"Maybe," Luke said. "It would be nice to have a reason we understood."

"But you don't think that's it."

"I guess not," Luke said. "When it comes to anything else, he's just too adventurous and confident, sometimes even reckless."

Noting that the *Falcon* was already drifting into a standard defensive formation while Juun's *XR808g* continued to speed ahead, Luke opened a tight-beam channel to both vessels.

"Not so fast, *Exxer*," he said. "Until we know what that battle was about—"

"There was a battle?" Juun gasped.

"Check your readouts," Han commed from the *Falcon*. When he received only dead silence in response, he added, "You *do* have the standard reconnaissance suite?"

"We have two pairz of electrobinocularz," Saba informed them, acting as the *XR808g*'s copilot. "And only one of us is small enough to use them."

As Han chided the Sullustan for this lack, Mara said to Luke, "Heads up. What's that?"

Luke checked his tactical display and found a torrent of Killik dartships streaming out of Qoribu's shadow. Frowning because he had not sensed any nests in that area, he turned to ask R2-D2 to double-check the readings—and found the little droid leaning against his interface arm, slowly twisting the information buffer back and forth in the socket. Alarmed at how the droid seemed to be deteriorating, Luke promised himself that he would schedule some maintenance time and looked out the forward viewport instead.

It took only a moment to see the sensors were not mistaken. An elongated oval of tiny white flecks was pouring into the gray shadows of the planet's penumbra, moving to position itself in front of the six moons where Luke *had* sensed Killiks.

"This isn't standard procedure," Juun said. The *XR808g* continued toward the Killik moons. "They must be nervous because of the battle."

"Then what are you doing?" Han asked. "Shouldn't we slow down?"

"The sooner they see us, the better," Juun said. "Once they realize we're only flying transports, they'll return to their usual routine. Insects are very advanced. They always follow standard procedure."

Luke wasn't so sure. He reached out to the dartships and sensed . . . nothing definite, only the same vague uneasiness that he had felt before the tower collapsed on Yoggoy. He knew that Mara felt it, too.

"Captain Juun, I think you should come back," Luke commed. "We can't feel those pilots in the Force."

"You place too much faith in your ancient sorcery, Master Skywalker," Juun said. "In *Running the Blockade: Escape from Yavin,* Captain Solo clearly illustrated the value of a confident approach."

"What'd I tell you about those history vids?" Han warned. "The Force isn't just some hokey religion. This stuff works."

"So does procedure, Captain Solo," Juun said. "That's why you're paying me the big credits. Let me do my job."

The dartships continued to stream out of the umbra, gathering in a wall of swirling, flickering orange between them and the Killik moons. The *XR808g* accelerated.

"Captain Juun, I think you should reconsider." Though Luke spoke more forcefully, he resisted the temptation to tell Saba to take control of the *XR808g*. The Jedi may have developed a ruthless streak during the war, but they still stopped short of fomenting mutiny. "After the attack on Yoggoy—"

"What attack?" Juun asked.

"The building collapse," Saba rasped.

"But that was determined to be an accident."

"Not by us, it wasn't," Han answered.

The *XR808g*'s running lights began to flash in ancient blink code. Luke looked to his display, but instead of the translation he had expected, he found only the blip-storm of approaching dartships.

"Artoo!"

R2-D2 emitted a surprised clunk, then trilled a short question.

"The *Exxer*'s blink code, that's what!" Luke said. "How about a translation?"

R2-D2 droned wearily, and the translation began to scroll across the screen.

This is the XR808g, flagship of JuunTaar Commercial, with

*two sister ships bearing supplies for the Jedi warriors. Please
signal your intention to provide safe escort.*

"*JuunTaar Commercial?*" Han complained over the comm.
"*Flagship?* I didn't think Sullustans *had* that much imagination."

Luke looked back to R2-D2. "Any answer from the Killiks?"
R2-D2 tweeted a sharp no.

The dartships began to stream toward the *XR808g*, bleeding a
swath of orange rocket flame through Qoribu's shadow.

"Juun, get out of there now!" Han's voice made the comm
speakers pop. "Time to cut and run . . . or you're fired!"

Juun was already swinging around, but the dartships put on a
burst of speed and shot across the last few kilometers in an eye-
blink, engulfing the *XR808g* in a whirling cloud of rocket light
and splinter-shaped hulls. Luke felt a sudden spike of Sullustan
fear and Barabel anger, then bursts of silver light began to erupt
around the transport.

Juun's voice came over the S-thread emergency channel. "Urgent, urgent." His voice was terrified but steady. "This is Captain Jae Juun of the *XR-eight-oh-eight-g* requesting immediate
assistance. We are under attack just off Qoribu in the Gyuel system, coordinates—"

"Enough procedure, already!" Han said over the normal comm.
"We *know* the situation."

"Copy," Juun said. The channel crackled as the *XR808g*'s
shields fell, then the comm erupted into a steady, deep rumble.
"Uh, we just lost our drives. Request plan update."

"I'll be there in a minute," Han commed. "Just sit tight."

"Cop—"

The signal disintegrated into a series of loud bangs, and the
Falcon started forward.

"We'll take this one, *Shadow*," Leia commed. "Hang here and
cover our stern."

"Why don't you cover *our* stern?" Mara suggested. "You're
better armed."

"Because the *Shadow* has *yacht*-class drive units," Han said.
"If you latch onto that transport, it'll take you a week to get
moving."

"You have us there," Mara admitted.

The *XR808g*'s blaster cannons began to fire indiscriminately, blowing whole swaths clear of dartships, and the anger that Saba had been pouring into the battle-meld turned to hunt-glee.

"We're going in," Leia commed. "Just keep your ion drives hot. We may have to scoot out of here in a hurry."

"Copy." Luke was just as worried about Han and Leia as he was about Juun and Saba. The *Falcon* packed a powerful punch and boasted military-grade shields, but her legendary speed would not be available if she was dragging along a transport almost as large as she was. "Just be as fast as you can."

"Check that," Mara said. "I think you're scaring them off."

Luke glanced at his tactical display and saw that the dartships were swinging away from the *XR808g*, leaving the *Falcon* a clear path to rescue Juun and Tarfang.

"Maybe those guys aren't as homicidal as we thought," Luke said. "Could this be a communications problem?"

"It wasn't a communications problem when that tower fell," Mara said. "And I don't like the way those dartship pilots feel."

"Shadowy," Luke agreed. "Like they're hiding in the Force."

The dartships hooked around and began a ferocious acceleration on a course opposite the *Falcon*'s, back toward the pitch blackness of Qoribu's umbra.

"They're sure in a hurry," Luke said.

He switched scales, searching for any sign that the Chiss were moving against the Killiks, or the Killiks gathering for an assault on the Chiss. Everything looked quiet on both fronts. The dartship swarm split into two groups, one accelerating at twice the rate of the other.

"I didn't know methane rockets could provide so much thrust," Mara said. "None of this makes sense."

R2-D2 beeped, then scrolled a message across their displays. *These Killiks are flying hydrogen rockets.*

By the time the *Falcon*'s tractor beam had caught hold of the *XR808g*, a two-kilometer gap had opened between the two sets of dartships. The swarms continued to accelerate toward the planet's umbra until the faster one was past the *Shadow*, then both groups pivoted around and came shooting back for a flank attack.

"Look sharp!" Luke warned. "They're coming back for us."

"See 'em," Leia replied coolly. "Thanks."

The *Falcon* began to accelerate, but hardly with her usual speed. She was dragging the *XR808g* along, drawing it in slowly because the two transports were so close in size. Working any faster, Luke knew, meant risking the tractor beam's grasp—or smashing the derelict into the *Falcon*.

The dartships continued to close, and it quickly grew apparent the *Falcon* could not outrun them without setting the *XR808g* adrift. Luke started to suggest that they let Juun and Saba go EV so the *Shadow* could pick them up on the way past, but the slow swarm suddenly stopped and began to form a wall between the *Shadow* and the *Falcon*. The second, faster swarm continued to pursue the *Shadow* from behind.

"*This* doesn't look good," Mara said. "Artoo, start plotting escape vectors."

The droid tweedled an acknowledgment and went to work.

"They drew us in," Mara said. "I'm ashamed."

"They're going to a lot of trouble to get us," Luke said. "What I want to know is why."

That was the question he held in his mind as he reached for Jacen and Jaina in the Force. Raynar had been unwilling—or unable—to discuss the Yoggoy attack honestly, but Luke felt sure his niece and nephew would prove much more open.

In reply, he received only an impression of confusion.

"Same story as on Yoggoy," Mara observed. "Nobody knows anything."

R2-D2 tweeted an announcement. The *Shadow* lacked enough current velocity to escape unscathed. No matter which way they turned, the fast swarm would have a thirty-second window of attack—and that assumed the *Shadow* suffered no damage to her drive units.

Nanna's voice came over the intercom. "Shall I take Ben to the docking bay?"

"Not yet," Mara said.

"I really think you should take Ben and flee in the StealthX,

Master Skywalker," the droid insisted. "The *Shadow*'s odds of survival are—"

"Certain," Mara growled. Her gaze slid across the mirrored canopy toward Luke. "Right?"

"Right," Luke said. They had rehearsed just this situation many times. "We're fine."

Closing his mind to external distractions, Luke began a focusing exercise, breathing in through his nose, filling his belly diaphragm with air, then exhaling slowly out his mouth. He barely felt the *Shadow* shudder as the first dartships began to pelt her shields with balls of primitive chemical explosives, and when Han's voice came over the comm, he heard the words only with his ears.

"Uh, why aren't you on an escape vector? Is Artoo on the blink again?"

"Negative that," Mara answered. She lowered the *Shadow*'s blaster cannon and began to fire indiscriminately into the cloud of swirling dartships. "We're okay."

"You don't look okay," Han said. "We'll cut the *Exxer* loose and circle back to—"

"Nega*tive*!" Mara snapped. "You do that, we'll never get free of these pests. Keep going—and don't look back. Luke has a trick up his sleeve."

"Copy." It was Leia this time. "If you're sure."

"We're sure." Mara closed the channel, then—as the *Shadow*'s shuddering worsened—added, "I think."

Luke was sure. By then, he had opened himself wide to the Force, and it was pouring in from all sides, filling him with a maelstrom of power, imbuing his whole body with its energy.

A bang sounded back in the engineering bay as a power circuit overloaded, then the lights dimmed as R2-D2 redistributed shield power. Luke felt a surge of anxiety from Mara, but pushed it to one side so he could concentrate on the task at hand. He formed an imaginary picture of the *Shadow*'s exterior, then expanded it into the Force, moving it from his mind out into the cockpit.

Mara turned around and inspected the image carefully, then said, "Looks good."

Luke continued to enlarge the image, extending it into every corner of the vessel, taking his time to absorb the attributes that made up the *Shadow*'s sensor signature. He began to grow tired, but ignored his fatigue and expanded the illusion until it covered the entire ship like an imaginary skin.

Another bang sounded in the engineering bay. This time, before R2-D2 could redistribute power, the sound was followed by the muffled thuds of several hull hits. Mara hit the crash alert, closing all airtight doors and activating the pressure stop-loss systems, then spoke over the intercom.

"Nanna, get Ben into his vac suit."

"I've already done that," the droid responded. "We're waiting at our evacuation station now. Perhaps you should come—"

"Nanna, you short-circuit!" Ben's voice said. "We're fine. Dad said so!"

Trying not to be distracted by his son—or by the steadily growing shudder of the barrage of dartship attacks—Luke brought to mind another image of the *Shadow,* this time with a black, star-speckled veneer that resembled the emptiness of deep space. Instead of absorbing the ship's sensor signature, however, he blanketed it with a layer of cold emptiness.

Once the illusory skins were in place, he carefully adjusted them, drawing the masking image tight against the hull here, pushing the counterfeit out a little there. The effort of maintaining both illusions began to deplete the energy running through him, so Luke opened himself up completely, using his fear for Ben's life, his anger at the insects that were threatening it, to draw more Force into himself. Every centimeter of his body began to nettle with its sting, and a faint aura arose from his skin.

A third bang sounded from the engineering bay.

"How about that decoy, Skywalker?" Mara asked. "Our shields can't take—"

Luke released the outer skin. "Go!"

Mara shoved the throttles to overload, then, half a second later, shut down the drives. The *Shadow* slid out of her double and—still masked by the dark veneer Luke had constructed— glided quietly away from the Force illusion.

The shuddering stopped. Luke continued to maintain both illusions, the Force pouring through him like fire, burning more fiercely every moment. He was drawing more energy than his body was conditioned to endure, literally burning himself up from the inside. It was not really a dark side act—to a modern Jedi, the dark side was more a matter of intent than deed—but it felt that way to him. According to Mara, this was what happened to Palpatine, and Luke believed her. He could feel himself aging—his cells weakening, the membranes growing thin and the cytoplasm simmering, the nuclei coming apart.

The air around him began to crackle with static.

R2-D2 extended a fire extinguisher and started toward Luke, squealing in alarm.

"It's okay, Artoo!" Mara said. "He knows how far to push it. He's not going to ignite."

I hope, she added silently.

On Luke's tactical display, the illusionary *Shadow*—the real one was not visible even to her own sensors—was slowly drifting toward the bottom of the screen, still surrounded by a cloud of attacking dartships. A small inset was counting down the seconds remaining until the Force-cloaked *Shadow* would be far enough from the dartships to restart the drives and flee. The way Luke was hurting, thirty seconds seemed like an eternity.

"We're bringing Juun and Saba aboard now," Leia commed. Her voice was filled with the concern that Luke felt in the Force. "Do you need help?"

They could not answer for fear that the dartships would notice the comm waves and discover the *Shadow*'s true position. Instead, Mara reached out to Leia through the Force, trying to assure her that everything was fine. Though the message would have been clearer coming from Luke, his body was starting to tremble and spark, and he needed all his concentration just to fight his exhaustion.

The *XR808g* began to drift away from the *Falcon* on the tactical display, and the Solos started a sweeping turn back toward the "battle." Luke felt Mara protesting through the Force, but the *Falcon* only began to pick up speed. Leia was angry with them for trying to be heroes; the situation wasn't *that* bad.

"Stang!" Mara cursed. "That—"

"Moommmmm!" Ben called, peeking around the corner. He was in his vac suit, with the helmet visor open. "Dad says we're not supposed to say *stang*."

"Your father's right," Mara said. "Aren't you supposed to be at your evacuation station with Nanna?"

"We were, but then the shuddering stopped and . . ." Ben's gaze drifted over to Luke's glowing, anguished form, and his eyes bulged with horror. "What's wrong with Dad?"

"Nothing. I'll explain later." Mara activated the intercom. "Nanna—"

The droid appeared behind Ben. "Master Ben!" She swept him up and retreated aft. "The drill is *never* over until we hear the all-clear."

Luke's skin felt as dry as a Tatooine lake, and tiny haloes of golden light were starting to appear around his fingertips. The *Falcon* was on a straight heading and accelerating toward the dartships. The inset on the tactical display showed three seconds, two . . .

Mara brought the sublight drives back online. Luke let the illusions drop and slumped into his chair, his skin prickling and his hair standing on end as the last of the Force energy left his body.

Han's voice came immediately over the comm. "What the blazes?" The *Falcon* made a hard turn away from the confused dartships. "Did you just tele—"

"Didn't I tell you not to look back?" Mara asked, her voice still that of a reproving mother. "Now fall in behind us and stay there."

"Uh, sure." Han sounded more confused by her tone than he had been by the sudden change in the *Shadow*'s location. "Whatever you say."

The comm went silent, and Mara let out a breath. "Chubba. Don't tell me I just talked to Han like he was a—"

"It's okay," Luke assured her. "At heart, he's just an overgrown kid anyway."

She activated a mirror section and looked back at him. "How're you feeling?"

"Like I grabbed a powerfeed," he said. "Why is that so much harder than pushing a Star Destroyer around?"

Mara smiled. "Just don't make a mess on my flight deck."

Feeling in danger of doing just that, Luke started to rise—then caught a glimpse of himself in the mirrored section of canopy. His face was puffy and wrinkled, his skin sallow and dry, his eyes sunken and baggy and rimmed in red. He was starting to look like Palpatine.

Not by half, Mara assured him through the Force.

"But get some rest," she said aloud. "If you push that stuff too hard, there's no telling what might happen."

FIFTEEN

The AWOL Jedi stood waiting in front of their makeshift squadron, a small eye of calm in a frenetic storm of insect activity. The Knights were still wearing their rumpled flight suits, staring at the *Shadow* and *Falcon* as they landed. Tesar and Zekk had the good grace to wear guilty expressions as well, but Jaina and Alema merely looked defiant. Jacen and Tahiri betrayed no emotion at all.

Mara took her time closing down the ship's systems, allowing their suspense to build—and giving herself a few moments to search the cavernous hangar for any hint of danger in the Force. There was no chance that Jaina or any of the others had been involved in the assault on the *Shadow,* but *someone* had attacked her family—and that someone had certainly *looked* like Killiks. Unlike Luke, she was utterly convinced that Raynar Thul would do anything he thought necessary to keep Jaina and the others in the Colony—even if that meant ambushing his old friends.

Finally, when she could not find even a hint of danger, Mara joined the others in the *Shadow*'s main cabin. Despite a twenty-minute rest trance, Luke still looked like an escapee from a spice mine, with sallow skin and red-rimmed eyes. Ben was bright-eyed and eager to meet his cousins. He kept looking from his father to the door.

Mara took his hand from Nanna. "Ben, you understand that we have important business with Jaina and the others, don't you?"

"I'm not a Gamorrean, Mom," he said. "I know we wouldn't come all the way out here if it was *unimportant* business."

"Good. You can say hello to your cousins, but then Nanna will take you to stay with Cakhmaim and Meewalh on the *Falcon.*" She looked to Nanna. "Ask them to lock down the ship—I don't care if it *does* offend the Killiks."

"I was about to suggest the same thing myself," Nanna replied.

Mara nodded, then opened the boarding hatch to the cloying, fuel-laced mugginess of the big hangar. Ben was off like a blaster bolt, racing down the stairs and throwing himself into Jaina's arms. She laughed and gave him a warm hug.

"Nice to see you, too, Ben," Jaina said. She stepped back and ran an appraising eye over him. "You've grown."

"It's been a whole year." He smiled mischievously, then added, "Boy, are you guys in trouble!"

Mara, who was still only halfway down the stairs, cringed inwardly, but Jaina only smiled.

"I imagine we are."

"Well, I hope they don't take away your lightsaber or anything."

This caused Jaina's eyes to flash, but Ben didn't seem to notice. He turned to Jacen, who had matured into a handsome man with a thick beard and brooding brown eyes, and seemed unable to decide what he should do next.

Jacen smiled and extended his hand. "Hello, Ben. I'm your cousin Jacen."

"I know you." Ben took the hand and shook it. "You went away when I was two. Did you find it?"

The question puzzled Jacen less than it did Mara. "Some of it," Jacen answered.

Ben's face fell. "So you're going back?"

"No." Jacen's tone changed to that of a person addressing an equal. "What I haven't found, I doubt I ever will."

Ben nodded sagely, then glanced toward the *Falcon,* only now lowering her boarding ramp. "I have to go, but we can talk later."

"Yes," Jacen said. "I'll look forward to that."

Ben took Nanna's hand and started toward the *Falcon,* leaving nothing but an awkward silence between Mara and the AWOL Jedi. Though Luke was the informal leader of the Jedi

Order, they had decided that she would be the one to confront them and put them on the defensive. That would leave Luke free to assume the role of judge, mentor, or friend—whatever was needed.

Mara stopped a few steps away and studied the young Jedi Knights in silence, meeting each of their unblinking gazes in turn, trying to gauge their moods but finding only the unreadable durasteel of veteran killers. She did not recall when they had grown so hard. The Yuuzhan Vong had come, and it seemed to Mara that they had gone almost overnight from being teenage Jedi-in-training to seasoned warriors. After what they had seen in battle—after what they had *done*—it seemed ludicrous to think of them being "in trouble."

Jaina tolerated the scrutiny for only a few seconds, then stepped forward to give Mara a tentative hug. "*This* is a surprise."

"I'm sure," Leia said, arriving from the *Falcon* with Han, C-3PO, and Saba. "Raynar didn't make it easy for us to find you."

The glance of silent thanks that Leia flashed to Jacen did not go unnoticed by Jaina or the others, but Mara saw no sign that anyone seemed upset by it.

"Raynar is afraid you'll try to take us back." Tahiri Veila said. Over the last five years, she had matured into a sinewy blond woman—so much so that Mara might not have recognized her, if not for her bare feet and the three vertical scars the Yuuzhan Vong had left on her forehead. "And isn't that why you've come?"

"It's good to see you, too, kid," Han taunted. "What do you say we let Luke answer that and just say hello?"

Tahiri's face melted into an expression of joy and chagrin. "Sorry—we were kind of in the middle of something." She opened her arms and went to Han, giving him a big, Wookiee-style hug. "It *is* good to see you, Han."

When she started rubbing her arms across his back, Han shuddered and looked vaguely nauseated. Tahiri released him with a grin and embraced Leia as well, and the awkwardness finally faded between the two generations of Jedi. Han and Leia hugged Jacen and Jaina long and hard, fondly telling them both they had a lot of explaining to do and making them promise to do so later aboard the *Falcon*. Then the group exchanged greetings all around, and when they were done, Jaina quickly seized the initiative again.

"So what *are* you doing here? Without us, I didn't think the council would have any Jedi to . . ."

The sentence trailed off as her eyes drifted back to Luke's weary face, and her expression changed to one of dismay and fear.

"What's wrong?" she asked. "Are you sick?"

"I'm fine—just a little worn," Luke said. "We came to, um, *talk* about what's going on here."

Jaina's relief was obvious—as was that of her companions. Only Jacen's expression did not change—and he had seemed unconcerned in the first place. He had been gone five years, and still he seemed less surprised than anyone by Luke's temporary appearance.

Though Mara was being careful not to stare, Jacen gave her a small smile, letting her know that he had sensed her scrutiny. There was nothing menacing in the gesture, but it sent a cold prickle down her spine. As Palpatine's assassin, her life had often depended on her ability to hide her thoughts—both physically and in the Force. Yet Jacen had sensed her attention casually, the way he might have caught a young woman studying him from afar.

Mara pretended not to notice and kept her gaze riveted on Jaina. "You've let down the entire order," she said, deliberately forcing the younger Jedi to try to excuse their actions. "Losing one of you would have been bad enough, but there's no way we could fill the holes left by all five of you."

As Mara had expected, Jaina would not be intimidated. "Then how could the order spare *four* Jedi to come 'talk' to us?"

"The council felt the situation warranted it," Luke said. "And now the order is short *nine* Jedi."

"Situation, Master Skywalker?" Tesar rasped. "Has something happened?"

"You first," Mara demanded. This was not the way the council normally dealt with its Jedi Knights, but she did not want this group taking advantage of Luke's patience—or his regret over the outcome of the Myrkr mission. "What, exactly, are you *doing* here?"

Jaina and the others shared a moment of silent communion, then, to everyone's surprise, Alema Rar stepped forward.

"We're trying to prevent a war," she said. "Isn't that what Jedi are supposed to do?"

Luke would not be baited into making this a discussion. "Go on."

Zekk spoke next. "You know about the call we'd all been feeling . . ."

Luke nodded.

And Tahiri continued, "It wasn't something we could ignore, especially at the last."

"We *had* to come," Tesar rasped. He looked to his mother. "It was like the Mating Call. We could think of nothing else until it was answered."

They stopped, as if that had answered the question.

"That explains *why* you came," Leia said. "It doesn't explain what you're *doing*."

A chest-high Killik with a green thorax and tiny wings came over and brushed Jaina's arm with an antenna, then thrummed something with its chest.

"She says the StealthXs are fed and rested," C-3PO translated proudly.

"Fueled and armed," Jaina corrected. She ran her arm down the Killik's antenna, then said to it, "Thanks. We'll be leaving shortly."

"Lowie had to go EV," Zekk explained. "We're getting ready to bring him back."

"With shadow bombs?" Mara asked. She pointed to a rack of proton torpedoes being dragged away from the StealthXs by several Killiks. Even from ten meters away, it was apparent that the propellant charges had been replaced with packed baradium. "That's not exactly rescue equipment."

"We might need to create a little diversion," Alema admitted.

"No kidding?" Han scoffed. "You mean to get past all those Chiss?"

"Nobody's going anywhere." Mara directed this to Jaina. "Not until we have some answers. Things are too far out of control."

Jaina's face grew hard. "I'm sorry, but I'm not leaving Lowie out there another minute—"

"Lowbacca has dropped into a Force-hibernation," Luke interrupted. His eyes were half closed, his chin raised. "He's safe for now."

Jaina scowled and looked as though she wanted to argue, but she knew better than to doubt her uncle's word.

"The sooner we get those answers, kid, the sooner we get to Lowbacca," Han said.

Jaina and the others exchanged a few tense looks, then she nodded. "Fine. You want to see what this is about, come with us."

She led the way deeper into the hangar cavern, past rack after rack of dartship berths. Stacked a staggering fifteen berths high, they were strewn with fueling lines and swarming with Killik technicians. Their technology was unsophisticated, but the insects were incredibly efficient, working a dozen at a time in cramped spaces that would have had just two human technicians throwing hydrospanners at each other. The fuel-tinged air was permeated by a low, rhythmic rumble that sounded like machinery, but Mara soon realized it was coming from the creatures themselves.

She turned to Tahiri, who was walking beside her, and asked, "That sound . . . are they singing?"

It was Alema—walking at Luke's side—who answered. "It's more like humming."

"They do it when they concentrate," Tesar added. "The harder they work, the louder it growz."

"It's their part in the Song of the Universe," Tahiri explained.

"Doesn't sound like any song *I've* ever heard," Han said from a step ahead of Mara. "In fact, I've heard more rhythm in a bantha stampede."

"That's because you can't hear the whole song," Zekk explained helpfully. "Only insect species hear it all."

"Yeah?" Han scowled and turned to Jacen. "Can *you* hear it?"

"No." Jacen flashed an imitation of Han's roguish smile. "Then again, I've only been here about a month."

"Relax, Dad," Jaina called from the front of the group. "We don't hear it, either."

Han let out an audible sigh of relief, then Jaina suddenly stepped into an empty berth and ducked down a waxy passage that led out the back.

C-3PO stopped outside the berth. "That doesn't look like a proper corridor, Mistress Jaina."

"You could always stay here, Threepio," Han said, watching six Killik workers carry a damaged dartship past. "I'll bet these guys are always looking for spare parts."

"I was just commenting, Captain Solo."

C-3PO dropped into an awkward crouch that was half squat and half hunch, and they all followed Jaina into the passage.

"Sorry about this," Zekk said from behind Mara. "They weren't thinking of larger species when they dug these tunnels."

"No problem. We're not that old." Mara was bent over nearly double, so Zekk had to be crawling on all fours. "Where are we going?"

"You'll see," he said. "We're almost there."

The Force ahead grew heavy with pain and fear, and the humid air began to smell of blood, burns, and bacta. A moment later, they emerged into a large oblong chamber lined by hundreds of hexagonal wall bunks. In the open areas of the room, hand-sized Killik healers were swarming over casualties from both sides, spitting antiseptic saliva into their wounds, spinning silk sealant into cracked chitin, slipping tiny pincers into torso punctures to pull shrapnel from internal organs. Low purrs of gratitude reverberated from the chest plates of the insect patients, but the Chiss—those who were still conscious—were staring at the creatures in horror.

As the rest of the group stepped into the chamber behind Mara, a green triage nurse rushed over and brushed its antennae across Jaina's arm, then looked at Luke and thrummed a question.

"Oh, dear," C-3PO said. "She doesn't seem to know what's wrong with Master Luke!"

"Nothing's wrong with him, Taat," Jaina said to the insect. "We're all fine. We just wanted to see the infirmary."

The triage nurse stepped closer to Luke and scrutinized him with its bulbous gaze, then clicked its mandibles doubtfully.

"I'm sure." Jaina glanced at Mara. "Right?"

"Oh, yeah," Mara said. Even had there been something wrong with him, she would not have trusted the insects to fix it—not after what had become of Raynar.

"I'm just a little burned out," Luke assured the Killik.

The nurse spread its antennae in doubt, then scurried off to hold down a screaming Chiss. The patient did not seem pleased to have three Killik healers rummaging around inside his torso.

"They are not being cruel," Tesar said. "But the Taat are very stoic. They don't use anesthesia themselvez."

"And when they have it available for other species, they never get the dosage right," Jaina added. "They've decided that it's just faster and safer to do without."

"I'll bet," Han said, eyeing the carnage. "Because it kind of looks like they're enjoying it."

"They're not," Zekk assured him. "The Kind are the most gentle and forgiving species I've ever met."

"They have no malice," Alema added. She pointed to a nearby bunk, where a trio of Killik nurses clung to the wall, hovering over a half-conscious Chiss, holding a casted leg in traction. "Once the fighting's over, they care for their attackers as their own. They don't even imprison them."

"I can't imagine that works very well with *Chiss*," Leia said. "What happens when the prisoners attack?"

"Their escortz bring them here for evaluation," Tesar rasped. "They think other speciez are aggressive only because they can't stomach pain. So they look for the *source* of the pain . . ."

"Eventually, the Chiss figure it out and stop attacking," Tahiri said.

"Yeah, well, a little bug-probing would stop *me*," Han said. His gaze was fixed on a Killik healer, whose four limbs were straddling a Chiss face as it extracted something from the patient's red eyeball. "At least until I could escape this creep show."

"Dad, the Chiss don't need to *escape*," Jaina said. "They're free to leave whenever they like, if they can find a way."

Han nodded knowingly. "There's always a catch."

"Always," Alema agreed.

"But it's not what you think," Zekk added.

"The Chisz won't take back their MIAz," Tesar finished.

"I'm sure," Mara said. The young Jedi Knights' habit of talking fast and completing each other's thoughts was beginning to make her edgy. It was almost as if they were sinking into a permanent battle-meld. "I can't imagine the Chiss are much for prisoner exchanges."

"Oh, we're not talking about exchanges," Jaina said.

"The Chiss won't take them back at *all*," Tahiri explained.

"Before we got here, they used to steal transports and try to go back on their own," Alema said. "The Chiss just turned them away."

"How awful for them," C-3PO said sympathetically. "What happens to prisoners now?"

"A few hitch rides out, then who knows what happens to them," Jaina said. "Most end up staying with the nest."

Alarm bells began to ring inside Mara's head. She glanced toward the heart of the chamber, where Tekli and several Chiss medics had set up a makeshift surgical theater beneath the jewel-blue glow of a dozen shine-balls, then looked back to Jaina.

"Doesn't that worry you?" Mara asked.

"No," Zekk said, frowning. "Why should it?"

"Because they're *Joiners*," Han said. "They don't have their own minds."

"Actually, they have *two* minds," Jacen said, speaking for the first time since entering the infirmary. "They still have their own mind, but they share the nest mind as well."

Han grimaced, but Mara was relieved. At least *Jacen* still sounded as though he were considering matters from outside the Killik perspective. Maybe his odyssey had given him an extra resistance to the Killik influence . . . or maybe he had just arrived later than the others. Either way, it made him an asset when dealing with the rest of the strike team.

After a moment, Han said, "You'd better not be trying to tell me this is a *good* thing."

"It's not a good thing or a bad thing, Dad," Jacen replied. "It just *is*. What disturbs you is that the Will of the nest mind is more powerful than the will of the individual mind. They appear to lose their independence."

"Yeah." Han's eyes flashed to Jaina and the other young Knights. "That disturbs me. A lot."

"And it would certainly disturb the Chiss," Leia said. "They would feel very threatened by anything that limits their self-determination."

"That doesn't justify speciecide," Jaina countered.

"Speciecide is a harsh accusation," Luke said. The calmness of his voice, and the fact that he had been even more quiet than Jacen so far, commanded the attention of the entire group. "It doesn't sound like the Chiss. They have very strict laws regarding aggression—especially outside their own borders."

"You don't *know* the Chiss." Alema's voice was full of bitterness. "They keep Kind prisoners in isolation cells in a free-drifting prison ship and starve them to death."

"How can you know that?" Leia asked. "I can't see the Chiss letting anyone inspect their prisons."

"A Chiss Joiner revealed it," Jacen explained.

"The prison ships I believe," Mara said. "But I can't see the Chiss starving *any* prisoner. Their conduct codes wouldn't bend that far."

"The starvation is incidental," Jacen said. "The Chiss are *trying* to feed their prisoners."

"It can't be that hard to figure out what bugs eat," Han said.

"Not what, Dad—*how*," Jacen said. Motioning the group after him, he started toward the infirmary's main entrance. "Come on. This whole problem will make more sense if I just show you."

Jacen led the group into a huge, wax-lined corridor bustling with Killik workers. Most were bearing large loads—beautiful jewel-blue shine-balls, multicolored spheres of wax, wretchedly small sheafs of half-rotten marr stalks. But some carried only a single small stone, usually quite smooth and brightly colored, and these insects moved slowly, searching for the perfect place to affix their treasure amid the scattered groupings on the walls.

"So this is how they make the mosaics," Leia commented.

"One pebble at a time," Jaina said. "Whenever one of the Killiks comes across a pretty stone, she stops whatever she's doing and rushes back to the nest to find the perfect place. It can take days."

Mara was surprised to hear a tone of awe in her niece's voice; normally, Jaina was too preoccupied with tactics or readiness drilling to even *notice* art.

"She?" Leia asked. "The males don't contribute to the mosaics?"

"There aren't many males," Zekk explained.

"And males only leave their nest when it's time to establish a new one," Alema added.

The corridor branched, then ended a short time later at the brink of a huge, sweet-smelling pit so dimly lit that Han would have plunged over the edge had Jaina not caught him with the Force and pulled him back. Mara and the other Jedi had more warning. The Force inside the chamber ached with a hunger so fierce that they instinctively hesitated at the entrance.

"This is the busiest place in the nest," Jacen said over the din of clacking mandibles and drumming chests. "The grub cave."

As Mara's eyes adjusted to the dimness, she saw that the chamber was swarming with Killiks, all carefully crawling over an expanse of hexagonal cells. Half the cells were empty, a handful were sealed beneath a waxy cover, and the rest contained the thick, squirming bodies of Killik larvae.

Each larva was being attended by an adult, who was either carefully cleaning its head capsule or feeding it small pieces of shredded food. As the group watched, a nearby larva ejected a brown, sweet-smelling syrup. The adult grooming it unfurled a long, tongue-like proboscis and quickly sucked up the fluid, then burped and turned to leave the chamber. A new Killik quickly took its place.

"Blast!" Han sounded as though he might imitate the larva. "Don't tell me that was dinner."

"It's not that unusual," Jacen said. He guided them to one side of the entrance, so they would not impede the constant flow of Killiks entering and leaving the nursery. "There are bees and wasps across the entire galaxy that feed this way. It produces a very stable social structure."

Han turned to Leia. "Didn't I tell you this would happen? We let him have too many weird pets when he was a kid."

"But it does explain why the Chiss captives are starving," Mara surmised, ignoring Han's joke. "Without larvae, the prisoners can't eat."

"You make it sound like an accident, and it's not." Zekk's voice was sharp with outrage. "The Chiss are trying to starve all of the Qoribu nests into leaving."

"But they can't leave." Alema's voice was bitter. "Even if they had someplace to go, each nest would need a vessel the size of a Star Destroyer, and it would take months to prepare. They'd have to build a whole new nest inside the ship."

"That's not the answer, anyway," Jaina said. "This isn't Chiss space. The Killiks are innocent victims here."

"Victims, possibly," Mara said. She was growing alarmed by the wholehearted naïveté with which her niece and the others appeared to be embracing the Killik cause. "But hardly innocent."

Jaina's eyes flashed at the challenge, but her voice remained steady. "You don't know the situation. This system—"

"I know that on the way in here, the *Shadow* was jumped by Killiks," Mara said.

"The trouble you had on the way in?" Jacen asked. "I've been wondering about that."

"So have we," Han said dryly.

"And you think it was Killikz?" Tesar asked.

"We know what a dartship lookz like," Saba said. "But these were better than the craft that met us at Lizil. These were powered by hydrogen rocketz."

"Hydrogen?" Zekk echoed. "That can't be right."

He exchanged a confused glance with the others, then Jaina explained, "We've been trying to get them to convert to hydrogen rockets, but they produce the methane themselves."

"What are you saying?" Leia demanded. "That those weren't

Killik dartships attacking the *Shadow*? Or that we're making this up?"

The young Jedi Knights all looked uncomfortable, then Tahiri finally said, "We're saying none of this makes sense. The Kind wouldn't attack you, you wouldn't lie, none of the Kind nests have hydrogen rockets—"

"And those blast craters in my hull armor didn't get there by themselves," Mara finished. She kept her gaze fixed on Jaina. "Do you think maybe you're wrong about these insects?"

Jaina met her gaze squarely. "That's just not possible." She motioned a passing Killik over, then asked, "Our friends were attacked by a swarm of flying hydrogen rockets. Are any of the nests—"

An earnest thumping began to resonate from the Killik's chest.

"She claims it was the Chiss, pretending to be Kind," C-3PO translated. "They're trying to make the Protectors leave."

"It *wasn't* Chiss," Mara said. "I could see the pilots. They were insects."

The Killik drummed a reply, and C-3PO translated, "There are a lot of space-faring insects in the galaxy. The Chiss could have hired some."

"Not very likely," Leia said. "The Chiss are arrogant . . . elitist."

"These were Killiks," Luke agreed. "We're not mistaken."

A series of sharp booms reverberated from the Killik's chest.

"She asks if there's *anything* you will believe?" C-3PO translated.

"The truth," Mara answered.

The Killik rumbled a short reply, then dropped to all sixes and started down the corridor at a trot.

"She said she doesn't know the truth," C-3PO said. "And she sees no reason to think of one, since you won't believe it anyway."

Luke turned to Jaina. "We've seen enough. Take us back to the hangar."

"Not yet," Jaina said. "You still don't understand—"

"We understand all we need to." Luke glanced at Mara and

Saba, silently asking if the council's representatives had reached a consensus. When they both nodded, he took a step back so he could address all of the AWOL Jedi. "The situation here is as confused as it is volatile, and your team has lost the neutrality required of Jedi Knights. The Masters ask for your return to Coruscant."

Mara cringed inwardly. Like Kyp, Corran, and several other Masters, she believed the Jedi Order should command the obedience of its Jedi Knights, rather than "ask" for it. Luke preferred to allow the Jedi Knights their independence, saying that if the Jedi Order could not trust the good judgment of its members, then the Masters were failing at their most important job. Being first among equals, Luke's opinion held sway.

Jaina was quick to seize on the opening, of course. "Is it *our* neutrality the council is worried about—or the Galactic Alliance's relationship with the Chiss?"

"At the moment, it's *you* we're worried about." Luke's voice was as warm as it was firm. "Any Jedi should recognize the importance of maintaining good relations with the Chiss. The sectors they patrol for us along the border are the *only* ones free of piracy and smuggling."

"The Jedi are not servants of the Galactic Alliance," Alema countered.

"No, we aren't," Luke agreed.

As he spoke, Killiks were beginning to gather in the corridor, clambering up onto the walls and ceiling. Mara did not sense anything threatening in the Force—it was closer to grim concern, if she was reading the insects' emotions correctly—but she reached out to Saba and Leia, subtly suggesting they move to a more defensible position.

"But a peaceful Galactic Alliance is the strongest pillar of a peaceful galaxy," Luke continued. "And the Jedi *do* serve peace. If the Reconstruction fails and the Galactic Alliance sinks into anarchy, so does the galaxy. The Jedi will have failed."

"What happened to defending the weak?" Zekk demanded. "To sacrificing for the poor?"

"Those are worthy virtues," Luke said. "But they won't stop

the galaxy from sinking into chaos. They aren't the duties of a Jedi Knight."

"So we abandon the Killiks for the good of the rehab conglomerates snapping up our part of the galaxy?" Jaina asked. "Isn't that how Pal—"

"Don't say it!" Mara stepped toward her niece, drawing a rustle from the ceiling and walls as the Killik spectators shrank back. "It's bad enough to desert your posts and make us come out here looking for you. Don't you dare make that comparison. Some things I won't tolerate even from you, Jaina Solo."

Jaina's eyes widened in shock. She stared at Mara for a long time, clicking softly in her throat, hovering between an apology and an angry retort that everyone present knew would open a rift between the two women that could never be closed again. To his credit, Luke did not intervene. He simply stood quietly, patiently waiting to see what decision Jaina would make.

Finally, Jaina's face softened. "That was a thoughtless thing for me to say. I didn't mean to suggest that Uncle Luke was anything like the Emperor."

Mara decided to take that as an apology. "I'm glad to hear it."

"And we're not going to abandon the Killiks." Luke glanced up as the Killiks thrummed their approval, then looked to the rest of the strike team. "But I'm worried about you—all of you."

"You've lost your objectivity and you've taken sides," Mara said, sensing what Luke wanted from her. "You're openly fighting on the Killiks' side—and that means you have no chance at all of solving the problem."

"Frankly, you're half Joiners now," Luke said. "I think you should to return to Coruscant with us at once. All of you."

The bitter scent of an alarm pheromone filled the air, and the corridor erupted into such a panicked din of drumming and clacking that Mara's hand went automatically to her lightsaber—and so did the hands of Leia and Saba. The color drained from Han's face, and he casually hooked his thumb in his belt above his blaster. But Luke's hands continued to hang at his sides, and the only sign that he showed of hearing the tumult was the patience he displayed in waiting for it to die down.

When it was possible to hear again, he continued as though

he had never been interrupted. "We saw what became of Raynar, and the order just can't afford to lose any Jedi Knights right now."

"What about the Killiks?" Tahiri asked. "Without us here, the Chiss will have a free rein to—"

"This one will stay," Saba said. "Until Master Skywalker can arrange to speak with Aristocra Tswek, she will let the Chisz know the Jedi are still watching."

"Alone?" Tesar asked.

Saba nodded. "Alone."

Tesar grinned, then thumped his tail on the floor and bumped skulls with his mother. "Good hunting."

Mara looked to Jaina. "And the rest of you?"

Jaina exhaled loudly, then looked from the floor to Leia. "You've been awfully quiet, Mother."

"I'm not a Master."

"I know," Jaina said. "So what do you think?"

Leia's brow rose, and she appeared almost as shocked as Mara felt. "You're asking *me* what to do?"

"Don't look so surprised," Jaina said. "I *know* how you and Dad feel about the Galactic Alliance. You're the only ones here who don't have an agenda."

"Oh, I have an agenda." Leia smiled. "Your father and I *did* come all the way out here to make sure you and Jacen are safe."

Jaina rolled her eyes. "Like *that's* going to happen. Just tell me what you think."

Leia didn't even hesitate. "Jaina, I think you're just making the situation here worse."

"Worse?" Alema demanded. Her lekku were writhing. "What do you know? You've only been here—"

Jaina glanced at the Twi'lek out of the corner of her eye, and Alema fell silent.

"Thank you," Leia said. "As I was saying, your presence is a provocation to the Chiss. They're only going to press harder, and you'll end up starting a war that might have been averted."

"Averted?" Tahiri asked. "How?"

"I don't know how—not yet," Leia admitted. "But I can tell

you how it *won't* be averted: by destroying Chiss task forces. They'll just start sending bigger flotillas."

"They already have."

Jaina turned to her fellows to discuss the matter—or so Mara thought. Instead, they merely looked at each other for a couple of seconds, then the Killiks suddenly let out a single disappointed boom and began to disperse. Tesar, Jacen, and Tahiri started up the corridor.

"We'll go," Tahiri said.

"So will Tekli," Tesar added.

"That's half," Mara said, raising her brow to Jaina and the remaining two. "What about you three?"

"We *four*," Jaina corrected. "You forgot to count Lowbacca."

SIXTEEN

Far below the *Falcon,* the golden expanse of Qoribu's largest ring swept past, a vast river of sparkling rubble that curved under the purple moon Nrogu and faded into the twilight murkiness of the planet's dark side. In the distance, just beyond the ghostly green crescent of the moon Zvbo, the first tiny darts of Chiss efflux were tracing a crazy lacework against the starflecked void.

"We're coming into visual range now," Leia reported. "It looks like the search is spreading. I see ion trails to all sides of the ring—some up to thirty degrees above."

"Wonderful." Han's tone was sarcastic. "The Chiss are going to be in a *great* mood."

"What leads you to believe that?" Juun asked. He was in the port-side passenger's seat, annoying Han by constantly peering over his shoulder. Fortunately, Tarfang had been sent back aboard the *Shadow,* where Tekli would be able to tend to his wounds. "Because they're having trouble finding survivors from their starship?"

"How'd you guess?" Han's voice was even more sarcastic.

"Procedure," Juun answered proudly. "They've increased their search radius, and why would Chiss search protocols be any different from our own?"

"You're one smart Sullustan."

"Thank you." Juun beamed. "Coming from Han Solo, that is an enormous compliment."

"Yeah," Han said. "Sure."

He pulled back on the yoke, and the *Falcon* began to climb

away from the ring. Immediately, Leia felt the curiosity of their escorts—Jaina, Saba, Alema, and Zekk—rise in the Force.

"Our StealthXs are wondering what you're doing," Leia reported. "To tell the truth, so am I."

"*We* don't have stealth technology," Han explained. "And as bad as things are going for the Chiss, if they catch us trying to sneak in, they're liable to blast first and not bother with questions."

"Like the Talu insertion in the Zsinj campaign," Juun declared. "The *Falcon* will act as a decoy while the StealthXs penetrate the enemy's perimeter."

"Not really," Han said.

"No?" Juun sounded crestfallen. "Why not?"

"Because you can't stuff a Wookiee into a StealthX cargo compartment," Han said. "So we're just gonna fly in there and fetch Lowbacca ourselves."

"And the Chiss are going to permit that?" Juun gasped.

"Sure." Han glanced over at Leia, then said, "Leia is gonna talk 'em into it."

"I am?" Leia waited for Han to elaborate, then finally realized he was counting on her to come up with a plan. "This should be interesting."

"Very," Juun said. "I'm looking forward to seeing how you do it."

"Me, too," Leia said.

Leia set her doubts aside and reached out to Jaina and the others in the Force, trying to lay out Han's plan without the benefit of words. Though she had participated in a handful of battle-melds toward the end of the war, she was not very practiced in the sort of empathic broadcasting used to communicate with StealthX pilots, and the sentiments she felt in reply ranged from confusion to concern. Growing more frustrated with each failure, she finally stopped trying and concentrated on two words: *Trust me.*

The four pilots seemed instantly reassured and spread out behind the *Falcon,* flying along the dark bands in the ring so their craft would not be silhouetted against the glittering rubble. Leia shook her head, thinking that she needed to spend more time practicing.

The Force filled with encouragement.

"Jaina and the others seem okay with the new plan," Leia reported. Though Saba was in charge of the Jedi in the StealthXs, Leia's bond with her daughter was so much stronger that the clearest communication came from her. "I think."

"Good." Han leveled off ten kilometers above the planet's ecliptic and took the *Falcon* into the gray dusk of its penumbra. "But doesn't all this seem a little easy to you?"

"Not really," Leia said. "We still haven't seen how the Chiss are going to respond, and—"

"Not them," Han said. "Jaina. She doesn't give up that easily."

"I'm sure she just realized you were right," Juun offered. "Any daughter would listen to a father of *your* experience."

"I'm afraid humans are more complicated than that," Leia said before Han could respond. Sooner or later, even a Sullustan would recognize the sarcasm in Han's voice, and she did not want to see Juun crushed again. It had been bad enough when they had shut off the tractor beam and let the *XR808g* float free. "And Jaina is more complicated than most. She's as stubborn as her father."

"Thanks." Han sounded genuinely proud. "She's got something up her sleeve, I know it."

"Probably," Leia agreed. "But at the moment, all that matters is recovering Lowbacca. After we've kept our end of the bargain, we can take her home by force, if necessary."

"By force?" Han looked down his nose at her. "We haven't had that option since she was ten. This is *Jaina,* remember? Sword of the Jedi?"

"I remember," Leia said. "But I'll always be her mother. I can still do what needs to be done."

Han studied her for a moment, then grinned and nodded. "Yeah, Princess, I'll bet you can."

"*We* can," Leia corrected. She could sense that Han did not entirely agree with her; that now *he* was the one hiding something up his sleeve. "We're in this together, nerf herder. This won't be like the time you left me to deal with that unwashed vent crawler she brought home."

"Honey, that was Zekk," Han said.

"I know who it was," Leia said. "If not for me, Jaina would have ended up living in the undercity with him. It was all I could do to get him into the Jedi academy so she'd stay there."

"Okay," Han said. "But Jaina's not thirteen anymore. She's older than you were when I met you, and twice as bantha-headed. If she doesn't want to go—"

"You're *not* suggesting we let her stay," Leia said. "I know you better than that."

"I'm *suggesting* we might not have a choice." Han took a breath, then spoke again in a calmer voice. "I don't get it, either. Why anyone would risk their neck to save a bunch of overgrown anthills is way beyond me. But Jaina really wants this. I saw it in her eyes when Luke asked her and the others to return home."

"Saw what?" Leia asked, wondering what Han was up to. This did not sound like the same man who had just flown across half the Unknown Regions to prevent his daughter from becoming a "bughugger." "Because all I saw was disappointment and defiance."

"Exactly," Han said. "She's not going to give this up. She's probably never felt anything this pure."

"You're not making any sense, Han."

"Look, Jacen and Jaina were raised on deals," Han explained. "They grew up watching us struggle to hold the New Republic together, making bargains and playing politics."

"Because *we* were the established order," Leia said, feeling a bit defensive. "It's more complicated to preserve the status quo than to overthrow it. You write your plans in shades of gray."

"That's what I mean," Han said. "Everything was a compromise for those kids. They never had anything simple to fight for."

"They had the Dark Jedi and the Diversity Alliance," Leia countered. "They had the Yuuzhan Vong. That was all pretty clear."

"And all of it was stuff to fight *against,*" Han said. "I'm talking about something to fight *for,* something pure to build. None of these young Jedi Knights has ever had that."

Leia was beginning to see what Han was driving at. "You mean they didn't have the Rebellion."

"Right," Han said. "The Killiks are peaceful underdogs, minding their own business in neutral territory, and the Chiss are trying to starve them out. I can see how Jaina might think that's a pretty clear-cut case of the weak needing protection from the strong. Heck, it almost makes *me* want to fight for them."

Leia frowned, wondering if her husband was showing the first signs of becoming a Joiner. "But you don't, do you?"

Han rolled his eyes. "I said *almost.*" His tone was a little sharp and defensive. "I'm just talking about how *Jaina* might see things."

"What a relief," Leia said. "I thought for a minute you were going to say we had to let her and the others stay with the Colony."

"When black holes shine," Han scoffed. "What I'm *saying* is we have to make them think it's *their* choice. I don't want to take that spark away. Jaina finally has the same look in her eye that you did when I rescued you from the Death Star."

Trying not to read anything into the word *did,* Leia objected, "You *didn't* rescue me." The debate was an inside joke with them, a way of reliving their past, when their own dreams had been so pure and uncomplicated. "You fell for Darth Vader's trick and led the Imperials straight to Rebel base at Yavin Four."

"No," Han corrected. "I lured the Death Star into the Rebel trap. If not for me, that thing would still be flying around the galaxy."

"Really?" Juun gasped from the navigator's seat. "They didn't mention *that* in *Special Delivery.*"

Han blinked slowly, then twisted around in his seat. "Are you still here?"

"Of course," Juun replied to Han. "A crew member never leaves the flight deck without permission."

"You're not a crew member," Han said.

Outside the forward viewport, Leia noticed a cluster of tiny blue halos beginning to swell in the darkness of Qoribu's shadow. She checked the tactical display and found two flights of Chiss starfighters heading their way.

"Han!" Leia grabbed Han's shoulder. "Company!"

By the time Han turned around, the halos were large enough to show the spidery silhouette of the clawcraft cockpits and weapons-arms.

"Finally." Han gestured at Leia's comm microphone. "What are you waiting for? Talk to 'em."

In the dream, Lowbacca was down in the Shadow Forest with his uncle Chewbacca, racing along the dark wroshyr branches toward the green wall that was the Well of the Dead. Though the Well's tangled boundary of foliage was no farther than two hundred meters ahead, the two Wookiees never reached it. They just kept running, tearing through curtains of sloth-moss, jumping the long kkekkrrg rro claws that swung up to slash at their ankles. Every dozen meters, Chewbacca would lay a mighty hand on Lowbacca's shoulder and rumble encouragement. But the words were never clear, and the only comfort came in the familiarity of his uncle's heavy touch.

But this time, the touch was not Chewbacca's. It was just as familiar, but lighter, and on the inside and it did not feel like a Wookiee at all.

It felt like a human. Like a *female* human.

Jaina.

When did she learn to climb wroshyr trees?

"You've what?" the Chiss voice demanded over the comm.

"I repeat," Leia answered, "we've come to assist your search for survivors."

"*Jedi* survivors?" the voice asked.

The six clawcraft had taken up escort positions behind the *Falcon*. With Leia occupied on the comm, Han had barely persuaded the Noghri not to hand-crank the as-yet-unrepaired cannon turrets around to face the starfighters.

"Negative," Leia replied. "All Jedi are accounted for. We've come to assist in the search for Chiss survivors."

"Really." The officer sounded disbelieving. "The Chiss Ascendancy has adequate resources in place. You may return to your own base at once."

Leia took a deep breath. She glanced over at Han and pointed at the throttles, signaling him to be ready to make a break for it, then said, "That's clearly not true."

There was a long pause, during which time the *Falcon* passed by Zvbo's ghostly crescent and slipped into the full darkness of Qoribu's umbra.

Finally, the Chiss asked, "Did you just call me a liar, *Falcon*?"

"We can see the search operation is going poorly," Leia said. "You've expanded your radius to an area your flotilla couldn't cover properly in a week, and the situation is rapidly growing worse. So please don't insult me by telling us you have the situation under control."

"Very well." The officer's voice turned icy. "Then I will simply instruct you to leave the area at once. Your assistance is not desired."

Han made a turning motion, but Leia shook her head. She was just getting started.

"Negative," she said. "We're continuing on to assist."

"Now you are the one insulting *me*," the officer said. "Whatever your interest is here, I doubt it is Chiss casualties. Turn back, or you *will* be fired upon."

"I really doubt that," Leia said. "If you don't know who flies the *Millennium Falcon,* I'm sure your superiors do. The Chiss are not going to fire on a former New Republic Chief of State and Luke Skywalker's twin sister—not over a few moons that aren't even inside their own territory."

A flurry of red cannon bolts flashed past and lit the *Falcon*'s canopy.

"Shouldn't we ob-b-bey?" Juun stammered. "He s-seems very serious!"

"You've got a lot to learn about security patrols," Han said. "If he had been serious, we'd be sucking vac right now."

"I see." Juun's tone was one of sudden enlightenment. "You have a copy of their procedural manual!"

Han let his chin drop and shook his head.

A moment later, the officer finally grew tired of waiting for Leia's protest. "That was your only warning. The next time, we fire for effect."

"Just how many Jedi *would* you like in this system?" Leia retorted. Her threat was far more empty than the officer's, since even if there had been enough Jedi Knights to carry it out, Luke would never use the Jedi in retaliation. "This is no longer an unauthorized operation. Master Skywalker has already taken half of our Jedi Knights and started back to the Galactic Alliance. I'm sure your superior wouldn't want my brother's report to the Jedi Order and Chief of State Omas to be influenced by another unfortunate incident. Wouldn't it be better to allow us to assist, as a gesture toward continuing to resolve this thing?"

There was a short silence, then the Chiss asked, "Which Jedi Knights departed with Master Skywalker?"

Leia smiled. It was an obvious honesty test, with the Chiss asking for information their spies had probably already supplied.

"Luke and Mara took Tesar Sebatyne, Tekli, my son Jacen, and Tahiri Veila," Leia said. "We plan to take the rest with us when we go."

"You give your word?" the Chiss asked.

"Certainly, if your commander will give *his* word that the Chiss will cease their attempts to force the Colony to depart Qoribu," Leia answered. She doubted the standoff would be resolved so easily, but it was worth a try. "In any case, we will be leaving a senior Jedi to monitor the situation."

There was another pause, then the Chiss said, "Obviously, I lack the authority to negotiate on behalf of the Ascendancy."

"Obviously," Leia said.

"But the offer will be passed to the appropriate Aristocra. Until then, we are honored to accept your offer of assistance. Please proceed to the coordinates I transmit and begin a two-kilometer grid search."

"Copy," Leia said. "And thank you for allowing us to help."

"My commander asks me to express his gratitude for your assistance," the officer replied. "Out."

The coordinates appeared on the navigation display.

"We're not going to find anyone up there," Juun complained. "That's practically out of orbit!"

"Juun," Han said. "You're supposed to be a smuggler."

"I *am* a smuggler." A catch came to Juun's voice. "At least I was until I lost the *XR-eight-oh-eight-g.*"

"Then you should know we're not going anywhere near there." As Han spoke, he was swinging the *Falcon* away from Qoribu's dark mass onto a heading that would carry them generally toward the area they had been assigned. "We just gotta make it look good."

Lowbacca opened his eyes to a vast banded darkness and was instantly back above Qoribu, shivering inside the cold stink of his EV suit, anchored to a ronto-sized hunk of ice and dust in the planet's ring system. The blackness around him was filled with blue needles of ion discharge—Chiss rescue ships still searching for survivors—and a steady rain of battle debris was plunging into the gas giant's thick atmosphere, igniting a spectacular display of crimson cloud-blossoms.

Jaina continued to touch Lowbacca through the battle-meld, helping him push back the loneliness and despair that she herself had experienced when she went EV at Kalarba. Alema assured him they would reach him soon. Zekk worried about his life-support status. The heads-up display inside Lowbacca's helmet showed low batteries, no water, and thirty minutes of air—three times that if he returned to a hibernation trance. Another presence urged him to stay alert and be ready.

Lowbacca thought for a moment this last presence was Tesar, but it felt older, fiercer, less familiar . . . *Saba!*

Be ready! There would be only one chance.

Lowbacca disengaged his tether-line safety sleeve and poised his thumb over the quick release gate. He was ready.

With his other hand, he pulled himself down to the iceball, then grabbed the anchoring bolt and used it to slowly spin around, looking for the telltale halo of an approaching vessel. He saw only the ion trails of craft passing on the oblique, and that puzzled him. Jaina and the others would be coming in StealthXs, but they were even more cramped than standard XJs. How were they going to pick him up . . .

The question vanished from Lowbacca's mind. There was a dark shape about a hundred meters ahead, its canopy and one weapons-arm protruding above the sea of iceballs that formed Qoribu's ring system.

It was probably just an empty wreck. Or maybe Lowbacca was seeing things. His EV suit was automatically holding his oxygen consumption at a minimum, feeding him just enough air to keep him functional, and hallucinations were common under such circumstances. Jaina had told him she spent several hours talking to Yoda when she went EV. Unfortunately, she had not been able to understand anything he said because he spent the whole time speaking in Gamorrean.

Lowbacca slowly spun himself toward Qoribu, keeping a careful watch at ring level. He found another dark shape about the same distance away, this time pointed in his direction, standing on edge with two weapons-arms protruding above the surrounding surface. A flash of entry fire on Qoribu briefly lit the cockpit, silhouetting a helmeted head.

The cold suddenly began to seep into Lowbacca's bones. He reached out with the Force, extending his awareness in all directions, and found himself surrounded by living presences.

Chiss presences.

Leia set their new waypoint and transferred it to Han's display. "There, I think."

Han glanced down at his screen. "You think, or you're sure?"

"Sure?" The word emerged from Leia's dry throat in a high-pitched croak. "What do you think? The coordinates just popped into my head."

The navigation schematic showed a yellow destination icon hanging on the inner edge of Qoribu's ring, about as far from the *Falcon*'s assigned search area as it was possible to get.

"Sorry for asking," Han said. "But we're only going to get one shot at this."

When Han continued on their current trajectory, Leia sighed

and reached out to her daughter, then began to recite the coordinates in her mind.

But Jaina was in no mood to be bothered. Leia sensed only an overwhelming urgency and determination—and perhaps an irritated admonishment to stop wasting time.

"Han, just go. Something's not right."

"Okay." Han swung the *Falcon* toward the new waypoint, then pushed the throttle forward and activated the intercom. "Battle stations back there. This might get rough."

"Battle stations?" Juun gasped. "Do you remember that your cannon turrets are nonfunctional? Your gunners won't be able to hit a thing!"

"Have some faith, Shortwave," Han said. "You'd be surprised what Noghri hit when they can't aim."

"This has happened before?"

"Sure," Leia said, only half listening. "It seems like something's always broken down just when you need it most."

To her surprise, the Chiss did not immediately demand to know why the *Falcon* had drifted off course. In fact, she detected no sign they had even noticed. Thankful that Raynar had not felt threatened by their sensor dish, Leia locked it on their destination and began a passive analysis of the vicinity.

"The Chiss are being awfully quiet," Han said. "Better take a sensor reading on our destination—but don't go active. We don't want to give away where we're going."

"Good idea," Leia said, vaguely affronted that Han had felt it necessary to tell her the copilot's job. "There are some unusual mass concentrations in the vicinity, but no EM or propulsion emanations."

Han glanced over and gave her a crooked grin. "You've been reading my mind again, haven't you?"

"Princess Leia does that?" Juun sounded worried—or embarrassed. "She reads minds?"

"Sure," Han said. He frowned at the Sullustan's reflection in the cockpit canopy. "All the best copilots do."

Leia found the Juun's embarrassment a little disturbing, but decided it was better not to contemplate the source. The Sullustan had probably been admiring her procedure or something.

"Speaking of mind reading, I can't get that infrared reading you were thinking about," Leia said. "Too much background radiation from Qoribu."

"Not good," Han said. "And the Chiss aren't sending—"

C-3PO clumped onto the flight deck. "Captain Solo, you seem to have forgotten about the cannon turrets when you declared battle stations," the droid said. "We should probably turn around now, before anything unfortunate happens. It would be much safer."

"Juun!" Han barked. "Do you know where the circuit breaker is on a threepio droid?"

"Of course."

"If he says another word about turning around or being doomed, trip it."

"Aye, Captain."

"Please don't," C-3PO said. "My poor circuits have already been overstressed by the deterioration of Captain Solo's reflexes, and the current folly isn't helping matters."

Juun stood on his chair.

C-3PO stepped away. "There's no need for that," he said. "I'll be the routine of bravery, I assure you. Go ahead. Fly us straight into that planet, and you won't hear another word from me."

"Tempting offer," Han grumbled.

Finally noticing the *Falcon*'s direction—or bothering to address it—the Chiss flight controller opened a channel.

"*Millennium Falcon,* this is Rescue One. Explain your course deviation."

Leia reached forward to open a reply channel, then thought better of it and lowered her hand. "Let's see if they're serious."

"The Chiss?" Han asked. "You want to see if the *Chiss* are serious?"

"I have a feeling," Leia said. "Just—"

"—trust me," Han finished. "I know."

Juun's eyes widened. "Does everyone on this ship read minds?"

"Why, no," C-3PO confessed. "I don't."

The *Falcon* continued toward the web of ion trails crawling across Qoribu's dark face for another second, then the Chiss controller's voice came over the comm again.

"*Millennium Falcon,* I ask again. Explain your course deviation."

Leia glanced over. Finding Han's eyes narrowed in thought, she knew they were thinking the same thing.

"They're afraid of scaring us off," she said.

Han nodded. "It's a setup."

"*Millennium Falcon,* if you fail to reply—"

"Sorry about that," Han said, activating his own microphone. "We've been kind of busy up here."

"Doing what?"

Before replying, Han glanced over and mouthed their daughter's name. Leia nodded and, allowing her alarm and suspicion to rise to the surface, reached out to Jaina.

"Uh, we think we've spotted some survivors," Han said into the comm. "That's why we weren't answering—been busy getting the recovery equipment ready."

"We haven't detected any survivors on your course," the Chiss said.

"We're closer," Han said. "And, uh, you don't have a Jedi on board."

"A *Jedi* found them?" There was a short pause, then the Chiss said, "Very well. Carry on with our gratitude."

Han closed the channel. "That does it—they're playing us," he said. "Did you warn Jaina?"

"She already knew." Leia's stomach felt as empty and cold as the darkness outside the canopy. "She doesn't care."

Lowbacca could not see the StealthXs, of course, but he could feel them. They were no more than a thousand kilometers away, converging on him from four sides, coming in fast and hard.

No! Lowbacca thought into the meld. He fixed his gaze on the nearest of the clawcraft, then imagined its laser cannons flashing to life as his rescuers swooped in to pick him up. *Ambush!*

Jaina's laughter echoed in his mind. But Saba seemed more curious. Lowbacca's meld-connection was not as strong to the

Barabel as it was to Jaina and the other strike team members, but he felt sure she was wondering how many clawcraft there were, whether the StealthXs could take them all. Lowbacca had never wanted to lie more than he did at that moment, to see a friendly face smiling down at him from a StealthX cockpit. But his rescuers had no chance of success. There had to be an entire wing of clawcraft hiding in the rubble around him, all waiting for a shot at the Jedi rescue team.

Jaina wished he would stop exaggerating, but Saba seemed sorry, and it was clear she did not like the thought of abandoning him. Lowbacca wasn't worried. Clearly, the Chiss knew where he was.

Jaina's frustration filled the Force, and Saba's anger rose in reply. But Lowbacca could sense Jaina still approaching, feel her arming her weapons and selecting targets, determined to draw the Chiss off en masse. The Sword of the Jedi was not one to give up easily, not while there remained one sliver of hope.

Lowbacca knew what he had to do. He turned his wrist up, then opened the safety cover on the inside sleeve of his EV suit and revealed the emergency beacon activator.

"This is going to be bad, Han," Leia said.

"How bad?" Han armed the concussion missiles.

"Worse than that."

Jaina had lost too much during the war—Anakin, Chewbacca, Ganner, Ulaha, and on and on. She was determined to lose no more.

Then the steady *ping* of an emergency beacon sounded from the *Falcon*'s emergency speaker, and Leia looked down to see a bright yellow EV designator blinking over their waypoint. The tactical display instantly grew white with clawcraft, and Jaina's frustration changed to shock.

"Lowie!" Leia gasped, saddened and relieved at once. "Thank you."

She experienced a brief moment of warmth through the Force, then the feeling was lost as Lowbacca grew distracted and broke contact.

Han looked over expectantly. "Well?"

"It's over," Leia said. She reached out to Jaina and sensed her daughter's disappointment—and Saba's lingering fury at having had her orders disobeyed. "They're on their way back."

"Sounds like a good idea." Han swung the *Falcon* around to join them, then added, "The rescue team did everything it could. I hope Jaina knows that."

"Me, too, Han," Leia said. "But I don't think—"

She was interrupted by the Chiss flight control officer. "*Millennium Falcon,* what is the status of your survivors?"

"Survivors?" Leia was confused for a moment, but that confusion quickly turned to anger as she recalled the excuse Han had made and realized she was being mocked. "I'm sure you've figured that out, Rescue One."

There was a slight pause, then a deep and familiar voice sounded from the comm speaker. "My apologies, Princess Leia. I just wanted to confirm my understanding of the situation."

Leia's jaw fell, and she looked over to find Han having trouble keeping his own mouth closed.

"Jag?" she gasped. "Jagged Fel?"

"Indeed," the reply came. "It wasn't our intention to gloat."

"Jag!" Han cried. "What are you doing here?"

"That would fall under the heading of military intelligence, Captain Solo," Jag replied. "But rest assured, the Jedi Wookiee has been recovered. He'll be treated with all the rights and privileges due any enemy combatant—as will the rest of your rogue Jedi, when we capture *them*."

SEVENTEEN

In every base, there was a place like this, someplace dark and hot and deserted where a Barabel could go to hunt and clear her mind, someplace filled with the smell of local soil and the rustlings of alien prey. Saba was deep below the Taat nest, creeping down a crevice at a speed only a reptile would recognize as motion, her darting tongue stinging with the acrid odor of Jwlio's fractured bedrock, her mouth filled with the bitter taste of Jaina's insubordination.

Master Skywalker had allowed his niece to take part in the rescue mission only on the condition that Saba was in command. Yet when matters had grown difficult, Jaina had submitted—as always—only to her own emotions. Saba did not consider herself worthy to question Master Skywalker's judgment, but she *did* fail to understand his wisdom in permitting the disorderliness that encouraged such behavior. Disobedience led to chaos, and chaos led to ineffectiveness.

The crevice opened into a cavity ahead, and the faint odor of meat that Saba had been following grew stronger. All her thoughts went instantly to the hunt, for the prey was often near its litter. She did not know what she was stalking, of course, but the smell suggested another predator. Herbivores rarely dragged fresh carcasses back to their lairs.

To her Barabel eyes, which saw well into the infrared spectrum, the entrance looked like a dark diamond opening into the cool gleam of Jwlio's bedrock. She crept another step forward and heard the soft scratch of movement inside the lair. She waited, every muscle tensed to pounce on anything that poked its head out. She had been careful to mask her own odor by rubbing her scales in crevice dust, but such efforts were never entirely successful—and a worthy quarry usually smelled the predator long before the final attack.

Another rustle sounded from the cavity. Saba started steadily forward, a tenth of a meter at a time. If the prey had not fled or showed itself by now, it was not going to. The musty odor grew stronger, with just a hint of Killik sweetness, and she came to the entrance. The edge dropped away into a cold darkness that gave her the impression of a sizable emptiness. She stopped there for ten heartbeats, listening and testing the air with her tongue, twenty, fifty, a hundred.

No more rustles.

Saba slipped over the edge and crawled down a fissured rock face into a three-meter hollow. She could not sense any other presences in the area, but the spines along her dorsal ridge had risen on end, and that usually meant something exciting was about to happen. She continued across a floor of jumbled stones, licking the air, following her tongue toward the musty odor ahead. A few steps later, Saba peered over a boulder and found the source of the rustles.

A flat stone ahead was littered with about two dozen cuticle exoskeletons, all empty and split down the spine from molting. They ranged in size from smaller than Saba's thumb to a little larger than her hand, and they were so light that even the unfelt movement of the cavern air made them quiver and rustle. Scattered among the empty shells were dozens of small bones, enough to make six or seven wabas. Most were stripped of their flesh and cracked open, but a handful in the center of the pile still had some meat on them.

Fresh meat.

Sensing that she was closing on her prey, Saba activated a glow rod and went over to the exoskeletons. They were a familiar dark blue, but with thick knobby chitin like that of Raynar's guards. Starting to feel puzzled—and therefore short-tempered—Saba blew aside several of the smallest ones and shined her light into a tail-width cleft that ran a meter down the center of stone. It had been precisely cut, as though by a laser saw—or perhaps a lightsaber.

Her prey was growing more interesting.

The cleft held four hexagonal cells, each about five centimeters in diameter and constructed of Killik spitcrete. One of the cells remained covered by a plug of dusty wax, but the other three were empty.

A soft rustle rose as the empty exoskeletons were stirred by an air movement so gentle Saba did not feel it. She flicked out her tongue and tasted a bitter hint of apprehension, but felt nothing in the Force except a faint stirring of her danger sense. Strange prey. Her tail twitching with anticipation, she scraped the last cell open, using the talon of her smallest finger to pluck out the insect egg inside. It was withered, gray, and dry—not worth eating.

The bitterness in the air grew stronger. The scales between Saba's shoulder blades rose in excitement, and she swept her tail around in a swift arc that ended in a knee-crunching impact. Her prey landed with the crisp slap of a practiced warrior, winning Saba's instant respect by not crying out in either pain or surprise. She spun on her haunches, snatching her lightsaber off her utility belt, bringing it around from the direction opposite her tail.

A crimson blade sizzled into existence and blocked, then a Force wave blasted her across the chamber into the wall opposite. The air left her lungs as her skull slammed against stone and a ring of darkness formed around the edges of her vision. She could see only her prey's red lightsaber and his seated silhouette. She felt nothing in the Force from him, only the same vague danger as before.

Now, *this* would be prey worth taking.

The shadow man returned to his feet and remained where he was, gathering himself to continue or arrogantly waiting for Saba to ask who he was. First mistake. Saba sprang, sissing in delight, ignoring the murk in her head, bringing her arms around in a vicious overhand slash. Her prey—she wasted no time wondering who he was—limped two steps back, then brought his crimson blade up and stopped her swing cold.

Saba brought a knee around, driving for his rib cage, and felt like she had struck a statue. He slipped a palm-heel under her guard and caught her in the chin, sent her staggering back.

Strong, too.

Saba kicked a fist-sized stone off the floor, then used the Force to hurl it at his head and followed it in with a cut at his knees. He pivoted past the stone and met her attack, catching her blade on his and sweeping it up in a disarming counterarc, power-fighting against a Barabel and *winning*.

At the top of the arc, Saba released her lightsaber and raked her claws down in a vicious one–two slash, the first strike opening her prey's face from temple to jaw, the second strike slicing an eye apart. He whirled away, still silent but screaming in the Force, and planted a spinning stomp kick in Saba's belly. She went with the blow, rolling into a quick backflip and losing half a meter of tail to his lightsaber.

This time, the shadow man gave her no time to recover. A fork of blue lightning crackled from his hand and caught Saba square in the chest. Every nerve in her body became a conduit of blazing agony, and she dropped her to her knees, teeth gnashing, scales dancing, muscles clenching—paralyzed.

Continuing to hold the Force lightning on her with one hand, the shadow man limped forward. In the light of his red lightsaber, Saba saw her prey clearly for the first time. Dressed in an amalgam of black plastoid armor and blue Killik chitin, he was surprisingly gaunt, with a sinewy frame and a twisted posture that looked ready to collapse beneath his humped shoulder. His face was even more melted and shapeless than Raynar's, just two eyes and a lipless slash in a scarred oval of flesh, and one of his arms was as much insect as human, turning tubular and chitinous at the elbow before ending in a hooked pincer.

Raynar and the Killiks had lied, Saba realized. Welk, at least, had also survived the Crash.

The Dark Jedi stopped a meter and a half away. Having learned the folly of hesitation, he brought his arm up quickly, swinging at Saba's neck—then pitched backward as her Force shove buckled his injured knee. His lightsaber scraped along Saba's skull, flooding her mind with a pain so hot and blinding that she could not tell whether the Force lightning had stopped. She sprang anyway and slammed into his chest, driving her prey the last half a meter to the ground, clutching blindly at his weapon arm, biting into his throat.

Her fangs barely sank two centimeters. She tried to rip the wound open, but lacked the strength to keep her jaw clamped and came away only with a mouthful of blood.

Still, the bite took her prey by surprise. She found herself in the grasp of the Force, flying back through the darkness. She reached out, calling her lightsaber to hand, and had it in her grasp when she hit the cavern wall.

Fighting off a black curtain of unconsciousness, Saba slid down the wall and landed on her feet. Her vision was blotchy at best, and she could not even hear the customary *snap-hiss* as she ignited her lightsaber. She sprang at her prey anyway, covering the distance in three short bounds, and nearly lost her balance when she landed in his blood.

Welk retreated two meters and leveled another fork of Force lightning at her. She deflected it with her lightsaber and pivoted past, sissing in excitement. It was turning into a good hunt, a *very* good hunt. She rushed to close the distance. He brought his lightsaber to a middle guard and retreated another step.

Saba attacked high, but her reflexes were fading and his lightsaber flashed up to block. He retreated another step. She launched a spinning advance, bringing her blade around in a shoulder slash, whipping her bloodied tail around at his legs.

She was smooth but slow. He blocked the shoulder slash and hopped over the tail sweep, then rolled his blade over Saba's in an *excellent* block-assault conversion.

The attack might have opened her throat, had there been a way for him to block Saba's trailing foot. As it was, she swept his feet from beneath him and continued into a second spin, bringing her lightsaber down across his pincer-arm, then planting a foot on his remaining arm and rolling her blade around to add a neck wound to the arm he had just lost.

That was when Saba's blotchy vision proved costly. She sensed something flying at her from behind and turned to look, but saw only dark against dark.

The rock slammed into her head wound, and then she was kneeling on the floor, her lightsaber in a high guard, with no recollection of how she had landed there. Her sight was worse than ever, narrowed to a tiny circle, and her senses of smell and taste had gone the way of her hearing.

This was becoming a hunt to remember.

Seeing nothing ahead but a narrow cone of rock, Saba stretched into the Force and felt more danger than before. It seemed to have her surrounded, as though her prey had extended his presence over the entire chamber. She began to weave her lightsaber in a blind defensive pattern and rose. Something spongy and warm landed on her shoulder beneath her head wound. She hoped it wasn't her brains.

Saba began to spin in a slow circle, and finally her narrow cone of vision fell on her quarry, fleeing toward the cavern wall at a fast limp, blood pouring from his neck wound, the cauterized stump of his severed arm waving useless in the air.

Good. The prey was weakening.

Saba shut down her lightsaber and bounded after him, her heart pounding in anticipation of the final kill. She reached the cavern wall three steps behind him . . . and hissed in surprise as something landed on her back and pierced her neck scales with a sturdy proboscis.

She reached over her shoulder and felt a creature about the size of her head. Cursing her fading senses, she pulled it off and found herself looking into the dark eyes of a small blue-black Killik.

It spread its mandibles, and a stream of brown fluid shot from its tiny mouth. Saba barely turned away in time to protect her eyes. The slime instantly began to eat away at her cheek scales.

Acid.

Saba felt her dorsal spines rise and knew another attack was coming. She dropped into a crouch, and a small boulder slammed into the slope above. She jumped out of the way as it rolled back toward her, then, holding the Killik at arm's length, glanced up to see Welk glaring down at her in disbelief. Saba jammed her lightsaber against the Killik's abdomen and activated the blade.

The discharge that followed was not quite an explosion. She

lost only two fingertips instead of an entire hand. The fireball did little more than scorch her scales and bedazzle her eyes, but . . . exploding Killiks?

When Saba looked up again, Welk had started climbing for an exit crevice. She sprang after him and collapsed to her knees two steps later, feeling weak and nauseous. She touched the bite on her neck and found it already swollen and oozing.

Venom?

What kind of bugs were these? Saba should have stopped and gone into a healing trance. But her prey was wounded and escaping, and if she let him go, he would only be that much harder to track and capture next time. She continued her pursuit.

Her muscles obeyed reluctantly, stiffly, as though she were dropping into a hibernation—without the sleep. She drew the Force into her, calling on it to strengthen her, to burn the poison from her body, and staggered after her quarry.

Saba was only three meters behind when a second proboscis pierced her leg. She glanced down and found another small Killik latched onto her calf. She plucked it off and, holding it so it could not release its corrosive bile in her direction, tossed it high into the air.

The insect extended two pairs of wings, then spread its mandibles and came diving back at her, weaving and dodging past her flashing lightsaber to alight on her chest. Before Saba could grab it, the Killik's head dipped, and its proboscis pierced her scales. She plucked it off and held it away from her, trying to decide how to kill it without losing any more fingers.

Saba sensed another boulder flying in her direction. Still holding the insect at arm's length, she pivoted around and reached for the stone in the Force, redirecting it up the hill toward her prey. Her effort was rewarded with a dull *thud* and a cry that seemed equal parts surprise and pain.

The little Killik drummed its chest, then began to squirm and flap its wings, trying to escape. Saba caught a handful of wing and tore it off, *then* tossed the insect into the air.

Her reflexes were so slowed by the paralyzing poison that, by the time she ignited her lightsaber, the insect had already hit the ground. It took three strikes before she finally detonated it.

Saba turned instantly upslope, but her prey had already vanished into his exit crevice. Feeling half dead from poison already and not wanting to take yet another shot of venom, Saba remained motionless for a long time, trying to listen through her deafness, trying to taste the air with her dead tongue, trying to see outside her narrow cone of vision. She felt nothing, only the dark loneliness of the underworld.

Recalling that there had been three cells and only two Killik attacks, Saba went to the escape crevice and peered inside.

Nothing.

Her prey was gone, and so was the third Killik.

Every Barabel instinct urged her to continue the pursuit, to follow the quarry's blood trail until she ran it to ground. But the rational part of her mind knew better. A hunter needed a quick wit and sharp senses, and Saba's injuries had taken a toll on both. She was slow and beginning to tremble, and soon she might not be able to move at all.

Besides, Saba had a sinking feeling that the third Killik had left the nest early, and she could think of only one reason it would have done so: the departure of *Jade Shadow*.

EIGHTEEN

"Ben!"

Mara's voice came over the *Shadow*'s intercom so sharp and loud that Luke nearly dropped the micropoint he was holding in R2-D2's deep-reserve data compartment.

"Ben, come to the galley this instant!"

"Uh, that might not be such a good idea," Luke said into the intercom. He flipped up his magnispecs and looked across the utility deck to where Ben sat, surrounded by crate covers and spacing rods, covered head-to-toe in servomotor lubricant. "At least not until he's had a good saniscrubbing. He's on the utility deck with me."

"Doing what?" Mara demanded.

Luke caught Ben's eye and pointed his chin toward the intercom wall unit.

"Working on my Killik," Ben said meekly. His expression struck Luke as both guilty and worried. "Nanna said I could."

"Stay where you are!"

Luke cocked a brow at his son. "It sounds serious."

Ben nodded. "I guess."

"Any ideas?"

Ben returned to working on his "Killik" droid. "Maybe."

Deciding they would *both* find out what was troubling Mara in a minute, Luke returned to the sequestered sector he had found on one of R2-D2's deep-reserve memory chips. Judging by the tarnished break in the service circuit, the fault had occurred years—maybe decades—earlier, and had been entirely benevolent until a microscopic sliver of casing bridged the break. Given that R2-D2 had been functioning well with the fault for most of his service life, Luke was wondering how long it had been since anything was written to the sector.

The access hatch iris opened next to Luke, and Mara stepped through with an empty gelmeat container in her hand. Her irritation was obvious in the briskness of her step—and in the turbulent aura she projected in the Force.

"Hold on a second, Artoo," Luke said, setting the micropoint on the workbench. "This looks important."

R2-D2 tweedled a worried response.

"Of course you're important," Luke said. "But I need a break anyway. I'll want to be sure my hands are steady."

R2-D2 whistled his encouragement.

Luke started across the deck toward his wife and son, where Ben was still sitting inside his crate-cover Killik shell, looking up at Mara.

"Did Nanna say you could have a whole can of gelmeat, young man?" Mara asked.

Ben's eyes grew round. "She said I could have a slice."

"Does *this* look like a slice to you?" She held the empty container down for him to see.

Ben shrugged—rather bravely, Luke thought. "I thought she meant one *can.*"

Luke felt Mara's patience snap. When she started to wave the container at Ben, he gave her a gentle Force tug and urged her to calm down.

Mara paused, collecting herself while she pretended to examine the container label.

"Nanna is the one who found the container, Ben," Mara said, handing it to him. "She says we've gone through a whole case since we left Jwlio—and I don't think anyone else eats this."

"Tesar might."

"Gelmeat?" Mara asked doubtfully.

"Maybe," Ben said hopefully. "He eats anything."

"Anything *alive,*" Mara corrected. "But we could ask him. Should I have him come down?"

Ben hesitated, then shook his head. "No."

"I didn't think so." Mara's voice softened. "Ben, I don't know how you can eat all this without making a mess of my decks, but you have to stop. It'll make you sick."

"It's okay, Mom," Ben said, sounding relieved. "You don't have to worry about that. I haven't been *eating* it."

"You haven't?" Mara asked. "Then what have you been doing with it?"

Ben's expression grew worried again, and he reluctantly said, "Feeding it to my Killik."

Mara was silent for a moment, then she asked, "Ben, what did we say about lying?"

Ben's eyes dropped. "That if I lie, I have to stay with Kam and Tionne the next time you and Dad go on a mission."

"Right," Mara said. "Let's remember that."

"Okay," Ben said. "I didn't forget."

"Good." Mara stooped down and took the empty container from him. "And no more gelmeat."

Ben's eyes grew wide. *"None?"*

"Not until we get home." Luke hoped he sounded stern. "You've had enough to last you ten trips."

As he and Mara returned to the engineering station, he continued to feel a general irritation from her.

"Okay, this wasn't just about gelmeat," he said softly. "What's wrong? Tired of hearing about how much Tahiri and the others miss Jwlio?"

Mara shook her head. "It's not that."

"Tired of growling Ewoks?"

"It's not Tarfang, either," Mara said. "I'm not sure yet whether the Killiks are enemies or just dangerous friends, but I *am* certain we need to learn everything we can about them."

Luke remained silent, sensing more was to follow.

"It's just this uneasiness I have," Mara said. "I keep feeling like we're about to be attacked again."

Luke paused and consciously opened himself to the Force. "I can sense it, too, but not as strong as you. We could do another stowaway sweep."

"And find something we missed the last six times?" Mara shook her head and smiled. "Go back to your droid, Skywalker. You're just trying to get me into our cabin again."

"I'm predictable that way," Luke said. "But pay attention to this feeling. Whatever's causing it, you seem to have a special connection to it."

"Lucky me." Mara opened the hatch, then looked over her shoulder before stepping through. "And about that cabin."

"Yeah?"

"Maybe later."

R2-D2 trilled a worried objection.

"Don't worry," Luke said, chuckling. "I'm a Jedi Master. I can still concentrate."

He picked up his tools and carefully repaired the break in R2-D2's deep-reserve chip. Once the solder was cool, he flipped his magnispecs up again and turned to the diagnostic display above the workbench.

"All right, Artoo. Let's see what your deep-reserve memory shows now."

A list of headings and numbers began to scroll down the screen, but suddenly stopped as it approached the location of the repaired sector.

"Don't stop," Luke said. "I need to see if you can access that sector."

R2-D2 whirred a moment, then the scrolling resumed. The missing sector number appeared, but the descriptive heading looked like nothing but random characters.

"Stop," Luke said.

The scrolling continued until the heading vanished off the top of the screen, then stopped.

"Now your *response* time is slow," Luke complained. "Bring it back."

R2-D2 piped a question.

"The sector I've been trying to repair. Two twenty-two."

The list scrolled down until the lower half of the entry appeared at the top the screen.

"And you're having *roll* problems." Luke sighed. "It looks like you've got a bug in your system. I may need to get out the blast degausser."

The entry dropped toward the middle of the screen, one letter in the heading changing with each line it sank.

"Stop! Why are you randomizing the heading?"

The droid whistled a denial.

"You are, too," Luke said. "I saw the letters change."

R2-D2 whirred a moment, then displayed a message on diagnostic screen.

It must be encoded.

"Encoded?" Luke began to wonder if perhaps the sector had been sequestered on purpose. R2-D2 had seen a lot of action even before the Rebellion, and Luke was always curious about what secrets the little droid might have locked away. "Then slice it."

R2-D2 grated an objection.

"Artoo, you're an *astromech* droid," Luke said. "You have enough computing power to slice a triple-key, double-blind randomizer. I think you can solve a simple substitution code."

The droid buzzed in resignation, then began to whir and hum. A few moments later, the heading vanished altogether. Luke waited for it to return in legible form, then finally gave up and groaned.

"Don't tell me you lost the heading."

R2-D2 trilled an apology.

"No problem," Luke said, losing his patience with the little droid's excuses. He lowered his magnispecs. "I'll just fuse it to a sector that *is* in the directory."

R2-D2 withdrew his interface arm from the data socket and whistled in protest.

"Then plug back in and stop making this difficult," Luke said. "Let me see what's in that sector."

The droid warbled a question.

"*This* one."

Luke touched the tip of his soldering filament to sector 222 and was astonished to hear a tinny female voice erupt from the droid's speaker.

"Anakin . . ."

Luke caught a glimmer of moving light on the workbench. He flipped up his magnispecs, expecting to find the images of Tahiri and his dead nephew, Anakin, sharing a personal moment R2-D2 had caught with his holorecorder.

Instead, Luke found himself watching a beautiful, hand-sized, brown-eyed woman whom he did not recognize. She walked across the workbench, then stopped beside a sinewy young man dressed, as she was, in nightclothes.

"What's bothering you?" she asked.

The young man continued to look away from her. "Nothing."

"Anakin, how long is it going to take for us to be honest with each other?"

Luke's heart rocketed into his throat. He had not immediately recognized his father. He wanted to call out to Mara, to share with Leia what he was feeling . . . but he was too stunned. He simply continued watching.

The young man—Anakin—turned to face the woman. "It was a dream."

"Bad?"

Anakin looked over her head. "Like the ones I used to have about my mother . . . just before she died."

The woman hesitated, then finally asked, "And?"

Anakin's gaze fell. "It was about you."

The hologram crackled to an abrupt end, and an ominous humming arose deep inside R2-D2's internal workings. Luke flipped down his magnispecs and peered in to find the recording head bumping against his soldering filament as it attempted to access sector 222.

"Artoo!" Luke reached for the droid's primary circuit breaker. "Wait!"

The recording head stopped moving, but Luke did not lift the soldering filament.

"What are you doing?"

The droid reinserted his interface arm into the data socket, and Luke had to flip up his magnispecs to read the message on the diagnostics screen. He continued to hold the soldering filament in place.

I need to reformat sector 222. Those data are corrupted.

"Nothing looks corrupted to me." Luke could not understand why R2-D2 would try so desperately to hide 222's contents, but he had no doubt that was exactly what the droid was doing. "Who was that woman with my father?"

R2-D2 whistled two notes.

"The woman in the hologram," Luke said irritably. "Show it to me again."

R2-D2's holoprojector obediently came to life, displaying the familiar, three-dimensional figure of an Alderaanian Princess in an elegant white gown.

"Help me, Obi-Wan Kenobi," the figure said. "You're my only hope."

"Not *that* woman," Luke said. "I know my sister. The one talking to *Anakin*. Is that . . . is she my mother?"

A message appeared on the diagnostics display.

I don't know what woman you're talking about. That sector is defective. It should be sequestered.

"It *was* sequestered—probably on purpose."

Luke studied R2-D2 carefully, touching him through the Force. With most other droids, any hope of sensing the truth would have been lost to the indecipherable Force static generated by its system routines. But R2-D2 had been Luke's close companion for nearly three decades. The little droid's static aura was as distinctive to him as was the presence of Mara or Leia or Han.

After a moment, Luke sensed the direction his questions should take. "It didn't look like they knew you were holorecording. What were you doing? *Spying?*"

R2-D2 let out a squeal that Luke took to be a protest of denial—until it ended in a sharp crackle and a surge of electricity melted the filament Luke was using to protect sector 222. He jerked the wire free and started to rebuke the droid for his stubbornness, but one whiff of the acrid fumes pouring from the access panel told him this much damage was nothing the droid would do to himself. Luke used the Force to trip R2-D2's primary circuit breaker, then opened a second access panel to vent the interior of the casing.

When the smoke cleared, he flipped his magnispecs down and saw that every circuit within a millimeter of sector 222 had been melted. Worse, a bead of hot filament had landed on the sector itself. Luke tore his magnispecs off and hurled them against the wall.

"Kriffing slicers!" He could not help feeling that *someone* had gone to a great effort to prevent him from discovering his mother's identity, but of course that was just his disappointment. Whoever had booby-trapped R2-D2's spyware had done it for their own reasons—reasons important fifty years ago, but that hardly mattered now. "Kriffing history!"

"Dad," Ben's voice asked, "what's kriffing?"

Luke turned to find his son standing at his side, mouth agape at his father's unaccustomed display of anger.

"Nothing—a bad word," Luke said, calming himself. With a little luck—and the proper equipment—the memory chip could be restored and the booby trap bypassed. Things were never as bad as they seemed. "Your mother won't be happy I said it in front of you."

"Don't worry. I won't tell." An innocent smile came to Ben's small face. "Maybe I can have a tube of nerfspread?"

NINETEEN

With the dance-field glowing in the iridescent light of Qoribu's reflection and a thousand Taat swirling through the intricate patterns of the Little Dawn Rumble, Leia felt as though she had stepped a thousand centuries into Alderaan's past, when the Colony still ruled the planet and human expansion remained a dark storm on the galaxy's horizon. The Killiks were "singing" their part of the Song of the Universe as they danced, chirping melody through their tiny proboscises, tapping time with their mandibles, drumming bass in their chest cavities. Alien and primal though the music was, the performance was as flawless as anything Leia had ever heard in Harmony Hall on Coruscant, a thousand instruments played by a single artist.

"Now *that* is just not right," Han said, adding his own special counternote to the concert. "Why didn't she marry Jag Fel when she had the chance?"

"Be careful what you wish for," Leia said, following Han's gaze. "If we don't get her out of here soon, she might be spending more time than we like with Jag—being interrogated in his . . ."

Leia saw what Han had been looking at and let her sentence trail off. On the near side of the swarm, Jaina, Zekk, and Alema were frisking through the dance steps amid an eddy of dancers. The three Jedi were holding their hands above their heads, waving them in unison with the Killiks' antennae. Every few seconds, Jaina and Zekk would bow forward with the entire nest and rub forearms with the antennae of whatever insect they happened to be facing. Alema bowed as well, but rubbed lekku instead of arms.

"It does look a little . . . unnatural," Leia admitted.

"Not at all," C-3PO assured them. "It's a bonding dance, welcoming the birth of the new day. They perform it once a week, before they go to the Harem Cave to mate."

Stomach tightening in alarm—or perhaps it was revulsion—Leia turned to Han. "We'll talk to them as soon as the dance ends. You're okay with the plan?"

"For what good it'll do," Han grumbled. "Kidnapping her would be easier—and we both know how well *that* would work."

Leia grew exasperated with his pessimism. "Since when did you start worrying about the odds? You're starting to sound—"

She was saved from uttering the lethal *like Threepio* by the thunderous reverberation of an alarm rumble. She turned and found all the Killiks looking toward one of the passage entrances that ringed the dance-field. The insects were holding their antennae vertical and motionless, and their mandibles were spread wide in menace. Most of the Joiners were mimicking the gesture to the extent that their various anatomies allowed, but Alema was the only Jedi doing the same.

"That doesn't look good." Han turned to scan the sky. "Chiss?"

"I'll be happy to ask," C-3PO said.

He shot a burst of squelch at a nearby Killik.

"The Taat speak Bocce?" Leia asked.

"Why, yes, Princess Leia. I've yet to discover a language the Killiks *don't* understand. It seems they learn every language their Joiners know." A second Killik turned and answered C-3PO's question with a series of mandible clacks. "For instance, that was just Snutib click code."

"And?" Han asked.

"It was quite fluent," C-3PO said. "Though that particular dialect predates—"

"We're more interested in *what* it said," Leia clarified.

"My apologies." C-3PO sounded disappointed. "I believe it concerns Jedi Sebatyne."

"Saba?"

"Apparently, she appeared in the depths of the nest rather badly injured."

A knot of Taat emerged from the tunnel, tumbling and staggering as they attempted to keep ahold of a flailing mass of scales. The rest of the Killiks turned as one to look in Han and Leia's direction, then thrummed their chests.

"In fact, Taat is rather hoping that you might help calm down Master Sebatyne so their healers can close the small hole in her skull."

Han took off at a sprint, with Jaina and the other young Jedi forcing their way across the dance-field behind him. Leia asked Meewalh to fetch the emergency medpac from the *Falcon,* then started running.

She arrived to find Saba strapped to a primitive stretcher, an elliptical slice of scalp and skull missing from one side of her head. Han was already standing at the Barabel's side, trying to quiet her.

"I know they're creepy looking," he was saying. "But settle down. They're trying to help."

"No!" Saba's eyes twitched as though she was trying to throw her head back and forth, but the head itself remained motionless. "Azzazzinz!"

Her lisp was more pronounced than usual—a bad sign, given the head wound. Leia also saw a number of other injuries—a circle of broken scales around her temple, some lost fingertips, a third of a tail missing, and some suspicious swelling on her neck and calf. Lying on the stretcher, strapped next to the injured tail, was something that hadn't come off Saba—a human bicep fused at the elbow to a chitinous Killik forearm.

A *blue* chitinous forearm.

The Killiks holding Saba drummed in protest.

"They point out that Jedi Sebatyne's brain is showing," C-3PO translated. "She's quite delusional."

C-3PO rose into the air and began to spin like a pinwheel.

"What? Stop! . . . Put me down, you overgrown newt!"

"Not . . . deluzional," Saba growled.

"Saba, it's okay." Leia reached out to the Barabel in the Force, trying to assure her that they did not doubt her. "We believe you."

C-3PO stopped spinning, and Saba's gaze shifted to Leia. The pupils of her eyes were hugely dilated. "Yezz?"

"Sure." Han let his gaze linger on the forearm. "*Something* happened to you. Anyone can see that."

"Why don't we take care of these wounds?" Leia wished Tekli had not left with Luke. She and Han had certainly patched up their share of wounds, but this was beyond their skill. "Then you can tell us about it."

"*Now*," Saba insisted. "This one will tell you . . . now."

"Okay." Leia gestured to the Taat healers cowering on the edge of the sled. "As long as you'll let them work on you while we talk."

Saba narrowed a pebbly eye. "This one . . . thought you believed her."

"Saba, some of your wounds are cauterized," Leia pointed out. "Does that mean you shouldn't trust anyone who carries a lightsaber?"

The Barabel snorted.

"Look, we've got some concussion missiles on the *Falcon*," Han said. "If they kill you, we'll blast the place."

"Blazt it?" Saba began to siss weakly. "You are alwayz joking!"

"He wasn't joking," Leia said. "Do we have a deal?"

Saba eyed the healers cowering on the edge of her stretcher, then nodded. "Deal."

She lowered C-3PO to the ground again.

"Thank goodness!" He clunked over to stand behind Leia, then said more softly, "They say she's been an impossible patient!"

A dozen Killik healers crawled onto her body and went to work, sterilizing her wounds and spinning silken bandages. As they labored, Saba recounted—in a halting voice—her discovery of the empty exoskeletons and the attack by Welk, then ended by noting that she had found *three* empty egg cells and killed only two immature assassins. She was worried that the third had left early to stow away aboard the *Shadow*.

One of the healers squatting over her opened skull purred an opinion, which C-3PO translated as, "Patients with head wounds often suffer from hallucinations."

"It waz no—"

"Allow me." Leia laid a calming hand on the Barabel's shoulder, then pointed to the arm lying next to Saba's truncated tail. "If it was a hallucination, how do you explain that?"

One of the Killiks holding the stretcher began to clack its mandibles.

"The healers sometimes make grafts for the injured," C-3PO translated. "In her delirium, Saba must have mistaken a Joiner for a Chiss. The nest is searching for his body now."

Saba raised her head. "It waz no—"

"Let us handle this, Hisser." Han motioned Saba down, then asked, "Then how'd she get delirious in the first place? Where'd all these wounds come from?"

It was one of the healers on her neck that answered.

"Oh, dear!" C-3PO exclaimed. "She says Saba must have fallen after she was poisoned."

"Poisoned?" Leia gasped.

"Did this one not mention . . . that?" Saba asked.

The healer on her head purred a comment.

"Head wounds often cause forgetfulness," C-3PO translated. The Killik on Saba's neck added, "And they're very sorry about the poison. They hope you won't blast the nest."

"Blast the nest?" Leia looked to the healer that had spoken. "What's that mean?"

It was the healer on Saba's leg that thrummed an answer.

"It's a powerful neurotoxic venom," C-3PO said. "It causes permanent paralysis—and they have no antidote."

Saba cocked her brow up at Leia. "Told . . . you."

"You're not dead yet," Leia said. "How do you feel?"

"Worze than . . . it lookz."

Wondering if Saba had any idea how bad she looked, Leia turned to Han. "She might beat it with a healing trance, but—"

"We've got to take her back."

He looked as worried and frustrated as Leia felt. There was no question of *not* taking Saba back. The Barabel was clearly in danger of dying or being permanently paralyzed, and Cilghal—the Jedi Master-healer—had an infirmary and a lab back on Ossus that would have the best resources to help her.

Han turned to Cakhmaim. "Catch Meewalh and start prepping the *Falcon*."

The Noghri nodded and raced off toward the tunnel that led down to the hangar.

"And don't wake Juun up!" Han yelled as an afterthought. "The last thing we want is a Sullustan slowing things down with procedure."

Leia motioned the stretcher bearers after Cakhmaim. "Let's get her to the *Falcon*."

"Not zo . . . fazt," Saba said. The Killiks paid no attention to her and started across the dance-field after Cakhmaim. "The third azzazzin . . . we muzt warn Mazter Zkywalker."

Leia exchanged a concerned look with Han, then said gently, "Saba, the *Shadow* is gone, remember? We won't be able to warn them until we reach Galactic Alliance space."

Jaina appeared alongside the litter with Zekk and Alema.

"Saba, are you *sure* about the assassins?" Alema asked. "It really doesn't sound like—"

The inquiry was cut short when the severed arm rose off the stretcher and hit the Twi'lek in the chest.

"Yezz . . . zure."

They reached the tunnel leading down to the hangar. Leia sent C-3PO on with the Killiks and Saba, then stopped at the entrance and turned to Jaina.

"How soon can you be ready?"

Jaina's jaw fell. "Ready?"

"Yeah, to leave," Han said, coming in on cue. "You can't have much stuff to pack."

Jaina continued to look shocked for a moment, then a shadow of her father's crooked grin came to her lips. "Nice try, guys."

"*Try?*" Han managed to sound outraged. "We had a deal!"

"You can't hold us to that!" Zekk cried.

Jaina raised a silencing hand to him. "Let me handle this, Zekk. I've had practice."

"Jaina," Leia said sternly, "we *did* go after Lowie."

"Don't try the Desilijic shift on me," Jaina said. "The terms were that we had to bring him back."

"Yeah, well, you should have told us your ex-boyfriend was sitting on him," Han countered. "You held back."

"Didn't know," Jaina said, "and it wouldn't matter if I did. Lowbacca's still out there. We're not going back without him."

As Jaina folded her arms, the gesture was simultaneously mimicked by the swarm of Killiks that had gathered around them. But Leia was not ready to give up.

"Jaina, you know you're only making the situation worse," she said. "The Chiss are escalating things because of your presence."

"That's right," Han said. "And you proved on the rescue mission that your judgment isn't exactly sound."

Jaina did a good job of maintaining a neutral expression, but Leia was too adept at reading faces to miss the glimmer of hurt that flashed through their daughter's eyes.

"Jaina, if you really want to help Lowbacca, you'll come back with us." Leia switched her gaze to all three Jedi. "You know the Chiss are an honorable people. Stop making the situation worse and give us a chance to work this out diplomatically."

Jaina and Zekk actually dropped their gazes, but Alema was ready with a response. "And while you're still trying to make contact, they'll send in a fleet of defoliators to finish what they began."

Jaina nodded. "Diplomacy is good," she said. "But it's better when there's something to back it up. Go ahead and make contact with the Chiss, but we're staying."

"That's one option," Leia allowed. "But I'm concerned that you really don't know who you're dealing with."

Jaina's scowl of confusion was mirrored by the other two Jedi.

"We're not talking about the Chiss," Han explained. "You three are in way over your heads here—unless you think Saba really *did* imagine those assassin bugs?"

Alema's eyes flashed at the word *bugs,* but she was the first to shake her head. "They were real."

"But they weren't Taat," Zekk added.

"That's one of the things we'll be working on," Jaina said.

"Until when?" Once again, Leia was unnerved by how easily the trio were finishing each other's sentences. "Until you become Joiners?"

Jaina and the others shared a glance, then Zekk said, "That depends."

"On what?" Han asked.

"On how quickly *you* convince the Chiss to stop," Alema finished.

"Maybe you'd better hurry back to the *Falcon*," Jaina finished. "Especially if Saba is right about where that third assassin went."

Leia's stomach grew hollow and worried. Jaina was right about that much, at least. They did not have a lot of time to waste trying to talk the three Jedi into coming home.

And Han knew it, too. He stepped close to Jaina. "Jaina, listen to me—"

"I don't have to listen, Dad," Jaina said. "I can *feel* what you're thinking."

"We all can," Zekk added. *"No daughter of mine—"*

"—is going to become a bughugger," Alema finished.

"Hey, no fair!" Han objected. "Just because I don't like bugs doesn't mean I'm wrong. There's something sneaky going on here—and Raynar's in it up to his neck."

"You don't know that," Jaina said.

"This is the third time we've been attacked," Leia reminded her. "And Raynar *did* tell us he was afraid we'd try to take you away."

"Then he can stop worrying, because we're not going anywhere until the Chiss leave," Jaina said. "So hurry up and make that happen."

She opened her arms to embrace Han, but he stepped back shaking his head. "No, Jaina, I'm not giving this my—"

"I wasn't looking for your blessing, Dad." Jaina's voice had grown hard—not angry, just hard. "And I guess I'd be foolish to hope for anything else."

"If you're going to be ronto-brained about this, yeah," Han said. "I'll tell you what. You take Saba back in the *Falcon,* and your mother and I'll stay here to handle the Chiss."

"And recover Lowie," Leia added.

"You'd let me fly the *Falcon* home?" Jaina asked, cocking her head in an all-too-Killik-like fashion. "Alone?"

"Well, with Alema and Zekk," Han said. "Sure."

Jaina scowled. "Who do you think you're talking to, Dad? I know how you feel about insects." She turned her back on Han and held her arms out to Leia. "Mother?"

"I wish you'd listen to your father." Leia's chest grew heavy, for she could see Han's frustration with Jaina turning to anger. "You do know *you* might be the real prize in this conflict? Raynar isn't the earnest young man who went to Myrkr with you. He's desperate and lonely. I wouldn't be surprised if he had instigated the whole border conflict just to draw you—"

"Mom, sometimes you think too much." Jaina lowered her arms, then turned and started away. "You'd better get the *Falcon* off this moon. I'll try to warn Aunt Mara through the Force."

"Jaina!" Han barked.

Jaina ignored him.

Zekk said, "Do what you can with the Chiss. We'll keep things in check here."

He turned and started after Jaina.

"This isn't over, you know!" Han said to their backs. "We're going to come back."

Jaina waved over her shoulder, but Alema remained where she was, in front of the Solos.

"I'll be going with you," the Twi'lek said to Leia.

Jaina and Zekk both stopped and whirled around in surprise.

"You will?" Jaina asked.

"We didn't expect this," Zekk said.

"They'll need a guide," Alema explained. "They can't go back the same way they came without stopping at Yoggoy, and that may not be a good idea—at least not until we know who's behind these attacks."

Jaina scowled at the unexpected change of plan, but nodded and turned to her father. "Do you have room on the *Falcon*?"

"Sure," Han said. "Why don't you all come?"

TWENTY

Even curled into the primal egg position on the *Falcon*'s med-bay bunk, staring dead ahead with glazed eyes, Saba looked more annoyed by her wounds than pained by them. Her pebbly lips were drawn back in a frozen sneer, with the tips of her forked tongue showing between her fangs, and the claws on her hands were fully extended. She held her bandaged tail wrapped tightly around her hindquarters, and if she was breathing at all, Leia saw no sign of it in her constricted nostrils and motionless chest.

"She looks like she's dying," Alema whispered over Leia's shoulder. "Is she dying?"

"I don't know." Leia checked the monitors and found a single spike on the cardio-line. There was a barely discernible upward slope on the respiratory chart. "I think it's just a healing trance."

"Well, she *looks* like she's dying," Alema said.

Saba's tongue shot out and snapped the air, drawing a surprised gasp from both Leia and Alema, then returned to its place between her teeth. The Barabel's eyes remained fixed and glazed.

"Healing trance," Leia concluded.

"Do you think she'll survive?"

Leia studied the silken bandage that covered half of Saba's skull. "With that head wound, anyone else would be dead already," she said. "But Saba's a Barabel. Who knows?"

Alema's only answer was a long, concerned silence.

After a time, Leia lowered the lights and told the medcomputer to alert her if anything changed in Saba's status.

As Leia drew the privacy curtain across the medbay, she

asked, "How about a nice mug of hot chocolate? We have some of Luke's special supply on board."

"Really? Hot chocolate!" Alema gasped. Always scarce, hot chocolate had become a true Hutt's pleasure after the Yuuzhan Vong reshaped seven of the eight planets capable of growing the rare pods necessary to produce it. "What about your duties in the cockpit?"

"Don't worry about that." Leia took the Twi'lek's arm and led her forward. The *Falcon* had just left Qoribu and was preparing to make its first jump to hyperspace, but Leia needed to find out what was really happening on Jwlio—and the sooner, the better. "Juun is filling in for me. Han's growing fond of the little guy."

Alema curled her lekku. "That's not the impression I get from Han."

Leia gave a knowing smile. "That's because *Han* doesn't realize it yet." They entered the main cabin. "Anyway, we have time. Have a seat."

Leia took several white, thumb-sized seeds from a storage box and placed them in the galley multiprocessor. She set the controls to DRY AND POWDER, then turned, placed a fist on her hip, and began to study Alema with the same slightly interested, slightly preoccupied expression that she had been using to soften up her subjects since her days as a junior Senator in the Old Republic.

Leia should have known it wouldn't work on Alema Rar. Lithe, beautiful, and averse to modest clothing, the Twi'lek was used to being stared at. She simply stared back, making Leia feel as though *she* were the one dressed only in a sideless chemise.

The multiprocessor chimed, allowing Leia to turn away gracefully. She added a lot of sweetener and a small amount of water, then set the controls to AGITATE AND HEAT.

"You have a complicated way of making hot-chocolate," Alema noted. "Usually, it just comes out of the dispenser nozzle."

"This is better," Leia said, turning back toward the Twi'lek. "Trust me."

"Of course," Alema said. "Is there a reason not to?"

Leia began to wonder who was being interrogated here. She

waited until it was time to add the milk, then instructed the multi-processor to heat slowly and joined Alema at the table.

"Okay." Leia assumed her best motherly tone and leaned in close. "So what is it?"

Alema frowned, but did not pull back. "What is *what*?"

"The reason you're here," Leia said. "We both know that Juun could have gotten the *Falcon* past Yoggoy."

Finally, a glimmer of doubt showed in Alema's face. Leia was tempted to probe her feelings through the Force, but suspected the Twi'lek would sense the intrusion and resent it.

Alema looked toward the multiprocessor. "Shouldn't you check the hot chocolate?"

"The unit will chime." Leia kept her gaze fixed on the Twi'lek's face. "I *saw* how Jaina and Zekk reacted, Alema."

"That doesn't mean—"

"You three could barely start a sentence without someone else finishing it," Leia said.

"It's the meld." Alema's answer came a little too quickly. "We really baked ourselves on the voxyn mission."

"That so?" Leia was far too experienced to miss the Twi'lek's attempt to change the subject, but she decided to play along—for now. "When did you start using the battle-meld with Killiks?"

Alema looked genuinely confused. "We haven't. What makes you think that? They're not even Force-sensitive."

"I know." Leia gave her a motherly smile. "But there *is* a mental connection, especially with you. I saw it at the dance."

Alema cast a hopeful look toward the multiprocessor, then seemed to realize that the bell would only delay the inevitable.

"Maybe there is," she said. "It's nothing you're aware of. You start feeling like you belong, then you sort of . . . suddenly you just seem to have a larger mind."

Leia began to wonder if there were any deprogrammers in the Galactic Alliance capable of handling eight Jedi.

"It's hard to describe." Alema must have sensed Leia's thoughts in the Force, because her tone was defensive. "You're aware of so much more. You see outside the nest when you're inside, or inside when you're outside. And what you feel—you feel *everything*."

"I've heard glitterstim is a lot like that," Leia commented dryly.

"This is even better," Alema said. "You don't get sick. It's completely harmless."

Leia was beginning to see why the Twi'lek's infatuation with Anakin had always made Han so nervous. Though the multi-processor hadn't chimed yet, she returned to the galley and took two empty mugs from the cabinet, then placed a sliver of tang-bark and a drop of orchid-bean extract in each.

"What's that?" Alema asked, joining Leia at the galley.

"Spice," Leia said.

Alema's eyes lit.

"Not that kind," Leia said. "Just flavoring."

The multiprocessor chimed. She filled both mugs, topped them with dollops of mallow paste—made from real mallow root—and handed one to Alema.

"You're wrong, you know," Leia said. "It's not harmless."

Alema glanced at her mug and looked confused.

"The Colony," Leia said. "Or have you forgotten the attack on the *Shadow*? And the tower collapse on Yoggoy?"

"You can't believe the Colony was responsible. Taat may not have healed Saba, but they saved her life."

"Taat's healers had to save Saba's life because someone else tried to take it."

"Not Killiks. Saba said she was attacked by . . ." Alema frowned, then finished, ". . . a man. You heard her."

"She thought it was Welk," Leia said, supplying the name Alema had not been able to recall. "Saba also said he was protecting a *Killik* nest. A nest with two dark blue Killiks." Leia paused, then demanded, "Who were they?"

"That part makes no sense," Alema said. "There are no blue Killiks—at least none we've seen here."

The denial would have been more convincing had Alema's eyes not slid away. Leia took a sip from her mug, savoring its silky sweetness as she pondered what the Twi'lek might be trying to conceal.

"It makes sense to *you*," Leia said finally. "But you don't want to tell me."

Alema took a sip of her drink, hiding from Leia behind the rim of her mug. "We're all upset about what happened to Master Sebatyne. Why would anyone hide information about that?"

"Obviously, because you're trying to protect the Killiks." Leia returned to the table and sat down, regarding the Twi'lek from across the cabin. "What I can't figure out is why you wanted to come with us. Are you afraid we're going to discover the secret they're trying to protect?"

"Very good." Alema raised her mug to indicate she was talking about the hot chocolate. "It *is* better this way."

Leia ignored the compliment. "Or maybe you're afraid that what happened to Master Sebatyne is going to happen to us?"

Alema raised her mug again, but she swallowed too quickly to enjoy what she was drinking.

"So that's it," Leia said. She could not help feeling a little hurt that her own daughter had not worried about her safety—but that was probably because Jaina knew that Leia and Han could take care of themselves . . . or so she told herself. "You're trying to protect us."

"Not at all." Alema came to join her at the table. "You don't need protecting—at least not from Killiks."

"The Chiss are afraid of *something*," Leia pointed out.

"Yes." Alema sat down next to Leia. "They're afraid the Galactic Alliance will learn what they've been doing in Qoribu."

"They're afraid of the *Killiks*," Leia said. "And you're hiding the reason. All of you are."

"There's nothing to hide," Alema said. "Chiss xenophobia is well documented. And where insects are involved, it's pure bigotry. Just because a life-form has six legs, they think they're free to smash it."

"Nice try," Leia said. "But we're not changing the subject."

The jump alert knelled softly, and the silky beverage in their mugs shuddered slightly as the *Falcon* slipped into hyperspace. Leia decided the time had come to start pushing.

"Alema, what were those insects Welk was protecting?"

Alema made a point of meeting Leia's gaze. "You know as much about that as anyone."

"Fair enough," Leia said. "I do have a theory. Those insects were exactly what Saba thought they were: Colony assassins."

Alema shook her head. "Why would the Colony need assassins?"

"Because Unu wants its own Jedi," Leia said. "And that means stopping *us*."

"No," Alema insisted. "The Colony would never murder anyone."

"Sure it would," Leia said. "That's why Raynar was willing to let us leave after we discovered Yoggoy's location. He didn't think we'd live long enough to reveal it to anyone else."

"He let you leave because he *trusted* you to keep the secret. Unu has nothing to do with the attacks on you and the *Shadow*. That was . . ."

Alema frowned again, as though she were trying to recall the name of Saba's attacker.

"Welk," Leia supplied. "I'm surprised you have so much trouble remembering the name of someone who betrayed you."

"It doesn't mean anything," Alema said. "You're flustering me with this nonsense about the Colony trying to kill you, that's all."

The excuse was just convenient enough to rouse Leia's suspicion. "I'm sorry. Maybe you can remember the name of Welk's Master? What was his name?"

"*Her* name," Alema said. "Good try, though."

"Do you recall her name?"

Alema thought for a moment, then asked, "What does this have to do with anything? They're both dead."

"Then it wasn't Welk who attacked Saba?" Leia asked.

Alema shook her head resolutely. "It couldn't have been. He died when the *Flier* crashed, along with . . . his Master."

Now it was Leia's turn to frown. The truth—at least Alema's memory of it—seemed to be changing before her eyes. "Then who was it?"

"It must have been a Chiss spy," Alema said.

"With a lightsaber?"

"He could have stolen it," Alema said. "Or found it."

"That's possible," Leia said carefully. "But wouldn't a simpler explanation be that Welk survived the Crash?"

Alema shook her head, and her tone grew ardent. "Raynar was the only one Yoggoy found at the Crash."

"That doesn't mean Raynar was the only one who survived," Leia insisted. "Didn't Jacen tell you? He was there. He saw Raynar pull both Welk and Lomi out of the crash."

"Jacen said that," she admitted. "But it's impossible. When the *Flier* crashed, he was on *Baanu Rass* with us. Or Vergere's prisoner on Coruscant."

"True," Leia said. "Still, he saw what happened at the Crash. I don't know how, but he did."

"He *said* he did." Alema stood and turned as though to leave, then whirled back toward the table. "That doesn't make it true."

Leia was puzzled by the strange reaction. "When I was at the Crash, he spoke to me—at the same time he was on Jwlio," she said. "So I tend to believe him."

"You would." Alema began to pace. "He's your son."

"And I've seen what he can do." Cautiously, Leia asked, "Why is it so important for you to believe Jacen is wrong?"

"Why is it so important for you to believe he *isn't*?"

"I'm trying to figure out who's been attacking us." Leia was speaking in a soft, nonthreatening voice . . . and wondering who exactly she was talking to. Maybe there had been more to that hopeful look than Leia imagined when Alema had mistaken the tangbark for glitterstim. "And I'm pretty certain Welk is involved. Possibly Lomi—"

"It doesn't matter what Jacen *thinks* he saw," Alema said. "They're both dead."

"And you know this?"

Alema nodded.

"How?" Leia asked.

"We . . ." Alema's face went blank, and she began to make loud clicking sound deep in her throat. "The Colony knows."

"The *Colony* knows." Leia made a point of letting her skepticism show. "Alema, what are you trying to protect us from?"

"Nothing!" The Twi'lek banged her fists on the table. "You have nothing to fear, if you will just do what we tell you!"

"We *who*, Alema?"

Alema's eyes widened, then she drew herself upright and stood at the table in shock, her mouth working but no sound coming from her lips. The Noghri appeared silently at the cabin entrance. Leia signaled them to wait with an eye flicker, then let the silence hang while she finished her hot chocolate.

Finally, she put the empty mug down and looked up. "Well, I'm happy to see you understand why that statement is so wrong."

"Of course," Alema said. "We . . . I . . . apologize."

She spun on her heel and left the cabin so quickly that the Noghri barely had time to step out of her way. Leia did not go after her. There would be plenty of time to tease the rest of the truth out of her on the trip back to Ossus, and Leia had learned enough for now. She closed her eyes and reached into the Force for Luke, hoping that this time her sense of him would be a little more solid, that she could impart to him some hint of the hidden danger that the *Shadow* might have carried back from Qoribu.

TWENTY-ONE

The four brains displayed above the medholo varied broadly in size and shape, the largest being oblong with only a slight downward bulge to join the brain stem, the smallest looking more like a withered pallie mounted on a pulsing mushroom stem. In three of the brains, bursts of activity were simultaneously blossoming in bright identical colors, then fading at exactly the same rate. Even more telling were the two-dimensional alpha waves crawling through the air beneath each hologram. Three of the patterns were indistinguishable, with matched frequencies and amplitudes. The fourth wave, located beneath the solid blue shape of a human brain, was alternating between dead flat and so wildly erratic that the peaks vanished into the holo above.

"Very funny, Jacen." Luke frowned toward the relaxi-chair where his nephew reclined, looking out through viewing window of a huge scanning hood. "Would you stop playing with the brain mapper?"

"Just making the point." The fourth brain went entirely white. "This won't tell you anything. You must decide for yourselves whether we can be trusted."

"Trust isn't the issue," Corran Horn said. Along with Luke, Mara, and several other Jedi Masters, he was standing in the isolation ward of the infirmary at the Jedi academy on Ossus, where they would be far from the prying eyes of the Galactic Alliance advisory council. "We're just trying to figure out what happened to you."

"It has nothing to do with Killikz," Tesar said.

"We overused the meld," Tahiri said.

"And now we can't stay out of each other's minds," Tekli finished.

Though Luke certainly knew about the problems the meld had caused the strike team survivors, he suspected these new symptoms had more to do with Killiks than the meld. Still, that was a judgment better made by the Jedi order's Master healer.

Luke turned to Cilghal. "What do you think?"

The Mon Calamari looked at him out of one bulbous eye. "I think they are . . . mistaken."

"Mistaken?" Kyp Durron asked with his usual lack of tact. "Or lying?"

Tesar Sebatyne started to push his scanning hood off. "This one does not—"

"Easy, Tesar." Luke flashed Kyp a look of irritation. Now was hardly a good time to be testing Tesar's patience. The Barabel had felt his mother get wounded less than twenty-four hours earlier, and the only thing anyone knew about the circumstances was a vague sensation that Luke had felt from Leia suggesting that she was caring for Saba—and that he and Mara faced the same danger on Ossus. "I'm sure Master Durron didn't mean to impugn your honor."

Ignoring the opportunity for an apology, Kyp continued to look at Cilghal. "Okay, why do you think they're . . . *mistaken*?"

"Because the activity is in the wrong places."

Cilghal keyed a command, and a blobby structure about the size of a thumbtip began to glow deep within the hologram of Tahiri's brain.

"With the meld, the hypothalamus responds to emotional reverberations in the Force," Cilghal said. The blob began to swell and grow red. "Prolonged use—or very intense use—can enlarge it and make it hypersensitive. Melders can become so attuned to each other that their minds begin to read the reverberations much as transceivers read comm waves. That's when the meld slips into telepathy."

"What about the mood swings?" Corran asked.

Cilghal keyed another command. What looked like a wishbone with two long, curling tails appeared above the image of Tahiri's hypothalamus.

"As use is continued, the effect spills over into the rest of the limbic system, and melders begin to alter each other's emotions."

The Masters watched for a few moments as the "wishbone" grew thicker and darker. They were all aware of the risks associated with the meld, but this was the first time many had heard Cilghal's theory concerning the actual mechanism. Luke had the sense that some were looking inward, trying to guess how sensitive their own limbic systems might be growing.

Finally, Corran asked, "And where is the other kind of activity occurring?"

Cilghal keyed another command. A fibrous, cap-like structure about ten centimeters long appeared above Tahiri's limbic system and beneath both her cerebral hemispheres. It was, Luke noted, in a perfect position to act as bridge among all major sections of the brain.

"The structure of the corpus callosum has changed," Cilghal said. As she spoke, the hypothalamus and limbic system paled, and a hazy yellow fuzz formed in their place. "That haze you see is composed of free-dangling dendrites. It suggests that Tesar, Tekli, and Tahiri are sending impulses directly from one brain to another."

"And Jacen?" Mara asked.

"That's difficult to say." Cilghal glanced at Jacen, who sat beneath his hood, playing color games with the hologram of his brain. "But probably not, since he was there only a fraction of the time the others were."

"What about these impulses?" Kyle Katarn asked. With brown hair, brown eyes, and a tan shirt tucked into brown breeches, he looked like a farmer about to return to his fields instead of one of the Jedi order's most famous and skilled members. "Are you talking about Force impulses?"

Cilghal shook her elongated head. "Probably not. From what Master Skywalker said, the Killiks don't appear to be Force-sensitive." She stepped away from the controls, then continued, "I suspect the impulses are moving through their auras."

"Their *auras*?" Kenth Hamner asked. A tall Jedi with a deeply lined face and dignified bearing, he had a keen mind and a habit of skeptical inquiry. "I've always had the impression that auras were so much Fallanassi nonsense."

"Not at all," Cilghal said. "Every being is surrounded by an aura of subtle energies—heat, electric, magnetic, even chemical—some extending as far as ten meters. I have a multi-band detector that can image your own, if you like."

"For now, we'll take your word for it," Luke said. At the moment, he was less interested in proof than in a working theory. "How confident are you?"

"Not confident at all," Cilghal said. "I'll have to perform some tests to verify my hypothesis."

"Tests are useless," Tekli said from inside her scanning hood. "They won't reveal anything."

"Our problem is the meld," Tahiri insisted.

"We need no testz to tell us that," Tesar agreed.

Luke and the other Masters exchanged uncomfortable glances, their mutual concern growing sharper in the Force. The trio's insistence on blaming the meld was beginning to sound irrational.

Finally, Corran said, "Cilghal, you said their corpus ca—er—whatever-it-was had changed. How did that happen? Was that also caused by the auras?"

"Probably not," Cilghal said. "Most insects rely heavily on pheromones to regulate their lives, so that's where my suspicions fall first."

"That makes sense," Mara agreed. "The nests were soaked with pheromones."

"You're saying a *smell* changed our Jedi's brain structure?" Corran asked.

"Pheromones aren't just odors," Cilghal said. "They're very powerful chemicals. They trigger a wide range of behaviors—and physical changes—in nearly every animal in the galaxy."

"And they change your brain?" Corran repeated, still unconvinced.

"*Everything* changes your brain," Cilghal said. "Whenever you learn something new, or develop a skill, or make a memory, your brain grows new connections to store and access information. Under the right stimulus, it's very conceivable that parts of it could be completely modified."

"So," Mara asked, "spend enough time in the pheromone bath, and your brain rewires itself?"

"Exactly," Cilghal said. "Especially if the pheromones work through the nose. In most species, smell is a direct input to the brain."

"And you're sure these Jedi Knights are just *mistaken* about what's happened to them?" Kyp asked, raising the question again for no good reason Luke could see. "They couldn't be lying?"

"We are not lying!" Tesar stood, pushing his hood up and pointing a talon in Kyp's direction. "We do not lie!"

Concerned that Kyp was sensing something he had not, Luke reached out to Tesar and the others in the Force. He felt outrage, confusion, even a small hint of a Joiner's double presence—but no dishonesty. As far as he could tell, the trio believed they were telling the truth.

Luke sent a gentle Force-nudge urging Kyp to apologize, but the shaggy-haired Jedi ignored it and returned the glare Tesar was shooting in his direction.

"Then prove it," Kyp said. "Tell us why you agreed to come back from Qoribu."

The tip of Tesar's forked tongue darted between his lips, and the anger in his slit-pupiled eyes slowly changed to admiration.

"Very good, Master Durron," Tesar said. "We did not see that coming at all."

"I'm glad I still have something to teach," Kyp said. "Are you going to answer?"

"Of course," Tahiri said, slipping out from beneath her own hood. "All you had to do was ask."

"So we're asking," Mara said.

"We came to persuade the council to help the Killikz," Tesar said. "The Colony can only stop the Chisz through war."

"And the Jedi can bring other pressures to bear," Tahiri added. "It's best for everyone."

"That will be for the Masters council to decide," Kenth said. "And when it does, will you abide by our decision?"

"We aren't wrong about this," Tahiri dodged.

"The Chisz are committing xenocide," Tesar added. "We must intervene."

"Immediately." Tekli pushed her hood up and came to stand with the others, leaving only Jacen's brain—currently gold and pulsing—displayed on the medholo. "Aren't we bound as Jedi to protect the weak?"

"Jedi are bound by a great many duties, often contradictory," Kenth said. "Which is why we call Masters' councils. I ask again, will you abide by our decision?"

The trio fell silent, then Tahiri and Tekli dropped their eyes, and Tesar said, "That dependz on what the decision is."

Kenth and Corran recoiled visibly.

But Kyp Durron smiled. "Well, it's an honest answer."

"As much as that is possible for them," Cilghal said. She turned to Luke. "I don't like to question their integrity, Master Skywalker, but anything they tell us is suspect. We must assume their judgment has been compromised by the same power that called them away in the first place."

Tesar glared openly in Cilghal's direction. "You are saying we cannot be trusted?"

She met his gaze evenly. "You're not to blame, but yes—that's exactly what I'm saying."

Tesar looked from Cilghal to Luke to Kyp and back to Luke, then thumped his tail and retreated to his relaxi-chair.

Tahiri took his place. "We don't deserve this." She glared directly into Luke's eyes. "You have no reason to treat us like we're Sith."

"Probably not," Kenth said. "But until those mysterious attacks on Yoggoy and at Qoribu are explained, there's no harm in being safe."

"By all meanz," Tesar rasped from his chair. "This one would not want you to fear us."

Luke turned to Cilghal. "Perhaps you'd explain your concerns?"

The Mon Calamari nodded. "It's very simple. The meld always comes from the outside—you *know* you're listening to someone else's thoughts and reacting to someone else's emotions. But this . . . this *joining* feels like it comes from inside.

The things our Jedi Knights see through it—or hear or smell or taste—seem like things they're sensing themselves. Even the thoughts they share seem to arise inside their own minds."

"So they don't know whether their thoughts are their own or someone else's?" Mara asked. Luke could sense that she was as concerned as he was, that she was afraid their young Jedi Knights were lost to the Colony already. "They can't just ignore outside thoughts, like we can in the meld?"

"I'm afraid that's correct," Cilghal said. "In all likelihood, it's impossible to know the difference."

The Masters studied Tahiri and the other young Jedi in silence, their faces betraying the same disappointment and concern and uncertainty that Luke felt. Cilghal could probably find a way to negate the changes to their brain structure. But the patients were clearly going to be uncooperative, and that would make recovery a long, difficult process.

Finally, Kenth said, "Well, that explains a lot. They certainly haven't been acting like themselves."

"Perhapz not," Tesar admitted. He leaned forward, being careful to remain seated and nonthreatening. "But that doesn't mean we are wrong about Qoribu."

"Ask Masters Skywalker," Tekli said. "They both saw Jwlio. *They* can tell you what the Chiss have done to the moon."

"Fair enough," Luke said. "Mara and I weren't on Jwlio long enough to gather many facts, but it *is* clear the Chiss are trying to drive the Killiks out of the system."

"And it's just as clear that the Killiks don't have the resources to leave," Mara added. "The way things are looking, the result will be war or extermination, probably both."

Tahiri beamed, Tesar assumed a reptilian grin, and Tekli brought her ears forward.

Then Corran asked, "Why?"

Tesar rose. "Why what?"

"Why are the Chiss doing this?" he asked. "They're xenophobic and secretive, but they're not expansionists. If they're trying to drive the Killiks away, they must have a reason."

"They are afraid the Colony will expand into their territory," Tesar said. "That is what their Joinerz say."

"There's more to it," Mara said. "If all the Chiss were worried about was border security, they'd just wait for a nest to pop up in their own territory, *then* attack."

"That's right," Luke agreed. "Something about the Killiks scares the Chiss so much they don't want them in the same sector as an Ascendancy system."

"You'd have to ask the Chiss about that," Tahiri said.

"We shouldn't need to," Kenth pointed out. "Isn't it the first duty of a Jedi to understand *both* sides of a conflict?"

Tahiri met his gaze with a raised chin. "We were occupied."

"Saving innocentz."

"And look what happened," Kenth said. "Both sides are closer to war than ever."

"Perhaps," Tekli said. "But our mistakes shouldn't condemn the Qoribu nests."

"And they shouldn't commit the Jedi to any action the Masters haven't authorized." Corran turned away from the trio and addressed the other Masters. "Our first concern must be the stability of the Galactic Alliance."

"No." Kyp Durron surprised everyone by stepping to Tahiri's side. "The Jedi are no one's mercenaries—not even the Galactic Alliance's. Our first concern, our only concern, is our own conscience. We must follow it wherever it leads."

Octa Ramis, who had remained silent until now, spoke up to agree with Kyp, then Kenth agreed with Corran, Kyp repeated his position, and the discussion degenerated into argument. Tahiri, Tekli, and Tesar remained silent, content to let their advocates argue their case. Luke glanced over at Jacen, who was continuing to create elegant swirls of light in his brain holo, and wished he were also free to ignore the argument. What he really wanted to be doing was looking for a slicer who could access that sequestered sector in R2-D2's memory, but personal business would have to wait. The argument among the Masters was rapidly growing more heated.

Luke eased his way into the middle of the knot.

"Enough." The tumult began to quiet, and he said, "This isn't the time for discussion. We're just here to have a look at Cilghal's tests and listen to our Jedi Knights' report."

An embarrassed silence fell over the room as the Masters contemplated their outbursts, then Kyp flushed and dropped his chin. "I let my emotions carry me away. I apologize."

"No need," Corran said, slapping his shoulder. "We were all a little excited."

"Master Skywalker is right," Kyle added. "We're just here to listen."

"You haven't listened to *me* yet."

Jacen sounded as though he were less than a meter from the group. But when Luke turned around, he found only the image of his nephew's brain floating above the holopad. Jacen himself remained seated in his relaxi-chair, eyes staring blankly out through the viewing window of his scanning hood.

"Okay, Jacen," Luke said. "We'd be very interested in hearing your report."

The hologram pulsed in a brilliant show of iridescent color, and the alpha line below it quivered in time to a deep, booming voice that was barely recognizable as Jacen's.

"Killiks are dangerous friends, but no one's enemy," the brain said. "The true danger lies not in *what* the Jedi do, but in their failure to act at all."

The effect was exactly what Jacen had intended. A thoughtful silence descended on the group, and the Masters' gazes turned inward as they searched for the deeper meaning in Jacen's words.

Luke walked over the control panel. "Very funny," he said, switching it off. "Didn't I tell you to stop playing with Cilghal's brain mapper?"

TWENTY-TWO

Han and Leia were alone in the cockpit, sitting together in one chair, watching the opalescent nothingness of hyperspace slide silently past. The jump was a long one, and there was no reason for them both to spend it on watch. But the flight deck was the one place on the suddenly crowded *Falcon* to find some discreet time together, and—after the way things had ended with Jaina—Han was glad they had. Somehow, it helped to know that Leia was as frightened for Jaina as he was—that she, too, was determined to find out what Raynar really had planned for their daughter, to return to Qoribu the minute they could, and to put a stop to it.

"You're in a better mood," Leia said.

"Talking to you, I guess," Han admitted. "How'd you know?"

"The humming. You never hum."

"Humming?" Han frowned. "I'm not humming."

"Really?" Leia cocked her head. "It certainly *sounds* like you are."

Han spun the seat around until he was facing the same direction Leia had been, then he heard it—a faint, undulating purr.

"That's not me." Han jumped up, dumping Leia onto her feet. "It's a coolant line!"

"A coolant line?" Leia slipped into the copilot's chair and began calling up status displays. "What happened to the alarm?"

"Good question." Han turned toward the back of the flight deck and started down the access corridor. "Disengage the hyperdrive and do a slow cool-down. I'll see what I can find out back in systems."

The hum grew steadily louder as Han advanced. By the time he entered the main cabin, it had risen to an irritating drone. He met the rest of his crew and passengers coming the other way. Cakhmaim and Meewalh were wide awake, but still pulling on their sleeveless robes. Alema and Juun were both bleary-eyed and dressed in their sleeping shifts, which, in Alema's case, was considerably more than she wore when she was awake.

C-3PO was also present and, of course, fully alert. "I don't believe I've ever heard the *Falcon* make a sound quite like this, Captain Solo. What is it?"

"Boiling coolant," Juun said through a yawn. He stretched his arms. "The hyperdrive must be—" The bleariness vanished from the Sullustan's bulbous eyes. "Bloah! The hyperdrive is overheating!"

A loud boom reverberated through the hull as the *Falcon* executed an emergency drop into realspace. The drone in the coolant lines became a loud, bubbling hiss.

Han pointed at Juun, then jerked a thumb toward the cockpit. "Take the navigator's station and get a fix on where we are. Threepio, take the comm station in case we need to send an emergency hail. Everyone else, with me."

Han led the way to the rear of the ship, then opened an access panel and peered in at the contorted tangle of valves and radiation-shielded conduits surrounding the unit itself. There was no need to ask for a thermoscanner to determine which lines were overheated. The lower inside conduit was bulging, glowing pale blue, and banging as if there were a profogg inside. Han activated the lighting and crawled into the sweltering cabinet, then traced the pipe up to the dark nook where it passed through the flow regulator. The diverter valve was stuck half closed, but Han could not see what had caused the malfunction—or why the sensor hadn't sounded an alarm.

"Meewalh, get me some burn gloves and a face shield."

Before he finished asking, the Noghri was passing the gloves and face shield into the cabinet.

As Han donned the equipment, Juun's voice came over the intercom. "Captain Solo, I haven't identified exactly where we are yet—"

"Well, keep working on it. I'm sure you can figure it out." Han rolled his eyes. "Let me know when you do."

"Of course," Juun said. "But I thought I should report—"

"Look, I'm kind of busy here," Han said. "So unless we're under attack, hold the reports until you're done."

There was a moment of silence, then Juun asked, "Do you want me to wait until we're *actually* under attack?"

"What?" Han turned, banging the side of his head on a strut. "Blast! What do you mean, *actually*?"

"Han, it looks like we're still in Colony territory," Leia said, breaking in. "We've got a swarm of dartships coming."

"Rodder!" Han nodded the Noghri toward the cannon turrets, then pulled on the second burn glove. "Okay, forget the cooldown. Recalculate the rest of the jump using three-quarter power and go. This shouldn't take long."

"You've found the problem?" Juun's voice was full of awe. "Already?"

"Even better." Han reached up to the regulator and shut down the damaged coolant line. "I've found a fix."

When Han pulled himself out of the cabinet, Alema was frowning down at him with her lekku crossed over her chest.

"Don't scowl at me," he said. "It gives you wrinkles."

The frown vanished at once. "Are you sure it's necessary to take this kind of risk?" she asked. "Those dartships are only coming to greet us. Their nest might even be able to help us make repairs."

"First, not all dartships are friendly." Han passed her his face shield, then pulled off his burn gloves. "Second, Saba can't wait for repairs—and maybe not Luke and Mara, either."

"And third?"

"There is no third."

"There's always a third," Alema said.

"Okay, third." Han passed her the burn gloves and, as the *Falcon* slipped back into hyperspace, concluded, "I'm the captain. It's safe if I say it is."

Alema shrank back. "Okay—just asking," she said. "Maybe we should check on Saba."

"You go ahead," Han said, wondering why the Twi'lek

thought he was needed to check on the Barabel. *Bugs and bug-lovers,* he thought, *you can't trust either of 'em.* He had a sudden image of Jaina and Raynar rubbing forearms and shuddered. He closed the access panel and started forward. "I need to keep an eye on things in the cockpit."

Han had barely stepped onto the flight deck when Juun reported, "We have to recalibrate the warp controller. The heat buildup caused a performance spike in the number two nacelle, and we veered off course by seven one-thousandths of a degree."

"We don't have time," Han said. Recalibrating meant days of trial jumps, then he'd have to do it all again when they returned to the Galactic Alliance and repaired the problem. "Just run a compensation program."

"A compensation program?" Juun was aghast. "But procedure mandates recalibration anytime—"

"It also mandates obeying the captain's orders," Han said, slipping into the pilot's seat. "Just run the blasted program."

Juun was silent for a moment, then asked in a subdued voice, "Was the malfunction anything I should account for?"

Han softened. "Good question." He considered for a moment, mentally reviewing the entire coolant system in his mind. An *underactive* diverter could cause another performance spike, but probably not a closed one—especially not if the hyperdrive remained below maximum power. "I don't think so."

"You don't *think* so?" Juun repeated. "Didn't you identify the malfunction?"

"Didn't have time," Han said, growing irritated again.

"But if you haven't identified the problem, how can you know it's safe—"

"I *know*," Han growled. "Now, are you going to stop bothering me and run that program, or do I have to do it myself?"

"I'd advise you to choose the first option," C-3PO said. "When Captain Solo's voice assumes that tone, he has a nasty habit of tripping primary circuit breakers."

"It's okay, Jae," Leia said. "Han knows what he's doing."

"Oh, I realize that, Princess Leia," Juun replied. "I was only asking because I'd like to understand how Han Solo makes decisions."

"Wouldn't we all?" Leia replied.

Juun ran the compensation program, then they jumped back into hyperspace and spent the next quarter hour riding in silence, watching status readouts and listening for the faintest hum in the coolant lines. Finally, Han felt confident enough to pronounce the emergency passed. He sent Juun back to tell the others they could return to their bunks, then looked over to find Leia staring raptly into her display, biting her lower lip as she double-checked Juun's compensation parameters against status readouts.

She wore the same enthralled expression she'd often had as New Republic Chief of State, poring over a report on an initiative to feed hungry natives on Gottlegoob, or as Rebel leader studying a cruiser buildup on Farbog. It was a look Han had not seen since the end of the war with the Yuuzhan Vong, when the challenge of combat had faded to the drudgery of reconstruction and they had retreated into the *Falcon* to build a smaller, more private life together.

It was a look Han missed, and one he felt responsible for losing. As much as he loved having Leia all to himself—finally—he knew she needed more out of life; she would never be happy flying around just having adventures. She needed to be doing important things, putting the galaxy back together and seeing to it that the megaconglomerates did not end up owning everything.

Seeming to feel the weight of his gaze—or perhaps sense it through the Force—Leia looked up from the columns scrolling down her display. "Something wrong?"

"Nothing," Han said. "I was just wondering . . ." He wanted to say *if you were happy,* but knew that would sound wrong—it would sound like *he* was unhappy. "Well, if . . ."

"Juun's parameters are very complete, if you're worried about that," Leia said. "We're not going to stay in the safety margin—but when do we ever?"

"Yeah," Han said. "That's kind of the point. Do you ever miss our old place back on Coruscant?"

Leia cocked her brow and remained silent, studying him like a worrt eyeing a kreetle.

"Having a whole bedroom suite to ourselves, and a real kitchen where we could cook real dinners?"

"That apartment is gone—along with everything else we might remember about that planet." Leia made a point of not looking at Han. "And I don't recall *you* doing much cooking."

"That doesn't mean I didn't like the food," he said. "And we could get another place. With the Reconstruction Authority trying to move the seat of government back—"

"What's this talk about moving into an apartment?" Leia asked. "I thought you loved living on the *Falcon*."

"I do," Han said. "But there's more to life than being happy!"

Leia frowned. "Han, you're starting to sound confused. Have you been seeing color flashes? Feeling dizzy? Having trouble hear—"

"I'm not having a stroke," Han interrupted. "I'm fine."

"Good." Leia returned to her status display. "So am I."

"And I'm *not* old," Han said.

"Did I say you were?"

Han activated his own display and went to work running sensor tests, trying to locate the fault that had prevented the safety system from detecting the coolant problem before it grew critical. An hour later, he had determined that all of the sensors on the coolant line were stuck at the optimum readings. It took another hour to determine that the number one nacelle readings were being repeated on the number two status bar. By itself, either malfunction was dangerous; together, they could prove catastrophic.

"I don't know where we serviced the hyperdrive last time," Han said, "but the next time we're in the neighborhood, remind me to send them a concussion missile."

"Bad coolant?" Leia asked. Corrosive impurities were the cause of most coolant problems.

"Yeah, and that's not all," Han said. "Some short circuit ran a double status feed from the number two nacelle."

"Really?" Leia grew thoughtful. "I wonder what the chances of making those two mistakes are."

"Approximately one hundred twelve thousand to one, Princess Leia," C-3PO said helpfully. "The hangar staff at the Jedi Temple are generally quite proficient."

"*That's* where we got our last coolant change?" Without waiting for a reply, Han turned to Leia. "Something smell bad to you?"

"Very," she said. "The Temple would know by now if it had been using bad coolant. Someone would have warned us."

"Yeah," Han said. "It's gotta be something else."

"Sabotage?"

"That'd be my bet," Han said. "Threepio, find out how Saba's doing—and have Meewalh and Cakhmaim do another sweep of the ship. Tell them to look for droppings and bug tracks. That may be the only way we know they're here."

"They?" C-3PO asked.

"Killiks," Han said. "Stowaways."

The droid left to obey. Han turned to find Leia staring out the viewport with a distant expression. It was the same look he'd seen a dozen times, as she reached out in the Force and tried to warn Luke about the assassin bugs Saba had found.

He waited until her attention returned to the cockpit, then asked, "Any luck?"

"Luke's preoccupied with something about our family. I think he thought I was trying to tell him about Saba." Leia shook her head. "And I just don't have a strong enough connection with Mara."

"What about Jacen?"

"I don't know," Leia said. "I can't tell if he doesn't believe me or just doesn't understand."

"Blast," Han said. "We could us a little help here. If this is sabotage . . ."

Han let the sentence trail off, for a faint thread of blue had appeared ahead, stretched horizontally across the pearly void of hyperspace.

"Leia, do you see that?"

"What?"

Han pointed at the thread, which had thickened into a line of mottled colors ranging from white to dark purple. "Colors."

"Very funny," Leia said. "I'm sorry I called you old."

"No, really." Han jabbed his finger toward the line, which was now a finger-width band darkening toward sapphire. "Look."

Leia looked, and her jaw dropped. "Should that *be* there?"

Fangs of blue light began to flash out from both sides of the sapphire stripe.

"No," Han said.

"Then why hasn't the proximity alarm dropped us out of hyperspace?"

"You don't want to know."

By the time Han had a hand on the hyperspace disengage, the sapphire stripe had thickened into a braided grimace of purple and white, and the tips of the blue fangs were flashing clear up to the canopy. He pulled the control lever back to emergency override . . . and a muffled bang sounded deep in the *Falcon*'s stern.

"Han!" Leia demanded. "What don't I want to know?"

"Tell you in a minute." The entire ship began to buck and shudder, and an eerie chorus of whirs hummed up the access corridor. "Blast!"

Han reengaged the hyperdrive. The ship stopped shuddering and the whirs faded to silence, but the crimson blue ahead reached out and closed around the *Falcon*.

"Tell me, Han. *What* don't I want to know?"

"What is this?" a reedy voice asked from the back of the flight deck. "Have we flown into a nebula?"

Han was vaguely aware of Leia turning toward Juun's voice—but only vaguely. The blue teeth had become the interior of a white-veined mouth, and most of his mind was busy trying to figure out what to do next.

"You've flown into a nebula before?" Leia asked Juun.

"Of course—many times," Juun assured her. "But usually I disengage the hyperdrive and fly right back out."

"Not an option." Han eased the hyperdrive control lever back until he heard the first hint of a whir. It didn't take much. "We'll blow that bad coolant line when the shutdown temperature spikes."

"I thought you fixed that!" Juun complained.

"So did I." Han glanced up at Juun's reflection in the canopy. "Someone unfixed it."

If Juun noticed the fear in Han's voice, he hid it well. "Well, you can't just keep going. The gas friction will distort the continuum warp."

"Distortion won't kill us," Han said. The *Falcon*'s stabilizers would probably keep their warp within safe parameters. "It's the dust shell I'm worried about."

"Oh, yes." Juun's voice was forlorn. "The dust shell."

"How long?" Leia asked.

She was too good a copilot to need to ask what would happen when a vessel traveling through hyperspace tried to punch its way through the striated layers of dust and debris that hung inside an expansion nebula.

"That depends on how old the nebula is," Han said. Two-meter circles of white began to flash ahead of the *Falcon* as the first dust particles blossomed against her forward shields. "But not long enough."

"This is a young one," Juun agreed. "A *very* young one."

The whir finally went silent, and Han eased the control lever back until he heard it again. He was only prolonging the inevitable, but sometimes stalling was the only move you had.

"Han." There was a tremor in Leia's voice, and she was staring straight out the forward viewport. "Tell me the truth—are we going to die?"

"Can you do that fog-parting trick you used on Borao again?" Han asked. "And extend it to about twelve light-years?"

"I doubt it," Leia said.

"Then, yeah, we're probably gonna die."

"What a pity Tarfang isn't here!" Juun said.

Han scowled into the canopy reflection. "I thought you *liked* that mattball."

"Very much!" Juun exclaimed. "And I'm sorry his name won't be listed among those who died with Han Solo."

"Not so fast," Leia said. The dust particles were blooming fast and furious now, turning hyperspace almost solid white with microscopic novae. "If we're going to die anyway, there's nothing left to lose."

"I hadn't thought of it that way," Juun said. "But—"

"Watch and learn," Leia said.

She activated the *Falcon*'s attitude control system, then—before Han could stop her—spun the ship around so that it was traveling backward through hyperspace.

The white blossoms vanished, and for a moment, the *Falcon* felt as though she were simply traveling through hyperspace backward.

Then the nebula turned red and started to spiral away from the viewport. Han's stomach turned somersaults faster than a Jedi acrobat, and the *Falcon*'s hull began to wail and screech like a rancor in full rut.

"Ke . . . b . . . ff!"

Han could not understand Leia above the terrible clamor, but it was easy to guess what she was yelling. He eased the lever back another centimeter. There was no question of listening for the humming coolant line, so he decided to count to thirty and do it again. What did it matter? They were going to die anyway.

Then Leia did something *really* foolish . . . she fired the sublight drives.

The shrieking and wailing stopped at once, and suddenly it was the *Falcon* spinning instead of space. Han felt as though his heart were going to fly out between his ribs, and he lost his last three meals.

But incredibly, he was still alive to know how bad he was feeling. He realized he had lost his count and eased the control lever back some more.

The whir returned. It occurred to him that the *Falcon* had fallen otherwise silent—which meant they weren't being pelted by dust particles, which meant the sublight drives were blasting a hole through the dust shell. Han looked over to congratulate Leia. Her face was a meter wide and five centimeters tall.

Nice try, he said. It came out *yiiiirt eeeeeciiiiN* in his own head. He doubted he would ever know how it sounded to Leia.

The whir vanished. He eased the control lever back. Leia's face went to a meter tall and ten centimeters wide. Something big exploded against the *Falcon*'s rear shields and the ship shook so violently that Juun—who had not strapped himself in—ended up splayed against the forward viewport.

Han eased the control lever back and took a long deep sniff, smelled only the sour barf of five different species—maybe a hint of verbobrain actuating gas—and eased the lever farther.

Leia's face shrank to half a meter on the diagonal, and Han said, *I love you, Princess, even if you drive like a . . .*

He didn't finish. The words came out *Eeeyyyyeeee wooooobe ooooooo,* which wasn't half bad, considering.

Han eased the control lever back again, and Juun slid down the canopy and disappeared behind the instrument console.

Then the proximity alarm went off, and the color outside the canopy went from blue to red to blue to whirling stripes of silver. Suddenly, Leia's face was the proper size and shape—still far too green, but at least oval and no more than twenty-five centimeters from chin to hairline—and Han felt even sicker than before.

That was when C-3PO came tumbling up the access corridor. "Doomed!" He crashed to a halt behind the navigator's chair, then fell to the deck, flailing. "We're doomed for sure!"

Han immediately knew they were going to make it. He took control of the *Falcon* and began to fire attitude thrusters, slowly bringing their spin under control. There was just a hint of coolant sweetness in the recycled air—enough to mean they would have to decontaminate the ship, but not so much they would die before they had a chance.

A pair of small hands appeared at the top edge of the control panel, and Juun pulled himself up to peer over the edge. "Real space?"

"Yeah." Han glanced out the viewport and saw nothing but the veined, red sky of a still-cooling nebula. "I think."

"It is," Leia said. "The proximity alarm dropped us out of hyperspace."

"And we survived?" Juun sounded almost disappointed. His sunken eyes swung toward Han. "That wasn't in any of the history vids. Did *you* teach her that?"

"No," Leia said. "And it hasn't worked yet. There's still one tiny problem."

"As long as it's tiny," Han said, eyeing the white static on his sensor screen.

"Well—not really tiny." Leia used the attitude thrusters to spin the *Falcon* around, bringing into view the green, rapidly swelling disk of the planet they were about to crash into. "It *was* big enough to drop us out of hyperspace."

TWENTY-THREE

Jacen dropped out of the tik tree to discover that even here, in the muggy heart of her private jungle garden, Queen Mother Tenel Ka was not alone. Seated in a small sunken courtyard with her rust-colored braids hanging down the back of her sleeveless frock, she was surrounded by twenty courtiers—mostly male and attractive, all attired in absurd, hand-tailored imitations of the Queen Mother's rustic fashion. Tenel Ka could have that effect on people.

Jacen crept up silently behind a camouflaged sentry who was patrolling the musky foliage along the garden wall—the last of the palace's many layers of security—and grasped the man's neck. The fellow tried to spin and yell the alarm, but went limp as Jacen sent a paralyzing jolt of Force energy through his spine.

Still alert to her Jedi instincts, Tenel Ka felt the disturbance and turned on her bench, revealing a classic profile even more stunning than the one in Jacen's memory. He expanded his presence in the Force so she would not be alarmed, then lowered the unconscious sentry to the ground and stepped out of the shrubbery.

Several courtiers cried out and sprang forward to shield Tenel Ka, and three more sentries emerged from the foliage along the garden wall. The two guards with clear angles zipped blasterfire in the intruder's direction, while the third called for help. Jacen deflected the bolts with his palms, then reached out with the Force and jerked the blaster rifles from their hands.

"Cease fire!" Tenel Ka ordered, a bit late. "Stand down!"

The guards, already rushing Jacen with their hand blasters

251

half free of their holsters, reluctantly obeyed. The nobles complied far less reluctantly.

Once Tenel Ka was satisfied her orders were being followed, she leapt onto the courtyard wall and, smiling warmly, opened her arms. Jacen was not surprised to see that the left one still ended above the elbow. After the sparring accident that had claimed the limb, Tenel Ka had refused an artificial replacement, keeping the stump as a reminder of the arrogance that had led to the mishap.

"Jacen!" she cried. "Welcome!"

"Thank you." It warmed Jacen's heart to find such an enthusiastic reception. "It's good to see you again, Queen Mother."

As Jacen stepped forward to receive her embrace, half a dozen burly Hapans blocked his way. One of them, an icy-eyed noble with neck-length blond hair and no left hand, glanced back at Tenel Ka. "This man is a friend of yours, Queen Mother?"

"Clearly, Droekle." Tenel Ka pushed between Droekle and an even larger noble missing an entire forearm. "Would I wish to hug him if he weren't?"

She pressed herself tightly enough to Jacen's chest for him to tell that a lot had changed in the last five years—all for the better. Jacen hugged her back and, noting the noxious glowers from her male courtiers, tried not to smirk.

"I apologize for entering this way," Jacen said. "But your social secretary refused to announce me. He kept telling me you were unavailable."

Tenel Ka released him and took a step back, her expression darkening. "Which one? I must see that he's corrected."

"No need." Jacen allowed himself the hint of a smile. "He has been."

"Is that so?"

Tenel Ka waited for him to elaborate. When he did not, she shrugged and took his hand, then jumped into the sunken courtyard to face her slack-jawed courtiers. Jacen was astonished to see that more than half had lost parts of their arms.

"Jacen is one of my oldest friends." She squeezed Jacen's hand, then looked up at him with a mischievous grin. "He was the boy who cut my arm off."

Though Jacen and Tenel Ka had long ago come to terms with that terrible accident and had developed a friendship bordering on romance, even he was taken aback by the bluntness of the announcement. The courtiers were left stammering—which was exactly what he sensed Tenel Ka wanted. Pulling him toward the far side of the courtyard, she slipped her arm through his and leaned her head against his shoulder.

"I would like to catch up with my friend," she called back. "Please amuse yourselves."

She guided him onto a stone path that wound its way through the jungle alongside a small stream. Though the lush foliage and gurgling water made it seem as though they were alone, Jacen could sense the guards shadowing them in the brush— and the courtiers following them down the path, just out of sight one curve behind.

Guessing this must be the normal state of affairs for Tenel Ka, Jacen said, "Thank you for taking the time to see me, Queen Mother."

"No—thank *you* for coming," Tenel Ka said. "You cannot know how refreshing it is to speak with someone who is not trying to win my hand or coax something out of me."

Jacen felt instantly guilty. "Actually, I *did* come to ask a favor. A big one."

"I know." Tenel Ka squeezed his arm and leaned closer to him. "That changes nothing I said. Hapan nobles never *ask*. They *arrange* or *contrive* or—if I am lucky—merely *persuade*. You would not believe what they do to curry favor."

Jacen raised his brow. "The amputations?"

"Fencing accidents." Tenel Ka snorted. The path came to a jungle pond, complete with a waterfall and a small island rising out of the green water. "To judge by the number of limbs being preserved in Hapan cryovats, most of my idiot nobles have no idea which end of a sword to hold."

They stopped at the edge of the pond, and Jacen leaned down so that his voice would not carry up the path. "You *do* know we're not alone, don't you?"

"Of course." Tenel Ka turned and raised her voice. "Be gone—or I will ask Jacen to take your other arms."

The nobles retreated quickly, but Jacen could sense the sentries continuing to lurk in the bushes.

Tenel Ka sighed. "There are some things even a Queen Mother cannot order." She slipped off her shoes, then turned toward the island. "Would you like to get your feet wet?"

"Why not?" Jacen eyed the twenty-meter distance to the island. "Only our feet?"

"Trust me." Pulling him along, Tenel Ka stepped out onto the water. Her feet sank only to the ankles. "Walk only where I walk, or it will be more than your feet."

Jacen did as she ordered and found himself standing atop a stone pier concealed just beneath the surface of the murky water.

"The Secret Way," Tenel Ka said. "It is an ancient Hapan defense—and it leads to the only place I can ever be truly alone."

"Why do you put up with them?" Jacen followed her along a jagged pathway of sharp, seemingly random turns. "Those idiot nobles, I mean?"

"They have their uses," Tenel Ka said. "I allow one to sit at my side, then watch to see who seeks him out."

"And that tells you what?" Jacen asked. "Who wants something from you?"

"Everyone wants something from me, Jacen." They reached the island and stepped onto a mossy path that, Jacen suspected, was rarely trodden by any feet but Tenel Ka's. "But the families who *don't* change alliances when I change favorites—I know those are the advisers I should listen to."

"It seems very . . . intricate," Jacen said.

"Calculated," Tenel Ka said. She led the way into a shielding copse of paan trees, then sat down on one end of the only bench. "It is the Hapan way, Jacen. There is a use for everyone."

Knowing it would not be proper etiquette to assume, Jacen did not sit on the other end of the bench. "Including me?"

Tenel Ka looked away. "Even you, Jacen." She patted the bench beside her, then said, "Now the houses of my suitors will be united against you. It would be wise to watch what you eat while you are here."

"Thanks," Jacen said. "But I won't be staying."

"Of course not." Tenel Ka continued to look away, but Jacen sensed tears in her voice. "What is it you need from us?"

"You felt Raynar's call?" Jacen asked.

"Yes. In the end, I had to keep myself locked in the palace. I didn't know who it was from. I thought maybe . . ." When Tenel Ka turned to face him, her gray eyes were clear and steady, but she had not bothered to wipe the tear tracks from her cheeks. "I have heard that a colony of Killiks is threatening Chiss space."

In that moment, the entire weight of the last five years' loneliness fell on Jacen's heart, and he wanted nothing more than to take Tenel Ka in his arms and kiss her.

Instead, he said, "It's a complicated situation."

Jacen went on to recount his journey into the Colony, from his arrival at Lizil to his exploration of the *Tachyon Flier* to joining Jaina and the rest of the strike team on Jwlio. Tenel Ka's gaze never strayed from his face, and he described his slowly dawning awareness that the Killiks shared a collective mind, what Raynar had become, and Cilghal's theories about how the pheromones altered the Joiners' minds. This drew a cocked brow from Tenel Ka, and for a while she seemed a young Jedi Knight again, her thoughts consumed by adventure and mystery rather than intrigue and politics. Jacen ended by reporting the mysterious attacks against his parents and aunt and uncle, and by noting that the Killiks claimed to have no memory of Lomi or Welk.

"The two of them just disappeared after the crash," Jacen finished. "The Killiks insist Raynar was the only one aboard the *Flier,* even though I *know* he dragged both Lomi and Welk out of the fire."

Jacen did not say exactly *how* he knew. There was no reason to go into the subtleties of Aing-Tii flow-walking right now. Tenel Ka sat in deep silence for several moments, then swung around, straddling the bench, and faced him.

"What became of Em Teedee?"

"Lowbacca's translator droid?" Jacen asked.

"He *was* on the *Flier* when it was stolen," she pointed out.

"I think he was destroyed in the fire," Jacen said. "I found a melted lump of metal that kind of looked like him."

Tenel Ka sighed. "Too bad. He could be a very annoying droid, but I know Lowie would have liked to have him back." Their gazes met, and neither hurried to look away. "So, you've come to ask me to leave here and help track down Lomi and Welk, before they create a whole legion of Dark Jedi?"

Jacen's heart leapt. "You could do that?"

Tenel Ka smiled, but her eyes turned sad. "No, Jacen. It was a joke."

"I see," Jacen said, also growing a little sad. "Am I required to laugh?"

"Only if you wish to avoid offending the Queen Mother."

"Never." Jacen laughed dutifully, then added, "You still have a lot to learn about jokes."

"So *you* say." Tenel Ka raised her hand and made an elaborate wave skyward. "Everyone *here* seems to think my jokes are quite funny."

"And you trust them?"

"Only the ones who don't laugh," Tenel Ka admitted. She swung her leg back over the bench and assumed a more regal pose. "All right, Jacen. I confess, I cannot guess. What is it you require of us?"

"A battle fleet," he said. "For the Colony."

Tenel Ka's face did not show the surprise that Jacen sensed from her in the Force. "That is a great deal to ask. The Hapes Consortium is a member of the Galactic Alliance."

"Does that mean the Galactic Alliance makes your decisions for you?"

Tenel Ka's gray eyes turned steely. "It *means* that we try to avoid angering Alliance friends."

"It's more important to prevent this war," Jacen said. "The Chiss are pushing too hard, and the Killiks couldn't withdraw if they wanted to. It's going to erupt into full-blown carnage, unless something happens to give the Chiss pause and the Colony a reason to be patient."

"And why should it matter to the Hapan people if a border conflict on the other side of the galaxy *does* become war?"

"Because it would end in xenocide, one way or the other," Jacen answered.

Tenel Ka turned and looked up into the paan trees, and Jacen sensed in the silence her Jedi instincts battling her duties as the Hapan queen.

"The Killiks are tied to the history of the galaxy in a way we don't understand yet," Jacen said. "They were living in cities before humans learned to build, and they were a civilization before the Sith were spawned. They were here when Centerpoint and the Maw were constructed—and they were driven from Alderaan by the beings who did it."

Though Tenel Ka's gaze remained in the treetops, her eyes widened, and Jacen knew he was reaching her.

"Tenel Ka, the galaxy will turn on what happens next," Jacen said. "And the Killiks are the pivot point. We need time to figure this out, because it could be total war—or true and lasting peace."

Tenel Ka finally turned to look at him. "What about the will of the Force, Jacen? Why not trust it?"

The reference to the Jedi's new understanding of the Force made Jacen think of Vergere—the lost Master who had opened their eyes to so much of that new understanding—and he smiled at the first truth she had taught him: *Everything I tell you is a lie.*

To Tenel Ka, he said, "Should I trust a river because it wants to run downhill?"

Tenel Ka frowned. "I am the one who asks the questions on Hapes, Jedi Solo."

Jacen chuckled. "Okay. The Force isn't a deity, Tenel Ka. It's not self-conscious, and it isn't capable of caring what happens to us. It's a flow. Its only will is to remove that which blocks it. When we facilitate that flow, when we allow it to run through us to others, we're in harmony. We're using the light side."

"And the dark side?"

"Is when we block that flow and turn it to our own ends," Jacen said. "We keep it from others. And when we release it too quickly, we turn it from a nurturing stream into a destructive flood."

"Didn't Vergere teach that our *intentions* make an act dark or light?" Tenel Ka asked.

"She did," Jacen admitted. "And she was telling the truth,

from a certain point of view. If you have good intentions, you tend to let the Force flow through you. If not, you tend to bottle it up inside, and it starts eating away at your good looks."

Tenel Ka looked at him from the corner of one eye. "I prefer my truths to remain true from *all* points of view."

"Sorry," Jacen said. "The Force is too big."

"And this is what you learned in the five years you were gone?"

"The core of it, yes."

Tenel Ka studied the ground for a moment, then looked back at him. "It took five years to learn *that*?"

"There was a lot of travel time," Jacen said.

Tenel Ka smiled and rolled her eyes, then asked, "What about our Killiks? Is the Force flowing through them, or into them?"

"Too early to say," Jacen said. "Raynar has grown incredibly powerful in a short time."

"And that doesn't scare you?"

"Of course it does," Jacen said. "But right now, he's trying to *avoid* a war. I'll be a lot more frightened when he stops."

Tenel Ka nodded. "Fact." She stood and extended her hand. "I think my suitors have had enough time to plot your death."

"I'm glad I could bring them together."

"Yes, you have been very useful that way." They started down the moss path toward the water. "I hope you will stay the night. It would be even more effective."

Jacen slowed. "Tenel Ka . . ." He did not need to wonder exactly what she was asking; he could feel it in the Force. "I didn't come here to . . . to become your paramour."

"You won't. Paramours are playthings." She stopped in full view of the pond's far bank and gave him a long, warm kiss. "And I would never play with you, Jacen Solo."

Jacen was beginning to feel very carried along—and spending the night could only help his chances of getting the fleet. "Then I'll stay," he said. "But it can only be one night."

"One night is fine," Tenel Ka said. "One night will be very useful."

TWENTY-FOUR

The observation deck was as stately, luxurious, and hushed as one would expect aboard the Bornaryn Trading Company's mighty flagship, the *Tradewyn*. A curving wall of transparisteel enclosed the cabin on three sides, offering an expansive view of the vast cargo fleet waiting permission to descend into the thin atmosphere of a dusty orange planet. In the distance, a starfighter security screen was scratching a grid of blue ions across a star-flecked backdrop.

The luxurious cabin was the kind of place that always made Tesar drool with nervousness. He drew air through his fangs to dry them, then followed his human escort past a long beverage bar toward a woman and two men waiting at the front of the deck. It was a long trip made longer by the fact that they had all turned to watch his approach—and by his fear of depositing a glob of saliva on the expensive wroshyr-wood floor.

Now that he was actually here, twenty steps from the Thul family, Tesar could not understand what had possessed him to track down the Bornaryn merchant fleet. He had overheard Master Skywalker and several others discussing how much should be told to Raynar's mother about her son's fate. A few hours later, Tesar had felt compelled to find Aryn Thul himself, and a few hours after that he had sneaked off Ossus in a Jedi StealthX. It had not begun to seem like a bad idea until he had arrived outside the *Tradewyn*'s docking bay, taking the ship's watch officer by surprise and causing the consternation that had scrambled the fleet's starfighter screen.

Tesar's escort stopped in front of the three humans and bowed

to the woman. "Madame Thul, may I present Jedi Sebatyne—
Tesar Sebatyne."

Dressed in a blue shimmersilk gown, Madame Thul was
gaunt and short, with long chestnut hair and a regal bearing. She
wore a sash striped with scarlet, yellow, and purple.

"Tesar was one of the Jedi Knights who accompanied Raynar
on the Mission." The escort stressed the word *Mission* just
enough to make clear that this was how they referred to Raynar's
disappearance. "He agreed to leave his weapons in a locker."

"Thank you, Lonn." Madame Thul lifted her chin and examined Tesar head-to-toe, lingering a moment on his brown Jedi
robe and the empty lightsaber clasp on his utility belt. "I know
the name."

Suspecting he was expected to speak now, Tesar drew more
air to dry his fangs—creating a small hiss that caused Madame
Thul to flinch. The dark-haired man behind her fingered the
hold-out blaster in his pocket and took a single step forward.

"Sorry. This one did not mean to scare you." Tesar felt a drop
running down his front fang and sucked air across his teeth
again. "It is very warm in here."

Madame Thul raised a carefully thinned brow. "Something to
drink?"

"Yes, that would be good."

Madame Thul waited a moment, then prompted, "Endorian
port? Bespin sparkle? Talhovian ale?"

"Do you have nerf milk?" Milk always slowed the drool.
"Which planet doesn't matter."

The shadow of a smile flicked across Madame Thul's lips,
then she turned to her servant. "Milk for Jedi Sebatyne, Lonn.
We'll have our usual."

The servant bowed and departed to collect the drinks.

Madame Thul gestured to the blond man at her side. "This is
my late husband's brother, Tyko." She did not bother to intro-
duce the bodyguard. "Now, what can Bornaryn Trading do for
the Jedi?"

"Nothing." Sensing he should probably not just blurt out the
news about Raynar to this frail woman, Tesar said, "This one is
here with newz."

"News?" Tyko asked.

"About Raynar."

Tyko scowled and slipped half a step forward, moving to shield his sister-in-law. "Raynar died at Myrkr."

"Yes," Tesar said. "After a fashion."

"After a fashion?" Madame Thul gasped. "You mean he's alive?"

"After a fashion, yes," Tesar said, happy he had broken the news gently. "That is what I—"

"My son is *alive*?"

Madame Thul's knees buckled, and she would have hit the floor had Tesar not reached out and caught her beneath the armpits. He waited while the stunned bodyguard jerked his hand from the blaster pocket, then laid her back into the man's arms.

"S-sorry." Tesar sucked more air to dry his fangs. "This one did not mean to touch her. When he saw her falling, he just—"

"It's . . . it's okay. Thank you." Madame Thul glanced up at her bodyguard. "Perhaps we should sit down, Gundar."

"Of course."

Gundar returned Madame Thul to her feet and guided her toward a chair. Tesar started to follow, but Tyko put a hand on his chest.

Tesar reacted as most Barabels would to being touched by a stranger. He grabbed Tyko's wrist and pulled it past his face, bringing the elbow into perfect biting position.

"Stop!" Tyko cried. "What are you doing?"

Tesar looked down at the man out of one eye. "You did not challenge this one?"

"N-no!" Tyko was up on his toes, being held so that his feet barely touched the floor. "I just wanted to talk to you!"

"We *were* talking," Tesar pointed out.

"Alone." Tyko's eyes slid toward the krayt-leather couches where Madame Thul's bodyguard had deposited her. "Quietly."

"My brother-in-law is being protective," Madame Thul explained from her seat. Her blue eyes shifted to Tyko. "That's hardly necessary, Tyko. I'm sure I can judge for myself whether *Jedi* Sebatyne has come selling starlight."

"If he *is* a Jedi," Tyko said. "I doubt anyone here can tell one Barabel in a robe from another."

Tesar saw the doubt flash through Madame Thul's eyes and realized he might be asking the Thuls to take a lot on faith. He released Tyko's arm and turned toward the bar, where the servant had gathered their drinks on a silvertine tray. Tesar reached out with the Force and lifted the tray out of the servant's hands, then floated it over to Madame Thul.

Her surprise quickly turned to approval. "Thank you, Jedi Sebatyne." She removed a small crystal goblet filled with burgundy liquid, then shot her brother-in-law an amused look. "I think that establishes Tesar's bona fides quite sufficiently."

Tesar floated the tray over to Tyko.

"It would be hard to argue." Tyko took a golden-rimmed snifter that contained a clear yellow liquor.

Tesar took his milk, then returned the tray to the astonished servant and followed Tyko over to Madame Thul. He sat down on a padded tail-stool the bodyguard offered.

"Now, Jedi Sebatyne, tell me about my son," Madame Thul ordered. "What does *after a fashion* mean?"

"The ship he was aboard crashed in the Unknown Regionz," Tesar began. "There was a fire."

"Oh." Madame Thul reached for her brother-in-law's hand. "Go on."

"He was taken in by a nest of sentient insectz," Tesar said.

"The Killiks?" Tyko glanced at Madame Thul. "Our agents have been hearing reports of an insect colony in the Unknown Regions."

"They call themselvez the Kind," Tesar clarified. "Raynar'z nest is the Unu. It is the Colony'z king nest, and he is the Prime Unu."

"That doesn't surprise me." There was a touch of pride in Madame Thul's voice. "Raynar has always been such a natural leader."

"Always," Tyko agreed. "What exactly is the Prime? The chairman?"

"*Voice* would be closer," Tesar said. He started to explain how other species sometimes joined the collective mind of the Killiks, then felt a restraining influence and decided to leave it for later, when the Thuls would be better able to understand. "He representz the Colony, and sees that itz Will is done."

Tyko nodded as though he understood exactly what Tesar meant. "The operating officer. Not quite as high as the chairman, but more important in terms of real power."

"That hardly matters, Tyko," Madame Thul said. "We'll groom him to take my place when he returns home."

Madame Thul may have missed the alarmed flash in Tyko's eyes, but Tesar did not.

"This one does not think Raynar will return," he said. Part of Tesar still wanted to bite Tyko's arm off, but another part realized that it was important to avoid making an enemy of the man—to be certain Tyko understood that Raynar did not threaten his position. "Raynar is too important to the Colony."

"Of course he is," Madame Thul said, addressing Tesar. "How long will it take him to groom a replacement?"

"This one is sorry," Tesar said. "He is not making himself clear. Raynar will not be returning. He has joined the Colony. He has become Unu. He has become the UnuThul."

"Are you really trying to tell me that my son has become an insect?" Madame Thul demanded.

"Not physically," Tesar said. "But, yes."

"By the Core!" Madame Thul studied him for a moment, then grew pale. "You're serious!"

Tesar nodded, and the purpose of his visit finally began to grow clear to him.

"Unu wishez to establish a relationship between the Colony and Bornaryn Trading," he said. "A *confidential* relationship."

"And *you're* the authorized agent?" Tyko asked.

Tesar considered a moment, then said, "For now."

Tyko accepted this with a nod, then turned to Madame Thul. "I've heard that there is large demand for the shine-balls and amber ale the independent smugglers are bringing back from the Unknown Regions."

Madame Thul seemed too shocked to reply. She merely nodded, then drained the contents of her goblet and held it up for the servant.

"Lonn—"

"Of course, madame." Lonn took the empty goblet and replaced it with a full one. "I shall keep them coming."

TWENTY-FIVE

Even full hazmat gear could not prevent Alema from appearing immodest and just a little bit debauched. The suit she had selected was two sizes too small, stretched so tightly over her svelte curves that it was apparent she had decided to leave her underclothes—if she owned any—aboard the crippled *Falcon*. Leia shook her head in weary amusement, wondering whom Alema was hoping to attract on the deserted planet that had jerked them out of hyperspace. Then again, had *Leia* spent her formative years as a dancing slave in a Kala'uun ryll den—or merely been a Twi'lek female—she, too, might have felt comfortable only when on display.

Alema glanced back, no doubt feeling Leia's scrutiny through the Force. "Is something wrong?"

"Not really." Leia dropped her gaze to the Twi'lek's seat area. "Just wondering if that suit is going to split."

Alema craned around to look, then gave a roguish smile. "Only if I bend over."

Juun came down the access corridor holding Alema's utility belt and lightsaber. "You forgot this, Jedi Rar."

"I don't think we'll be needing weapons," Leia said. "The scan showed no animal life at all."

"Better to be safe," Juun said.

"Why, thank you, Jae." Alema raised her arms and let him buckle on the belt. When the short-armed Sullustan had to press his face against her stomach, she smiled and added, "You're always so considerate."

Silently cursing the Sullustan's growing infatuation with

Alema, Leia had C-3PO fetch her own belt and buckled it on herself. After a thorough inspection of the *Falcon* had revealed no trace of insect stowaways, the Solos had been forced to turn their suspicions in other directions. Their plan had been to keep Alema separated from her weapons until Leia figured out whether she was the one who had been sabotaging the *Falcon*—but no one had told that to Juun, of course. He was the only other suspect.

Leia passed the Twi'lek four twenty-liter buckets, then lowered the boarding ramp. A cool wind was hissing across the marsh grass, carrying on its breath the fragrance of a carpet of nearby blossoms. Not far beyond, a ribbon of open water purled past, vanishing into the dark wall of a distant conifer forest.

"It's stunning!" Leia led the way down the ramp, carrying four empty buckets of her own. "It reminds me of Alderaan— unspoiled and beautiful."

"Yes, it's very . . . natural." Alema was looking above the forest, at a single jagged mountain silhouetted against the veined ruddiness of the nebular sky. "Not a bad place to crash—"

"Nobody crashed," Han said over their headsets. "And nobody's going to be marooned, either—if you two will get under the drive unit with those collection buckets."

"On our way." Under her breath, Leia added, "Hutt."

"I heard that."

"Good."

When Leia stepped off the ramp into the grass, the ground felt soft and spongy under her feet. She parted the grass and found water seeping up around her boot.

"We'll have to make this fast," Leia reported. "The ground's a little soft here."

"Ready when you are," Han replied.

Leia pulled on her hazmat hood and ducked under the *Falcon*. She tromped down the grass beneath the hyperdrive hull-access panel, then positioned her collection buckets under likely-looking leak points. Only when she finished did she notice that Alema was out beyond the boarding ramp, kneeling over a magenta blossom the size of a Wookiee's hand.

"Alema, we're kind of in a hurry here." Leia wondered if the Twi'lek was intentionally dawdling, hoping the *Falcon* would sink in the soft ground—and then she put the idea out of her mind. This was going to be dangerous enough without Alema sensing her suspicion through the Force. "We can look at flowers later."

"Sorry." Alema glanced in her direction, but did not rise. "Are you sure there are no animals here? No insects or birds or flying mammals?"

"The scan didn't reveal any," Leia said. "And I've seen nothing to suggest it was wrong."

"Interesting." Alema plucked the flower off its stem and brought it over to Leia. "If there are no insects or animals, what pollinates the flowers?"

Leia studied the blossom. Its structure was much the same as flowers across the galaxy, with a stamen, anther, and pollen.

"Good question," Leia said, surprised the Twi'lek had noticed. "I didn't think Ryloth had any true flowers."

"We have sex," Alema replied. "And males who want sex bring—"

"I get the picture," Leia said. "The answer is I don't know. Wind seems pretty inefficient, and that's about the only pollen-transfer agent I can see."

Han's voice came over their headsets. "If you two are done talking about the birds and the bees, I'd like to change out this coolant line—*before* the *Falcon* sinks to her belly."

"It's my fault." Alema's voice assumed the same purring quality she used with Juun. "I hope you can forgive me."

"That remains to be seen," Han said.

Leia winced at Han's cool tone, but saw no sign that Alema had sensed truth beneath his words. The Twi'lek simply retrieved her own buckets and positioned them beneath the *Falcon,* then curled her lekku into her hood and pulled it on.

"Ready."

Han grunted, and one corner of the hyperdrive hull panel sagged open. Toxic red coolant began to pour out. Leia quickly moved one of the buckets into position to catch the primary flow, then placed three others beneath adjacent drips.

It took only a minute to fill the first bucket. Alema passed an empty to Leia and moved the other one out of the way. They repeated the process four more times, carefully placing the filled buckets five meters away, where they were unlikely to be accidentally overturned.

Finally, the flow slowed to a drip, and Han said, "We're done. Just catch those last drips, and we'll be ready."

"Affirmative." Under her breath, Leia added, "For all the good it will do."

"Relax," Han said. "I can handle this repair. No problem."

The final drops of coolant fell from the hull panel. When they moved the last buckets aside, Leia was surprised to find the first little bit that had fallen on the flattened grass was evaporating before her eyes.

"Look at that," Leia said.

"It killed the grass," Alema observed. "That's to be expected."

"It should have killed a lot more," Leia replied. "And look at how fast it's drying up. It's not that hot—or dry—around here."

Alema shrugged. "Maybe the grass is absorbent." She glanced at the vast field surrounding the *Falcon,* then added, "I don't think we need to worry about the environmental damage."

They carefully wiped the access panel down with absorption pads, then Leia reactivated her throat mike.

"Okay, it's clean. You can close up now."

The panel hissed into place, then Han asked, "How much did you get?"

Leia eyed the buckets. "About a hundred and twenty liters."

"That's all?"

"Maybe one thirty," she said. "No more."

A disappointed sigh came over the headsets. "It'll have to do—but don't spill a drop. We need it all."

"Copy." Leia picked up a bucket, using both hands on the handle, and started for the *Falcon*'s ramp. "We'd better take it in one bucket at a—"

A liquid *thunk* sounded behind Leia, and she turned to find Alema holding a broken handle. At the Twi'lek's feet lay three overturned buckets, an eighty-liter pool of hyperdrive coolant slowly spreading across the ground.

"Alema!" Leia was trying to feel genuinely surprised, rather than disappointed, to avoid giving Alema any hint that this was exactly what she had expected. "What happened?"

"The handle broke," Alema said. "I'm—"

The Twi'lek's eyes grew large behind her faceplate, and suddenly she sprang toward the *Falcon*'s prow in a diving roll. An instant later, Meewalh and Cakhmaim dropped out of the ship's far-side air lock, their blaster rifles spraying stun bolts at the place Alema had just been standing.

Blasted Jedi danger sense.

Alema came up on her knees, her hazmat-gloved hands fumbling for her lightsaber.

"Did they get her?" Han asked over the headset.

Leia and Alema answered together. "No!"

The Noghri spun toward the *Falcon*'s prow and opened fire again, but Alema was already leaping behind a landing strut. Leia dropped her own bucket and started to circle behind the Twi'lek, fumbling at her lightsaber through the thick hazmat gloves.

"Wait!" Alema cried. "What's this about?"

"Spilled coolant," Han replied over the comm.

"It was an accident!"

"Sorry, kid," Han said. "We were watching on the hull cam. You broke the handle."

The four remaining buckets of coolant rose and went flying toward Meewalh and Cakhmaim. The Noghri dodged easily, but the maneuver gave Alema time to pull off her hood and gloves and snap her lightsaber off her belt.

Blasted telekinesis.

Leia pulled off her own gloves and hood, then grabbed her lightsaber and continued toward the prow. Though she felt certain that the Colony was behind Alema's treachery, Leia could not help feeling hurt, angry, and confused. Somehow, the Twi'lek's vulnerability felt like a betrayal in itself, and Leia could not help wondering whether Jaina had really been as surprised as she seemed when Alema announced her plans to return aboard the *Falcon*—or if her own daughter had known of the plan and kept silent about it.

Alema glanced in Leia's direction, but then Cakhmaim and Meewalh were fanning out toward her flanks, firing as they ran. The Twi'lek spun from her hiding place, her silver blade deflecting the Noghri's stun bolts back at them as she ran.

Han continued to chatter at Alema over the headsets. "What we can't figure out is *why*. What'd we ever do to you?"

"We told you," Alema insisted. "It was an accident!"

"You *kicked* over two buckets," Han said.

"We had no . . . choice." Alema launched herself through the air, flipping and corkscrewing closer to Cakhmaim, turning bolt after bolt in Meewalh's direction. "You betrayed the Colony!"

"*We* betrayed *them*?" Han was incredulous. "Saba's the one lying up there half dead."

"You see?" Alema landed. "You blame the Colony! We can't—" She directed one of Cakhmaim's stun bolts into Meewalh's chest. "—let you poison the Masters' council against us!"

Meewalh dropped to her knees, but kept firing. Leia ducked under the *Falcon*'s prow, ignited her own lightsaber at midguard, and raced to attack.

Alema did not even show Leia the respect of turning around. She simply raised a leg and planted a hazmat boot squarely in Leia's stomach and sent her flying back into a landing strut, then directed a second stun bolt into Meewalh and turned all her attention to Cakhmaim.

"How's it going down there?" Han asked.

"Aaaag . . ." Leia answered, trying to suck some air back into her lungs. "Ooog . . ."

"That good?"

Seeing that his blaster rifle was doing him more harm than good, Cakhmaim tossed it aside and drew his favorite weapon, a thin durasteel club connected by a hilt cord to a short sickle. Alema continued her advance more slowly, her lightsaber weaving a silver shield in front of her.

Leia really didn't want to turn this into a killing fight, but neither did she want to die marooned on an empty planet. She pointed to the bucket she had left near the boarding ramp and used the Force to send it flying at Alema, then pointed at Cakhmaim's discarded blaster rifle and sent *that* flying as well.

Alema pivoted away from the bucket and ducked the blaster rifle.

Then Cakhmaim was on her, club-and-sickle whirling, lashing sickle-low and club-high, then sickle-high and club-low, hands flashing as he switched from one weapon to the other. Alema fell back jumping, skipping, ducking, trying to land just one parry with her sizzling blade and send her attacker's weapons spinning away. Cakhmaim's reflexes were too quick for her. Every time she turned her wrists to intercept an attack, he reversed his whirling weapons and hit her where she was unprotected, clubbing her in the ribs, slashing her across the thigh, always forcing her to retreat.

Han continued to speak over the headsets. "Hang tight, Leia." His voice was strained, which was not surprising, given the length and diameter of the twisting access tunnel that led to the hyperdrive coolant drain. "Be there . . . anytime now!"

Leia pushed off the strut and rushed Alema with a heavy heart. Though she still intended to capture the Twi'lek alive if possible, she knew a killing fight when she found herself in one. She reached striking range and, activating her blade, swung for the head.

Alema had no choice but to drop to her haunches. Cakhmaim was all over the Twi'lek, catching her weapons-hand with the sickle and whipping it around, slashing the tendons that controlled her fingers. The lightsaber deactivated and went tumbling away. Cakhmaim brought his club around for a temple strike, but at the last instant must have glimpsed the sorrow in Leia's face and dropped it below the ear for a knockout blow.

Alema took full advantage of the switch, turning to take the strike on her lekku, then continuing around, bringing the palm of her good hand up under the Noghri's chin, putting the power of the Force into the blow and driving him off his feet. Cakhmaim's head hit the underside of the *Falcon* with a dull *clang,* then he dropped limply into the smashed marsh grass.

Leia slammed the butt of her lightsaber into Alema's head, striking to subdue but striking hard. The Twi'lek staggered and looked as though she might pitch forward. Leia cocked her arm to strike again . . . and felt one of the Twi'lek's legs catching her across the ankle, swinging through to sweep her off her feet.

Leia landed on the back of her head so hard that, even with the soft ground, her vision began to narrow. She braced a hand by her hip and instantly brought her feet under her, but Alema was already rolling to her feet, facing Leia, her good arm reaching out to call her lightsaber.

Leia reached out in the Force and tried to wrench the weapon away, but her head was spinning, and the lightsaber floated straight into Alema's hand. With both Noghri lying limp and helpless in the grass, Leia was on her own. She didn't like her odds. Her ankle was beginning to throb, and she wasn't sure she'd be able to stand on it.

"Han?"

"Almost . . . out."

A frightening darkness came to Alema's eyes, and she took one step toward Leia. "Put down your weapon, Princess. There's no need for us to fight. Without coolant . . ." The Twi'lek stopped midsentence, apparently realizing how she had been tricked, then said, "You have extra coolant."

Leia shrugged. The gesture felt like it would split her head. "We had to find out."

"You can still lay down your weapon," Alema said. "It would be better if you did."

Leia eyed the unconscious Noghri. If they had failed to take Alema by surprise, it seemed unlikely that Leia could win a lightsaber duel—even if Alema would be fighting with her off hand.

"You're right about one thing," Leia said. "There's no need for us to fight. I've been reaching out to Luke in the Force."

Alema remained where she was, about five steps from Leia— safely out of attack range, but close enough to spring.

"And?"

"And the Masters already know that something happened to Saba," Leia said. Her vision had returned to normal, but now her head was throbbing worse than her ankle. "They know the Skywalkers might have had a stowaway, too. My guess is they'll assume the Colony is responsible."

"You're lying."

"You're a Jedi Knight," Leia said. "You *should* know I'm not."

Alema's eyes narrowed, and Leia felt the Twi'lek probing her mind, searching for any hint of deceitfulness.

Leia made no attempt to resist. "The Colony's best chance to win the Masters' support—its *only* chance—is for you to go to Ossus *now* and explain what really happened."

Alema's lightsaber crackled to life.

"You won't win any friends for the Colony that way," Leia pointed out.

Alema shrugged.

"It doesn't *matter* to you?" Leia began to drag the Force into herself, preparing to pull herself to her feet the instant the Twi'lek even *looked* like she was going to advance. "I thought you sabotaged us because . . ."

Leia let the sentence trail off, suddenly realizing how badly she had misunderstood the situation. Alema did not *know* why she had sabotaged the *Falcon*. She thought she was protecting the Colony when she was actually damaging any chance it had of winning the Masters' sympathies . . . and why?

"Luke and Mara! Or . . . *Ben*?" Leia's heart felt like it would burst with rage. "You ungrateful—"

Alema sprang.

Leia activated her lightsaber and blocked the Twi'lek's first attack, then stretched out with the Force and used it to pull herself to her feet a dozen paces away. Alema started after her, coming fast but under control, and that was when a muffled *thud* reverberated from inside the *Falcon*—Han finally dropping out of the hyperdrive access tunnel into the aft service corridor.

Alema glanced up, and Leia had an idea.

"Han, I think she's figured us out!" Leia screamed into her headset. "She's looking toward the drive exhaust."

"The drive exhaust?" Han managed to make his confusion sound like alarm. "Well, stop her! If she cuts one of those—"

"Han!"

"Yeah?"

"Enough!" Leia said. Han certainly knew his own ship well enough to realize that the aft escape pod discharged a couple of meters forward of the drive exhaust, and she would just have to trust him to figure out the significance of that. "She has a headset, too. Remember?"

"All right . . . just stop her!"

Leia raised her lightsaber and charged. Alema looked first puzzled, then worried; then finally she pivoted away and blocked as Leia swung at her head.

Leia kicked wildly at the Twi'lek's leading foot, forcing her to step back, then swung again at the head. Alema blocked and stepped into the attack, trying to work her way past Leia to strike at the drive exhaust.

Leia attacked hard, smashing her knee into Alema's ribs, forcing herself not look toward the escape pod hatch, to not even *think* about it . . .

Alema surprised Leia with a spinning hook kick that caught her across the shins and sent her sprawling onto her face just centimeters from a pool of spilled coolant.

Han's panicked voice came over the headset. "Leia! Stop her!"

Leia looked up to find Alema racing past, only three steps shy of the pod hatch but a full meter off to one side. She locked her blade into the activated position, then rose to her knees and threw her lightsaber at the Twi'lek's shoulder.

Whether Alema sensed or heard the blade coming did not matter. She dodged away—and that was when the escape pod's outer hatch blew, catching the Twi'lek along her whole left side, buckling her knees and leaving her lying motionless in the grass.

By the time Leia scrambled to her feet and raced over to make sure Alema would not be getting up again, C-3PO was already riding the rear cargo elevator down with a hypo full of tranquilizer in his hand.

"Well done, Mistress Leia!" C-3PO said. "Captain Solo said all along that experience—"

"Give me that!" Leia snatched the hypo from the droid's hands and knelt down to inject the Twi'lek . . . then nearly fainted as a terrible pain shot up her leg. "Blast! If I'm going to make a habit of this, I really have to practice more."

TWENTY-SIX

At the near end of the academy training grounds, the youngest students were practicing Force leaps, stepping to the mark with knitted brows, then launching themselves one after the other over a three-meter cross ray. Most cleared the red beam with a simple arcing dive, then dropped into the landing area headfirst, relying on the safety repulsors to break their falls. But a few—especially from the more agile species—executed graceful somersaults and came down on their own feet. Some of the children in line noticed Luke and Mara emerging from the access tunnel and began to point and whisper, so Luke made a show of nodding approval as the next few jumpers cleared the beam.

"These are the Woodoos," Luke explained to their guest, Aristocra Chaf'orm'bintrani of the Chiss Ascendancy. "They're our youngest students."

"Your youngest?" A few centimeters shorter than Luke, the Aristocra was relatively small for a Chiss, with a blue angular face just beginning to sag with age. "How young are they?"

"The Woodoos are generally between five and seven years old, Formbi," Mara said, calling the Aristocra by his core name. "Though that varies by species—some mature at markedly different rates."

"Yes—well, we wouldn't have that problem in the Ascendancy." Formbi folded his hands behind his back and peered across the running track at the children. "Which one is your son?"

Luke felt the pang in his wife's chest as clearly as the one in his own, but when Mara answered, her voice betrayed no hint of her emotions. "Our son doesn't attend the Jedi academy."

"How strange." Formbi continued to watch the Woodoos. "My file lists his age as seven."

"Ben is withdrawing from the Force right now." As much as it pained him, Luke had no intention of hiding the fact. That would have implied he was ashamed, and he was not. "We don't know why."

Formbi turned. "I didn't know children could do that."

"Most can't," Mara said. "Ben demonstrated exceptional power from birth. This only confirms how gifted he is."

"I see," Formbi said. "I'm sorry, then, that he is choosing not to develop his potential."

"We're not," Luke said. He felt Mara's ire rising, but the smile on her face remained polite. Winning Formbi's cooperation was going to be difficult enough without allowing Chiss manners to become an issue. "Children must *want* to be at the academy to succeed. We don't force anyone to attend, and we do everything we can to encourage them to enjoy their time here."

"We can even arrange employment for their parents on Ossus—some are assistant trainers here at the academy," Mara said. "And we encourage students to develop at their own pace. So when Ben *is* ready, his natural capabilities will allow him to establish himself very quickly."

"I have no doubt." Formbi turned back to the training grounds, looking past the Woodoos to where the Rontos were practicing telekinesis by smashing giant bean bags against each other. "But I'm sure you didn't summon me here to discuss Jedi training techniques."

"As a matter of fact, we did," Luke said. They had also asked Soontir Fel to come, but he had politely declined, explaining it would not do for anyone on the Defense Fleet general staff to consort with Ascendancy enemies. "We want you to understand what goes into the training of a modern Jedi."

"Hoping to impress me so much that I'll persuade the Ruling Circle to let you handle the Qoribu problem?" Formbi asked.

"Precisely," Mara said. "And it was an invitation, not a summons."

"Funny," Formbi said. "Your message mentioned the Brask Oto."

"That's right," Luke said. The Brask Oto was a Chiss battle station he and Mara had saved during an earlier trip into Ascendancy territory. "We wanted you to know it was authentic."

Formbi smiled. "As I said—a summons. We Chiss always repay debts of honor." He waved a hand toward the interior of the training complex. "Please, impress me."

Luke led the way across the running track to the slidewalk that circled the inner fields, then heard an alarmed whistle behind them. He glanced back to find R2-D2 traversing a banked turn, one tread off the ground and perilously close to tipping over.

"Your droid seems rather intoxicated," Formbi observed.

"A memory fault is playing havoc with his systems." Luke reached out in the Force and carried R2-D2 over to the slidewalk. "I don't want it repaired until we find a way to extract some information stored on the chip."

Formbi watched with an amused expression as the droid settled onto the slidewalk behind him. "And this information is so valuable you must keep the droid with you at all times?"

Luke thought for a moment, then said, "Yes." The truth was that R2-D2 kept scheduling himself for a chip replacement, so Luke had decided to keep him nearby until the Galactic Alliance's best slicer, Zakarisz Ghent, arrived to bypass the security program protecting the memory chip. "It could solve a very old mystery for us."

"Then I wish you luck," Formbi said. He pointed to a circle of twelve-year-olds—Banthas—sitting cross-legged around a single happy-looking nerf, waving their fingers and sending the contented beast waddling back and forth among them. "What in space are they doing?"

"Mind tag," Mara explained. "It's how they develop their persuasive abilities."

Formbi gave her a sharp look. "I trust that's not how you intend to persuade me?"

"The technique only works on the weak-minded," Luke said.

"And no Jedi would ever consider a Chiss Aristocra to be weak-minded."

"Good," he said. "I was given to believe Jedi Knights are rarely fools."

"We generally try to train that out before anyone becomes a Jedi Knight, yes," Mara said.

"Then why do you insist on involving yourselves at Qoribu?" Formbi's voice was casual, as though it were only an idle question. "The conflict is of no concern to the Galactic Alliance."

"The Jedi serve the Force." Luke was keeping an eye on R2-D2, making sure he did not wander off. "Our concerns reach well beyond the Galactic Alliance."

Formbi's gaze grew hard. "Into the Ascendancy?"

"Into the Colony, at least," Luke said.

Formbi looked away, focusing his attention on a group of fourteen-year-olds who were using their lightsabers to bat live blaster bolts back and forth. These students had no nickname; once students built their first lightsabers, they were known simply as apprentices.

"You understand nothing about the Colony," Formbi said, almost absently. "If you did, you would leave it to us."

"We understand that what you're doing at Qoribu comes close to violating Chiss law," Mara said. "Unless the Ascendancy has bent from a thousand years of tradition?"

"A lot has changed in the Ascendancy." Formbi's voice grew resigned. "But not that. It remains unlawful for the Chiss to be the aggressor people."

"I've always admired that about the Ascendancy," Luke said.

"In truth, I find it rather quaint," Formbi replied. "But, having no desire to find myself exiled, I'll follow the law—even if it means the destruction of the Ascendancy itself."

A line of ten-year-old students appeared ahead, racing toward Luke and the others against the flow of the slidewalk. Formbi started to step aside so they could pass, but Mara used the Force to gently tug him back.

"Please, Aristocra," she said. "They'll be disappointed if we rob them of their chance to show off."

Formbi eyed the chubby Kitonak girl at the head of the line, then cocked his brow when she suddenly sprang off the slide-walk, turned a Force flip over his head, and landed gracefully—if somewhat heavily—behind him. The rest of the students followed suit, beaming in pride as they somersaulted over Luke and the others. Once Formbi grew accustomed to the game, he even encouraged the students by pretending to flinch before each one jumped.

"Thank you for indulging them, Aristocra," Luke said. "The dining halls will be buzzing tonight with how they actually drew a reaction from you."

"My pleasure," Formbi said. "As long as they understand the difference when they become Jedi Knights."

"They will," Mara said. "Chiss courage is legendary around here—which is why I'm so puzzled about your fear of Killiks."

"If you are puzzled, it is only because you are ignorant of the Colony's true nature."

"Then enlighten us," Luke said. "The sooner the Jedi understand the situation, the sooner we will find a solution and end our presence at Qoribu."

"And if there is no solution?"

"It would be better to discover that now," Luke said, "before any more of our Jedi become like Raynar."

Formbi frowned. "Who is Raynar?"

"Raynar Thul," Mara said. "He went MIA during the war. He was presumed dead, but apparently his ship crashed inside the Colony."

"A nest of Killiks rescued him and saved his life," Luke said.

"Saved his life?" Formbi sounded surprised. "When did this Raynar come up missing? About six years ago?"

"Close." Luke began to have a sinking feeling. "It was a little over seven."

"I see." Formbi's gaze turned inward. "That explains it."

"Explains what?" Mara demanded.

"The Defense Fleet reconnaissance corps has been watching the Colony for centuries," Formbi said. "It has been slowly expanding over time, but it wasn't considered a threat."

"Until recently," Mara surmised.

"Correct," Formbi said. "The insects—Killiks, as you call

them—are clearly intelligent, but they've customarily shown little concern for life. When one was injured, its companions would simply abandon it, and when food grew scarce, whole columns would just wander off to die."

"And that changed six years ago," Luke said.

Formbi nodded. "The first satellite nests appeared on our border, and we began to notice an exponential population increase. Imagine our surprise when we learned that now they had hospitals to care for their ailing and were using interstellar trade to alleviate the cyclic food shortages that once kept their populations in check."

"And *that* frightened the Ascendancy into sending your defoliators to give nature a helping hand?" Mara asked.

"No." Formbi accepted the criticism in her question without visible emotion. "We didn't make that decision until later—after we had discovered how dangerous they were."

The slidewalk carried them past a sunken basin, where a group of adolescent apprentices stood meditating under the watchful eye of a training Jedi Knight. They were surrounded by twenty grown adults, who were shouting insults at them and pelting them with missiles ranging from kitchen leftovers to sting balls.

"My word!" Formbi gasped. "What kind of drill is that?"

"It's a centering exercise," Luke said proudly. He was counting on this part of the tour to persuade Formbi to speak on their behalf on the Chiss capital world, Csilla. "Young Jedi must learn to detach themselves from their emotions, to remain focused regardless of whatever they are feeling at the time."

"There are several other versions," Mara added. "A five-day fast while the rest of the academy feasts around them, a three-day swim in a warm bubble pool, an all-night tickle where they're forbidden to laugh."

"That may sound silly, but that's actually the most difficult test," Luke said. "And if they fail, they repeat the other exercises."

Formbi stared at them as though they had told him they were Sith Lords. "You people make the Ssi-ruuk look kind!"

"Jedi Knights often find themselves in tumultuous situations," Luke replied. "Their judgment must remain sound, no matter what they are feeling."

"Sound judgment is a warrior's best weapon," Formbi agreed. "Though I don't understand what the Jedi have against laughing."

The slidewalk carried them past the centering exercise, and R2-D2's presence began to fade. Luke looked back and, finding the confused droid facing the wrong direction, used the Force to lift him back to the group.

Mara was already grilling Formbi again. ". . . convinced the Ascendancy the Killiks are dangerous?"

Formbi hesitated a moment, then asked, "Do you recall our first meeting, when I welcomed you aboard the *Chaf Envoy* to examine the wreck of the Outbound Flight?"

"How could we forget?" Luke said. "The whole mission was a gambit to lure the Vagaari into attacking, so you could carry the war to them legally."

"The choice was theirs," Formbi said defensively. "But yes. And do you happen to remember how many ruling families there were at the time?"

"Nine," Mara said instantly. When it came to politics, she rarely forgot a fact. "But five years later, when we visited Csilla, the number was four. I assumed the discrepancy to be a result of a war with the Vagaari."

"Not directly," Formbi said. "But the Third Vagaari War did leave us with a labor shortage, and *that* led to the discrepancy."

"I'm afraid I don't understand," Luke said. "Were the losses of some families so heavy—"

"Several families began to hire entire nests from the Colony. It seemed the perfect solution. The insects were plentiful, industrious, and not averse to risk. This was a couple of years before your Raynar arrived, and they began to care about surviving." Formbi winced at how that sounded, then hastened to add, "Of course, we were careful not to take advantage."

"Of course." Luke had the unhappy feeling that he saw where this was leading. "Didn't you know about the Joiners?"

"We took precautions," Formbi said. "Very stringent precautions."

"That still didn't work," Mara surmised.

"They worked," Formbi replied. "Until someone started sabotaging them."

"The Killiks?" Luke asked.

Formbi frowned. "We value fools no more than the Jedi, Master Skywalker. The precautions remained solely under our control."

There was a moment of silence, then Mara asked, "And?"

"We don't really understand," Formbi admitted. "It may have been interfamily rivalries. All we know is that the precautions broke down, and before we realized it, two entire families had become Joiners."

"Only two?" Luke asked. "What about the other missing families?"

"Three of the families had become critically dependent on insect labor," Formbi replied. "There was a dispute over the best course of action."

"The Ascendancy had a civil war?" Luke gasped.

"Chiss do not have civil wars, Master Skywalker," Formbi replied. "We have disagreements. The matter was resolved before your visit to Csilla—though I do believe you were witness to some reverberations."

"The attack on Soontir Fel?" Mara asked. "I thought that concerned the aid he provided the Galactic Alliance against the Yuuzhan Vong."

"It is easy to disagree with the policies of someone who has destroyed your family," Formbi said. "Fel has a habit of being too merciful for his own good."

The slidewalk carried them to the training field that had been Luke's destination all along, a jumbled course full of traps, hazards, and obstacles. Two teams of senior apprentices—one team large and strong, the other small and quick—were running back and forth through the course, using long-handled rackets, stunblasters, and Force telekinesis to pass half a dozen crackling jetballs to each other through the air. In the midst of the crashing bodies and acrobatic power plays, a single referee was struggling to maintain order.

Motioning Formbi and Mara along, Luke stepped off the

slidewalk—then reached out with a mental hand and pulled R2-D2 to his side. Luke did not launch into a description of the game, however; he still had some questions about the trouble the Killiks had caused the Chiss Ascendancy.

"I'm beginning to see why the Ascendancy doesn't want the Colony encroaching on its frontier," Luke said. "Were the Killiks also responsible for the destruction of the Empire of the Hand?"

Formbi turned and, in a surprised voice, asked, "What makes you think the Empire of the Hand has been destroyed?"

Luke wasn't fooled for a moment. He could feel the Aristocra's dismay through the Force—and so could Mara.

"Baron Fel, for starters," she said. "He wouldn't have abandoned his duties while the Empire of the Hand stood."

"Perhaps it was merely absorbed," Formbi suggested.

"*After* being battered into nothingness," Mara said. "We know that Nirauan has been abandoned. Something must have happened."

Formbi sighed in resignation. "The Empire of the Hand served the purpose Mith'raw'nuruodo intended—though it was not against the Colony, as you suggest."

"The Vagaari, then?" Mara pressed. "The Yuuzhan Vong?"

"That's really all I am at liberty to say," Formbi answered wearily. "Except, perhaps, that the Colony is only one of the Terrors remaining to the Unknown Regions. Do not be surprised to see the Empire of the Hand rise again, when there is need."

"I see," Luke said, saddened to have confirmed what he had only suspected until now. "I know that three of the Fel children survived, but what of Chak—"

"Only *two* survived," Formbi said. "Jagged and Wyn. Chak, Davin, and Cherith are all dead."

"I'm sorry to hear that," Luke said. "I liked Chak very much."

"But what of Cem?" Mara asked, picking the question off the top of Luke's head. "Was she killed, too?"

"Cem?" A sly smile came to Formbi's mouth. "*Cem* is a son's name."

"Excuse me," Mara said. "We never actually met."

"I should think not." The smile grew wider and shiftier. "Cem would be the Fels' shadow child."

"Shadow child?" Luke asked.

"Publicly unacknowledged," Formbi explained. "Secret, in fact. It's a common Chiss precaution to keep enemies from wiping out an entire ruling family."

Luke began to have a guilty feeling in his stomach. "How secret?"

"Quite," Formbi replied. "In fact, this is the first time I've heard of a Cem Fel. I imagine *you* heard the name from Wyn."

"Jacen did," Mara replied. "How could you know?"

"Wyn is notorious for spilling secrets," he said.

"And now we've compounded it," Luke said. "I hope you'll hold the name in confidence."

"Of course." Formbi's voice was sincere. "And you shouldn't feel bad—Soontir Fel is a clever one. I often suspect that Wyn reveals only what he wishes her to."

"Thank you."

Luke returned the smile, hoping to conceal his doubt about the Aristocra's reassurances. He waved at the training field, where the small team had won control of all six jet-balls and was driving deep into opposition territory. "And now, perhaps you'd allow me to explain the game we're watching."

"Please," Formbi said. "It looks refreshingly riotous."

"We call it Skorch," Luke explained. "It's actually the referee who's being trained. Each team has a set of secret goals—such as collecting three balls or sending two into one goal and one into another—and it's the referee's job to discover those goals and see that both sides win."

"*If* that's possible," Mara said. "In some Skorch scenarios, the goals are mutually exclusive. Then the referee must see that both teams achieve an equivalent level of victory."

The referee, a black-furred Defel with eyes as red as Formbi's, popped up from behind a wall and sent a small Rodian sprawling. He intercepted the jet-ball that had been coming in her direction and sent it sailing toward the other end of the course.

"The referee can also arrange complete losses for both

sides," Luke said. "Though that's a last resort. It's considered barely adequate."

"What an odd game," Formbi said.

R2-D2 emitted a discordant series of beeps, then raised his transceiver antenna and began to move off.

Luke scowled and called, "Artoo, come back here." When R2-D2 continued toward the Skorch field, Luke excused himself and caught up to the droid. "Didn't you hear me? We're in the middle of some very important business."

R2-D2 whistled a sharp reply.

"I'm sure your business is important, too," Luke said. "But you'll have to conduct it over there, with us."

R2-D2 pivoted on a tread, then tweedled a question.

"If it can't wait, you'll have to," Luke answered. "You're in no condition to wander around the training grounds alone."

Another question.

"Yes, on Ossus," Luke said. "Where did you think we were?"

R2-D2 gave a confused sigh, then reluctantly returned with Luke. Mara was explaining the theory behind Skorch as two players—a Wookiee and a Squib—wrestled with the Defel referee in an attempt to keep him from interfering with the game.

"The only rules are the ones the referee can persuade the players to accept," she was saying. "And his only rule is that he can't use his lightsaber on any of the players."

"It sounds like a dangerous game," Formbi observed. "How many students are killed playing it?"

"These are senior apprentices," Luke said. "They can take care of themselves."

"And there are always healing trances," Mara added.

"Healing trances are good," Luke agreed. "The idea is to teach our Jedi Knights to look for secret agendas and develop solutions that work for everyone." He turned to Formbi. "That's what we hope to do at Qoribu."

"Very noble." Formbi turned away from the game. "But I have seen nothing to convince me that you understand the Killiks any better than we do. Quite the opposite, in fact."

"We haven't had as long to study them as you have," Mara retorted. "But our senior scientist has already developed a theory about how Joiners are created—"

"And about how the Killiks' collective mind functions," Luke said.

"Which is?" Formbi asked.

Luke sensed that the question was a test. "We believe Joiners are created when Killik pheromones alter the basic structure of the corpus callosum," he said. "Those changes allow the Joiners to receive signal impulses directly from the Killik brains, which—we presume—have a similar capacity."

"And what is the transfer agent?"

Luke hesitated. He could sense that they were close to winning Formbi's support, but they were crossing from theory to guesswork here, and he did not want to undermine their progress by making a wild-sounding assertion.

Mara disagreed. He could feel her through their Force-bond, urging him to take the chance.

"We think the impulses are transferred through auras," Luke said. "But we're having trouble identifying exactly which part."

"All of them," Formbi said. "Heat, electric, magnetic, probably chemical—at least that's what *our* scientists think. But that doesn't explain the Will."

"The Will?" Mara asked.

"As far as we know, only individuals from the same nest share a truly collective mind," Formbi said. "Our scientists describe it as a sort of very advanced telepathy, where an individual has access to the thoughts and sense impressions of the entire nest."

Luke nodded. That was just as Tekli and Tahiri described the experience—though he was not going to admit *that* to Formbi. "That's what our investigations suggest."

"But insects from different nests must communicate with each other via language, just as we do," Formbi said. "The collective mind doesn't seem to extend far beyond the confines of the nest."

"Which is exactly what you'd expect, if the communication medium is their aura," Mara said. "To participate in the collective mind, an individual would always have to be within range of another insect's aura, and that one would have to be close to another—"

"Precisely," Formbi agreed. "The collective mind can extend over quite a large area, as long as the chain of insects remains unbroken."

R2-D2 began to beep for attention.

"Not now, Artoo," Luke said. He did not want to give Formbi time to reconsider what he was about to tell them. "Please continue, Aristocra."

Formbi glanced at the droid, then nodded. "But the entire *Colony* seems to be subject to a single Will. We've noticed that nests all across the sector are acting in concert, pursuing a single, unified purpose."

"Let me guess," Luke said. "Expanding the Colony."

"Very good," Formbi said.

"And this Will appeared about six years ago?" Mara asked. "When they started to develop hospitals and interstellar trade?"

"Right again," Formbi replied. "And, frankly, we're puzzled."

"How so?" Luke asked. "Perhaps we can help clear something up for you."

Formbi smiled. "Yes. Soontir suggested you would respond well to an information exchange, and we believe this mystery to be particularly well suited to the Jedi."

"We'll do what we can," Mara said, leaving out what exactly she meant by *can*. "Though, as I said before, we haven't had as long to study the Killiks as you have."

"That has been to your advantage, I assure you," Formbi said. "If you were wise, you would leave our part of the galaxy to us and avoid the Colony at all costs."

"We Jedi try to be brave as well as wise," Luke replied mildly. "Now, how can we be of service?"

"Our scientists are having trouble understanding how the Will exerts its hold over the entire Colony," Formbi said. "The distances involved are too great for it to function through their auras, as the collective mind does."

"Killiks aren't Force-sensitive, if that's what you're thinking," Luke said. "At least not the ones we've met."

"Would they need to be?" Formbi asked. "If each nest had

just one Joiner who could feel the Will, wouldn't the entire nest be subject to it?"

"Possibly," Mara allowed. Luke felt her alarm growing as clearly as his own; it was growing all too obvious that Unu—Raynar's nest—was the source of what the Chiss were calling the Will. "But this central Will would have to be magnitudes stronger than the wills of the individual nests."

"And it could be," Luke said, recalling how powerful Raynar had grown in the Force. "A gifted Joiner might be able to draw on the Force potential of his entire nest."

"I thought you said that the Killiks aren't Force-sensitive," Formbi said.

"He did," Mara answered. "*Force-sensitive* means you have the ability to tap into the Force. *Force potential* is just another way of saying 'life energy.' "

"All living things generate Force energy," Luke explained. He was beginning to see that Formbi had played them—just as he had during the investigation of the Outbound Flight wreck. "But I suspect you already know that. The information is readily available on any HoloNet terminal in the Galactic Alliance."

"But it *is* good to have our theory vetted by the experts," Formbi said, still trying to maintain his charade. "And it seems a reasonable exchange, considering what I gave you."

"It would have been, if that's all you had come for." Luke turned back to the Skorch field, buying himself a moment to contain his rising emotions. The anger he felt was at himself, for failing to see Formbi's game early on, before they had told him about Raynar. "But you came looking for a name—for the source of the Will."

Formbi spread his hands and stepped to Luke's side. "You were the ones who summoned *me*."

On the Skorch field, the small team once again had control of all six jet-balls and were racing toward the large team's goal. The Defel referee was limping after them with one furry arm synth-glued to his knee.

"You have what you came for," Mara said. "But it wouldn't be wise to act on the information."

Formbi looked at her in surprise. "Are you threatening me?"

"She's telling you that killing Raynar won't return the Colony to what it was," Luke said. "If you assassinate him, all you're going to have are a trillion angry insects who don't care if they die. The Jedi won't be able to save you."

"Actually, we weren't counting on that," Formbi said. "The Jedi have no business—"

R2-D2 emitted a piercing shriek, then began to bang back and forth on his treads until Luke looked down.

"Artoo, I said—"

R2-D2's holoprojector activated, and fuzzy image of Leia appeared on the ground in front of him. For a moment, Luke thought that it was the old message she had recorded for Obi-Wan—then he noticed that she was dressed in a white jumpsuit instead of a ceremonial gown, and her hair was falling loose down her back instead of being gathered in those ear-buns she used to wear.

"Luke?" Her voice was scratchy and barely audible. "Are . . . there?"

"Yes." Luke answered. "Artoo, where's this coming from?"

R2-D2 tweedled a sharp reply.

"I *know* it's being relayed through the Academy HoloNet transceiver," Luke said. He dropped to his knee. "Leia, where are you?"

"Luke?" Leia's image said. "Can't . . . you. But . . . important . . . Killik attacked Saba . . . stowaways on . . . think . . . after you and . . . maybe Ben."

"Stowaways?" Mara gasped. An image of their son holding an empty container of gelmeat flashed from her mind to Luke's, then she was racing toward the exit. "Ben!"

". . . careful," Leia's image said.

The image grew motionless, obviously waiting for a reply.

"Tell the comm officer to acknowledge and ask for a repeat," Luke instructed R2.

". . . tell if . . . ," Leia said. ". . . again later."

The image winked out, leaving R2-D2 buzzing in frustration.

"It's okay, Artoo. We heard enough." Luke turned to find Formbi eyeing him with an expression halfway between smugness and concern. "I'm afraid we'll have to cut our tour short."

"Of course," Formbi replied. "It sounds as though you'll be quite busy . . . as will I."

"Is that so?" Luke used the Force to summon a pair of apprentices out of the Skorch game to escort Formbi and look after R2-D2. "Can the Jedi be of any assistance?"

"Not really," Formbi said. "Chief of State Omas was kind enough to send an escort to accompany me to his office on Coruscant."

"I see," Luke said. "I assume you'll be discussing the situation at Qoribu."

Formbi smiled and dipped his head in acknowledgment. "*Discussing* would be the wrong word, I'm afraid."

TWENTY-SEVEN

Leia had heard it said that no captor could imprison a Jedi longer than the Jedi wished to be imprisoned, and she was beginning to understand how true that was. Even with Alema lying unconscious in the number two hold, with all four limbs shackled to cargo tie-downs and two angry Noghri guarding her with T-10 stun blasters, Leia constantly found herself limping back with a new way to confine their prisoner. Her head and ankle were throbbing harder by the minute, and the last thing she wanted was to start fighting the Twi'lek again.

Now Leia was holding a pair of LSS 1000-series Automatic Stun Cuffs from the security locker—highly illegal, of course, but standard equipment aboard the *Falcon*. After checking the vital-signs monitor on Alema's wrist to make sure the Twi'lek was still unconscious, Leia limped around behind her head.

A sudden shudder ran down Alema's lekku. Her eyes started to move beneath their lids, and she began to mumble in a frightened, high-pitched voice. At first, Leia thought the Twi'lek was crying out incoherently in a dream, but then she recognized a couple of Twi'leki words—those for "night" and "herald"—and realized Alema was actually talking in her sleep.

Leia turned toward the intercom panel. "Threepio, activate audio recording in hold two."

"As you wish, Princess," he said. "But I will need to leave Master Sebatyne unattended for a few moments."

"As long as she's still stable," Leia said.

"Oh, she's quite stable," C-3PO said. "Her vital signs have been hovering close to zero for hours."

A moment later, a red light activated on the intercom panel. Alema continued to mutter in her native language—something about "the Night Herald"—and her limbs began to jerk against their restraints. Leia glanced at the vitals monitor and saw that the Twi'lek had slipped into the REM state. She motioned for the Noghri to cover her, then squatted on her haunches and clamped the stun cuffs on Alema's lekku.

"You're a hard woman, Leia Solo," Han said, stepping into the hold. "I kind of like it."

"Just being careful," Leia said. She set the power to maximum, then slowly rose and backed away. "I doubt we could trick her twice."

"Sure we could," Han said. "Teamwork and treachery will beat youth and skill every time."

"Alema isn't that young—and I'd say she beats us hands-down in the treachery department," Leia said. She crossed the hold—emptied so Alema would have nothing to fling with the Force—and stopped at Han's side. "I thought you and Juun were plotting the next jump."

"We've been trying," Han said.

"Trying?" After repairing Alema's sabotage, they had emerged from the nebula to find themselves staring into the creamy heart of the Galactic Core, no more than twenty light-years from the Galactic Alliance. "You said we'd be on the Rago Run in one more jump."

"We will," Han said. "But every time we engage, the navicomputer detects a mass fluctuation and shuts us down."

"You're sure we're in the right place?" Leia asked. Worried about the possibility of an escape, she had insisted on supervising the security precautions while Juun filled in as copilot. "Jae didn't plot a bad jump?"

Han shook his head. "It's definitely the same place we stopped on the way out. Rago is five light-years ahead, and the star charts match what we stored in the navicomputer. The only difference is the fluctuation."

Leia cast a nervous glance at Alema, who was continuing to mumble and thrash against her restraints, then asked, "Could it be something coming down the Run toward us?"

"Sure," Han said. "If it had the mass of a battle fleet."

"I see what you mean."

Leia studied Alema for another moment, then checked the Twi'lek's vital signs again. The monitor showed her deep in the REM state, but Leia remained suspicious. She withdrew a hypo of tranqarest from her jumpsuit pocket and pressed it to Alema's neck.

"Whoa!" Han said. "She has a head wound!"

"She's young." Leia hit the injector and held it down until the hypo stopped hissing. "A little coma won't hurt her."

"Remind me not to get on your bad side," Han said.

Alema stopped thrashing and fell silent, and her vital signs dropped into the coma range. Leia thumped the Twi'lek on the eyelid just to be sure, then nodded when there was no reaction.

"Let's go see if we're still having that mass fluctuation."

Han raised his brow. "You think *she* was—"

"I don't know," Leia said. Leaving instructions for the Noghri to blast the Twi'lek at the first sign of trouble, she left the hold. "But it never hurts to be careful."

"You don't think you're overdoing it?"

"Han, she sabotaged the *Falcon* and gave me a beating," Leia said. "And there's every chance my message didn't get through to Luke and Mara. If the *Shadow* had a stowaway aboard—or if Tahiri and the others are as far gone as Alema—we might be too late already."

"Okay, there's that," Han said. "But—"

"Han, you *do* understand how good Alema is?" Leia stopped and turned him to face her. "How lucky we were to knock her out?"

"Yeah, I understand." There was barb to Han's voice. "But we've still got to keep her alive."

"Even if it means she might escape and blow us all to stardust?"

"Yeah, even if it means that," Han said. "Because what happened to her is probably happening to Jaina and Zekk, and maybe Cilghal can learn something from Alema to help us fix it."

"*That's* why you're so worried about her?" Leia was glad to hear the ruthlessness in his voice, to know that so many decades of strife and danger had only made him shrewder and more stubborn. "I was starting to think you'd gone soft."

She took Han's arm and started up the access corridor. They had lost so much during the war that it was impossible to believe they had come out stronger or happier. But they *had* emerged together, with a better understanding of each other and a bond that had survived the deaths of a son, a close companion, and more friends than Leia could name. No matter how alarming this latest crisis, no matter how frightened they were for Jaina, they would face it together—and together they would do whatever was necessary to prevail.

They reached the flight deck and found Juun staring at the navigator's display, so engrossed in star plotting and continuum calculations that he did not notice the Solos' presence. Leia could see that he was attempting a broad-spectrum variable analysis with a ten-decimal accuracy parameter. With his eyes bulging and his cheek folds flared in frustration, it looked like he would blow a circuit before the navicomputer did.

Leia brought her mouth close to Han's ear. "I hope you've been backing up our navigation log."

"You bet," Han said. "I knew what you were thinking the minute we realized we were coming down on an abandoned planet."

"Really." Actually, Leia had been too busy trying to cold-fire the repulsor engines to be thinking much of anything, but she wasn't going to admit that to Han. She didn't want him thinking Juun was a better copilot than she was. "Pretty sure of yourself, aren't you?"

"Yep." Han flashed a cocky grin. "*And* I charted everything in sensor range on the way out." The grin grew larger and cockier. "There might be another dozen stars inside the nebula."

"A dozen?" Leia gasped. Then, not wanting Han to see just how well he really did know her, she assumed a more subdued tone. "So there might be another five or six habitable planets, plus a few moons, if we're lucky."

"Five or six? There'll be a dozen—even two!" The indignation in Han's voice faded quickly to concern. "But will anyone *want* to colonize there? It's still outside the Galactic Alliance, and it's not easy to reach."

"The Ithorians will go right away," Leia said. "The world we came down on is perfect for them. And—given how they feel about violence—it's about the only chance they have of getting around the Reclamation Act."

"As long as the rehab conglomerates don't steal it out from under us again."

"The Reclamation Act doesn't apply outside the Galactic Alliance," Leia said. "Besides, who's going to tell them?"

Han nodded quietly at the navigator's station, where Juun was mumbling to himself and shaking his head in frustration. Finally, he banged the side of his fist into his temple and whined something in Sullustan that Leia did not quite catch.

"We'll just have to keep him close," she whispered. "At least until we've relocated the Ithorians."

Han let his chin drop. "You really know how to spoil the moment." He stepped on the flight deck and, peering at the display over Juun's shoulder, asked, "So, what have—"

Juun jumped out of his seat, the top of his head avoiding Han's chin only by virtue of his short stature, then spun to face them.

"What are you doing, sneaking up like that?"

Han raised his hands. "Easy. I wasn't trying to give you a power surge."

"Actually, Jae, we've been standing here talking for a couple of minutes." Leia leaned down to look at the display. "It appears you've been hard at work."

Juun relaxed somewhat. "I've been running a full gravitational analysis, per emergency troubleshooting procedure."

"Come up with anything besides a headache?" Han asked.

"Nothing that makes sense." Juun returned to his seat and began to call up columns of stellar deflection observations. "Light is definitely being distorted at a steadily increasing rate, which means that either there's a very large, completely invisible rogue body dead ahead—"

"Or something big is about to come out of hyperspace," Leia finished. "Did you do a rate-of-change analysis?"

"Of course." Juun typed a command and brought up a graph plotting angle of deflection against time. "According to this, space-time should be separating just about—"

Leia's hair stood on end, then an iridescent flash lit the interior of the cockpit, and tiny snakes of static electric began to drag-race down her neural pathways. The proximity alarm blared to life. She hurled herself toward the copilot's seat, but lost her footing and hung in midair for a moment, her eyes aching with the brilliance of the silvery flash ahead, her stomach swirling inside her like water down a drain.

Then Leia stumbled into the copilot's chair and found herself staring out the viewport at an immense, cylinder-studded crevice of durasteel whiteness. Her stomach rose toward her throat as Han put the *Falcon* into an emergency climb, and her ribs began to throb from an impact she did not remember receiving.

"What is it?" Han yelled.

Leia activated her tactical display and found the top half rapidly filling with transponder codes. It took her a moment to find the *Falcon*'s own code, surrounded as it was by others of a similar color.

"I . . . I think it's a battle fleet," Leia reported.

"Whose?"

A jagged line of familiar white ellipsoids appeared along the bottom edge of the viewport. Interspersed among them were about twice as many thin white arrows.

"Hapan." Leia did not bother to confirm her conclusion with a code search. She had seen the distinctive ships too many times— at Dathomir, Corellia, and even Coruscant—to need corroboration. "Those are Novas and Battle Dragons."

"Yeah," Han agreed. "What are they doing out *here*?"

"Going to Lizil," Juun said. "What else?"

The comm channel crackled to life, and a voice with a thick Hapan accent said, "This is Hapes Battle Dragon *Kendall* hailing Galactic Alliance transport *Longshot*. Heave to and prepare for temporary impoundment."

"Impoundment!" Han maintained his course. "Better let them know who we really are."

Leia was already reaching for the transponder controls.

"*Longshot,* this is your last warning—"

"Battle Dragon *Kendall.*" Leia activated the *Falcon*'s true transponder code. "This is Leia Organa Solo aboard the *Millennium Falcon.*"

The Hapan voice grew more uncertain. *"Millennium Falcon?"*

"Yes," Leia said. "Sorry for the confusion, but we usually travel incognito. I'm sure you understand."

"Of course," the voice said.

"Good. If you'll assign us a safe vector, we'll move through and let you be on your way."

"I'm sorry, Princess. We have orders—"

"Then I suggest you let me speak to whoever issued them," Leia said. "Queen Mother Tenel Ka has been a frequent guest at my dinner table. I'm sure she would be unhappy to learn we were detained as a matter of . . . procedure."

A new voice came over the comm channel. "Princess Leia Organa Solo?" he asked. "The mother of Jedi Jacen *Solo?*"

"That's correct." Disturbed by the way the man had emphasized Jacen's last name, Leia reached out in the Force and was relieved to feel no sense that her son was anywhere in the fleet. "To whom do I have the honor of speaking?"

"Forgive me," the man replied. "I am Dukat Aleson Gray, ninth cousin to the Queen Mother and Duch'da to Lady AlGray of the Relephon Moons."

"Thank you," Leia said. "I'll remember you to the Queen Mother the next time we meet."

"You're very kind." Gray's tone was polite but doubtful. "I'm certain we can trust you to hold our encounter here in the strictest confidence."

"Of course," Leia replied. "We wouldn't want to jeopardize the Colony's reinforcements."

The comm fell silent.

"Blast, you didn't have to say *that,*" Han groaned. "We know where they're going."

"But not *why,*" Leia said. "If a war is breaking out, we need to know."

"Why?" Han asked. "We won't be able to tell anyone if we're stuck in the belly of a Battle Dragon."

Gray's voice came over the comm again. "Actually, our mission is closer to peacekeeping than reinforcing."

Leia shot Han a smug grin, then said, "Yes, that's what I was given to understand. Do you need navigation data to the Colony gateway?"

"That won't be necessary," Gray responded. "We have a course to the Lizil nest, and your son assured us that someone would be waiting—"

"Our *son*?" Leia interrupted.

"Yes." Gray sounded confused. "The Queen Mother's new consort. He was the one who, uh, *convinced* her to intervene."

A loud smack sounded from the pilot's seat. Leia glanced over to find Han holding his palm to his brow.

"You think you know him," Han said, shaking his head. "And then he tries to start a war."

TWENTY-EIGHT

The door slid aside, revealing the clean-lined interior of the Skywalkers' uncluttered Ossan cottage. Mara had grown so accustomed to the vague uneasiness she had been feeling in the Force that the sensation barely registered as she crossed the foyer. But this time she paid special attention, closing her eyes and letting her feet carry her toward where it seemed strongest.

"Mom!"

Mara opened her eyes and found Ben standing before her, on the other side of low table that was the living room's only furniture. The sliding wall panels that partitioned the house into rooms were all closed, so it was difficult to tell where he had come from. He pointed at her feet.

"Your shoes!"

Mara glanced down and saw she had neglected to leave her dusty boots in the foyer, as was the custom on Ossus.

"Never mind my shoes." She started around the table toward Ben. "Did you bring a pet back from Jwlio?"

Ben's eyes grew round. "A pet?"

"A Killik," Mara said. The uneasy feeling was as strong as ever, but she could not pinpoint a location. It seemed to be coming from Ben and from all around her. "Is that what you've been doing with all that gelmeat and nerfspread?"

"Aren't Killiks smart?" Ben asked.

"Smarter than I thought. Why?"

" 'Cause then she'd be a friend, not a pet."

Mara cocked an eyebrow. "*She,* Ben?"

Ben's mouth fell open, and he backed toward the kitchen. "I, uh . . . they're all—"

"Stay here." Mara started around the table. "Don't even *think* of moving."

"But, Mom—"

"Don't argue," she ordered. "Your father will talk to you later."

Mara stretched her awareness into the kitchen and sensed only Nanna inside, but that did not stop her from pulling her lightsaber.

"Mom, don't—"

"Quiet!"

Mara used the Force to slide a wall panel aside and found Nanna down on her knee joints, quietly brushing morsels of gelmeat onto a sheet of flimsiplast. The rest of the room appeared deserted.

"Nanna?"

The droid looked up, but was so flustered she continued to brush morsels, missing the flimsiplast and spreading them across the floor.

"Yes, Mistress Skywalker?"

Mara's eyes went to the three gelmeat containers lying empty on the preparation island.

"Don't worry," Nanna said. "Ben didn't eat all that."

"I hope not," Mara said. "That would be a good way to earn a memory wipe."

There was too much YVH droid in Nanna to be intimidated. "That won't be necessary. My nutritional programming is very up to date."

Mara pointed the handle of her lightsaber at the wrappers. "Then who ate that?"

The droid peered up at her. "I'm sorry. I can't say."

"Then how can you be sure it wasn't Ben?"

"I'm afraid you're misunderstanding," Nanna replied. "I know who ate the gelmeat. I'm the one who opened the food locker. I just can't tell you."

"*What?*" Mara used the Force to jerk the droid off her knees. "Explain yourself."

"It's a *secret*," Ben said from the edge of the kitchen. "You promised, Nanna."

"You can't have secrets from me," Mara said, holding the droid in the air. "I'm his mother."

"Under normal circumstances, of course not," Nanna agreed. "But where there is a danger to the child, my programming—"

"Danger to the child?" Mara demanded. "*What* danger?"

Nanna lowered her feet to the floor. "Ben said you would kill him if you found out what he was doing," the droid explained. "And I must say, considering how angry you are now, his fear certainly seems warranted."

"Ben?" When he failed to answer, Mara glanced back and found an empty doorway. She turned to go. "Ben! I said—"

Nanna started after her. "I'm sorry, Master Skywalker, but until you calm down I really must—"

Mara whirled on the droid. "Stand down, Beautiful Blaster."

The override code stopped the droid midstride, darkening her photoreceptors and dropping her chin to her chest.

"I'll handle this myself."

Mara continued into the living room and went straight to Ben's room, where he was busy pushing the closet panel closed.

"Ben, come away from there . . . now!"

Ben pressed his back to the closet. "It's not what you—"

Mara reached out with the Force and pulled him to her side, then grabbed his wrist and—keeping one eye on the closet door—knelt at his side.

"Ben, we just received a holo from Aunt Leia," she said. "She was worried that a Killik assassin might have stowed away aboard the *Shadow*. So if all that gelmeat you've been taking is for—"

"Gorog's no assassin!" Ben said. "She's my best friend."

"She's an insect, Ben."

"So? *Your* best friend's a lizard."

"Don't be ridiculous." Mara rose and pushed him behind her. "Aunt Leia is my best friend."

"Doesn't count," Ben said. "She's family. Saba is a lizard."

"Okay, maybe my best friend's a lizard."

Mara was both repulsed and terrified at the thought of her son developing a relationship with a Killik—especially given what Cilghal was learning about the Joiner bonding mechanism. But she was also beginning to worry about the psychological damage Ben might suffer if she slew his "friend" in front of him.

"If Gorog's your friend, tell her to come out nice and slow. We'll talk this—"

The muffled groan of a sliding wall panel sounded from two rooms over. Holding her lightsaber at the ready, Mara used the Force to open Ben's closet—and nearly ignited her blade when an empty exoskeleton tumbled into the room. It was about a meter high, with thick blue-black chitin and barbed mandibles half the length of Mara's arms.

"Ben!"

"I told you it wasn't what you thought."

"Stay here!"

Using the Force to slide the wall panels aside in front of her, Mara rushed two rooms over and found six black limbs—two legs and four arms—sticking out from under the low table that Luke used for a writing desk. The mandibles were protruding from one end, and the whole piece of furniture was trembling as though there were a groundquake.

Ben rushed up beside Mara.

"I told you to stay in your room," Mara said.

"I can't," Ben said. "Gorog's scared."

"Okay. Tell her to come out. Everything will be all right."

A low rumble reverberated from under the table.

"She doesn't trust you," Ben reported.

Mara actually looked away from the bug. "You speak Killik?"

"I don't speak it. I just understand it." Gorog drummed again, and he added, "She says you're a killer."

Coming from her son, the words felt like a vibroblade to the heart. "We talked about that, Ben. Sometimes I have to kill. Many Jedi Masters do."

Gorog rumbled something else, and it seemed to Mara that there was something sharp in the insect's rhythm, something spiteful and malevolent.

"Mom, what's cold blood?" Ben asked.

"Is that what she's saying?" Mara squatted down so she could look Gorog in the eye. Instead, she found herself staring at a dark sheaf of mandibles and mouthparts. "It means you kill when you don't have to. I don't do that."

The Killik slowly moved away, carrying the table along on her back and drumming incessantly.

"She says you killed lots of people when you didn't have to, for Palpytine," Ben said. "Mom, who's Palpytine?"

"Palpatine," Mara corrected automatically. She felt as though the Emperor were reaching across time to her yet again, as though to prove how foolish she had been to believe she could ever truly escape him. "A bad man I used to know. How does Gorog know his name?"

A stream of brown saliva shot out from under the table. Mara's reflexes were too quick for it to come near her face, but in the quarter second it took her to draw away, the insect came flying at her with the table still on its back. She activated her lightsaber instinctively—and heard Ben crying out over the crackle of the igniting blade.

"Don't!" Ben cried. "Please!"

Mara deactivated the blade in a pang of motherly concern and whirled into a spinning back kick instead, her foot landing high because she had to lift her leg above Ben's head. Instead of launching the Killik across the room, the attack simply knocked off the table and drove the insect to the floor.

A soft sizzle sounded from the wall beside Mara, and a sour, acrid smell filled her nostrils. She put down a hand to push Ben back, and Gorog slammed a mandible into her ankles, sweeping her from her feet.

Mara hit the floor flat on her back. The Killik stabbed a pair of sharp pincer-hands down on her shoulders and brought her head around, a hypo-shaped proboscis pushing out between the mandibles, venom dripping from its tip. Mara smashed her lightsaber handle into the tube, folding it over and drawing a boom of pain from the Killik's chest cavity.

"Mom!" Ben cried.

"Go to your room!" Mara hooked her elbow around the arm on her shoulder and pulled, dropping Gorog to an elbow. "Now!"

The Killik reached for Mara's neck with its *other* two hands.

Mara drove her free hand up under the insect's jaw, then bridged on her shoulders and flipped it onto its back. She sprang instantly to her feet—and the Killik flexed a wing and flipped instantly to its feet.

Ben remained in the doorway, on the opposite side of the Killik from Mara.

"Ben, I'm very disappointed in you." Mara's shoulders were throbbing where the pincers had pierced them, and blood was running down the front of her jumpsuit. She could sense that Luke was only a couple of minutes behind her, but a lot could happen in two minutes—too much to be sure that she would not have to kill Ben's friend. "You need to start obeying me and go find your father."

"But you said to go to my—"

"Ben!" Mara brought her lightsaber up and started to circle toward him. "Just do as I say. You're in enough trouble already."

Ben's face grew pale, and the Killik began to pivot with Mara, keeping itself between her and her son. She thought for a moment the Killik meant to use Ben as a hostage, but it was careful to stay away from him—as though it, too, were worried he might be accidentally injured.

"Ben, I think Gorog wants you to leave, too."

Ben glanced at the Killik, then asked Mara, "Are you going to kill her?"

"Ben, *I'm* the one who's bleeding here."

"But you're a Jedi Master," Ben said. "It doesn't matter if a Jedi Master bleeds."

"You've been watching too many action holos," Mara said. Nevertheless, she hung her lightsaber on her belt. "But, okay, I promise—*if* you leave right now."

Gorog rumbled something that caused Ben to scowl.

"Maybe you should just be nice," he said to the Killik. "Then maybe Mom would let you stay."

Gorog thrummed, and Mara began to wish C-3PO were here to translate.

"She doesn't *always* lie," Ben protested. "Not even most—"

Gorog raised two hands and shooed him toward the door.

Ben sighed and left the room.

Mara waited until she heard the front door slide open, then said, "Thank you for that."

The Killik spread its mandibles and sprang. Mara caught it in the Force and slammed it into a support post. There was a sharp crackle, and when the insect dropped to the floor, one of its wings jutted out at an angle.

"I don't understand why you want to fight," Mara said. "Because you have *no* chance of winning—"

Gorog jumped across the room, mandibles snapping at head height. Mara rushed to meet the attack, then dropped into a slide, catching both ankles as she passed beneath the insect, spinning to her belly, twisting its legs around and slamming the Killik down on its back.

The insect flexed its good wing and landed back on its feet, but Mara was already driving an elbow into a tubular knee. The leg snapped with a sickening crackle, and the Killik dropped to the floor.

Mara grabbed the Killik's good leg and stood, jerking it up more or less upside down, then snake-locked her leg over the insect's and shoved against the joint.

"All right, that's enough," she said. "I promised Ben I wouldn't kill you—but I didn't say anything about hurting."

The Killik clacked its mandibles wildly, then released an acrid, foul-smelling vapor that filled Mara's eyes with cloudy tears and turned her stomach queasy and rebellious. She snapped the joint and attempted to launch herself out of danger with a departing thrust-kick, but the insect was already rolling into Mara's leg.

She landed facedown, her kicking leg trapped beneath the Killik. Four pincer-hands grabbed hold of her calf and began to pull, dragging her foot toward the clacking mandibles. Mara's own hand drifted toward her lightsaber, but she stopped short of pulling it free. This bug was not going to make a liar and a killer of her in her son's eyes. She reached forward, clawing at the wooden floor, trying to pull free, and only slipped farther beneath the insect.

Then Mara saw the table, lying on its side where it had fallen when Gorog attacked. She reached out with a mental hand, turned it end-on, and brought it sailing into the Killik's head.

The table connected with a spectacular *pop,* and Gorog's grasp loosened. Mara scrambled free and Force-sprang to her feet, then spun around to find the Killik collapsed on its belly, all six limbs trembling and shaking in convulsions. She rushed to its side and pulled the table away, revealing a ten-centimeter dent in the head where the edge had cracked the chitin.

"Stang!"

Mara pulled the comlink from her pocket and started to call for medical assistance—then noticed the Killik slowly drawing its trembling arms in toward its body, gathering itself to spring.

Mara slipped forward and brought her heel down on the dented chitin. "I said that was enough!"

Gorog collapsed again, unable to do anything but lie on the floor and tremble. Then Mara felt Luke urgently reaching out to her, warning her to be careful, urging her not to kill it.

Mara eyed the insect with spite in her heart. "What is it with you?"

A few seconds later, Luke came rushing in the door with half a dozen senior apprentices at his back.

"Mara, are you—"

"I'm fine, Skywalker." She took the hand he offered and glared down at the trembling insect. "But I'm getting awfully tired of people telling me not to squash that bug."

"Sorry about that, but the comm center just finished reconstructing some of Leia's message." Luke motioned the apprentices to secure the Killik, then added, "She says it could explode."

TWENTY-NINE

Reclining in long diagnostics chairs with their heads hidden beneath scanning helmets and their bodies swaddled in sensor feeds, the subjects of the experiment—Tahiri and the other Joiner Jedi Knights—reminded Luke of captives in an Imperial interrogation facility. It did not help that the Killik and Alema Rar, who had arrived aboard the *Falcon* just hours before, were heavily sedated and strapped in place with nylasteel bands. Even the isolation chambers in which the subjects were located— dark, gas-tight compartments with transparisteel doors—looked like detention-center cells.

"I'm sorry it's so dim in here, Master Skywalker," Cilghal said. She was standing behind a semicircular control station in a white laboratory smock, studying a data-holo comparing the brain activity of her subjects. "But it's better to have as little background stimulation as possible. It helps isolate their responses."

"I understand." Luke did not bother denying his revulsion. Cilghal could certainly sense his feelings through the Force, just as Luke could sense the excitement that had caused her to comm him in the first place. "And it's more than the darkness. The whole lab raises unpleasant associations."

"Yes, it does have a certain Imperial utilitarianism," Cilghal said. "I wish there had been time to design something less dismal, but this configuration was the quickest to assemble."

"Speed is important," Luke assured her. "It will only take Han a few days to repair the damage to the *Falcon,* and I'd like to have this thing figured out before he and Leia start back to the Qoribu system."

Cilghal studied him out of one bulbous eye. "You can't convince them to wait until we learn more?"

"Not with Jaina still there, not after what happened to Saba."

"Saba will recover, and Jaina . . ." Cilghal turned up the palms of her fin-like hands. "If Jaina would not return before, what makes them think she will listen to them *now*?"

"I don't know," Luke said. "But they're convinced we need to return to Qoribu as soon as possible . . . and I think I agree with them."

Luke had heard reports of Jacen's visit to Tenel Ka and rumors of unexplained Hapan fleet maneuvers, and Leia had told him flatly that the balance of power at Qoribu was about to shift. He and the other Masters were still debating if that was a good thing or bad, but events were clearly moving faster than the order's ability to deal with them. Whether the Jedi understood the Killiks or not, they had to take action soon.

After considering Luke's words for a moment, Cilghal said, "Then I should just tell you what I need and not waste time reporting failures."

Luke frowned at the hesitation . . . shame . . . he felt from the Mon Calamari. "If you think that's best," he said cautiously.

Cilghal turned to her assistants—a trio of apprentice healers—and sent them out of the room.

"That bad?" Luke asked.

"Yes." She pointed at the chambers holding Alema and Gorog. "I need to hurt them."

"*Hurt* them?"

"Inflict pain," she clarified. "Torture them, in truth. Not for long, and nothing that will injure. But it must be intense. It's the only way to test a critical hypothesis."

"I see."

Luke swallowed and forced himself to look through the transparisteel doors at the two prisoners. There was a time when he would not even have considered such a request—and when Cilghal would never have made it. But now that the Jedi had elected to embrace *all* of the Force, to utilize the dark side as well as the light, nothing seemed off limits. They deceived, they manipulated, they coerced. To be sure, it was all done in the name of a higher purpose, to promote peace and serve the Balance, yet he occasionally felt that the Jedi were losing their way; that the war with the Yuuzhan Vong had turned them from their true path. He sometimes thought this must have been how Palpatine started, pursuing a worthy goal with any means available.

"Perhaps we should back up a little," Luke said. "Have you made any progress at all?"

"Of a sort." Cilghal pointed to her data-holo, which was basically a flat grid plotting each subject's name against various brain regions, with colored data bars above each square. As the level of activity changed, the bars rose and fell, changing colors and glowing more or less brightly. "As you can see, all of our subjects display similar levels of activity in their sensory cortices, which suggests they're experiencing the same physical sensations."

"And they shouldn't be?"

The corners of Cilghal's lips rose in a broad-mouthed grin. "Not really. The environment in each chamber is different—hot, cold, rank, fragrant, noisy, quiet."

Luke raised his brow. "Doesn't that confirm your theory about the corpus callosum receiving impulses from other brains?"

"It does." Cilghal pointed at four red bars near the end of Alema's and Gorog's data rows. "But look at this. The hypothalamus and limbic system are the center of the emotions. Alema's is correlating to Gorog's."

Luke noticed that this was true only of Alema and Gorog. The hypothalami and limbic systems of Tesar, Tekli, and Tahiri remained independent. Jacen's readings were, as usual, completely useless. He was playing with the brain scanner again, moving his color bars up and down in a rhythmic wave pattern. It was, Luke knew, a not-so-subtle form of protest; his nephew believed that the Jedi order should have more faith in its Jedi Knights than in Cilghal's instruments. Under normal circumstances, Luke would have agreed—but circumstances were not normal.

"Alema and Gorog are in a meld?" Luke asked.

Cilghal shook her head. "No. They're not *perceiving* each other's emotions, as Jedi do in a meld. Alema and Gorog are *sharing* emotions, the same way Tesar and the others are sharing sensations. This takes the collective mind a step deeper than we have seen before."

Thinking of the Will that Formbi had described, Luke reached out to Gorog in the Force and felt only the vague sense of uneasiness that—after the battle in the Skywalkers' cottage—he had come to associate with the blue Killiks that had been attacking them. But the data bars matched to Gorog's hypothalamic and limbic systems brightened to orange and started rising. So did Alema's.

"Interesting," Luke said. "This Killik is Force-sensitive."

"After a fashion," Cilghal said. "I believe she and other Gorog can use the Force to hide their presence—not only from us, but from other Killiks as well. What I need to find out is whether they can also use the Force to pass neural impulses to other members of the Colony—even those outside their own nest."

"And that's why you need to inflict the pain?" Luke asked.

Cilghal nodded. "I'll neutralize the numbing agent, but leave Gorog and Alema unable to move. If the pain is severe enough, Gorog will be motivated to reach out to the others, and we'll see the results on their graphs."

"And this will tell us . . . ?"

"Whether Gorog is also able to influence the others," Cilghal said. "We need to know that before we can begin thinking about countermeasures."

Luke's heart sank at the word *begin*. If Cilghal had not yet started to think about countermeasures, it seemed unlikely she would have any ready before the *Falcon* was repaired. And if Luke asked her to find some other way to test her hypothesis, unlikely became almost impossible.

Feeling just a little more lost inside, Luke nodded. "If there's no other way . . ."

"There isn't." Cilghal's sad eyes grew even sadder. "Not in the time we have."

She activated the electromagnetic shielding between the

cells, and all the sensory cortex readings returned to independent levels. Alema's hypothalamic and limbic systems remained the same color and brightness as Gorog's, however.

Cilghal entered another command. A hypo dropped down from the ceiling panel and injected the neutralizing agent into a soft spot just below the Killik's mouthparts. A few seconds later, the insect's cortex activity began to fluctuate as its physical sensations returned. The hypo ascended back into the ceiling, and a flat-tipped probe took its place. Gorog's hypothalamic bar turned brilliant white, shooting to the top of the data-holo and staying there. So did Alema's.

"Gorog is angry with us," Cilghal observed.

"I don't blame her," Luke said.

He wanted to look away, but forced himself not to. If he was willing to sanction torture, then he had to make certain it never became easy.

Cilghal brought the probe down to where one of Gorog's upper arms joined the thorax, then sent an electrical charge through it. All six limbs—even the two casted legs—extended straight out and began to quiver. All of the insect's data bars brightened to white and rose to the top of the holo. Alema's limbic system continued to mirror the Killik's, but her sensory cortices remained quiet.

When the other subjects did not show a similar rise in the activity of their hypothalamic or limbic systems, Luke asked, "Is that enough?"

"Not yet. She must believe it will never end."

The Killik's mandibles clacked close, and its antennae began to whip madly back and forth. Luke reminded himself that this was the insect that had tried to turn his son against his wife, but that did not make torture feel right. Mara was spending every waking minute with Ben, trying to make him understand how the things that Gorog had said could be true and still not mean she was an evil person, and Luke knew that even *she* would not have approved of the insect's suffering.

Mara reached out to him in the Force, worried about Ben and curious about what was happening to Gorog.

Luke's stomach grew hollow with fear. Ben and Gorog were

clearly joined—perhaps not as completely as Alema, but too much. A part of Luke wanted to kill the Killik right now, to punish it for trying to use his son against him, to sever the connection before it grew any stronger.

But a bigger part of Luke wanted to protect Ben, to spare him the anguish of knowing that his friend was in pain. He started to tell Cilghal to turn off the probe—then Tesar's hypothalamic bar began to rise. Tahiri's limbic system also began to show more activity, and Tekli exhibited steep rises in both.

A moment later, the trio's data bars vanished as they pushed off their scanning helmets and began to peel electrodes off their bodies. Unlike Alema and Gorog, they were not restrained.

"Okay, turn it off," Luke said. He could feel Mara growing more concerned about Ben. "There's no sense—"

Cilghal held up a hand. "Wait."

Gorog continued to clench her limbs to her chest and whip her antennae. Tekli, who as a healer was a little faster at extricating herself from the equipment, emerged from her chamber first.

"I'm sorry," she said, marching straight for the exit. "I need to use the refresher."

"Of course." Cilghal swiveled a dark eye in Luke's direction, and he felt her interest growing. "Take your time."

Tahiri emerged next. "You need to give us a break sometimes," she complained, walking over to the console. "I'm beginning to feel like I'm on a weeklong X-wing jump."

Tahiri's gaze drifted to the data-holo and lingered for a moment on Gorog's bars. Then she turned to Luke with her mouth twisted into a brutal grin.

"Looks like I'm not the only one who came out of the war part Yuuzhan Vong," she said. "What's next? Jedi tattoos?"

The comment stung Luke more than it should have—in large part because he could feel his wife growing more worried and angry as the experiment continued.

"This isn't for fun," Luke said. "We're—"

"Tahiri, are you feeling any pain?" Cilghal interrupted. "Is that why you came out here?"

Tahiri looked at the Mon Calamari as though she were a

dimwit. "Cilghal, I'm half Yuuzhan Vong inside. The only thing pain would cause me is a religious experience."

"You're sure?" Cilghal asked. "You don't feel any at all?"

"This one feelz no pain, either, but that does not excuse what you are doing." Tesar emerged from his compartment trailing a dozen broken sensor wires. "This one is through with your gamez. He will not be party to a breaking."

He tore a handful of electrodes off his chest, threw them on the floor, and started toward the exit.

Tahiri watched him go, then looked back to Luke with the hardness of a Yuuzhan Vong in her green eyes. "Tesar and I must not be completely joined," she said. "*I'd* kind of like to stay."

"I think we're through," Luke said, wondering if the revulsion he felt was for the Yuuzhan Vong in Tahiri's personality, or for himself. "Isn't that right, Cilghal?"

"Yes, I have seen everything I need to."

She cut the power to the probe. Gorog's data bars returned to normal, and Mara gushed relief through the Force.

"We're through for today," Cilghal said to Tahiri. "Thank you."

As Luke watched the young Jedi Knight leave, he began to feel increasingly disappointed. He had no doubts now that Tesar and the others were completely under Raynar's control; that they had agreed to return to the Galactic Alliance only so they could sneak away from the academy—as they had all done at one time or another—and seek support for the Colony.

After the door had hissed shut, Luke shook his head and dropped onto a bench in front of the control panel. "I guess that tells us what we needed to know," he said. "They're all under control of the Colony's Will."

"Of a Will," Cilghal corrected. "Not *the* Will, as the Chiss believe."

Luke looked up. "You've already lost me."

Cilghal came out from behind the control console. "Like the Force itself, every mind in the galaxy has two aspects." She sat next to Luke on the bench. "There is the conscious mind, which embraces what we know of ourselves, and there is the unconscious, which contains the part that remains hidden."

Luke began to see where Cilghal was headed. "You're saying that since the war, the Colony has developed *two* Wills, one conscious and one subconscious."

"Not subconscious—*unconscious*," Cilghal corrected. "The subconscious is a level of the mind between full awareness and unawareness. We're talking about the *unconscious;* it remains fully hidden from the part of our mind that we know."

"Sorry," Luke said. "It's complicated."

"Just like every mind in the galaxy," Cilghal said. "This is an analogy, but it fits—and our experiment demonstrates just how closely. Alema and Gorog are controlled by the unconscious Will—the correlation of their emotional centers makes that clear."

"And Tekli, Tesar, and Tahiri are controlled by the Colony's conscious Will?" Luke asked.

"*Influenced* by," Cilghal said. "They have not fallen under the Colony's complete control. They still think of themselves as individuals."

"Then why did they end the experiment?"

"How often do *you* do something without truly understanding why?" Cilghal countered. "In every mind, the unconscious has a great deal of power—some psychologists even think it's absolute. So when Gorog was in pain, the Colony's unconscious Will influenced its conscious Will to end the experiment. Suddenly, Tekli had to use the refresher, Tahiri had to stretch—"

"And Tesar became angry with us."

"Exactly," Cilghal said. "Of the three, he was the only one who had even a vague understanding of his motivations. Barabels are usually in touch with their unconscious."

Luke thought of the mysterious attacks on him and Mara, and of the Killiks' absurd insistence that they had not occurred. "And the conscious Will wouldn't be aware of the unconscious Will, would it?"

"It *is* the nature of the unconscious mind to remain hidden," Cilghal said. "That is why the Gorog are so hard to sense in the Force. They use it to hide—not only from us, but from the rest of the Colony as well."

"Gorog is part of a secret nest," Luke said, making sure he

understood what Cilghal was telling him. "The Colony wouldn't be aware of it—"

"And might well fool itself into believing it doesn't exist," Cilghal said. "We've more or less proved that, and it explains the Killiks' reaction to the attacks on you."

"It all makes sense, except for one thing—why does the secret nest keep attacking us?" Luke asked. "Raynar seemed to *want* our help."

"But Lomi and Welk are threatened by you." It was Jacen who asked this, his voice coming from the data-holo. "And *they're* the ones who control the Gorog nest."

"You know that for certain?" Luke turned toward the data-holo and, finding himself being addressed by a row of colored bars, frowned in irritation. "And I thought I told you to stop playing with Cilghal's brain scanner. Come out here, if you're going to be part of this conversation."

"I know that Raynar dragged Lomi and Welk out of the burning *Flier*." Jacen pushed the scanner helmet up and, now projecting his voice into the air in front of Luke, began to remove the electrodes attached to his body. "And *we* know that Saba was attacked by a disfigured Jedi Knight—almost certainly Welk. I'm willing to take a leap of faith and guess that Lomi survived, too."

"Yeah," Luke said. "I guess I am, too."

"Then only one question remains," Cilghal said. "Why did Alema join the Gorog, while the rest of you—"

"*Them,*" Jacen corrected. "In case you haven't noticed, *my* mind remains entirely my own."

"Very well," Cilghal said. "Why did Alema join the Gorog, while everyone else joined the Taat?"

Luke knew the answer to that, and he wished he didn't.

"Because of Numa." He was remembering the time he had stood outside Alema's bacta tank, awash in the guilt the Twi'lek felt for allowing the voxyn to take her sister. "When Numa was killed, Alema turned a lot of her anger inward—and anger has always been fertile ground for the likes of Lomi Plo."

"You saw this coming, didn't you?" Jacen asked. He stepped

out of the isolation chamber, pulling his tunic over his head. "Even before the mission to Myrkr, I mean."

Luke turned to look at the unconscious Twi'lek, held prisoner by nylasteel and tranqarest. "Not this—not Gorog," he said. "But I knew Alema would fall."

THIRTY

"Elders, welcome," Leia said, bowing.

She stepped away from the door and waved her Ithorian guests into the Rhysode Room. With a costly roo-wood serenity table surrounded by extravagant flowfit armchairs, the chamber was a conspicuous departure from the sparse décor of the rest of the Jedi academy. Being the designated receiving area of an institute that cordially discouraged visitors, it was also one of the least used rooms in the facility—and one that reflected the sensibilities of its Reconstruction Authority builders far more than it did those of the order itself.

"I hope you'll forgive the room," Leia said as the Ithorians filed into the foyer. "It's the best I could do under the circumstances."

Ooamu Waoabi—the eldest of the Ithorian elders—politely swung his ocular nodes around the room, his small eyes blinking gently as they observed the automated beverage dispensers, the state-of-the-art holotheater, the transparisteel viewing wall that overlooked the academy's training grounds and low-slung instruction halls.

"Your presence would make any room pleasant, Princess Leia." Waoabi spoke out of only one of the mouths on his throat, a reflection of the poor medical care aboard the Ithorian refugee cities. "But we thank you for your concern."

"And thank you for coming to Ossus." Leia could barely contain the excitement she felt—nor her fear that the Ithorians might balk at settling outside the Galactic Alliance. "I know it was an unexpected journey. But Han and I must return to the

Unknown Regions as soon as the *Falcon* is ready, and there is something I wanted to discuss . . ."

Leia let her sentence trail off as a pair of black-clad Galactic Alliance bodyguards stepped into the foyer behind the Ithorians. The two women were not armed—only Jedi were permitted to carry weapons on Ossus—but their sinewy builds and supple grace suggested they did not need to be. Leia's hand dropped to her lightsaber, and she slipped between Waoabi and another Ithorian elder to confront the newcomers.

"May I help you?" she said.

"Yes." The first woman's cobalt eyes darted past Leia, scanning all corners of the chamber. "You can clear the room."

As the first woman spoke, the second was slipping past behind her, waving the feathery antennae of a threat scanner at various pieces of furniture and artwork. Leia glanced toward Han, but he was already placing himself squarely in the bodyguard's path, studying the scanner with feigned interest.

"Is that one of those new Tendrando Arms multisniffers Lando was telling me about?" Han pushed his head between the delicate antennae, pretending he wanted to see the data display—and ruining the instrument's calibration. "I've heard they can smell a gram of thermaboom at fifty meters."

Leia waited until the first bodyguard finally stopped looking past her, then said, "I'll be happy to clear the room when our meeting is finished. Until then, feel free to wait in the reception—"

"We have no time to wait." Cal Omas entered the room wearing a rumpled travel tunic as red as the veins in his bloodshot eyes. "This matter has taken too much of my time already."

"Chief Omas!" Leia's diplomatic skills must have been degenerating from disuse, for she could not quite conceal her shock. "What a surprise to see you here."

"I imagine." Omas started for the beverage station, walking straight past the Ithorian delegation and failing to acknowledge them. "Where's Luke?"

"I really don't know." Leia began to fume at the way he had slighted her guests. "Chief Omas, allow me to present Ooamu Waoabi and the Council of Ithorian Elders. We were about to begin a meeting—a meeting for which they have traveled a long distance on short notice."

Taking the hint, Omas set aside the glass of bwago juice he had been filling and returned to the Ithorians. "Elder Waoabi, a pleasure to see you again."

He bowed formally to Waoabi, then greeted each of the other elders by name, stumbling only when he came to the young Jedi liaison, Ezam Nhor. For a moment, Leia was impressed enough to recall why she had helped elect Cal Omas to the Chief's office in the first place.

Then Omas returned to the beverage station. "Forgive me for pushing in like this." He retrieved his bwago juice and took a sip. "But I've asked the senior Jedi to meet me here to discuss a matter of vital importance."

"And I'm afraid you're going to be disappointed," Luke said. He entered the room with Mara and, pausing to bow to the Ithorians, approached the Chief of State. "Most senior Jedi aren't available. Perhaps if there had been more notice . . ."

"If you hadn't been hiding here on Ossus, perhaps I would have been able to provide it." Omas gave Luke an icy glare. "As it is, *you* will have to do. Aristocra Formbi is demanding to know why the Galactic Alliance has sent a battle fleet to the Colony."

"Have we?" Luke's gaze remained fixed on Omas, but Leia felt his mind reaching in her direction, wondering what this had to do with her vague warning about the shift of power in the Colony. "I wasn't aware of that."

"Neither was I," Omas fumed. "Yet a Hapan battle fleet was seen at someplace called the Lizil nest."

"In the Colony?" Corran Horn asked, stepping into the room. "What's it doing there?"

"I was hoping someone *here* could explain." Omas's gaze swung to Leia. "Perhaps *you*?"

"I'm afraid not." Leia had been half expecting this. In the convoluted politics of the Hapan Royal Navy, there was sure to be some ambitious spy who saw an advantage in reporting the fleet's encounter with the *Falcon* to Galactic Alliance Intelligence. "They were in no mood to answer questions."

"*Who* was in no mood to answer questions?" Kyp asked, joining the group. He nodded to the Ithorians, from him the equivalent of a full diplomatic salutation, then ignored Omas and came to stand with Leia and Han. "The Hapans?"

"Yeah," Han said. "They wanted to intern us."

"*Intern* you?" Omas knitted his brow. "You *encountered* this fleet?"

Leia began to have a sinking feeling. "You didn't know?"

"No." Omas's voice was icy.

"I apologize," Leia said. "We gave our word not to reveal their presence."

"And you *kept* it?" Omas demanded.

"Some of us still honor our promises," Han said. "I know it's old-fashioned, but there you have it."

"The Galactic Alliance can't afford your promises right now," Omas retorted. "I only hope they haven't started a war."

"Leia had no choice," Luke said. "The word of one Jedi to another is binding."

Omas let his chin drop. "*Don't* tell me there were Jedi aboard those ships!"

"It was Tenel Ka's fleet, and *she* is a Jedi," Mara said. "Leia's word is as binding to Tenel Ka's agent as it would be to the queen herself."

The assertion was a stretch, since being honest with other Jedi was more of an unwritten policy than a formal code. And the concept of extending it to a Jedi's representatives was a new innovation entirely, but Leia appreciated the support. She started toward the conference area, initiating a subtle migration that she hoped would result in a shift of mood as well as location. Once she arrived, she turned and watched in silent amusement as Omas instinctively searched for the head seat at a round table. Now would have been a good time to ask the Ithorians to wait in the reception area, but she was not about to sanction the rude way Omas had burst into the chamber. If he did not want to discuss this in front of the Ithorians, *he* could be the one who asked them to leave.

"If you didn't know about our encounter with the fleet, Chief

Omas, why did you think Han and I could tell you what it was doing in the Colony?" Leia asked.

"Because of your son." Omas finally took a chair across from her, his gaze lingering on the concentric black-circle, white-star inlay that repeated itself on the table's surface in ever-smaller renditions. "I thought Jacen might have told you why he arranged this."

"Jacen?" Han asked. He sat at Leia's right. "Last time I checked, he wasn't king of anything."

"No, but Tenel Ka dispatched the Hapan fleet shortly after his visit." Omas waited as Luke, Mara, and the other Jedi Masters also took seats at the conference table, allowing his gaze to linger on the Ithorians, then finally seemed to accept that the Jedi were not going to ask them to leave and simply turned back to the conference table. "I doubt it was a coincidence."

"It wasn't," Jacen said, breezing into the room. "I asked her to send a fleet to the Colony's aid."

Omas twisted around in his chair. "Why in the blazes would you do something like that?"

Instead of answering, Jacen stopped and greeted the Ithorians fondly, addressing several by name, then excused himself to go over to the conference area. The Ithorians, as perceptive as they were gentle, remained in the foyer area, awkwardly greeting Kenth Hamner, Cilghal, and the other Jedi Masters as they continued to trickle in.

Jacen took a chair at Omas's side, then said, "I am a Jedi. All you need know is that my reasons were sound."

The calming aroma of the roo wood must have been working, because Omas remained in his seat and looked across the table toward Luke. "I didn't realize Jacen was a Master."

"The opinions of all Jedi are valued in this room—even those who don't consider themselves members of the Jedi Order." Luke looked to Jacen. "Perhaps you'd explain to the Masters present?"

"If you like." Jacen's tone was cordial. "I was trying to prevent a war."

"*Prevent* one?" Omas demanded. "The Chiss—"

"Understand only power," Jacen interrupted. "And now the Killiks have some. The Hapan fleet will buy us the time we need to resolve this conflict."

"At the Galactic Alliance's expense," Omas said. "The Chiss are already threatening to withdraw their security patrols if we don't bring our Jedi under control."

Mara's eyes—and those of several other Masters—flashed at the word *our,* but Omas did not seem to notice. He turned back to Luke.

"And that's exactly what I want you to do, Master Skywalker," he said. "By force, if necessary. I want all of our Jedi, and the Hapan fleet, back inside Galactic Alliance borders by this time next month."

"Wouldn't it be better for *you* to talk to Queen Tenel Ka?" Leia asked. "She is, after all, the leader of a Galactic Alliance republic."

"*And* a Jedi," Omas countered. He lowered his eyes, then continued in a softer voice. "Frankly, she refuses to listen to me. She insists she is only doing what is right, and the discussion ends there."

"And perhaps ours should end here," Kyp said. He sat at Leia's left, looking across to where Luke sat at one tip of the conference table's largest inlaid stars. "Jedi don't answer to politicians."

"What?" This from Corran, who sat on the other side of Kyp. "Then who *do* we answer to? Ourselves?"

"Of course," Jacen replied calmly. "Who else can we trust to wield our power? We must follow our own consciences."

"That's very arrogant," Kenth Hamner said. He placed his hands on the table and leaned forward, looking Jacen directly in the eye. "It concerns me to hear *any* Jedi say such a thing . . . but you, Jacen?"

"It *is* sound public policy to place powerful factions like the Jedi under the control of a civil authority." Leia kept her voice reasonable and conciliatory. Whether Jacen knew it or not, he was digging at an old wound among the Masters, and she did not want the meeting to descend into another of the shouting matches that Luke had described over the Jedi's proper relationship to the government. "Even in those with the best of intentions, power corrupts."

"And so we place the burden of remaining pure on lesser shoulders?" Jacen pressed. "Mother, you've watched two governments collapse under the weight of their own corruption and inefficiency, and the third is sagging. Do you really believe Jedi should be the tools of such frail institutions?"

Leia was at a loss to respond. Jacen's question was almost rhetorical. He had been there when she declared that she was done with politics forever, and he knew better than anyone— probably even Han—how disheartened she had been by the ineptitude of the New Republic government. In truth, she almost agreed with what he was saying . . . and probably would have done so openly, had she known of a better way to run a galactic republic.

When Leia failed to answer, Jacen turned to Omas, who was flushing in speechless anger, and said, "I'm sorry if this offends you—"

"It offends *me*," Corran said. "The Jedi exist to serve the Galactic Alliance."

"Our duty is to the Force." Kyp's voice was calmer than Corran's, but harder. "Our *only* duty."

Kenth Hamner held his hand out toward Kyp, fingers forward in a conciliatory fashion. "I think what Corran is saying is that it's our duty to serve the Galactic Alliance, because serving the Alliance serves the Force."

"That so?" Han asked. He usually avoided ethics debates like the black holes they were, but this time even he could not restrain himself. "Because Corran made it pretty clear he thought the Jedi were just a bunch of Reconstruction Authority cops who ought to take their orders from Chief Omas like everyone else."

He winked at Jacen—which was exactly the wrong thing to do at that moment.

Corran glared blaster bolts at Han. "I think we are answerable to Galactic Alliance authority, yes."

"Even if it means war in another part of the galaxy?" Mara

retorted. "Because Jacen's right about this. The Force extends beyond the Galactic Alliance—and so does our responsibility."

"Then let the rest of the galaxy pay your bills," Omas snapped. "Until that happens, I expect the Jedi to put Galactic Alliance interests first."

A sudden silence fell over the conference table, with Corran and Kenth casting accusatory glances at Kyp and Mara, and Kyp and Mara studying Omas with knowing sneers.

After a moment, Luke said, "When the Alliance offered its support, it was with the explicit understanding that there were no conditions."

"In an ideal galaxy, that would still be true," Omas said. He met Luke's gaze without flinching—and with no regret or embarrassment for breaking his pledge. "But Galactic Alliance finances are stretched thin as it is. If we must suddenly replace the Chiss security patrols, the only way to afford the cost would be to slash the Jedi budget."

Kyp planted his elbows on a wedge of black tabletop and ran his gaze around the circle of Masters. "Well, at least the question is out in the open now. Are we mercenaries, or are we Jedi?"

Corran's eyes bulged, and the debate deteriorated into an open quarrel, with Corran and Kenth still arguing fiercely that the order's first obligation was to the Galactic Alliance, and Kyp and Mara stubbornly contending that Jedi should strive to bring justice and peace wherever the Force summoned them. Cringing at what the Ithorians must think of such a contentious display, Leia glanced over at the foyer area and found them standing there in polite silence, as overlooked and forgotten by the Jedi as they had been by the Galactic Alliance government for the last five years . . . and that was when a terrible thought struck her.

Leia had a solution to the Colony problem—a solution that meant cheating the Ithorians yet again.

The Masters' voices were growing sharp and loud, but Leia remained quiet. Her plan would please Omas more than it did her, and that in itself was almost enough to make her reject it. Once, she had held the Chief in high regard and helped place the war against the Yuuzhan Vong in his hands. But peace was often harder to manage than war. Over the last five years, Omas had made too many compromises, bowed to the demands of the moment so many times that he could no longer hold his head up high enough to see what was coming on the horizon.

And if Leia proposed her solution, she would be guilty of the same thing. She didn't know if she could do that, if peace would be worth seeing the defeated eyes of Cal Omas in her own face when she looked into the mirror every morning.

Finally, Luke had heard enough. "Stop!"

When Kyp and Corran continued to argue, he stood and sharpened his voice without raising it.

"Stop," he repeated.

Kyp and Corran slowly fell silent.

"Is this how Jedi resolve their disagreements?" Luke asked.

Both of the Masters' faces went red with embarrassment, and Corran said, "I'm sorry."

He was apologizing to Luke instead of Kyp, but that was more than Kyp did. He simply sank into his chair and, being careful to avoid Corran's eyes, stared blankly at the table's star-within-a-star inlay.

"Too bad," Han muttered. "I haven't seen a good lightsaber fight in ages."

Leia was about to kick Han under the table when he exclaimed, "Ouch!"

"Sorry." Mara looked past Han to Leia. "Just stretching."

"No problem," Leia said. Han's joke was too true to be funny; the rift in the Jedi order had been widened today, and she was beginning to wonder if it could ever be closed. "I was feeling a little cramped myself."

Luke allowed a tense silence to fall over the room, then sat down and turned to Omas.

"It may take some time to reach a consensus on your request, Chief Omas. As you can see, our decision is complicated by the fact that the Chiss are acting against the Killiks not because of what they *have* done, but because of what they *might* do."

Omas nodded gravely, his irresolute gaze gliding around the table, silently taking the measure of the Jedi who had defied him, trying to judge the resolve of those who had not. Finally, he came to Luke and stopped.

"Master Skywalker, I quite simply do not care," he said. "The Chiss's trouble with the Colony is no concern of ours. We can't put Galactic Alliance lives at risk just because a few Jedi feel bound by a quaint morality no one else understands."

Kam Solusar and Tionne arrived on the heels of the exchange. It had been over a year since Leia had seen either of them, but they looked much the same, Kam still wearing his white hair cropped close to the head and Tionne allowing her silver-white tresses to cascade over her shoulders. They had barely cleared the door before they drew up short, recoiling from the animosity in the Force with the horrified expressions of someone who had just stumbled upon a pair of mating Togorians.

Leia had not realized until she saw their alarm just how noxious the atmosphere in the room had grown. The rift in the council was widening before her eyes, opening a chasm that would only grow increasingly difficult for prideful Masters like Kyp and Corran to cross. Assuming that her idea was viable, and she felt sure it was, she had it in her power to close that rift—at the price of her own conscience.

Kam and Tionne took seats next to each other, on the opposite side of Cilghal from Luke.

"We were just discussing the situation at Qoribu," Luke said to them. "Chief Omas has informed us that Tenel Ka has dispatched a Hapan battle fleet to aid the Colony."

Tionne's pearlescent eyes grew wide. "That doesn't sound good."

"It gets worse," Corran said, scowling at Jacen. "A *Jedi* is responsible."

"He followed his conscience," Kyp said. "Which is more than I can say for half—"

"Actually," Leia said, cutting off Kyp's insult before it could be finished, "there may be a way for the Jedi to stop the war *and* earn the trust of the Chiss."

Han groaned, but everyone else turned to her with a mixture of relief and expectation in their eyes.

"Han and I discovered—"

"Uh, sweetheart?" Han grabbed her forearm. "Can I talk to you a minute?"

This did not please Omas. "Captain Solo, if you have discovered something useful to the Galactic Alliance—"

"Excuse me, Chief." Leia spun her chair around, placing her back to the table, then waited as Han did the same. "Yes, dear?"

Han's eyes bulged. "What in the blazes are you doing?"

"Stopping a war," Leia whispered. Knowing Han would only grow stubborn if he realized how much this was going to hurt her, she tried to hide her dismay. "Saving billions of lives, keeping the council together, preserving the Galactic Alliance. That kind of thing."

"Yeah, I know." Han jerked a thumb toward the Ithorians. "What about them? That world we found was perfect—"

"And it's perfect for the Killiks, too." She had a familiar queasiness inside, a heavy feeling that used to come whenever she was forced to make an unfair choice as the New Republic Chief of State. "We'll take care of the Ithorians another way."

"How?" Han asked. "Ask Omas to give them a planet?"

"No," Leia said. "*Make* him."

She turned around and smiled across the table at Omas.

"On the way home, Han and I discovered a small group of uninhabited planets." Leia waited for the murmur of surprise to fade, then said, "I think they might make a good home for the Qoribu nests."

A wave of disappointment filled the Force, and Leia could not help looking past Omas toward the foyer. The Ithorians were all staring silently in her direction, their eyes half closed in resignation—or perhaps it was sorrow. Still, when Leia met Waoabi's gaze, he merely tightened his lips and gave her an approving nod. No Ithorian would want to live on a world that had been bought with someone else's blood.

Leia directed her attention to Luke. "I propose that we move the Qoribu nests to these planets."

"How?" Jacen asked. "There are four nests in the system, each with at least twenty thousand Killiks, and you don't just

move a Killik nest. You have to rebuild it inside a ship, lay in stores—"

"I'm sure Tenel Ka will instruct her fleet to help with that," Leia said. "In fact, I'm rather counting on it."

Jacen's jaw fell, then he closed his mouth and nodded. "That could work."

"And it will look as though it's what the Jedi intended all along," Omas added. "Brilliant!"

"You're sure about this planet?" Luke asked Leia. "It's completely deserted?"

"We should stop on the way back to the Colony and do a thorough sector scan." Leia glanced at Han, who nodded, then added, "But I'm sure. The astrobiology there is . . . unique."

"Well, then." Luke glanced around the circle, seeking and receiving an affirmative nod from each of the council Masters. "We seem to have reached an agreement."

The bitterness began to fade from the Force, and the tension drained from the faces of the Masters.

"We'd better prepared to deal with the Dark Nest," Mara said. "It might not like this idea."

"Dark Nest?" Omas asked.

"The Gorog nest," Luke explained. "The Colony seems completely unaware of it, so we've started calling it the Dark Nest."

"It's attacked us several times," Mara said.

"Why?" Omas asked.

Mara hesitated, clearly unwilling to tell the chief about the nest's personal vendetta against her, so Leia answered.

"We're not sure," she said. "The nest doesn't seem to want us involved with the Colony, so it's a good bet it will try to stop us."

"Maybe the Dark Nest *wants* war," Jacen suggested. "It sounds like the Colony was pushing up against Ascendancy territory even before their own worlds began to grow scarce. There must be a reason."

"I don't understand," Omas said. "I thought you persuaded Tenel Ka to send her fleet because the Colony is trying to *avoid* a war?"

"The *Colony* is," Cilghal said. "But the Dark Nest—"

"May have its own reasons to want a war," Leia said. She did not want to complicate Omas's view of the issue with a lengthy explanation of the Colony's unconscious motivations—or give him reason to doubt the Jedi's ability to resolve the crisis. "There's a bit of a, um, power struggle going on inside the Colony."

"Isn't there always?" Omas said, nodding sagely. Power struggles were something that every government official understood well. He turned to Luke. "Is this going to be a problem for us?"

"Only finding it," Mara said. "The Gorog are pretty secretive. So far, we've seen them on Yoggoy and Taat, but we have no idea—"

"Not a problem," Han interrupted. "I can find their nest."

"I don't know if that's even possible," Cilghal said. "The Gorog social structure may be quite different from other nests'. They may have parasite cells hidden among all the other—"

"I can find 'em—at least the, uh, *heart,*" Han said, following Leia's lead in not mentioning Lomi and Welk by name. "Trust me."

"Fine." Luke turned to Chief Omas and added, "But we'll have to take along a Jedi team large enough to neutralize the nest. The Chiss will be alarmed—and nothing you say is going to reassure them."

"They'll be reassured when the Killiks leave Qoribu. I'll handle them until then—just don't take too long." Omas braced his hands on the table and rose. "Speaking of which, I'll be on my way—"

"Not so fast, Chief," Han said. "We haven't told you what this is going to cost."

"Cost?" Omas looked to Luke, who merely shrugged and directed the Chief back to Han. "Of course, the Galactic Alliance will be more than happy to compensate you for any expenses the *Falcon* incurred—"

"We're talking a lot more than that." Han pointed at Omas's chair, motioning him back down. "You see, Leia and I had something in mind for that group of planets, and we're not about to give that up just because you're afraid of what the Chiss think."

Omas scowled. "I'm sorry, I don't understand what you're saying."

"Borao," Leia said. "We want you to annul RePlanetHab's claim in favor of ours."

"You see, we were there first, and they kind of claim-jumped us," Han said. "It's been scorching my jets ever since."

"You want me to give you a *planet*?" Omas gasped. "In the Inner Rim?"

"Not us." Leia pointed over Omas's shoulder toward the Ithorians. "Our clients."

Omas spun in his chair, slowly, and faced the Ithorians—who were looking considerably less glum.

"I see," he said. "If the decision were mine alone—"

"Han, do you remember the coordinates of the new planet group?" Leia asked. "We were having that trouble with the navicomputer, and I'm not sure we made a backup of—"

"I'll see what I can do," Omas said, rising again. "But, you understand, I can't just *do* this. The Recovery Act is law—I'll have to push a special exception through."

"Then I suggest you hurry," Corran said, leaning back in his chair. "The Qoribu problem is time-sensitive, and I'm sure the Solos will want this matter resolved before they leave."

"That's quite impossible," Omas said.

When Corran merely shrugged, Omas turned to Kenth—who suddenly seemed far more interested in the training fields outside than in the Chief of State.

Omas sighed, then said, "But I *can* block RePlanetHab's claim." He turned to the Ithorians and added, "It may take a month or it may take ten, but I'll push this through. By this time next year, you'll have a planet of your own again. I give you my word as Chief of State."

"That's not much," Han said, also rising. "But it'll have to do."

"To the contrary, Captain Solo." Waoabi started forward, holding out his long-fingered hand to shake Omas's and accept the promise. "It is more than we have now. Thank you."

Waoabi's courtesy should have made Leia feel better, but it did not. Instead, she felt sad and sickened and a little bit soiled by the trade-off she had been forced to make.

Like it or not, she was suddenly back in politics.

THIRTY-ONE

A weight lay across Jaina's chest, and the inside of one ear was being warmed by a soft, pulsing growl. The dormitory air was filled with a comforting mélange of refresher soap and body smells from a dozen different species, but the predominant odor, familiar and musky and strongest, was human.

Male human.

Zekk.

Jaina reached down and felt his arm across her, and his leg a bit lower, then slowly turned her head. Through a lingering fog of membrosia excess, she saw the familiar chiseled features surrounded by a frame of shaggy black hair. Thankfully, he was still clothed.

The previous night came flooding back to her: Unu's arrival at Jwlio, the Dance of Union, the Taat drifting off into the Harem Cave, the Joiners leaving in twos and threes and fours, her hand in Zekk's . . .

Zekk's green eyes opened, and the smile on his face was replaced by a confused squint. He blinked two or three times, then glanced at the lightly-clothed female body over which he'd draped himself and raised his brow. Jaina sensed a distinct *click* in the back of his mind. His eyes slid away from hers, and she felt his emotions swinging from disbelief to bewilderment to guilt.

"Well," Jaina said, hoping to set a casual tone. "Interesting night."

"Yeah." Zekk pulled his arm and leg off of her body. "I—I thought it was a dream."

Jaina cocked her brow. "You're saying it wasn't?"

Zekk's eyes widened. "No, it was fun!" he said. "Great, even. I just . . . it just didn't feel real . . ."

Zekk let the sentence trail off, sharing his thoughts and emotions with Jaina directly via the meld—or perhaps it was the Taat mind—instead of trying to explain. He had loved her since they were teenagers, and he had imagined waking at her side countless times. But last night had not felt like *them.* They had been carried along on a wave of Killik emotion. He had sought her out in the rapture of the dance, even when he knew she did not share his feelings, and found himself leading her down into the dormitory with all the Joiners—

"Zekk, we didn't do anything," Jaina said. She could have answered him more quickly and clearly just by thinking, but right now she needed the sense of separation that came with speaking—even if it *was* an illusion. "It was just a little cuddling between friends. You have a problem with that?"

"No!" Zekk said. "I just feel like I took advantage."

Jaina clasped his forearm. "You didn't." She was genuinely touched by his concern—and truly relieved that it had been handsome, muscular, familiar Zekk who had taken her hand instead of Raynar. "We lost control there for a minute, but we got it back. I'm just glad Alema went home with Mom and Dad."

Zekk remained quiet.

Jaina propped herself up on an elbow. "Hey!" She punched him in the shoulder. "I know what you're thinking!"

"Sorry."

Zekk blushed and turned away, and Jaina felt him closing down emotionally.

"Zekk, you can't do that," she said. They had to keep the meld open between them, to constantly draw on each other's strength and resolve to remain their own little entity within the greater Taat mind. "And will you stop apologizing?" Jaina rolled her eyes, then reached for her jumpsuit. "I think I'm getting dressed now."

She sat up and, sensing someone behind her, pivoted to find Raynar on the busy walkway at the head of their sunken bed. Dressed in scarlet and gold and surrounded by his usual retinue of assorted Killiks, he was squatting on his haunches, staring down into the hexagonal sleeping cell with no discernible expression on his melted face. A sense of overwhelming awe arose inside Jaina—Taat's reaction to UnuThul's presence—and she felt her mouth broadening into an adoring grin.

She managed to wipe it away by reminding herself that this used to be *Raynar Thul*.

"Raynar—good morning." Jaina pushed her feet into the jumpsuit and continued to dress without embarrassment. There was not much sense in being modest when several thousand nestmates had access to your innermost thoughts. "Come down to see how the drones live?"

Raynar lowered his stiff brow. "Why do you call us Raynar when you know Raynar Thul is gone?"

"Raynar's still in there somewhere," Jaina said. "I can feel him."

Raynar glared down at her, then said, "Perhaps you are right. Perhaps a little Raynar Thul remains in us still." A glimmer of sadness appeared in his cold blue eyes. "And he will be sorry to see you go."

Jaina felt Zekk's alarm at the same time as her own.

"Go?"

"Your task here is done," Raynar explained.

"Really?" Jaina thrust her arm through a sleeve. "I hadn't heard the Chiss were gone."

As she said this, the image of a clawcraft reconnaissance patrol appeared in her mind—the scene being relayed to one of the tactical monitors in the Taat control room. The ships were silhouetted against Ruu's amber disk, flying just above the plane of Qoribu's golden ring system.

"It looks like they're still here to me," Zekk said, no doubt seeing the same thing in his mind's eye as Jaina did in hers. "So why would the Colony want us to leave *now*?"

"We wish you to return to the Galactic Alliance," Raynar said, dodging the question.

"What about our mission?" Jaina rose and closed her jumpsuit. "You brought us here to keep the peace."

Raynar stood. "Your starfighters are being fueled. We thank you for coming."

"You seem eager to be rid of us," Zekk said, zipping his own suit. "What's going on?"

"It's the Chiss." Jaina could not tell whether her inference came from her own mind, Zekk's, or Taat's, but she *knew* it was correct. "They're going to attack."

A short, very Raynar-like sigh escaped Raynar's lips. "There's nothing more you can do here. And we don't wish to involve Jedi in this fight."

"There isn't going to be a fight," Zekk said. "Jaina and I will turn them back."

"Not this time," Raynar said. "The Chiss intend to bring this to an end, and they won't be intimidated by Jedi tricks."

"There's no harm in trying." Jaina summoned her utility belt and began to buckle it on. She did not understand why the Chiss were suddenly changing strategy and launching a major assault, but in a war, some things you just did not have time to figure out. "Where are you expecting them? Zekk and I will—"

"No. We don't wish to risk the lives of our friends in this matter."

"What do you think we've *been* doing?" Zekk asked, buckling on his own belt. "We're here to keep the peace, and we're not leaving—"

"There is no longer a peace to keep," Raynar said. "And you *are* leaving."

Suddenly his voice felt like it weighed a thousand kilos, and the urge to do as he ordered grew almost overwhelming. There was more going on here than Raynar was telling.

Ambush.

The thought had barely flashed through Jaina's mind before a Taat in Raynar's retinue began to drum its chest. Raynar listened intently, then met Jaina's gaze and shook his head.

"You have always been too headstrong for your own good, Jaina. Do not try to figure this out, or—"

"It won't work," Zekk said, leaping to the same conclusion as Jaina. "If you destroy the Chiss fleet, the next one will only be bigger."

Raynar let his chin drop in another old-Raynar gesture. "Now you've done it." The urge to depart suddenly vanished. "Now you must stay."

"We weren't leaving without Lowbacca, anyway." Jaina sounded more certain than she was; Raynar's will had felt like it was more than a match for her stubbornness. "And Zekk is right. The Colony isn't strong enough to destroy the entire Chiss space force."

"That won't be necessary," Raynar said. "We only need to hold them off until the Hapans arrive."

"Hapans?" Jaina climbed out of the sleeping cell onto the walkway with Raynar, causing a soft clatter as his retinue scrambled to make room for her. "What are Hapans doing out here?"

"Defending the weak," Raynar said. "Jacen convinced Tenel Ka to send us a fleet."

At least now Jaina understood why the Chiss were attacking. They wanted to destroy the Qoribu nests before reinforcements arrived to complicate the job.

"Jacen convinced Tenel Ka, or *you* used Jacen to convince her?" Jaina was thinking of how Raynar had nearly forced her to leave just a few moments earlier—and of the irresistible call that had summoned her and the others to the Colony in the first place. "Your touch can be very compelling."

"Perhaps, but even *we* are not strong enough to control Jacen," Raynar said. "He has moved beyond our control—or anyone else's. You know that yourself."

Jaina could not argue. During Jacen's five-year journey, she had felt him growing steadily stronger in the Force—but also more distant and isolated, like a hermit retreating to his mountaintop. At times, he had seemed to vanish into the Force entirely, and at other times she had sworn he was floating just above her shoulder.

To tell the truth, it had given her the creeps. She had started to feel like she was sharing a twin bond with a different brother every few weeks—or like he was practicing to be dead or something.

"Jacen wouldn't send you a fleet," Zekk said. He jumped up onto the adjacent side of the sleeping cell, into the middle of a steady line of Joiners streaming past toward the communal re-fresher. They smoothly detoured down another walkway, and both the conversation and the morning parade continued unabated. "That could start a war between the Chiss and the Galactic Al-liance."

"Or prevent one between us and the Chiss," Raynar coun-tered. "Perhaps he is willing to run the risk."

"Even Solos don't like odds *that* long," Jaina said. "When Chiss feel threatened, they don't back off. They get mean and aggressive."

"You can't do this," Zekk added.

"What we cannot do is allow the destruction of the Qoribu nests." Raynar's retinue abruptly started for the exit, and he turned to follow. "Once the ambush begins, you will be free to fight or leave, as you wish. Until then, you remain our guests."

Jaina started after him. "Raynar!" When a pair of knobby-shelled bodyguards moved to cut her off, she used the Force to shove them into a sleeping cell, then said, "This is madness!"

Raynar continued moving away from her. "It is self-defense." Again, his voice grew heavy and commanding, and this time it contained an edge that suggested he would abide no more argu-ment. "You will return to your proper barracks and remain there until the battle begins."

Jaina felt an overwhelming urge to obey, but there was a darkness in his tone that alarmed her, a hint of brutality so ut-terly alien to Raynar Thul that she knew it was not him alone speaking. She planted her feet on the walkway and, drawing on Zekk for the strength to resist the compulsion to start toward the barracks, touched Raynar in the Force.

The murky presence inside him was so caustic that she re-coiled and would have lost contact had Zekk not bolstered her through their meld. Jaina began to feel her way through the bit-ter darkness, searching for Raynar's pride and idealism, trying to find the core of him that she sensed was still there.

"*They* want this war," she said. "They're the ones who con-vinced you to establish your nests so close to Chiss territory."

Raynar stopped, but did not turn around. "*They? Who is they?*"

"Your shipmates on the *Flier*." Zekk stepped past Jaina and, shuffling along the walkway, started toward Raynar. "Lomi and Welk."

"Lomi and Welk are dead."

Jaina found something pure and compassionate inside the Prime and touched it. "Then who attacked the *Shadow* on her way in?"

"Insect mercenaries hired by the Chiss," Raynar answered instantly.

Zekk stopped a step behind Raynar. "You have proof?"

"We have no time to look for proof." Raynar reluctantly turned around, and his retinue of insects began to file back toward the discussion. "We are too busy defending our nests."

Jaina sighed inwardly. It was the same circular logic they encountered every time they tried to investigate the mysterious attacks.

"What about the attack on Saba?" Zekk pressed. "I suppose you're going to tell me she attacked a Joiner by mistake, and he took her lightsaber away and wounded her?"

"Yes," Raynar replied. "That is the best explanation."

Jaina tightened her hold on the core of benevolence she had found. "Raynar, they're blinding you to the truth. The best explanation—"

"We are tired of telling you!"

The murky presence welled up inside Raynar and swallowed the pure center that Jaina was holding, and she found herself suddenly adrift in a void of biting darkness. Instinctively, she reached for Zekk and opened herself to their meld, but instead of his strength, all that came to her was cold, stinging shadow.

"Raynar Thul is gone," Raynar said.

Jaina felt herself turning. She tried to fight the compulsion, to lock her gaze on Raynar and keep it there, but she simply did not have the strength to fight him. She stepped away and started for the barracks.

"We are all that remains."

THIRTY-TWO

A long, golden arrow curved through the heart of the hologrammic flight control display, tracing the route of the stolen skiff from the repair hangar to its current location on the edge of Ossus's gravity well. The reckless manner in which the skiff had cut through the approach zone of the planet's primary spaceport suggested the pilot had been eager to get away from the Jedi academy as quickly as possible. But Luke had already known that. Escapees liked to move fast.

"Thirty seconds before she can jump," a flight controller reported. A large-headed Bith with an auditory data feed in one ear, he was seated at one of a dozen control stations surrounding the hologrammic display. "She still won't acknowledge our signal."

"Keep trying," Luke said. He could feel the anxiety of the XJ3 pilots trailing the skiff—a pair of young Jedi Knights flying their first security rotation. They were worried they would have to blast it out of space. "Do we know yet whether she has company?"

"Not with certainty," said the Bith's supervisor, a blue-skinned Duros woman named Orame. She stepped to an empty terminal and clacked a few keys. An inset of a repair hangar security vid appeared at the base of the flight control display. "But we did find this."

The inset showed Alema Rar striding through a darkened repair bay, two cases of food goods floating through the air ahead of her.

"We think that shadow—"

"Enhance the cases," Mara said. Along with Han, Leia, and several others, she had accompanied Luke up from the hangar floor as soon as the stolen skiff had streaked skyward. "Bring up a label, if you can."

The Duros typed a command, and the carton label filled the image.

"NUTROFIT GELMEAT," Mara read.

"She's stealing Gorog!" Ben cried.

The skiff's trajectory began to flatten as Alema prepared to enter hyperspace. The XJ3 pilots commed for permission to open fire, and Luke reached out to them in the Force, urging them to avoid disabling the vessel.

"Permission granted," Orame said over the comm channel. "Open fire."

The pilots hesitated. "But—"

"You heard the order," Luke said, still reaching out to the pilots through the Force, urging them let the skiff go. "Open fire."

The skiff's trajectory began to weave and wobble as it began evasive maneuvers.

"She's getting away!" Ben cried. "Stop her!"

"They have to be careful, Ben," Mara said gently. "Or they might hurt Gorog."

Ben considered this, then sighed and took her hand. "Let them go. I don't think Gorog wanted to stay anyway."

The skiff's trajectory reached the edge of Ossus's gravity well and vanished. The flight controller reported that the stolen skiff had entered hyperspace.

Han let out a sigh of relief. "Right on sch—"

"Not now," Luke interrupted, raising his hand to silence Han. He turned to Ben. "How did you know Gorog didn't want to stay? Do you still feel her in your mind?"

Ben closed his eyes, then nodded. "Sort of. She wants me to be happy."

Luke felt his own dismay mirrored in Mara. If Ben remained in touch with Gorog after she had entered hyperspace, it could only be through the Colony's Will. He was part Joiner—Dark Nest Joiner.

Mara had reached the same conclusion. Luke could feel her alarm and anger through the Force, and she was as quick as he was to realize that they could not discuss their plans in front of their son.

"Ben, maybe Nanna can take you to the pilots' lounge for some Fizzer," Mara said. "We have some things to discuss, then we'll find you there before we leave."

Ben made no move toward the door, where Nanna and C-3PO were waiting.

Luke frowned. "Ben, I'm sure you heard your mother."

Ben nodded. "I heard. But why do I have to stay behind on Ossus?" Without waiting for an answer, he turned to Han. "Is there going to be another war?"

Han grimaced, then said, "Not if we can help it, kid."

"And certainly not in this part of the galaxy," Mara added. "Why are you worried about that?"

"Because this is what you *do* when there's a war," Ben said. "You just dump me someplace with Masters Tionne and Solusar and then never even come to visit."

The accusation struck a pang in Luke's heart, and he felt Mara wince as well. They often wondered how much Ben's refusal to use the Force had to do with the separation anxiety he had suffered during the war with the Yuuzhan Vong, and Ben knew this particular complaint had an effect on them.

Even so, Mara refused to be manipulated by an eight-year-old. "Don't exaggerate, Ben. We had to keep you safe, and you know we came to see you every chance we had."

"Besides, they won't be gone long this time," Jacen said, stepping out from behind Han and Leia. "There isn't going to be a war."

Ben frowned. "How do you know that?"

"I *know*." Jacen flashed a crooked Solo smile. "Trust me."

Luke felt a sudden qualm in Mara, and though her eyes remained fixed on Ben, he sensed that her thoughts were on Jacen.

"Besides, you're not going to be alone," Jacen added. "I'll be here, too."

"You're not going back?" Ben asked.

"Not yet. The Masters are worried that *some* of us have spent too much time with the Killiks already."

"Tell me about it," Ben answered, rolling his eyes.

"So maybe you and I could hang out together?" Jacen glanced at Mara. "If that's all right with your mother."

"Of course." Mara answered with no outward hesitation, but Luke detected just a hint of apprehension, as though she did not quite trust the "new-and-improved" Jacen. "As long as Master Solusar thinks Ben is keeping up with his schoolwork—"

"No problem!" Ben's smile was as broad as a Hutt's. "School's easy."

"*And* as long as you obey Masters Tionne and Solusar," Mara warned Ben. "No secrets with Nanna, either."

"I can't do that anymore," Ben said. "Dad altered her program."

"Good." Jacen took Ben's hand and started for the door. "Why don't we get that Fizzer now?"

"Can I have kyleme?" Ben asked, not looking back. "A Blue Giant size?"

As soon as they were out of earshot, Han said, "Jacen has a knack with kids. Go figure."

"It's his empathy," Leia said. "I'm glad to see it's intact."

Leia left unsaid what Luke knew she was thinking: that after the war—after all Jacen had suffered at the hands of Vergere and the Yuuzhan Vong—she was surprised he had *any* empathy left.

Luke turned to Han. "Sorry to interrupt you earlier, but we don't know how much the Dark Nest might be able to glean from Ben's mind."

"No problem," Han said. "I got a little carried away when I saw how well the plan was working."

"I don't know why you're surprised," Leia said. "Alema is still a Jedi. Once Cilghal let her regain consciousness, there was never any question she could escape. The tricky part is going to be following her."

"How did you know which vessel she'd steal?" Mara asked.

"We didn't," Leia said. "We bugged them all."

"Speaking of bugs, we'd better get going," Han said. "That

transmitter only has a subspace range of fifty light-years. We can't be too far behind when Alema hits Colony space, or we'll be stuck guessing where she went."

Luke followed Han and the others toward the door. Their intention was to follow Alema to the core of the Dark Nest, then undermine its influence over the Colony by eliminating Welk and—assuming she had survived the Crash—Lomi Plo. Cilghal and Jacen were convinced that at least Welk had survived—and that a Dark Jedi now led the Gorog in much the same way Raynar led the Unu. It was a somewhat ruthless plan, especially in the way it placed Alema's life at risk without her consent. But it seemed to Luke to be consistent with the nature of modern Jedi themselves. The war with the Yuuzhan Vong had taught the Jedi the folly of valuing sentiment over effectiveness, the wisdom of striking quickly and fiercely at the heart of a problem. Sometimes, Luke wondered whether it was a lesson the Jedi had learned too well; whether in defeating their enemies they had not become a little too much like them.

At the door, Han ran headlong into a short, gawky man with a heavily tattooed face and unruly blue hair. Without apologizing for—or even seeming to notice—the collision, the newcomer pushed past Han and stopped in front of Luke. R2-D2 followed close behind.

"Here you are," the man said. "I've been looking everywhere."

"I don't understand why, Ghent," Mara said. "We told you we were leaving on Jedi business."

Ghent furrowed his brow. "You did?"

"Several times." Luke saw Han tapping his wrist impatiently. "And we have to leave soon."

"Oh." Ghent's eyes dropped, then slid back toward R2-D2. "I guess this can wait."

"*What* can wait?" Leia asked. Luke had told her about the holo hidden in the sequestered sector in R2-D2's memory, and she was as eager as he was to learn more about the mysterious woman. "Did you find something?"

Ghent shook his head. "Just a few seconds of holo that I managed to relocate before I tripped a security gate. What I wanted to ask is if I could—"

"Holo of what?" Luke asked. "A brown-eyed woman?"

"That's right," Ghent said. "But it's really not very much. If I can—"

"Can you show it to us?" Leia sounded even more excited than Luke felt. "Before we leave?"

Ghent frowned. "Of course."

An uneasy silence fell as Luke and the others waited.

"Ghent, we want to see the holo," Mara said. "Now. As Luke said, we haven't got much time."

Ghent's brow rose. "Oh."

He squatted and inserted the plug of a homemade diagnostics scanner into one of R2-D2's input slots, then hastily typed a command.

"Show them."

R2-D2 piped an objection, and Han groaned and looked at his chrono.

"Don't make me scramble your sector tables again," Ghent warned. "This time, I won't restore them."

R2-D2 let out a long, descending trill, then activated his holoprojector.

The hand-sized profile of the same brown-eyed woman that Luke had seen before appeared on the control room floor. She seemed to be standing alone, facing someone outside the hologram.

"Has Anakin been to see you?" asked a male voice.

"Wait a minute," Han said. "That guy sounds familiar."

"He should," Luke replied. The voice was much younger than when they had known him, but there was no mistaking its clarity and resonance. "That's Obi-Wan Kenobi."

Ghent tapped a key on his diagnostics scanner, stopping the holo. "Do you want to see this or not?"

"Of course—we're sorry," Leia said. "Please continue."

Ghent punched the key again, and R2-D2 restarted the holo from the beginning.

"Has Anakin been to see you?" Obi-Wan's voice asked.

"Several times." The woman smiled, then said, *"I was so happy to hear that he was accepted on the Jedi Council."*

"I know." Obi-Wan walked into the hologram, wearing a Jedi cloak with the hood down. He was still young, with a light brown beard and an unwrinkled face. *"He deserves it. He's impatient, strong-willed, very opinionated, but truly gifted."*

They laughed, then the woman said, *"You're not just here to say hello. Something's wrong, isn't it?"*

Obi-Wan's face grew serious. *"You should be a Jedi, Padmé."*

The name shot an electric bolt of excitement through Luke—and he could sense it had done the same to Leia.

"You're not very good at hiding your feelings," Padmé said.

Obi-Wan nodded. *"It's Anakin. He's becoming moody and detached."* His holoimage turned half away. *"He's been put in a difficult position as the Chancellor's representative, but I think it's more than that."* The image turned back to Padmé again. *"I was hoping he may have talked to you."*

Padmé's expression—at least what could be seen of it in the small hologrammic image—remained neutral.

"Why would he talk to me about his work?"

Obi-Wan studied her for a moment. *"Neither of you is very good at hiding your feelings, either."*

Padmé frowned. *"Don't give me that look."*

Obi-Wan continued to look at her in the same way. *"I know how he feels about you."*

Padmé's eyes slid away. *"What did he say?"*

"Nothing," Obi-Wan answered. *"He didn't have to."*

Padmé's face fell, and she turned and walked out of the hologram. *"I don't know what you're talking about."*

"I know you both too well." Obi-Wan followed her out of the frame. *"I can see you two are in love."*

There was no answer, and the hologram ended.

Luke could see Han biting his tongue, forcing himself to remain patient while the distance grew between them and Alema's skiff, but this was important—at least to him and Leia.

"That's all?" Luke asked.

Ghent nodded and tapped R2-D2's silver dome. "Artoo's

blocking me. When I tripped that security gate, he encrypted the rest of the data."

R2-D2 whistled an objection.

"It's not your place to decide what is good for Master Luke," C-3PO said. "You're only a droid."

R2-D2 trilled an angry reply.

"No, I *don't* know the secret you're keeping," C-3PO answered. "And if I did know, I'd tell Master Luke instantly."

R2-D2 responded with a low, slurpy buzz.

Luke frowned at the exchange, but turned back to Ghent. "Look. We've got about two minutes before we have to launch. Is there any way to see the rest now, without Artoo's cooperation?"

Ghent sighed. "Sure." He pulled his scanner plug out of R2-D2's input socket. "All I have to do is overwrite his personality sectors—"

The rest of Ghent's explanation was lost to R2-D2's screech of objection.

"Don't expect me to translate that," C-3PO said. "That's what happens to arrogant droids like you. I suggest you extend your cooperation immediately."

R2-D2 trilled a sad refusal.

Luke glanced at the droid, then asked, "I mean *without* a personality wipe."

"Not in two minutes—and maybe not in this lifetime," Ghent said. "This droid hasn't had a memory wipe in decades. His circuits are one huge personality fault."

"I know that," Luke said. "What about the spyware?"

Ghent looked confused. "Spyware?"

"The spyware that's keeping me from accessing those memories." Luke was losing patience with the programmer. "The memories concerning the woman we just saw?"

"Oh, *that* spyware," Ghent said. "There isn't any."

"There isn't?" Luke frowned. "Then how come Artoo won't give me access?"

Ghent sighed, sounding as exasperated as Luke felt. "That's what I'm trying to explain—"

"Maybe you can explain on the way to the pilots' lounge,"

Mara interrupted. She motioned them out the door. "We can finish talking on the way. We've still got a Twi'lek to catch, remember?"

"Right."

Luke was so excited by the hologram that he had let it overshadow their mission for a moment. Anakin—his father—had been in love with a beautiful woman named Padmé. And Padmé did not look so different from Leia. Did they finally know their mother's name? He could sense that Leia thought so—but she was too afraid to say as much out loud. So was he.

Luke fell in beside Ghent. "You were explaining why Artoo won't let me access those memories?"

"Because he thinks he's protecting you," Ghent said. "He's a very stubborn droid."

"But you can get around that, right?" Leia asked. "I've seen you slice codes on units far more sophisticated than Artoo's."

Ghent turned around and looked at Leia as though she had asked for the name of the last girl he had tried to pick up in a cantina—they *never* told him their name.

"No," he said. "Artoo units were designed to military standards. That means their security protocols will destroy the data before they let it fall into unauthorized hands. If you try to force access, a doomsday gate will reformat the entire memory chip."

"And there's no way to beat that security without wiping Artoo's personality first?" Luke asked.

"I didn't say *that*," Ghent said. "There's a way—but you'd have to help me, and you probably can't do it."

"Try us," Han said.

"Okay," Ghent said. "Bring me the Intellex Four designer's datapad."

"What for?"

"Because *he* had to have a way to access the data when his prototypes developed glitches like these," Ghent said. "And if he's like most droid-brain designers, that hatch became part of the Intellex IV's basic architecture. It's a very complicated computer unit, so there'll be a long list of passwords and encryption keys on that datapad."

"That shouldn't be too difficult, assuming it wasn't destroyed in a war," Luke said. "Who was this designer?"

Ghent shrugged. "Your guess is as good as mine. The Artoo was originally an Imperial design, and the Imperial Department of Military Research kept the identities of its top scientists secret."

"You must be joking," Leia said. "You want us to find this guy's datapad without knowing anything about him?"

"It's not quite that bad," Ghent said. "Do you remember when Incom's design staff defected to the Rebellion with the X-wing prototypes?"

"Of course," Leia said cautiously.

"Well, this guy was consulting with them on the Artoo interface," Ghent said. "And after the defection, Industrial Automaton never made another design modification to the Intellex Four."

"They were afraid to," Han surmised. "Because this guy was the only one who could do it right, and he had defected with the X-wing designers."

"No, not because he had defected," Leia said. She was studying Ghent intently. "If he had, we'd know who he was. Right?"

"Right," Ghent said. "He just disappeared."

Luke had a sinking feeling. "When you say disappeared, do you mean—"

"Nobody knows." Ghent turned to Leia. "That's what *disappeared* means, right? Nobody knows."

THIRTY-THREE

The sky had been dark for hours beneath clouds of dartships, roaring into the Taat nest to refuel and refresh life-support systems, roaring back out to await the arrival of the Chiss assault fleet. Jaina had given up trying to estimate how many craft the Colony had assembled for the ambush, but the number had to be over a hundred thousand. The Taat hangars alone were servicing six swarms an hour, and there were three other nests in the Qoribu system.

It makes us proud, Zekk said through the Taat mind. *No other species could mount such an operation.*

The Chiss will be surprised, Jaina agreed. Somewhere deep in her mind, she knew that this was a bad thing, that it would make her mission as a Jedi more difficult—but it did not feel that way to Taat. To Taat, it felt like their nests were finally going to be saved. *They will pay a terrible price.*

Good, Zekk said.

Good, Jaina agreed.

The roar of arriving dartships faded to a mere rumble, and the kilometer-long oval of a top-of-the-line Gallofree medium freighter descended out of the rocket smoke. The well-maintained hull was finished in the scarlet-and-gold flames of the Bornaryn Trading Company, with an escort of corporate E-wings providing security.

Jaina wondered what the vessel was doing so far from home, but Taat did not know. Unu wished the nest to welcome *Roaming Ronto,* and so Taat welcomed *Roaming Ronto.* Taat had heard, though, that similar vessels had landed on Ruu and Zvbo carrying a big surprise for the Chiss.

As the *Ronto* neared the nest, it adjusted course, heading out over the plateau toward the freight yard, where a swarm of Taat workers were already assembling to unload it. Jaina thought briefly about going to see the cargo, but Unu did not want that. Unu wanted her to enjoy the beauty of the nest from the veranda of the Jedi barracks.

That freighter should alarm us, Jaina said to Zekk. *It can only make war more likely.*

It's too late to stop the war, Zekk replied. *But we should try.*

Jaina started to rise, then suddenly felt too tired and dropped back onto her seat. *Maybe later.*

"Yeah," Zekk said aloud. *We'd rather sit here.*

There was something wrong with that, Jaina knew. Jedi were supposed to be dauntless, resourceful, resolute. They were supposed to accomplish the impossible, to keep trying no matter how difficult the mission.

They were supposed to have indomitable spirits.

Jaina felt a stirring deep down inside, in the place that had always belonged to her brother Jacen, and she knew he was with her, urging her to fight back, to throw off her lethargy, to break the Colony's hold on her and reach for that part of her that was just Jaina.

Jaina stood.

Where are you going? Zekk asked. *It doesn't feel like you need the refresher.*

"Get out of our—*my*—mind," Jaina said.

Jacen was urging her to remember how Welk and Lomi Plo had tricked the strike team on *Baanu Rass,* how they had stolen the *Flier* and abandoned Anakin to die. And now Jaina was allowing them to control her mind.

Jaina did not understand how that could be. The entire Colony knew that Raynar Thul was the only survivor of the Crash.

But Jacen seemed so sure. A black fury rose in Jaina's mind, the same black fury to which she had succumbed when she went to recover Anakin's body, and finally she felt able to act.

She wanted to find Welk and kill him. She wanted to find Lomi Plo and make *her* wish for death.

But first, there was duty. To let anger distract her was to let the Dark Jedi win. First, Jaina had to stop the war—*then* she could kill Lomi and Welk.

Jaina turned toward the hangar.

"Where are you going?" Zekk whined from his bench. "We can't do anything. It's too late."

Jaina opened herself to their meld, then reached out to him and let her anger pour from her heart into his.

I won't surrender to them. *I'm going to stop this war.*

Zekk's eyes widened, then turned a bright, angry green. He slammed his palms down and pushed himself to his feet.

"I'm with you," he said, catching up. "How are we going to do this?"

"Tell you later," Jaina said. She did not yet have a plan—and she had no intention of developing one until after they were away from the Taat nest. "For now, let's just concentrate on getting to our StealthXs."

They stepped into the sweet dampness of the wax-lined access tunnel and started down toward the hangar. As they progressed, Taat began to fill Jaina's mind with doubts about her intentions, to make her wonder if she would really be stopping the war—or merely sparing the Chiss a much-deserved defeat.

Jaina thought of Anakin, and her doubts vanished in the black fire of her anger.

Taat workers began to pour into the tunnel, all scurrying up a passage that led only to the Jedi barracks. Jaina and Zekk threatened them with word and thought, but the Killiks continued to clamber past, slowing the pair's progress to a crawl.

Zekk took the lead and began to muscle forward, using the Force to shove aside the Killiks ahead of him. More Taat poured into the tunnel, convinced they had some urgent errand in the Jedi barracks. Zekk continued to push ahead. Jaina added her Force powers to his, and the entire stream of insects began to slide backward down the tunnel.

The Killiks dispersed, and a strange resistance began to rise inside the two Jedi, a cold hand pushing at them inside their own bellies. Their limbs grew heavier, their breathing became labored, their pulses pounded in their ears. They leaned against the cold hand, and still it grew harder to move. Soon, their legs were too heavy to lift, their lungs were ready to burst, their drumming hearts drowned out their own thoughts. They came to a stop, hanging parallel to the floor, and the harder they tried to move forward, the more impossible it became.

They hung there for several minutes, testing their wills against that of the Colony, and only grew more tired. Jaina thought of how Lomi and Welk had betrayed Anakin, and she grew more determined than ever to avenge him—and less able to move.

Jaina began to despair. Her anger was no match for the Will of the Colony. She had to find another way.

The seed of a new plan came to Jaina, a plan that relied not on anger, but on love instead.

Jaina did not nurture that seed. Instead, she buried it deep down in her mind, in that part that was still *I* instead of *we*.

Keep trying, she urged Zekk. *Don't stop, no matter what.*

Never! he assured her.

Good.

Jaina let the pressure push her away from the hangar, back up the passage.

"Hey!" Zekk's voice was strained. "Where are you going?"

"The barracks," Jaina said. "I'm giving up."

"What!"

"I'm not as strong as you." It irked Jaina to say this, but it was the one way to be sure Zekk would continue to struggle. "I'll see you later."

As Jaina retreated up the passage, the pressure gradually diminished. Finally, she was able to simply walk back to the barracks. She could sense Zekk down near the hangar, feeling puzzled and angry and a little bit abandoned, but he remained determined not to quit, to show Jaina he was as strong as she believed.

Once Jaina reached the barracks veranda, she returned to her bench and began to contemplate the beauty of the Killik mind. Every member of a nest worked flawlessly with all the others, executing unbelievably complex tasks—such as refueling and restocking several thousand rocket ships an hour—in near-perfect harmony. There were seldom any of the accidents or shortages or confusion so common to any military operation—and there were never arguments or disagreements or territorial spats.

Would it truly be so bad if there *was* a war, and the Colony won? For once, there would be true galactic peace—no vying for resources, no clashes of interest, no territorial conquests, just all the peoples of the galaxy working together for the common good. Was that so wrong?

Jaina supposed that the fact that she did not see anything wrong with that meant she had become a true Joiner. She was only worried that the Colony could never win a war against the Chiss.

The Colony would have help, Taat assured her. An image came through the nest mind of the *Ronto* being unloaded. A dozen long streams of Killiks were pouring in and out of its cargo bays, working together to off-load the huge, telescoping barrels of at least a dozen turbolaser batteries.

The Chiss were going to be *very* surprised when they attacked. Maybe the Killiks could win this war after all.

Jaina decided to wait there on the veranda until Unu called for her. Sooner or later, there would be a mission that only a Jedi in a StealthX could do, and Jaina would be ready.

Then, when her mind finally went quiet and she knew that Taat and Unu were no longer paying her any attention, she pictured the handsome, square, scarred face of Jagged Fel. She held the image in her mind and performed a series of breathing exercises, focusing on the feelings they had shared while they were fighting the Yuuzhan Vong together—and during those few times they had managed to rendezvous after the war—then turned roughly toward where the Chiss staging area would be, somewhere outside the orbit of Qoribu.

While Jag was not Force-sensitive, Jaina had touched him through the Force many times while they were together, and she felt sure he would recognize the sensation of her presence brushing his. But he wouldn't trust her. He would think she was just another Joiner trying to lure him into a mistake. So she would have to convince him that he was discovering the ambush on his own—and she would have to do it before Taat realized what she was doing.

Jaina reached out to Jag in the Force and found his presence—distant and dim—somewhere ahead on Qoribu's orbital path, exactly where he would be if he was guarding the staging area for a Chiss assault fleet.

Come get me, lover boy, Jaina sent. Jag would not understand the words, of course, but he would recognize the sentiment. She had used the same taunt many times when they sparred. *If you can.*

Jaina felt Jag start in surprise, then she caught a flash of anger as he recognized her touch. This wasn't a game! This was war, and . . .

His irritation suddenly changed to concern as it dawned on him why she had picked *that* particular day to reach out to him. Jaina sensed a rising tide of alarm, then lost contact as Jag drew in on himself.

THIRTY-FOUR

Qoribu's brightly striped orb hung sandwiched between the flat, twinkling clouds of two sizable space fleets. For now, both sides seemed content to avoid a battle, each hiding from the other behind the gas giant's considerable bulk. But they were also maintaining aggressive postures, keeping their sublight drives lit and their shields up, dropping reconnaissance patrols through the planet's golden ring system like airspinners from a Bespin raawk trawler.

"Good news," Han said, decelerating hard. As they had half expected, the homing beacon aboard Alema's stolen skiff had led them straight back into the middle of the Qoribu conflict. Though the standoff between the two fleets was certain to complicate their plans, Han could not have been more thrilled. After they destroyed the Dark Nest, he could track down Jaina and have her safely away from the Taat nest within hours. "We're just in time for the war."

"Why is that good news?" Juun asked from the navigator's station. "Are we planning to go back into smuggling?"

"No!" Leia said. She keyed a command on the copilot's console, and the tactical display began to light up with mass readings and vector arrows. "Han's smuggling days were over a long time ago."

Tarfang, still regrowing his fur after the head-to-toe clipping that had preceded a lengthy stay in the bacta tank, chittered a rude-sounding question.

"Tarfang wishes to inquire whether Princess Leia always answers questions on Captain Solo's behalf," C-3PO said.

Han did not bother to answer. He had brought Tarfang along only because Juun would not come without him, and he had brought Juun along because he was actually considering taking the Sullustan on as a copilot. After seeing how deftly Leia had resolved the crisis between the Jedi and the Galactic Alliance, it had finally grown clear to Han that he was blocking fate. Leia had been born to run things, and the wretched state of the Galactic Alliance Reconstruction was evidence enough of how badly she was needed. Thus he had made up his mind to step aside so she could follow her destiny . . . again.

Tarfang jabbered something else, which C-3PO translated as, "Tarfang says it is quite unfortunate that old age has broken your spirit, Captain Solo. Wars are good for smugglers. You might have been able to earn enough to replace the fine ship you tricked Captain Juun into sacrificing on your behalf."

This was too much. "First, I'm not old, and my spirit is fine." Han twisted around and wagged his finger at Tarfang. Without any fur, the Ewok reminded him of a womp rat with a short nose and no tail. "And second, *I'm* not the one who told Juun to out-fly his cover. Getting that rustcan blown out from under him probably saved his life."

Tarfang started to yammer a reply.

"Later, you two," Leia interrupted. "Luke and Mara will be arriving soon, and we have work to do."

She pointed at the tactical display, which now identified the fleet hovering above Qoribu's northern pole as Hapan and the one at the southern pole as Chiss. While the Chiss appeared to be outnumbered more than two to one, Han knew appearances were deceptive. In all likelihood, they had a much larger force waiting just inside Ascendancy territory, ready to jump into battle the instant the enemy attacked. He only hoped that Dukat Gray—or whoever commanded the Hapan fleet—understood the basic deceptiveness of Chiss war doctrine.

Across the center of Qoribu ran a thick band of yellow bogey symbols.

"Dartships?" Han gasped.

"That's how it looks," Leia said. "The spectrograph suggests a methane-based fuel."

"There must be a million of 'em!"

"Closer to a hundred and fifty thousand, Captain," Juun said from behind him. "Plus a handful of freighters, blastboats, and four KDY orbital defense platforms."

Han raised his brow. "I wonder where *those* came from?"

Tarfang offered an opinion, which C-3PO reported as, "Smugglers."

Han ignored the Ewok and asked Leia, "Where's Alema?"

"Still working on that," she said. "I could use a little help."

"Yeah, sure," Han said. "All you have to do is ask."

A grid appeared over the bright band of bogey symbols strung across Qoribu's equator.

"Alema's skiff has to be somewhere in there, or we would have picked her up by now," Leia said. A quarter of the grid turned red. "Do an efflux search on the areas I'm assigning you. She's only a few minutes ahead, so her ion drives must still be active."

The homing beacon they had planted on the stolen skiff was only accurate to within a light-month, which left a lot of territory to search via normal sensors. Han brought up the first grid square and began to look for a telltale plume of hot ions. At this scale, the band of dartships resolved itself into a lumpy strand of swirling dots, with the gray disk of one of Qoribu's moons hanging just beneath the main area of activity.

After a moment of study, Han switched to the next grid and found several bogey symbols that turned out to be a Gallofree freighter and a pair of patrolling blastboats. As soon as he brought up the third grid, he was tempted to move immediately to the next one. The dartships in this area were spread so thin that he could make out the thin gold line of Qoribu's ring system and the irregular nugget of a small ice moon. But the thin Killik defenses here just did not feel right. Han brought the moon, Kr, to the center of his display and enlarged the scale.

A blue circle the size of a fingertip appeared in the screen center, slowly growing smaller as it traveled toward the moon.

"Got it!" Han began a mass analysis to confirm his suspicions, but he was sure enough of himself to transfer an inset to

Leia's display. "This one's still moving insystem. It has to be her."

"Very good." Leia leaned across and kissed his cheek. "You win the reward."

"That's my reward?" Han complained. "I get that every day."

"That could always change, flyboy."

"Come on. You know you can't help yourself." Han flashed her his best arrogant smirk, then activated the intercom. "Battle stations back there. We might be going anytime."

"We know," Kyp replied. "We're Jedi."

"Oh, yeah." Han looked at the ceiling and silently cursed Kyp's arrogance. "I must be getting forgetful in my old age."

Meewalh informed him that she and Cakhmaim were also ready. Noghri were always ready.

When the mass analysis finally confirmed Han's guess, he turned to face Juun. "You two had better head to your battle station, too. You remember how it works?"

"Of course—you went over the procedure several times." Juun popped his datapad out of his vest pocket. "And I've recorded all your instructions right here, in case I forget."

"Uh, great." Han glanced away so Juun would not see him wince. "That makes me real confident."

"I'm happy to know that," Juun said. "But I do have one question."

Han counted to three, reminding himself that it was better for the Sullustan to ask his questions now rather than later, when they were being dive-bombed by a thousand dartships.

"Okay, shoot."

"Has this ever been tried before?"

Han and Leia exchanged looks of surprise, then Leia said, "I don't see how it could have been, Jae."

"Oh." Juun was silent for a moment, then said, "I have another question."

"No kidding," Han grumbled.

"Maybe we should make this the last one," Leia said. "I just felt Luke and Mara emerge from hyperspace."

"Of course." The Sullustan slipped out of his chair, and Tarfang did the same. "How do we know it's going to work?"

"Good question," Han said. He turned forward again and placed a tracking lock on Alema's skiff.

After a moment, Leia explained, "It was Han's idea, Jae."

"Oh, I see." Juun sounded satisfied. "Of course it will work."

Tarfang growled something doubtful, but Juun was already leading the way back toward the engineering station.

A moment later, the irregular, matte-black body of two StealthX starfighters pulled alongside the *Falcon,* and Han saw Luke's and Mara's helmet-framed faces looking over from the cockpits of phantom craft. Leia closed her eyes for a moment, reaching out to them in the Force, trying to get some sense of their intentions. After the Dark Nest attack on the *Shadow,* they had decided to return with only the *Falcon* and a couple of StealthX escorts. Since the *Falcon* was not equipped to carry fighters, Luke and Mara had been taking turns with the other two Jedi Masters on the mission—Kyp and Saba—ferrying the star-fighters through hyperspace.

Luke and Mara happened to be in the cockpit when the time came for the final jump to Qoribu, but Han suspected that Mara would have insisted on being one of the pilots to follow Alema into the Dark Nest. She was taking the whole assassin thing pretty personally.

Leia opened her eyes, then Luke and Mara accelerated away toward Kr. They remained visible for a moment, a pair of dark X's silhouetted against Qoribu's bright stripes, then shrank into invisibility.

"Luke wants us to hold here until they find the nest," Leia reported. "Then—"

"Excuse me," C-3PO interrupted. "But we have an unfortunate situation. We're being hailed by both Dukat Gray of the Hapan fleet *and* Commander Fel of the Chiss."

"Put Gray on first," Han said. "Fel is just going to—"

"No, shift them to a conference channel," Leia said. "Maybe we can promote a dialogue."

"Or a war," Han grumbled.

Gray's voice came over the speaker first. "Princess Leia, I demand an—"

"Who's this?" Fel demanded.

"Dukat Aleson Gray, Duch'da to Lady AlGray of the Relephon Moons," Gray responded.

There was a long silence.

"To whom am I speaking?" Gray demanded.

"Commander Jagged Fel," Fel replied. "Of the Chiss Expansionary Defense Fleet."

Another long silence.

Finally, Gray said, "I was attempting to comm Princess Leia and her crew. Have you boarded their vessel?"

"I was wondering if *you* had," Fel said.

"Of course not. Why would I comm a vessel I had boarded?"

"I don't know that you *are* comming them," Fel countered suspiciously. "Your signal is coming from the *Falcon*."

"*Your* signal is coming from the *Falcon*," Gray accused. "I warn you, I won't fall for any of your Chiss—"

"Pardon me, gentlemen," Leia said. "Your concern is touching, but I assure you, the *Falcon* remains under Han's command. Will you both activate Idol Smasher?"

Idol Smasher was an old encryption system the allies had used in the war against the Yuuzhan Vong. Outdated though it was, it was almost a certainty that both fleets would still have the decoding hardware available in their code room archives. Military cryptographers were notorious pack rats.

After a short pause, Gray said, "We'll need two minutes."

"We'll need one." Fel's tone was superior. "Please notify us when you're ready, Dukat."

Han glanced back at C-3PO, who was already plugging the necessary module into the comm station, and smirked.

"The *Falcon* is ready now."

The transmission light went out, then Leia said, "Trouble, Han."

Han looked back to the tactical screen and immediately began to warm the ion drives. The moon Kr was fast vanishing behind a cloud of dartships. As he watched, the spectrograph identified their propulsion as hydrogen-based.

"Dark Nest," he said. "Anything from Luke and Mara?"

"A little anxiety—they're not calling for us, yet."

"Tell them not to push it," Han said. "They're too old to play hero."

"Han, they're younger than you were at the Battle of Yuuzhan'tar."

"Yeah, well, I've got my luck," Han said. "All they have is the Force."

Fel's voice came over the comm. "Checking encryption."

"Well done, Commander!" C-3PO answered. "That took only thirty-three point seven seconds."

"Thirty-three point *four*—you neglected the transmission lag," Fel corrected. "I wanted to have a word with the Solos before Dukat Gray joined us."

"Jag, we're not going home." Han was keeping one eye on the tactical display and one on Leia, ready to start toward Kr the instant it looked like Luke and Mara were in trouble. "Jaina's in there, and—"

"Yes, I know," Fel said. "I think . . . actually, I'm *convinced* she saved our fleet."

Leia's jaw fell, but her voice betrayed no hint of her shock. "You find that surprising, Jag? The Jedi are here to stop a war, not choose sides."

"We've never doubted your intentions, Princess Leia," Fel said. "Only your province in being here—and your ability to resist the Colony's Will."

"Then Jaina has changed your minds?"

"She has opened *mine*," Fel corrected. "But that is very different from convincing Defense Fleet Command that the Jedi can neutralize the Killik threat."

"We understand your concern," Leia said. "Perhaps Defense Fleet Command would believe us if the Colony withdrew from Qoribu?"

There was a moment of stunned silence. On the tactical display, Kr had vanished beneath a yellow swarm of dartship symbols. Han shook an inquiring finger in the moon's general direction, but Leia shook her head. Luke and Mara still did not want any help.

Finally, Fel asked, "The Jedi can arrange that?"

"Testing encryption," Gray's voice broke in. "You've been talking without me."

"Encryption confirmed." In a tone that mimicked Gray's peevishness, C-3PO replied, "Though you *are* somewhat late."

"It was only two minutes twenty," Gray complained. "That's no excuse—"

"We were just catching up on old times," Leia said. "You may not be aware of it, but Commander Fel came *very* close to becoming our son-in-law."

As Leia spoke, her eyes grew wide, and she began to gesture frantically out the forward viewport. Han slammed the throttles forward, and the *Falcon* leapt toward Qoribu.

"Commander Fel, Dukat Gray, your tactical officers are about to tell you that the *Falcon* is accelerating toward the moon Kr at maximum power." Though Leia's face was pale, her voice remained calm. "I wanted to inform you both of the reason."

Leia briefed them on the Jedi discovery of the Dark Nest and their theory about the power it held over the rest of the Colony's collective mind. She even revealed the Order's fear that the nest was being controlled by the two Dark Jedi who had abducted Raynar Thul on *Baanu Rass,* keeping secret only the fact that the Dark Nest was also attempting to absorb Alema Rar.

"You're telling us that the Colony is ruled by a hidden nest?" Fel asked, incredulous.

"Only in the sense that any sentient mind is ruled by its own unconscious mind," Leia said. "*Influenced* might be a better term—though in the Killiks' case the influence is very heavy. We're fairly sure the Dark Nest is responsible for the Colony's decision to inhabit Qoribu."

"For what purpose?" Fel asked.

"To start a war," Han said. "And so far, you guys are playing right into their snappy little pincers."

"It would be foolish to assume you know our plans, Captain Solo."

"Your plans were clear enough when the Fleet of the Glorious Defender Queen arrived," Gray said. "You were maneuvering to attack."

"Obviously, I cannot discuss our plans with any of you," Fel said. "I assume that the Jedi have located this Dark Nest on Kr and intend to break its hold over the Colony?"

"You could say that," Han said. Kr was visible to the naked eye now, a fuzzy blue nugget about the size of a thumb. "If blasting it to bug parts counts."

"With just the *Falcon*?" Gray asked.

"We have more than the *Falcon*," Leia said. "Luke and Mara have already found the entrance to the nest."

"That explains the activity on Kr," Fel concluded. "The dartships seem to be swarming something."

Though the *Falcon*'s tactical display showed no indications of weapons activity, Han had no doubt that the Skywalkers were busy dodging dartships. He could see it in the tautness around Leia's eyes.

"Master Skywalker is under attack?" There was more excitement in Gray's voice than concern.

"There's no need for alarm, Dukat!" Leia commanded. "Luke and Mara can easily—"

A pair of Hapan Novas began to slip down the tactical display toward Kr. Han's heart rose into his throat.

"Uh, what are you doing there, Dukat?"

"Sending support," Gray said. "Queen Mother Tenel Ka would not be pleased if I allowed this Dark Nest to kill Master Skywalker and her husband—"

"Recall your vessels at once, Dukat," Fel said. "We cannot permit any Hapan capital ship to approach the orbital plane."

"It's a small force," Gray said. "Any fool can that see it poses no threat to—"

"Only a fool would allow his enemy to establish a forward position under the current circumstances," Fel replied. A Chiss Star Destroyer and half a dozen cruisers started upward to meet the Hapan trio. "And we Chiss are not fools."

"Oh, boy," Han said under his breath. "I've got a—"

"—bad feeling. I know," Leia finished. "Dukat Gray, leave this to us. We'll let you know if—"

A chain of tiny orange flashes suddenly flared along Kr's long axis as someone on the moon opened fire.

Two more Battle Dragons, accompanied by a dozen Novas, began to descend toward Qoribu's rings.

"The queen's fleet will not stand idly by while Master Skywalker is viciously attacked," Gray declared.

"Dukat Gray—"

That was as much as Leia could say before Fel started to talk over her.

"The Chiss have no wish to see Master Skywalker and his wife injured, either." A dozen Chiss cruisers joined the growing migration toward Kr. "But the Dark Nest is on *our* side of the rings. Allow *us* to support him."

"Out of the question!" Gray shot back. Han had known even before the reply that Fel's offer would never reach orbit. Gray cared more about being able to claim credit for rescuing Luke and Mara than whether they actually *needed* to be rescued. "The Chiss have made it clear they didn't want the Jedi here in the first place. We have no assurance that you wouldn't kill them yourselves."

"Perhaps not," Fel returned coolly. "But if you don't recall those vessels, I *can* assure you—"

"Dukat Gray," Leia said. "Sparking a clash with the Chiss is *not* going to win the Queen Mother's favor. I suggest you recall your vessels and wait until your aid is truly needed."

Another string of explosions lit Kr's face. "It's apparent to me that our aid *is* needed," Gray said. "And if we must fight the Chiss to deliver it, we will."

He closed the channel.

"Stubborn rodder!" Leia cursed. "Jag, you understand—"

"I'm sorry, Princess Leia," Fel said. The Chiss fleet began to stream upward on all sides of the planet. "But my superiors refuse to take the chance that this isn't a ploy. I suggest you avoid getting caught in the crossfire."

THIRTY-FIVE

A pillar of orange rocket exhaust arced out of Kr's frozen tangle of ethmane crystals, emerging from an ice-lined shaft more than a kilometer across. This column was far larger than any others Luke and Mara had seen, its heat raising a wall of steam as it bent toward the Skywalkers and streaked low over the moon's frozen surface.

Confident they had finally found what they were looking for, Luke and Mara banked away and began to accelerate, drawing the orange column after them. Luke would have liked to make a reconnaissance pass to be certain the huge shaft was the hangar opening he believed it to be, but Kr's tortured terrain and icy blue light neutralized the speed and camouflage of their StealthXs, and both of their starfighters had already taken too much of a beating to risk another confrontation.

Two seconds later, Luke's R9 astromech unit—sitting in for an operationally challenged R2-D2—sounded an attack alarm. Luke felt a start from Mara as an explosion rocked her StealthX; then his own starfighter gave a sharp double buck. The R9 pointedly informed Luke they were being ambushed by Gorog dartships, and the tactical display showed half a dozen of the little craft behind them, rising from the sensor-blocking depths of the frozen ethmane jungle.

Luke continued toward the *Falcon,* flying low over Kr's feathery jungle of ethmane crystals. Ideally, he would have climbed for open space where their StealthXs would have full advantage, but the tactical display showed a second swarm of dartships flying top cover, in perfect position to stop them.

The Skywalkers had traveled barely a kilometer when another column of dartships rose out of the ethmane jungle ahead.

Luke sensed Mara's alarm almost before his own. They had stayed a little too long, and now Gorog was boxing them in. The swarm spread out before them, creating an orange wall of rocket exhaust. The Skywalkers began to pour cannon fire into the swirling mass, trying to clear a lane for their StealthXs.

It was like trying to blast a tunnel through a cloud. Every time they created a hole, it filled instantly.

As the Skywalkers drew closer, the orange wall resolved itself into a pattern of fiery whirling disks, each with the black dot of a dartship at its heart. Mara continued to fire, and Luke followed her lead. The tactic clearly had no chance of success, but Mara had a plan. Luke was almost sure of it.

Finally, when the swarm was so close that the dartships had grown into tiny cylinders, glowing streaks of missile propellant began to reach out toward the Skywalkers. Mara took the lead and pulled up, a loose wing stabilizer shuddering under the strain. The two nearest swarms—the one blocking their escape and the one pursuing from behind—nosed up to give chase.

Stick close, she warned.

Suddenly Mara dropped the nose of her StealthX. Luke followed so quickly that he almost beat her, but the Dark Nest was not fooled. The dartships simply leveled off and continued to close on the Skywalkers.

Luke expected Mara to pull up again and outclimb their pursuers, gambling that the StealthXs could withstand a barrage of Killik chemical explosives long enough to fight through the top-cover swarm. Instead, she continued to dive. The ice jungle's feathery canopy came up rapidly. Luke began to wonder when she intended to pull up.

She did not.

A flurry of cannon bolts lanced out from Mara's StealthX, instantly superheating the ice crystals in front of her and filling Luke's forward view with brown steam. He switched to instrument flying and followed her through the cloud into the snarled depths of the ice jungle. Flash-frozen spires of ethmane stood at all angles, glowing translucent blue with Gyuel's distant light, reaching out to embrace each other with delicate arms of hoar-frost.

Mara flipped her StealthX up on edge and slipped between two ethmane pillars, then crashed through a curtain of frost and sent up a glittering cloud of ice particles. Luke ducked under a frozen arch, then shot ahead of Mara into the lead.

He offered his apologies through their Force-bond, along with an image of the loose stabilizer he had seen on her wing.

Whatever, she answered.

Luke felt a sudden compulsion to swing back toward the nest and wondered if his wife had gone crazy.

Mara urged him to think. Gorog expected them to run for the *Falcon.*

Luke quickly brought them around. It would be safer to go in the opposite direction . . . and sneak a look at the nest. He focused all his attention on the frozen jungle ahead and began a Jedi breathing exercise, allowing his mind to race forward through the ethmane spires, to find its own route down the twin-ing passages and rolling channels. Time seemed to slow. He sur-rendered his steering arm to the Force, and his hand began to move of its own accord, guiding the StealthX into one shimmer-ing gap after another, bobbing over blue curtains, ducking be-neath long fronds of frost, blasting holes through impassable walls of ice.

Mara stayed close on his tail, almost joining her hand to his through their Force-bond, and thirty seconds later they shot through a small icy portal into an irregular blue shaft barely broad enough for Luke to bank the StealthX into a tight inside spiral.

Stang!

Luke felt Mara's fear through the Force, and his heart jumped into his throat. Then, as he continued his own spiral around the small shaft, he saw the jagged hole where her StealthX had bounced off the icy wall. His tactical display showed her still on his tail, but weaving badly.

Mara?

Fine! she answered.

Luke continued to bank, setting the StealthX up on one wing

so that he could look up out one side of the cockpit and down out the other. He estimated they were about two kilometers deep, though that was impossible to confirm with instruments. This far down inside the frozen moon, the StealthX's sensor range extended only as far as the walls of frozen ethmane.

Below, the shaft continued to narrow and curved back under itself, concealing the nest entrance—assuming it was down there—behind a wall of blue ice. Aside from the walls, which had been polished smooth by the heat-and-freeze cycle of countless rocket launches, there was no sign of dartships.

Mara seemed worried by how quiet it was.

Luke didn't like it, either. Gorog would have left *something* to defend the nest. The hair on his neck began to rise, and he decided they had seen enough.

Mara, now directly opposite him on the other side of the shaft, agreed and started to climb. Her shields were flickering, and that loose stabilizer was flapping around beneath her wing.

Luke fell in behind her; then an attack alarm sounded and a laser cannon began to fire blue bolts up the shaft. He felt another jolt of emotion from Mara, this time anger, as her StealthX took a trio of hits. Her shields went down with the second, and the ends of both starboard wings vanished with the third.

Luke did not waste time looking at his tactical display. He simply dropped the StealthX into a dive and started firing and *then* saw the nose of Alema's stolen skiff, just slipping back out of sight. He continued to fire for a second longer, pouring his rage and disbelief at her through the Force, until the bend in the shaft vanished behind a curtain of ethmane steam. He sensed no shame or sorrow in the Twi'lek, only the enormous, murky presence of the Dark Nest.

When no more cannon bolts rose out of the fog, Luke pulled up into a tight banking turn that would allow him to keep an eye on the shaft in both directions. Mara was still above him, her StealthX crawling around the shaft in a wobbling circle, both starboard engines shut down and the stumps of her starboard wings vibrating badly.

Mara?

Everything good, she reported.

It didn't look good. Luke was about to tell her to try climbing when the mouth of the shaft—two kilometers above—began to brighten with the orange glow of dartship rockets.

Mara brought her StealthX out of its circle and fired at the icy wall, trying to punch through into the ethmane jungle beyond.

The stumps of her starboard wings tumbled away in a cascade of sparks and mini-explosions. Then she slipped into a spin and flashed past Luke, vanishing into the ethmane steam below.

Luke felt her stretching out to him, clinging to their Forcebond as she fought to bring the StealthX under control. He poured reassurance into their bond, trying to let her know that he would not abandon her, that he was coming right behind her. Then he reached for Leia in the Force, pouring out his alarm and picturing a crashing starfighter, and dived after Mara.

He caught up to Mara on the other side of the fog. She was using a combination of the Force and power manipulations to keep the StealthX under control, corkscrewing down the shaft in an ever-tightening spiral, pushing the damaged craft to its limits and a little beyond to stay ahead of the approaching dartfighters.

The shaft twined its way another seven kilometers into the ice moon, growing ever smaller and more twisted. Finally the squarish, cave-like opening of a launching bay appeared at the bottom of the shaft, perhaps a kilometer away.

Luke armed a pair of proton torpedoes, then urged Mara to do the same. They would need to give the *Falcon* something to look for.

With pleasure!

Mara stabilized her spin just long enough to send a pair of proton torpedoes streaking toward the cavern mouth. Under other circumstances, Luke might have felt a pang of concern knowing that Alema's skiff had entered the hangar only a short time before. But under these conditions—even understanding that she was under the control of the Dark Nest—he felt nothing. Whatever happened, the Twi'lek had brought it on herself.

A brilliant flash filled the cavern mouth as Mara's torpedoes detonated inside, and suddenly the last five hundred meters of shaft were filled with glittering ice shards. Luke activated his targeting computer, but between Mara's wildly gyrating StealthX and interference from the ethmane ice, he was unable to get a lock.

Mara. Luke moved his finger to the torpedo trigger. *Stay left.*

The first barrage of turbolaser fire fanned down from the Hapan batteries, and Kr was suddenly veiled behind a curtain of crimson energy. The Chiss answered with a volley of missiles, and a thousand propellant trails rose to bar the way forward. Han pulled up short and rolled the *Falcon* away from the sudden fury.

"No!" Leia's eyes were fixed on her display, where a navigation lock had been guiding them toward the detonation site of the Skywalkers' proton torpedoes. "Luke and Mara need help."

"And they won't get it if we fly into that mess," Han said. In fifty years of flying, he had never seen a battle this compact before. There had to be a hundred capital ships fighting over a moon only eighty kilometers long. "Even I'm not that good."

"Yes, Han, you are."

"Look, I'm not leaving," Han said. "We just have to find another way in."

Leia's voice grew sober. "Han, I think they're down."

"Down?" A leaden ball formed in Han's stomach. "What do you mean, *down*?"

"Crashed," Leia said. "They may need—"

Han swung the *Falcon* around and started back toward Kr.

"—extraction," Leia finished.

"How did that happen?" Han demanded. Space ahead had become a flashing sheet of turbolaser fire, striped at irregular intervals by growing lines of missile flame. "They're *Jedi*, blast it! In *StealthXs*! They were just supposed to find the nest and call *us*."

"Things go wrong even for Jedi." Leia's eyes were fixed out the viewport. "Threepio, break out the EV suits."

"EV suits?" C-3PO squealed. "If we go EV out *there,* we're

doomed! The odds of surviving are . . . why, they're entirely incalculable!"

"Still better than with no suit," Han said. "Do as she says. We may need suits to recover Luke and Mara."

"As you wish, Captain Solo," C-3PO said. "But I really don't think we're going to survive long enough to reach them."

The sheet of flashing energy ahead brightened rapidly as the *Falcon* drew closer, and the canopy tinting darkened. Han looked to his instruments and found nothing but electromagnetic static, its density increasing as space ahead grew more brilliant.

"Sweetheart," Han asked as casually as he could manage, "do you think you can do that Jedi thing—"

"Quiet." Leia was already staring out the forward viewport with a faraway expression in her eyes. "I'm concentrating."

Han waited for instructions. Leia continued to concentrate.

A web of tiny efflux trails—all that was visible of the Chiss and Hapan starfighters vying for control of the attack routes— began to lace the darkened canopy. Even that faded when the *Falcon* entered the battle zone.

A shudder ran through the decks as Meewalh opened up with the belly turret against some hazard Han could not see. Then the attack alarms shrieked as cannon fire pounded their lower shields.

"Who was that?" Han demanded over the intercom.

Meewalh informed him it was a starfighter, but she had no idea whose. All she had been able to see was a blurry tail of ion exhaust.

"Uh, sweetheart?"

"Concentrating!"

The invisible fist of a turbolaser blast glanced off the *Falcon*'s port side, instantly overwhelming the shields and sending her spinning out of control. The cockpit erupted with damage alarms, and Leia began to scream.

It took Han a moment to realize she was finally giving him instructions. "Port! Go port!"

He steadied the *Falcon*—relieved to see that he still could— then swung hard to port.

"Threepio, give me a damage report."

The droid dropped an EV suit on the deck. "We'velostourauxiliaryaccelerationcompensator!" he babbled. "Andourport-dockingringiscompromised. We'llnevergetoutofthisinonepiece!"

"The damage is minor," Saba said over the intercom. "This one will see to it."

Han frowned. Saba still had a piece of skull missing under that thick hide of hers. She had talked Luke into bringing her along only by threatening to come anyway, but he knew better than to protest. It just wasn't smart to question a Barabel's ability to do *anything*.

Leia ordered, "Climb!"

Han pulled back on the yoke and felt the *Falcon* buck as something exploded under her.

"Dive!"

Han pushed the yoke forward and was nearly thrown out of his seat as a turbolaser blast blossomed just to their stern.

"Starboard, gentle."

Han swung to starboard, and the red streak of a missile shot past the *Falcon*'s blackened canopy.

"Dead ahead, fast."

Han pushed the throttles into overdrive. The canopy grew suddenly transparent again, and still he could not see anything. There was only a thick brown fog, blossoming here and there with cannon fire and laced with the blue trails of starfighter ion drives.

"They melted it!" Han gasped. "They melted an entire—"

"Instruments, Han!"

Han glanced down and found the reassuring sight of a space battle on his tactical display. What looked to be about ten dozen squadrons of starfighters were whirling around Kr, maneuvering for position and pouring laserfire at each other. A single Chiss cruiser was sliding quietly around the moon's bulk, playing a game of moog-and-rancor with a pair of Hapan Novas.

Kr's surface, a sensor-blocking layer of frozen ethmane, was literally disappearing before their eyes. Every time a stray cannon blast struck ground, a thumb-sized area of ice vanished from Han's display.

Leia found the fading rad signature of the Skywalkers' proton torpedoes and reestablished their navigation lock. Han slipped the *Falcon* under the moon, streaking toward their destination only a hundred meters below Kr's jagged belly. Their goal lay about ten kilometers ahead of the Chiss cruiser, so he chose a slow, direct route that would take them past its weapons turrets at a respectable distance. In a battle like this, the only way *not* to get shot at was to make clear you were no kind of threat.

As the *Falcon* neared the cruiser, a flight of clawcraft dropped out of the fog to look her over.

C-3PO opened an emergency channel. "This is the *Millennium Falcon* hailing all combatants. We are neutral in this conflict. Please direct your fire away from us! I repeat: we are neutral!"

The clawcraft dropped back into the kill zone behind the *Falcon* and hung there. The navigation lock slowly drifted toward the center of the screen.

The stolen skiff was floating amid the rest of the wreckage, a pile of flattened durasteel flickering in the light of Mara's two functioning spotlights. There was no way to tell whether Alema and Ben's Killik "friend" had been aboard when the proton torpedoes eviscerated the launching bay, but Mara was betting the pair had escaped. So far, she had seen no signs of the Twi'lek's body among the scorched pieces of chitin tumbling past her canopy, and Alema was a *Jedi*. She would have sensed what was about to happen and raced for shelter.

Mara guided her ailing starfighter through a jagged breach in the launching bay's rear wall. Her spotlights stabbed through a dusty cloud of floating rubble, illuminating a maintenance hangar with a bank of shattered dartship berths on the far wall. She sealed her EV suit and dropped her StealthX to the deck, skidding to a lopsided landing between the broken remnants of two egg-shaped storage tanks.

Knowing that Luke would be covering her from his own craft, Mara sprang out of the cockpit and tumbled all the way to the ceiling, coming to a rest beside a spitcrete ridge that would have served the Gorog as a sort of upside-down catwalk. When no attacks came, she exchanged her lightsaber for her blaster and covered Luke while he landed.

A large part of her—the part that was Ben's mother—would

have preferred him to rejoin the *Falcon* and come back with the Solos and the heavy artillery. But she had known from the moment her R9 died that would never happen; Luke would no more have left her alone than she would have him. Besides, this wasn't so bad. It had been her and Luke against a world more times than she could count, and they always won.

Luke took cover inside the shattered base of a storage tank, then Mara pushed off the ceiling and joined him. They were taking care to stay out of their StealthXs' spotlights, but there was enough ambient light to see his lips pressed tight together through his faceplate.

"What do you think?" Mara spoke over their suit comm. She wanted to keep her Force-senses clear for alerting her to danger. "Try to squeeze into your Stealth and sneak out?"

Luke shook his helmet. "There won't be any slipping past that dartship swarm out there. As a matter of fact . . ." He turned toward his StealthX and commed his R9. "Arnie, go find a dark corner and—"

The command came to a sudden end as the orange glow of rocket exhaust lit the launching bay entrance. Mara grabbed Luke's arm and kicked off the floor, using the Force to pull them toward a ruptured door membrane in the back of the maintenance hangar. Arnie started to tweedle a question, but the comm channel abruptly dissolved into static as a trio of bright flashes lit the chamber.

There was no boom, of course, but Mara suddenly grew uncomfortably warm inside her vac suit, and the shock wave hurled her and Luke headlong through the door membrane into the darkened utility passage beyond.

With no gravity or friction to slow them down, they did not stop until they slammed into a wall two seconds later. Mara hit back-first, driving the air from her lungs but not breaking anything she could feel. A sharp crack over the comm suggested that Luke had impacted on his helmet. She started to ask if he was okay, then sensed him wondering the same thing about her and knew he was.

"Check air and suit," Luke said, righting himself.

The reminder was unnecessary. The heads-up status display

inside Mara's faceplate was already glowing, though she did not remember activating it.

"I'm good," she said. "You?"

"Have a hisser," he reported, indicating a small air leak. "But we'd better look for it later."

He pointed back toward the maintenance hangar. Thirty meters away, the orange glow of rocket exhaust was flickering against a section of curved tunnel, dimming and brightening as dartships landed and shut down their engines and more poured into the hangar behind them.

"I don't recall seeing any EV suits in the Taat hangars," Mara said hopefully.

"No—but a carapace is a good start on a pressure suit."

"Killjoy." Mara turned her wrist over and entered a four-digit code on her forearm command pad. The StealthX's self-destruct alarm began to gong inside her helmet, and the heads-up display on her faceplate began a twenty-second countdown. "Come on, Skywalker. Let's stay on the move until we hear from the *Falcon*."

Mara turned away from the hangar and started into the frozen darkness ahead.

THIRTY-SIX

The walls and floor were coated in a frozen black wax that absorbed the light from Luke's helmet lamp and made the passage seem even darker and murkier than it was. Every few meters, a fissure caused by the tunnel's sudden decompression ran all the way to the moon ice, sometimes exposing a short length of spitcrete piping or power conduit. There were none of the shineballs that illuminated other Killik nests, nor any sense of order to its convoluted plan. The passages seemed to meander at random, twining around each other like vines, branching off at arbitrary intervals and rejoining the main passage without crossing any obvious destination between.

At the speed he and Mara were sailing through the darkness, using the Force to pull themselves along through the zero-g, Luke was growing badly disoriented. He no longer had any sense of whether they were traveling deeper into the moon or back toward the surface; whether ten meters of ethmane ice separated them from the hangar or a thousand. Were it not for the frozen beads of vapor that his leaky vac suit was leaving behind, he wasn't even sure he could have found his way back down the same passage.

Mara suddenly grabbed a crack in the wall and brought herself to a stop. Luke did the same and found himself looking at one of the bulging hatch membranes that Killiks used instead of air locks. A pull chain hung to one side of the hatch, attached to a set of valves positioned to spray sealing gel over the membrane before anyone tried to push through.

Mara didn't reach for the pull chain, and neither did Luke. Both their spines were prickling with danger sense, and they were all too aware of how difficult it was to sense Gorog in the Force.

"Ambush," Mara concluded. "They're starting to come after us."

"Starting?"

Luke looked around, and his helmet lamp illuminated a torrent of dartship pilots pouring around the bend, at most thirty meters away. Wearing their dartship canopies like carapaces, they were scurrying along every available tunnel surface, with their legs and arms sheathed in a shimmering fabric that bunched and gathered at the joints. They had no weapons other than their six limbs—but that would be enough if the swarm ever caught up.

There was no question of using the Force to hide. Whenever the Gorog lost sight of their quarry, they simply spread out, scrambling over every surface in every direction, literally hunting their quarry down by feel.

Luke began to pour blasterfire into the front ranks. Most bolts ricocheted off the canopies, while those that hit a limb simply activated a safety seal at the nearest joint. The insects just kept coming.

"Trouble," Luke said over the suit comm. Lightsabers would be more effective, but he *really* didn't want to go hand-to-hand with who-knew-how-many bugs. "Big trouble, in fact."

"Maybe not that big," Mara said.

"No?"

"They can't *all* be dartship pilots," Mara said. He felt rather than saw her nod at the bulging hatch membrane. "So they won't *all* be wearing pressure suits."

"You're right," Luke said. The first pilots were less than ten meters away now, but he holstered his blaster and grabbed his lightsaber. "Not that big."

They ignited their lightsabers, then pressed themselves against the tunnel wall and slashed a large X across the center of the hatch. The membrane blew apart, and their would-be ambushers went tumbling past on a tide of explosive decompression, crashing into the pilot swarm and bringing its advance to a tumbling, confused halt.

Once the torrent slowed, Mara floated through the tattered

membrane into a corridor filled with flash-frozen Killiks. Luke followed a few meters behind, using the Force to pull himself along, shouldering aside Gorog warriors with heads painted in the dark spray pattern of decompression death.

"How's that hisser?" Mara asked.

Luke checked the heads-up display inside his faceplate. He was down to just fifteen minutes of air, and the loss rate was increasing.

"Fine for now."

He turned his helmet lamp back through the burst hatch and was relieved to illuminate only a small portion of the throng that had been pursuing them so far. About fifty of the insects were still coming, pushing their way up the body-choked passage toward him and Mara. The last dozen or so were scurrying in the opposite direction, vanishing into the darkness behind the hundreds of pilots that had already started back toward their dartships.

"But the next time we come to a pressure hatch, let's try to leave it intact," Luke said. "I think our rescue party is about to be delayed."

The navigation lock finally reached the center of the display. Relieved to note their Chiss escorts were still behind them—the cruiser was less likely to blast the *Falcon* to atoms that way—Han began a slow, spiraling descent into Kr's thickening fog. He would have liked to drop into a power dive and go screaming down to find Luke and Mara, but that would have looked suspicious. And when Chiss grew suspicious, they killed things.

"Let's see what it looks like inside that fog," Han said. "Activate the terrain scanners."

Leia brought the scanners online. Unlike ethmane ice, ethmane fog was almost as transparent to sensors as air, and a moment later the mouth of a broad funnel-like pit appeared on Han's display. The hole appeared to be a deep one, descending more than two kilometers before finally curving out of sight.

"Any sign of rescue beacons?" Han asked.

Leia shook her head. "None." She closed her eyes. "They're too deep."

"Deep?"

"Inside Kr," she said. "I think they're in the nest."

"*In* the nest?" Han felt like he was going to choke on his heart. "That's not funny, Leia."

"It gets less funny," she said. "Luke seems to think we'll meet a reception committee."

"You don't say." Han smiled. "Good."

"Good?" C-3PO demanded. "I don't see anything good about this situation at all. There's every chance that both Master Sky-walkers will be killed by our baradium missiles!"

"Not really." Han pushed the *Falcon*'s nose down and dropped into a steepening dive. "For that to happen, we'd have to actually *fire* the baradium missiles."

"You don't intend to fire them?" C-3PO asked, growing even more alarmed. "Not even one?"

"No." Leia's tone was relieved. It had been her idea to bring the baradium missiles along, but she had spent most of the trip worried about how they were going to keep Alema clear when they fired the weapons at the nest. Han had not been quite so worried. "Not with Luke and Mara inside."

"But you won't be able to clear the nest!" C-3PO objected. "Without those missiles, the odds will be—"

"Easy, Threepio." The last thing Han wanted to hear was how bad the odds were. He was already having to hold the yoke tight to prevent his hands from shaking. "I wasn't counting on the missiles anyway."

"You weren't?"

"Of course not," he said. "They're baradium. You *never* get to shoot the baradium missiles."

"Oh." C-3PO grew calmer. "That's true. I have no record of one ever actually being launched."

They descended a thousand meters into the fog, then a Chiss voice crackled over the comm.

"*Millennium Falcon,* be advised that if you attempt to evade us, we *will* open fire."

"We're not evading," Han answered. "We're going in . . . and you're welcome to follow."

"Going in?" The ethmane ice was already beginning to make the comm signal scratchy. "Clarify."

"We have two Jedi pilots down inside the nest," Leia explained. "We're going to extract them."

The clawcraft reappeared on the *Falcon*'s tail. "We've detected no other craft—"

"Do you ever?" Han interrupted. "She said they were *Jedi* pilots—Luke and Mara Skywalker, to be exact. You coming or not?"

There was a moment's silence, then the two clawcraft began to drop back. "Your request lies outside our mission profile, but we have been authorized to wish you good luck."

"Thanks for nothing," Han grumbled.

"You're welcome," the Chiss replied. "We could have shot you down."

The *Falcon* continued to descend, then finally broke out of the fog into a twisting, ice-walled shaft that was much narrower than it had appeared on the terrain scanner. Han gasped and pulled the ship in a spiral so tight it was almost a spin.

"Oh, dear!" C-3PO cried.

"Relax, circuit-brain." Han spoke between clenched teeth. "I've got us under control."

"That isn't what concerns me, Captain Solo. We have a safety margin of point—"

"Threepio!" Leia barked. "What *does* concern you?"

C-3PO's golden arm stretched toward the viewport. *"That."*

It took a moment for Han and Leia to see the faint orange glow building in the depths of the shaft.

"Okay." Leia sighed. "That kind of concerns me, too."

"Relax. Everything's under control." Han activated the intercom. "Juun, you ready back there?"

There was a short delay, followed by the electronic screech of someone speaking too close to the intercom microphone. "Yes, Captain, if you think this is going to work."

"It's going to work," Han said. He checked the power levels on the *Falcon*'s tractor beam and saw that they were holding at maximum. Still, he asked, "Are you *sure* you're ready?"

There was a short pause, then Tarfang jabbered something sharp.

"Tarfang assures you that he and Captain Juun are very prepared," C-3PO translated. "He adds that if your geejawed plan fails, it's your own fault; you shouldn't try to blame it on them."

"It's going to work," Han said.

He started to address the rest of his passengers, but Kyp cut him off.

"Of course we're ready." Kyp's voice came over the comm channel rather than the intercom, an indication that he was already in his vac suit and buttoned up tight. "We're Jedi."

Han glanced over at Leia. "I *hate* it when he does that," he growled. "*You* ready?"

She nodded gravely. "As soon as you tell me how you're going to get past that swarm."

Han grinned. "Who says I'm going to?"

They rounded a bend and, about two kilometers below, saw the first haze of the dartship swarm filling the shaft. Han pointed the *Falcon*'s nose at them and accelerated.

"Han?"

"Yeah?"

"You don't have to impress me." Leia pinched her eyes shut. "I've never thought you were fainthearted. Not even once."

Han chuckled. "Good. Just want to keep—"

Juun's voice came over the intercom. "Captain Solo, I have a question."

"*Now?*" Han asked. The swarm of dartships had thickened to a gray-and-orange cloud. "*Now* you have a question?"

"I can't find the activation safety," Juun said.

"There isn't one!" Han said. "Just activate . . . *now!*"

"But the CEC maintenance manual clearly states that every freight-moving apparatus shall have—"

"Flip the kriffing switch!" Leia yelled.

The shaft's blue walls vanished behind the swarm, and bolts of red energy began to streak down into the shaft as Cakhmaim and Meewalh cut loose with the quad laser cannons.

"That's an order!" Han added.

Juun flipped the switch.

The cabin lights dimmed, and every display on the flight deck winked out as cockpit power dwindled to nothing. Even the quad lasers started to dribble beams of blue light.

"Han?" Leia's voice broke with fear. "We don't have any status displays. I can't monitor our shields. Is it supposed to do that?"

"You bet," Han said proudly. "When I reversed the polarity of the tractor beam, I had to feed it every spare erg of power I could find."

All Han could see ahead was the cloud of dartships, so close now that he could make out individual exhaust trails curving toward the *Falcon*'s nose.

"But not the shields, right?" Leia said. Canopy bulges began to appear atop the closest dartships, some with antennae waving inside, and propellant trails began to stab out from the swarm. "Please tell me we're not drawing on the—"

A cone of iridescent energy shot out from beneath the *Falcon,* swallowing both the Gorog missiles and the swarm beyond. A series of fiery blossoms erupted as the missiles interpreted the repulsion beam as impact and detonated. The dartships were harder to defeat. The pilots increased power, and the cloud of ships hung in stasis, still struggling to ascend the shaft.

But as the *Falcon* continued to descend, the beam grew stronger. Soon the Killiks' primitive rocket engines began to overload and explode. Some dartships fell out of control and crashed, while others began to tumble back down the shaft. For several moments, Han and Leia continued to catch glimpses of dartships rolling around inside the beam, smashing into each other, spontaneously exploding, erupting against the pit's icy walls.

Han slowed their descent until the eruptions grew less frequent. Finally, the boiling cloud of rubble dispersed, and nothing lay below them but a jagged star of darkness that had once been a dartship launching bay. He brought the *Falcon* to a full stop and activated the intercom.

"Okay, Juun, you'd better shut down before something blows up." Han looked over at Leia and winked, then added, "And shift that power diverter back to the shields."

THIRTY-SEVEN

The Battle Dragon and its escorts were floating nose-down above Qoribu's blast-tattered rings, trading fire with two Chiss cruisers as the Great Swarm swept down to join the fight. Jaina's and Zekk's cockpit speakers crackled to life with Hapan comm officers demanding explanations and Colony Joiners outlining Unu's plan, but the two Jedi paid the exchange little attention. They were two hundred kilometers behind the Swarm, with a third StealthX slaved to Jaina's controls, and their mission was completely independent of the Killik assault. UnuThul was still angry about the spoiled ambush, and he had planted one notion firmly in their minds before allowing them to launch: Jaina and Zekk were to find Lowbacca and leave.

The Great Swarm reached the Hapan fleet and swallowed it in a flickering cloud of rocket exhaust, then streamed past to engulf the maelstrom of starfighters battling for the crucial space midway between the two sides. The Chiss cruisers redoubled their fire. Brilliant bursts of crimson and sapphire blossomed inside the Great Swarm, three or four a second, but the Colony continued to descend, a dozen dartships vanishing every time a turbolaser struck. The Killiks did not even break formation.

Hoping to locate Lowbacca before they entered hostile territory, Jaina and Zekk quieted their minds and reached into the Force . . . and were so surprised that they gasped. Together.

That feels like Master Skywalker, Zekk said through their shared mind.

Both of them, Jaina confirmed. *And Mother and Kyp and others . . . hard to tell. Pretty shut down.*

Trying to hide, Zekk agreed. *But having a bad time. Wonder if Unu knows?*

UnuThul must know, Jaina replied. Though she and Zekk were hundreds of kilometers from the nearest Taat, and not currently in touch with the larger collective mind, they could still feel the Colony's Will. UnuThul was too powerful *not* to know when so many Jedi entered the system. *Wonder why Unu hid it from* us.

Unu's will began to press down on them, and their thoughts turned back to Lowbacca.

After a few moments of searching, they found their friend, groggy and confused and barely conscious, down below Qoribu's southern pole in the heart of the Chiss command group.

Drugged, Zekk said in their thoughts. *Not surprising.*

Predictable, Jaina agreed, growing impatient. *We'll have to move fast.*

Unu's will pressed down, and their hands grew too heavy to lift toward their throttles. Their turn would come later—once the Great Swarm prepared the way.

By the time the Colony's command ship—an outdated *Lancer*-class frigate operated by the Unu—appeared, the first dartships were closing with the cruiser escorts. Jaina's and Zekk's tactical displays turned white with propellant trails and did not darken again. The Chiss escorts flickered and vanished one after the other, and the Killik barrage fell on the cruisers themselves. Both vessels lost shields within seconds and withdrew under fire.

The lead cruiser took a drive hit and was overtaken. Its turbolasers continued to fire for another few seconds, then it suffered a hull breach and began to belch flame. Once its weapons had fallen silent, the Great Swarm stopped attacking and streamed after the surviving cruiser.

The Hapan squadron started to follow, moving to secure the hole the Killiks had opened in the enemy's lines, but Jaina and Zekk were in no mood to wait. They needed to retrieve Lowbacca *before* the Chiss withdrew to Ascendancy space.

Unu's will grew lighter, and Jaina and Zekk shot past the

nearest Hapan Nova, passing so close to the bow that they saw the bridge pilot squinting at the shadowy silhouettes of their StealthXs.

The passage opened into a murky vault too large for Mara's helmet lamp to illuminate; the beam merely reached into the darkness and vanished. She shined the light at her feet and found a dark, ribbed slope strewn with membrosia balls. In places, the balls were heaped a meter high. Her spine felt prickly and cold, but that was nothing new. Her danger sense had been on overload since the moment they entered the nest.

Luke's blaster flashed behind her. A distant *peew-peew* sounded through Mara's helmet, suggesting that air pressure had been restored to at least this part of the nest. A quick check of the heads-up display inside her faceplate confirmed her guess.

"At least my hisser's no problem now." Luke opened his faceplate and continued to fire. "One less thing to worry about."

Mara glanced back and found a wall of six-legged dartship canopies scurrying up the passage. She used the Force to shove all but one of the insects back down the passage, clogging the tunnel while Luke concentrated on the leader. Half a dozen shots later, the canopy finally cracked, and a blaster bolt burst the pilot's head.

Mara allowed another Killik to come forward, and she and Luke repeated the maneuver once more before the insects in back turned around and started down the tunnel.

"Time to go," Mara reported, still speaking over her suit comm. "Trying to flank us again."

Luke finished the insect they had isolated, then they floated out into the weightless darkness. Fifteen meters in, Luke stopped and began to shine his helmet lamp around the chamber.

"Might be a good place to make a stand," he said. "Room to maneuver. With the Force, we'll have an agility advantage."

Mara swept her own lamp around the vault. Once in a while, she glimpsed a stretch of shapeless wax or a few membrosia balls resting on a dark, sloping wall. Otherwise, they seemed to be floating in empty air.

"Sounds good." Mara shined her light back into the passage from which they had come. She was surprised to find it completely empty. The dartship pilots were nowhere in sight. "Just one problem."

Luke turned to look as well. Mara sensed him reaching into the Force, then he said, "Han and Leia must be drawing them off. I think the *Falcon* is inside the nest."

Mara equalized her suit pressure, then retracted her faceplate and nearly gagged on the cloying rankness of the air. "You could have warned me," she complained. "What *is* that smell?"

"Maybe it's better not to know," Luke said. "Something rotting, I think."

"And I thought Lizil smelled bad."

As Mara spoke, a ball of membrosia drifted past, "falling" at an angle toward her knees. In contrast to the clear amber syrup of the Lizil and Yoggoy nests, this liquid looked dark and muddy inside its wax container, with stringy clots of solids silhouetted in the glow of her helmet lamp.

Mara looked up toward the ceiling and thought for a moment she was only looking at an area of burnished wax. Then, as her eyes grew more accustomed to what she was seeing, she began to make out several speeder-sized Killik heads. All were deep, dark blue, and all were facing a two-meter tunnel opening.

"What the blazes?" Mara reached for her lightsaber. "Queens?"

"I don't think so," Luke said, sounding a little disgusted. "Membrosia givers. Look at the other end."

Mara ran her light along one of the Killiks' bodies, past a thorax clamped to the ceiling by six tubular legs running to a hugely swollen abdomen. About the size of a bantha, it was oozing cloudy beads of dark membrosia and crawling with tiny Gorog attendants, which carefully slurped up each drop and redeposited it in a waxy ball extruded from their own abdomens.

"Appetizing," Mara commented dryly. Neither the membrosia givers or their attendants seemed inclined to attack—no doubt because they were entirely lacking in combat ability. "What now? Start back?"

As Mara asked this, Alema Rar appeared in the tunnel above,

still dressed in the skintight flight suit she had been wearing when she stole the skiff back on Ossus. Now the material was stained and rumpled in a way Alema would never have permitted before.

The membrosia givers extended short feeding tubes and began to clack their mandibles for attention, but Alema ignored them.

"Sorry," she said to Mara. "We can't let you leave."

"You can't *let* us?"

The sight of their betrayer made Mara's blood boil. She tried to remind herself that Alema was not entirely responsible for her actions—that the Twi'lek had unwittingly fallen under the Dark Nest's influence—but it didn't make her feel any less angry. She pulled her lightsaber from its belt hook, then glanced toward the empty tunnel that led back toward the hangars.

"From where I stand, you're in no position to stop us."

Alema gave a sly smile. "We believe we are."

A muffled rustling rolled up the tunnel, and a wall of Gorog warriors appeared in its mouth. Though they lacked the canopies that had protected the dartship pilots, they were much larger and armed with both tridents and electrobolt assault rifles. The rifles, Mara knew, were relatively feeble weapons, cheap and reliable but requiring three or four hits to take down most targets. Unfortunately, she did not think the Killiks were going to have any trouble massing their firepower.

A shrill chorus of *squeck-squecking* began to spread outward from the dark corners of the chamber, the sound of hundreds of Killik feet rushing across the sticky wax that lined the nest. Mara swept her helmet lamp over the walls and found them crawling with Gorog warriors, and the anger she felt toward Alema assumed an acid taint.

"Tell your masters they're about to wish they *had* died in the Crash." Mara slipped a fresh power pack into her blaster pistol. "We're coming for them."

Alema smirked, and Gorog warriors began to pour out of the tunnel behind her. "You will need more than lightsabers and blaster pistols, we think."

* * *

The *Falcon*'s darkened air lock slid silently open. The four YVH "bugcruncher" war droids—on loan from Tendrando Arms and specially programmed to Han's specifications—jumped into the pitch-black hangar. Next went the four Jedi—Kyp, Saba, Octa Ramis, and Kyle Katarn—in their combat-rated vac suits. Han was just glad he had convinced Meewalh and Cakhmaim to "help" Juun and Tarfang guard the *Falcon,* or he and Leia— bringing up the rear in standard-issue EV suits—would have had to follow *them,* too.

"I'm the captain of *Millennium Falcon,*" Han grumbled into his faceplate. "That used to mean something."

A moment later, Leia took his wrist, and they jumped out of the air lock. She drew him along through the weightless darkness, using the Force to move them away from the *Falcon* so they would not need to activate their jet belts and make targets of themselves. To Han, it was like making his way through a cargo hold during an all-systems failure. He kept bumping into stuff, and stuff kept bumping into him.

Finally, the YVHs gave an all-clear and activated their thrusters, briefly illuminating the airless, flotsam-choked launching bay before they shot through a hole in the rear wall. Conversing through the Jedi battle-meld if at all, Kyp and the other Masters activated their green combat lamps and used the Force to pull themselves after the war droids. Leia drew Han by the wrist and followed. He felt like a little kid being dragged through a bad dream, what with all the loose bug heads and chunks of thorax chitin floating around.

As they passed through the hole, Leia's helmet lamp came on. Han activated his own light and found himself in a small repair hangar. The YVHs led the way into a small utility tunnel filled with Gorog bodies. Most of the insects had burst eyes and dark strings of tissue extruding from the breathing spiracles on their thoraxes—signs of a quick-but-painful decompression death.

Kyp motioned the rescue party forward, then activated his belt thruster and led the way up the passage. Glad to finally be under his own power, Han started his own thrusters and followed at Leia's side. The accumulation of insect bodies grew thicker as they advanced, and soon the group almost seemed to be swimming through them.

Han touched his helmet to Leia's so they could speak without breaking comm silence. "Luke and Mara did all this?"

"Kyp seems to think so."

"Huh." Han started to wonder who might need rescuing more—the Skywalkers or the bugs. "Nice of them to leave us a trail."

They passed through the tattered remains of a hatch membrane and continued deeper into the twisting warren of tunnels, following a steady trail of dead Gorog and gouged walls. Han began to think the Skywalkers had decided to hunt down Welk and Lomi Plo on their own.

The rescue party came to another hatch, this one intact, and progress slowed to a crawl as the bugcrunchers pushed through one by one. Kyp and Octa Ramis followed the droids, and suddenly the membrane grew bright with battle flashes.

"Enemy located," Bug One reported, terminating comm silence. "Engaging now."

Han armed the T-21 repeating blaster he had brought along as bug repellent, then started toward the membrane.

Leia put out a hand to stop him. "Not yet," she said over the comm. "Kyp's suit has been punctured."

She did not need to explain further. With Kyp's suit damaged, it would not be smart to draw more fire in the hatch's direction.

"Well, tell 'em to hurry up," Han said. "My trigger finger is getting itchy."

Leia's eyes slid away from Han's, looking past his shoulder back down the corridor.

Then Saba's faceplate suddenly loomed up behind Leia's head, her pebbly lips broadening into a huge, fang-filled smile.

"It will not itch for long, this one thinkz."

Han spun around, and his stomach sank.

Dozens of dartship canopies on legs were racing up the tunnel toward them. Han raised his T-21 and opened fire. One canopy shattered, but most of the bolts ricocheted off, melting holes into the walls and filling the passage with an ever-thickening cloud of ethmane vapor.

Han slid over to stand shoulder-to-shoulder with Leia.

"Sweetheart . . ." He lowered his aim and began to blast Killik legs. ". . . did I ever tell you how much I hate bugs?"

THIRTY-EIGHT

The Chiss were retreating in disarray, spiraling down below Qoribu's south polar region in a tangled vortex of ion trails, lacing space behind them with a ragged net of turbolaser fire. Jaina and Zekk spotted an opening and swung their StealthXs toward it. Before they could dart through, a pair of frigates managed to shift their fire and string the hole with streaks of energy.

Jaina and Zekk peeled away, the StealthX slaved to Jaina's controls lagging half a second behind. Silhouetted against the white backdrop of Qoribu's south pole, they were visible to any sensor operator with a tracking telescope, and it would be folly to attempt a penetration when they had so clearly been spotted. If they wanted to reach Lowbacca alive, they would have to try another approach.

Not as disorganized as they look, Jaina observed.

This is a show, Zekk agreed.

Jaina and Zekk checked their tactical displays. The screen showed only the portion of the battle not hidden behind Qoribu's mass. But what it did show clearly revealed the Chiss falling back in a crooked, disjointed line that was barely managing to stay ahead of the swarm's dartships. A couple of frigates and light corvettes were blinking with damage, but most of the cruisers, and all of the Star Destroyers and fighter carriers, were safely below Qoribu, milling about in the heart of the fleet.

A Bothan fade, Jaina remarked.

The Chiss probably have a different name for it, Zekk pointed out.

Probably, Jaina agreed.

They swung around in a crooked, uneven curve, ducking behind blossoming turbolaser strikes and changing their approach frequently to throw off anyone trying to track them by sight. But Qoribu's polar region was as vast as it was bright, and their StealthXs remained silhouetted against its whirling white clouds.

We should warn UnuThul, Zekk suggested.

Our help isn't wanted, Jaina replied. That fact made them feel sad and rejected and horribly, utterly alone. *Our mission is to—*

—retrieve Lowbacca and leave, Zekk finished. *But we're Jedi.*

Our first mission is prevent a wider war, Jaina agreed.

They were deliberating more than discussing, weighing both sides of the argument in a single shared mind, and an unhappy thought occurred to them.

What if they did nothing?

The Great Swarm would be destroyed—perhaps even the Hapan fleet, which was advancing behind the safety of the Killik dartships. Without the means to defend the Qoribu nests, the Colony would be forced to abandon them, or to find a way to evacuate. In either case, the Chiss would no longer feel threatened, and a greater war would be averted.

UnuThul might be killed, Zekk pointed out.

Would the Colony return to normal? Jaina wondered.

Impossible to know.

Impossible, Jaina agreed. *But maybe not a bad thing.*

Jaina and Zekk waited, expecting to feel Unu's Will pressing down on them, driving them to act in the Colony's best interest.

But they were out of contact with the Taat mind—cut off from it by distance as well as by Unu's anger—and UnuThul was too busy coordinating the overall battle to join their combatmeld. Jaina and Zekk's mind was their own—for now.

A hole appeared in the turbolaser net, and they accelerated toward it, aiming for a quartet of tiny blue circles that their R9 units assured them was a cruiser's sublight drive. If they could sneak up close enough, they could slip into the heart of the Chiss fleet by hiding near its exhaust nozzles, where the glare would blind anyone peering in their direction.

This feels wrong, Zekk said. *Like we're betraying the Colony.*

And UnuThul, Jaina added. *But we're Jedi.*

Jedi do what is necessary, Zekk agreed. *To prevent war.*

To keep the peace.

The cruiser was so close now that they could see the boxy outline of its engine skirt enclosing the bright disks of its four huge thrust nozzles. Turbolaser beams stabbed out all around them, but never close enough to suggest that the StealthXs had been spotted again. Jaina and Zekk continued to close the distance.

Then another unhappy thought occurred to them. *Welk.*

If UnuThul dies . . .

The possibility was almost too terrible to consider. If Unu-Thul died, Welk—or Lomi Plo, if she had survived—might become the new Prime Unu. They did not know what that would mean for the Colony, but it would certainly be bad for the rest of the galaxy. The Dark Jedi would use the Killiks for their own ends, perhaps even to draw the entire galaxy into a single collective mind.

Need to protect UnuThul, Zekk concluded.

Better warn him.

Jaina and Zekk were relieved. It was what they had wanted anyway. Maybe they had even convinced themselves it was the best thing when it was not, but their mind was made up. They reached out to UnuThul in the Force, urging him to open himself to their combat-meld.

Unu's will pressed down on them. Suddenly, rescuing Lowbacca seemed more important than stopping the Colony's attack. If Jaina and Zekk did not rescue their friend quickly, he would perish along with his captors when the Great Swarm destroyed the Chiss fleet.

Jaina and Zekk pushed back, but—being out of touch with the Taat mind—they had no way to explain the Chiss trap. All they could do was pour their alarm into the Force and urge Unu-Thul to join the combat-meld.

Unu's will grew heavier, and they began to believe it was not so important to reach UnuThul after all.

Afraid we're trying to trick them again, Zekk surmised.

Only the knowledge that Unu was wrong gave them the strength to resist, to continue reaching into the Force.

Finally, someone reached back—but it was Jaina's mother, not UnuThul. Jaina and Zekk stretched out toward her, inviting her into their battle-meld, and the situation grew a little clearer. Leia and the others were under attack. An image of dozens of blue-black Killik soldiers appeared inside their mind, swarming up a dark tunnel, pouring electrobolt fire toward them.

Jaina and Zekk were alarmed, but Leia did not seem frightened or worried. Why should she be? She and Han had been trapped in worse situations a hundred times.

Now Jaina and Zekk were really worried—and confused. They did not know of any blue-black Killiks in the Qoribu system—nor of any nests with such gloomy walls.

Kr, Leia explained. *Secret nest.*

A nest could not be secret. Unu would know about it.

Welk? Leia reminded them. *Saba?*

Now Jaina and Zekk understood. Every time they had tried to investigate the assault on Saba, the Taat—and later UnuThul—had turned them aside. The Barabel had mistakenly attacked a Joiner, it was claimed, or she had fought a Chiss assassin.

Perhaps UnuThul had been attempting to hide the secret nest all along. Or maybe he just did not want to believe it existed.

Either way, the situation was worse than Jaina and Zekk had realized. They wanted to go to Kr to help Leia and the others, but if UnuThul died, the Dark Jedi would be close by, waiting to take over.

Leia seemed to understand. She was already withdrawing from the meld, urging them to be careful, assuring them that Luke and the other Masters had things well in hand on Kr.

When she was gone, Jaina and Zekk still felt no hint of Unu-Thul.

Have to do this the hard way, Jaina said.

Go back and make contact with Taat, Zekk agreed. *Then the Colony will know what we're thinking.*

Jaina and Zekk hesitated. Unu's will was a bantha sitting on their shoulders, pushing them toward Lobacca, toward the heart of the Chiss fleet.

Lowie can wait a few more minutes, Jaina said. *We'll come back for him.*

Lowie would understand, Zekk agreed. *Lowie is a Jedi.*

Jaina and Zekk rolled into simultaneous wingovers and reversed direction, pointing their noses back toward the Great Swarm. Unu's weight sank to their stick hands.

Only one problem with this plan, Zekk observed.

Jaina could feel Zekk fighting, as she was, to keep his controls dead center.

Not really. Jaina released her stick. "Sneaky, take us in."

The astromech took control of the StealthX, then chirped a question.

"To Unu's squadron." As Jaina spoke, Zekk was giving the same orders to his own astromech. The Taat were flying escort for UnuThul's flag frigate, so all the two Jedi needed to do to was rejoin the swarm, and the Taat mind would know everything they did. "And that command is non—"

"There is no need to desert our friend." UnuThul's gravelly voice reverberated over their comm speakers, but when Jaina and Zekk checked their reception meters, they discovered that their transceivers were not receiving a signal. "We will listen to your plea, but Unu will never let you stay. You have betrayed the Colony's trust—"

"It's not about us." Jaina was not quite certain what form of reply UnuThul could hear, so she simply spoke the words aloud. "We need to warn you."

"You're flying into a trap," Zekk added.

They took control of their StealthXs again, turned back toward the Chiss cruiser they hoped to use for cover. Lowbacca would not have to wait after all.

"This *is* about you," UnuThul insisted. "You are trying to save the Chiss fleet. Again."

"We're trying to save you," Jaina replied.

"It's a Bothan fade," Zekk added. "The Chiss are drawing you into the open."

"You studied battle tactics on Yavin," Jaina said. "You know what's going to happen when the fight moves beyond Qoribu's gravity well."

The boxy outline of the cruiser's engine skirt was again visible ahead. UnuThul remained silent as the brilliant circles of the thrust nozzles continued to swell in front of the StealthXs. Jaina and Zekk began to hope that they had convinced Unu of the danger.

Then UnuThul said, "It must be a coincidence. There were no Chiss in our tactics classes."

Jaina and Zekk knew better than to waste time pointing out the flaws in Unu's argument. Killik logic did not follow the same rules as that of most species—in fact, it did not follow rules at all.

Instead, Jaina asked, "Can the Colony really afford to take that chance?"

"When the Great Swarm reaches Qoribu's south pole, take a minute to regroup," Zekk suggested.

"You remember what will happen if we're right?"

"Of course," UnuThul said. "We have an excellent memory."

The comm speakers fell silent, leaving Jaina and Zekk feeling alone and shunned again, worried their pleas would go unheeded. The first tendrils of the cruiser's exhaust tail began to lick at their forward shields. Jaina and Zekk dropped below it and closed to within three hundred meters of the ship's stern. Their canopy tinting darkened to solid black, and they flipped their bellies toward the ion stream to protect the delicate sensor windows on top of the StealthXs' nose cones.

For the next thirty seconds, they remained on the fringes of the exhaust stream, following the cruiser toward the heart of the Chiss fleet. Jaina and Zekk tried to keep an eye on their tactical displays, but the ion interference rendered their screens almost unreadable. To discern anything, the R9s had to use a complicated algorithmic analysis to separate interference from true sensor returns.

Jaina and Zekk were beginning to think Unu had ignored their warning when the R9s announced that the Great Swarm had slowed. The eyes of the two Jedi Knights went to their tactical displays, desperately trying to infer a picture from the static on the screens. The astromechs reported that the Chiss retreat appeared to be growing even more disorganized.

Trying to tempt the enemy, Zekk observed.

Hope Unu sees that. To Sneaky, Jaina said, "Give us a simple schematic—"

Sneaky interrupted with a series of concerned tweets. Jaina looked out the canopy to see the cruiser swinging back toward Qoribu.

Baiting the trap, Jaina observed.

With our camouflage, Zekk complained. *Too many eyes watching now.*

Better find something else to follow in, Jaina agreed.

They dropped out of the exhaust stream. As their canopies grew transparent again, they found themselves surrounded by durasteel hulls ranging in apparent size from that of a finger to something closer to a Wookiee's arm.

Already deeper than we thought, Jaina observed.

Yeah, Zekk agreed. The static began to clear from their tactical displays. *But is that a good thing or—*

Blossoms of turbolaser fire lit the space around them. Jaina and Zekk surrendered their hands to the Force, and their StealthXs began to weave and bob, swinging wide before a strike exploded in front of them, climbing away from a beam even as it lanced out behind them.

Jaina's hand pushed the stick forward. The third StealthX— the one slaved to her controls—followed her into a dive and slammed into a blossom of fire behind her. Her R9 let out a sad whistle as it received the final data burst from its counterpart, then Jaina jinked starboard and Zekk juked port, and a trio of turbolaser strikes burst into a miniature sun between them.

Our boyfriend means business, Zekk observed.

Don't know that it's him. And it's old *boyfriend.*

Right. We're so over *him.*

We?

Jaina and Zekk dropped the line of thought there. It was just getting too creepy, with Zekk sharing everything that Jaina *still* felt for Jag, and Jaina sharing everything that Zekk still felt for her, and it didn't help matters that, at the moment, Jag was doing his best to kill them both.

He's just following orders, Zekk consoled.

He has to, Jaina agreed. *He's Chiss.*

They continued to dodge through the barrage, angling first one direction, then another, always working deeper into the fleet. Despite the loss of the third StealthX, they could still rescue Lowbacca. Zekk's storage compartment was filled with oxygen tanks, and there was an air feed running into the empty torpedo bay below his seat. Unfortunately for Jaina, she was the only one small enough to fit inside.

The Chiss brought more ships to bear, stringing kilometer-wide screens of crimson energy ahead of the StealthXs, hoping the elusive starfighters would simply fly into a strike. Jaina and Zekk rolled away from one beam and found another crossing their noses. Jaina pulled up hard, her astromech screeching alarms as the inertial compensator strained to keep the ship together. Zekk dropped his nose and squeezed past underneath, his StealthX shuddering and bouncing as its shields crackled and overloaded.

Enough! To her droid, Jaina said, "Sneaky, give us a one-second fuse and drop a shadow bomb . . . now!"

The droid tweeted its alarm, but obeyed.

Jaina gave the bomb an aftward Force shove, and a silver flash filled the space behind them. The shock wave hit an instant later, slamming both StealthXs forward and pushing their tails down. Jaina and Zekk did not right themselves. They simply poured on the power and shot away, doing anything they could to change course and location before the Chiss eyes tracking them recovered from the blinding flash of the shadow bomb.

The Chiss brought even *more* turbolasers to bear—but well behind and below the StealthXs. Jaina and Zekk were close enough now to feel Lowbacca's presence aboard a heavily armored Dreadnaught escorting the flagship. They closed formation and swung toward it, then finally had time to check their tactical displays.

Unu had listened to their warning. The Great Swarm remained at Qoribu, spread out just beneath the southern pole, with the Hapans taking a supporting position behind the dartships. Meanwhile, the Chiss had given up trying to draw out the

Colony and were smoothly dispersing into their own defensive wall, three layers deep and just out of Hapan turbolaser range.

Could have timed this better.

Going to be hot as a nova getting through that picket field, Zekk agreed.

The Dreadnaught's ion drives suddenly brightened, then Jaina and Zekk's heart sank as the ship turned and accelerated away from the fleet. The Chiss were not fools. Having lost track of their quarry, they had decided to remove the bait.

Could have timed this a lot *better.* Jaina's vision blurred with welling tears, and she and Zekk reached out to Lowbacca, trying to reach him through the stupor in which his captors were keeping him, trying to assure him that they would find him, urging him not to lose faith.

They felt a question struggling toward the top of Lowbacca's mind, then anger; then the Dreadnaught vanished into hyperspace and they felt nothing at all.

THIRTY-NINE

The chamber was choked with dead Gorog, and still more came, pushing through the bodies and floating globules of gore to press their assault, their electrobolt rifles stringing the darkness with bright ropes of silver. Luke was tumbling through the rancid air, somersaulting over forks of crackling energy and spinning away from thrusting tridents, his lightsaber tracing a green cage around him as the blade moved smoothly from defense to offense, from diverting electrobolts to cleaving dark chitin. Mara was twisting along three meters behind him, connected by an invisible Force tether, firing her blaster with one hand and wielding her lightsaber with the other. They were sinking deeper into a battle trance, becoming one with their weapons, becoming the hands of death . . . and drawing ever closer to Alema Rar.

Luke felt the warm prickle of danger sense and glimpsed a large band of Gorog gliding through the bodies to his right, the electrodes on their rifles already charged and glowing. Still rolling and twisting, fighting off attacks from every direction, he pointed at one of the membrosia givers on the ceiling and used the Force to pull it down—legs flailing and chest booming—into their line of fire.

Alema tried to wrench the creature free, but her grasp was no match for Luke's. The membrosia giver remained in the thick of battle, a shrill screech rising from its feeding tube, long gobs of membrosia shooting from its abdomen.

Alema spat a Twi'leki curse and ignited her lightsaber. Luke's chest tightened with cold anger—he had not thought her foolish enough to come for him—and he steeled himself to do what was necessary.

But Alema went straight to the membrosia giver, stunning Luke by sinking her lightsaber deep into the insect's thorax and dragging the blade along the insect's entire length. The two halves of the huge body drifted apart, and a deafening volley of electrobolt fire lit the darkness.

The Skywalkers ducked away, Luke protecting them with his lightsaber while Mara's blaster added more dead Killiks to the shell of bodies already shielding them.

"Getting dangerous . . . in here!" Mara observed.

"Looks like."

"Time to carry the fight to them." Mara stopped firing and reached for a fresh power pack. "Time to go after Welk." She slipped the pack into her blaster and resumed firing. "And Lomi Plo."

Luke risked a glance toward Alema, who was clearly in no hurry to engage the Skywalkers directly and was gliding back toward her tunnel.

"Hoping to wear us down," Mara observed.

Luke shook his head. "Protecting something," he said. "Or someone."

Take her, Mara ordered through their Force-bond. "I'll cover."

Luke moved to intercept, no longer dodging or twisting, just shouldering past Killik corpses and going after Alema. He was shocked by her ruthlessness, but hardly surprised. The line she had crossed was an invisible one, a matter of degree and intention rather than principle. Had another Jedi Knight made a similar sacrifice pursuing a Jedi goal, Luke might have condoned the act, even tried to console the individual and reassure her that it had been the best choice available.

And that made him wonder more than ever what the Jedi had become.

A trio of Gorog warriors zeroed in on Luke, forcing him into somersaults until Mara took them out. He arrived at the cutoff point after Alema, but close enough on her heels that she had to turn and face him. She showed no emotion on her face or in the

Force, but she raised her lightsaber into a middle guard—the best initial defense for an outmatched fighter.

Luke continued to bat electrobolts aside, his lightsaber weaving a green cage around him, but he made no move to attack.

"Alema, this doesn't have to happen," he said. "You still have a home with us. Gorog persuaded you to betray the Jedi, but we *can* forgive you." Luke did not like what the war had done to the Jedi—what it had done to *him*—and he was determined to start *undoing* that right now. "Alema, reach out to me. I can help you find the way back."

"We don't want to come back!" Alema sprang, flying at Luke behind a whirling onslaught of slash and backslash. "Stop . . . interfering!"

Luke blocked and redirected her momentum, sending her tumbling into the body-choked darkness—and placing himself between her and the tunnel she had been guarding. He felt an inquiry from Mara, then glimpsed her pointing her blaster at the Twi'lek's back. He shook his head.

Be quick! Mara broke their Force tether, then launched herself into a wild gyre of sweeping blade-light and flashing blasterfire. *Han and Leia . . .*

Luke could sense the rest for himself. Han and Leia were almost there—and they would not be so forgiving. He began to retreat toward the tunnel, weaving and dancing as the electrobolts flew thick and fast around him. Alema started after him and had to slow down to dodge and block herself.

"Alema, your anger has made you vulnerable," Luke said. "Your sister's death made you angry, and the Gorog are using that anger to hold you."

"Numa was a warrior!" Alema snarled, readily shifting topics—as Luke had known she would—to the still-open wound of her sister's death. "She would defend the Colony!"

This time, she came at Luke under control, combining the flashing blades of a speed attack with the driving stomp kicks of a power assault. He switched to a one-handed grasp, parrying her strikes with his own lightsaber, slipping her kicks with a deft trunk twist, deflecting electrobolts with the palm of his free hand.

"Numa was wise." Luke continued to fall back, spinning around to slash open a pair of Gorog warriors foolish enough to charge him from behind. "She would have been the first to warn you against your anger."

Luke reached out for the Twi'lek, trying to embrace her in the Force and shield her from the Dark Nest's touch. "She would have been disappointed to see how you have surrendered to it."

Alema was too far gone. She attacked all the more furiously, shrieking her grief and rage in Twi'leki, slashing low and high, kicking right and left, her words as hard and angry as her blows. Time and again, Luke forced her to leave her body open for a killing blow he did not want to deliver, and time and again she failed to notice his mercy and spun around in another wild attack.

Then Luke felt an icy jolt of fear. He looked past Alema to see Gorog warriors closing on Mara from all sides, silver rays crackling at her so fast and furious she could not block them all. The first bolt burned a fist-sized hole in the thigh of her vac suit and filled the air with the stench of scorched durafiber. The second caught her in the chest, and Luke did not see the third. By then he was driving forward, pressing the attack and forcing Alema back toward Mara.

Suddenly the Twi'lek stopped, determined to stand her ground. Luke tapped her lightsaber aside, then used the Force to pull her hand toward him, drawing her off balance onto his own weapon. Her eyes widened, and the blade sliced down through her clavicle, deep into her shoulder.

Luke brought his boot up under her chin, snapping her head back, sending her arms flying out to her sides. She began to backflip away, her lightsaber slipping from her open fingers.

Luke summoned the weapon into his empty hand and continued toward Mara, who had disappeared inside a knot of Gorog. Her weapons were still flashing inside the snarl and her presence was burning hot in the Force, and that gave him hope. He reached out to Leia, urging her to hurry, then fell on the jumble with both lightsabers whirling.

The battle erupted into a tempest of hissing blades and shrieking blasters and crackling electrobolts. Luke opened a dozen thoraxes in a dozen strokes, then his back spasmed with the paralyzing heat of an electrobolt strike. Mara fired from somewhere inside the tangle of limbs and mandibles, and the acrid stench of melted chitin rose behind him. Luke stretched out with the Force, dragging Killiks away from Mara, hurling them into their fellow warriors or impaling them on crooked forks of energy.

Luke pulled himself toward a glimpse of red-gold hair, his lightsabers opening a path, filling the air with globules of insect gore. Twice, a mandible slipped through his defenses, one stabbing deep into his thigh, the other slipping a barb inside the face opening of his helmet. Both times, he slashed off the attackers' heads and moved on.

Finally, Luke came to Mara's whirling figure. Her vac suit had been burned to tatters, and she had half a dozen black circles where electrobolts had hit her. A faint aura of gold had arisen around her, a sign she was drawing on the Force to keep her exhausted, wounded body going.

Mara briefly locked gazes with Luke, then her green eyes slid away, looking overhead. Luke followed her line of sight and was surprised to see Alema Rar pulling herself into the tunnel mouth. Her left arm was floating at her side, a deep, gaping V where she had been cleaved.

Mara lowered her gaze again and continued her defensive whirl.

She batted away an electrobolt, then groaned, "This isn't really taking the fight to *them*."

"Not too late, though." Luke sent a flurry of electrobolts screaming back toward the Killiks that had fired them. "Got them overconfident now."

"Better make it look good, then."

Mara sent a dozen bolts screaming toward the Twi'lek. Luke did not see whether any hit. By then, the Gorog were pressing the attack again, and he was too busy defending himself and Mara to worry about Alema.

Leia's arms had become deadweights fifteen minutes into the fight, and she was able to wield her lightsaber now only by virtue of the strength Saba was lending her through the Force. Han had run out of power packs—she had not noticed when—and traded his T-21 for a pair of captured assault rifles, which he had taken to firing one in each hand. The bugcrunchers had taken so many hits that Bugs One through Three had exhausted their laminanium repair ingots. With the exception of Saba—who only seemed to grow quicker, stronger, and more joyful as the battle wore on—even the Jedi Masters were slowing, if the tattered condition of their combat vac suits was any indication.

And the Gorog just kept coming, blocking the way ahead, clattering out of side passages, rumbling up the tunnel behind the rescue team. A limitless swarm.

"Han!" Leia's lightsaber swept down to divert an electrobolt streaking toward his knee, then swung up to block one coming at her own head. Her arms were so numb she did not even feel them move. "Do those bugcrunchers have thermal detonators on them?"

"What do you think?"

"Use 'em."

"In *here*?" The assault rifle in Han's left hand ran low on power and began to shoot sparks. He let it float free. "That's crazy! If we blow a hole in this ice cube—"

"Use 'em!" Leia used the Force to pull a rifle out of a dead Gorog's hands and floated it up the corridor to Han. "I don't think we're going to reach Luke and Mara in time. And we're not doing very—"

"YVH bugcrunchers," Han said over the combat channel. "Go BAM. Use your detonators."

"BAM status requires authorization—"

"Do it!" Han shouted so loudly that his voice reverberated out of five other helmets. "Do it *now*!"

"Authorization code *do it now* accepted," Bug One said. The soft crump of the droid's grenade launcher sounded from the head of the line. "*By Any Means* status—"

A brilliant flash lit the corridor, and the rest of the report was lost to the earsplitting crackle of a thermal detonator.

The rescue team surged forward into the crater, and Bug Four called, "Proceed with all haste." A soft *crump* sounded as the droid launched his detonator. "Explosion imminent."

Leia and the others barely had time to start forward before a brilliant flash filled the corridor behind them. Leaving Bug Four to handle rear-guard duty, they followed Kyp and the other Masters forward. Another *crump* sounded from the front of the line. Another detonator exploded. The tunnel behind them filled with Gorog, and Bug Four launched a detonator.

"Blazt!" Saba shut down her lightsaber. "Where is the fun in that?"

Moving much faster now, they passed through another crater and started around the next corner—then stopped short when a deafening storm of electrobolt fire sent Bug One tumbling back into the adjacent wall. His armor was blasted down to the frame and his internal systems were hanging out, sparking and shooting green lubricant.

"Major eneeemyyy conceeeee . . ." He raised his arm, and a detonator floated out. "Deeeeee . . . eee . . . e . . ."

His systems shut down, leaving the detonator floating in front of him, its red warning light blinking the countdown.

"Misfire! Misfire!" Bug Two started toward the detonator. "Please seek—"

"Stand fast!" Leia ordered.

She raised her finger toward the detonator, but Saba or Kyp or someone had already sent it sailing around the bend. It detonated with a brilliant flash, then Bug Two led the charge forward.

When the rescue team followed, they found themselves entering a vast, murky vault filled with Gorog warriors. Leia could sense Luke and Mara a dozen meters above, hidden in a tangle of insects so thick and large she could not see the glow of their lightsabers.

"How about it, Saba?" Han asked. "That enough fun for you?"

Before the Barabel could answer, some of the Gorog recovered their senses and fired a volley of electrobolts. Leia's lightsaber came up automatically, as did those of Kyp, Saba, and the other Masters, but there were just too many strikes to block. She took a scalding hit in the shoulder and heard Han curse as he took one, then a pair of *crumps* sounded as Bug Two and Bug Three launched more detonators.

"Careful!" Kyp warned. "Master Skywalker—"

The rest was lost to a pair of earsplitting crackles, and Leia's sight flashed to white. The air shuddered as the bugcrunchers opened up with their blaster cannons. By the time her vision cleared, both droids had activated their thrusters and were shooting toward the combat tangle above. Kyp and the other Masters were close on their heels.

Leia looked over at Han. A hand-sized expanse of blistered flesh showed through a hole in the stomach of his vac suit.

"You all right?" he asked.

"Fine," Leia said. She started to remark that Han's wound looked worse than hers, but stopped when Jaina and Zekk touched her through the battle-meld, wondering what the blazes was happening and assuring her that help was coming. She grabbed Han's wrist. "Han, there's something I should tell you."

"Now?" He leaned down and kissed her on the lips. "I love you, too, but maybe—"

"Not that," Leia said. "I mean, it's Jaina. She's on her way."

"Here?" Han scowled. "Good thing or bad?"

Leia could only shrug and shake her head. "I'm pretty sure she and Zekk are Joiners."

Han let his chin drop. "Just shoot me—"

A volley of electrobolt fire crackled up the tunnel behind them. Bug Four retreated around the corner, armor smoking, a deep melt-crease along one side of his head.

"Okay—I didn't mean that."

Han dropped one of his electrobolt rifles and grabbed Leia around the waist, then activated his belt thrusters. They jetted toward the combat above, plowing through an ever-thickening morass of blood globules and drifting bodies. The largest part of the Gorog swarm had turned to face Kyp and the other Masters, but Luke and Mara were still trapped a few meters above the main combat, their lightsabers weaving brilliant snakes of color as they spun and slashed and killed.

Leia and Han were about halfway to the fight when she noticed that no Gorog were firing in their direction. Faced with a line of Jedi Masters and bugcruncher droids, apparently Leia and Han just did not seem like much of a threat.

Leia *hated* being underestimated.

"That way!" Leia reached across Han's face, pointing away from the battle at an angle. "Flank 'em!"

"I was just about to think of that." Han turned in the direction Leia had indicated, then dropped his second assault rifle and drew his trusty DL-44 blaster. "Take the stick!"

Before Leia could ask for clarification, Han braced his blaster hand across his free arm and pointed the emitter nozzle at one of the Gorog attacking Luke and Mara.

"Are you crazy?" Leia cried. "You can't shoot into a hand-to-hand fight!"

"No kidding?" Han replied. "I didn't know that."

Leia grabbed Han in the Force and, as they continued to approach the battle, tried to steady him. He squeezed the trigger, and a bolt streaked up to blast a Gorog's head apart. He fired again, and an abdomen exploded. The third shot burned a hole through a warrior's thorax.

Han began to fire more rapidly now, always aiming for the perimeter of the battle. The two Masters used the Force to shove targets into his line of fire, and it was only a few seconds before the only Gorog between them and the Solos were dead ones.

Han stopped firing and waved them down. "Come on! Let's get outta—"

Luke and Mara shook their heads, then turned toward the ceiling and vanished into a tunnel surrounded by the five largest, ugliest Killiks Leia had ever seen.

"Hey!" Han yelled, still trying to wave them back. "The ship's *this* way!"

FORTY

Jaina and Zekk knew they were getting close to the launching bay when the broken cylinders of derelict dartships began to appear in the ethmane fog. They could feel Leia and the other Jedi somewhere beyond, deep within Kr, awash in a battle whirl of anger and fear and pain.

They followed the shaft around a bend and, in the fog below, saw the hazy star of a blasted-out launching bay. From inside came the silver flicker of a small-arms barrage, punctuated at intervals by the brilliant bursts of laser cannons. Jaina and Zekk stretched their Force-awareness into the battle. They felt only four living presences aboard the *Falcon,* the Noghri and two others they did not recognize.

As their StealthXs slipped through the entrance, forks of white energy began to crackle across their forward shields. Jaina and Zekk activated their forward floodlights. The launching bay was filled with wrecked dartships and drifting insect parts. In the heart of the carnage floated the *Millennium Falcon,* taking fire from dozens of positions concealed in the flotsam. Perhaps two dozen insects in the chitin-and-insulfiber carapaces that served as Killik pressure suits had slipped inside the *Falcon*'s shields. They were blasting it with electrobolts at point-blank range, melting fist-sized pits into the hull armor.

Jaina and Zekk paused, struggling to grasp what they saw. Despite what they had sensed from Leia through the Force, they still found it difficult to believe that a nest of Killiks would attack the *Falcon* without reason . . . and all too easy to believe the *Falcon* might have provided a reason. Only the memory of the unprovoked attacks on the *Shadow* and Master Sebatyne earlier— and of the illogical explanations provided by the Colony—gave them the resolve to open fire.

Their laser bolts were blindingly brilliant in such a narrow space, and their canopy flash tinting went to black. Jaina and Zekk instinctively reached into the Force to locate their targets, but the only presences they felt were aboard the *Falcon*. They had to settle for counterfire, allowing their R9 units to control the laser cannons and target the source of each electrobolt.

It took longer, but the result was the same. The positions in the flotsam fell silent, leaving only the Killiks on the *Falcon*'s hull to contend with. Jaina and Zekk sealed their vac suits and moved their StealthXs deeper into the launching bay.

Before they could pop their canopies, the *Falcon*'s rear cargo hatch opened and two Noghri in vac suits dropped out of the vessel with a pair of T-21 repeating blasters. The hatch closed behind them, and they turned in different directions, twisting and spinning like Jedi, working their way around the hull, burning the Killiks off the ship. As much as it pained Jaina and Zekk to watch the deaths of so many Kind, they had to admire the artistry.

The Noghri had almost completed their hull cleaning when the *Falcon*'s ion drives glowed to life. Jaina and Zekk stretched their awareness into the ship again, trying to figure out why the two presences aboard would do such a thing.

They did not like what they felt.

"Help!" C-3PO's voice came over the emergency channel. "This Ewok is a criminal! He has the death mark on ten planets, and now he's attemptttiiiing . . . tooooo . . . steeeeeeaa . . ."

C-3PO's plea trailed off into a deep rumble as someone tripped his primary circuit breaker.

The *Falcon* spun her bow toward the exit. Still fighting the Killiks, the Noghri were thrown from the hull and began to drift.

Jaina swung her StealthX in behind her father's beloved freighter and armed a proton torpedo.

Zekk began to wonder if this was not overkill.

The specifications of the *Falcon*'s military-grade shields rose to the top of their mind, and Zekk understood. He armed a torpedo of his own.

They activated their targeting computers.

The *Falcon* stopped spinning—no doubt as target-lock alarms filled the cockpit.

A nervous Sullustan voice came over the comm channel. "This is Jae Juun, second mate of the *Millennium Falcon,* requesting the two unseen craft to deselect us as targets."

Jaina and Zekk did not comply.

The glow died from the *Falcon*'s ion drives. "This is Jae Juun, second mate of the *Millennium Falcon.* See-Threepio was mistaken. Our only intention was to move the ship out of . . . the line . . . What the bloah is *that*?"

Jaina and Zekk did not need to see past the *Falcon* to know what Juun was talking about. They could feel it in the growing pressure of Unu's will, in the growing weight inside them.

The *Falcon* slipped away from the exit, exposing the old *Lancer*-class frigate now blocking the way outside. A small, well-armed launch was gliding silently through the jagged entrance, nosing aside ruined dartships and tumbling pieces of Killik.

Unu's will grew crushing, compelling Zekk and Jaina to answer honestly—even before they sensed the question.

Who did this?

Mara and Luke were ten meters down a sticky, wax-lined tunnel, and every time Mara made the mistake of breathing, she came close to retching. The dank air stank worse than a Sarlacc's belch, a cloying mélange of decay, spice, and free ethmane. And the smell was only growing worse as they advanced.

"At least it keeps you from thinking about the burns," Luke said.

Mara's awareness of her wounds—half a dozen aching circles where electrobolts had burned thumb-sized craters into her flesh—returned. She drew a little more of the Force into herself, using it to reinvigorate exhausted muscles, to keep her pain-crippled body functional.

"That's what I love about you, farmboy," she said.

"I always look on the bright side?"

"Not really." Mara assumed a cynical tone. "You always know how to make a girl feel better."

The tunnel finally opened into a large vault where the air was so humid and hot that their faces grew instantly moist. An eerie whine permeated the chamber, barely loud enough to hear above the pounding of her own heart, and the Force grew heavy with the pain of the nearly dead.

Mara followed Luke into the vault, and suddenly she forgot the eerie sound, the horrible smell, even her own fiery pain. The entire chamber was lined by large hexagonal cells, some sealed with a wax cap, some containing a paralyzed Chiss captive curled around a Gorog larva. Many of the prisoners were dead and mostly devoured, with the barbed mandibles of a nearly developed larva protruding half a meter above the cell walls. Just as many remained alive, groaning weakly as larvae gnawed at their immobile bodies.

"I'm beginning to understand the Chiss point of view," Luke said. "I wonder if Raynar knows about this?"

"Maybe, on some—"

Mara's neck prickled with cold, and she spun around to find the wrong end of an electrobolt rifle illuminated in her lamp beam. Behind it, sighting down the stock, was a blue face framed by a pair of Twi'lek lekku.

Rather than taking half a second to ignite her lightsaber and another half a second to block, Mara pointed and released the Force energy she had been using to keep herself going. Her body erupted into pain and muscle tremors, but blue lightning shot from her fingertips and blasted the rifle, driving the stock back into the Twi'lek's mangled shoulder and crackling deep into the wound. Alema cried out and let the weapon slip from her hands, then went limp and floated away into darkness.

Mara felt a hint of uneasiness in Luke. "What?"

"Nothing," Luke replied. *Just thinking—*

Luke's lightsaber crackled to life and droned past Mara's ear, blocking what sounded more like blasterfire than another electrobolt. She sensed a second attack coming and activated her own blade, sweeping it up behind Luke's to bat away another string of bolts.

The blasterfire fell silent, but not before Mara could swing her helmet lamp toward its source. She glimpsed a hump-shouldered man with a half-melted face and one chitinous insect arm grafted to his shoulder; then he slipped out of the light.

"Force lightning." The man's voice was raspy and sharp. "We had thought Skywalker's Jedi considered themselves above that."

"We make exceptions." Again, Mara sensed a certain apprehension in Luke. She ignored it and swung her helmet lamp toward the voice, and again the dark figure slipped out of the light. "Especially in your case, Welk."

As Mara spoke, she and Luke moved apart, positioning themselves just within each other's reach, where they could still take advantage of overlapping fields of defense.

A soft flutter sounded above Mara's head.

"Hear that?" Mara asked.

"What?"

"I was afraid you didn't." Mara reached out in the Force but felt only a shadowy sense of danger, so vague and ambiguous she could have been imagining it. "There's something flying around over here."

"Welk?" Luke asked.

A string of blaster bolts erupted from Luke's other side, directly opposite the fluttering. He brought his lightsaber around and sent the bolts tearing back toward the source.

"I don't think so," Mara concluded.

She brought her own blade up, slashing through the darkness above her head, finding only dank air. Another flutter sounded behind her. She spun to attack and suddenly found herself in the Force grasp of someone else, twirling across the room and accelerating. Mara reached out, searching for her attacker. She felt only the horror and anguish that permeated the entire room.

Then she came to the wall, and a piercing agony blossomed low in her back. She looked down to find ten centimeters of mandible tip protruding from her abdomen, and the pain spread across her entire belly.

"Roddddder!"

The second mandible closed, driving a pair of barbs deep into the flesh above her hip.

"That *hurts*."

Mara reversed her grip on her lightsaber, and a flutter arose in the darkness at her side. Suddenly the handle grew stinging cold, then the blade started to sputter, flicker, and fade. Mara attacked anyway.

The blade sank two centimeters and sizzled out. The larva began to shake its head back and forth, its mandibles tearing at her inside.

"Mara?" Luke had activated his second lightsaber—the one he had taken from Alema earlier—and was advancing on Welk, batting the Dark Jedi's blaster bolts back at him. "Need the spare—"

"Fine here!" Mara returned her useless weapon to its clip. "Just take care of Welk."

Welk broke into an evasive tumble, firing as he moved and seldom going astray. Luke deflected a chain of bolts, but finished with his blades out of position and had to somersault away.

Trying.

Mara drew her blaster and put a bolt into the larva's head. It shook even harder, drawing an involuntary cry from her as a barb scraped something inside. She fired a second time, then heard a soft throb in front of her and brought her weapon around.

The handle grew icy cold, then a depletion alarm sounded. When she squeezed the trigger, she heard only the soft *pop* of a gas charge moving into the XCiter chamber.

"Neat trick," Mara said to the darkness. "It isn't going to save you."

The air pulsed above Mara's left shoulder. She swung her helmet lamp toward the sound and—as always—saw nothing. Then a prickle of danger sense raced up her spine, and she looked in the opposite direction. Gliding out of the darkness, just at the edge of her light, was a meter-high Gorog with thick chitin armor and overlong mandibles.

Even had she not seen the splint fused to its broken leg, Mara would have known that this was the assassin she had fought on Ossus. Much smaller than a typical Gorog warrior, it was coming at her in a fury, mandibles clacking, thorax drumming, crooked proboscis foaming.

Mara finally hesitated, confused, unsure, angry. The nest would be reaching out to Ben now, using the Force to share all that was happening here, to make him feel every Gorog death.

A puff of dank air brushed Mara's face. Her helmet grew biting cold and the lamp dimmed to darkness, then a soft *phoot* sounded from the direction of the approaching assassin bug. A glob of caustic-smelling acid hit the front of her ragged vac suit, and her flesh erupted with a new kind of burning.

Ben would have to get over it.

Opening herself completely to the Force, using her resolve to draw it in, Mara lifted her hand toward the assassin bug and squeezed. It popped with a long, sharp crackle and the rotten smell of dissipating methane.

A pair of blue bolts flashed up from Welk's direction and streaked into the smashed body. Mara had just enough time to push out with the Force and create a small bubble of protection before the assassin bug exploded.

In the orange light, floating just beyond arm's reach, she glimpsed a pale oval with little to suggest a face, only a few dark areas where there might have been a mouth and nose and eyes. Mara swung her hand toward it, but the blast light faded and the apparition was gone.

Luke barely felt the heat of the explosion, but the shock wave sent him cartwheeling into darkness. He kept his helmet lamp fixed on Welk's tumbling form and brought himself to a halt a few meters later. Welk slammed into a sealed cell and crashed through the wax cap.

Luke Force-plucked the blaster from Welk's hand and started toward him. He could feel that Mara was wounded but, at the moment, no longer under attack. The best thing he could do was keep the enemy too busy to worry about her—at least until Han and Leia arrived with the rest of the team.

Luke was still five meters away when Welk pulled his twisted body free of the cell. His black armor was smeared in yellow pulp, and the lipless slash of his mouth hung agape with what was either fear or disdain.

Luke reactivated his lightsabers.

The soft whiffle of wings sounded to his right, and the air suddenly grew as thick and heavy as water. He twisted toward the noise, but his body seemed to move in slow motion, and by the time he turned there was nothing to see but darkness.

A crimson blade ignited a few meters ahead, and Luke knew Welk was coming. He brought his lightsabers around in a cross guard and looked back toward the attack. Again, his actions seemed to take forever, and the glow of the crimson blade drew within striking range long before Luke was ready to defend.

The fight was about to get interesting.

Luke extended himself toward the glow, slamming his Force presence into Welk. It was like trying to push Qoribu out of orbit. Welk continued to come, bringing his blade around in a brazen full-reach attack.

Luke didn't even try to block. The Dark Jedi was strong— even stronger than Saba had said—but great strength was like great power. It seduced those who had it, lulled them into relying on might when other tools were better. Luke reversed tactics, pulling his attacker toward him. Welk tumbled forward, his hoarse voice croaking in alarm, his scarred face dropping toward Alema's silver blade.

The low throb of wings sounded overhead, and the hilt of Alema's lightsaber grew painfully cold as the thing causing the sound—he wondered if *that* could be Lomi Plo—drained the energy from its power cell. The blade sputtered and died.

Welk slammed into Luke headfirst, sending them both into an uncontrolled tumble. The Dark Jedi's crimson blade flashed past Luke's leg and burned a gouge into his shin, sending a fiery shaft of pain straight to the heart.

Luke righted himself, but he was still moving in slow motion, and Welk was already coming again. Luke reached out in the Force, bringing his thumb and forefinger together.

Welk's lipless mouth fell open. Dire gurgling sounds began to rise from his throat—and then Luke remembered Alema's sacrifice of the membrosia giver. Had *he* grown that casual about killing? So accustomed to the power he wielded that he would use it to kill when he had other means to defend himself?

Luke opened his fingers and released Welk.

The Dark Jedi's breathing returned to normal, but he stopped where he was, rubbing his throat and eyeing Luke in suspicion.

Skywalker! Mara's voice was a screech in the Force, but when she spoke aloud, it sounded weak and pained. "Are you crazy? Finish him!"

"Not that way," Luke answered. "The Force may have no light or dark side, but we do. We must choose."

"Right *now*?" Mara asked.

"*Especially* now."

Luke caught Welk's gaze, then—still moving slowly—raised his remaining lightsaber to high guard.

"Are you ready, son?"

"We are not your son!"

The Dark Jedi sailed forward, bristling at the condescension, striking at the flank Luke had left open.

Moving even slower than was necessary, Luke pulled his guard around and rotated away. A soft flutter sounded behind him. The hilt of his lightsaber grew cold—as Alema's had a moment earlier—and the blade died.

By then Luke had already released the weapon and accelerated to his best speed, slipping forward even as he twisted away from the attack. The sudden speed change caught Welk by surprise. Luke trapped the Dark Jedi's wrist in an X-block and continued to pivot smoothly away, forcing those hands into a tight circle and driving the lightsaber back up into Welk's stomach in one not-so-fast motion.

Welk let out a bloodcurdling scream and tried to deactivate the lightsaber, but Luke had his hand over the switch and now *he* was the strong one. He wrenched the handle free and ripped the blade out the Dark Jedi's side, then turned to face the attack he felt certain would be coming from Lomi Plo—and went spinning out of control when the air suddenly grew light and thin again and he could once more move at normal speed.

Luke saw the wall flashing past, coming up fast, barbed

mandibles protruding where he was about to hit. He deactivated the lightsaber, then reached out in the Force and jerked the larva from its cell, slammed into it in midair, and tumbled off in a new direction.

This time he managed to stop himself before he hit another wall. He reignited Welk's lightsaber and spun around with the crimson blade swinging—then felt a jolt of alarm and sensed Mara approaching out of the darkness.

"Hey, it's me!" Mara used the Force to push the weapon down. "Don't you recognize your own wife anymore?"

. Luke deactivated the blade. "Sorry."

Being careful to keep the beam below her chin so he didn't blind her, Luke turned his helmet lamp in Mara's direction. Her Force aura had subsided to a mere blush, and the charred circles on her body reminded him of how much his own electrobolt wounds ached. But it was the jagged, triangular puncture wound in her right abdomen that he found most alarming. About the size of three fingers bunched together, it was smeared with grime and oozing dark blood.

"How are you feeling?"

"About as good as I look." As Mara spoke, her eyes were searching the darkness around them. "But I'll last until we can find Alema. Any idea where she's—"

A series of dull thuds reverberated through the chamber, followed by the fading light and dying crackle of the thermal detonators that had just discharged inside a wall across the chamber. An instant later, a pair of Han's YVH bugcruncher droids rode into the chamber on the blue-white tails of their propulsion thrusters and quickly swung toward the Skywalkers.

"Remain calm!" one ordered in its ultradeep, ultramale voice. "Remain stationary! Help is coming."

FORTY-ONE

The bolt burns had been smeared with bacta salve, the puncture wounds were covered with actibandages on both sides, and there was enough stericlean in the air to disinfect half the nest. All that could be done in the field, Leia had done, and still she did not like how her sister-in-law looked. Mara had an ashy complexion and a hint of blue in her lips, and her eyes were so sunken they looked like crash craters.

"We'll get you to the *Falcon* soon," Leia said. They were back in the membrosia chamber, where the worst of the battle had taken place, waiting for a pair of fresh vac suits for Mara and Luke. "Bug four should be returning anytime now."

"No hurry." Mara squeezed Leia's hand. "I've been hit worse than this."

"It's not *you* she's worried about," Han said. "If I don't get out of this place soon . . ."

Han let his sentence trail off, and Leia turned to find him shining his helmet lamp into the haze-filled darkness. The beam extended only about ten meters before terminating in a wall of floating Gorog corpses.

"What, Han?"

"I don't know." Han pointed into the carnage, then swung his helmet lamp away to reveal a faint golden glow snaking through the corpses and floating blood globules. "Trouble, maybe."

Leia reached out in the Force and felt a swarm of Killiks approaching in the company of three Joiners.

"It's Jaina and Zekk!" she said. "With Raynar."

"Like I said," Han muttered. "Trouble."

The golden glow resolved itself into a line of shine-balls being carried by a long column of Killiks in chitinous pressure suits of many different configurations. At the head of the procession came the hulking form of Raynar Thul, his vac suit helmet tucked under one arm, his scar-frozen face red with fury. Half a meter behind, Jaina and Zekk followed, looking more nervous than angry.

Leia waited as they approached, then bowed to Raynar. "Unu-Thul, I'm sorry we must meet—"

"So are we," Raynar said. The battle-pitted form of Bug Four drifted out from among the mass of Unu following him. The droid's photoreceptors were dark, the seams of his body shell were smeared with soot, and he was surrounded by the acrid stink of scorched circuits. "Your droid murdered Unu."

Giving Leia no chance to respond, Raynar floated around her to the sides of Luke and Mara, and several hand-sized Killik healers poked their tiny heads up past the collar of his pressure suit. Leia started to go after him, but was stopped by a gentle Force tug.

"Wait with us," Jaina said from behind Leia. "Trying to explain now will only make Unu angrier."

"Thank you for the advice." Leia turned to face Jaina and caught the flash of several tiny eyes peering out of her collar, too. "Looks crowded in there."

Jaina stared into Leia's eyes. "Not really."

"It grows on you," Zekk said. He reached over and rubbed the backs of his fingers down Jaina's cheek.

"To tell the truth, we kind of like it," Jaina added.

"Oh," Leia said. "I would have thought all that creeping inside your suit would feel, um, *uncomfortable*."

Jaina and Zekk shook their heads in unison.

"Not at all," Jaina said.

"It makes us feel whole," Zekk added.

The trio spent an awkward moment looking at each other, Jaina and Zekk softly humming and clicking to themselves, Leia hiding her feelings behind a polite smile. Though she had already sensed in the Force what had become of her daughter and Zekk, actually seeing them behave like Joiners was almost more than she could bear. Her heart was dropping with every beat.

Finally, Jaina asked, "What are you doing here, Mother?" Little Killik healers began to crawl out of her suit and launch themselves into the darkness. "We thought you were going to open negotiations with the Chiss."

"I had another idea," Leia said. "One that might actually work."

Jaina and Zekk waited patiently for her to elaborate.

"There's no sense explaining it twice," Leia said. "Let's wait until Ray—er, UnuThul is available."

A hurt look came to the faces of Jaina and Zekk. Leia felt a pang of regret, but she did not apologize. Too much depended on her plan, and she could not risk having the pair speak against it before she had a chance to present it to Raynar.

"What about Dad?" Jaina asked quietly. She glanced toward Han, who remained with Luke and Mara but was looking over at his daughter and Zekk. "Is he still going to cut our tether for staying?"

"It may take some time for your father to accept this," Leia said. "He still has nightmares about whatever happened to him after that misunderstanding with the Kamarians."

"We're not Kamarians," Jaina objected. Zekk absentmindedly rubbed his forearm along the back of her neck, and Han made a sour face and looked away. "We're still his daughter."

"Just give your father some time," Leia said. She did not know how to explain—without offending Jaina and Zekk—what she knew in her heart: that Han was not as disappointed with Jaina as he was angry in himself; that he blamed himself for not protecting her from what she had become. "This is going to be hard for him."

"It will be hard on us all, we think," Zekk said.

Raynar slipped away from Luke and Mara—who were now crawling with Killik healers—and returned to Leia. He fixed his gaze on her, and suddenly her vision darkened around the edges. His blue eyes seemed the only lights in the chamber, and she felt an enormous, murky presence pressing down on her inside.

"*Now* you can explain this slaughter, Princess Leia," Raynar said. "Why did the Jedi kill all these Kind?"

"Quite simply, we had no choice," Leia said. "They were attacking Luke and Mara."

This drew a round of suit-muffled chest pulsing from the entourage of Unu.

"Strange," Raynar said. "This does not look like the Skywalkers' nest. Are you sure *they* were not the ones attacking?"

"It's complicated." Leia started to suggest they come back to that in a moment, but the presence in her chest grew heavy, and she found herself explaining more about the mission than might have been wise. "This nest was drawing the Colony into a devastating war. We hoped to undermine their influence so you would consider our peace plan."

Han's jaw fell. "Leia! How about a little tact?"

"We prefer her candor," Raynar growled. His burning eyes continued to hold Leia's gaze. "But this slaughter was pointless. Eliminating this nest can only turn us against your plan."

"Unfortunately, we had no choice." By the sound of Luke's voice—Leia remained unable to see anything but Raynar's eyes—he was floating over to insert himself into the conversation. "They were trying to eliminate *us*. It was self-defense."

"*Self-defense?*" Raynar sounded outraged. "The Kind fight only when *they* are attacked."

"Yeah," Han said. "You're a lot like the Chiss that way."

Raynar turned to glare at Han. Leia's vision returned to normal, and she found Han sneering confidently back at Raynar, looking as though he were staring down an Aqualish bar brawler instead of the leader of an interstellar civilization.

Leia slipped between the two. "Let me show you something." She addressed herself not only to Raynar, but to the entire Unu entourage. "You need to understand something about this nest, and then we can talk about whether the Colony truly wants peace."

Without waiting for permission, Leia turned toward the ceiling, leading Raynar, Han, and the Unu through the body-filled darkness toward the nursery entrance. Luke and Mara, who had stopped using the Force to compensate for their injuries, remained behind at the insistence of the Killik healers, and Jaina and Zekk stayed with them. Leia did not understand why, but there was a lot about her daughter and Zekk that she did not understand right now.

After a few moments, they reached the cave that Bugs Two and Three had blasted through the ceiling, and the smell of decay grew sickening. Kyp and the other Masters were inside the nursery gathering Chiss survivors and searching for Lomi Plo, so Leia opened herself to the battle-meld and urged them to have the bugcrunchers stand down.

"Bugcrunchers?" Raynar said.

Leia was a little surprised, since she could not sense Raynar's presence in the meld, but Han was nonchalant.

"No offense. We had to call 'em something."

Halfway through the cave, they found Saba waiting. Her vac suit and face scales were smeared with wax and offal from pulling Chiss out of larval cells, and the stench rising off her was enough to send a rustle of revulsion through the Unu.

Saba allowed Raynar and the entourage to stare at her for a moment, then said, "This one is sorry for her smell. The work in here is meszy."

"What *is* your work?" Raynar asked.

Saba looked to Leia before answering.

"It will be better if we just show you," Leia said, directing her comment more to Saba than Raynar. "Any sign of Alema yet?"

"None," Saba said. "Perhapz she was disintegrated in a detonator explosion."

"Maybe." Having seen for herself how acute the Twi'lek's danger sense was, Leia had her doubts. "What about Lomi Plo?"

Saba turned her palms up. "Vanished."

"Lomi Plo is dead," Raynar said, as if by rote. "She died in the Crash."

Saba glanced his way, gnashing her fangs, then looked back to Leia. "You are sure about this?"

Leia nodded. "Unu needs to see this." Silently, she added that it was *still* the only way to break the Dark Nest's hold on the Colony.

Saba shrugged, then led Leia and the others into the darkness of the nursery. The air was hot and dank and so filled with the stench of decay that Raynar gulped and the Unu rumbled their thoraxes. Kyp and the rest of the rescue team were working along the far side of the chamber, the beams of their helmet lamps sweeping across the wall but revealing little more than the hexagonal pattern of the nursery cells.

A few meters in, Leia stopped and swung her helmet lamp toward the nearest wall. The beam illuminated the half-devoured corpse of a Chiss prisoner, still curled around a squirming Gorog larva.

Raynar gasped, and the nearest Unu brought their mandibles together in shock. Han shined his helmet lamp on a second cell, and Saba a third. Both of those cells also contained the bodies of Chiss captives.

"What is this?" Raynar demanded.

"Looks pretty clear to me," Han said. As more Unu poured into the room with their shine-balls, the chamber brightened rapidly, and the true extent of the horror grew more apparent. "Kind of makes a fella see how the Chiss might have a point, doesn't it?"

Raynar whirled on Han. "You think *we* did this?"

"Not *you*, exactly," Leia said, silently cursing Han's biting humor. "The Dark Nest did it. The Gorog."

"Gorog?" Raynar's gaze drifted back to the gruesome sight in the cells. "What is this Dark Nest?"

"*This*." Saba waved her arm at the murk around them. "The nest that keepz attacking us. The one that has been feeding on Chisz captivez. The one that made you build more nestz at Qoribu."

Raynar glowered at the Barabel. "The nests do not lead Unu. Unu leads the nests."

"Really?" Leia cocked her brow. "Then all this is *Unu's* doing?"

"No." Raynar's voice grew sharp. When his entourage began to clack and drum, he added, "This is not even a Colony nest. We do not *have* a nest on Kr."

Han looked around pointedly. "Funny. Looks a lot like that nursery on Jwlio—except for all the Chiss captives, of course."

"Actually, it can be a Colony nest," Leia said to Raynar. "And you *wouldn't* remember."

This drew an even louder protest from the Killiks, but Leia spoke over it. "Cilghal thinks the Dark Nest serves as a sort of unconscious for the Colony's collective mind. It would be able to influence the Kind without you knowing—just as the unconscious mind of most species influences *their* behavior."

"Impossible," Raynar said, far too quickly. "There are no Gorog in the Kind. How could the nest influence us?"

"The same way *you* influenced Jaina and the others when you called them to help the Colony," Leia replied. "Through the Force."

Raynar's voice grew soft. "Through the Force."

"That's right," Leia said. "The same way you convinced Tesar to visit Bornaryn Trading. The same way you convinced Tahiri and Tekli to argue the Colony's case to the Jedi Order."

Raynar's eyes flared in understanding, but Unu's protest rose to a crescendo. He closed his eyes as though trying to concentrate, but Leia could see in the twitching muscles of his face some internal struggle, some insect argument she would never understand. She began to have the unpleasant feeling she was attempting the impossible.

Leia glanced over at Saba and mouthed Welk's name. The Barabel's eyes narrowed, but she nodded and quickly slipped away.

At last, the insect din quieted, and Raynar opened his eyes.

"Even if you are right about the Dark Nest, conquering is not our way," he said. "The Kind seek only to live in harmony with the Song of the Universe."

"Yeah, well, you don't have to conquer something to take it over," Han said. "And the Dark Nest had more in it than just Killiks."

"I assume you remember the Dark Jedi," Leia pressed. "Raynar fought them as a young man at Yavin Four. And Welk and Lomi Plo abandoned the strike team on *Baanu Rass.*"

Raynar studied her for a moment, then nodded. "We remember. And you think . . ." He let the sentence trail off as the Unu began to rustle and clack; then his voice grew stubborn again. "But you must be wrong. Welk and Lomi Plo died in the Crash."

"Then who is this?" Saba asked.

She emerged from shadows dragging Welk's badly slashed body. He was still dressed in his chitin-and-plastoid armor, with a new insect arm grafted to his shoulder. His face looked even less human than Raynar's, but he clearly wasn't Chiss.

Saba sent the corpse gliding toward Raynar's chest.

Han waited until the thing hit, then said, "He's got some pretty bad burn scars, but that tells you something right there."

Once it was in front of him, Raynar seemed riveted by the corpse, his blue eyes slowly sliding back and forth beneath his scarred brow, his breath coming in ever-raggeder rasps.

"Jacen investigated the Crash," Leia said. "He saw you pull Welk and Lomi out of the flames."

The Unu fell deathly quiet, and Raynar's gaze swung to Leia. "*Saw* us?"

"Through the Force," she clarified.

"Yes—we remember." Raynar nodded and closed his eyes. "He was there . . . on the bridge . . . for just a moment."

"You saw *Jacen*?" Han gasped.

"That's impossible," Leia said. "He would have had to reach across time—"

"We *saw* Jacen. He gave us the strength to continue . . . to pull them . . ." Suddenly Raynar stopped and turned toward the center of the nursery. "Where is Lomi?"

He had barely asked the question when the Unu entourage began to disperse across the nursery, their shine-balls illuminating the vault in a spray of whirling light.

"Where is Lomi?" Raynar repeated.

Relief washed over Leia like a Rbollean petal-oil shower. She had broken through to Raynar's memory. "Then you recall saving her?"

"We remember," Raynar said. "She was afraid that the Yuuzhan Vong would find us again, or that Anakin would come looking for her, or Master Skywalker. She was afraid of many things. She wanted to hide."

"Well," Han said, "that sure confirms Cilghal's theory."

"What theory?" Raynar asked.

"The way Cilghal sees it," Han said, "when a Killik nest swallows up someone who's Force-sensitive, the nest takes on some of his personality."

"In your case, the Yoggoy absorbed the value you place on individual life," Leia said. "They started to care for their feeble and provide for the starving, and it wasn't long before their success led to the creation of the Unu."

"That's much how we remember it," Raynar allowed. "But it has nothing to do with the Gorog."

"You said you remember pulling Welk and Lomi Plo out of the fire," Han pointed out. "But then they just disappeared."

"You said Lomi was afraid and wanted to hide," Leia added. "That was what Yoggoy absorbed from her. Isn't it possible that she also created a nest of her own—a nest hidden from everyone else?"

As Raynar considered this, the color seemed to drain from his face. "*We* caused this?"

"That's not what we're saying," Leia said. "Only that the Dark Nest is influencing—"

"If we saved Lomi and Welk, we are responsible."

An eerie tempest of clacking and muffled booming rolled through the nursery as the Unu again started to protest. Raynar turned from Leia and the others and slowly glided along the wall, peering into each cell he passed and shaking his head in despair.

"If we saved Lomi and Welk—"

Han caught up and took Raynar by the arm. "Look, kid, you couldn't have known."

Amazingly, Raynar did not send Han tumbling across the room or silence him with a gesture or even pull away. He merely continued to float along, seemingly unaware of Han at all, staring into the cells.

"If we saved Lomi and Welk, *we* did this."

"You should get a medal for saving them," Han said. "What happened later, that's not your fault."

That got Raynar's attention. He stopped and turned to Han. "This is not our fault?"

"No way," Han said. "All you did was save their lives. That doesn't make you responsible for what they did later."

"We are not responsible." Raynar's voice was filled with relief, and Unu's clacking died away. "That's right."

The spray of shine-ball light slowly began to contract back toward Raynar, and Leia felt Kyp reaching out to her, demanding an explanation, but she could not sense what he wanted explained.

"Maybe this is a Chiss ruse," Raynar said, talking more to himself than Han now. "It must have been a trick to convince the Jedi that the Colony is in the wrong."

Saba shined her helmet lamp into one of the cells. "To this one, it lookz like the trick was on the Chisz."

"The Chiss are ruthless," Raynar said. There was an ominous note of insistence to his gravelly voice. "They would sacrifice a thousand of their own kind to turn the Jedi against us."

"That doesn't explain the Gorog that attacked us on the way in," Leia said. She was alarmed by how Raynar was trying to reshape reality, by how he seemed to be searching for a story that worked. "They weren't Chiss—and neither are all these larvae."

"Yes, it was a very insidious plan," Raynar said. "The Gorog must have been brain-slaves. They were *forced* to fight—and to feed on Chiss volunteers."

"Perhaps," Leia allowed carefully. In a human mind, she would have called Raynar's thought process a psychotic break; in the collective mind of the Colony, she didn't know what to make of it. "But there is another explanation."

"The Chiss are creating Killik clones?" Raynar asked.

"I don't think so," Leia said.

The Unu entourage began to return, many of them drawing the helpless, wide-eyed forms of the Chiss survivors that the rescue team had been pulling out of the cells. Kyp and the other Masters were also approaching, pouring their displeasure into the battle-meld. Saba reached out to them, urging them to stand by, assuring them Leia was in control.

Thanks a lot, Leia thought.

"Do you remember what we were talking about?" Leia asked, continuing to address Raynar. "The Dark Nest?"

"Of course. Our memory is excellent." Raynar's eyes turned bright and angry. "Han said we were not responsible."

"That's right," Leia said. Her vision began to dim around the edges again, and the heavy presence she had experienced before returned to her chest. "But that doesn't . . . mean . . ."

The murky weight inside grew heavier, and Leia began to understand that Raynar had been damaged as much on the inside as on the outside. Hopelessly marooned, in unimaginable anguish, dependent on a bunch of insects—the shock had just been too much. Raynar had dissociated from the situation, literally becoming UnuThul so he would not recall all the terrible things that had happened to Raynar Thul.

"We understand what *not responsible* means," Raynar said. "It means that just because the Dark Nest exists, we are not the ones who created it." He pointed to the nearest captive, a frightened-looking male wearing the black shreds of a CEDF gunnery officer's uniform. "The Chiss did."

The officer's face paled to ash, and his eyes grew even wider—the only signs of fear that his paralyzed body could still exhibit.

"What we do *not* understand," Raynar said, "is the purpose of this nest."

An unintelligible groan rose from the Chiss's throat, so weak and low that Leia took it to be more of a pained whimper than an attempt to speak.

"Tell us!" Raynar commanded.

The officer moaned again, but the noise sounded even less like words than before.

"We know you are lying." Raynar's tone was ominous, and the officer's face grew white. "Do not insult us."

"I don't think he means to," Leia said. She felt certain that the officer had not said anything at all; Raynar's shattered psyche was just imposing its own meaning on the Chiss's incoherent groans. "I'm sure he doesn't even know that the Chiss created this nest."

Raynar turned back to Leia. "You are *sure*?"

"Perhaps *confident* is a better word," Leia corrected. Again, the weight pressed down inside, and she knew she had to tell Raynar something he wished to hear—something that would make him agree to her plan. "What if the Chiss didn't even *know* they created the Dark Nest?"

"How could they create the Dark Nest without knowing it?" Raynar's voice was doubtful. "We don't see how that could work."

"By *accident,*" Han said, picking up on Leia's plan. "That's the only way it could happen. The Chiss would never intentionally do something like this to themselves—not even to volunteers. They have too many honor codes."

"That's right," Leia said. The weight inside was decreasing. "Chiss society is defined by war. They're always fighting—against the Vagaari, the Ssi-ruuk, even each other."

"And the Qoribu nestz are filled with Chisz Joinerz."

Saba let the statement hang, leaving it to her listeners to draw their own conclusions. Under normal circumstances, it would have been perfect persuasive technique. But with Raynar, Leia did not want to take any chances. There were too many dangerous turns available to a dissociative mind—especially a dissociative *collective* mind.

"Remember what Han said about Cilghal's theory?" Leia asked. "She believes that when a Killik nest absorbs a Force-sensitive being, the nestmates assume a portion of that being's personality."

"When the Yoggoy absorbed you," Han added, "they started to value individual life. When they absorbed Lomi Plo and Welk, they assimilated the desire for secrecy and—"

"We are not responsible for the Dark Nest!" Raynar protested. "Lomi Plo and Welk died in the Crash!"

"That's right," Leia said, cringing inwardly. "Welk and Lomi Plo died in the Crash."

It was growing more apparent that dragging Welk and Lomi Plo out of the burning *Flier* had been just too much for Raynar to bear; that whenever he remembered it, he also remembered how much *he* had suffered—and all that he had lost—by doing it.

Leia continued, "But the Yoggoy absorbed your respect for living things, and it wasn't long before their success led to the creation of the Colony."

"That is how we remember it," Raynar agreed. "But we do not see what that has to do with the Dark Nest—"

"Everything!" Saba waved her scaly arm at the nursery again. "Look at how many Chisz Joinerz they had!"

Raynar's eyes brightened with anger. "The Kind are not cannibals. Our nests do not feed on our own Joiners."

"*Something* happened in this nest," Saba pointed out.

"And the Chiss are bloodthirsty warriors," Leia added. It was a wild exaggeration, but one that Raynar would be eager to believe. "Really, I'm surprised this hasn't happened to the other Qoribu nests."

"This?" Raynar shook his head. "This could not happen to another nest of Kind."

"It happened here," Saba pointed out.

"Maybe there's some sort of balance point," Han added, feigning contemplation. "When a nest gets too many Chiss Joiners . . ."

He let the sentence trail off and turned toward Raynar, his expression growing steadily more concerned.

Raynar finished the thought. "It becomes a Dark Nest?" The Unu broke into a distressed drone, and he nodded. "That could explain what happened here."

"The Chisz *are* great believerz in secrecy," Saba offered helpfully.

"Yes." Raynar spoke with an air of certainty. "The Kind will take no more Chiss into our nests."

"That's one solution," Leia agreed. She caught Han's eye, and they shared one of those electric moments of connection that made her wonder if he was Force-sensitive after all. "But what are you going to do with all your prisoners?"

A nervous clatter rose among the Unu, and Raynar asked, "Prisoners?"

"*Chisz* prisonerz," Saba said. "As the war spreadz, you will have hundredz of thousandz. *Millionz.*"

"Only one thing *to* do." Han shook his head in mock regret. "Of course, that'll only make the rest of the Chiss fight that much harder."

Raynar turned to glare at Han. Leia found herself holding her breath, hoping she had not made a mistake reading Raynar's warped psyche—that he had not grown ruthless enough to accept Han's suggestion.

At last, Raynar said, "The Colony does *not* kill its prisoners."

"No?" Han returned the glare for a moment, then shined his helmet lamp on a half-eaten body. "That'll change soon enough."

The Unu entourage erupted into an angry buzz, but Raynar said nothing.

"Maybe it will not be so bad for the Colony," Saba said. She turned to address the Unu. "Soon, *all* your nestz will be like the Gorog. The Kind will become great fighterz."

"We do not wish the Kind to be great fighters," Raynar said. "We have seen what happens to great fighters. *Anakin* was a great fighter."

A pang of grief struck Leia, but she forced herself to continue. "I'm sorry, UnuThul. I don't see how you can avoid it."

"Too bad there's going to be a war," Han said. "If there wasn't, the Colony could set up some sort of buffer zone and keep the Chiss away from their nests."

"That might work," Leia said. "But Qoribu is too close to Chiss territory. The nests are bound to keep coming into contact with Chiss exploration and mining crews. Sooner or later, they'll reach the balance point."

"Qoribu is too close," Saba agreed. "The Colony would have to move itz nestz."

"Impossible," Raynar said. "It cannot be done."

"That's very unfortunate." Leia said this to the Unu entourage. "Because Han and I found this paradise world—"

"Several worlds, probably," Han added. "All empty, lush with foraging grounds, just waiting for a species to come along and claim them."

The entourage began to rustle with interest.

"Tell us more," Raynar said.

"It's in a subsector on the edge of Colony territory," Leia explained. "We didn't have time to do a complete survey, but the world we visited would be perfect for the Taat nest. There were at least two other habitable planets in the same system, with another dozen systems nearby that gave every indication of being just as profuse."

"We were thinking the Colony would want to have a look," Han said. "But if you guys aren't interested, there are still plenty of displaced species in the Galactic Alliance—"

"We are interested," Raynar said. "We always have need of new territory."

"Good," Leia said. "I'm sure the Chiss could be persuaded to stand down long enough for you to organize a relocation."

The corners of Raynar's mouth turned down. "I've told you, that is impossible. There's no way to transport the Qoribu nests. They are too large."

"Really?" Han flashed a smug smile, then asked, "So large they couldn't be temporarily rebuilt in the hangars and launching bays of, say, a few Hapan Battle Dragons?"

Raynar's jaw dropped. "The Hapan fleet would help us escape the Chiss?"

"Sure, why not?" Han retorted. "That has to be easier than *defending* you."

"And they would let us build *nests* in their Battle Dragons?"

"This one thinkz they would." Saba sissed in amusement. "In fact, she is *sure* of it."

The Unu thrummed their chests and tapped their mandibles for a long time, then Raynar finally said, "We understand what you are doing. You're just as bad as Jaina was."

"Was?" Han scowled and looked back toward the other room—the one he had departed without even greeting his daughter. "If you've—"

"Relax, Han." Leia touched Jaina through the Force, then said, "She's fine. She's still with Luke and Mara."

"Of course she is," Raynar said indignantly. "We *meant* that Jaina is no longer welcome in her nest."

Han raised his brow. "I've been kicked out of a few saloons in my time, but a nest? What'd she do?"

"She's too much like you," Raynar said. "She is stubborn and tricky, and she cared about nothing but preventing a war."

"You don't say." Han smiled proudly, then asked, "Does this mean she'll stop being a bughugger?"

Raynar's eyes flashed in anger, and Leia began to have visions of her carefully crafted peace initiative falling apart.

"Han," she said. "Remember, UnuThul hasn't agreed to our proposal yet."

"Well, he hasn't *disagreed,* either." Han turned to Raynar. "What's it going to be, kid? A nasty war and a Colony full of Dark Nests, or a free ride to a free world?"

The Unu erupted into a riot of chest drumming and antenna waving, but Han ignored them and kept his eye fixed on Raynar. The entourage kept the racket up for a few moments longer, then abruptly fell silent and began to stream out of the vault.

Leia frowned. "Are we to take that as a yes?"

"Of course," Raynar said. He rubbed his arm down the antennae of a small, red-eyed Killik about half the size of an Ewok, then turned and started after his nest. "Wasn't it *our* idea?"

EPILOGUE

At the far end of the long, slanting cylinder of spitcrete storage cells, a single Taat was clinging to a patch of durasteel wall, peering out through the hold's lone observation bubble at the golden-ringed mass of the planet Qoribu. With *Kendall's* decks shuddering beneath the power of her sublight drives and the departure alarms chiming over the intercom, the other members of the nest were perched atop the cell covers, thrumming a soft, mournful song that made the hair rise on the back of Han's neck.

"Enchanting song," Mara said.

Peering in through the hatch with Han, Luke, Leia, and several others, she was seated in a hoverchair she probably did not need. The Killik healers had tended her goring wound so well that the Hapan surgeons had sent her straight to the bacta ward. Between her own healing trances and the month she had spent in the tanks, the only signs that remained of the fight on Kr were the dark circles beneath her eyes and a general haggardness—both of which, according to Leia, had less to do with her injuries than with having to call so heavily on the Force to keep herself going during the battle.

"It's an ancient Killik tune that goes back to the creation of the Maw," C-3PO said. "I'd—"

"Hold on," Han said. "The Killiks were there when the *Maw* was created?"

"Of course," C-3PO said. "According to their histories, they were the ones who built it."

"The Killiks?" Dukat Gray gasped. He took an unconscious step away from the hatch. "Truly?"

"I wouldn't count on it," Leia said. "Killik memories can be rather, uh, flexible."

"What about the song?" Mara asked again. "Can you translate, Threepio?"

"Of course," C-3PO said. "The air tides move us to a different place, the air—"

"Not quite, Threepio," Jaina said.

"It's more like this," Zekk added.

Together, they sang:

The cold wind carries us far from our nest,
The cold wind sweeps us where it may.
Cold wind, bear us out of danger,
Cold wind, carry us home again.

An uneasy silence fell over the group; then the underway alarms fell silent. *Kendall* gave a small jolt, and the bands of Qoribu began to grow smaller as the Fleet of the Defender Queen moved off. Han resisted the temptation to check on the *Falcon*'s status; she was isolated in a capture hangar, safely secured alongside the Jedi StealthXs and being guarded by two Noghri and the surviving pair of YVH droids. She would ride safely until the fleet reached the Killiks' new home.

Zekk said, "We are going to miss them."

"Them?" Han asked. He recalled what Raynar had said about Jaina and Zekk no longer being welcome in their nest, but the Colony's attitude about a lot of things had softened in the last month, and Jaina and Zekk had been spending most of their time with the Taat, helping build the temporary nest aboard *Kendall*. "The rings of Qoribu? The moons?"

"The *Taat*, Dad," Jaina said. "Our mission in the Colony—"

"—is over," Zekk finished.

"No kidding?" A smile as wide as a door crept across Han's mouth. "Great! That's just—" He felt his eyes growing watery, then threw his arms around Jaina and Zekk and pulled them close so they would not think he was going to cry. "I'm happy as a Jawa in a junkyard."

"Dad!" Jaina lifted her chin. "You didn't let us finish!"

"We're not coming home until . . ."

Zekk let the sentence trail off when a Hapan adjutant appeared at the edge of the group with a portable holocomm.

"Until when?" Han demanded.

"Later." Jaina nodded at the adjutant. "I think this could be important."

"Indeed." Gray turned toward the adjutant with an air of expectation. "Is the passenger aboard?"

The adjutant's reply was drowned out by a thundering Wookiee bellow from the other end of the access corridor. Lowbacca came bounding up the passage, his furry arms spread wide. Jaina and Zekk started to race off to meet him, but stopped a step away to look back over their shoulders.

"Dad, about that *until*," Jaina said, smiling.

"Just forget it," Zekk finished.

Then Lowbacca was on them, picking them up in his arms and complaining about the food in Chiss prisons.

Once the noise had died down a bit, the adjutant said, "Pardon me, Your Grace, but we're being hailed."

"Hailed?" Gray repeated. "Out here?"

"By the Chiss, Your Grace. Ship-to-ship."

Gray sighed. "Very well. I'll take it in—"

"I'm sorry." The adjutant looked as though he expected to be hit. "But the Aristocra wishes to speak to Master Skywalker."

Gray scowled at Luke, then swung his scowl over to the adjutant. "What are you waiting for?"

The adjutant paled, then knelt in front of Luke and activated the holocomm. The image of a Chiss of about Han's age appeared above the pad.

"Aristocra Formbi," Luke said immediately. "What a surprise."

"It shouldn't be," Formbi retorted. "Did you think Jagged Fel was overseeing this operation?"

"Not really," Luke said. "What can we do for you . . . that we haven't already?"

"Absolutely nothing," Formbi declared. "Commander Fel informs me that your sister was responsible for persuading the Killiks to depart Qoribu."

"For *negotiating* a truce," Leia said, stepping into the holocam's view. "The Chiss also made certain guarantees."

"Of course. A border guarantee and a promise of nonaggression. All Chiss doctrine, anyway."

"Explicit guarantees, nonetheless," Leia said.

Noting that Qoribu had now shrunk to a size such that the whole planet could be seen through the Taat's observation bubble, Han caught Leia's eye and made a winding motion with his finger.

Leia nodded, then said, "What is it you wished to say to me, Aristocra? We have time left before the fleet enters hyperspace, but we should be aware of it."

"Of course—forgive me," Formbi said. "First, I wished to congratulate you on your success. Without your talents, I fear this matter would have come to war."

"Thank you, Aristocra," Leia said. "But it took the involvement of a great number of people to resolve this conflict—Jagged Fel among them."

"Commander Fel will receive a promotion in recognition of his judgment here," Formbi said. "But is you who deserves our thanks. You have achieved peace in our time."

"The *Jedi* achieved this peace, Aristocra. I was just one of many who were involved." Qoribu's bands were now a colorless mass, and its rings looked like tiny ears protruding from the fattest part of its sphere. "And the second thing? We don't have much time."

"I wanted you to know that Commander Fel is responsible for the return of your Wookiee," Formbi said. "Had it not been for his objections—his very *vigorous* objections—the prisoner would have remained interned until we could be certain this peace is going to hold."

"Then it's a good thing you listened to Jag," Han said. "Keeping the Wookiee would have been a bad mistake."

"Yes, so Commander Fel informed me," Formbi replied calmly. "Be that as it may, I thought you should know that Commander

Fel guaranteed your Jedi Knight's parole personally. We don't expect to see *any* Jedi back in our neighborhood soon, but if Lowbacca were to return, the Fel family would be responsible for repaying any damages he caused to the Ascendancy—and a Wookiee Jedi can cause quite a lot of damage, if our prison ship is any example."

"That's very kind of Commander Fel," Leia said. "Please thank him for us."

Jaina and Zekk appeared at Han's back. Lowbacca was towering over them from behind, more of an appendix to their pair than a third member.

"Dad," Jaina whispered.

"We'd like to talk to Jag," Zekk finished.

Han cringed at the thought of Zekk being a part of that particular conversation, but nodded and spoke into the holocomm.

"Is Jag there? We have someone here who wants to say thanks personally."

"Jaina, I presume." Without waiting for confirmation, Formbi said, "Let me check his availability."

Formbi turned and said something they could not hear to someone they could not see. A moment later, Jagged Fel's rugged face replaced Formbi's above the holopad. Han and the others stepped aside to let Jaina—and Zekk—move into the holocam's field.

"Jaina." He frowned, a little confused, and his gaze reluctantly shifted to Zekk. "And Jedi Zekk. I'd like to express my personal gratitude for . . . everything you did. Your efforts helped avert the war."

"You owe us no thanks for that," Zekk said.

"We were acting on everyone's behalf," Jaina said.

"Yes . . . of course." Jag's gaze drifted to Zekk again, and he seemed even more uncertain of himself. "Congratulations, then. You did it very well."

Han glanced out the observation bubble and saw that Qoribu had shrunk to a flattened, silver disk about the size of his thumb. He leaned down next to Jaina's ear.

"Get to the point," he whispered. "The jump is coming."

Jaina and Zekk nodded, then Jaina said, "Thanks for getting Lowbacca released. We were worried that we might have to come break him out."

"So were we." Jagged's tone remained deadpan. "I was not looking forward to that meeting."

"Neither were we," Zekk said.

"But we do look forward to seeing you again sometime soon," Jaina said.

"Under better circumstances," Zekk added.

"Both of you?" Jagged's gaze slipped back and forth between them. "Yes, I will look forward to that." He glanced away, his scarred brow betraying his disappointment—or perhaps it was revulsion. "Now, if you will excuse me, duty calls."

"Of course," Jaina said. "We'll be entering hyperspace soon ourselves. May the Force be with you."

"And with you." Jag shifted his gaze to Zekk. "*Both* of you."

The holocomm blinked out, then Jaina and Zekk turned away, the same crestfallen expression on both their faces. A shudder ran down Han's spine, but he did his best to hide it.

"Kind of sticks in the ol' throat, doesn't it?" he asked, flashing his best crooked, fatherly smile.

"Like we're going to choke on it," Jaina answered.

"But we'll survive." Zekk rubbed his forearm along Jaina's, and she began to make low clicking sounds in her throat. "We have each other."

Han had to look away.

Qoribu was a tiny, oblong circle of light now, glinting in the light of its blue sun, and the Taat's song was growing more forlorn and haunting by the minute. It seemed to him that he could actually feel their sadness himself, and he wondered if this was what it was like to sense something in the Force: to know a thing more clearly in one's heart than in one's head.

Zekk and Lowbacca stepped through the hatch into the temporary nest and began to rub their arms along Taat antennae.

Jaina lingered behind. "We think it will be better to say goodbye now," she explained. "It will only be harder if we wait until they make the new nest."

"Go on," Han said. "I don't have to watch."

Jaina smiled and kissed him on the cheek, then followed Zekk into the hold.

Dukat Gray irritated Han by coming to stand behind him and Leia. For a few moments, the Hapan seemed content to simply watch the two Jedi saying good-bye to their nest, but then he finally decided to ruin the moment completely.

"Aristocra Formbi may have been right about one thing, Princess."

"I find that hard to believe, Dukat," Leia said. "But perhaps I'm mistaken."

"If you will forgive me for saying so, I think you are," Gray said. "It *is* a pity you're not serving in the Galactic Alliance government. A diplomat of the talent and skill you displayed here could be of great service to the new government."

"Thank you, Dukat," Leia said. "Coming from you, that's a very informative suggestion."

Gray beamed, and Han's heart fell. The time had finally come for him to stop being selfish, to suggest that Leia return to her first love.

"Listen," he said. "I know you've missed being in the middle of things. Maybe it's—"

"Yes, it's time for a change," Leia said, cutting him off. "But *not* that way, Han. The last thing I want to do now is join a government—the Galactic Alliance's or anyone else's."

Han began to grow confused. "No?"

"No," Leia said. "I'm sick to death of compromising, of finding the workable solution instead of the right one."

"Okay," Han said cautiously. "What do you have in mind?"

"Following my heart—for a change," Leia said. She turned to Luke. "I've seen many changes in my life—"

"And brought about most of them," Luke said.

"Perhaps," Leia said. "And I've worn some very high titles."

"You deserved 'em," Han said, wondering where this was going.

"That wasn't what I was getting at. After all that, after all that I've seen and done, it always comes down to this." She pulled the lightsaber off her belt and hefted it in her palm. "To one

Jedi, to one blade, standing against the darkness." She turned to Han. "I think it's time that I chose a new path."

"New path?" Han asked, growing worried now. "What do you mean, *new path*?"

"I've loved being your copilot, really," Leia said. "But the galaxy has changed. *I* need to change."

"Define *change*," Han said. "Because if this is about the snoring—"

"Don't you dare stop that *now*—I wouldn't be able to sleep!" Leia laughed, then turned to Luke. "I'm beginning to understand the Jedi's place in the galaxy—and to see my place in the Jedi."

Luke smiled. "You want to assume your place in the order."

Leia shook her head. "No—I want to *earn* my place in the order." She turned to Saba Sebatyne, who had been standing at the back of the group in typical reptilian silence. "I want to dedicate myself to becoming a proper Jedi."

"You *are* a proper Jedi," Saba said. "You have done more for the galaxy than any *ten* Jedi."

"You're not listening," Leia said. "Diplomacy didn't stop this war. *Jedi* did. I want to complete my training—and I want you to be my guide."

Saba's scaly brow rose almost as high as Han's, and Luke's, and Mara's.

"You want *this* one to guide *you*?" Saba asked carefully.

Leia nodded. "If you would consider it."

"*This* one?" Saba repeated.

"Yes," Leia repeated. "I want someone who will challenge me in unexpected ways. I want someone who will teach me what I *don't* know."

Saba's diamond-shaped pupils grew narrow as slits, and her forked tongue began to flick between her pebbly lips. She studied Leia for several moments more, then began to siss so hard that she had to grab her sides.

"That is a good one, Princesz. You really had this one—"

"I'm *not* joking," Leia interrupted.

Saba's hissing stopped. "Truly?"

Leia nodded. "Truly."

"Well, then." Saba glanced at Han. "It seemz this one has no choice."

"Not really," Han said. "And it's a lot better than the alternative."

"What alternative?" Saba asked.

Before Han could answer, the jump alarms chimed. A shudder ran through *Kendall*'s decks, then Qoribu's distant pinpoint of light winked out of existence. The Taat's mournful song came to an abrupt end, and the velvet light outside the observation bubble paled to the colorless blur of hyperspace.

YLESIA

WALTER JON WILLIAMS

Nom Anor suppressed a shiver at the sight of the Shamed One Onimi leering from the doorway. Something in him shrank at the appearance of the lank creature with his misshapen head and knowing smile.

Onimi's grin widened.

Nom Anor, distaste prickling, pushed past the Shamed One and entered. The rounded resinous walls of the chamber shone with a faint luminescence, and the air bore the metallic scent of blood. In the dim light Nom Anor made out the magnificently scarred and mutilated form of Supreme Overlord Shimrra, reclining on a dais of pulsing red hau polyps. Onimi, the Supreme One's familiar, sank into the shadows at Shimrra's feet. Nom Anor prostrated himself, all too aware of the scrutiny of Shimrra's rainbow eyes.

The Supreme Overlord's deep voice rolled out of the darkness. "You have news of the infidels?"

"I have, Supreme One."

"Stand, Executor, and enlighten me."

Nom Anor repressed a shiver of fear as he rose to his feet. This was Shimrra's private audience chamber, not the great reception hall, and Nom Anor was absolutely alone here. He would much rather be able to hide behind his superior Yoog Skell and a whole deputation of intendants.

Never think to lie to the Supreme One, Yoog Skell had warned.

Nom Anor would not. He probably *could* not. Fortunately he was well prepared with the latest news of the infidels' efforts against the Yuuzhan Vong.

"The enemy continue their series of raids against our territory. They dare not confront our might directly, and confine themselves to picking off isolated detachments or raiding our lines of communication. If a substantial fleet opposes them, they flee without fighting."

The Supreme Overlord's head, the sum of its features barely discernable as a face with all its scars and tattoos and slashings, loomed forward in the shadowy light. "Have your agents been able to inform you which of our conquests are being targeted?"

Nom Anor felt a cold hand run up his spine. He had seen what happened to some of those who disappointed the great Overlord Shimrra, and he knew his answer would be a disappointment.

"Unfortunately, Supreme One, it appears that the new administration is giving the local commanders a great deal of latitude. They're choosing their own targets. Our agents on Mon Calamari have no way of knowing what objectives the individual commanders may select."

There was a moment of silence. "The new head of state, this infidel Cal Omas, permits his subordinates such freedom?"

Nom Anor bowed. "So it appears, Supreme One."

"Then he has no true concept of subordination. His rule will not trouble us much longer."

Nom Anor, who thought otherwise, chose not to dispute this analysis. "The Supreme One is wise," he said instead.

"You must redouble your efforts to infiltrate the military and provide us with their objectives."

"I shall obey, Supreme One."

"What news of the Peace Brigade?"

"The news is mixed." The collaborationist Peace Brigade government had been established on Ylesia, and had grown sufficiently large and diverse to have divided into squabbling factions, all of which competed ferociously in groveling to the Yuuzhan Vong. None of this cringing actually aided the creation of the Peace Brigade army and fleet, which, when built up to strength and trained, were to act as auxiliaries to the Yuuzhan Vong.

"Perhaps it should be admitted that infidels so disposed as to join an organization called the 'Peace Brigade' may not be temperamentally inclined toward war," Nom Anor said.

"They need a leader to exact obedience," Shimrra concluded.

"That role was to be assigned to the infidel Viqi Shesh, Supreme One," Nom Anor said.

"Another leader shall be assigned," Shimrra said. His eyes shimmered from blue to green to yellow. "We should choose someone who has nothing to do with these factions. Someone from outside, who can impose discipline."

Nom Anor agreed, but when he searched his mind for candidates, no names occurred to him. "We are having better luck with infidel mercenaries," he said. "They have made no true submission and possess no loyalty, but they are convinced they have joined the winning side, and are content to obey so long as we pay them."

"Contemptible creatures. No wonder a galaxy that spawned such as these was given by the gods to us."

"Indeed, Supreme One."

Shimrra shifted his huge form on his dais, and one of the polyps beneath him burst under the pressure, spraying the wall with its insides. An acid reek filled the room. The other polyps at once turned on the injured creature and began to divide and devour it.

Shimrra ignored the clacking and slurping. "Speak of our visitor from Corellia."

Nom Anor bowed. "He is called Thrackan Sal-Solo."

"Solo? He is related to the twin *Jeedai*?"

"The two branches of the family are estranged, Supreme One."

A thoughtful rumble came from the dais. "A pity. If otherwise, we could hold him hostage and demand the twins in exchange."

"That is indeed a pity, Lord."

Shimrra waved one huge hand. "Continue, Executor."

"Sal-Solo is the leader of a large political faction on Corellia, and has been elected governor-general of the Corellian sector. He says that, with our support, he can assure that the Corellian system—five planets—is detached from the infidel government.

Once this is done, he can assure its neutrality, including the neutrality of the Centerpoint weapon that so devastated our force at Fondor. Then, as diktat, he will sign a treaty of friendship with us."

Shimrra shifted thoughtfully on the pulsing bed. The dismembered polyp twitched and fluttered as its siblings consumed it.

"Is this infidel trustworthy, Executor?"

"Of course not, Supreme One." Nom Anor made a deprecatory gesture. "But he may be useful. He gave us the location of the Jedi academy, and that information was correct, and led to our colonization of the Yavin system. Corellia is a major industrial center, where many weapons and enemy ships are built, and its neutrality is desirable."

"What is our information on the Centerpoint weapon?"

"Sal-Solo did not come alone. He brought with him a supporter and companion, a human female called Darjeelai Swan. While I interviewed Sal-Solo, we took his companion and interrogated her. According to this person, the Centerpoint weapon is not functional, though efforts are being made by New Republic military forces to rehabilitate it."

"So this Sal-Solo offers to trade us what he does not have."

"True. And—also according to Darjeelai Swan—it was Sal-Solo himself who fired the Centerpoint weapon at our fleet at Fondor."

Shimrra's hands—giant black taloned things, each implanted from a different carnivore—made massive fists. "And this creature has the effrontery to bargain with me?"

"Indeed, Supreme One."

Onimi piped up,

> *"Fetch him to our presence, Lord,*
> *And bring us all into concord.*
> *I wish it known and made a rule*
> *That I am not the only fool."*

Shimrra's vast frame heaved with what might have been laughter.

"Yes," he said. "By all means. Let us meet the master of Corellia."

Nom Anor bowed in response, then hesitated. "Shall I bring his guards, as well?"

Contempt rang in Shimrra's answer. "I am capable of defending myself against anything this infidel should attempt."

"As you desire, Supreme One."

Like most humans Thrackan Sal-Solo was a thin, ill-muscled creature, with hair and beard growing white with age. His eyes widened as he entered the chamber and perceived, in the darkness, Shimrra's burning rainbow eyes. Nevertheless he summoned a degree of swagger, and approached the Supreme Overlord on the pulsing polyp bed.

"Lord Shimrra," he said, crossed his arms, and gave an all-too-brief bow.

Nom Anor reacted without thought. One sweep of his booted foot knocked the human's legs out from under him, and a precise shove dropped the startled Corellian onto his face.

Onimi giggled.

"Grovel before your lord!" Nom Anor shouted. "Grovel for your life!"

"I come in peace, Lord Shimrra!" Sal-Solo protested.

Nom Anor drove a boot into Sal-Solo's ribs. "Silence! You will wait for instruction!" He turned to Shimrra and translated the human's words.

"The infidel says that he comes in peace, Supreme One."

"That is well." Shimrra contemplated the splayed human figure for a moment. "Tell the infidel that I have considered his proposals and have decided to accept."

Nom Anor translated the overlord's words into Basic. Sal-Solo's face, pressed against the floor, displayed what might have been a trace of a smile.

"Tell the Supreme Overlord that he is wise," he said.

Nom Anor didn't bother to translate. "Your opinions are of no interest to the Supreme Overlord."

Sal-Solo licked his lips nervously. "The only way I can guarantee the success of the plan is to be given a free hand in Corellia," he said.

Nom Anor translated this.

"Tell the infidel he misunderstands," Shimrra said. "Tell him that the only way the plan will succeed is if *I* am given a free hand in Corellia."

Sal-Solo looked startled as this was translated, and his lips began to frame a protest, but Shimrra continued.

"Tell the infidel that we will give his associates in the Centerpoint Party all assistance necessary to gain control of the Corellian system. He will direct them to cooperate with us. Once Centerpoint Station is taken by his people and surrendered to our forces, the Centerpoint Party will rule Corellia in a state of peace with the Yuuzhan Vong."

Sal-Solo's eyes widened as he listened to Nom Anor's lengthy translation. The executor did not bother to state the fact that, in the Yuuzhan Vong language, *peace* was the same word as *submission.*

Sal-Solo would find that out in time.

Sal-Solo licked his lips again, and said, "May I stand, Executor?"

Nom Anor considered this. "Very well," he said. "But you must show complete submission to the Supreme Overlord."

Sal-Solo rose to his feet but didn't straighten, instead maintaining a sort of half bow toward Shimrra. His eyes ticked back and forth, as if he were mentally reading a speech before giving it, and then he said, "Supreme One, I beg permission to explain the situation on Corellia in more detail."

Permission was given. Sal-Solo spoke about the complex political relations at Corellia, the Centerpoint Party's desire to cast off the New Republic. As he spoke he seemed to grow in confidence, and he paced back and forth, occasionally raising his eyes to Shimrra to see if the Supreme Overlord was following his argument.

Nom Anor translated as well as he could. Onimi, from his posture at Shimrra's feet, watched with his upper lip curled back and one misshapen fang exposed.

"I shall have to return to Corellia immediately in order to undertake the Supreme One's plan," Sal-Solo said. "And regretfully I must warn that it will be difficult to gain cooperation once it is known that the Yuuzhan Vong plan to seize the Centerpoint weapon after we evict the New Republic military."

"The answer to that difficulty is a simple one," Shimrra said through Nom Anor. "*Do not tell* your associates that the Yuuzhan Vong are destined to control the weapon."

Sal-Solo hesitated only a fraction of a second before he bowed. "It shall be as the Supreme Overlord desires," he said.

Shimrra gave an appreciative growl, then turned to Nom Anor. "Is the infidel lying?" he said.

"Of course, Supreme One," Nom Anor said. "He will never voluntarily relinquish a weapon as powerful as the Centerpoint device."

"Then tell the infidel this," Shimrra said. "It will not be necessary for him to return to Corellia—he will simply inform us which of his Centerpoint Party associates we should contact in order to deliver his orders and our assistance. Tell the infidel that I have a much more important duty for him to perform. Tell him that I have just appointed him President of Ylesia and Commander in Chief of the Peace Brigade."

Nom Anor was struck with admiration. *Now* that *is truly inventive vengeance,* he thought. Thrackan Sal-Solo had destroyed thousands of Yuuzhan Vong warriors at Fondor, and now he would be publicly linked with a Yuuzhan Vong–allied government. His reputation would be destroyed; he would be at the mercy of those whose warriors he had killed.

Sal-Solo listened to the translation in horrified silence. His eyes ticked back and forth again, and then he said, "Please tell the Supreme Overlord that I am deeply honored by an appointment to this position of trust, but because this would make it impossible for his plans for Corellia to be realized, I regret that I must decline the appointment. Perhaps the Supreme Overlord doesn't realize that the Peace Brigade is not admired by all Corellians, and that anyone identified as Peace Brigade wouldn't be able to command the respect necessary to win power in Corellia. It is, furthermore, absolutely necessary that I be in Corellia to coordinate the Centerpoint Party, and . . ."

Sal-Solo went on at some length, long enough so that Nom Anor began to feel toward him a thorough contempt. Sal-Solo, convinced of his powers to charm others, thought that once he could get in the same room with Shimrra, he could talk to him, one politician to another, and convince him of the rightness of his schemes. As if he could lobby the Supreme Overlord of the Yuuzhan Vong the same way as he might lobby some miserable Senator from his homeworld!

"Executor," Shimrra said conversationally, as Sal-Solo continued to speak, "is there a place where one might strike a human in order to cause immobilizing pain?"

Nom Anor considered the request. "There are organs known as 'kidneys,' Lord. One on either side of the lower back, just above the hips. A strike there causes considerable anguish, often so severe that the victim is unable to cry out. Or so I am given to understand."

"Let us find out," Shimrra said. He made a slight gesture, and Onimi rose from his place at the foot of Shimrra's dais. In the dim light Nom Anor saw, coiled in the Shamed One's hand, a batron of rank, the officers' version of the amphistaff. He was shocked to discover that Shimrra permitted his familiar to carry weapons.

But who else would be more trustworthy? Nom Anor thought. *Onimi must know that if Shimrra is killed, his own death will surely follow.*

Onimi stepped behind Sal-Solo and flung out his lank arm. The whiplike batron froze into its solid form, now a lean staff, and Onimi with a single efficient swing slashed the weapon into Sal-Solo's left kidney.

The human opened his mouth in a silent scream and fell like a bundle of sticks, hands scrabbling at the floor. Nom Anor stepped to the helpless man, bent, and seized him by the hair.

"Your resignation is declined, infidel," he said. "We shall see you are transported immediately to Ylesia, where you may take your place as head of the government. In the meantime, you will give us the names of your associates on Corellia, so they, too, may be given their instructions."

Sal-Solo's face was still distorted by an unvoiced shriek, and

Nom Anor decided that his information regarding a human's vulnerable kidneys was true.

"Nod your head if you understand, infidel," Nom Anor said. Sal-Solo nodded.

Nom Anor turned to Shimrra. "Does the Supreme One have any further instructions for his servants?" he asked.

"Yes," Shimrra said. "Instruct that human's guards well."

"I shall, Lord."

Nom Anor prostrated himself beside Sal-Solo's shuddering body, and then he and Onimi carried Thrackan Sal-Solo to his guards, who managed to stand the man upright.

"I believe I address you as 'President' from this point," Nom Anor said.

Sal-Solo's lips moved, but again he seemed unable to utter a sound.

"By the way, Your Excellency," Nom Anor continued, "I regret to say that your companion Darjeelai Swan died while furnishing the Yuuzhan Vong information. Is there anything you wish done with the body?"

Sal-Solo again voiced no opinion, so Nom Anor ordered the body destroyed and went about his business.

The pale form of the cruiser *Ralroost* floated in brilliant contrast to the green jungles of Kashyyyk below, the immaculate white paint of its hull a proof that the assault cruiser served as the flagship of a fleet admiral and was maintained to the standard that befit his rank. Around the cruiser were grouped the elements of an entire fleet—frigates, cruisers, Star Destroyers, tenders, hospital ships, support vessels, and flights of starfighters on patrol—all formed and ready for their next excursion into Yuuzhan Vong–controlled space.

Jacen Solo watched the swarming fleet elements through the shuttle's forward viewport. The outlines of the warships seemed too *hard* somehow, too defined, a little alien, lacking the softer outlines of the organic life-forms he had grown accustomed to while a prisoner of the Yuuzhan Vong.

"Bets, anyone?" came his sister's voice. "Where's the next raid? Hutt space? Duro? Yavin?"

"I'd like to see Yavin again," Jacen said.

"Not once you see what the Vong have done to it."

He turned at the bitter tone in Jaina's voice. She stood slightly behind him, her intent gaze directed toward *Ralroost*. A major's insignia was pinned to the collar of her dress uniform, and a lightsaber hung from her belt.

Yavin was our childhood, Jacen thought. And the Yuuzhan Vong had taken that childhood away, and Yavin with it, and left Jaina a grown woman, hard and brittle and single-minded, with little patience for anything but leading her squadron against the enemy.

Sword of the Jedi. That's what Uncle Luke had named her at the ceremony that had raised her to the rank of Jedi Knight. *A burning brand to your enemies, a brilliant fire to your friends.* That's what Luke had said.

"I think it will be Hutt space myself," Jaina said. "In Hutt space the Yuuzhan Vong have had their own way for too long."

Yours is a restless life, and never shall you know peace, though you shall be blessed for the peace that you bring to others.

Luke had said that as well. Jacen felt an urge to comfort his sister, and he put an arm around her shoulders. She didn't reject the touch, but she didn't accept it either: he felt as if his arm were draped around a form made of hardened durasteel.

It didn't matter, Jacen thought, if she accepted or rejected his help. He would make his aid available whether she wanted it or not. Luke had offered him a choice of assignments, and he had chosen the one that would place him near Jaina.

When Anakin had died, and Jacen had at the same time been made a prisoner of the Yuuzhan Vong, Jaina had allowed herself to be overcome by despair. The dark side had claimed her, and though she had fought her way out of that abyss, she was still more fragile than Jacen would have liked. She had grown fey, haunted by death, by the memories of Chewbacca and Anakin and Anni Capstan and all the many thousands who had died. To his horror Jaina had told him that she didn't expect to survive the war.

It wasn't despair, she insisted; she'd beaten despair when she conquered the dark side. It was just a realistic appraisal of the odds.

Jacen had wanted to protest that if you expect death, you won't fight for life. And so he volunteered for duty with the fleet at Kashyyyk, determined that if Jaina wouldn't fight her utmost to preserve her life, he would fight that battle on her behalf.

"I think Yavin is a good bet for the next strike," another voice said. "We've had squadrons clearing Yuuzhan Vong raiders off the Hydian Way, as if they're preparing a route for us. We might soon find ourselves moving in that direction."

Corran Horn stepped to the viewport. The Rogue Squadron commander wore a battered colonel's uniform that dated from the wars against the Empire.

"Yavin," he said, "Bimmiel, Dathomir . . . somewhere out there."

A polite hissing signaled a disagreement. "We forget the enemy are behind uz," hissed Saba Sebatyne. "If we take Bimmisaari and Kessel the enemy will be cut in two."

"That would bring on a major battle," Corran said. "We don't have the strength to fight one."

"Yet . . ." Jaina said, and through their twin bond Jacen felt the fierce power of her calculation. She had probably reckoned to the day when the New Republic would have the power to shift to the offensive, and could hardly wait.

The Sword of the Jedi wanted to strike to the enemy's heart.

The shuttle swept into Ralroost's docking bay and settled onto its landing gear. The droid pilot, a metal head and torso wired onto the instrument console, opened the shuttle doors. Its head spun clean around on its shoulders to face them.

"I hope you enjoyed your ride, Masters. Please watch your step as you exit."

The four Jedi stepped out of the shuttle onto Admiral Kre'fey's pristine deck. Scores of people bustled about, rode hovercarts, or worked on starfighters. Most were furred Bothans, but among them were a fair number of humans and other species of the galaxy. Jacen was suddenly conscious that he was the only person present without a military uniform.

They stepped toward the bulkhead, with its open blast doors

that led forward to the ship's command center. Above the open doors was a sign:

HOW CAN I HURT THE VONG TODAY?

This was what Admiral Kre'fey called his Question Number One, which everyone in his command was to ask her- or himself every day.

In a few moments, Jacen thought, he'd hear an answer to that question.

Jacen craned his head as he passed through the blast doors, and on the other side he saw Kre'fey's Question Number Two.

HOW CAN I HELP MY OWN SIDE GROW STRONGER?

The answer to *that* question was going to be a little harder to find.

The four Jedi reported to Snayd, Admiral Kre'fey's aide, who took them to a conference room. Jacen followed the others into the room, and in the dim light he first saw the Bothan admiral Traest Kre'fey, who stood out by virtue of the unusual color of his fur, the same brilliant white as *Ralroost*'s paint. As Jacen's eyes adjusted to the room's darkness he saw other military officers, including Commodore Farlander, and another group of Jedi who were quartered on the cruiser. Alema Rar, Zekk, and Tahiri Veila. Jacen felt the welcoming presence of the others greeting him in the Force, and he sent his own warm reply.

"Greetings!" Kre'fey returned the salutes of the three military Jedi, and stepped forward to clasp Jacen's hand. "Welcome to *Ralroost,* young Jedi."

"Thank you, Admiral." Unlike other military commanders, Kre'fey had been happy to work with Jedi in the past, and had sent a specific request to Luke Skywalker for more Jedi warriors.

"I hope you'll be able to help us in this next mission," the admiral said.

"That's why we're here, sir."

"Fine! Fine." Kre'fey turned to the others. "Please be seated. We'll begin as soon as Master Durron joins us."

Jacen seated himself in an armchair next to Tahiri Veila, the soft, smooth leather embracing his body. The little blond Jedi gave him a shy smile, her bare feet swinging clear of the carpet beneath her.

"How are you faring?" he asked.

Her wide eyes turned thoughtful as she considered the question. "I'm better," she said. "The meld is helping a lot."

The fierce, impulsive Tahiri had loved Jacen's brother Anakin, and had been present at Myrkr when Anakin had met his hero's death. Devastated by Anakin's passing, her fiery character had come close to being snuffed out. She had withdrawn, and though she had continued to function as a Jedi, it was as if she were only going through the motions. Her impetuous personality had vanished into a subdued, ominously quiet young woman.

It had been Saba Sebatyne, the reptilian leader of the all-Jedi Wild Knights Squadron, who had suggested that Tahiri should be sent to join Admiral Kre'fey at Kashyyyk. Kre'fey wanted as many Jedi as possible under his command, to form a Jedi Force-meld in combat, all the Jedi linked together through the Force and acting as one. Saba insisted that the Force-meld would help a wounded mind heal, by drawing a Jedi in pain toward light and healing.

Apparently Saba had been right.

"I'm glad to know you're doing better," Jacen said. His own experience with the meld, on Myrkr, had been more ambiguous: if it amplified Jedi abilities, it also enlarged any disharmony that existed among them.

Tahiri gave Jacen a quick smile and patted his arm briefly. "I'm glad you're here, Jacen."

"Thank you. I wanted to be here. It seemed to be where I was needed."

He wanted to experience the meld again. He thought it could teach him a great deal.

The doors slid open, Kyp Durron entered, and at once the mood of the room seemed to shift. Some people, Jacen thought, carried a kind of aura with them. If you met Cilghal, you knew at once you were in the presence of a compassionate healer, and Luke Skywalker radiated authority and wisdom.

When you looked at Kyp Durron, you knew you were seeing an enormously powerful weapon. If only Jacen didn't know how erratic that weapon had been.

The dark-haired, older Jedi wore a New Republic–style uniform without any insignia, to show that he led an all-volunteer squadron that fought alongside the military forces but was not formally a part of them.

Kyp and his unit, the Dozen, had always gone their own way. They flew with Kre'fey not because they were under orders, but because they chose to.

Kyp and the admiral exchanged salutes. "Sorry I'm late, Admiral," Kyp said. He showed the datapad he carried in one hand. "I was getting the latest intelligence reports. And, uh—" He hesitated. "—some of the data were kind of interesting."

"Very good, Master Durron." Kre'fey turned to the others. "Master Durron has submitted a plan for action against the enemy. As it's fully in line with our operational goals as established by Admirals Sovv and Ackbar, I've given it my tentative approval. I thought I would place it before my senior commanders, and you squadron commanders, to see if you might have anything to add."

Jacen looked at Tahiri, startled. She was a squadron commander? Her feet would barely reach the foot controls in a starfighter cockpit.

And then, as what he'd heard struck home, he exchanged a quick glance with his sister. Kyp Durron's plans, in the past, had been aggressive in the extreme; at Sernpidal he'd tricked Jaina and the New Republic military into destroying a Yuuzhan Vong shipwomb, thus stranding untold numbers of Yuuzhan Vong in intergalactic space and dooming them to a cold, lingering death.

Kyp was said to have changed in the months since then, and had been appointed to the High Council that advised the Chief of State and oversaw Jedi activities. But Jacen was prepared to examine carefully any plan put forward by Kyp Durron before he could bring himself to approve it.

Kre'fey surrendered his place at the head of the room and

seated himself on a thronelike armchair. Kyp nodded to the admiral, then swept the others with his dark eyes. Jacen sensed Kyp's firmness of purpose, his conviction.

He also thought that it was a good idea to be wary of Kyp's conviction.

"When the Vong struck at us," Kyp said, "their way had been prepared for them. They had agents already in place, both disguised Yuuzhan Vong and traitors like Viqi Shesh. And after our first encounters with the Yuuzhan Vong, the enemy found there were tens of thousands of people who were willing to collaborate with them in attacking and enslaving their fellow galactic citizens."

He gave a shrug. "I'm not willing to speculate why the Peace Brigade and their ilk chose to work with the invaders. Maybe some are simply cowards, maybe some were bought, maybe some were given no choice. I suppose most of them are opportunists who think they're on the winning side. But I know this—up until now there's been no real penalty for being willing to betray the New Republic and work with the invaders." The amber room lights glowed in Kyp's eyes. "I propose we inflict a penalty," he said firmly. "I propose that we strike the Peace Brigade right in the center of their power. I say we raid Ylesia, their capital, destroy the collaborationist government, and show everyone in the galaxy that there *is* a penalty for collaboration with the Yuuzhan Vong, and that the penalty is a dire one."

There was a moment of silence, and Jacen again turned to Jaina. *You were right,* he thought. *Hutt space after all.*

Corran Horn raised a hand. "What kind of opposition might we expect?"

Kyp pressed the datapad in his hand, and a number of surreptitiously taken holos were projected on the wall behind him. "We have no permanent intelligence presence on Ylesia," he admitted, "but Ylesia's most profitable export is glitterstim spice, and a number of New Republic agents have scouted the planet while posing as crew from the merchant ships. They report few Yuuzhan Vong warriors—most of the Vong on the ground seem to be members of the intendant class, who help the Peace Brigade run their government.

"There haven't been any Yuuzhan Vong fleets in orbit since the original conquest, though sometimes Vong fleet elements, mostly coralskippers and their transports, transit the Ylesia system on their way to somewhere else. What we have instead is the Peace Brigade military itself—the Yuuzhan Vong are trying to build up the Brigaders as an 'independent' government, with their own fleet. They're also using glitterstim revenues to hire mercenaries. Here are the agents' estimates of what we might be up against."

More figures flashed on the screen. "Mostly starfighters, a mixed bag," Kyp continued. "There are a dozen or so capital ships—Intelligence thinks they were probably in dry dock in places like Gyndine and Obroa-skai when the Vong captured them. The Vong then completed the repairs with slave labor and handed the ships to their allies."

"It looks easy," Tahiri said softly in Jacen's ear. "But I don't believe in easy anymore."

Jacen nodded. He couldn't bring himself to believe in easy, either.

Kre'fey rose from his chair. "Excellent, Master Durron!" he boomed. "I will commit fleet resources to this, including interdictor ships—enough to assure that this so-called fleet can't escape! Fifteen squadrons of starfighters! Three squadrons of capital ships—we'll outnumber the enemy three to one!" He held up a white-furred hand and then drew the fingers together, as if capturing an enemy fleet in his fist. "And then we'll sit above the enemy and obliterate their capital from orbit."

Jacen felt a mental hesitation from every Jedi in the room. Even Kyp Durron's face reflected uncertainty.

Tahiri's voice piped up instantly. "What about civilian casualties?"

Kre'fey made a deprecatory gesture. "The population of Ylesia is very scattered," he said. "The civilians were slaves of the Hutts, working in glitterstim packing plants scattered over the countryside, and now they're slaves of the Vong—or of the Peace Brigade, it's hard to say which. The town the Peace Brigaders are using as their capital used to be called Colony One, but now it's Peace City, and there are few slaves there. Most of the city's inhabitants are collaborators, and they're guilty by definition."

Kyp Durron gave a solemn glance to his datapad. "The latest reports have slave barracks all over Colony One. They're constructing palaces for the leaders of the Peace Brigade, and a building to house their Senate." He paused. "And they were excavating one very large shelter, just in case of orbital bombardment."

"Destruction would be awfully random," Tahiri said.

Kre'fey nodded, then stepped toward her and looked at her with what seemed to be great respect. "I esteem the Jedi traditions of compassion for the innocent, and of precise personal combat with an enemy," he said. "But my own people don't have your training. It would be too great a danger to send them to the planet to sort out the innocent from the guilty, and I don't want to lose good troops in a ground fight when I could accomplish the mission from orbit in safety." Kre'fey turned to Kyp. "All that shelter would require is increased firepower, and then we get *all* of them in one go." His eyes traveled from one Jedi to the next. "Remember who we're dealing with. They destroyed entire worlds by seeding alien life-forms from orbit. Just think what they did to Ithor. What we're doing is merciful by comparison." He shook his head sadly. "And those slaves would be dead anyway, within a year or two, just from overwork."

Jacen could see the logic in Kre'fey's argument—and he had to admire a powerful, important fleet admiral who would bother to engage in a serious debate with a fifteen-year-old—but he could also see the reverse of Kre'fey's position. Killing civilians was something *the enemy* did. The fact that the civilians were slaves made their deaths even more unjust—the New Republic forces should be *liberating* the slaves, so that even if the Hutts returned they would have no workers for their wretched factories . . .

"Let's capture the government instead," Jacen said, the idea occurring to him even as he spoke it aloud.

Kre'fey looked at him in surprise. "Jacen?" he said.

Jacen turned his face up to Kre'fey. "If we *captured* the Brigaders' government, and put them on trial and exiled them to some prison planet, wouldn't that be more of a propaganda coup than simply bombing them?" He forced a smile. "They'll all be in one shelter, right? As you say, that should make it easy."

"Jacen has a point," Kyp said, from over Kre'fey's shoulder. "If we destroy Peace City, we make an announcement and then it's forgotten. But if we put the traitors on trial, that would be on the HoloNet for *weeks*. Anyone thinking of switching sides would have to think twice, and any collaborators would be shaking in their boots."

"Not only that," Jacen said, "but a team could be landed in Peace City to become our permanent intelligence presence in the enemy capital, and perhaps to organize the underground there."

Kre'fey's long head turned from Jacen to Kyp and back again. He tugged at his white-furred chin in thought. "This requires a more elaborate mission—perhaps you do not realize *how* much more elaborate. With the original plan there's very little that can go wrong. We transit to the system, engage, win our victory, and leave. If the enemy are too strong, we run without a fight. But with Jacen's idea we'd need transports, dropships, ground forces. If things go wrong on the ground, we'll take a lot of casualties just getting our people away. If things go wrong above the planet, the forces on the ground may be stranded there."

"Sir," Jaina said, "I volunteer to lead the ground forces."

The Sword of the Jedi, Jacen thought, *thrusting straight to the heart.*

Kyp turned to Jaina, his voice hesitant. "I, uh—" For once in his life Jacen was privileged to watch Kyp Durron embarrassed. "I really don't think that would be a good idea, Sticks."

Jaina's eyes flashed, but her voice was very controlled. "You don't have to be so protective of me, Master Durron," she said.

Surprise rose in Jacen. He sensed history here, something between Jaina and Kyp that he hadn't known existed.

Now that's *interesting.*

"Ah, that's not it," Kyp said hastily. "It's just that—" He looked at his datapad. "The latest news from Ylesia indicates that you have a personal relationship with, ah, one of our potential captives." And, as Jaina's indignation increased, Kyp turned to Jacen as his embarrassment deepened. "And Jacen, too, of course."

"Jacen, too?" Jaina demanded, outraged.

Kyp looked at the datapad again and shrugged. "The Peace Brigade just announced their new President. He's, ah, your cousin Thrackan."

Confusion swept Jaina's face. "That doesn't make any sense," Jacen said immediately.

"Sorry," Kyp said, "I know he's a member of your famly, but—"

"No," Jacen said, "that's not it. I'm not going to defend Thrackan Sal-Solo because he's a distant *cousin*—"

"A cousin who's vicious as a slashrat and slippery as an Umgullian blob," Jaina added.

Jacen took a breath and continued, intent on making his point. "I was only going to point out," he said, "that it doesn't make any sense because Thrackan is a human chauvinist. He's always wanted to run Corellia so he could throw the other species *out.* He'd never make a deal if that meant he'd have to collaborate with an alien species."

Kyp looked dubious. "I suppose the story could be false," he said, "but it's all over the HoloNet, complete with pictures of your cousin taking his oath of office in front of the Peace Brigade Senate."

Jacen saw Jaina's face harden. "Right," she said, "now I've *got* to be with the ground party."

"Me, too, I guess," Jacen said. "It'll be . . . enlightening . . . to see cousin Thrackan again."

Traest Kre'fey looked from Jaina to Jacen and back again.

"I must say," he said, "that the two of you belong to the most *interesting* family."

Admiral Kre'fey continued his show of reluctance, but eventually he set his staff to "exploring" the possibility of a landing to capture the Peace Brigade leadership. By the time Jaina entered the shuttle that would take her party back to their quarters on the old Dreadnaught *Starsider,* she was already calculating her deployments for the battle—she'd leave Tesar in command of

Twin Suns Squadron and take Lowbacca onto the ground with her. She'd like Tesar with her, too, but a Jedi would have to stay with the squadron and keep it connected to the meld . . . and keep her new pilots from doing anything foolish, as well.

Before the operation she'd get her squadron as much practice as she could fit into their schedule. The military had taken half her veteran pilots to use as a cadre around which to build new squadrons, filling their slots with rookies, inexperienced pilots who needed all the drill Jaina could give them.

The New Republic's industries were finally on a war footing and pouring out war matériel by the millions of tons. All the personnel losses the military had suffered in the war had been replaced—but with raw recruits. What had been lost was *experience.* Jaina was terrified of Twin Suns Squadron being committed to a major battle before her new pilots were ready.

That's why she was a supporter of Kre'fey's current strategy of raiding the enemy only where the Yuuzhan Vong were vulnerable. His raids were staged only against weak targets, building morale and experience against an enemy guaranteed to lose.

She could only hope the Yuuzhan Vong didn't move against Kashyyyk, or Corellia or Kuat or Mon Calamari—a place where the New Republic would *have* to fight. That would be a conflagration in which Twin Suns Squadron would be lucky to survive . . .

"Odd to think of Tahiri as a squadron commander."

Jacen's comment interrupted Jaina's thoughts.

"Tahiri's doing all right," Jaina said.

"She's not a crack pilot, though."

"She's more experienced than most of her pilots—almost all of them are green—and she fought well at Borleias. Kre'fey's given her a good executive officer to help her with organization and red tape." She smiled. "Her pilots are very protective of her. They call themselves Barefoot Squadron."

Jacen smiled also. "That's good of them."

Jaina sighed. "The Barefoots' real problem is the same one most of us have—too high a percentage of rookie pilots." She looked at Saba and Corran Horn. "*Some* commanders get all the luck."

Horn's mouth gave a little quirk. "Saba has the true elite force here. What I wouldn't give for a roster made up of Jedi . . ."

Saba's eyes gave a reptilian glimmer, and her tail twitched. "A pity you humanz lack the advantage of hatchmatez."

Horn raised an eyebrow. "*Hatching* Jedi. Now *that's* an interesting idea."

Saba hissed amusement. "I can testify that it workz."

"I hope you enjoyed your ride, Masters." The head of the droid pilot spun on its neck. "Please watch your step as you exit."

A few minutes later, after they'd separated from their companions and begun walking toward their quarters along one of *Starsider's* avenues, Jaina turned to Jacen.

"Kre'fey will give you a squadron," she said. "I'm surprised he hasn't asked you already."

"I don't want one."

"Why not?" Jaina asked, more snappishly than she intended. Jacen had always been on a quest for the deeper meaning of things, and that meant that occasionally he'd give something up just to find out what it meant. For a while he'd given up being a warrior, and he'd given up use of the Force, and for all intents and purposes given up being a Jedi . . . now he was giving up being a *pilot*?

The one thing he hadn't given up was being exasperating.

"I can pilot and fight well enough," Jacen said, "but I'm rusty on military procedure and comm protocols and tactics. I'd rather fly for a while as an ordinary pilot before I'm given responsibility over eleven other lives."

"Oh." Jaina was abashed. "You could fly with Tahiri, then. Another Jedi in her squadron would be a boon to her."

"But not this next mission," Jacen said. "Not Ylesia. I want to fly with you, since we're both going on the landing party."

Jaina nodded. "That makes sense," she said. "We'll find a slot for you."

Jacen seemed uneasy. "What do you think about Kyp Durron's plan?" he asked. "Do you see a secret agenda here?"

"I think Kyp's past that sort of thing. It's *your* plan that worries me."

Jacen was taken aback. "To capture the Brigader leadership? Why?"

"Kre'fey was right when he said there was a lot that could go wrong. We don't have enough data on Ylesia to make certain the landings will go as planned."

"But you agreed to join the ground party."

Jaina sighed. "Yes. But now I wonder if we oughtn't leave Ylesia alone until we have a more seasoned force and better intelligence."

Jacen had no answer to this, so they plodded up the corridor without speaking, stepping carefully past a droid polishing the deck. The scent of polish wafted after them. Then Jacen broke the silence.

"What's with you and Kyp Durron? I sensed something a little odd there."

Jaina felt herself flush. "Kyp's been feeling a little . . . sentimental . . . toward me lately."

Jacen looked at her in solemn surprise. It was that solemnity, Jaina decided, that she disliked most about him.

"He's a little old for you, don't you think?" Jacen asked. Solemnly.

Jaina tried to throttle her annoyance at this line of questioning. "I'm grateful to Kyp for helping me come back from the dark side," she said. "But with me, it's gratitude. With Kyp . . ." She hesitated. "I'd rather not go into it. Anyway, it's over now."

Jacen nodded. Solemnly. Jaina came to her cabin door and put her hand on the latch.

"Good," Jacen said. "Because you've been conquering a bewildering number of hearts while I was away. First Baron Fel's son, and now the most unpredictable Jedi in the order . . ."

Supremely irritated, Jaina opened the cabin door, stepped inside, and in the darkness of the cabin was seized by a pair of arms. Pressure was applied in an expert way to her elbow joints, and she was whirled around. A familiar scent, a spicy aroma from the Unknown Regions, filled her senses, and a hungry mouth descended on hers.

A moment later—and the length of that moment was something she would not forgive herself—it occurred to her to resist.

Her arms were securely pinned, so she summoned the Force and flung her assailant across the room. There was a crash, and items tumbled off a shelf. Jaina took a step to the door and waved on the lights.

Jagged Fel lay sprawled across her bed. He touched the back of his head gingerly.

"Couldn't you just have slapped me?" he asked.

"What are you doing here?"

"Conducting an experiment."

"A *what*?" Furious.

His brilliant blue eyes rose to meet hers. "I detected a degree of ambiguity in your last few messages," he said. "I could no longer tell what your feelings toward me might be, so I thought an experiment was in order. I decided to place you in a situation that wasn't the least bit ambiguous, and see how you reacted." An insufferable smile touched the corners of his mouth. "And the experiment was a success."

"Right. You got thrown into the wall."

"But before you remembered to be outraged, there was a moment that was worth all the pain." His eyes turned to the door. "Hello there, galactic hero. Your mother told me you'd escaped."

"She mentioned she'd met you." Jacen, in the doorway, turned his owlish expression to Jaina. "Sis, do you need rescuing?"

"Get out of here," Jaina said.

"Right." He turned back to Jagged Fel. "Nice seeing you again, Jag."

"Give my regards to the folks," Jag said, and sketched a salute near his scarred forehead. The door slid shut behind Jacen. Jag looked at Jaina and removed from his lap some of the objects that had fallen from her shelf.

"May I stand up?" he said. "Or would you just knock me down again?"

"Try it and see."

Jag elected to remain seated. Jaina folded her arms and leaned against the wall as far from Jag as the small cabin would permit.

"Last I heard you were clearing Vong off the Hydian Way," she said.

He nodded. "That's where I met your parents. It's important work. If the routes from the Rim to what's left of the Core were broken, the New Republic would be broken into—well—into even smaller fragments than it is now."

"Thanks for the lecture. I never would have guessed any of that in a million years." She frowned down at him. "So you left this important work in order to sneak into my cabin and conduct your experiment?"

"No, that was by way of a bonus." Jag swept a hand over his dark short-cropped hair. "We're here for routine maintenance. Since my squadron flies Chiss clawcraft that aren't in the New Republic inventory, it's difficult to find maintenance facilities geared to our requirements. Fortunately Admiral Kre'fey's Star Destroyers have all the equipment necessary to maintain Sienar Fleet Systems TIE fighter command pods, and their machine shops should be able to create anything we need for our Chiss wing pylons." He smiled up at her. "A lucky coincidence, don't you think?"

Jaina felt herself softening. "I've got six rookie pilots," she said. "And there's an operation coming up."

He gave her an inquiring look. "You weren't planning on taking them out on an exercise at this very moment, were you?"

"I—" She hesitated. "No. You've got me there. But there's a ton of administrative work, and—"

"Jaina," he said. "Please allow me to observe, one officer to another, that it is not necessary to do all the work yourself. You absolutely must learn to delegate. You have two capable, veteran lieutenants in Lowbacca and Tesar Sebatyne, and not only will it aid *you* if you share the work with them, it will aid *their* development as officers."

Jaina permitted herself a thin smile. "So it's to the benefit of my officers and pilots to spend the evening in my cabin alone with you?"

He nodded. "Precisely."

"Do you play sabacc?"

Jag was surprised. "Yes. Of course."

"Let's have a game, then. There's a very nice sabacc table in the wardroom."

He looked at her mutely. She broadened her smile and said, "I played your little game, here in the darkened cabin. Now you can play mine."

Jag sighed heavily, then rose and stood by the door. As she walked past him to open the door, he clasped his hands behind his back.

"I should point out," he said, "that if you chose to kiss me at this moment, I would be absolutely powerless to prevent you."

She regarded him from close range, then pressed her lips to his, allowed them to linger warmly for the space of three heartbeats. After which she opened the door and led him to the wardroom, where she skinned him at the sabacc table, leaving him with barely enough credits to buy a glass of juri juice.

Her father, Jaina thought, would have been proud.

Jag contemplated the ruin of his fortunes with a slight frown. "It seems I've paid heavily for that stolen kiss," he said.

"Yes. But you've also paid in advance for others."

Jag raised his scarred eyebrow. "That's a good thing to know. When might I collect?"

"As soon as we can find a suitably private place."

"Ah." He seemed cheered. "Would it be precipitate to suggest that we go immediately?"

"Not at all." She rose from the table. "Just one thing."

He gained his feet and straightened his impossibly neat black uniform. "What's that?"

"I think you're right about my not doing all the work. I intend to delegate a fair share to you."

Jag nodded. "Very good, Major."

"I hope this will contribute to your development as an officer."

"Oh." He followed her out of the wardroom. "I'm sure that it will."

Thrackan Sal-Solo looked out his office viewport at the squalid mess that was Peace City—half-completed construction covered with scaffolding, muck-filled holes in the ground, slave barracks boiling with alien life—and he thought, *And all this is mine to command* . . .

If, of course, he could avoid being murdered by one of his loyal subjects. Which was the topic of the present discussion.

He turned to the black-haired woman who sat before his desk and contemplated the suitcase he'd opened on the desktop. The suitcase that contained a kilogram of glitterstim.

"You get one of these every week," he said.

She looked at him with cobalt-blue predator's eyes, and flashed her prominent white teeth. "And how many people do I have to kill to earn it?"

"You don't have to kill anyone. What you have to do is keep *me* alive."

"Ah. A *challenge*." Dagga Marl steepled her fingertips and looked thoughtful. Then she shrugged. "All right. It'll be more interesting work than all the boring assassinations the Senate has been handing me."

"If I ask you to kill anyone," Thrackan said, "I'll pay you extra."

"Good to know," Dagga said as she closed the case and stowed it neatly under her chair.

He stepped from the viewport to his desk, then grimaced at the stitch in his left side. He massaged the painful area, feeling under his thumb the scar from Onimi's nasty little batron. Thrackan swore that if he ever caught up with Onimi, that malignant lop-headed little dwarf was going to lose a lot more than a kidney.

The first thing he'd done on Ylesia was be sworn in as President and Commander in Chief of the Peace Brigade.

The second thing he'd done on Ylesia was to meet with the chiefs of the Peace Brigade, an experience that left him undecided whether to laugh, cry, or run in screaming terror.

The Peace Brigade had originally owed its allegiance to something called the Alliance of Twelve. Maybe there had been twelve of them at one point, but there were around sixty of them now, and they called themselves a Senate. One horrified look had shown Thrackan what they were: thieves, renegades, turncoats, criminals, slavers, murderers, and alien scum. The people who had betrayed their galaxy to the terror that was the Yuuzhan Vong—and it wasn't as if they'd done it out of conviction in the rightness of their cause. They made the Hutts who had built the original colony look like a congregation of saints.

The Hutts were dead: the Yuuzhan Vong had made a clean sweep of the whole caste, then installed the Peace Brigade in their place without altering any of the Hutts' other arrangements. The flayed skin of the Hutt chief was still on display in front of the Palace of Peace, where the Senate met, just in case anyone was tempted to grow nostalgic about the old order.

Most of the population of the planet were slaves, and most of these, oddly enough, were volunteers—religious ecstatics who worked themselves to death in the glitterstim factories in exchange for a daily blast of bliss directed at them by the Hutts' telepathic t'landa Til henchmen. The t'landa Til were still very much a part of the picture, having exchanged one overlordship for another.

Thrackan didn't like slavery—at least for humans—but he supposed there was no alternative under the circumstances. The Yuuzhan Vong wouldn't allow the use of droids, so *someone* had to dig the ditches, build the grand new buildings of Peace City's town center, and process the addictive glitterstim that made up the entirety of Ylesia's gross planetary product.

The son of Tiion Gama Sal had been raised on an estate, as a gentleman, with an army of droid servants. In the place of droids, he needed *someone* to see to his comforts.

Just as he needed someone to keep him from being murdered by the Senate and their cronies. They'd been madly conspiring and committing quiet violence against one another over control of the glitterstim operation, but now they'd united against their new President.

Thrackan decided that he needed to find the most cold-blooded, ruthless, efficient killer among them, and win that person to his side. And one look at Dagga Marl had convinced him that she was exactly what he was looking for.

She was completely mercenary and completely without morals, something Thrackan thought was to his advantage. She made her living as a bounty hunter and an assassin. She'd killed people for the Peace Brigade, and she'd killed Peace Brigade on behalf of other Peace Brigade. She seemed perfectly willing to kill Peace Brigade on behalf of Thrackan, and that was all he asked.

The most important thing about Dagga was that she was smart enough to know when she was well off. Others might offer her a large sum to kill Thrackan, but they weren't going to offer her a kilo of spice per week.

The spice was the only thing on Ylesia that passed for money. The Yuuzhan Vong intendants in charge of running the supposed economy hadn't even seen a *need* for money. Their chief economic principle was that those who obeyed orders and did their work without question would be rewarded with shelter and food. It hadn't occurred to them that a person might want a little *more* than organic glop to eat, a membranous cavern to live in, and an overgrown fungus to sit on. A person might prefer to live in marble halls enjoying a bath with golden fixtures, and the latest-model atmosphere craft.

Dagga looked up at him. "Is there anything you'd like me to do right now?"

Thrackan sat, fingers stroking the smooth polished surface of his desk. "Evaluate security here in my office, and in my residence. If you can't fix whatever's wrong, tell me and *I'll* fix it."

She flipped him a casual salute. "Right, Chief."

"And if you can recommend any reliable people to assist you . . ."

She tilted her head in thought. "I'll think about it. Reliability isn't one of the more common Peace Brigade virtues."

"Did I say Peace Brigade?"

Dagga seemed startled by the vehemence of Thrackan's words.

"I said *reliable*. I'll import someone if he's good enough. Though," he admitted, "I prefer them human."

A white smile flashed across Dagga's features. "I'll put together a little list," she said.

There was a knock on the door. Dagga made a slight adjustment to her clothing to enhance her homicidal capabilities, and Thrackan said, "Who is it?"

It was his chief of communications, an Etti named Mdimu. "Beg pardon, sir," he said, "but the advance party for the joint maneuvers has entered the system."

"When are they scheduled to arrive?" Thrackan asked.

"They'll be landing at the spaceport in approximately two hours."

"Very good. Send the quednak to the spaceport now, and I'll follow in my landspeeder at the appropriate time."

"Ah—" Mdimu hesitated. "Sir? Your Excellency?"

"Yes?"

"The Yuuzhan Vong—they don't like machinery, sir. If you arrive at the spaceport in a landspeeder they may consider it an insult."

Thrackan sighed, then explained slowly and simply so that even an alien like Mdimu could understand. "I'll arrive *before* the Vong and then send the landspeeder back to its docking bay. I will return with the Vong on the riding beasts. But I will *not* ride those stupid six-legged flatulent herbivorous lumbering ninnies to the spaceport *when I don't have to.* Understand?"

Mdimu hesitated, then nodded. "Yes, sir."

"And please tell the construction gangs to keep their machinery out of sight while the Vong are in town."

"Yes. Of course, Your Excellency."

Mdimu left the room. Dagga Marl and Thrackan exchanged looks.

"Of this I build a nation," he said.

The Yuuzhan Vong frigate analog, which looked like a large brownish green lump of vomit, arrived escorted by two squadrons of coralskippers, which looked like rather uninteresting rocks. Thrackan's official bodyguards—whom he would not have trusted to guard his body if they were the last on Ylesia, and who were most likely in the pay of various factions of the Senate anyway—shuffled into line and presented their amphistaffs.

Amphistaffs. One of the Yuuzhan Vong's most annoying and dangerous exports. Thrackan gave his official bodyguards a wide berth, as experience had shown they weren't very good at controlling the weapon their Yuuzhan Vong sponsors had so graciously given them. The previous week he'd lost two guards, bitten during practice by their own weapons' poisonous heads.

Followed by his *real* bodyguard, Dagga Marl, Thrackan marched to the frigate analog and waited. Eventually a part of the hull withdrew somehow, and an object like a giant, wart-encrusted tongue flopped down to touch the landing field. Down this ramp came a double file of Yuuzhan Vong armored warriors with amphistaffs—which *these* warriors looked as if they knew how to use. Once formed on the pavement, they were followed by Supreme Commander Maal Lah, architect of the Yuuzhan Vong capture of Coruscant.

Maal Lah's appearance was presentable, for a Yuuzhan Vong. Unlike Nom Anor, with his brand-new plaeryin bol implant—this eye replacement even larger and nastier than the one he had lost—or Shimrra, who was so scarred and mutilated that his face looked as if it had gone through a threshing machine, Maal Lah's regular features were still recognizable as features. He'd restrained the impulse to carve himself up in honor of his vicious gods, and for the most part settled for red and blue tattoos. Thrackan could actually look at him without wanting to lose his lunch. If he let his eyes go slightly out of focus, the tattoos formed an abstract pattern that was almost pleasing.

He made a note to try to keep his eyes slightly out of focus for the rest of the day.

"Greetings, Commander," he said. "Welcome to Ylesia."

Maal Lah had fortunately brought a translator along, a member of the intendant caste who had cut off an ear and replaced it with a glistening, semitranslucent sluglike creature the function of which Thrackan preferred not to contemplate.

"Salutations, President Sal-Solo," Maal Lah said through his translator. "I come to remind you of your submission and to bring your fleet to its obedience."

"Er—quite," Thrackan said. *A fine way with diplomacy these Vong have.* "The intendants on Ylesia have . . . grown . . . your damutek. Would you care to see it?"

"First I will inspect your guard."

Thrackan stayed on the far side of Maal Lah as the warrior inspected the Presidential Guard, hoping that if Maal Lah were accidentally sprayed with poison, Thrackan himself might have a running head start before Yuuzhan Vong warriors began to massacre everyone present. Fortunately no fatalities occurred.

"A shabby lot of useless wretches, totally without spirit or discipline," Maal Lah commented as he walked with Thrackan to the riding beasts.

"I agree, Commander," Thrackan said.

"Discipline and order should be beaten into them. What I wouldn't give to see them in the hands of the great Czulkang Lah."

Now that *might be fun,* Thrackan thought, though without knowing who or what Czulkang Lah might be. Thrackan always enjoyed a good thrashing, provided he wasn't the one on the receiving end.

"I'll dismiss their commander," he said. Their commander was a Duros, and therefore expendable. He'd replace the Duros with a human, provided he could find one who might conceivably be loyal.

"I trust the Peace Brigade fleet is ready?" Maal Lah said.

"Admiral Capo assures me that they are fully trained and alert, and eager to serve alongside their gallant allies, the Yuuzhan Vong." Actually Thrackan had no great hope for the motley force that was the Peace Brigade fleet. In fact he rather hoped that Maal Lah would be so disgusted as to execute the Rodian Admiral Capo, thus providing another vacancy Thrackan could fill with a human.

Again, if he could find one to trust. Here that always seemed to be the problem.

Reflecting that he was a little old for this sort of thing, Thrackan followed Maal Lah up the vine ladder to the purple-green resinous tower atop the six-legged form of a Yuuzhan Vong riding beast. The quednak's moss-covered scales reeked of something that needed flushing down the nearest sewer. At the urging of its intendant handler, the beast lurched to its feet and set off for Peace City at a slow walk. Thrackan hoped the motion wouldn't make him ill.

A pair of swoop analogs—open-cockpit fliers with a crew of two and sped along by dovin basals—rose to take position on either side of the riding beast. Maal Lah wasn't trusting his life entirely to guards who moved on foot.

Thrackan cast a glance at the double file of Yuuzhan Vong warriors trotting along in the big lizard's wake. By the time they traveled the twenty-two kilometers to Peace City, perhaps even the fabled Yuuzhan Vong would be tired of the pace.

"Now that we have more of your people on the planet," Thrackan ventured, "I wonder if we might better provide for their spiritual needs."

Maal Lah's answer was dry. "How would you do that, Excellency?"

"There are no temples to your gods here. Perhaps we could provide one for your people."

"That is a generous thought, Excellency. Of course, it is *we* who would have to provide the template for the structure, and, of course the priest."

"We could donate the ground, at least."

"So you could." Maal Lah considered for a moment. "As with many of my clan, I have always been a devotee of Yun-Yammka, the Slayer. It would be an act of devotion to foster his worship on a new world. Of course, the worship requires sacrifice . . ."

"Plenty of slaves for that purpose," Thrackan said, as heartily as he could manage.

Maal Lah bowed his head. "Very good. So long as you are willing to donate one from time to time."

Thrackan waved a hand dismissively. "Anything we can do for our brothers." At least he could make sure none of the victims were human. "I have a piece of land already in mind," he added.

He certainly did. The land in question was adjacent to the Altar of Promises, where the t'landa Til administered to the slaves their daily dose of telepathic euphoria. The t'landa Til were said to have powers over all humanoid species, and Thrackan was inclined to wonder if that included the Yuuzhan Vong.

The sight of the Yuuzhan Vong rolling about in ecstatic bliss would certainly be a pleasing one. The sight would be even more pleasing if he could get the mighty warriors *addicted* to their daily blast of cosmic communion, as were the slaves.

It seemed worth sacrificing a few aliens to have a whole regiment of Yuuzhan Vong addicts willing to do anything Thrackan suggested in return for a daily ecstatic thunderbolt from their god.

Thrackan chuckled to himself. And Shimrra thought *he* was an expert on the taking of vengeance.

So agreeable did Thrackan find this vision that he almost missed Maal Lah's next statement.

"You should prepare yourself and the Senate for a special visitor in the next few days."

It took Thrackan a few seconds to realize the import of this. All his pleasing fantasies vanished like vapor before the wind.

"Shimrra's coming *here*?" he gasped.

Maal Lah snarled at him. "The *Supreme Overlord*," he corrected savagely, "will remain in his new capital until the gods tell him otherwise. No, it's *another* who will soon be paying you an official visit. With this one you will sign a treaty of peace, mutual aid, and nonaggression." A smile snarled its way across the warrior's face. "Prepare yourself to meet the Chief of State of the New Republic."

The streaming stars flashed and nailed themselves to the heavens, and the Ylesia system leapt into life on Jacen's displays. Alarms bleeped at the realization that the ships in orbit around the planet were enemy. Jacen closed up on Jaina, the formation leader, his X-wing tucked in neatly behind his sister's fighter.

"Twin Suns Squadron, check in!" Jaina's voice on the comm.

"Twin Two," said Jaina's Neimoidian wingmate, Vale, "in realspace with all systems normative."

"Twin Three," another pilot said. "In realspace. All systems normative."

The pilots all checked in, all the way to Jacen, who had been added to Jaina's flight as Twin Thirteen. He made his report, the Force filling his mind, and through it he felt the Jedi: fierce, loyal Lowbacca and the exhilarated Tesar near at hand; Corran Horn distracted by his own pilots' checklist; the cold-blooded exhilaration of Saba Sebatyne and her Wild Knights. And, more distantly, other elements of the fleet, the concentration of Tahiri, the melancholy determination of Alema Rar, the confidence of Zekk, and the sheer *power* of Kyp Durron, a power very much akin to rage.

And, most clearly of all, Jacen felt the presence of Jaina, her mind ablaze with machinelike calculation.

The Jedi meld filled Jacen's mind, a psychic feedback mechanism between himself and the other Jedi. He was impressed by the meld's power, and by how it had grown since he'd last experienced it on Myrkr. There, it had been a mixed blessing, but then the Jedi war party at Myrkr had been divided among themselves. Here, they were united in a single purpose.

Jacen's sensitivity to the Force had grown within the meld, and he was aware of the other lives around him, the non-Jedi pilots of Twin Suns Squadron, and others nearby, particularly the disciplined minds of Jagged Fel's Chiss squadron, which flew to port and slightly behind them. Jag had volunteered his squadron for this fight, even though they weren't technically a part of Kre'fey's command. Once Kre'fey had been reminded that Jag's veterans had originally been a part of Twin Suns Squadron before being split off, he'd accepted Jag's offer.

"Listen up, people." Jaina's voice came again on the comm. "I know we outnumber the enemy, but that doesn't make the ordnance they'll shoot at us any less real. This isn't a drill, and you can get killed if you're not careful. I want everyone to stick with their wingmate and keep an eye open for an enemy maneuvering to get behind you. Streak," she said to Lowbacca, "I want your flight to our right, a couple of klicks behind. Tesar, you're flying above and behind."

Above was a meaningless term in space, but it was easier than saying "ninety degrees from my and Lowbacca's axis," and Tesar knew what she meant, anyway.

"Copy," Tesar said, and Lowbacca gave an answering roar.

"Remember that Jag Fel's to our left. Understood?"

There was a chorus of acknowledgments.

"Right then," Jaina said. "Let's teach these traitors a thing or two."

Jacen was impressed. He hadn't realized Jaina had become such an effective leader. Her performance was even more impressive because, through the Jedi meld, he could also sense her scanning her displays while she was talking, minding her comm channels, and worrying about her inexperienced pilots while trying to work out tactics that would keep them from killing themselves.

Jacen kept his fighter tucked into formation behind Jaina's, an extra wingmate for Twin Leader. His eyes scanned the displays and saw that Kre'fey's entire armada had by now entered realspace, three task forces grouped as close to Ylesia as the planet's mass shadow would permit. Each of the three groups was the equal of the entire Peace Brigade fleet, and they had the enemy force trapped between them. The only hope for the enemy commander was to leave orbit instantly and attack one of Kre'fey's task forces, hoping to smash through it before the others arrived to overwhelm him.

Moments ticked by, and the enemy commander made no move. His only real hope was slipping through his fingers.

And then the enemy fleet moved, choosing as its target Twin Suns Squadron, and the task force behind it.

The Chief of State of the New Republic was in the middle of his address to the Ylesian Senate when one of Thrackan's aides—the human one, fortunately—came scuttling down the aisle of the Senate building and began to whisper in Thrackan's ear. Maal Lah, who was watching the speech from another seat nearby, suddenly became very preoccupied with talking into one of the villips he wore on the shoulders of his armor.

Thrackan listened to the aide's agitated whisper, then nodded and rose. "I regret the necessity of interrupting," he began, and saw the Senate's malevolent gaze immediately turn in his direction. "A fleet from the New Republic has appeared in Ylesian space." He watched the august Senatorial heads turn to one another in growing panic as a buzzing filled the hall. Thrackan turned to the Chief of State of the New Republic.

"You didn't tell anyone you were coming, did you?" he asked.

If it weren't a dire emergency in which he might be killed, Thrackan might almost enjoy this.

"These are rebels!" the New Republic Chief of State proclaimed. "Rebels against rightful authority! They wouldn't dare fire on their leader!"

"Perhaps," Thrackan suggested, "you'd care to get on the comm and order them to stop."

The Chief of State hesitated, then came down from the podium. "This is the sort of misunderstanding that can only be cleared up later. Perhaps we should, umm, seek shelter first."

"An excellent idea," Thrackan said, and turned again to the Senate. "I suggest that the honorable members proceed to the shelter." As a few bolted at top speed for the exit, he added, *"In an orderly manner!"*—as if it would do any good. His words only seemed to accelerate their flight, desks overturning as the founders of the noble Ylesian Republic jammed shoulder to shoulder in the doors.

Thrackan turned to Maal Lah and suppressed a shrug. These people hadn't betrayed their own galaxy out of an excess of courage, and he couldn't say he was surprised by their behavior.

The Yuuzhan Vong commander was barking into his little shoulder villip. His translator sidled up to Thrackan.

"Commander Lah is ordering the forces that were already in transit for the joint maneuvers to come at once."

"Very good. Will the commander be going to his command ship?"

"The distance to the spaceport is too great."

Especially if you're traveling at the pace of a fat ugly Hutt-sized reptoid, Thrackan thought.

"I can offer the commander room in our shelter," Thrackan said.

"The commander has no need of the shelter," the translator said. "He will instead take charge of the troops here in the capital."

"Excellent! I'm sure we're in good hands."

Maal Lah finished his one-sided conversation and stalked toward Thrackan, his fingers curled around his batron of rank. "I will need to take command of your Presidential Guard and your paramilitaries."

"Of course," Thrackan said. "Be my guest." He feigned

thought, and added, "It's a pity the Yuuzhan Vong gods are so opposed to technology. If they weren't, we'd have installed planetary shields and be perfectly safe."

Maal Lah gave him a murderous glare, and for a moment Thrackan's kidney tingled at the thought that he'd gone too far.

"Will you lead your forces into battle, Excellency?" Lah demanded. "Or will you seek shelter with the others?"

Thrackan raised his hands. "I regret that I have no warrior training, Commander. I'll leave all that to the professionals." He turned to Dagga, who had been waiting politely behind him all this time. "Come, Marl."

He left the room at a rapid but dignified pace, Dagga falling into step by his side and half a pace back. "Will you be going to the shelter, sir?" she asked.

Thrackan gave her a sidelong smile. "I know better than to hide in a hole with no back door," he said.

Her cold grin answered his own. "Very good, sir," she said.

"I'm going to the docking bay in back of the Presidential palace and take my landspeeder on the fastest route out of town."

Dagga's smile broadened. "Yes, sir."

"Can you drive fast, Marl?"

She nodded. "I can, sir. Very fast."

"Why don't you drive, then? While I make use of the razor I've stored in the backseat, and change into the fresh clothes I stored there."

"Shadow bomb away." Jaina's voice came over Jacen's headphones. "Altering course, thirty degrees."

"Copy that, Twin Leader," Jacen said.

Jacen remained tucked in behind Jaina's X-wing as the fighter lifted out of the way of the enemy fleet, which was set to come rampaging through this part of space in about ten seconds, and he used the Force to help Jaina push the shadow bomb on ahead, toward its target, a *Republic*-class cruiser that was spearheading the Peace Brigade escape attempt.

"Enemy fighters ahead. Accelerating . . ."

Jacen had already felt the enemy pilots in the Force. He opened fire at where he knew they would be, and was rewarded with a flash that meant an enemy pilot hadn't powered his or her shields in time. Jacen shifted to another target and fired, another deflection shot, but the bolts slammed into shields and flashed away. The target formation burst apart like a firework, each two-fighter element weaving away from Twin Suns' attack.

At that moment Jaina's shadow bomb hit the enemy cruiser, and its bow blossomed in a blaze of fire.

Jacen was following Jaina after the corkscrewing enemy fighters—E-wings—and the Jedi meld rose in his perceptions. He felt Corran Horn making a slashing run at an enemy frigate, the Wild Knights methodically destroying a flight of B-wings, but the knowledge wasn't intrusive—it didn't demand attention, or take away from his piloting, it was just *there,* in the back of his mind.

"Stay close, Vale," Jacen told Jaina's wandering wingmate.

"Oh! Sorry!"

"No chatter on this channel," Jaina admonished. "I'm breaking right . . . *now.*"

Vale wandered even farther from her assigned position during this maneuver, and through the Force Jacen sensed the intense concentration of an E-wing pilot trying to get her into his sights. Jacen deliberately wove out of his assigned place in an S-curve, and as he did so he was aware through the Force-meld that Jaina knew exactly what he was doing, and why.

"Turning left thirty degrees," Jaina said, which swung her fighter and Vale's into what the enemy pilot certainly thought was a perfect setup . . .

Except that it led the enemy right into Jacen's sights. He touched off a full quad burst of laserfire and saw the E-wing's shields collapse under the concentrated barrage. Jacen fired again, and the E-wing disintegrated.

Jacen's heart gave a leap as the E-wing's wingmate chanced a deflection shot and scored a triple laser burst on Jacen's shields—which held—and then Jacen wove away, the E-wing in pursuit, until Jaina's own fighter swirled through a graceful, un-hurried series of arcs, and she and Vale blew the Brigader and his craft to atoms. As she overtook Jacen he could see Jaina's grim satisfaction through the cockpit, and she waggled her wings at him as he slid once more into position.

Then he sensed her mood shift, and he knew she was receiving orders on the command channel.

"Twin Suns," she said. "Regroup. Re-form on me. We're going to cover the landing party."

Jacen knew she was reluctant to leave the combat once it had begun, but he also knew that the fight was going well for the New Republic. The forces were evenly matched in numbers, but the Peace Brigade personnel simply weren't up to the mark. Some mercenary pilots in starfighters were giving a good account of themselves, but the capital ships weren't fighting very well, and some of them were shedding escape pods even though they hadn't taken critical damage. A pair of enemy starfighter squadrons were fleeing the battle as fast as they could, with A-wings in pursuit. Kre'fey's two additional task forces would soon be on the scene, decisively tilting the odds even farther toward the New Republic, and at that point Jacen wouldn't be surprised to see some of the Peace Brigade ships surrender.

It was good to feel the enemy in the Force again, Jacen thought. The Yuuzhan Vong were an emptiness in the Force, a black hole into which the light of the Force disappeared. These Peace Brigaders at least registered as a part of the living universe, and because he could feel them in the Force, Jacen could anticipate their actions. Compared to the Yuuzhan Vong, these people were easy.

Easy to destroy. He tasted a whiff of sadness at the necessity—these targets shouldn't *be* targets; they should be fighting on behalf of the galaxy against the invaders. Instead they had chosen to betray their own, and Kyp Durron and Traest Kre'fey were determined they pay the penalty.

Twin Suns Squadron re-formed, and Jag Fel's Chiss squadron fell into place on their flank. The blue-and-white sphere of Ylesia grew closer. Jacen saw the landing force separating itself from the closest of Kre'fey's task forces.

"We're going to take out the spaceport," Jaina said. *And also to draw fire,* Jacen knew, so they could learn where the defenses were and knock them out before the ground forces, in their lightly armored landing craft, attempted their assault.

"Configure your foils for atmosphere," Jaina said.

The X-wings took on an I-shape as the foils drew together to become wings. The blue planet rolled beneath them . . . and then they saw a patch of green, one of the small continents coming up, and Jaina tipped her fighter toward it, with Jacen and the others after.

Jacen's craft rocked to the buffets of the atmosphere. Flame licked at his forward shields. If he looked over his shoulder he could see sonic shock waves rolling over his foils like spiderwebs. The green land drew closer.

Then new symbols flashed onto his displays, and his own voice echoed Jaina's cry. "*Skips!* Coralskippers, dead ahead!"

The enemy fighters were rising from the spaceport, two squadrons' worth, their dovin basals yanking them clear of the planet's gravity. And in their wake came a much larger target, a frigate analog. The Yuuzhan Vong were clearly aiming for the landing force, which was swinging above the planet in high orbit, guarded by a pair of frigates and the Screamers, a rookie squadron of X-wings under a twenty-three-year-old captain. The escort could probably handle the attackers—eventually—but in the meantime the Yuuzhan Vong could cut up the landing force badly.

"Accelerating! Maximum thrust!" Jaina called, and Twin Suns poured power to their engines. They were in a good position to bounce the enemy as the Yuuzhan Vong clawed their way up through the atmosphere. Jacen looked at his displays and calculated angles, trajectories . . .

"I've got a shadow bomb, Twin Leader," he said. "Let me take a run at the frigate."

Through the Jedi meld he felt Jaina duplicating his own calculation. "Twin Thirteen," she decided, "take your shot."

Jacen dipped his nose and aimed for the patch of air he thought the frigate would pass through in another twenty standard seconds or so. The moment of release was difficult to judge—he couldn't find the frigate analog in the Force, and Jacen would have to make a guess based on how it appeared on his displays.

Suddenly he felt the power of the Force swell in his body,

as if he'd just filled his lungs with pure universal power. Calculations stormed through his mind, faster than he'd thought possible. And distantly, he found he *could* detect the enemy ship—not as a presence in the Force, but as an absence, a cold emptiness in the universe of life.

There were Jedi nearby that hadn't yet engaged the enemy—Tahiri, Kyp Durron, Zekk, and Alema Rar. Since they hadn't been distracted by combat, they had just *loaned* him their power through the Jedi meld, sending him strength and aiding his calculation.

He felt the cold metal of the bomb-release mechanism in his fist, and he pulled it. "Shadow bomb away." And then, as he pulled back the stick and fed power to the engines, he fired a pair of concussion missiles.

The shadow bomb was a missile without propellant, packed instead from head to tail with explosive, and would either drift toward its target or be pushed with a little help from the Force. The lack of a propellant flare made the bomb hard for the Yuuzhan Vong to detect, and the extra explosive gave it tremendous punch when it hit.

The two concussion missiles were intended as a distraction for the Yuuzhan Vong—if the enemy were paying attention to the two missiles, coming in on a different trajectory, then they'd be less likely to see the shadow bomb dropping toward them.

Thanks, Jacen sent into the meld. And then he felt the others fade from his perceptions as first Kyp, then the others, entered combat.

The three parts of Kre'fey's fleet had just united, Jacen thought, with the Peace Brigade forces trapped between them. The Brigaders were about to lose their whole fleet.

The nose of Jacen's X-wing pointed higher, toward the distant glowing exhaust ports of Jaina's squadron. This put the frigate below in a perfect position to shoot at him, the fire heading practically up his tail. He saw the plasma cannon projectiles and missiles coming, and he jinked wildly for a few seconds, until his shadow bomb hit the Yuuzhan Vong ship and blew its nose off. Along with the nose went the dovin basals that were being used for defense, so even the two concussion missiles slammed home.

What doomed the Yuuzhan Vong frigate wasn't the damage, but the aerodynamics. If the frigate had been in the vacuum of space it probably would have survived, but its fate was sealed by Ylesia's atmosphere. The frigate began to weave through the air like an out-of-control skyrocket as the wind seized hold of its torn bow section. Parts tore off and flew away, spinning downward; and then the frigate lost control completely and began a death spiral toward the planet below.

Jacen's attention was already on the combat above him. Jaina and Jag Fel had bounced the coralskippers and had killed at least three of them, their wrecked hulls plunging downward in the atmosphere with tails of flame, but now the battle had become a melee. Again aerodynamics worked to the advantage of the New Republic: a coralskipper had all the aerodynamics of a brick, but the X-wings, with their foils closed, made decent, maneuverable atmosphere craft. Still, Jacen sensed Jaina's tension through the Jedi meld: half of Twin Suns Squadron were still rookies, easy meat for an experienced enemy; and the Yuuzhan Vong were flying like veterans.

An X-wing trailing fire plunged past Jacen as he climbed, and he saw a flash as the pilot ejected. Fragments of burning yorik coral crashed onto Jacen's shields as he climbed: that meant another coralskipper accounted for.

He would be at too much of a disadvantage if he climbed straight into the fight, so he avoided the battle and got above the furball before rolling his craft into a dive. He felt control surfaces biting air as the X-wing accelerated, and found a target ahead, a coralskipper maneuvering onto the tail of an X-wing that seemed to be wandering around randomly, like a dewback looking for its herd—doubtless one of Jaina's rookies. Jacen chanced the deflection shot, quadded his lasers, and opened fire, and only when he saw the coralskipper explode behind him did the rookie panic, flinging his fighter all over the sky to avoid a menace that Jacen had already destroyed.

Jacen flew on, saw a coralskipper being chased by a Chiss clawcraft, the Yuuzhan Vong's dovin basal snatching the pursuer's bolts from the air as he flew. It was another chancy deflection shot, but Jacen carefully pulled the fighter after the enemy, a smooth curve . . . then found that he was falling short, the enemy dancing just ahead of his shots. Frustration sang in his nerves, and he was on the verge of ordering his astromech to check his controls when he realized it was all the fault of the air—the atmosphere had slowed the fighter too much. He triggered a concussion missile then, and was rewarded by seeing it slam home on the Yuuzhan Vong's flank. The tough coralskipper kept on flying, but its dovin basal was distracted and the Chiss pilot's next shot flamed it.

Jacen's heart leapt as he realized he was in danger, and he jerked his stick to the right as shots flared past his canopy. He'd spent too long lining up his last target and an enemy had jumped him. He corkscrewed through the sprawl of swirling fighter craft and managed to lose his pursuer, and when he stopped his dodging there was an enemy right in front of him, flying right into his sights while lining up on a clawcraft. Jacen blew him apart with a quad laser burst.

He was through the furball now, and pulled back the stick to climb and repeat his maneuver. The others had slowed down to maneuver, and were easy targets for anyone diving in from above. He doubted that he could manage three hits on every pass, but there was no reason not to try.

Jacen made a lazy loop while he scanned the fight through his cockpit, then he half rolled upright and fed power to the engines. A sudden cry came over the comm. "I've just lost rear shields! *Anyone!* This is Twin Two—I've just lost an engine! *Help!*"

Twin Two was Vale, Jaina's rookie wingmate—probably lost, and without cover. He felt Jaina's rising tension through the Force-meld as she searched for Twin Two, and he scanned the mass of weaving fighters as he approached, seeing one madly dancing X-wing with a tail of flame, a pair of skips weaving after her.

"Break left, Twin Two," he called. "I've got you."

"Breaking left!" Panic and relief warred in Vale's reply.

Jacen hit the atmosphere brakes and the X-wing slowed as if

it had hit a lake of mercury, and then he crabbed his jouncing fighter around into a shot on the lead coralskipper. His laser bolts blew the canopy away and sent the craft in an end-over-end spin for the planet below. The second enemy dodged his lasers, and Jacen yanked his fighter into an even tighter turn, the atmosphere jolting the craft, dropping its speed. The enemy swallowed his concussion missile into the singularity of its dovin basal and caught the laser bolts as well, but Jacen saw Vale dart away into safety while her pursuer was preoccupied. And then enemy rounds were hammering on Jacen's shields, and he released the atmosphere brakes and tried to roll away, punching the throttle.

He'd slowed down too much, losing speed and maneuverability and choice. An enemy had found him and was hovering off his tail, hurling round after round after him while he tried desperately to regain speed and the ability to maneuver . . .

Jacen's astromech droid chittered as the aft shields died. And then there was a crash that Jacen felt through his spine, and the stick kicked against his gloved hand. The X-wing slewed abruptly to the left. It slowed so much that the pursuing coralskipper overshot, passing within meters of Jacen's canopy, and his head swiveled on his neck as he looked frantically in all directions, trying to spot any additional threats . . .

And there it was. On the end of Jacen's left foils, its claws dug into the paired laser cannons, was a grutchin, one of the winged, insectoid, metal-eating creatures that the Yuuzhan Vong sometimes released with their missiles. A grutchin whose malevolent black-eyed gaze stared back at Jacen, before it turned to its work and took a leisurely chomp out of the upper left foil.

Jacen dived to gain speed, working the controls frantically to keep the X-wing balanced as the weight and drag of the grutchin threatened to destabilize it. As speed built he was rewarded by the grutchin digging its claws more firmly into the foil, hunching against the battering it was receiving from the atmosphere. Jacen felt his lips draw back in a harsh smile. He'd hoped the wind would strip the grutchin away, but this was the next best thing: the creature couldn't eat his ship as long as it was spending all its strength just to hang on.

Then Jacen pulled back on the stick and fed power to the engines. The only way to get rid of the grutchin was to open the canopy and shoot the thing off his wing, but he couldn't open the canopy and stand up as long as he was in Ylesia's atmosphere—the wind would tear him right out of the craft and send him tumbling toward the planet below with half the bones in his body broken.

An interesting dilemma, he thought. The grutchin couldn't eat his craft as long as Jacen was flying at speed through the atmosphere, but he couldn't get rid of the grutchin until he got out of the atmosphere altogether. This would call for fine judgment.

"This is Twin Thirteen," he said into the comm. "I've got a grutchin on my wing. I'll be back after I deal with it."

"Copy," came Jaina's voice. He could hear the strain of combat in the terse expression, and feel her stress in the Force.

Jacen kept his eyes on the grutchin and his throttles all the way forward. He kept the nose tipped as far as he could without losing speed, and slowly the buffeting of the atmosphere eased as the air thinned. When the grutchin was able to lift its head and take another bite of the upper port laser cannon, Jacen stood the X-wing on its tail and fled straight up into space. The grutchin shifted its grip and took another bite, and the laser cannon tore free and spun away into the darkening sky. Jacen reached for his blaster and loosened it in its holster. The whisper of wind on the canopy was almost gone. The second laser tumbled into the sky, and the grutchin turned, its claws clamped firmly on metal, and walked methodically along the two united foils, heading for the engine.

Jacen extended the foils into the X-position, hoping to shake it free or slow it down, but without success. Instead he felt, rather than heard, a crash as the grutchin's head drove like a metal punch into his engine cowling.

Better do *something,* he thought. He threw the cockpit latch; as the cockpit depressurized, force fields snapped into place around him, preserving his air. The sound of flight vanished, though he could still feel the vibration of his craft sounding up his spine. Red lights were flashing on his engine displays. He nudged the controls to the cockpit servos, lifting it slightly open. When he felt no turbulence he opened the cockpit all the way.

He summoned the Force to guide the fighter's controls as he stood in the cockpit and pulled his blaster from its holster. As he leaned out of the cockpit he saw the upper left foil fly away spinning, eaten away at the root. There was a flash of fire in the engine and it died.

Surely, he thought, the flameout was enough to cook the grutchin. He leaned farther out, bracing one arm on the cockpit coaming, and thrust out the blaster.

The grutchin's beady eyes stared back at him with malevolent purpose. And then the creature's wings extended, and Jacen's heart gave a lurch as he realized the grutchin was going to leap straight for his face.

He fired while mentally rehearsing the move necessary to snatch his lightsaber with his free hand in case the blaster didn't do the job. He fired again, and again. The grutchin reared, its clawed forelegs pawing the airless space between them, and Jacen fired twice more.

The grutchin's head tumbled away into the emptiness. The rest of the grutchin then followed.

Blasters work, Jacen reminded himself as he eased back into the cockpit and sealed the canopy.

His astromech droid had already prepared a damage report. Rear shields down, both port lasers gone along with the port upper S-foil; the other port foil damaged, and one engine destroyed.

Jacen thumped a frustrated fist on the cockpit coaming. The X-wing's aerodynamics had been wrecked—if he went into the atmosphere to aid Jaina now, his craft would go into a spin that would end only when he hit the ground.

He had come here to aid Jaina, to make certain that she would never be without his support. Now he was leaving her in a desperate fight with the enemy.

But once he had time to listen on Twin Suns' comm channel, it appeared that Jaina no longer needed his aid. She was ordering her squadron to regroup.

"Twin Leader, this is Twin Thirteen," he said. "The grutchin's dealt with."

Jaina was all business. "Twin Thirteen, what's your status?"

"I'm going to need to get a new fighter before I can rejoin. What's *your* condition?"

"The fight's over. Kyp and Saba came to help us. We're regrouping to hit the spaceport and cover the landing."

"And the Brigaders' fleet?"

"Surrendered. That's how Kyp and Saba were free to join us." There was a pause. "Twin Thirteen, Twin Two has lost an engine. I need you to escort her to rejoin the fleet."

"Understood," Jacen said, "though considering the state of my fighter, Vale may end up escorting *me*."

He heard snickers over the comm. Through the meld Jacen felt his sister bearing the humor with patience.

"Just get her there, Twin Thirteen," she said finally.

"Understood," Jacen said, and rolled his fighter so that he could spot Vale approaching from the planet below.

"Inertial compensators," Thrackan said as he contemplated the wreck of his landspeeder. "What a *good* idea."

It had taken Thrackan and Dagga Marl longer to escape Peace City than he'd expected, largely because so many others were fleeting on foot and had gotten in the way. Barely had they emerged from Peace City's ramshackle limits than a colossal spiraling chunk of yorik coral had come tumbling down out of the sky like a grayish green lump of cosmic vomit and impacted on the road just ahead of them.

The explosion had thrown the landspeeder off the road and spinning into a patch of trees, where, between tree trunks and flying chunks of yorik coral, it had been comprehensively destroyed. But the deluxe landspeeder—built originally for a young Hutt, to judge by the fittings—had been equipped with inertial compensators, and these had failed only after the vehicle had come to a complete halt. Thrackan and Dagga emerged from the wreck unscathed.

Thrackan turned to look at the shattered Yuuzhan Vong frigate lying in fragments beneath a thick cloud of smoke and dust.

"I don't think Maal Lah's forces are doing very well," Thrackan said. There was a horrific smell of burning organics, and he remembered that the frigate had actually been alive, that something akin to blood had pulsed through its hull.

He turned to Dagga. "You wouldn't have private means of getting us off the planet, do you?"

"No, I don't."

"Or knowledge of a landspeeder anywhere nearby?"

Dagga shook her head. Thrackan shrugged.

"That's all right. One will come along in a minute, stop to work out how to get around the wreckage—and then we'll steal it."

Dagga flashed him her shark's grin. "Boss, I like the way you think."

They crouched for some time in the trees by the road, but no landspeeder came. The explosion, with its cloud of smoke, had discouraged anyone from fleeing in this direction.

Thrackan shrugged. "I guess we walk."

"Where are we walking *to*?"

"Away from the city that's about to be pounded into gravel." Thrackan began picking his way through the debris field. There was relatively little left to burn—most of the frigate had been *rock*—and the smoke was dissipating.

He and Dagga fled back into the cover of the trees as a flight of fighter craft howled out of the sky and shrieked along the road toward Peace City. The fighters were distinctive, with ball cockpits and weird jagged pylons on either side. Thrackan was annoyed.

"TIE fighters? We're being attacked by the *Empire* now?" He glared. "I call this excessive!" He shook his finger at the sky. "I call this overkill on the part of Fate!"

He waited a few minutes, then rose from his crouch among the bushes and scanned the sky carefully. "I guess they're gone. But let's stay in the trees and—"

Dagga cocked an ear to the sky. "Listen, boss."

Thrackan listened, then ducked into the bushes again. "This is outrageous," he muttered. "Haven't these people anything better to do?"

Another squadron of fighters—X-wings this time—blasted along the road, their wakes sending the last of the debris smoke swirling out to the sides in huge corkscrew whirls. Then out of the smoke came a phalanx of whining white landing craft that settled onto the huge scar created by the falling frigate. The last wisps of smoke were flattened by the repulsorlift fields as the landers neared the ground, and then the great forward hatches swung open and whole companies of armored soldiers floated out on military landspeeders that bristled with armament.

"Right," Thrackan said as he and Dagga tried to dig themselves into the turf. "We wait till they've gone on to the city, and then we steal one of the transports and head for home."

Dagga gave him a look. "Home had better be pretty close. Those transports won't have hyperspace capability."

Thrackan ground his teeth. This was *not* working out.

The soldiers briskly secured a perimeter, and more craft whined to a landing. It looked as if the soldiers had landed in at least regimental strength.

"I think we're in trouble," Dagga said.

The soldiers' perimeter had expanded as new craft landed, and troopers were now quite close. An officer with a scanner had spotted the two life-forms in the trees, and at his command a pair of landspeeders swung toward the wooded area where Thrackan and Dagga were hiding.

"Right," Thrackan said. "We give ourselves up. First chance you get, you break me out and we steal a ship and head for freedom."

"I'm with you there," Dagga said, "right up to the point where I take *you* with me. I don't think you're going to have access to a weekly kilo of spice after this."

"I've got more than spice," Thrackan said. "Get me to Corellia, and you'll find I'm stinking rich and willing to share—"

His words were interrupted by an officer's amplified order.

"The two of you in the woods. Come out slowly, and with your hands up."

Thrackan saw Dagga's cold eyes harden as she calculated her chances, and his nerves leapt at the thought of being caught in a crossfire. He decided he'd better make up her mind for her.

"Darling!" he shouted. "We're saved!" And then, as he scrambled to his feet, he whispered, "Leave your weapons here."

He pasted a silly grin to his face and came out of the trees, his hands held high. "You're from the New Republic, right? Bless you for coming!" The officer approached and scanned him for weapons. "We saw those TIE fighters and we thought maybe the Emperor was back. Again. That's why we were hiding."

"Your name, sir?"

"Fazum," Thrackan said promptly. "Ludus Fazum. We were part of a refugee convoy from Falleen, got captured by the Peace Brigade and enslaved." He turned to Dagga, who was walking carefully out of the trees with her hands raised. "This is my fiancée Dagga, ah—" He coughed, realizing Dagga might have a warrant out for her. "—Farglblag." He gave her a grin. "Whaddya think, darling?" he asked. "We're rescued!"

She managed a smile. "You bet!" she said. "This is great!"

Dagga was scanned and came up clean. The officer gave them a searching look from under the brim of his helmet. "You look pretty well fed for slaves," he said.

"We were house slaves!" Thrackan said. "We just did, ah . . ." His invention failed him. "House things."

The officer turned to look over his shoulder. "Corporal!"

Thrackan and Dagga were marched to an open area under the guard of the corporal. The area, gouged dirt scattered with hot, crumbling yorik coral, had been reserved for captured civilians, but Dagga and Thrackan were, for the moment, its only two occupants.

"Farglblag?" she grated.

"Sorry."

"How do you *spell* it?"

Thrackan shrugged. He looked at the troopers in their white armor, ready for an advance on Peace City, and wondered what they were waiting for.

The answer came in the form of a pair of X-wings that hovered to a stop right over their heads, not knowing the large open space had been reserved for civilians. Thrackan and Dagga were forced to move to one side as the two craft settled onto their repulsorlifts. Thrackan spoke under cover of the engine whine.

"You've got a hold-out, right?"

"Sure. I always carry a weapon that'll get past a scanner."

The engines whined to a halt, and the cockpits lifted. A ginger-haired Wookiee stood in the cockpit of the nearest and lowered himself to the ground. "Good," Thrackan said, lowering his voice. "It's a Wookiee. They're not very bright, you know. What happens now is that you clip the Wookiee, then we both hop in the fighter and rocket out of here."

Dagga raised an eyebrow. "You can fly an X-wing?"

"I can fly anything Incom makes."

"Won't it be a little crowded?"

"It'll be uncomfortable, yes. But it won't be nearly as uncomfortable as prison." He gave her a significant look. "You can take my word on that last part."

And if the cockpit seemed to be too small for them both, Thrackan thought, he'd just leave Dagga behind. No problem.

Dagga gave the matter some thought, then nodded. "It's worth a try."

She turned to examine the situation more closely just as the second pilot stepped around the Wookiee's craft. Thrackan saw the slim, dark-haired form and felt all the color drain from his face. He turned away abruptly, but it was too late.

"Hi, Cousin Thrackan," Jaina Solo called. "However did you know we've been looking for you?"

"I wonder if you can remember when *you* held *me* prisoner," Jaina said cheerfully.

Thrackan Sal-Solo tried to fashion a smile. "That was all a misunderstanding. And long ago."

"You know . . ." Jaina cocked her head and pretended to study him. "I think you look younger without the beard."

General Tigran Jamira, the commander of the landing force, whirred up in his command vehicle, rose from his seat, and gave Thrackan a careful look. "You say this is the Peace Brigade President?" he asked.

"That's Thrackan all right." Jaina looked at the black-haired woman who had been with Thrackan. "I don't know who this is. His girlfriend, maybe."

Thrackan seemed a little indignant. "This is the stenographer the government assigned me."

Jaina looked at the woman and her cold eyes and bright white teeth, and thought that clerical assistants were certainly looking carnivorous these days.

Thrackan approached the general and adopted a pained tone. "You know, there's a family vendetta going on here." He pointed at Jaina. "She's got it in for me over something that happened *years* ago."

General Jamira gave Thrackan a cold look. "So you *aren't* the Peace Brigade President?"

Thrackan threw out his hands. "I didn't *volunteer* for the job! I was kidnapped! The Vong were getting even with me for killing so many of them at Fondor!"

Lowbacca, who had been listening, gave a complex series of moans and howls, and Jaina translated. "He says, 'They got revenge by making you *President*? If you killed more of them, they'd make you *emperor*?' "

"They're *diabolical*," Thrackan said. "It's a *very elaborate piece of revenge*!" He jabbed a finger toward the small of his back. "They destroyed my kidney! It's still bruised—you want to see?" He began pulling up his shirt.

Jaina turned to the commander. "General," she said, "I'd put Thrackan on the first landspeeder into town. He can guide us to our objectives." She turned to her cousin and winked. "You'll want to help us, right? Since you're not Peace Brigade after all."

"I'm a citizen of Corellia!" Thrackan insisted. "I demand protection from my government!"

"Actually you're *not* a citizen anymore," Jaina said. "When the Centerpoint Party heard you'd defected, they expelled you and sentenced you in absentia and confiscated your property and—"

"But I *didn't* defect! I—"

"Right," General Jamira said. "On the first landspeeder he goes." He looked at Thrackan's companion. "What do we do with the woman?"

Jaina looked at her again, cogitated for a moment, and moved. In a couple of seconds she had the woman's wrist locked and had relieved her of her hold-out blaster.

"I'd put stun cuffs on her," Jaina said, and handed the blaster to General Jamira.

"How did you know she was armed?"

Jaina looked at Dagga Marl and thought about why she'd made her decision. "Because she was standing like a woman who had a blaster on her," she decided.

Dagga, her wrist locked and her elbow hoisted above her head, snarled at Jaina from under her arm. Troopers came to cuff her and put her under guard.

"Let's get moving," Jamira said.

Jaina marched Thrackan to the first landspeeder and sat him in front, next to the driver. She herself folded down a jump seat and sat directly behind him.

The operation was going better than she'd expected. Jamira had landed most of his force here, to drive on Peace City, but he'd stationed blocking forces on all routes from the capital to catch any Brigaders trying to flee. The fight in the atmosphere had delayed things a bit, but it had also wiped out the only Yuuzhan Vong ships in the system. Still, a wary alertness prickled along Jaina's nerves. There was plenty that could yet go wrong.

She turned to Thrackan. "Now, you be sure and let us know where your side's first ambush is going to be," she said.

Thrackan didn't bother turning to face her. "Right. Like they'd tell me."

The first ambush took place on the outskirts of the city center, Peace Brigade soldiers firing from atop flat-roofed buildings on the landspeeders below. Blaster bolts and shoulder-fired rockets sparked off the landspeeders' shields, and the soldiers aboard returned fire from their heavy vehicle-mounted weapons.

Jaina, crouched behind the bulwark in case something got through the shields, looked at her cousin, who was crouched likewise, and said, "Want to order them to surrender, President?"

"Oh shut up."

Jaina ignited her lightsaber and sprinted to the nearest building, a two-story block of offices. Lowbacca was on her heels. Rather than burst in through a door, which was what defenders might expect, Jaina sliced open the shuttered viewport and hurled herself through the gap.

There were no Peace Brigaders, but there was a mine set up to blast anyone coming in through the door. Jaina disarmed it with the press of a button, then cut the wire connecting it to the door for good measure.

Lowbacca was already roaring up the stairs, his lightsaber a brilliant flash in the dark stairwell. Jaina followed him to the roof exit, which he smashed open with one huge furry shoulder.

Whatever the dozen or so defenders on the roof might have expected, it wasn't a Jedi Wookiee. They fired a few bolts at him, which he deflected with his lightsaber, then before Jaina even emerged they fled, dropping their weapons and crowding for the wooden scaffolding that supported a part of the building that was being reinforced. Lowbacca and Jaina charged them and were rewarded by the sight of several of the enemy simply diving off the building in their haste to escape. When Jaina and Lowbacca reached the scaffolding, with the eight or nine soldiers still clinging to it and lowering themselves to the street, Jaina looked at Lowbacca and grinned, and knew from his grinning response that he shared her idea.

Swiftly the two sliced the lashings that held the scaffold to the building, and then—with Lowbacca's Wookiee muscles and an assist from the Force—they shoved the scaffolding over. The Brigaders spilled to the ground in a splintering crash of wood and were swiftly rounded up by more of Jamira's troopers, who had sped around the ambush to outflank it.

Jaina looked up. Enemy on the next roof were still firing at the landspeeders below, unaware their comrades had been captured.

She and Lowbacca had worked together so long they didn't need to speak. They trotted ten paces back from the edge, turned, and sprinted for the parapet. Jaina put a foot on the edge and leapt, the Force assisting her to a soundless landing on the roof.

The squad of Brigaders were turned away, firing into the street below. Jaina grabbed one by the ankles and tipped him over the edge, and Lowbacca simply kicked another over the parapet. Jaina turned to the nearest as he was reacting, sliced his blaster rifle in half with her lightsaber, then punched him in the face with the hilt of her weapon. He sprawled over the parapet unconscious. Lowbacca deflected a bolt aimed for Jaina, then caught the rifle with the tip of his lightsaber and flung it into the air. Jaina used the Force to guide the flying rifle to a collision with the nose of another Brigader, which gave Lowbacca time to heave his disarmed enemy into the street below.

That took the fight out of them, and the rest surrendered. Jaina and Lowbacca chucked the captured weapons to the street, then turned them over to a squad of New Republic troopers who came storming up the stairs.

The shooting was over. Jaina looked ahead to see the large, new buildings of the city center. She saw no reason to return to the landspeeder—she could guide the military to their objective from her vantage point on the rooftops. She leaned over the parapet and gestured to General Jamira that she would go ahead over the roof. He nodded his understanding.

Jaina and Lowbacca took another run and leapt to the next roof, checking the building on all sides to make certain that no ambush lurked in its shadows. They then sprang onto the next building, and the next.

Across from this last was what was probably intended to be a wide, impressive boulevard, but which consisted at the moment of a muddy excavation half filled with water. The air smelled like a stagnant pond. Beyond were some large buildings that would be very grand when finished. Jaina knew from her briefings that a large shelter had been dug behind the largest building, the Senate house, and subsequently covered over by the plantings of what was supposed to be a park.

The whole expanse was deserted. Smoke rose from several areas on the horizon. Jaina called the Force into her mind and probed ahead. The others in the Force-meld, sensing her purpose, sent her strength and aided her perception.

The distant warmth of other lives glowed in Jaina's mind. There were indeed defenders in the Senate building, though they were keeping out of sight.

Sending thanks to the others in the Force-meld, Jaina clipped her lightsaber to her belt, hurled herself off the building, and allowed the Force to cushion her fall to the duracrete below. Lowbacca followed. They trotted back to General Jamira's command speeder. There they found the general conferring with what appeared to be a group of civilians. Only on approaching did Jaina recognize Lilla Dade, a veteran of Page's Commandos who had volunteered to lead a small infiltration party into Ylesia in the aftermath of the battle and set up an underground cell in the enemy capital.

"This is your chance," Jamira told her.

"Very good, sir." She saluted and flashed Jaina a grin as she led her team into the nearly deserted city.

Jamira turned to Jaina, who saluted. "There are defenders in the Senate building, sir," she told him. "A couple hundred, I think."

"I have enough firepower to blow the Palace of Peace down around them," Jamira said, "but I'd rather not. You might see if you can get your cousin to talk them into surrendering."

"I'll do that, sir." Jaina saluted and trotted back to the lead landspeeder. "The general's got a job for you, Cousin Thrackan," she said.

Thrackan gave her a sour look. "I'll give diplomacy my best shot," he said, "but I don't think Shimrra's going to give Coruscant back."

"Ha ha," Jaina said, and jumped into the landspeeder.

Jamira's forces advanced on the government center on a broad front, repulsorlifts carrying them over the boggy, torn ground, their heavy weapons trained on the half-finished buildings. Starfighters split the sky overhead.

The landspeeders halted two hundred meters from the building. Jaina looked at what she'd thought was a tarpaulin stretched over some construction work, and then realized it was the flayed skin of a very large Hutt. She nudged Thrackan.

"Friend of yours?"

"Never met him," Thrackan said shortly. At Jaina's instruction, he stood and picked up the microphone handed him by the landspeeder's commander.

"This is President Sal-Solo," he said. "Hostilities have ceased. Put down your weapons and leave the building with your hands in plain sight."

There was a long silence. Thrackan turned to Jaina and spread his hands. "What did you expect?"

And then there was a sudden commotion from the Senate building, a series of yells and crashes. Jaina sensed the soldiers around tightening their grip on their weapons. "Repeat the message," she told Thrackan.

Thrackan shrugged and began again. Before he was half finished the doors burst open and a swarm of armored warriors ran out. Jaina started as she recognized Yuuzhan Vong. Then she saw that the warriors had raised their hands in surrender, and that they weren't Vong, just Peace Brigade wearing laminate imitations of vonduun crab armor. In their lead was a Duros officer, who ran up to Thrackan and saluted.

"Sorry that took so long, sir," he said. "There were some Yuuzhan Vong in there, intendants, who thought we should fight."

"Right," Thrackan said, and ordered the warriors into the hands of the landing force. He turned to Jaina, his look dour. "My loyal bodyguard," he explained. "You see why I decided to head out on my own."

"Why are they dressed in fake armor?" Jaina asked.

"The *real* armor kept *biting* them," Thrackan said acidly, and sat down again.

"We need you to lead us to the bunker where your Senators are hiding," Jaina said. "And to the secret exit they'll use for their escape."

Thrackan favored Jaina with another bitter glare. "If there was an escape hatch from that bunker," he asked, "do you think I'd be *here*?"

The bunker turned out to have a huge blastproof door, like a vault. Thrackan, using the special comm relay outside the bunker to talk with those inside, failed to persuade them to come out.

General Jamira was undeterred, sending for his engineer company to come down from orbit and blast the door off the bunker.

Jaina felt time slipping away. None of the delays so far had been critical, but they were all beginning to add up.

Maal Lah restrained the instinct to duck as another flight of enemy starfighters roared overhead. The villip in his hands retained the snarling image of the dead executor he'd used to try to command President Sal-Solo's useless bodyguard, and whom the Presidential Guard had killed rather than obey.

The cowards would be thrown in a pit and crushed by riding beasts, he promised himself.

The damutek grown on the outskirts of the capital to house his troops had been destroyed early in the attack, fortunately after he'd gotten his warriors out. But since then they'd been forced to remain in cover, pinned down by the accursed starfighters that patrolled at low altitude overhead. Fighter cover had been so heavy that Maal Lah had been unable to move even a few of his warriors toward the city center to guard the Peace Brigade government.

He gathered that the Peace Brigade fleet had surrendered— more candidates for the pit and the riding beasts, Maal Lah thought. His own small force of spacecraft had at least gone down fighting. And now, he suspected, Ylesia's government was about to fall into the hands of the enemy.

But even considering these developments, Maal Lah found himself content. He knew that the New Republic forces were about to suffer a surprise, and that the surprise should draw the heavy fighter cover away.

And once he could safely move his warriors, there would be more surprises in store for the raiders of the New Republic.

And many blood sacrifices for the gods of the Yuuzhan Vong.

Jacen and Vale brought their limping X-wings aboard Kre'fey's flagship *Ralroost*. By the time Jacen powered the fighter down he knew that the Peace Brigade forces had folded like a house of cards, both in space and on the ground, and that the New Republic forces were digging the last of the leadership out of their bunker.

Those who had nothing in common but treason, he thought,

had no reason to trust one another or fight on one another's behalf. There was no unifying ideology other than greed and opportunism. Neither was likely to create solidarity.

He dropped to the deck, breathing gratitude that the raid was a success. It had been his idea to capture the heads of the Ylesian government, and his fault that Jaina had volunteered to go in with the ground forces. If the mission had gone wrong he would have been doubly responsible.

Jacen first checked out Vale to make certain she was all right, then inspected their X-wings. Both would require time in a maintenance bay before they would fly again.

"Jacen Solo?" A Bothan officer, very much junior, approached and saluted. "Admiral Kre'fey requests your presence on the bridge."

Jacen looked at Vale, then back at the officer. "Certainly," he said. "May Lieutenant Vale join us?"

The Bothan considered the question, but Vale was quick to give her own answer.

"That isn't necessary," she said. "Admirals make me nervous."

Jacen nodded, then followed the Bothan out of the docking bay toward the forepart of the ship.

And then he felt the universe slow down as if time itself had been altered. He was aware of how long a time it seemed to take for his foot to reach the floor, aware of the long space between his heartbeats.

Something had just changed. Jacen let the Jedi meld that had been sitting quietly in some back room of his mind come to the fore, and he felt surprise and consternation in the minds of the other Jedi, a confusion that was soon replaced with grim resolve and frantic calculation.

Jacen's foot touched the deck. He took a breath. He was aware that a Yuuzhan Vong fleet had just entered the system, and that his plan for the Battle of Ylesia had just gone terribly wrong.

"I think we'd better hurry," he told the startled Bothan lieutenant, and began to run.

* * *

The huge cutting beams of the engineers' lasers were chopping the vault door into scrap. Jaina shrank away from the bright light and heat. She could sense panic through the vault doors, panic and flashes of desperate readiness from those preparing themselves for hopeless resistance. A few blaster bolts came spanging out of the torn vault, but the lasers were shielded and the blasters did no damage.

Jaina looked at the troopers preparing to storm the Senate bunker, and she thought that was a lot of firepower to subdue a group who might be no more prepared to resist capture than their army or fleet. She found General Jamina and saluted.

"Sir, I'd like to be first into the vault. I think I can get them to surrender."

Jamira took barely a second to consider the request. "I'm not going to tell a Jedi she can't be the first into a tight spot," he said. "I've seen what you people can do." He nodded. "Just be sure you call for help if you need it."

"I will, sir."

She snapped the general a salute and trotted back to the vault door. The cutting was almost done. Melted duralloy had frozen on the floor of the anteroom in the shape of a waterfall. Jaina stood next to Lowbacca, who gave her a significant look as he unclipped his lightsaber. Jaina grinned. Without a word he'd shown he understood her plan, and approved.

Jaina ignited her own lightsaber as the laser finished its final cut. With a shove of the Force she pushed the final chunk of the vault door into the interior, where it rang on the floor. Blaster bolts flashed out of the hole, and someone inside shouted, *"You people keep out!"*

Jaina leapt through the door headfirst, tucked into a somersault, came out on her feet. The blasterfire sizzled after her, allowing Lowbacca to follow through the hole without being targeted.

The room was bare duracrete, with no furniture and few fixtures: the Peace Brigade Senators were huddled in corners, shrinking away from those who were determined to fight for their freedom. Blaster bolts came at Jaina thick and fast. She leapt for the nearest shooter, parrying blasterfire with her lightsaber.

Bolts ricocheted off the hard walls and ceiling, and someone cried out as he was hit. The shooter was a big Jenet, and snarled at Jaina as she came for him.

She sliced the blaster apart with her lightsaber, then kicked the Jenet in the teeth with an inside crescent kick. She followed through with a heel hook that dropped the Jenet to the floor.

She saw Lowbacca grab a couple of other shooters, a pair of fighting Ganks, and bang their heads together. Peace Brigade Senators scuttled and huddled for cover. Another blaster went off, and Jaina parried the bolt back into the shooter's knee. The Force powered a jump that took her the six meters to the Ishi Tib shooter, where she kicked the blaster out of her hand; and then the Force seized the blaster and smashed it into the face of another shooter. His own bolt went wild into the crowd of Senators, and there was a scream. Lowbacca leapt on him from behind and smashed him in the head with one massive furry hand.

There was silence, except for the sobs of one of the wounded. The room stank from the ozone discharge of weapons. Armored New Republic troopers began to enter the room, weapons directed at the Brigaders.

Jaina brandished her lightsaber over the cowering group, its loud *thrummm* echoing in the small room, and called, "Surrender! In the name of the New Republic!"

"On the contrary," a commanding voice said. "In the name of the New Republic, I call on *you* to surrender."

Jaina looked in surprise at the tall, cloaked figure that rose from a huddled group of Brigaders, at the arrow-shaped head and writhing face-tentacles.

"Senator Pwoe?" she said in surprise.

"*Chief of State* Pwoe," the Quarren corrected. "Head of the New Republic. I am present on Ylesia in order to negotiate a treaty of friendship and mutual aid with the Ylesian Republic. I call upon New Republic forces to cease these acts of aggression against a friendly allied regime."

Jaina was so taken aback that she barked out a surprised laugh. Pwoe, an avowed foe of the Jedi, had been a member of Borsk Fey'lya's Advisory Council. When Fey'lya died in the ruin of Coruscant, Pwoe had declared himself Chief of State and began to issue orders to the New Republic government and military.

He might have gotten away with it if he hadn't overplayed his hand. When the Senate reconvened on Mon Calamari—ironically, Pwoe's homeworld—they'd issued an order calling on Pwoe and all other Senators to join them. Instead of obeying, Pwoe had issued an order *to the Senate* calling for them to join him on Kuat.

The Senate had been offended, formally deprived Pwoe of any powers, and conducted their own election for Chief of State. Eventually—and after a full measure of the usual skulduggery—the pro-Jedi Cal Omas was elected. Since then, Pwoe had been traveling from one part of the galaxy to another, trying to rally his ever-diminishing number of supporters.

"This peace treaty is vital to the interests of the New Republic," Pwoe went on. "This typical Jedi violence is on the verge of spoiling everything."

Jaina's grin broadened. Apparently Pwoe had grown so desperate that he'd decided that he could only regain his prestige and following if he came to Mon Calamari waving a peace agreement.

"I'm very sorry to disturb any important treaties," she said. "Perhaps you would care to step outside and speak to General Jamira?"

"That will not be necessary. I call upon the general and the rest of you to leave Ylesia at once."

The Ishi Tib, lying at Jaina's feet, began a gradual movement aimed at freeing a weapon concealed somewhere within her robes. Jaina stepped on her hand. The movement ceased.

"I think you should speak to the general," she said, and turned to the dozen soldiers who had been quietly entering the room during the course of this discussion. "Please escort Senator Pwoe to the general." Two armored troopers marched to either side of Pwoe, seized his arms, and began carrying him toward the vault door.

"Take your hands off me!" he boomed. "I'm your Chief of State!"

Jaina watched as Pwoe was carried away. Then she bent to relieve the Ishi Tib of her hidden blaster, and straightened to address the rest of the Brigaders.

"And the rest of you"—she raised her voice—"should file out of the room one by one, with your hands in plain sight."

Soldiers searched and scanned the Brigaders, then cuffed them, before they were allowed out of the vault. Engineers entered and began preparing explosives to destroy the bunker once it had been evacuated. Jaina and Lowbacca waited in the bare room as the Brigaders slowly left.

They were aware of the change in the Jedi meld at the same time, the sudden vast surprise at the appearance of a new enemy.

Here's where it all goes wrong. The thought sang at the back of Jaina's mind.

She looked at Lowbacca, and knew that the Wookiee shared the knowledge that their time on the ground had run out.

Maal Lah gave a roar of triumph as the patrolling starfighters suddenly throttled up their engines and pointed their noses to the sky. The arrival of a Yuuzhan Vong fleet had given the infidels better things to do than cruise the air above Peace City.

It was time to meet the enemy, but Maal Lah knew that the battle was lost at the city center. There was no point in reinforcing the Peace Brigade's failure.

Another course recommended itself. The commander also knew where the New Republic forces were at the present. He knew that eventually they would have to retreat to their landing zones outside of town.

Between these two places he would make his killing ground. And conveniently, the quednak stables happened to be nearby.

He called into the shoulder villip that communicated with his warriors. "Our hour has arrived!" he said. "We will advance to meet the enemy!"

Jacen arrived breathless on *Ralroost*'s bridge to find Admiral Kre'fey already making his opening moves. An enemy fleet had leapt out of hyperspace, and Kre'fey was placing his own ships between the Yuuzhan Vong and the ground forces on Ylesia.

"Welcome, Jacen," the white-furred Bothan said, his eyes still fixed on the holographic display that showed the relative positions of the fleets. "I see you understand there's been a new complication."

"How many?" Jacen said.

"Their forces are roughly equal to ours. But so many of our personnel are inexperienced, I would prefer not to engage." He raised his eyes from the display. "Fortunately my opposite seems in no hurry to begin a fight."

Indeed this was the case. The Yuuzhan Vong weren't moving to attack, but were instead hovering just outside Ylesia's mass shadow.

"Can you give me a starfighter?" Jacen asked.

"I'm afraid not. Our fighter bays were packed with operational craft only, plus their pilots—we carry no spares."

Frustration snarled in Jacen as Kre'fey's attention snapped back to the display. "Ah," the admiral said. "My opposite is moving."

The Yuuzhan Vong had detached a part of their force and were extending it to one flank, perhaps intending a partial envelopment.

"Easily countered," Kre'fey said, and ordered one of his own divisions to extend his own flank, matching the enemy movement precisely.

Jacen stalked around the room in a brief circle, angry at his own uselessness. He considered returning to his X-wing and flying to Ylesia to Jaina's aid, and then realized that his wounded craft wouldn't be an asset, but a liability—she'd have to detach pilots to look after him, pilots who would have many better uses in an engagement than escorting a crippled ship.

He finally surrendered to the fact he was going to spend the rest of the battle aboard *Ralroost*.

Jacen found a corner of the bridge out of everyone's way and let the Jedi meld float to the surface of his mind. If he couldn't be of any direct use in the upcoming battle, he could at least send strength and support to his comrades.

Jaina and Lowbacca, he sensed, were in motion, speeding

toward their fighters. The other Jedi were waiting in their cockpits, waiting for the battle to begin. Jacen could sense them in relation to one another, an array of intent minds focused on the enemy.

Through the meld, he sensed the Yuuzhan Vong fleet make another move, another division shifting out onto the flank, extending it farther into space. Only half a minute later did he hear Kre'fey's staff announce the move, followed by the Bothan admiral's counter.

The Yuuzhan Vong kept moving to the flank. And Jacen began to wonder why.

Pwoe and Thrackan Sal-Solo, cuffed, were keeping each other company in the back of the landspeeder. Neither of the illusory presidents seemed to have much to say to the other, or to anyone else, at least not since Thrackan's muttered, "Do I really have to sit with the Squid Head?" as Pwoe was directed into the vehicle.

As it turned out there was no room for Thrackan or anyone else to sit. The landspeeders were standing room only, packed with soldiers, prisoners, and refugees.

The vehicles moved as fast as possible toward the landing zone, though they were being slowed by crowds of refugees, slaves, and other unwilling workers begging for transport off-planet. As many as could fit into the landspeeders were pulled aboard. In their withdrawal to the landing zone the speeders hadn't gotten onto the roads in any particular order, and the speeder that Jaina shared with Lowbacca, Thrackan, and Pwoe was more or less in the middle of the column.

The column had reached the outskirts of the city, which at this point consisted of a strip of buildings on either side of the main road, all surrounded by wild country, unaltered terrain.

Jaina turned at the sound of an explosion behind her, a concussion followed by a shock wave that she could feel in her insides. Smoke and debris jetted high over the surrounding buildings. The engineers had just destroyed the Brigaders' bunker, as well as the Palace of Peace and other public buildings.

Jaina turned to face forward just as a giant, lichen-colored beast stepped from behind a building into the road in front of the column. Jaina's heart thundered as the lead landspeeder crashed into the animal, enraging the beast even though the inertial dampeners on the machine saved the crew and passengers. Another speeder smashed into the first from behind, preventing it from reversing. The beast reared onto its hind legs, and Jaina saw Yuuzhan Vong warriors clinging for dear life to their basket on the beast's back. Shields sparked and failed as the quednak's first four feet dropped massively onto the speeder. Jaina could hear the screams of the passengers as they died.

Jaina reached for her lightsaber, then her blaster, then hesitated. None of her weapons could kill this animal.

Vehicle-mounted weapons split the air as they opened fire on the riding beast. The quednak screamed and charged forward, crushing the forepart of a second landspeeder and brushing aside a third. One of its riders was hurled from his seat and flew, arms windmilling, into the side of a nearby building.

"Back! Back! Take a side street out of here!" The officer in command of the landspeeder barked orders to the driver. And then Jaina felt a shadow fall over her, and she turned.

Another riding beast was being driven out into the road behind Jaina's speeder. Her lightsaber leapt into her hand and she took three long jumps to the back of the landspeeder and launched herself for the riders on the quednak's back.

The Force seemed to catch her by the spine and fling her onto the creature's back, and she gave silent thanks to Lowbacca for the assist as she landed on the broad, flat haunches. She was poised atop the middle pair of legs, her balance uneasy with the creature's lurching, swaying motion. The two riders sat in a shell-shaped box forward. Jaina ignited her lightsaber and charged, her boot driving for traction on the moss-covered surface of the beast's scales.

One of the Yuuzhan Vong in the box leapt out to face her while the other continued to guide the beast. The air reeked of the quednak's stench. Landspeeders dodged from beneath its clawed feet. Panicked gunners at the tail of the column were opening fire, scorching the creature's massive sides, but the quednak remained under the control of its driver.

Jaina's opponent thrust out his amphistaff, its head spitting poison. Jaina slapped the poison out of the air with a Force-generated wind and sprang forward to engage, thrusting right for the Yuuzhan Vong's tattooed face. His circular parry almost tore the lightsaber from her fingers, but she managed to disengage in time, and now she made a less impulsive attack.

Jaina's violet blade struck again and again, but the Yuuzhan Vong parried them all, an intent look visible under the brim of the vonduun crab helmet. He was concentrating solely on defense, on keeping her off the driver until he could trample the maximum number of landspeeders under the beast's claws. Frustration built in her as she redoubled her attack, the violet blade building into a pattern that would result in the amphistaff being drawn out of line and opening the Yuuzhan Vong for a finishing thrust.

Unexpectedly Jaina threw herself flat on the quednak's back. A bright red-orange bolt from a blaster cannon ripped the air where she'd been half a second before. The Yuuzhan Vong hesitated, blinking, dazzled by the flash, and then Jaina rose on one hand only and lashed a foot forward, sweeping the warrior's feet. He gave a cry of pure rage as he tumbled off the creature's sides.

Jaina hurled herself toward the driver in his box, but another cannon opened fire, and the box disappeared in a flash of flame, the heat scorching her face. Frantically she looked for a way to control the creature. The quednak gave a cry of absolute fury and began to back, trying to turn to get at the source of the blaster bolts that were tormenting it.

A volley of bolts slammed into the beast and blew Jaina off the creature's back. She tumbled free, calling on the Force to cushion her landing on the duracrete. Even so the impact knocked the breath from her lungs, her teeth clacking together on impact. From her position on the ground she saw Lowie dragging wounded civilians from a wrecked landspeeder, other intact speeders milling amid a swarm of confused refugees and stunned prisoners, and the death agonies of the other quednak, which had finally succumbed to heavy weapon fire.

Then the second beast, the one she'd ridden, took a cannon

bolt to the head, and reared as it began to die. Jaina saw the slab-sided wall flank begin its fall, and she scuttled like a crab out of the way as the creature came down in a wave of stench and blood. An agonized thrash of its tail threw a pair of landspeeders against a wall, and then the giant lizard was dead.

Dead riding beasts now blocked the road at either end, trapping the column between rows of buildings. Overhead came a pair of swift flyers, swoop analogs, that dived over the street, plasma cannons stuttering. Jaina rolled away from fire and flying splinters as superheated plasma ripped the duracrete near her.

The worst threat from the swoop analogs wasn't their cannons, however. Each had a dovin basal propulsion unit in its nose, and these living singularities leapt out to snatch at the landspeeders' shields, overloading them and causing them to fail in a flash of frustrated energy.

Jaina rose to her feet, her head swimming with the magnitude of the disaster. There was nothing she could do against the aircraft without her X-wing, so she staggered across the duracrete to aid Lowbacca in helping injured civilians. With the Force she lifted rubble from a wounded Rodian.

Concentrated fire from the soldiers blew one of the swoop analogs apart. The other, trailing fire, was deliberately crashed by its pilot into a landspeeder, and both craft were destroyed in an eruption of flame.

It was then that Jaina heard the sudden ominous humming, and her nerves tingled to the danger as she swung to face the sound, her lightsaber on guard.

A buzzing swarm of thud and razor bugs sped through the air, racing for their targets—and then Yuuzhan Vong warriors swarmed out of the office buildings on the south side of the street, while from either end of the street they came pouring like a wave over the bodies of the dead riding beasts. From five hundred throats came the chorused battle cry, *"Do-ro'ik vong pratte!"*

There were screams as scores went down before the flying wave of deadly insects. Jaina slapped a thud bug out of the sky with her lightsaber, and neatly skewered a razor bug that was making a run for Lowie's head. The Yuuzhan Vong warriors slammed with an audible impact into the stunned, milling crowd in the street. The New Republic soldiers were so hampered by the swarms of noncombatants that they were barely able to fire in their own defense. The Yuuzhan Vong leapt right aboard the landspeeders that had suffered the loss of their shields, slashing through screaming civilians and prisoners in order to reach soldiers so tightly packed they couldn't raise a weapon.

Jaina parried away an amphistaff that was swung at her head, and let Lowie, thrusting over her shoulder, dispose of the warrior who wielded it. The next warrior went down before a pair of lightsabers, one swung high, one thrust low. Jaina readied a cut at a figure that lurched toward her, then realized it was one of Thrackan's bodyguards in his preposterous fake armor. A shrieking human female, bloody from a razor bug slash and helpless with her hands cuffed, stumbled into Jaina's arms, and died from the lunge of the snarling Yuuzhan Vong warrior who was willing to run her through in order to reach Jaina. Jaina shuffled away from the thrust in time, and then, before the warrior could clear his weapon from his victim, her point took him in the throat.

The two halves of a razor bug, sliced neatly in half by Lowie's lightsaber, fell on either side of Jaina. She and Lowbacca were able to protect themselves against the buzzing horror, and the troopers were at least armored, but the civilians had no defense and were being torn to shreds. The handcuffed prisoners were even more helpless. "We've got to get these people into the buildings where we can protect them!" Jaina shouted to anyone who could hear. "Get them moving!"

With shouts and gestures, Jaina and Lowie rounded up a group of soldiers who helped to herd the civilians into the buildings on the north side of the street. This gave other soldiers, and the few landspeeders that were still in operation, a clearer field of fire, and the Yuuzhan Vong began to take more casualties.

In the midst of the confusion Jaina saw General Jamira staggering backward with a group of his troopers around him. All of them seemed wounded; a squad of Yuuzhan Vong were in pursuit, their amphistaffs rising and falling in a deadly, urgent rhythm.

"Lowie! It's the general!" The Jedi charged, lightsabers swinging. Jaina hamstrung one enemy warrior, then ducked the lunge of another to drive her lightsaber up through the armpit, the one part unprotected by armor. A third Yuuzhan Vong was knocked to his knees by a Force-aided double kick, after which one of Jamira's troopers shot him with a point-blank blaster bolt.

Two of the soldiers grabbed Jamira under the arms and hustled him to one of the buildings on the north side of the street, a restaurant with booths by the viewports and a bar against the back wall. There, other soldiers firing from the viewports had clear fields of fire and were able to score hits on any pursuers. Lowie and Jaina covered the retreat, blocking one shot after another with their lightsabers before rolling backward through the viewports.

The room was filled with stunned people, most of them civilians slumped at the tables. Jaina recognized Pwoe standing tall among them, his face bloody, one tentacle sliced neatly off by a razor bug.

The Yuuzhan Vong were still fighting, trying to get into the buildings. Jaina and Lowbacca each chose a viewport, cutting and parrying through the opening while the soldiers fired continuously at the attackers.

It was flanking fire that eventually drove the attackers away. The Yuuzhan Vong had ambushed only the first half of the returning convoy. The rear part of the column was largely intact, though unable to maneuver its speeders over the dead riding beast that blocked the road. Instead Colonel Tosh, in command of the rear guard, pulled his soldiers off the landspeeders and sent them climbing up the massive flank of the dead quednak. From its summit the troopers commenced massed volley fire on the street below, a fire intense enough to cause the Yuuzhan Vong to fall back to the buildings on the southern side of the street.

Jaina extinguished her lightsaber and gasped for air. It was amazing how fast things had gone wrong.

Time was running out. And with it, lives.

General Jamira stood gasping for breath, one arm propping him against a wall while he talked into his comm unit. Blood stained his white body armor. He looked up. "What's behind us?" he said. "Can we pull back to the north, then rendezvous with the landspeeders?"

One of the soldiers made a quick check, then returned. "It's uncleared forest, sir," he reported. "The landspeeders couldn't get through it, but we could move through on foot."

"Negative." Jamira shook his head. "We'd lose all cohesion in the woods and the Vong would hunt us to death." He turned to look out the shattered front viewport. "We've got to get back to the landspeeders somehow, then take another route around the roadblock." He looked grim, and pressed a hand to a wound on his thigh. "Tell Colonel Tosh he's got to give us covering fire as we break out. But we're still going to lose a lot of people once everyone gets into the street."

Jaina became aware that her comm unit was bleeping at her. She answered. "This is Solo."

"This is Colonel Fel. Are you in difficulty? The other Jedi seemed to think so."

Relief sang through Jaina at the sound of Jag's voice, though the relief was followed immediately by embarrassment at its intensity. She struggled to keep her voice calm and military as she answered. "The column's run into an ambush and has been pinned down," she said. "What's your location?"

"I'm with Twin Suns Squadron in orbit. We're on standby, waiting for you and Lowbacca to rejoin us. An enemy fleet has appeared and the situation has grown urgent. It's imperative that the landing force return to orbit as soon as possible."

"You don't say," Jaina snapped, her relief fading before annoyance at Jag's pompous tone.

"Stand by," Jag said. "I'll lead the squadrons on a bombing and strafing run and blast you out of there."

"Negative," Jaina said. "The Vong are right across the street, too close. You'd hit us, and we've got civilians here."

"I still may be able to help. Stand by."

"Jag," Jaina said, "you've got too many rookies! They'll never be able to stay on target! They're going to splatter a hundred civilians, not to mention the rest of us!"

"Stand by, Twin Leader," Jag said, insistent.

Annoyance finally won over relief. Jaina looked at General Jamira in exasperation. "Did you hear that, sir?"

Jamira nodded. "Even if he can't do a strafing run, starfighters might keep the Vong's heads down. We'll wait."

"General!" Pwoe's commanding voice rang from the back of the room. "This is absolute folly! I demand that you allow me to negotiate a surrender for these people before those fire-happy pilots blow us all to pieces!"

The Quarren stalked forward. Jamira faced him, straightening, and winced as he put weight onto his wounded leg.

"Senator," he said. "You will oblige me by remaining silent. You are not in charge here."

"Neither are you, it appears," Pwoe said. "Your only hope, and the hope of all under your command"—with his cuffed hands he made a gesture that encompassed the soldiers, the civilians, and the prisoners—"is to surrender at discretion. I shall undertake the negotiations entirely at my own risk."

"Surrender at discretion." Jaina was surprised by Thrackan's sarcastic voice coming from the back of the room. Her cousin rose from the chair he'd occupied and limped forward. She could see that the long muscles of his back had also been sliced open by a razor bug.

"Up until now I'd thought the *Jedi* were the most pompous, annoying gasbags in creation," Thrackan said. "But that was before I met *you*. You take the prize for the most preposterous, self-important, prolix fiasco I have ever seen. And on top of that—" He stared at close range into Pwoe's indignant eyes. "On top of that, sir, you are a *fish*! So sit down and shut up, before I take a *harpoon* to you!"

Pwoe drew himself up. "Your display of rank prejudice is—"

Thrackan waved a hand. "Can it, Chief. Nobody's listening to your speeches now. Or will ever again, I guess."

Pwoe returned Thrackan's glare for a long moment, and then his gaze fell, and he retreated. Then Thrackan turned his scowl on the others—Jaina, Jamira, and the rest. "I'm not a Vong collaborator, no matter what the rest of you think. And I'm not about to let a subaquatic imbecile sell us out to the enemy."

With an air of painful triumph, Thrackan dragged himself to his seat.

From above came the peculiar creaking roar of a claw fighter, passing slowly overhead. Jaina could imagine Jag in the pilot's seat, flying the clawcraft inverted to give himself a better view of the scene below. When Jag's voice returned, it was thoughtful.

"Our forces are on the north side?"

"Yes, but—"

"The Yuuzhan Vong are regrouping—they'll be launching another assault in a few minutes. I'll commence a bomb run with our two squadrons to break up the attack. Tell your people to stay under cover, and be ready to run."

"No!" Jaina said. "I know my rookie pilots! They don't have the experience!"

"Stand by, Twin Leader. And tell those soldiers standing on the dead animal to take cover."

Jaina almost dashed the comlink to the ground in frustration. Instead she gave a despairing look to General Jamira, who was looking at her with a furrowed, thoughtful expression. Jamira raised his own comlink to his lips.

"Fighters are about to make a run. Everyone is to get under secure cover, and prepare to run for the landspeeders on my command. Tosh, get your people off that creature and under the speeders' shields again."

And then, with weary, silent dignity, General Jamira took shelter beneath a table. The others in the room did their best to follow suit.

The roar of starfighters floated through the broken viewports. Jaina, remaining on her feet, stepped to the viewport and took a quick look out.

Black against the western sky was the Chiss squadron, the craft flying nearly wingtip to wingtip, echeloned back from the leader in a kind of half wedge.

Of course, Jaina thought in admiration. Jag Fel would be in the lead, flying along an invisible line down the battlefield between the Yuuzhan Vong and the New Republic troops. The others were echeloned onto the Vong side of the line—as long as they maintained their alignment on the leader, their fire *couldn't* hit friendly forces.

Laser cannons began to flash on the Chiss leader, then on the others. Bolts fell on the street and on the roofs of the buildings opposite, a clatter of high-energy rain. Jaina dived under the nearest table and found Lowie already taking up most of the room.

"You know," she said, "sometimes Jag is really—"

Her thought was left unfinished. The first wave seemed to suck the air from Jaina's lungs, then transform it into light and heat that Jaina could feel in her long bones, her liver and spleen and bowel.

Twenty-one more detonations followed the first as the Chiss unloaded. Whatever was left of the restaurant viewports exploded inward. Storms of dust blasted in from the street, and bits of debris. And then there was a silence broken only by the ringing in Jaina's ears.

Slowly she became aware that her comlink was talking at her. She raised it to her lips.

"Say again?"

"Hold your positions," came the faint voice. "Twin Suns is next."

Tesar would be in the lead position, with the rest echeloned in the same formation Jag had used. Jaina had no fear that any of the fire would go astray.

"Hold your positions!" Jaina called. "Another strike coming!"

There were sixteen runs this time, two from each of the X-wings remaining. Jaina coughed as wave after wave of dust blew in the viewports.

Again there was silence, broken only by the sound of sliding rubble from the buildings opposite. As she blinked dust from her lashes Jaina could see General Jamira rise painfully from his position under one of the tables, then raise his comlink to his lips.

"Soldiers, take up positions to cover the civilians! All non-combatants to the speeders—and then the rest of us follow!"

Hands tore the rubble off him, and Maal Lah saw the sky where he had thought he would never see the free sky again. He wheezed as he coughed dust out of his lungs. "It's the commander!" someone called, and a host of hands joined to rip the debris away, then lift Maal Lah free of the wreckage.

Maal Lah gave a gasp at a sudden, nauseating wave of pain, but he clenched his teeth and said, "Subaltern! Report!"

"The infidels made their escape after the bombing, Supreme Commander. But they've left hundreds of dead behind." The subaltern hesitated. "Many of them our Peace Brigade allies."

Pain made Maal Lah snarl, but he turned the snarl into one of triumph. "The treacherous infidels deserved their fate! They should have died fighting, but instead they surrendered and left it to us to give them an honorable death!" He managed to turn another grimace of pain into a laugh. "The invaders feared us, subaltern! They fled Ylesia once they had felt our sting!"

"The Supreme Commander is wise," the subaltern said. Dust streaked the subaltern's tattoos, and his armor was battered. His eyes traveled along Maal Lah's body. "I regret to say, Supreme Commander," he said slowly, "that your leg is destroyed. I'm afraid you're going to lose it."

Maal Lah snarled again. As if he needed a young infant of a subaltern to tell him such a thing. He had *seen* the duralloy beam come down like a knife, and he had felt the agony in the long minutes since . . .

"The shapers will give me a better leg, if the gods will it," Maal Lah said.

He turned his head at a series of sonic booms: the infidel landers leaping skyward from their landing field.

"They *think* they've escaped, subaltern," Maal Lah said. "But I know they have not."

Before the enemy fire blew the building down on him he had been in contact with his commanders in space, and devised a strategy that would give the enemy another surprise.

Was it possible to die of surprise? he wondered.

As a tactician, he knew that it was.

Jacen stood in silence and held the Jedi meld in his mind. The last of the landing party was leaving Ylesia, with Jaina and Lowbacca, and the enemy commander still had not made his move. Instead he continued to extend his flank, shifting a constant trickle of ships into the void. Admiral Kre'fey matched each enemy deployment with one of his own. Both lines were now attenuated, too drawn out to be useful as a real battle line.

But why? Why had the enemy commander handicapped himself in this way, drawing out his forces until they were no longer able to fight cohesively? He had similarly handicapped Kre'fey, that was true, but he wasn't in a position to take advantage of it. What he should have done was attack immediately and try to trap the ground forces on Ylesia.

In Jacen's mind he could feel the Jedi pilots in their patrolling craft, scattered up and down the thinned-out enemy line. He felt their perceptions layered onto his, so he knew as well the positions of most of the fleet. And through their unified concentration on their own displays, he understood where they were in relationship to the enemy.

Why? Why was the Yuuzhan Vong commander maneuvering this way? It was almost as if there were a piece missing.

A missing piece. The piece fell into place with a *snap* that Jacen felt shuddering in his nerves. With some reluctance he banished the Force and the comforts of the meld from his mind, and he called up his Vongsense, the strange telepathy he had developed with Yuuzhan Vong lifeforms during his captivity.

An immeasurably alien sense of *being* filled his thoughts. He could feel the ememy fleet extending its wing out into space, the implacable hostility of its every being, from the living ships to the breathing Yuuzhan Vong to the grutchins that waited packed into Yuuzhan Vong missiles . . .

Jacen fought to extend his mind, extend his senses deep into space, into the void that surrounded the Ylesia system.

And there he found what he sought, an alien microcosm filled with barbarous purpose.

He opened his eyes and stared at Kre'fey, who was standing amid his silent staff, studying the displays.

"Admiral!" Jacen said. *"There's another Vong fleet on its way!"* He strode forward among the staff officers and thrust a pointing finger into the holographic display. "It's coming right *here*. Right behind our extended wing, where they can hammer us against the other Yuuzhan Vong force."

Kre'fey stared at Jacen from his gold-flecked violet eyes. "Are you certain?"

Jacen returned Kre'fey's stare. "Absolutely, Admiral. We've got to get our people out of there."

Kre'fey looked again at the display, at the shimmering interference patterns that ran over Jacen's pointing finger. "Yes," he said. "Yes, that has to be the explanation." He turned to his staff. "Order the extended wing to rejoin."

A host of communications specialists got very busy with their microphones. Kre'fey continued staring at Jacen's pointing finger, and then he nodded to himself.

"The extended wing is to fire a missile barrage *here*." Kre'fey said, and gave the coordinates indicated by Jacen's finger.

The capital ships on the detached wing belched out a gigantic missile barrage, seemingly aimed into empty space, and scurried back to the safety of the main body. When the Yuuzhan Vong reinforcements shimmered into realspace the missiles were already amid them, and the new arrivals hadn't yet configured their ships for defense, or launched a single coralskipper.

On the displays Jacen watched the havoc the missiles wrought on the startled enemy. Almost all the ships were hit, and several broke up.

Kre'fey snarled. *"How can I hurt the Vong today?"* We've answered that question, haven't we?"

One of his staff officers gave a triumphant smile. "Troopships report the landing party has been recovered, Admiral."

"About time," someone muttered.

Since the wing was contracting inward anyway, Kre'fey got the whole fleet moving in the same direction. The newly arrived Yuuzhan Vong were too disorganized, and too out of position, to make an effective pursuit. The first arrivals charged after

Kre'fey, but they were strung out while Kre'fey's forces were concentrating, and their intervention had no hope of being decisive.

But even though Kre'fey had assured the escape of his force, the battle was far from over. The Yuuzhan Vong commander was angry and his warriors still possessed the suicidal bravery that marked their caste. Ships were hard hit, and starfighters vaporized, and hulls broken up to tumble through the cold emptiness of Ylesian space, before the fleet exited the traitor capital's mass shadow and made the hyperspace jump to Kashyyyk.

"I don't want to do *anything* like that again," Jaina said. She was in the officers' lounge of *Starsider,* sitting on a chair with a cup of tea in her hand, her boots off, and her stockinged feet in Jag Fel's lap.

"Ylesia was like hitting your head again and again on a brick wall," she went on. "One tactical problem after another, and the solution to each one was a straightforward assault right at the enemy, or straightforward flight with the enemy in pursuit." She sighed as Jag's fingers massaged a particularly sensitive area of her right foot. "I'm better when I can be Yun-Harla the Trickster," she said. "Not when I'm playing the enemy's game, but when I can make the enemy play mine."

"You refer to sabacc, I take it," Jag said, a bit sourly.

Jaina looked at Jacen, sitting opposite her and sipping on a glass of Gizer ale. "Are you going to take Kre'fey up on his offer of a squadron command?"

Jacen inhaled the musky scent of the ale as he considered his answer. "I think I may serve better on the bridge of *Ralroost,*" he said finally, and thought of his finger floating in Kre'fey's holo display, pointing at the enemy fleet that wasn't there.

"Ylesia," he continued, "showed that my talents seem to be more spatial and, uh, coordinative. Is *coordinative* a word?"

"I hope not," Jag said .

Jacen felt regret at the thought of leaving starfighters entirely. He had joined Kre'fey's fleet in order to guard his sister's back, and perhaps that was best done by flying alongside her in an X-wing. But he suspected that he'd be able to offer a higher order of assistance if he stayed out of a starfighter cockpit, instead using the Jedi meld to shape the way the others fought.

"Look," Jag pointed out, "Jaina's got it wrong. Ylesia wasn't a defeat. Jaina's downed pilots were rescued, and so were mine. We hurt the enemy a lot more than they hurt us, thanks in part to Spooky Mind-Meld Man, here." He nodded toward Jacen. "We destroyed a collaborationist fleet and captured enough of the Peace Brigade's upper echelon to provide dozens of splashy trials. The media will be occupied for months."

"It didn't *feel* like a victory," Jaina said. "It felt like we barely escaped with our necks."

"That's only because you don't have a sufficiently detached perspective," Jag said seriously.

Mention of the Peace Brigade had set Jacen's mind thinking along other channels. He looked at Jaina. "Do you think Thrackan's really innocent?"

Jaina was startled. "Innocent of *what*?"

"Of collaboration. Do you think the story he told about being forced into the Presidency could possibly have been true?"

Jaina gave a disbelieving laugh. "Too ludicrous."

"No, really. He's a complete human chauvinist. I know he's a bad guy and he held us prisoner and wants to rule Corellia as diktat, but he hates aliens so much I can't believe he'd work with the Yuuzhan Vong voluntarily."

Jaina tilted her head in thought. Jag's foot massage had put a blissful expression on her face. "Well, he *did* call Pwoe a Squid Head. That's a point in his favor."

"If Sal-Solo wishes to prove his innocence," Jag said, "he need only volunteer for interrogation under truth drugs. If his collaboration was involuntary, the drugs would reveal it." Grim amusement passed across his scarred features. "But I think he's afraid that such an interrogation would reveal how he came to be in the hands of the Yuuzhan Vong in the first place. *That's* what would truly condemn him."

"Ahh," Jaina said. Jacen couldn't tell if she was enlightened or, in light of the foot rub, experiencing a form of ecstasy.

Jacen, sipping his ale, decided that whatever the truth of the matter, it wasn't any of his business.

* * *

Thrackan Sal-Solo paced across the durasteel-walled prison exercise yard, his mind busy with plans.

Tomorrow, he'd been told, he would be transferred to Corellia, where he would undergo trial for treason against his home planet.

He'd accept the transfer peacefully, and behave as a model prisoner for most of the way home. But that was only to lull his guards.

He'd catch them at a disadvantage, and bash them over the head with an improvised weapon—he didn't know what exactly, he'd work that out later. Then he'd take command of the ship— he hoped it was an Incom model, he could fly anything Incom made. He'd crash the ship into a remote area of Corellia and make it appear he died in the flames.

Then he'd make contact with some of the people on Corellia he could still trust. He'd reorganize the Centerpoint Party, strike, and seize power. He would *rule the world*! No, *five* worlds.

It was his destiny, and nothing could stop him. Thracken Sal-Solo wasn't meant to be condemned to a miserable life on a prison planet.

Well. Not more than *once,* anyway.

AT LAST!
THE STORY OF THE OUTBOUND FLIGHT PROJECT IS REVEALED

STAR WARS®:
OUTBOUND FLIGHT

By TIMOTHY ZAHN,
New York Times bestselling author
of *Heir to the Empire*

Finally, Timothy Zahn discloses the full story of the mysterious Outbound Flight Project—and reveals the first encounter with the alien warlord Thrawn, the future archenemy of the New Republic!

Before the Clone Wars began, a group of Jedi led by the legendary Master Jorus C'baoth lobbied the Republic Senate to fund a project to search for intelligent life outside the known galaxy. Six Jedi Masters, twelve Jedi Knights, and fifty thousand crew boarded an incredible starship and left on their adventure . . . only to disappear without a trace. Until now, the details of the tragic mission have only been hinted at in Zahn's *Heir to the Empire*.

AVAILABLE IN BOOKSTORES EVERYWHERE

A DEL REY®/LUCASBOOKS HARDCOVER
WWW.READSTARWARS.COM